PENGUIN BOOKS

THE STILLNESS THE DANCING

Wendy Perriam, born in 1940, graduated in History Honours from St Anne's College, Oxford, and later studied at the London School of Economics. She worked as a waitress, nanny, barmaid, artist's model, carnation de-budder and researcher in the British Museum before embarking on a successful career in advertising which she combined with writing poetry and short stories. She now writes full time.

Her previous novels – *Absinthe for Elevenses* (1980), *Cuckoo* (1981), *After Purple* (1982; Penguin, 1983) and *Born of Woman* (1983; Penguin, 1984) – were acclaimed for their explosive combination of sex and religion, humour and hang-up, as well as for their sheer exuberance and energy.

D1388328

WENDY PERRIAM

THE STILLNESS
THE DANCING

PENGUIN BOOKS

Penguin Books Ltd, Harmondsworth, Middlesex, England
Viking Penguin Inc., 40 West 23rd Street, New York, New York 10010, U.S.A.
Penguin Books Australia Ltd, Ringwood, Victoria, Australia
Penguin Books Canada Limited, 2801 John Street, Markham, Ontario, Canada L3R 1B4
Penguin Books (N.Z.) Ltd, 182–190 Wairau Road, Auckland 10, New Zealand

First published by Michael Joseph 1985
Published in Penguin Books 1986

The author and publishers would like to thank the following for
permission to quote extracts: Faber & Faber (*The Waste Land* and
Four Quartets by T. S. Eliot); Northern Songs ('Can't Buy Me Love' by
Lennon & McCartney); Gerald Duckworth ('The Early Morning'
from *Complete Verse* by Hilaire Belloc).

Typeset, printed and bound in Great Britain by
Hazell Watson & Viney Limited,
Member of the BPCC Group,
Aylesbury, Bucks

Typeset in Plantin

So the darkness shall be the light, and the stillness the
    dancing
Whisper of running streams, and winter lightning.
The wild thyme unseen and the wild strawberry,
The laughter in the garden, echoed ecstasy
Not lost, but requiring, pointing to the agony
Of death and birth.

T. S. Eliot
'East Coker'

1

Morna checked her watch. Less than half a minute, including foreplay. The still puffed-up male pigeon had already clambered off its mate, leaving it free to forage again. It seemed relieved, had simply endured the copulation, crouching tense and pinioned while the male bird perched on top of it, fluttering and tipping.

Morna threw more seed, ducked away from the thrash of wings as the pigeons swooped, every beak jab-jabbing, total concentration on the food. There seemed no pleasure in it, more a fierce rush and frenzy, bodies barging into each other, tails brushing heads, heads used as battering rams. The birds were running in tiny circles on their pink mincing feet, beaks open, orange bead-eyes swivelling and searching. A few intrepid sparrows, dwarfed by larger beaks and bodies, snatched mouthfuls where they could. A herring gull wheeled down, stood alone with wings outstretched, apart from all the rest. Morna edged a little closer. She had never seen a gull before in her mother's garden. It looked out of place, a gatecrasher, needed pounding waves and surf-flecked sand to frame it, not prissy rockery, pocket-hankie lawn. It scorned the crust she threw, soared away, white wings merging with white cloud.

She turned back to the pigeons, who were still scavenging, but less intently now, their circles larger and more leisurely as they mopped up the stray grains. Two were paler than the others, streaked and splotched with white; the rest dull grey with a gleam of green and purple on their necks. Strange that her mother should be fond of pigeons when they were all the things she disapproved of – drab, common, dirty and over-sexed – at least the males. Yet Bea bought seed for them in hundredweight sacks, fed them every morning, six o'clock in summer, eight in winter.

Morna glanced at her watch again. Half past nine. She wondered if the birds realized she was late and were judging her as her mother might have done – were Bea not at this moment stretched out on an operating slab. The surgeon would be just inserting his scalpel, Bea unrecognizable without make-up, clothes, teeth. Morna had never seen her naked and rarely naked-faced. Bea was always coiffed, rouged, powdered, smartly dressed. Earrings in the house, gloves and hat outside. Morna tried to picture her in a hospital gown, tied at the back with strings like a baby's nightdress, bloodstained now, perhaps. She took a step towards the house as if to grab her car keys, drive pell-mell to the hospital and snatch the body up, bring it back unscathed. Her mother had endured enough without this operation, this new scar. Yet Bea seemed unruffled when she took her in the previous afternoon, left her with a pile of magazines, a quart of orange juice, returned to her mother's house.

'Someone has to feed the birds.'

Bea's last words. If she died under anaesthetic, would her daughter have to scatter seed for ever, until she died herself, or feel guilt if she declined?

The puffed-up pigeon was still pursuing the same female, a thin and scraggy bird which kept trying to elude it, dodging away, running in the opposite direction. Morna watched. She had translated a paper once on the copulation of birds. The majority of species had no external reproductive organs, so mating was quite a feat. There were problems of contact, overbalancing. She had been translating from the German and the terms were tricky. (*Die*

8

Mündung, die Papille, die Fortpflanzung.) Most female birds were non-responsive, needed elaborate courtship displays to activate their hormones, rouse their interest. She was much the same herself. Except that even with the courtship, she had often remained unmoved. She watched the pigeon try a different mate, strutting and self-satisfied, neck throbbing with its hoarse and throaty love-song. That female was equally reluctant, made its escape in a comic hurried run.

Easier for pigeons. No one criticized them, made them feel inadequate, used words like frigid or non-orgasmic, urged them to see therapists or mug up manuals on technique. It was only two seconds, anyway. Over two hours with Neil. She tried to picture her ex-husband with wings. It would have been less uncomfortable. He had always pressed down on her, eleven stone of him grinding her into the bed springs. Neil was nowhere in her mother's house. Bea didn't recognize divorce, so once he had left, she removed both his photos and his memory, expunged him from her mind and conversation. Her daughter was bereaved as she herself had been, thirty odd years ago. Bea was right. Divorce *had* felt like a death. Neil had left at forty, the age she was herself now. Her birthday had come and gone and nothing changed. But Neil was a vain man. Forty probably hurt. Was that why he had found a new-model wife, thirteen years his junior and responsive to display, to throaty love-songs?

Morna closed the garden door, walked through into the sitting room, her own younger face reflected back at her from mantelpiece and sideboard. All the photo frames were full of Morna – Bea's exclusive Morna. Morna in shawls, rompers, frocks or fancy dress; Morna hairless, toothless, shoeless, Neil-less. Legs and pigtails growing longer. Smile less certain. Grim school hat pulled down over blue confining uniform. Blue for the Blessed Virgin.

Morna sat down at the table, sorted through her papers. At school she had had ambition – to cure lepers, save souls,

9

sway super-powers, change people's hearts and minds. To be a Florence Nightingale fused with Gandhi, with a dash of Bertrand Russell and Lord Reith. In fact, she worked part-time and intermittently. Translator sounded grand – almost as glamorous as interpreter. She had friends who were interpreters – simultaneous transmission at a packed United Nations, their fluent rendering picked up by satellite across the world. More likely jobs for her were low-grade advertising brochures plugging dog food or double glazing; long-winded articles on pig disease or bridge construction. She was lucky at the moment, working on something literary, in verse. She scored her biro through the first two lines. What had flowed before her breakfast coffee now sounded coy and stilted. Poetry was the most difficult of all. Did you retain the rhyme but force the sense and syntax, or sacrifice it in the cause of accuracy and then risk an uninspired rendering which was exact in letter only, not in spirit? Even in prose there were few exact equivalents. You could finish a job, post off the faithful English version of your client's French or German, and know that it still lied. You had to be two people – first the foreign one, and then the English – thinking differently with different idioms, a different way of framing concepts, coining words. She tried a rhyme, crossed it out again. She was used to a touch of schizophrenia even in her private life. It still felt strange to be a divorcée and a convent girl, Bea's daughter and Neil's ex-wife.

The wedding itself had been something of a strain – what the Catholic Church condemned as a mixed marriage. All her mother's Catholic friends had prayed for Neil's conversion. They had no idea that she, too, was an unbeliever, had lost her mother's God and put Neil in His place. She hadn't dared confess, had hidden the sham in ten yards of white tulle. A registry office would have killed her mother. At least she had been a virgin – technically. Fellatio didn't count, so Neil assured her. She hadn't even known the word. The nuns had compiled their own (shorter) dictionary omitting all the words they disapproved of, including 'sex' itself. Other, vaguer terms like 'sins against the sixth and ninth commandments' or 'occasion for procreation' had left her highly nervous. All through university she had remained intact, allowing men to kiss her, even fondle her, only to change her mind and rush away, shut herself up with her books. Neil was different, dominant, not a greenhorn student but an advertising executive. She had met him at a party in her final year. He had taken her to dinner, dazzled her with charm and Mouton Rothschild, insisted that she pay him back – in bed. The more she demurred, the more ardent he became. Virgins of twenty-one were rare, especially pretty ones. This was a challenge and his pride was on the line. So was her entire moral code. In the end he proposed. Later, she wondered if he would have done, had her standards been less strict. Did he only want her because he couldn't have her, because she was the first girl proof against his blandishments?

The cake was made, the dress bought, every last detail of the wedding fixed, when he finally seduced her. They were returning from a party in his red MG. He had drunk too much, missed a lorry by inches.

'Do you think you ought to drive?' she asked.

'No,' he said. He drew up in a layby. 'I think I ought to fuck you.'

She had flushed, as much from fear as from embarrassment. He sounded angry.

'Look, darling, it's only a week now. That's not long and . . .'

'Too fucking long.'

He had unzipped his trousers and she stared at the swollen red-faced stranger rearing up beside her.

'Suck it,' he demanded. His words were slurred.

She shrank away.

'I said "suck it".'

'I *can't*, Neil. I . . .'

He had pulled her down, held her face over his crotch. She smelt a whiff of stale urine.

'Open your mouth.'

Her mouth wasn't big enough. Every morning for eleven years she had opened it to receive the body of Christ. Christ was tiny, didn't gag.

'Put your heads well back, girls, and open your mouths wide.' Reverend Mother had coached them before their first Communion. 'Keep your eyes closed and your hands joined.'

Morna shut her eyes. The tears ran under the lids, dripped into her mouth. You weren't meant to cry when your fiancé made love to you. Love? He came in less than half a minute and she swallowed him. You didn't spit God out. He kissed her then, the other way up, and the taste of whisky disguised the taste of semen. Later, he apologized.

'It doesn't matter,' she had said. How could she tell him how . . . how *banal* it had been. Eleven years of prohibition, dire warnings about damnation, fornication classed with murder, and then twenty seconds and a spurt of slimy dribble in her mouth. You could be damned for that, pitched into hell for all eternity.

It was Neil himself who had cleared away the pitchforks, damped down the flames of hell, built her world anew for her with his own rational commonsense. He had taught her not to mortify the flesh but to pamper and indulge it, to squander cash on earth rather than save souls in purgatory. He had vanished now, but left his views behind, his comfortable agnostic way of life.

Morna took a sip of coffee. The hand on the cup jangled with his eighteen-carat white gold bracelet; the other wore his Longines jewelled watch. She put her cup down, picked up the German verse. There were at least a few advantages in being on her own. She could work in peace, for one thing.

Neil had hated competition. *He* was the achiever, the careerist; her rôle simply to admire. She was also free from his constant demands in bed – though she still felt guilty about using the word demands, still judged herself a failure. She had 'dropped' sex now, as simply as her daughter had dropped physics or geography at school. She was a daughter herself again, returned to the house she had grown up in, sleeping in a single bed while her own child, almost a woman, was away for the whole summer improving her French in Les Lecques. She glanced across at the postcard on the mantelpiece which had arrived just that morning, the first since Chris had left a week ago.

'It's not bad here. Madame is very strict but I like Monsieur. The kids stay up till nearly midnight. We visited a liqueur factory and were given half an inch to try. Hope Grandma is okay.'

Morna hoped *Monsieur* was okay – not the type who took advantage of seventeen-year-old au pair girls. Chris already had a boyfriend, a steady one, but he was in Hayling Island, not Les Lecques. Problems there, as well, Morna chewed her pen, saw Martin's long lean legs, restless, never still, his dark and wary eyes. She liked the lad in some ways, even quite admired him, but paired off with a precious only daughter . . .

She scribbled three more lines, toning down the high-flown adjectives which worked better in the German than the English. One or two of the fancier ones were Chris's. They had worked on the poem together just before Chris left. She was glad her daughter was good at languages – one of the few things they had in common. Morna had taught her French as a child, spoken it with her, bought her *Elle* and *Marie-Claire* instead of *Honey*. It had paid off. Chris had just sat her A levels – French, German, English – and had already been offered a place at both Bristol and St Andrews to read Modern Languages. She had one more term at school in which she would aim higher still, try for Cambridge. Neil had pushed for that – five thousand miles away. A self-made man himself, he relished the idea of his only daughter at Girton or even King's.

Morna shook her hair back, as if trying to shrug Neil off. It was difficult to work in her mother's house. Bea, like her ex-husband, disapproved of working mothers. Thoughts kept intruding, anyway – thoughts of Chris, Neil, Martin, operations. She kept worrying about her mother. Was Bea all right? No complications, crises? She ought to phone the hospital. A different body would be on that slab now – her mother stitched and sponged, back in bed. The phone was in the hall, without a chair. Morna slumped against the wall, heard the semolina voice dollop out its bland and soothing clichés.

'Yes, it all went very well. Your mother's come round from the anaesthetic now and is taking sips of water. She's quite comfortable. In fact, we're going to . . .'

The surge of sweet relief was followed by a twinge of disappointment. Your mother refused surgery, suddenly leapt up from the operating table, and is now running naked on the hospital roof. Your mother jumped a plane to France and is touring the liqueur factory, drunk on Benedictine. Your mother is sitting up in heaven throwing manna to the birds.

'Fine. I'll be in tomorrow. Is half past three all right?'

Twenty-nine and a quarter hours to fill. Morna straightened a saggy rose in a formal flower arrangement, plumped up a cushion on the sofa. Her mother's house had changed little over forty years – the same antique furniture which had come from Edward's family, the same faded but precious Persian rugs over highly polished parquet. Both she and her mother still lived in the homes bought and furnished by their husbands; kept them up when the men in question had died or disappeared. Both had been spared the financial blows at least. Edward had been well-to-do, left his widow with an investment income and a fully paid-up house – small but

14

elegant. Neil had always admired Bea's style. He was an ambitious type, keen to outgrow his own G-Plan and Formica parents who semi-lived in a semi-detached in Penge. Had he married her for her background, Morna often wondered. An ex-Marlborough squadron leader father-in-law killed on active service counted for more than a no one still alive. Her mother might talk about economy, but she spoke with the right accent, owned portraits and good furniture, genuine family pieces which combined age with breeding and which she would never dream of selling, even now, when inflation had reduced her income and she was forced to skimp on other things. Neil had eclipsed them all – lived in a mock-Italian villa in one of the classiest suburbs of Los Angeles, with new wife, new child, new job, new car, new smile.

Morna stood at the window, appraising her mother's crew-cut hedge and well drilled lupins, watching the sunlight fidget on the lawn. She felt fidgety herself, no longer in the mood for tragiromantic German verse. She went to fetch a duster, could find no use for it. The house was always immaculate and Bea had spent the day before her hospital admission improving on the perfect. Perhaps she should walk the dog. Service to bird and animal was service to her mother.

'Joy!' she called. Her mother's dog was an aggressive and irascible Yorkshire terrier bitch. (Bea had never had a male dog.) Joy nipped friends, maimed postmen, and was redeemed only by her name. She minced in, snapped at Morna's hand as she tried to buckle on her tartan coat, barked hysterically when the phone rang.

'Damn,' said Morna. It would be another of her mother's pious female friends. Three had rung already. 'Please tell Bea we're saying a novena for her.' 'Father Clarke offered Mass for her today.' 'I made my Holy Communion for her this morning.'

The voice was male.

'Hallo, Father Clarke here. That's Morna, isn't it?'

'Yes, hallo.' She refused to add 'Father'. Father Clarke had married her and Neil. In twenty years she had gone from virgin to bride to mother to divorcée, while he remained unchanged – smug, stubborn, petty, ever-virgin, closed to all new ideas, only his joints stiffening, his hair receding.

'How's your mother?'

'She's . . . er . . . quite comfortable.'

'Good, good. Why I'm phoning, my dear, is that there's going to be a summer school later on this month and I thought Beatrice might . . .'

Summer school? Bea had never studied anything, never taken a job. She had been a full-time widow and an overtime Catholic. It was she herself who attended summer schools, to dilute the isolation of her work, make her feel more of a professional. Father Clarke was coughing. He smoked too much – a pipe. He cleared his throat.

'Well, it's really a retreat – but not just prayer and silence. They're inviting a few speakers from outside this time – a little bit of history, a talk on religious poetry – you know the sort of thing.'

'I see.' Morna tried to disguise her disappointment. She would have liked to have seen her mother mugging up Old Norse or having a crack at morris dancing.

'I know Beatrice hates to be unoccupied, so I thought she might . . .'

Beatrice. Father Clarke avoided abbreviations as he avoided sloth and slovenliness. If you were sloppy over words, lazy about spelling out a name, it was all too easy to become sloppy over more important things – morals or good manners. He and Beatrice kept their standards high in both.

Morna realized she was slouching, stood up straighter. 'When exactly is it?' she asked. 'Mummy may not be well enough to . . .'

'That's just the point. I thought she might regard it as a sort of convalescence. The programme's very relaxed and it's not even far to travel. It's less than half an hour from here, in a delightful little village on the Surrey/Hampshire borders. The house itself is set in thirty acres of grounds, so she'll have peace and quiet and country air and someone to cook the meals and . . .'

'*I'm* cooking the meals.'

There was a short uneasy silence.

'I mean I'm staying with her all summer, Father, looking after her. Chris is away in France, so . . .'

'Why don't you come as well, then? I mean, it's . . . er . . . not exclusively Catholic. There's an Anglican vicar speaking and an ecumenical discussion on the church and disarmament.'

He was offering lollipops. She already regretted the 'Father'. It had merely been a sop because she'd sounded rude. She had been to confession to Father Clarke twenty years ago. Another sham. 'Father, I have eaten meat on Friday.' It was no longer a sin, and even at the time, she had trotted it out to conceal her graver lapses.

'Why I'm phoning now is . . .' The priest's voice was engulfed a moment in another burst of coughing. 'If . . . If you want to come, you'll have to book more or less immediately. They're almost full already.'

'Right, I'll tell my mother. I'll be seeing her tomorrow.'

'Good. Give her my regards – and prayers, of course.'

'Of course.'

Morna put the phone down. Joy was still trailing her lead. She took it off, unzipped the tartan coat. She didn't feel like service any more.

2

'Push,' the midwife shouted. 'Push!'

Bea couldn't push, hadn't any muscles. Hadn't any body at all. There was just her head, hugely blindly throbbing, and then a vague, hollow, floating blur below it. They must have given her gas and air, or one of those new-fangled epidurals.

There was a nurse still in the room, heavy clumping shoes punishing the lino, voice Irish-shrill and hurting.

'Wake up, Mrs Conyers.'

Stupid girl. She wasn't asleep. You didn't doze off in the second stage of labour. She could even feel the contractions now, the faintest griping somewhere at her outer edges. Tears were streaming down her cheeks. She was crying because her husband wasn't there, would never see his baby.

'*It's a little girl.*'

Edward had wanted a girl, chosen only girls' names – romantic fancy names – Miranda, Roxanne, Morna. Morna meant 'beloved'. *He* was her beloved. They had sent back his remains. Not bones or flesh or even ashes. Just his medals and a pile of books and papers, and a few limp pathetic clothes which still smelt of brilliantine and pipe-smoke. They had even sent his pipes back. Or two of them. His favourite one had crashed with him. Bits of briarwood, bits of body exploding over Hamburg. A seven-hundred-and-forty-strong bomber raid. Thirty planes had never returned, fifty others damaged, over two hundred young and plucky aircrew lost in one short night.

'Wakey-wakey!'

That nurse again. Why did she talk as if the place were Butlins? Always did in hospitals. Or treated you as pre-school.

'Come on, Mrs Conyers. Let's get you sitting up, then.'

Hot heavy arm around her shoulders, freckled face looming close to hers. Bea tried to struggle up, then fell back again, supported by the arm. She hadn't wanted drugs. They only made you fuddled, turning childbirth into nightmare.

'Your daughter's here.'

Bea nodded. She hadn't felt a thing. Yet her baby was a big one. Eight pounds seven ounces; eyes screwed up in fury, fuzz of Titian hair. They would lay her in her arms soon. Red face, red hair, white shawl. And she'd cry again because she wanted Edward in her arms, not a wailing infant.

'Let's comb your hair then, shall we? Make you look pretty for your visitor.'

'I'm not a child.' Her voice surprised her, loud and petulant. She was suddenly awake, squinting against the cruel beam of sunlight lasering from the window. The nurse was too close, breath fierce with peppermints. Bea seized the comb herself, tried to make her hands work.

'What . . . What time is it?'

'Half past three, my dear. High time you woke up.'

'You mean the . . . the *afternoon*?'

'Yes. Tea time. They've brought your tray already. Chocolate cake.'

Bea could see a metal teapot glinting in the light, a face distorted in it. She had lost another half-a-day then, as well as yesterday. The day had dawned for other people, dragged or busied, wept or shone, but she had had no part in it.

'You were awake this morning. We even got you up. Don't you remember?'

Bea didn't answer. Infants and idiots forgot things. You were always both in hospital.

The nurse was sponging her face. Nanny O'Riley. She'd had a nanny once, but not an Irish one. She remembered her as dark, casting shadows everywhere she went. Nurse O'Riley was ginger. She could see tiny auburn hairs glinting on her arms, even on her thumbs.

'Shall I fetch your daughter now?'

Bea nodded. It wasn't just a day she had lost, but a thousand thousand, while the daughter grew from a bundle in a shawl to a clever distant stranger, passing exams, speaking foreign languages, marrying a man who didn't believe in God or . . .

'Mummy darling.'

The lips barely grazed her cheek. Morna always kissed so warily. Hadn't as a child. When she had picked her up from infant school, there had been long wet eager smacking kisses, both arms flung around her neck.

'How you feeling?'

'Not too bad, dear.'

'I brought you some freesias.'

'Lovely.' Their scent was sickly like the gas. Her friends had sent more flowers. Fragile tiger lilies which looked pale beneath their speckles, blood-coloured roses with more thorn on them than bloom.

'And grapes.'

'You're spoiling me.' The grapes were black and plump and slightly mottled as if someone had tried to shine them up, but left smears on them instead. She couldn't eat. The numbness was throbbing into pain now. Pain everywhere, even in her throat, scratchy when she swallowed. They must have put some tube down.

'Bring that chair up, darling.' The scrape of wood on lino

etched an extra line of pain across her head. She picked up the freesias, cradled them in her arms. They were damp at the bottom like a baby. 'And why don't you have my tea? I don't want it.'

'Aren't you meant to drink?'

'I'll have a glass of orange. I prefer it.'

The chair yelped back again. Clink of jug against glass. Good girl, Morna – pouring orange, bringing flowers, looking after house and dog.

'How's Joy?'

'She rolled in something unspeakable last night and this morning she refused to eat her veal, but apart from that . . .'

Bea put her glass down. It hurt to laugh, but they had to make a joke of Joy. She knew Morna didn't like her much. She and Neil had never had a dog.

'It's best if you do a rota. Veal one day, then beef or chicken the next. She gets bored, you see, if you don't vary it a bit.' She had left all the different dishes in the freezer, clearly marked with dates. Simpler than opening a tin. You couldn't trust those tins. They were dog themselves, so Mrs Miller said.

'Are you managing to walk her?'

'Yes, of course. We've been twice today already. To the woods.'

Her daughter's hair looked different – still longish at the back, but layered around her face. Pretty. Her father's hair. The same rich auburn colour. Not ginger like that nurse's, a different class entirely. Edward would have been grey now, had he lived. Morna's first grey hairs had appeared about six months ago, though they seemed to have vanished for the moment. She must have pulled them out or been persuaded at the hairdresser's into one of those colour rinses which gave you cancer. She seemed a trifle subdued, not her usual chatty self. Was she simply being thoughtful, trying not to tire her, or sickening for something?

'Are you eating properly, Morna? I left plenty in the larder.'

'I know. Provisions for a year of siege.'

'Have that chocolate cake, darling. It might taste better than it looks.'

'No, really, I had a late lunch. Have you seen the doctor yet?'

'Not since the op. He's coming later on, I think.' Embarrassing to be inspected by a man there. Huge gloved hand thrusting up inside you; the booming public way he spoke about highly private things. *'Nothing to worry about, my dear. The bladder wall's beginning to sag down a bit into your vagina, so we're going to tighten you up . . .'*

Bea blinked the surgeon away, fixed her attention on her daughter. Morna was running through the phone-calls – Vera, Norah, Agnes, Father Clarke. A Mass for her recovery, a retreat in late July. Bea tried to think of God, but like the doctor, He had kept His distance since the operation. The ornate and gilded photo frame where she kept Him bright and polished in her mind was strangely blank – the first time in half a century. She had always seen God clearly – not an old man with a beard or a Middle Eastern gentleman with grubby robe and sandals, but a tall clean-shaven Englishman, some-one like her husband's Air Vice-Marshal, whom she had only met the once, but who had impressed her with his spruce good looks, his steel-and-velvet voice. He'd had a ten-column-inch obituary when he died, just two years after Edward. Bea clutched the end of the counterpane. God couldn't die, could He? Or only for clever wilful daughters. Not for her.

'What d'you think, then, Mummy?'

Bea wiped clammy palms on the sheet. 'Wh . . . What about?'

'The retreat of course. D'you fancy the idea?'

'When exactly is it? And what sort of retreat – a silent one or . . .?'

'Wake up, Mum! I've just been telling you about it. Didn't you hear?'

'I'm s . . . sorry, Morna. It's difficult to concentrate.'

'It's just a week – starting on 22nd July. And mainly silent, but with talks and things as well. Well, what's the verdict? Shall I book you in?'

Bea hesitated. You needed legs to go places and hers were still two humps beneath the blanket, with neither bone nor muscle. It was an effort to keep sitting up at all, keep smiling. Her lips ached along with all the rest.

Morna inched her chair up. '*I*'ll come with you, if you like. Father Clarke seemed to think I'd quite enjoy it.'

Was her daughter mocking her? Morna classed Father Clarke with Joy – both her mother's creatures who had to be treated with respect, fed and cossetted, but never actively sought out. Morna hadn't been to Mass (or priest) for years, but perhaps she was missing them, groping back to some meaning in her life.

'Well, if you'd *like* to go, darling . . .'

'Would *you*, though, Mummy?'

Bea took a sip of orange, glanced around the small quiet uncluttered private room. Her son-in-law paid her BUPA subscription, even now, half a world away. She tried to like Neil for it, failed. At least she was grateful, though. Norah Miller had been in a public ward, seen it all – women of all colours without teeth or shame or even please and thank you. Bea sank back on the pile of clean white pillows, laundered by someone else, closed her eyes. All she really wanted was a week of total rest. She had planned to take her convalescence at home, with Morna acting nurse. But was that fair on Morna? Perhaps her daughter would prefer a retreat to another week in Oxshott, another round of chores. At least there'd be some outside company, someone more stimulating than a doddery mother and her dog.

She tried to scan her daughter's face for boredom or

23

resentment. Neither showed. They didn't reveal their feelings, either of them. Probably safer not to. Yet if . . . if anything should happen to her, an accident or . . ., then so many things would be left unsaid. There were new lines around her daughter's eyes, eyes not the clear no-nonsense blue her own were, but a soft smoky colour, neither grey nor blue but somewhere in between. That fine fair skin didn't wear too well – perfect at eighteen but complaining at forty. She felt angry with the lines, longed to lean across and wipe them off her daughter's face as she had mopped up her tears, scrubbed at sticky cheeks. You couldn't do that any more. Daughters grew up, kept their distance. The older your child became, the nearer you were yourself to . . . to . . . Bea broke off a grape, forced it down with the fear, reached out for Morna's hand. 'I'll do what *you* want, darling.'

'Don't be silly. It makes no difference to me.'

Bea was silent. Ludicrous to want to cry because a daughter sounded sharp. 'Hail Mary,' she murmured under her breath. Prayer was always calming. At least it would stop her snivelling, embarrassing her daughter. She was only weeping because of the anaesthetic. The nurse had warned of that. 'Full of grace . . .' Morna was full of grace, pretty still, young, for heaven's sake, might even remarry. A decent man this time, with principles, faith in something greater than himself. Except remarriage was forbidden by the Church. Perhaps God would understand, though, make an exception in her daughter's case, grant one of those complicated annulments. She glanced at the photo frame again. Still empty. 'The Lord is with thee.' Was He? How could you ask Him favours if He wasn't there?

She crammed in three more grapes, heard the pips crunching in her head, gripped her daughter's hand. 'Let's go, please – both of us.'

3

Morna pushed open the heavy wooden door, held it for her mother. The garden scents of new-mown grass and lime trees gave way to convent smells – polish, incense, piety, cabbage cooked to punishment. A tall bony woman in a navy skirt and blouse with a plain metal cross around her neck was standing behind the desk.

'Good afternoon. Nice to meet you both. I'm Mother Michael.'

Morna forced a smile. There had been a Mother Mary Michael at her school. Chief of persecutors. This nun wore semi-mufti, her short blue veil revealing a fringe of grizzled hair, her skirt reaching only to her calves. Yet she had the earlier Mother Michael's piercing gaze – one which could bore through brick, excuses, lies.

'Names, please.'

'Mrs Conyers and Mrs Gordon.'

Morna watched her scan the list, tick their names off. She hoped nobody would ask about *Mr* Gordon. Should she have said 'Miss'? Ms was impossible – suggested permissiveness and feminism – both strictly banned in convents. Names had always been a problem. Her Reverend Mother had refused to call her Morna because it was not a saint's name and therefore unsuitable for any Catholic girl.

'Have you got a second name, my child?'

'No, Reverend Mother.'

A frown. 'What about your confirmation name? You *are* confirmed, I hope?'

'Yes, Reverend Mother.'

'Well, what name did you take?'

'Joachim, Reverend Mother.'

Joachim was the Blessed Virgin's father, and since she had no father of her own, it had seemed logical at the time, as well as original. Most of her classmates chose Thérèse after the Little Flower, who spent a lifetime doing Little Things, or Francis because he was the patron saint of animals and they were all dog- and pony-mad.

The frown deepened. 'We can hardly call you Joachim. How about Anne – Joachim's wife and the mother of Our Blessed Lady? That's simple, pretty and far more suitable than a pagan name like Morna.'

'But we've got three Annes in our class already, Reverend Mother.'

'Doesn't matter. There are five Marys in the fourth form and no one muddles *them*.'

It was she herself who had been muddled. She was often slow in answering to Anne. It seemed disloyal to her father who had chosen Morna himself and who was like another sort of God in that she had never seen him because he lived in heaven. She wore his photo in a locket round her neck, though only in the holidays. Jewellery was forbidden in the convent, save for the small gold crucifix she had received at her First Communion. She felt uneasy when she took it off at the end of term, replaced the lean and naked Christ with a braided medalled squadron-leader. She tried to compromise and wear them both at once – two cold dead father-gods swinging round her neck.

'I've put you on the ground floor, Mrs Conyers. I know you haven't been well. You're further up, Mrs Gordon. Number sixty-three. Sister Ruth will show you to your rooms.'

26

Sister Ruth was older, wore the full old-fashioned habit. Morna turned to follow her, was suddenly a child again, dwarfed by the wide winged wimple, the yards of flowing robe. She could almost feel the blue school hat, bought big as an economy, sitting on her eyebrows, blinkering her view as she trotted to keep up. 'Give me a child before he is seven,' the Jesuits always said. The nuns had got hold of her at seven and three-quarters, swiftly made up for lost time. She had swapped her mother for Reverend Mother, said goodbye to Bea in a vast and echoing London terminus, trains rattling through her tears, farewells cut short as cold fingers grabbed her wrist, steered her towards the train.

'Only babies cry, Morna.' A stiff white handkerchief which smelt of church was jabbed into her eyes. 'Pull yourself together.'

Mother Mary Michael was the first nun she had seen. She had sat beside her in the carriage, folds of musty black flapping against her bare and shaking knees. Mother Michael didn't have knees herself, nor lap nor breasts nor arms. Even her eyes were dead and tombed in spectacles. She had cried again in bed that night, stifled her tears in the pillow. Crying was forbidden. She hardly slept that week at all, heard strange frightening noises from the grounds, flutterings and rustlings, a screech of a bird in pain. Her mother had gone forever, swallowed up at Charing Cross – a blur through the steamed-up window of the train, a tiny speck dwindling into nothing.

It was pitch dark when the bell rang in the morning. A different nun was standing at the foot of the bed, black on black, chanting something she couldn't understand. She discovered later it was a prayer in Latin – a prayer for rising in a dead language. She soon learnt to make the right response in matching Latin, rise instantly and modestly from sleep, holding her nightie down with one hand so that it wouldn't show her legs and crossing herself with the other, to scare the Devil in case he had been lingering by her bed.

'Right, Mrs Conyers, this is your room. I'm afraid I can't put you near your mother, Mrs Gordon. These ground-floor rooms are reserved for nuns and invalids. But if you'd like to follow me . . .'

'No!' Morna almost shouted. She must cling on to her mother, refuse to let go her hand at Charing Cross. She took a step inside the room. 'Shall I . . . er . . . help you with your unpacking, Mummy, before I . . .?'

'No, dear. You go up. I can manage.'

Never contradict a nun, was what her mother meant, never keep one waiting. Morna slowly backed away, tagged after Sister Ruth. A younger version of the nun was standing over her desk, blocking out the light while she struggled with her first letter home, tears splashing on the paper.

'Darling Mummy, it is very nice here . . .'

The lie didn't matter, because her mother would never read it. She hadn't got a mother any more. God was mother and father now, Mother Michael had told her. But God was like the nuns – didn't have a lap and wasn't allowed to laugh and could see you through the ceiling. She was ten before she stopped resenting Him.

Morna walked faster, caught up with Sister Ruth. 'It's . . . er . . . a lovely day,' she said. She had to break the silence, prove she wasn't seven still.

'Yes, beautiful.' The nun sounded as if she begrudged the weather, would have regarded hail and thunder as more suited to man's sinfulness. Nothing else was said until they reached the top floor.

'That's it,' said Sister Ruth, stopping at the end room. 'The bathroom's down those stairs there. No smoking in your room, please, and make sure you switch all lights off at night.' She glided off back along the passage.

Morna stared at the strip of room, almost like a cell – bare white walls, low confining ceiling. The bed was two-foot-six, the mattress thin. Everything was thin – walls, blankets, curtains, skinny scrap of rug stranded on the khaki squiggled lino. The 1930s wardrobe didn't match the fifties chest of drawers, except that both were battered. The only ornament was a living-colour crucifix positioned above the bed. Neil had always abhorred what he called the mascot of the Catholic Church – a naked convicted criminal hanging on a gibbet. She turned her back to it, came face to face with Our Lady's disapproving eye staring directly into hers. She was caught between the Madonna and her Son – one expiring, one rebuking.

She removed her jacket, stared down at her scarlet-poppied skirt. There was no mirror in the room, but she knew already she was wrongly dressed. Her make-up was too obvious, her hair a slightly deeper shade of auburn than the one she had been born with. The three or four retreatants she had glimpsed so far were all females of uncertain age in Crimplene frocks and home-knit cardigans, pious souls who accepted the face and hair which God had handed out to them without presuming to make improvements. Morna kicked off her high-heeled shoes, opened her case – Neil's case – which looked too fancy with its elaborate zips and straps. Thank God she had packed sandals and a fairly basic navy skirt. Blue to match the Virgin on the wall. She changed into the skirt, tugged it well below her knees. Even their games shorts (which the nuns had called divided skirts) had been worn below the knee at school.

Dearest Mummy,
Today we had to kneel in rows on the floor and Sister Emelda went up and down the rows measuring our shorts with a metal ruler. If the hems didn't touch the floor, she rapped our knees with the ruler and we had to miss tea and let them down. I missed tea. It's swiss roll on Saturdays. I hope you are well.
Love, Morna.

She remembered that swiss roll – the only cake they had all week and cut so thin it was probably also measured out with Sister Mary Emelda's metal ruler. Morna grinned. This wasn't school, for heaven's sake. She had left all that behind more than twenty years ago. It was a holiday, a rest for Bea, a breath of country air. She walked to the window to admire the view, looked out on a stretch of slated roof, a length of rusty guttering. Why had they stuck her right up here, three floors from her mother? Had Father Clarke leaked her loss of faith, her lack of lawful wedded husband, so that they feared her as a contaminant?

Ridiculous. She was getting paranoid. Even simple harmless things like her bag of salted peanuts, her *Woman's Journal*, now seemed to scream aloud. Magazines and snacks would have been confiscated at school as evidence of worldliness and greed. Sister Ruth had probably tiptoed back again and was hovering just outside, hand outstretched waiting for the nuts. Morna flung open the door, came face to face with a jolly red-faced woman in her sixties.

'Hi, there! I was just about to come and say hallo. We're the only two who've arrived yet on this floor. The name's Joan.'

'H . . . Hallo. I'm Morna.' She didn't add 'Come in.' The woman had a cross around her neck.

'Nice rooms, aren't they? The last retreat I went to we had to sleep in dormitories. I've even got a wash-basin.'

'Congratulations.'

'Are you coming down to supper?'

Morna frowned. 'Supper? *Now*? It can't be much past five.'

'It's ten to six. Six o'clock sharp they said we eat, so we've time for the first talk afterwards and Holy Mass.'

Holy Mass was a giveaway, a nun's phrase, definitely. Morna followed Joan down the stairs, winced as a gong vibrated through the hall.

'That's the supper bell. Shall we sit together?'

'I'll just go and fetch my mother. Her room's a little further on.'

'Oh, you're with your mother, are you? Nice.'

Morna didn't answer. She could think of better ways of spending the last week of July. She and Neil had always flown to the sun and then avoided it in their air-conditioned hotel rooms. Neil had seemed to weigh more in the summer – heaving on top of her in strange foreign beds in Antibes or Marbella or Capri, their bodies stuck together with sweat. Mustn't think of sex, not here. Anyway, why did she keep harping back to Neil? She made sure to boot him out before she entered Bea's room, which was much larger than her own and looked out to lawn and flowers. Reward not just for Bea's nine days in hospital, but for her seventy years of faith.

'It seems a really friendly place, dear. I've just been having a chat with Reverend Mother and she says I can have tea in bed most mornings.'

'Lucky you! We'd better hurry or we'll miss our other tea. I refuse to call it dinner when it's only five fifty-nine.'

It wasn't dinner either, or not by Morna's standards. There was one sausage roll apiece (cold), served with a brown bog of baked beans, once hot but now congealing. The bread was thin-sliced and barely buttered. The tea was strong and came in a huge metal teapot with twin handles, which was passed from table to table, scalding into the thick white china cups.

Morna glanced around the rows of faces, all female save for three token men, one with a CND badge and open sandals, one a monk complete with rope and tonsure, and one near octogenarian.

Joan had saved her a place. She *was* a nun – Sister Emmanuel – but she had changed over to her ordinary Christian name in the progressive 1970s. Morna watched

31

with fascination as she shovelled in baked beans, mopped ketchup from her chin. She had never seen a nun eat. The nuns at school had had their living quarters in the basement, out of sight for meals and sleep. She had assumed as a child that their only daily sustenance was the tiny wafer of bread they received from the priest each morning. Later, when she was older and what the nuns described as impudent, one of the younger sisters confided that she had become a vegetarian.

'You can't be,' Morna retorted. 'Not if you go to Communion. That's Christ's flesh and blood.'

Six months later, she was doubting it. The so-called Real Presence became increasingly unreal for her, unleashed a flood of doubts which she was unwise enough to confide to Mother Michael.

'Life is nothing without your faith, and you're throwing it away, Anne.'

'I'm not, Mother. I *want* to believe. It's just that . . .'

'The sin of pride. Thinking we know best. Before God we are fools. Fools and worms. And yet you dare to question Him.'

'I only want to know if . . .'

'You shouldn't want. You must aim to crush your wants, bend your will to His.'

'Yes, but . . .'

'No buts. "But" is the Devil's word. I'm sorry to say it, Anne, but you are getting far too friendly with the Devil. Once you give him the smallest crack to put a claw in, he's got you hard and fast, fouling up your mind and then your body.'

She had seen a programme once about bacteria – microbes swarming on cheese, or crawling into every pore. Devils were as prolific and as dangerous – festering in your body, making dirty footmarks on your soul. She stopped writing home. She was infected and contagious. Bea might open the

32

envelope and find demons pouring out. Her mother had never doubted. God was as real for her as her kitchen stove or bed.

Morna smiled across at her now. Bea looked tired but cheerful, was talking to the only under-twenty in the room – a shy doe-like girl who stared down at her plate, mumbled yes and no. At least the silence hadn't started yet. Modern retreats broke you in more gently. The first evening was for relaxing, introductions. They had all swapped the briefest of biographies – name and job, address. Most of the jobs were worthy ones – school teachers and social workers, even a JP; spinsters looking after mothers, a scattering of nuns; people with a goal in life, a God. Was that why she felt so alien, the only one without a real purpose? Nonsense. She had work herself, a daughter, a lovely home. She picked up her spoon, scraped off the tobacco shreds of nutmeg grated too large atop her pink blancmange. It looked like a pink and fleshy breast, a large one, C-cup, wobbling in her dish. The Devil was especially fond of breasts, not that the nuns had ever used the word. Chest was safer.

'Are you a charismatic?' the woman opposite was asking – a housewife with six children who still found time to help with the handicapped.

'Er . . . no,' Morna said. Charismatic sounded like a disease. She stuffed her mouth with blancmange to fend off any further questions, especially religious ones. When did you make your last confession, how many times did . . .?

'More pudding?' Joan was asking. That was safer. She nodded, held out her dish while Joan dolloped in a second breast. She ate it fast, could see the demons swarming on her spoon. She was still hungry. There were no extras, no cheese and biscuits, no crusty rolls, nothing to drink save lukewarm water in the sort of dwarf-sized plastic tumblers which came free with Mobiloil. At translators' conferences you downed four-course meals with sherry first and brandy afterwards and decent intervals between the Camembert and Cognac and the first serious talk. Here, you were harried from refectory to lecture room, swapped one hard chair for another with barely time to wash your hands. At least the priest looked reasonable, a Father Colin Fenton – a tall rugged man, his face softened by wisps of silver hair. He stepped up to the podium, waited for silence, which was near-instant and respectful.

' "I will remove the heart of stone within you",' he recited. ' "And give you a heart of flesh instead." '

Ezekiel. Morna recognized the verse, felt a sudden soaring of her spirits. Perhaps she had been right to come. She could forget the pettiness, the bad food, stodgy company, if she were offered something else. Her heart had been stone too long. She had hardened it since Neil left, tried to block out all emotion, not to feel at all. She fixed her whole attention on the priest.

'We have seen enormous material progress in our lives. Now we need to catch up on the spiritual side, go on a voyage of spiritual discovery . . .'

She liked the phrase. It suggested new horizons, a new start. Neil had ensured the material progress; it was up to her to initiate the spiritual. It needn't be a voyage to God – and certainly not the nuns' God. There must be other routes which bypassed Him.

'We have been living in the dark,' the priest continued. 'The light is there, a light which can illuminate the world for us, if we will only crawl out of our gloom and hibernation.'

Morna closed her eyes to concentrate, felt the first few watts of weak new light surprising on her lids.

4

Three days later, they were back to demons. Morna fidgeted in her seat as a short fierce swarthy Irish priest warned about the 'Evil One' who still roamed the modern world. They no longer called him 'Devil', but the end product was the same – shame and guilt.

'Beware of a diet of dessert,' Canon O'Connor urged. 'A bland, hollow, pretty-pretty religion which pretends there is no sin, allows us to indulge ourselves, makes us spiritually flabby.'

Morna pressed her hands against her stomach. The double helping of orange jelly was still squelching there, blob of synthetic cream quivering on the top, reward for the first course of greasy mutton stew. She could still taste the mutton, felt clogged with it as if the fat had hardened and formed a white shiny scum across her body. She glanced at her watch. Only ten to three. The afternoons always seemed to slouch. It wasn't just the silence. That was oppressive, yes, but by no means total – broken up with lectures and discussion groups and with the services themselves. It was the fact that the silence was for God, every talk and prayer and sentiment for God, which made her feel so alien, like being tone-deaf at a concert, or paraplegic at the Olympic Games. Religion was like sex in that respect. If you were orgasmic, a believer, then the time flashed by because you were totally involved. If not, you found yourself staring at the ceiling or the altar, making Christmas lists or playing mental chess, whilst the ecstatic rest had eyes and ears only for the Beloved.

The evening Masses were the worst, interminable because everyone but her joined in, swelling out the standard service with personal petitions, individual confessions of sin. The sins were all venial, pathetically so, in fact. She found herself almost hoping for a real offence, a full-blooded theft or murder, or at least something graver than the endless petty recital of white lies, lost tempers, unkind thoughts. She even doubted those. Everyone was so unwaveringly good-natured, it grated on her nerves. Even in the silence, they managed to pour out the full-cream milk of human kindness, swapping smiles, squeezing hands, offering seats or hymn-books, exuding so much earnest feeling it made her squirm. They were all one happy cosy family – God's family – sisters and brothers in Christ with no hint of anything as crude or rude as sibling rivalry or incest.

She crossed her legs, uncrossed them, fiddled with her hair. Even trivial things were beginning to annoy her – the shapeless woman in front who wore two clashing shades of mauve and kept nodding her head at everything the priest said, Sister Joan's stupid tickly cough. She could accuse herself of sins enough – total lack of charity and, if not murder, murderous thoughts. She tried to concentrate. The Canon was quoting statistics now, to prove the decline in Christianity.

'The Devil is still evangelizing the world. Only ten per cent in Belgium and fourteen per cent in France still follow their religious duties . . .'

France. Morna wondered how her daughter was, whether *Madame* was dragging her off to church. Had she deprived her only child by not including a religion along with all the other goodies – the private school, Seiko watch, ten-speed racing bike? Chris felt very far away, further than Les Lecques, almost as far as Neil in California. She would be eighteen next birthday, official adulthood – seemed far too young for it; tall, but undeveloped still, like a lanky plant which needed fertilizer. Yet she would leave next year for university; home only in vacations (or bits and pieces of them) until she married, disappeared for ever. Morna hated the thought of that. Yet she couldn't cling, couldn't even say 'I love you, darling' without her daughter squirming away embarrassed. Chris could be cool at times – a coolness which hid blame, perhaps. 'Would my father have left a different sort of woman?'

Morna didn't care to answer that, sometimes also wondered if Neil would have left a son. He had always wanted a boy, prematurely christened his daughter Christopher, shortened it to Chris when she was still two months off full-term. She had hardly bothered with a name herself. The baby wasn't real. She was too young to have a baby, didn't want one yet. She blamed Neil's constant itch, transferred some of the resentment from his bulge to her own. When it turned out female, Neil refused to change the name. He hated being wrong. He had already lost a tenner on a wager with his friends – something to do with virility again. Men produced men.

'All right,' he had said, picking up the sallow screaming scrap. 'Christine.'

'Oh, no.'

'Well, Christabel. That's nice.'

'No, dear.' It was Bea this time who shook her head. Christabel was fancy and therefore vulgar; too close to what Bea called plumbers' children's names – Jason and Samantha. Even Morna was a little too unusual for her taste, and only Edward's death had won him his own way. Something plain and dignified like Jane, she urged. Morna felt too tired to argue. The labour had been long and painful and she was always tense when her husband and her mother were thrown together.

37

'Decided on a name yet?' asked the nurse, who appeared at dawn with the protesting baby and a tepid cup of tea.

'Yes,' said Morna. 'Christine Jane.'

'Pretty,' said the nurse, passing over the wailing ugly child.

'Hi, Chris!' said her father, when he blazoned in that evening scattering dolls, rattles, chocolates, and brandishing a sheath of flowers so tall they had to be cut down before they would fit any of the standard hospital vases. And Chris she remained.

Neil had a son now, not Christopher, but Dean. Four and a half and beautiful.

Morna jumped as the woman beside her pushed her chair back. The lecture had finished and she was still in the maternity ward. She tried to look alert, as if she had absorbed every word and was now spiritually nourished. There was another talk straight afterwards, so no chatting was allowed, but people were clearing throats and stretching legs, smiles switched on again.

'How's your mother?' someone whispered to her.

'Not too bright today,' Morna whispered back. It felt ludicrous conversing *sotto voce* as if they were conspirators. The setting was all wrong for that cloak-and-dagger stuff – a chintzy room with rose-sprigged wallpaper, bright sun streaming in.

'She's resting at the moment. I think she overdid it yesterday, so I persuaded her to spend the day in bed.'

'Very wise. Let her know we're praying for her, won't you?'

Morna nodded, tried to match the golden-syrup smile. She felt exposed without her mother. Bea was a buffer, a guarantee of her own religious pedigree, and even with Bea in bed, she couldn't miss the talks. Her mother had requested a complete résumé of the day's proceedings.

Father John was next. He was what was styled progressive,

but she knew already it would be only the outward wrappings that were different. It depressed her really, the way she was hearing the same old arguments which had been trotted out at school. Twenty years had passed, years of so-called progress, yet everything the same. Women fawning on their priests, arguing over petty points of ritual when the huge central questions were still shouting out for total reappraisal. She glanced up and down the rows of eager faces, simple children settling back on their hard school chairs to wait for Teacher – or still sitting on their Father's knee, open-mouthed and credulous, making sense of the senseless, adding up the infinite. Or maybe *she* was wrong? Not only arrogant, uncharitable, but still stuck in religious adolescence, searching for a Meaning to Life when most of her acquaintances left that to Monty Python or Woody Allen. Neil had tried to teach her that only cranks or bores brought God to the dinner table. There were more important things – whether unit trusts were superior to equities, or German Brie to French. Even her own woman friends regarded religion as irrelevant. Some had beliefs, even passionate beliefs, but more in feminism or unilateralism than in any Higher Being. Yet, at university everyone had agonized about meaning and morality, the purpose of life, the fact of death. Why should such questions have any less urgency when they were all now twenty years closer to that death?

Father John strode in. He had a long untidy beard, a denim jacket. She knew the type. He believed in a God-in-jeans who had failed his CSEs and called him Johnny – but he still believed. She was the only one whose heaven was empty. The talk was on love – *Agape* rather than *Eros*, though she guessed he would use words loosely, as the other speakers had done. As a translator, she was pained by their mishandling of the language, the way they shelled out words like pretty-coloured pills without realizing their more serious side-effects.

'Love is metaphysical gravity,' Father John began.

Morna winced at the lax analogy which followed, made with no respect for either physics or metaphysics. In Johnny's world, both love and gravity held things together or moved one object or person towards another.

She raised her hand. The priest had said he welcomed interruptions. 'I don't think that's quite exact,' she said. 'Surely gravity is a law – something which *must* happen and always does. Gravity can't fade or die or turn to its opposite, as love can.'

The priest laughed, as if to prove how lightweight her objection. 'Love is a law as well,' he insisted, beaming still. 'A universal law – Christ's law. Listen, my friend, let me try and . . .'

Morna didn't listen, banged back in her seat. She *wasn't* Johnny's friend. That, too, was sloppy language. Friend signified relationship, prior knowledge, and she had never set eyes on this priest before, never would again, if she were lucky. She wasn't friend to any of these worthy pious people who only needed God because they were too plain or plain simplistic to find other satisfactions. She let the talk drone on, hardly listening, slipped out before the questions at the end. At least she had an alibi. They would all assume she was checking on her mother. She trudged along the passage, stopped at what was called the bookshop. God-shop was more accurate. The only books on sale were holy ones – books on the sacraments, the Gospels, Christian marriage, death; 'God's Creatures' greetings cards in excruciating taste. She picked up a card with a cutesy bunny on it, sitting on its haunches with its front paws cocked to heaven. 'I tried God and He works,' the rabbit was saying, with the same simpering smile she had seen all week. She slotted it back, caught her elbow on the stand as she stalked away, watched in horror as a shower of pious puppies and crusading chimpanzees cascaded to the floor. 'Damn!' she said, falling on her knees to pick them up. 'Damn, damn, damn, damn, damn . . .'

'May I help?'

Morna started, glanced up at the tall lean man standing over her. God! Not a priest! Not with her swearing, crawling on hands and knees around the floor. He was one of the semi-progressive types who left off their dog-collars but still dressed all in black, and one who believed in priestly poverty judging by his balding corduroys. His shirt was deeper black, open at the neck, revealing dark tangled chest hair. The hair on the head was grey, surprisingly, since the face beneath it was younger than her own. She scrambled to her feet. Any priest under forty with even reasonably good looks was rare at Hilden Cross.

'I'm sorry,' she said. Extraordinary how priests made you guilty – instantly, invariably. 'I'll say three Our Fathers, shall I?' She had meant it as a joke, but it came out petulant. The priest said nothing, was on his knees as well now, helping her retrieve the cards.

She pounced on a poodle with a tartan lead saying 'All roads lead to God', suddenly started to laugh. He didn't join in. She could feel new spasms of laughter hurting in her chest, threatening to burst out; fought to get control. She was behaving like the worst of her daughter's friends – scatty adolescents who got the giggles in class or even school assembly. It must be a reaction to all those hours and hours of silence, sitting still, forcing down heretical thoughts, playing the role of devout retreatant. She had blown it now, though. The priest was looking pained, trying to cover his embarrassment by sorting through the fauna.

She glanced past his shoulder at a leggy giraffe – 'I'm sticking my neck out for God' – struggled to suppress another squall of laughter, tried to find her voice again, keep it steady, serious.

' . . . I assume you're one of the sp . . . speakers?'

He nodded.

'What's your s . . . subject?'

'Miracles.'

He was obviously not as progressive as he looked. You could never tell these days. Father Fenton had been the most genuinely revolutionary and he had worn both dog collar and cassock.

The priest stood up, brushing down his trousers. 'Or let's say the miraculous.'

Morna doubted if it would make a lot of difference. Simple faith required again, seeing God's finger in what Neil and Co. could explain by natural means.

'Do we get a demonstration – maybe water into wine? That would cheer up supper.' Facetious again. Her mother would be shocked. She tried to make amends, play the pious Catholic daughter rôle.

'Look, I'm sorry. Let me introduce myself. I'm one of the retreatants – Morna Gordon.'

He smiled for the first time, shook her outstretched hand. 'You must be from over the border with two Highland names like that.'

'No, I'm an out-and-out Sassenach.'

'Really?'

'Mm. My maiden name was Conyers.'

'So your husband's the Scot, then?'

'No – well, maybe way way back, but his family have lived in south-east London as far as anyone remembers.' She tried to dodge away from Neil. Divorce was still a red rag to Catholic priests. 'The Morna bit was chosen by my thoroughly southern English father. He liked it because it means beloved.'

The priest shook his head. 'No, I don't think that's quite right.

'Morna,' he repeated slowly, as if he were weighing up the name. 'The Gaelic *mùirn* means joy or cheerfulness, or natural affection or regard. I presume Morna must be a sort of anglicized post-medieval invention from the corresponding adjective *mùirneach*, or maybe from one of the female diminutive forms like . . .'

Morna stared at him, annoyed as well as fascinated. Most people said 'What?' when they heard the name and then went on to call her Lorna. Yet what right had he to demote her, turn her father's choice of name into that of her mother's dog? She had been beloved for forty years – trust a priest to spoil that.

'Hold on! My father found it in a book of Christian names – quite a reputable one – something like *The Oxford Book of* . . .'

'They're often very lax, those books. It was a brave try, I suppose, but . . .' He shrugged. 'I assume they were trying to imply that *muirne* is a past participle. But it's not, you see. It's not even a correct form. The accent on *mùirn* is important because . . .'

She was impressed by his scholarship – few priests at Hilden Cross ventured far beyond their own narrow field of theology and morals – yet she also felt an irrational resentment that he was doing her father down. She had always been sensitive about the stranger in the locket, ever since her schooldays – the only one in her class without a father, though it had seemed worse at times not to have a pony. The two were linked. Fathers bought you ponies and party frocks, unless they were unfeeling enough to fall out of the sky before they had ever seen you. Mothers on their own couldn't afford ponies, only school fees. She had wondered as a child if her father had ridden horses as well as piloted planes. Planes and death and party frocks had all been mixed up with something called The War, which meant that sweets were scarce and people made you dresses out of musty velvet curtains because they couldn't get new material.

The priest was still expatiating. Her name appeared to

have brought him to life. He was gesturing with both hands, brow creased in concentration as he explained the complexities of Gaelic grammar. She wished she could contribute something to the conversation.

'What's *your* name?' she asked at last, and lamely.

'David Anthony.'

Not a lot she could do to demolish that. 'With a hyphen?' she inquired.

'I beg your pardon?'

'I mean is Anthony your second first name?'

'No, surname. David Francis Anthony.'

Almost as correct as Anne. English, Christian and conventional. Morna felt vaguely disappointed. He looked foreign, even Jewish, a victim of the pogrom or the ghetto. It was something about his eyes – deep-set and suffering. She glanced up at him again. If you talked about flesh and bone, it was the bone you noticed, not the flesh – cheekbones prominent, lips thin, brow high and proud, eyes restless dark. She had expected an exotic name with fire in it, or pain.

'How come you know Gaelic?'

'I've been spending some time on a tiny Scottish island. They're all Gaelic-speakers there. And since I'd already learnt Old Irish – for my work – at least I started out knowing what sort of language Gaelic is, and how it's organized.'

'What *is* your work?' Morna asked. Most of the other lecturers had been run-of-the-mill parish priests or members of some teaching order who spent their days indoctrinating small boys.

'I'm working on the life of a seventh-century Celtic saint, St Abban.'

'Oh yes?' Morna had never heard of him, wondered if she should have done. This man seemed to be showing up her ignorance on several different fronts. 'I'm afraid he's new to me. I don't even know the name.'

'There were three or four St Abbans, actually, but there's a lot of confusion about them because one or two were very shadowy figures. The first one – Abban of Cell-Abbáin – died at the end of the fifth century and is said to have known St Patrick. The medieval hagiographers muddled him with St Abban of Mag-Arnaide who died a century later and posited just the *one* St Abban who was supposed to have lived three hundred years. Actually, there *were* some similarities. I mean both were members of the Irish royal family of Leinster and . . . Then there was a third Abban who lived in England – in fact, some books say he gave his name to Abingdon in Berkshire, but that's not true. The name means . . .'

'And he's yours?' Morna interrupted. She was getting confused herself now.

'No, no. He's *very* tenuous. I'm far luckier with mine. He was the latest of them all – didn't die till the 690s and is comparatively well documented. He was born in the south of Ireland but went off to the Hebrides and then to France. He eventually returned to Ireland, but only for a year or two. These Celtic saints were tremendous travellers, you know – and all before the days of Thomas Cook. He set out for the Scottish coast again in his potty little boat and sailed from island to island until he eventually decided that God had called him to found a monastery on the one we call St Abban's now, and there he stayed until the last six months of his life when he moved to a tiny rockstack and lived as a hermit cut off from everyone.'

David paused a moment, but only to return his pile of cards to the rack. Shy and almost taciturn at first, he was now warming to his theme. A true scholar, Morna suspected, with no time for small-talk, but who could elaborate for ever

45

on his work. She wished it were a subject she knew more about. She had never heard of St Abban's island either.

'Is the . . . er . . . island very remote?' she asked.

'Not so much remote as inaccessible. The coast's so treacherous, it's difficult to land there. That's why it's hardly known, except to a handful of archaeologists or crazy scholars like myself. Yet in St Abban's day, it was quite a famous monastery. Pilgrims came to visit it from as far away as northern Italy – or so the legends say.'

'And you're writing his Life? It sounds as if it'll run into several volumes!'

'I wish it would. Two hundred pages, if I'm lucky, and a lot of those sheer speculation. You can't really write the life of an early saint. One just doesn't have the evidence and what you do have is often very slanted. I suppose all I'm doing is trying to put together a jigsaw puzzle which has half its pieces missing and no picture on the box.'

'Did the saint write his own Life?'

'No, unfortunately. He was said to have written a few prayers and sermons and even verses, but not a single word's come down to us. The first biography, if you can call it that, is a ninth-century Life in Latin by one of Abban's successors, Abbot Dubhgall.'

'So why the Old Irish, then?'

'Well, a lot of the place names and proper names appear in Old Irish – or a sort of Latinized version of it. And it was Dubhgall's own first language, so I really need to know it to get into his mind – if you know what I mean.'

Morna nodded. That she did know.

'There seem to be some other names – Pictish or North-British – which can cause a few problems. In fact, there are problems all the way.' He smiled, turned the smile to frown, as if smiles required more effort. 'You see, the Life was copied several different times in later centuries, but with bits left out or new chunks written in, or corrections added in another hand or notes written in the margins which seem to refer to another saint entirely. You have to be a sort of Sherlock Holmes to see through the myths and propaganda. And then there's the confusion over spelling which . . . I'm sorry –' He broke off. 'I'm boring you.'

'Not at all. I'm fascinated. I'm a bit of a linguist myself, in actual fact.'

'Oh, really? What d'you do?'

'Nothing very grand. Sort of freelance translator, I suppose you'd call it. I translate anything and everything I'm given, though I must admit I haven't had a saint's Life yet, and nothing earlier than the nineteenth century.'

He laughed. 'Which languages?'

'French and German mostly – and a smattering of Italian.'

'You know the problems, then. What is it the Italians say – *traduttore traditore*?'

She nodded, felt a sudden bond with him – a man who spent his life with words, knew their slipperiness.

'I envy you the French,' he said. 'I'm struggling with about three hundred pages of very flowery French, written by a Breton professor who was working on the Irish saints who travelled to Brittany in the sixth and seventh centuries. He included quite a bit on Abban who spent some time in what's now St Brieuc. Sadly, he died a year ago, but I was lucky enough to get hold of all his papers. Le Goff, he's called, Yves Le Goff. You may have even heard of him. One of his works was translated into English a few years back – something on the sixth-century wine trade.'

'Er . . . no.'

'I only wish *this* one was translated. My own French is pretty rusty. And what makes it worse is that Le Goff employed his own strange brand of shorthand.'

'I'd be interested to see it. Does he use the . . .?'

There was a sudden tramp of feet along the passage.

Question time was over, the retreatants streaming out. The priest checked his watch.

'Gosh, I'd better get a move on. I've only just arrived and I haven't booked in yet – or whatever they call it here.'

Morna liked the 'gosh'. It made him boyish, vulnerable. She picked up one last forgotten rabbit, matched its grin. 'Well, see you later, then.'

'Yes . . . of course.'

She didn't see him later. She looked out for him at supper – white fish in a white sauce with a white soup to start with, which also tasted fishy, and then white ice cream to finish, semi-melted. The only new male face in the refectory was Father John's, attracting all the females with his metaphysical gravity. Father Anthony obviously preferred seclusion. He didn't appear for the talk on disarmament, nor at what was called the 'toilet break' which followed it and preceded evening Mass. Morna felt strangely disappointed. He had lifted her depression, if only for five minutes, made her feel alive, in touch with another mind. She found herself thinking back to what he had said, hearing his words instead of the ban-the-bomber's, recalling his hunched shoulders, restless hands, the way he spoke slowly and yet intently as if each word had been individually hacked out like iron ore. There was some kind of energy about him, some vehemence and force which he appeared to be struggling to rein in, trying to keep hidden behind that shy exterior. Even his hair, though grey, suggested a sort of rebellious vitality – not meek anaemic wisps like Father Fenton's, but a wildly curling outcrop which looked as if it might defy all normal combs. She wondered how long he would be staying. Most of the outside speakers came only for the day, or spent just one night at Hilden Cross before or after their talk, which meant he would be gone again by tomorrow afternoon. A pity. She would have welcomed some conversation which moved beyond Sacred Hearts or prayer groups.

She regretted really that they had come to the retreat at all. Bea would have been better off in bed at home, and she herself had been unprepared for the effect the place had had on her. It was as if she had been plunged back to those bitter teenage years when everyone around her was a living breathing Catholic, she the only non-believer, the only non-Communicant. She decided to skip Mass, couldn't face remaining in her pew again, an outcast and a sinner, whilst all the rest trooped up to receive the morsel of wheat-and-water they called their God.

She dodged into the garden, concealed herself amongst the trees. The weather was still perfect, the air heady with the scent of stocks, blue shadows lazing on an emerald lawn. The service had begun. She could hear the singing, wafting shrill-voiced through the open chapel windows. '*Oh Purest of Creatures.*' So what had changed? Same words, same tune, same ideal of spotless purity you could never emulate. They had reached the second verse now.

> *Deep night hath come down on*
> *this rough-spoken world*
> *and the banners of darkness*
> *are boldly unfurled.*

She could feel the darkness somewhere deep inside her. There had been total blackout when she left the church and it was threatening to engulf her once again. Easy to make jokes about the nuns, send them up for Neil's sake, but the pain had been real, the darkness terrifying. Neil had switched the lights back on, but she knew now those were only artificial lights – stylish spotlamps from Habitat and Heal's, cleverly angled to show off his possessions – and they, too, were extinguished when he left. If one had been exhorted all one's girlhood to live for God alone, then how could one have purpose if He vanished?

Even her current work seemed trivial – dribs and drabs thrown to her with no continuity, one-off jobs which meant little to her personally. She envied Father Anthony working on a saint he called his own, totally involved for years at a stretch. *And* with a God as well – the same God as St Abban's, still shining bright despite the thirteen centuries which divided them. Morna snapped off a branch, used it to scythe the tall tangled grasses which edged the copse, trailed back towards the house, the lawns now swallowed up in deeper shadow, the birds less garrulous. A soft bluish light muffled house and garden, smudging greens and greys together, softening stone.

She shut the twilight out, switched on the hall lights, her footsteps echoing in the deserted corridor. There was no television lounge, no games room, and she was reluctant to return to her cell upstairs when it was not yet ten o'clock. She walked on to her mother's room, opened the door a crack. The light from the passage fell on Bea's sleeping face, her scraggy neck, usually well-camouflaged beneath a smart silk scarf, now exposed and vulnerable, her unlipsticked mouth half-open. She remembered the shock she had felt as a child the first time she had caught her mother asleep. It was as if both of them were dead, Bea's closed lids a barrier shutting her out, denying her existence. She had grabbed her mother's arm, shaken, almost pummelled her awake. 'I'm here,' she shouted, 'I'm here!' She *was* there once her mother woke, gave her back identity. She hadn't even minded that Bea was cross. Anger proved that both of them existed. She longed to wake her mother now, be child again, return to the smug safety of her religion. Bea had barely stirred. She looked peaky, needed rest. Softly, Morna closed the door, trailed upstairs to her own bed.

*

Four hours later, she was still awake. The water-pipes ran through her room, disturbed her with their grumblings, broken up with sudden belches, long gargling moans. The bed was pushed right against the wall, and so narrow that she had grazed her hand on the rough-cast plaster as she tossed and turned. She had tried reading, counting sheep, still felt on edge and far from sleep. She heaved out of bed again, pulled on her skirt and blouse. She needed a breath of air. It was a close sultry night but at least it would be less claustrophobic in the grounds. She picked out an apple from what she called her tuckbox, a secret store of goodies smuggled out of the refectory or bought in the local village shop. She still felt guilty about eating in her room. The walls were so thin, she was sure Joan could hear her chewing two doors down. Less inhibiting to munch out of doors in the privacy of the garden. She crept downstairs, paused by the chapel. The door was half ajar and she could see the red glow of the sanctuary lamp flickering by the altar. Strange how churches continued to attract her, even with their Owner out of residence. She walked slowly up the aisle, knelt in the front pew. The stained glass windows were dark like her own extinguished faith, the dull lead outlines shaping only blank and bloodless forms. She stared at the flowers, the candlesticks, blurred shapes in the gloom – all trappings of a mystery she could no longer celebrate. Her apple looked somehow profane, sitting beside a hymnbook on the bench – too red and round and shiny for a church. She caged it in her pocket, clasped her hands. She longed to pray – for her mother's health, her daughter's happiness – sat with her eyes closed, mumbling words which had long since lost their meaning.

There was a sudden noise behind her. She swung round, saw a shadowy figure rising from its knees at the very back of the church, padding softly to the door, head bowed.

'Wh . . . Who's that?' She could hear the tremor in her

voice. Stupid to be frightened. It was probably only one of the nuns completing her night vigil.

'I'm sorry, I didn't mean to startle you. I . . .'

A *male* voice – and one she recognized. 'Father Anthony!'

'*David* Anthony.'

Christian names already. A true progressive. 'Couldn't you sleep?' she asked, without the David.

' . . . er . . . haven't tried yet. Look, we'd better talk outside.'

She wondered whom they were disturbing, followed him along the passage, trying not to stumble in the gloom. David stopped, waited for her to catch up.

'I was . . . going to make a cup of coffee, actually. Would you like one?'

'Coffee? Now?' It was hard enough to get it after lunch, let alone in the wee small hours. She assumed he had access to priests' privileges.

'There's a little room off this passage somewhere with an ancient kettle in it and a jar of Nescafé. I spotted it earlier on. At least I *think* it was this passage. The house is so rambling I keep on getting lost.'

They tried the first four doors. No coffee. Morna fought an urge to laugh again. There was something distinctly comic about the two of them tiptoeing in and out of ghostly rooms, conversing in whispers, bumping into things.

'Ow!' she said. 'That hurt.'

He pushed the offending wooden chest back against the wall. 'Stupid of them to leave it sticking out like that. Are you all right? Sit down and rest a minute.'

They had reached the room where the nuns arranged the altar flowers – a tiny room empty save for an old-fashioned china sink and shelves and shelves of vases. Morna blinked in the glare as David switched the light on, pulled up the one small stool. She perched on the edge of it, examined her bruised shin. She was suddenly aware of her bare legs, skimpy skirt. She tugged the skirt down, tried to distract attention from the leg.

'Oh look! Are those orchids? Aren't they strange.' She poked her finger in a soft green mouth, stroked the spotted tongue. Most of the other flowers were dying – crimson roses bleeding petals, white phlox browning as if someone had singed them with an iron.

'They're paphiopedilums. They grow in Asia – right across from India to New Guinea – about fifty different species in all, I think there are. You can raise them here in England, actually, if you've got a greenhouse and some patience. Perhaps one of the nuns is an orchid-nutter.'

Morna smiled. So he knew about plants, as well as seventh-century Celtic saints – even about grazed shins. He had wrung out a dishcloth in cold water, made a compress of it.

'Here, hold that against the bruise.' He sounded embarrassed now, kept his eyes cast down, beyond the leg.

'Th . . . Thank you.'

She felt as awkward as he looked, all too conscious of the strange bulge in her pocket. She had nicked that apple from yesterday's lunch. Pudding *or* fruit was the rule – not both. Another three Our Fathers if he found her out. Best to return him to the subject of his work.

'Is your book nearly finished, Father, or just . . .?'

'*David.*'

'I'm sorry. It's automatic – years of childhood conditioning. I suppose modern kids are brought up to use priests' Christian names instead of saying "Father", but in my day it would have been unthinkable. And my mother still abhors it.'

'I'm . . . er . . . *not* a priest, though.'

'But you said you were.'

'I . . . I didn't, actually.'

Morna stared at him, perplexed. Surely he had said . . .?

Anyway, only a priest would be lingering in the chapel in the early hours – a priest or a fanatic. She removed the compress, stared down at her brief and crumpled skirt. Her attire seemed somehow even more unsuitable now she knew he was a secular. She wished she had taken the trouble to put on something flattering, or at least combed her hair. Not that he was looking at her. He was slumped against the sink, fiddling with a piece of chicken-wire. Just their luck to end up somewhere weird again – first a God-shop with no chairs, now a room no bigger than a cupboard which smelt of rotting foliage.

'We . . . er . . . had a room like this at my convent school. Out of bounds, of course, unless you were what was called a Flower Prefect.' She laughed. 'Doesn't that sound absurd?'

'Not really. I went to a Catholic school myself. We had things called Candle Boys.'

'What were they?'

'The male version of your Flower Fairies, I imagine, but candles instead of flowers. We had to see to the candles on the altar.'

'Was yours a boarding school?'

'Oh yes.'

'A strict one?'

'Pretty strict.'

'Daily Mass and all that?'

'Twice daily if you were in the choir – and I was.'

'And Benediction every evening – five o'clock?'

'*Six* o'clock.'

'And confession once a fortnight?'

'Once a week. And exposition.'

'What?'

'You know, Holy Hour – adoration of the Blessed Sacrament.'

'Oh yes, I'd forgotten that.' Morna giggled suddenly. Neil had gagged on all those technical terms – exposition, transubstantiation, temporal punishment. David would have imbibed them with his mother's milk. Odd to think they had so much in common. Whilst Neil was catching jackpike or riding his bike no-hands, she and David would have been on their knees picking over their sins or reciting the Sorrowful Mysteries of the rosary. If you had been to a Catholic boarding school, you saw the world in a completely different light, shared a bond with all other detainees, could swap ordeals and scars.

'Remember Guardian Angels?' she asked. 'I presume boys had those as well?'

'Oh yes.'

'Mine was what my daughter would call a wimp – you know, big blue eyes and golden curls. I got so used to sort of feeling him hovering just over my right shoulder, I still turn round sometimes and wonder where he's gone. Mind you, I don't think he *was* a he. Men were strictly forbidden in the convent.'

David laughed, yet she saw him tense almost imperceptibly. She had broached a dangerous subject. Mother Mary Michael had banished her to her dormitory for a whole weekend, because she had asked what sort of bodies angels had when they came down to earth on errands. She hadn't dared go into details, use words like breasts or . . . or . . . worse, but she had seen pictures of those statues in museums, men with dangly bits between their legs, in marble. Did angels come complete with those and, if not, had God cut them off with his Golden Scissors or simply made their bodies differently from those of normal beings? Had David also puzzled about such things? She doubted it. Head Prefect, probably, as well as Candle Boy.

'When's your talk?' she asked him, moving on from the tricky topic of gender.

'Tomorrow morning, nine o'clock.' He glanced at his

watch. 'In fact, I ought to go and do a bit of preparation for it.'

She cursed herself for mentioning it, was reluctant to end the conversation, spend the rest of the night in her lonely room. She had to admit she was keener on his company now she knew he wasn't a priest; had even felt a crazy jolt of pleasure when he had renounced Father for plain David. Priests blocked you off, kept you distant and subordinate, but David might even be a friend. She must do her best to keep him there at least a little longer. 'What's your angle going to be?' she asked. '*Belief* in miracles, or . . .?'

'Well, a lot of it springs directly from my work. Those early Lives of the saints are two-thirds miracles. The biographer's first duty was to prove his subject's sanctity.'

'You mean they invented the miracles, simply to . . .?'

'No, not quite invented. There was a tradition going right back to the Gospels. Any saint worth his salt was expected to do as Christ had done – cure lepers, restore sight to the blind, calm the odd storm or two.'

'So they just lumped them in, you're saying, regardless of whether that particular saint had actually . . .?'

'It's not as simple as that. You've got to understand the whole context. Miracles were the currency of the age. And don't forget they were trying to convert the pagans and win over local chieftains, so they had to prove themselves every bit as powerful as the old gods – show that a handful of earth which had soaked up St Oswald's blood or a chip of wood from a post which St Aidan had leant against could work the same wonders as the pagans' holy rivers or magic charms. And then there was the whole business of prestige. Each individual monastery wanted its own saints' miracles shouted loud and clear, to win it fame and new recruits, or grants of land.'

'It sounds so . . . so calculating.'

'Not at all. It was just a completely different point of

view. Those biographers weren't like our modern ones, dipping into their Freud and showing up every wart and weakness. If their subjects were holy men, then the key word was holy and they were out to prove it.'

'But surely you can't defend that, David? It's hypocritical, like those Victorian biographies where any whiff of sex or scandal was totally suppressed so you get only a public face.'

David shook his head. 'It really *wasn't* the same – except in the sense that both were trying to set an example, I suppose – make the man a sort of moral exemplar. Anyway, we suppress things, too. We pride ourselves on dragging out every last sexual secret and being frank and open and adult, or whatever we call it, but we ignore other areas of life every bit as vital.'

'How d'you mean?' Morna glanced across at him – dark eyes narrowed, expression almost arrogant. It was still difficult to accept him as plain David. He had some quality of being set apart, set above the purely secular – or was she just romanticizing?

'Well, take the miraculous itself.' David stared down into the sink, as if he could see it there. 'In our society, we try and explain it away – wrap it up neatly with scientific theories or explode it with a blast of commonsense. We've booted out mystery and the supernatural and the whole . . .'

'But you were saying a minute ago that half the miracles were just standard stories trotted out to . . .'

'No, I wasn't saying that. In fact, what really comes across in those early centuries is the total acceptance of other dimensions, a sort of everyday acquaintance with the super- natural which we've lost – to our cost. The pagans had it, too. One of the reasons the Early Christian saints weren't snuffed out in a wholesale martyrdom was that they not only recognized pagan rituals and pagan sensibilities – besides being pretty clever diplomats – but they even shared certain beliefs with them. The Druids, for example, probably believed in life after death. All right, I grant you it was a very different sort of concept from the Christian one, but at least they *had* the concept. We're in danger of losing it. Yet we see that as an advantage, call it progress, congratulate ourselves on being free-thinking rationalists, no longer deluded like those cranks in their white robes. I'm not so sure. Rationalism can shrivel certain faculties.'

David was torturing the piece of chicken-wire, contorting it out into Giacometti shapes, then contracting them back again. Morna watched his hands, never still, as if the force of his arguments was too strong to be contained and was throbbing out into his fingers. She clasped her own hands, rocked back on her stool. 'But where do you draw the line? I mean, if we don't develop some sort of rational logical stance, we'd be back to superstition or . . .' She stopped. She was using Neil's old arguments, the ones he had used with her, twenty years ago.

David gestured with his wire. 'There's a great fund of wisdom in superstition. We've lost that, too. *And* in folk-medicine. That's beginning to creep back a bit, thank God, but on the whole we're so defensive about our four-square blinkered view of things, we fail to see what's just beyond us, or just below or . . . We put everything in categories – fixed and timid ones: If something doesn't fit, it's simply dropped, or shoved under the carpet. We need to be more open to . . . to what you'd call the numinous, I suppose – though I hate the word – but the whole element of mystery, the dimension beyond reason or materialism or . . .' He suddenly crumpled up the chicken-wire, tossed it into the sink. 'D'you realize it's almost three o'clock? In just six hours I'll be stepping on to that platform to give my talk and I've hardly even planned it yet.'

'It sounds as if it's all there – reams and reams of it.'

David flushed. The embarrassed, almost defensive look

returned. 'I'm sorry. Once I get on my hobby-horse, I tend to forget that other people find the subject boring.'

'Not at all. It's fascinating. In fact, you make me realize just how . . . how . . .' Morna groped for the words. Neil had closed heaven off like a draughty attic which wasted heat and was safer insulated. She had gone along with him, following his straight and simple path of rational common-sense, suddenly wanted to tear off the rolls of Insulwrap, feel the bracing air of a higher rarer atmosphere blowing through her skull. She slipped down off the stool, turned into the passage as he held the door for her.

'What about your coffee?' she asked, as they retraced their steps along the corridor, passing all the kettleless rooms.

'I think I'll have to leave that now. We could spend half the night searching the place for a jar of Nescafé which will probably turn out empty anyway, or full of miraculous medals.'

Morna laughed. She could think of worse ways of passing the time. As it was, he would be gone in just two seconds. They had already reached the ante-chapel, a chill and frowning space with a high ceiling, polished floor, a gigantic crucifix bleeding on one wall.

'You must be hungry. You missed supper, didn't you?' Morna was whispering again, as if in deference to Neil's naked criminal. She averted her eyes from the gobbets of plaster blood, rummaged in her pocket. 'Here, have an apple.'

David shook his head. 'No, thanks.'

Morna bit into it angrily herself. Her daughter was always refusing food. Refusals were a putdown. 'I've got some nuts, if you prefer, or . . .'

'No, nothing, honestly.'

She took another bite. The apple was soft and pappy like all the food at Hilden Cross – limp and pulpy cabbage, meat

minced or sauced, milky puddings which slithered down –
food for spiritual babies, invalids.

'I suppose you went out to dinner? I don't blame you!
The meals here are pretty basic. In fact, if you've found a
halfway decent restaurant, I'd be glad to know where. I
could do with a nice rump steak.'

'No, I . . . er . . . didn't.'

'The CND man goes to the pub most evenings. Do you
know if they serve meals there?'

'I'm afraid I don't, no.'

'So it's Mars bars in your room, is it?'

He stared down at the floor. 'I'm . . . er . . . fasting at the
moment, actually.'

'Fasting?'

'Mm. It's part of my research. St Abban used to fast for
weeks on end and I'm trying to work out if the visions he
described had a physiological cause – you know, due to near
starvation or low blood sugar or some change in body
chemistry – or were more genuinely spiritual. It's hardly
scientific, I admit, but . . .' He shrugged. 'I find it interesting. It's all part of what I've just been talking about – the
need to jolt ourselves out of our fixed routines. Most people
eat their three standard meals a day for sixty or seventy
years, so they've no idea what it feels like to be hungry, or
even go beyond that and experience sort of out-of-the-body
states or . . .'

'Have *you* experienced those, David?'

He looked guarded. 'Not this time, no.'

'How long have you been doing it?'

'Eight days.'

'Eight *days*! What, eating nothing?'

'Just water. And an occasional cup of coffee when they
don't hide the jar!'

'And how do you feel?'

'A little tired.'

60

'Hungry?'

'No, surprisingly.'

'Visions?'

'None at all. I must confess I'm a little disappointed. I'm afraid St Abban was a better man than I am and he certainly had more willpower. He could fast for months at a time.'

'David, you'll kill yourself if you try to copy that.'

He didn't answer. Morna regretted her words. She must have sounded like her mother – fretting, petty-minded, making clean socks and cooked breakfasts the touchstone of right living. In fact, her feelings were more complex – divided between admiration and some strange annoyance she could hardly understand. She was certainly impressed by David's dedication, his total involvement in his work; stunned also by his self-control. Neil had got peevish if dinner were delayed for half an hour, regarded one missed meal as near disaster. As a child, she had always admired those saints who starved themselves or slept on beds of nails; had tried out her own pale imitation of them – pebbles in her shoes, bread without butter. Then Neil had come along and piled cream and jam on top of butter, all spread double-thick; banished those of life's privations which could be smoothed away with cash. That had attracted her, as well – the power of it, the cock-a-snooking of the nuns. Wasn't David somehow allied with the nuns, punishing the flesh along with Mother Mary Michael? He'd be donning a habit next, sackcloth with a rope around the middle.

'I don't know how you do it,' she said. 'Especially if you've got to work. I couldn't lecture if I was starving.'

'St Abban managed. Once, he'd eaten nothing for a fortnight and the crowd mobbed his cell, begged him for a sermon. At first he was reluctant to interrupt his prayers, but eventually he came out and spoke to them, and seven hours later, when the sun went down and it was freezing cold, he was still preaching and not one of his listeners had moved or stirred. I promise not to do that. Fifty minutes maximum and then questions from the audience.' He turned to face her. 'Perhaps you'd ask a question, would you, Morna? I hate that pin-drop silence when they say "And now if anyone would like to . . ."?'

'Yes, of course.' She knew nothing at all about the seventh century, would have to stay up, too, thinking out some questions which didn't sound too crass. Why not stay up together? Couldn't she mention, casually, that she would be interested to see his work? Maybe their rooms were close together which would make it less contrived.

'Which floor are you on, David?'

'Ground floor.'

'Sister Ruth said that was reserved for nuns and invalids.'

'Well, there you are . . .'

Morna forced a smile. Maybe it was just as well. He was shy enough already, might freeze completely if she invaded the privacy of his room. There was always tomorrow, and even if he didn't come to meals, she might still snatch a pre-breakfast walk or chat. At least he had used her name – the first time since she'd given it.

'It's sinners at the top,' she grinned, pocketing her apple core. 'I'm in the attic, more or less.'

'Well I hope your leg's up to that long trek. How is it, by the way?'

She had forgotten all about it. 'Fine,' she said, striding three steps up. 'Good luck for your talk! I'm looking forward to it.'

5

'And now if there are any questions from the audience . . .'

Morna stood up. All the questions she had laboriously prepared the night before now seemed footling and inadequate in light of David's talk. He had ranged from prehistoric standing stones to sub-atomic physics, from shamans and witch-doctors to biofeedback and auto-hypnosis; considered miracles as metaphor, miracles as symbol; linked pagan art and folklore with Christian cure and vision. Her mind felt full and churning, as if she had crammed it with a ten-course meal, washed down with heady wines. She needed time to digest the talk, yet here she was rising to her feet with some mere petty point of phrasing to propound.

'I wonder, Mr Anthony, if it might be better to use different terminology? I mean the word miracle is so loaded now, it sets up a reaction which leads people to expect . . .'

Strange to be addressing him so formally and in a public lecture room. She had preferred their private talk which she had contrived two hours before by walking up and down the path which flanked his room on her early-morning stroll. At last, he had drawn his curtains.

'David!' (Surprise.)

'H . . . Hallo.'

'It's a glorious morning. Why don't you join me for a lap or two?'

It was so obvious, so unsubtle, yet he appeared to have enjoyed the walk. She had even elicited a brief biography, rejoindered with some items from her own. She tried to return her attention to the dais. She should be listening to David's exposition of the Latin verb *mirari*, not mulling over the fact that he still lived with his parents in the Midlands, apart from occasional forays to the London libraries; had been thirty-five last birthday and had an (elder) brother who worked in Africa. His family was neither Jewish nor exotic. His mother came from Shrewsbury, his father from a small and sleepy village close to Stafford.

Morna glanced at his dark eyes again as she sat back in her seat. It was their intensity which was foreign, perhaps, rather than their colour. She kept her gaze on him as he dealt with further questions from the floor – timid lapdog questions from pious ladies whose idea of miracle was strictly limited to Lazarus or Lourdes. David was wasted on this audience, she felt, but he couldn't be too fussy. He had told her he took what lecturing he could, to supplement his research grant. She waited until he had dealt with stigmata, Holy Relics, the problems of the Turin Shroud, then rose to her feet again, tried to deepen the discussion, make it worthy of him. She could see the retreat director anxiously checking his watch as she and David parried arguments. The lecture had already run over schedule and was now cutting into the coffee break. David had talked for longer than his promised fifty minutes, seemed to have lost all shyness as well as his sense of time, displayed a confidence and force which half surprised her.

She watched him now, accepting a vote of thanks and loud applause, already mobbed by females as he stepped down from the dais. It was impossible to get near him in the crowded coffee-room. She could see his head above the clamouring circle of permed and grizzled ones, looking trapped as it was plied with questions, biscuits, homage. She pushed a little closer, watched him take a custard-cream, hold it in his hand uneaten, almost an encumbrance, until he used it as a teaching aid to gesture with. It finally crumbled to pieces in his palm as he made some point too fiercely, stood shedding crumbs, enlightenment.

'Did you enjoy the talk, my dear?'

Morna swung round, was lassooed by the female JP's smile.

'Oh yes, very much.' She could still see David if she moved a fraction, craned her neck.

'I thought he sailed a bit close to the wind, though. I mean, that thing about the afterlife was near heretical.'

'I loved the animal stories, didn't you?' That was the spinster social worker. 'They were really quaint, particularly the otters and that tame stag which . . .'

'If you want to know what I think, he's unsound. I mean it's all very well opening your mind to any opinion going, but . . .'

Morna murmured her excuses, edged her way to the door. She couldn't bear to have David's talk dissected and diluted with these waffling pieties, her new elation punctured. She pranced along the passage feeling aroused, exhilarated, as she had done when she first went up to university and swapped Mother Michael's blinkered world for a wider and more dazzling one. She tried to suppress her stupid smile as she tapped on her mother's door.

'Mummy, it's me, Morna. Are you awake?'

'Yes, dear. Come on in.'

'How d'you feel?'

'A wee bit better now.'

'Good. Anything you want?'

'No thanks. Sit here on the bed. That chair's lost half its springs. I'm glad you've ditched that dreadful navy skirt, darling. You're looking really smart.'

Morna flushed. She had changed it in David's honour for a paler prettier one, added a real silk blouse. Stupid to have bothered. He would hardly notice things like that when his mind was on Abban's angelic apparitions or on St Cuthbert's body found uncorrupt and shining eleven years after he had died. She smoothed the skirt around her on the bed. 'We've just had the most astounding talk.'

'What on, dear?'

'Miracles.'

'Oh yes.'

'No, not what you think. It was more like philosophy or history or . . .'

'Pass me that woolly, darling, will you? It's none too warm in here.'

'It's boiling. Let me draw the curtains. The sun's blazing down outside.'

'No, I hate it. It gets in my eyes.'

'Come on, just a crack.' Morna wanted the sun to stream in, rival her own radiance. She glanced around the room. Bea had turned it into a sickroom – jars of pills, bottles of Lucozade, a smell of liniment, stale air. It wasn't like her mother to sit moping in the dark. Bea was seventy next birthday, but rarely used the word old. Maybe her spell in hospital had softened her, given her a taste for playing invalid. The rôle did have its payoffs – attention, sympathy, an opting out of life. Many of the retreatants were looking after aged parents. Morna admired their unselfishness, but it was easier to admire than emulate. Impatiently, she turned back to the bed. A finger of light was pointing across the counterpane, cutting her mother's face in half. Bea had tried to put on lipstick without a mirror, now had a double mouth, one wrinkled pale, one scarlet. Morna leaned over, kissed the pallid cheek. Hardly fair to judge her mother when she had barely had time to recover from the surgery. Why not be honest and admit she was only restive because she wanted to return to David? He was unlikely to attend the next event – a workshop on the Missions – so once the coffee break was over, she could maybe snatch an hour with him. Yet if Bea were really poorly . . .

'Look, Mummy, if you're feeling bad, why don't I phone the doctor?'

'Whatever for? I'm fine. I want to hear about this talk. What did the good priest say, then?'

'He wasn't a priest.' That stupid smile again.

'What, another of those unwashed poets?'

Morna laughed. 'Oh no.' They'd had a talk on Gerard Manley Hopkins from an ex-Beatnik in a scruffy smock and open sandals. 'This one even wore a tie.' A narrow stringy brown one, a different brown from his shirt – the same alopeciaed corduroys. Certainly not unwashed, though. You felt with David he had been scrubbed and sanitized, inside as well as out.

'And did he believe in miracles?'

Morna hesitated. 'Difficult to say. He gave all the different approaches, one by one – the gullible, the sceptical, the strictly scientific . . .'

Bea took a sip of Lucozade. 'How d'you mean?'

'I'll give you an example. He's researching a seventh-century saint whose life was one long miracle, more or less. I mean, he saw bright lights in the sky and balls of fire which *he* interpreted as Signs from God, but David said . . .'

'*Who*, dear? Was David the saint?'

'No, no – the speaker – David Anthony. He told us you *could* explain them by something like an electric storm which would have filled the sky with lurid lights and shadows and even sound effects. I mean, that's the natural explanation.' The sort which Neil would have insisted on, Morna added to herself. 'But there's more to it than that. You see, those balls of fire go back to the pagans who had heroes called the Shining Ones and . . .'

Bea shook out a shower of hair-pins from her hair, reached across for her comb. 'I remember one of those storms – a

67

really dreadful one. You were four and a half at the time –
or was it five? We were staying down in Devon, near the sea
and the whole . . .'

Morna picked up a stray hair-pin from the floor. It wasn't
going to be easy to give Bea a résumé. The whole thing was
too complex, too far-ranging. She tried again.

'It's really a question of – well – how we see the world. I
mean, he said the miraculous was close to the absurd in that
both sort of bring us up with a start and shake us out of
our . . .' Morna broke off. How could she explain the
Absurd to someone like her mother, make Bea see it was not
irrelevant for David to have brought in Lear, Ionesco, even
Alice Through the Looking Glass? He had reserved his greatest
passion for St Abban, talked of him like a friend or even
lover, kept returning to his life, quoting from his sayings.
'We don't know much about him,' he had told her yesterday,
and then proceeded to fill a morning with him – his ideas,
ideals, his prophecies, his visions. She had been stupid
enough to feel a twinge of jealousy – though crazy to be
jealous of some seventh-century anorexic whose idea of bliss
was to stand up to his neck in icy water. Wasn't that the
trouble, though? David was attracted by such extremes of
self-denial and she could hardly rival them herself. She had
been peeved at breakfast just because the toast was burnt,
compensated with double Sugar Puffs. She glanced down at
her thighs spreading on the bed, the swell beneath her
blouse. Too much unpunished flesh.

Bea was combing out her hair, coiling it up again. 'Well,
I'm glad you enjoyed it, darling. It's nice to see you smiling.
You've been a wee bit . . . mopish, recently.'

Morna shifted on the bed. 'It's only this place. It gets me
down a bit.'

'No, I meant before that – long before. You haven't really
been yourself since the . . . er . . .'

'Divorce?'

Bea nodded. She never used the word. 'You don't mind me saying, do you, darling?'

'N . . . No. Of course not.' Morna escaped to the window, tweaked the curtain back. She *did* mind. Why should her mother probe old wounds just when she was feeling good for once? Bea, like the priests, could always make her feel guilty, simply for turning out a disappointment. She should have been a different sort of daughter, one who would have filled the gaping hole of Bea's own widowhood, provided her with the horde of Catholic babies she couldn't have herself; one like her friend Anne – a *real* Anne who also boasted three other Catholic names – Anne Patricia Mary Thérèse. You couldn't get more orthodox than that. Anne still had her husband and her God, shared her life between them – Mass on Sunday mornings, golf Sunday afternoons, evening prayers at the bedside before her nightly rites with John. She had produced six children so far, took them all to tea with their Grandma twice a week. That would have made Bea's life – a devout Catholic son-in-law to drive her to church, eight bowed heads beside her in the pew.

Morna stared out at the green enamelled grass. Why were all close relationships mined and strafed by guilt – mothers, daughters, husbands, even dogs? She saw Joy's reproachful eyes again as she left the lead hanging where it was, switched on 'Panorama' in preference to a walk.

She unlatched the window, opened it an inch, let the scent of crimson glories cut across the fug; watched a squirrel streak towards the copper beech, turn tree trunk into lift shaft.

'It's a pity Joy's not here,' she said, returning to the bed. Dogs were safer than divorce. 'She'd make mincemeat of those squirrels.'

Bea removed a clutch of hair-pins from her mouth. 'I miss her. I couldn't sleep last night worrying about her meals. That Vera doesn't bother.'

Another stab of guilt. Morna had opened tins for Joy herself, watched with a sort of triumph as the dog wolfed soya chunks and gristle with far more obvious relish than Bea's home-cooked breast of chicken. It was Chris who wasn't eating well. She had complained in her last letter that *Madame*'s cooking was as lousy as her English. Was Chris unhappy? Hungry? Aching to come home? Her period was due this week and she always suffered badly. She had had her very first one just a fortnight after her father left – had connected them with crisis ever since. As if to bear her out, the periods were painful – stomach cramps and floodings every month. Morna had taken her to three separate doctors, but none could find anything physiologically wrong. Chris called menstruation the 'curse' and meant it. Both words had been forbidden at Morna's school. 'Curse' was wicked because every period meant the chance of bearing another soul for God, which was a blessing not a curse; and 'menstruation' sounded blatant and unladylike. 'Monthlies' was the permitted term.

Morna scooped up another hair-pin, bent it out of shape. Perhaps she should have written to *Madame*, explained the situation, asked if Chris could have some time off during 'monthlies', but her daughter would have hated that. She tried to force the thoughts down. She didn't want to be a mother at the moment, but friend instead – one of those intense ardent adolescent friendships where you stayed up all night to thrash out life-and-death questions and dilemmas: did mind exist, and, if so, how did it relate to soul or brain; or how, if everything were both relative and subjective, could one ever reach any truth at all? David would excel at those.

She wished her watch was larger, so she could check the time without her mother noticing, read the tiny figures. What was David doing? Surely the workshop would have started now? He might well decide to leave whilst the coast

70

was clear, dodge all those fond farewells. If she didn't slip out soon, she might never see him in her life again, miss her chance to say her own goodbye. Bea was discussing Joy's digestive problems. She was more worried about David's. This was the ninth day of his fast.

'Look, Mummy, if you're really feeling better, why don't you get up and come and meet him?'

'Who, dear?'

'The speaker. Mr Anthony.'

'Whatever for? He wouldn't want to see me.'

Her mother was probably right. Would he want to see her, either? It suddenly seemed imperative that Bea should make his acquaintance. 'You could . . . er . . . ask him a question.'

'But I didn't hear his talk.'

'Doesn't matter. Ask him anything.'

Bea smoothed the counterpane, clasped her hands on top of it. 'You're just trying to get me up, dear, aren't you – like those nurses at the hospital? Every time I closed my eyes, it was "Rise and shine".'

Morna grinned. 'Come on, then – rise and shine.' A nice phrase – one which expressed her mood exactly. 'Put on your greeny dress. I want you to look nice. You can ask him if he thinks Joy has a soul.'

Was she crazy, dragging her mother off to see a man she hardly knew and who preferred seclusion anyway? She had never behaved like this before, running after people, acting like a teenager. In the five years since Neil had left, she had been wary of men, tried to keep her distance, stay uninvolved. Her confidence was bruised enough without risking a second wound. If a partner of fourteen years' standing deliberately sought out another mate, in bed or out of it, why should any other man desire his reject? She was surprised, then, when they pestered – even her girlfriends' husbands, or other married men whom she had naïvely regarded as loyal and faithful souls, now expecting her to leap between the sheets with them simply because Neil had disappeared. It made her still more uneasy, more confused. She had weakened only once – and that time with a widower – a disastrous affair which had started off with snapshots of the deceased, and ended up with demands that she do it in the marital bed wearing the dead wife's nightgown. Since then, she had kept herself to herself. Safer and less hurtful.

She pulled the covers back, coaxed Bea out of her bed. So why change now, risk problems, complications, inflict herself on a man who was obviously as wary as herself? Except this was different, another thing entirely. It was David's mind which attracted her – the sheer range and reach of it – the excitement she felt hearing him explode new and startling subjects into life, or watching him push back the fences round the world. He had breached her own defences, got through to her own mind, kindled it, aroused it, made her realize how long it had been since she had enjoyed the cut and thrust of intelligent conversation – not just since the divorce, but years before it. Neil had had no patience with speculation, theorizing, what he called intellectual waffle. Her daughter was bright enough, but often reticent, saving her discussions for her peers, perhaps.

She fetched Bea's towel, ran some water for her in the basin. It was ironic, really. When she *had* been adolescent (and even afterwards), she had done her best to keep all male friends as far away from her mother as she could. Too few ever passed Bea's scrutiny – certainly not Neil. Yet here she was, actually pressing David on her. She had no choice. Either she stayed in this stuffy sickroom and David slipped away for ever, or she took her mother with her and gleaned one more conversation before he put a hundred odd miles between them. The real twist was that David was the only man she had ever met who might actually win the Conyers' Seal of Approval – the product of a devout Catholic family

72

and a minor Catholic public school, well spoken, well mannered and with a good degree from Cambridge. Neil had left his secondary modern at fifteen, and his parents were low Anglican which didn't count in Bea's book. Maybe her mother could even break David's fast, suggest they all had lunch together.

'Now you're up, Mummy, why not stay up and eat in the refectory? You've had enough of that soup and stuff on trays. You need something solid for a change.'

'What *is* for lunch? Did you see the menu?'

'Toad in the hole.'

'Well that should be solid enough, judging by their last attempt at batter.'

'And jelly to follow.'

'What, again?'

'Don't be fussy, Mum. We're going to celebrate and jelly's better for that than sago. You'll have to imagine the champagne.'

'Celebrate *what*, I'd like to know?' Bea was struggling with her stockings, rolling them over pale and veiny legs.

Morna looked tactfully away. 'Anything. Everything. Your getting up. Miracles, if you like.'

Or maybe just the simple fact she felt better for the first time in five years.

'So what did you think of my mother?'

'She's . . . charming.'

'She missed you at lunch. She saved you a piece of toad-in-the-hole with more toad in it than hole. That's quite a feat here.'

David smiled.

'Still fasting?'

'Mm.'

'Fancy another walk?' Morna weighed his hesitation. Perhaps he was too weak to walk. Wouldn't fasting sap his energy? Yet he had seemed fit enough this morning, showed no sign of any fatigue. 'Just a very short one. I know you've got to leave soon. I wanted to ask you another question, actually.' Intellectuals could rarely resist a question, especially one in their own field. 'If you've got the time, that is?'

'Yes, of course.'

'Well, you know you said the Druids believed in an afterlife? I wondered if you could explain how . . .'

Was it just his mind which attracted her? If so, why was she so aware of him as man, noticing every detail – the fact that he had removed his tie, had Biro on his fingers, an almost faded scar running down his left thumb; aware of his body, tall, stooping slightly, overshadowing hers. She tried to walk slowly, to save him extra exertion. She had sausages to fuel her, mushy peas; he only ideas. Yet he appeared to be the energetic one – kept striding ahead, then slowing down to wait for her, only to accelerate again as if to keep up with the outflow of his words.

'You see, Morna, the Romans were very different in that respect. *They* regarded death as something which brought an end to the troubles of this life, whereas the Druids looked forward to a paradise, not in a gloomy underworld, but somewhere in the setting sun or . . .'

They had left the house behind, passed the orchard and the vegetable garden, reached the wilder part of the grounds where the grass was tangled and untidy, the trees no longer pruned and tamed. David was still talking.

'Shall we have a breather?' Morna asked at last. Could he really be fasting and still have so much stamina? It was an effort to keep up with him, both literally and intellectually. She could feel her thighs perspiring, chafing together beneath the full skirt, breasts sticky in the heat. She flattened a patch of grass, lay back against the bank. He squatted down beside her, still developing his argument. He seemed

74

almost unaware of his surroundings, was sailing with the Druids to the Happy Isles.

'I'm sure that's one of the reasons why the pagan Celts understood the Christians' love of lonely island sites. They must have seen them as sort of . . . stepping stones which led to their own Blessed Isles.'

She had to bring him back, lure him away from the cold Atlantic Ocean. She saw him ready to run on again, jumped in first. 'When's your train?' she asked, leapfrogging fifteen centuries.

'3.19.'

Less than fifty minutes. 'Are you going home or only back to London?'

'Home.'

She picked a plantain, decapitated it, tossed the head away.

David was still squatting on his heels. 'Actually, I'll only be there for another couple of months. You see, I've finished most of my researches now and I'm almost ready to write them up, start on the actual book. I've decided to do that on the island.'

'What, St Abban's?'

'Mm. I need complete peace and quiet for it, and I can't think of anywhere less distracting. Also, I've never been there in the winter – always stuck to the summer months. That's a bit of a cheat. I mean, how can I understand what it was like for Abban and his monks, if I don't experience the cold and gales myself? I've booked the cottage from late September. That'll give me a month or so to acclimatize myself before the real squalls blow up. Mind you, you can't be too exact with dates. It's a question of when wind and tide are right. I've known people hang around for weeks waiting for a boat. It's a treacherous coast with riptides and . . .'

'Does anybody live there, or will it be just you and your dead saint?'

'Six brave souls. There's the crofter and his wife who are renting me the cottage, another elderly couple, a retired spinster schoolmarm, and a fierce old man who lives on his own and is reputed to be mad. They're all well over sixty. It's the same on most of the islands. The young people leave. They're too cut off and the life's too hard for them. There are no roads, no shops, not even electricity. The crofter has a boat, but half the year the weather's too moody for him to take it out very far.'

Morna pierced the plantain stalk with her fingernail. Not a hundred miles – five hundred – and a wild sea flung between them. David seemed already lost to her. He needed no friend, had already found his soul mate, his companion in prayer and fasting – a seventh-century monk. He might be David rather than Father, but his life was still vowed to Abban as exclusively as a priest's was to his God – a life full enough without her – recording miracles, translating prayers, poring over ruins, structuring a book. Someone believed in him enough to fund him. He believed in himself and his saint enough to subsist on a primitive island, starve and freeze in the cause of history. She lived in the smug and glossy suburb Neil had selected as reflecting credit on him, ate three balanced and nutritious meals a day, yet she was the one who was starving. Only David had made her see it. She felt restless, somehow, dissatisfied. Her own work couldn't compare. There were frequent barren spells, especially in the summer, when no one seemed to want her services. And even when she landed a job, it was often something vacuous. She had no boss, no office, no fixed routine – just herself sitting in Neil's ex-study trying to Polyfill the gaps between different languages.

She lay back again, feeling the long grasses tease and prick against her neck. Right, she had forty-seven minutes left of

76

David – less than that, if she subtracted the time he'd need to get to the station. She had better make the most of them.

'You don't look too comfortable,' she said, squinting up at him against the sun. 'Why not sit down for a moment? The grass is so dry here, it's almost turned to hay.'

He sat, reluctantly. His body looked awkward, even clumsy – long legs sticking out in front of him, one shoelace half undone. She watched a meadow brown spiral between white clover and blue harebells; heard the muted boom and sob of the chapel organ descanted by a thrush's song. It was a lazy languorous day, too hot to walk or work, a day for simply lolling on the grass, watching the play of sun and shadow, or closing one's lids and seeing black kaleidoscope to scarlet as the sun beat down on them. David seemed to contradict the mood. He was sitting bolt upright still, one hand clenched, the other threshing through the grass, dishevelling daisies. There was a tiny burr sticking to his corduroys. She wished she could be free enough and friend enough to reach across, remove it, but his shyness seemed infectious. Couldn't he simply relax, open up a bit? She longed to know more about him, exchange confidences, opinions, but she had noticed on their earlier walk how quickly he clammed up once she moved to matters personal. She searched for a neutral subject.

'They're . . . er . . . marvellous grounds, aren't they?'

'Mm.'

'Do *you* have a garden, David?'

'My parents do.'

'That's what I meant.'

Silence.

What was wrong with him? Was she that much of a drag? All right, she couldn't match his intellect, but at least she had a degree, an eagerness to learn. And as far as looks were concerned, she wasn't downright hideous. In fact, if they had run a Miss Hilden Cross contest for the retreatants (instead of a Chain of Prayer), she would have won it sash and crown. She might be five years older than he was, five pounds overweight, but she didn't wear yellow plastic hair-slides, or have swags of flesh drooping from her upper arms or a full moustache, like some of the females here. The woman JP had even called her beautiful.

She watched David shade his eyes against the sun, tried again. 'Don't you like the heat?'

'Not really.'

'They say our summers are gradually getting hotter. It's something to do with pollution, I think I read.'

He didn't answer, suddenly jumped up. 'I'm sorry, Morna, but I ought to turn back now. I haven't packed my bag yet.'

That couldn't take him long. A toothbrush and pyjamas. Or perhaps his notes and books.

'Do you have your work here?' she asked, still sprawling where she was. 'You know – that stuff in French you were telling me about?'

'Oh, no. It's all at home.'

'Pity. I'd have liked to have had a look at it.'

David had turned back towards the path, was waiting for her to catch up. Reluctantly, she struggled to her feet, brushed her skirt down. Go *on*, she urged him silently, why not say you'll send me a few pages, suggest I help you with it? He said nothing, even when she joined him, just strode ahead again, his long brown back blocking off the sun. They were skirting the orchard now, trees bandy and distorted, the clustering apples mostly green, unripe. She had bitten into one the day before, spat it out, grimacing. In two months' time they would be rotting underfoot or already pulped in pies or jams. And Chris would be back from France, already back at school; she, returned from her mother's to be a mother in her turn; David, one of seven benighted souls cut off by an ocean. What could she say to

78

him? Keep in touch, give me your phone number, send me a postcard from an island with no shop?

'Hey, David . . .'

'What?'

'I've just thought – perhaps I could help you with that French. I . . . I'd find it very interesting. And I haven't got much work on at the moment. You see, the summer's always fairly . . .' She was filling his silence with words. Couldn't he at least give her an answer, even if it were no? He was embarrassed to say no. She watched him frown, bite his lip.

'The . . . er . . . problem is, Morna . . . I mean, I'd love your help – of course I would – but I . . . can't really afford a translator's fees.'

'*Fees*?' She ducked to avoid an overhanging branch.

'Well, of course I'd pay you. It's just that my . . . er . . . budget's rather tight at the moment. I'm having to watch every last penny.'

'I wouldn't dream of taking money, David.' She was embarrassed now herself. He would think she was touting for work, trying to earn herself an easy cheque. 'I never meant that for a second. I'm just interested – not only in the French, but in your saint as well. It's a completely new period for me. At school, history started with the Normans – 1066 and all that.'

'That's scandalous. You can't understand the Normans without the . . .'

Morna cursed silently. If they sidetracked to the Vikings or the Saxons, she would never get her papers. Why didn't she just leave it, stop pestering, behaving in the same pushy, insensitive fashion as the men who plagued her after Neil had left? That was the trouble, though. David was so different. Those bores had been all booze and bun-fights, regarding her simply as a woman on her own who needed a replacement stud; whereas he was diffident, reclusive, had a finesse and vulnerability she valued for its rarity. She sensed a bond between them. They shared the same background, had been brought up with the same God, the same prohibitions, rituals. Did he still worship that God, celebrate those rituals? How did he square them with the tide of new knowledge, the explosion of new thinking, with which he had dazzled her this morning? There was so much she longed to know. Yet they were less than a hundred yards from the house now, five minutes from goodbye. *Adieu*, not *au revoir*. David stooped down to tie his shoelace, was silent for a moment. The shoes looked worn and battered as if their owner overworked them. She could see him about to speak.

'W . . . Why don't I give you my address?' she suddenly blurted out, still staring at the shoes. 'Then you can send me a few pages.'

David brushed his trousers down, stood up straight again. 'Well, if you're absolutely sure it's no trouble . . .'

'No, really, I'd enjoy it. Got a pencil?'

He fumbled in his pocket, produced a leaky Biro. 'No paper, I'm afraid. Have you got anything?'

Morna shook her head. She had left her handbag in her room, had no pocket in this skirt. She glanced around for a scrap of litter. None.

'Don't worry. I'll jot it on my hand.' David stopped, leant against a tree, held one palm flat and rigid like a notebook.

'That's what my daughter does. She keeps a whole address book on both hands.'

David laughed. 'Why not? Right, fire away.'

'Mrs Morna Gordon,' she spelt out. Why had she said Mrs? Simply force of habit, or because if she had a daughter, then she ought to have a husband? She had mentioned Neil already, without explaining he was ex; was always wary of being classed as a divorcée. She had soon learnt that divorcées were considered easy prey, and she had been forward enough with David as it was. Anyway, it really made no difference. It was his work she found so fascinating, the sheer range of his mind.

She was surprised to see him writing her name in full, instead of just initials. It took up his whole palm.

'5 Elmwood Drive,' she continued. He moved down to his wrist, wrote carefully, laboriously, tongue poking between his teeth like a child.

'Okay?' he asked, when he had finished at last – included even the postcode and the phone number which spread right down his forearm – and holding the arm up for her to check.

She nodded. 'Yes, that's it.' Felt a sudden stab of excitement as she saw her name – bold, indelible – imprinted on his flesh.

6

It was a golden day, the noon sun shimmering on yellow potentillas, golden rod; a burst of reddish gold chrysanthemums flaming by the hedge. Wasps were buzzing round the plums, golden plums, yellow greengages; a blackbird boasting on a topmost branch. Morna strolled into the garden, bare-armed, bare-legged – sniffed the late summer cocktail of monbretia and dianthus, cloying carnations, almost sickly sweet, musky helenium. There were other scents – warm grass, cut grass, rotting grass cut a week ago and mulching on the compost-heap; a faint tang of things over-ripe, creeping towards decay; blooms too full, colours already fading in the insistent sun.

She fetched the ladder, dragged it towards the apple trees. The Worcesters were ripe, but not the russets yet. Neil had planted the Worcester Pearmains, bought them as mere saplings, watched them grow, crunched their first perfect apple in his perfect teeth, then left them, along with everything else in house and garden.

Morna set the ladder steady, climbed up to the apples, filled two baskets with them. She carried them back to the house, picked out the best and biggest for her daughter's room, piled them in a bowl. She had already filled the room with flowers, bought a welcome-home card. Chris was expected back that afternoon. She felt excited and keyed up as if she were on holiday; had missed her daughter more than she'd expected. She did a quick check around the room, straightening books, tidying shelves – stopped in front of a photo of Chris and Martin. Bea was right – there was no such thing as divorce. Neil was still around. Bea might ban his photos in her house, but his eyes, hair, even something of his character, had transferred themselves to Chris. Both were lean, dark, ambitious, obstinate, though Neil's spare sallow wiriness worked better on a man. Chris had boyish hips, timid breasts. Her hair was as dark and straight as her father's but looked lank instead of sleek. His grey eyes seemed less steely and imperious when transferred to her pale and fragile face. She had his perfect teeth, but since she rarely smiled, no one could admire them.

Morna suddenly longed to see her in the flesh – tight mouth, wary eyes and all – longed to restitute her with all the things she should have had, but hadn't – beauty, security, serenity, a father. It was somehow Neil's fault that she hadn't grown more beautiful. If he had stayed around, she would have ripened in his honour. But since he wasn't there to notice, she simply hadn't bothered to fill out; was mourning him still, scowling even in her picture.

Her boyfriend also looked restive – another thin, dark, gangling type; mouth vulnerable, slick of hair falling into Bournville eyes. All the smiles were Neil's. Chris still kept her father in her room – three of him, cajoling and posturing from three separate photo frames. Morna always had to steel herself before entering her daughter's room, coming face to face with Neil in his endless beaming prime – face unlined, hair youthful dark. The room was full of his munificence – lavish presents sent over from the States: a giant-sized Donald Duck from Disneyland, dressed in rakish cap and waistcoat, an onyx musical box which played 'God Bless America', five scarlet satin cushions which spelt the letters of Chris's name; even an elaborate ice cream sundae complete with cherries, wafer and whipped cream, all in multi-coloured plastic. The clock was his as well – a jokesy one in the shape of an owl with eyes which swivelled back and forth. Morna wound it up, put it right. Five to one. Chris would still be in France – just – drawing into Calais on the coach. An hour to hang around, an hour to cross the Channel, two hours on the road from Dover to Victoria, an hour or less from there. Still half a day to go. She longed to shorten the day, hack into it, go up and meet Chris at Victoria, shout and wave as the coach drew in. But that was the boyfriend's privilege. Morna traced her finger along the glass-framed leather jacket, the long denimed legs; wished she felt more for Martin. He was a nice enough lad in his way, and on his own, but he wasn't right for Chris. Bea had used the same phrase about Neil. Perhaps all mothers used it – no one ever right.

Bea was out for the day, had left that morning – returned to Hilden Cross for a Women's Crusade of Prayer. She had made a friend there at the July retreat who not only shared her interests but also ran a car. Morna was pleased for her mother, relieved for herself. It helped to ease her burden of being the only chauffeur, left her more free time for David's work.

David had been grudging at first, sent her only a few pages, badly photocopied – although at least he had sent them promptly. They had been waiting on the doormat when she returned from the retreat-house on the last day of July. She had pounced on them, devoted every spare moment since to deciphering the shorthand, bringing the French to vivid thrusting life. She had returned to stay at Bea's again until just two days ago, working at the same inlaid walnut table she had used as a student. It was like being back at college, slaving away all hours, trying to impress her tutor – except this time he was five years younger instead of more than forty older. David had certainly been impressed, or so he said in his letter which arrived with a further four chapters of the manuscript. Now she had the whole three hundred pages; was nowhere near finished yet, but was finding it one of the most absorbing jobs she had ever taken on. Other translations she had always done alone. This time she had a collaborator, one she never saw, but who wrote or even phoned, discussed phrasing with her, shades of meaning, filled in the background, quoted the Latin Life. They had argued about money – David insisting on paying her in some way, she equally insistent that she wouldn't take a penny. They had finally let the matter rest, spent their time on more important matters, such as the dating of the second Latin manuscript or the extent of the borrowings from earlier classical writers.

She ran down to Neil's old study, settled herself at the desk. Better to get another chunk completed than waste the time fretting about her daughter. You couldn't hurry ferryboats or trains – nor translations, either. There were still passages she wasn't happy with – one in particular where the French professor had used the word '*l'esprit*' nine times in as many pages. She had translated it as 'soul' at first, though that was strictly '*l'âme*'; then, less sure, she had substituted 'mind'; considered spirit, essence, mentality. None was quite exact. The French suggested all of them, whereas every English equivalent seemed to rule the others out. That passage had given her more problems than any other she had tackled. It was more speculative and philosophical than the rest, language matching thought with a string of abstract nouns which sounded less pretentious in the French. She had still not succeeded in ironing out the lumpiness, bringing it alive, though David had written that he understood the gist of it which was surely all that mattered. She disagreed. Translation was art as much as craft, and she hated to give him something stilted and imperfect when his own standards were so high.

She picked up her pen, found a virgin piece of paper. '*L'esprit*,' she wrote, sat staring at it, frowning. 'Psyche' was a possibility, though Freud had spoilt the word. 'Superego' was far too modern; 'pneuma' sounded like a tyre. Perhaps she'd leave it for a moment, try and improve the general feel and flow. She read through the whole section, crossing out words and substituting others. 'Ambivalence' was better than 'ambiguity' in that particular context, and why use 'veracity' when simple 'truth' would do every bit as well? Only now did she realize that it was simplicity it lacked. David was right. He needed clear unequivocal meaning above all else. She had sacrificed it for effect, let the professor's highfalutin French distort her own style. She would have one more try, using a simpler English which was still faithful to the French but without its frills.

She scribbled on, forgetting lunch. She had come to like the French professor, even to share his and David's passion for their saint. Impossible to resist Abban's full-blooded Celtic charm – his extremes of feeling, hot temper, love of birds and animals. He converted stags and even fieldmice, as well as pagans, rebuked donkeys for their stubbornness or foxes for killing hens, was fed by two black crows when starving in a wilderness. The miracles both astounded and amused her – spanning, as they did, both the sublime and the near ridiculous. One in particular made her feel uneasy. It concerned a married woman who had long ceased what Le Goff described coyly as *rapports intimes*, since she longed to be a nun. Abban prayed. Two weeks later, the husband died a holy and painless death. The widow, both grieving and rejoicing, departed to a desert place to found a convent, using her late husband's riches to endow it. A less credulous age might have suspected foul play, Morna reflected, as she tried to find a better English equivalent for *lieu sauvage*. St Abban, like Mother Mary Michael, regarded the married state as unquestionably inferior to the monastic one; exhorted married couples to abstain from sex as long and often as they could. A pity, she thought, she hadn't had the saint around to help her temper Neil's demands.

She got up to stretch her legs, make a cup of tea; was still watching the kettle when the phone rang in the hall. The line was bad, sounded like long-distance. Maybe it was Chris, just arrived at Dover.

'Hallo. Can you speak up, please. I'm sorry, I can't hear at all. Oh, it's *you*, David! How are you? Funnily enough, I was just hoping you'd ring. I'm having a few problems with that . . . What? In London? Oh, I see. Next week? But why so soon?'

She slumped down on the settle. All the time she had been translating David's work, she had somehow managed to block out the fact that he would be leaving for the island. Late September was always weeks away – even now, when the month was already eight days old. But he had brought it forward, planned to leave next week; had been offered a lift to Oban in a colleague's car which would save him expensive rail fares, solve the problem of transporting all his books. She tried to sound pleased for him, steel herself against saying stupid things like she would gladly drive him to Oban herself, so long as he didn't leave so soon. They were only casual acquaintances, after all.

David was speaking again, his voice still muffled as if he were phoning from a far and distant country. In fact he was in London, only twenty miles away from her, staying with a cousin. He had come down just two days ago, to make some last-minute forays to libraries and bookshops before he left for Scotland. He also needed his translation. Was there any chance of fetching it, he wondered, any chance of seeing her? Perhaps he could come right now, if it wouldn't be a nuisance, catch a train to Weybridge, maybe take her out to dinner as a tiny return for all her . . .

Damn, she thought. She would have jumped at the invitation had it been any other day. David would hardly relish a teenage daughter and her boyfriend tagging along as well, quite apart from the expense. She had planned to take Chris and Martin out herself – partly as a little celebration and partly to prevent the dinner spoiling if Chris were, in fact, delayed. She had booked a table at Roxy's – Chris's favourite place – a noisy crowded dive where you had to shout against the rock music and the waitresses wore minis and muddled up the orders. She couldn't see David there. She checked her watch, still dithering. Even if he came to tea, how could she get rid of him before Chris and Martin arrived? She didn't *want* to get rid of him, had been hoping all through August to set eyes on him again. Why couldn't he have rung before – last night, or even this morning? They could have had lunch together then, or a whole evening to themselves, before Chris was even back.

'Hallo? Are you still there, Morna?'

'Yes – sorry. There's just a minor problem. My daughter's expected home from France today, so . . .'

'Oh, I see. Of course I shan't butt in then. I'm afraid I shan't see you, though. I'm returning home tomorrow and I'd planned to catch a fairly early train. Would it be an awful chore for you to post the stuff? If you send it first class, it should arrive before I leave for Oban. Or take your time and send it direct to the island. The post's a bit sporadic there – depends on the crofter's boat. But at least it's summer, more or less, so he should be able to get across to the mainland.'

Morna jabbed her foot against the settle. Summer was over. It was winter in her mind, a cold sea crashing between them, cutting her off.

'No, David, I really ought to see you. There's . . . er . . . various things I need to explain and . . . Look, why not come down here as you suggested and I'll cook dinner for us all?'

'*All*?' He sounded wary. She had managed to explain

about the divorce, included it matter-of-factly in one of her letters – almost as an aside. He had never brought it up, never mentioned it at all. Did he imagine now there was someone else?

'Only Chris's boyfriend. They're more or less inseparable. He'll be going up to meet her.'

'B . . . But won't I be in the way? I mean, your daughter's first night back and . . .'

Morna was worried about that herself, nervous about a foursome. Chris had never seen her with any man but Neil. 'Tell you what – she should be back before six. Why don't you come at seven thirty? Then I'll have had a little time with her on my own.' Time enough to explain who David was – employer, odd acquaintance. 'We can eat at eight and . . .'

'But are you sure it's no trouble?'

'No, I'd enjoy it.'

She already felt excited – not just her daughter back, but David in her house as guest and friend. She sprinted upstairs for purse and car keys, drove to the supermarket, her elation only ebbing as she stood dithering in the aisles, wondering what to cook. How on earth could she please the three of them, turn out something suited to them all? Chris had recently become a vegetarian and ate nothing much but salads, anyway. Martin dismissed salads as rabbit fodder, demanded solid stodgy food – chips with ketchup, suet puddings with custard – which seemed entirely wrong for David. If he were eating at all, it would probably be a diet like St Abban's – herbs and water or a thin potage of lentils. Perhaps she'd make some pasta dish – that was fairly basic – but Martin disliked what he called messed-up food, preferred straight steak or chops. It was Friday, though, and supposing David ate only fish on Fridays? The church had long since dropped its rule of abstinence, but *he* might still observe it, hark back to some earlier age when standards were less lax. She walked towards the fish counter. She could make Chris a separate salad while the rest of them ate halibut or trout or . . . No – Martin hated fish, except fish fingers, and she was damned if she'd serve those and turn a celebration dinner into kids' tea.

She stood blocking the aisle with her trolley, running through her cook books in her mind. Cook books didn't cater for guests as disparate as hers. Perhaps it would be simplest to prepare three separate meals – salad for Chris, fish for her and David, steak and chips for Martin with all the trimmings.

She returned with loaded baskets, worrying now that she had done a Neil and bought too much – not just sole and T-bone, but wine, strawberries, four different cheeses, three sorts of bread. She stood staring at the pile of food swamping the kitchen table. St Abban would regard it as belly worship, self-indulgent greed. There were even problems with the table setting. If she used her best bone china, Chris would object. When Martin had first come round, she had been jumpy and on edge.

'Don't fuss, Mum. I don't want things too fancy. He's not used to it. They eat in the kitchen.'

Neil had pulled himself out of the kitchen and now his daughter was returning to it.

'No one has fish knives, Mum. It's phoney.'

The fish knives and forks had been a wedding present from her mother's sister, Maud. Real ivory handles, silver filigree blades. Works of art. Neil had treasured them. Fish knives were part of his promotion – from office boy to assistant account executive to director of his own agency. She wondered if they had fish knives in Los Angeles.

She took two out from their velvet-lined mahogany box, laid them on the table, snatched them up again, replacing them with ordinary stainless steel; then removed that in its turn, whisked off the damask cloth, folded it in the drawer, started again from scratch. She got out her oldest place mats, swapped the crystal glasses for plain no-nonsense tumblers, banged the ketchup bottle down by Martin's place. No wonder saints were wary of material things, stuck to a habit or a uniform, ate beans or bread-and-water off bare boards, built even their monasteries to a standard plan. Whatever crockery or house or clothes you chose expressed some value, outraged some canon, involved you in some statement about dress or taste or status.

She stared around the kitchen. She had never noticed before how much Neil had put his stamp on it, even while purporting to follow her superior taste in furnishings and furniture. He had insisted on all the machines. Machines declared prosperity, success. Everything her mother or the nuns had done patiently and laboriously by hand – making coffee, chopping onions, washing clothes or dishes – she did swiftly, courtesy of Neil's machines. He had left them all behind. She was never sure whether through simple generosity, or guilt, or because it was too expensive or too complicated to ship them to the States. Now it was Martin who used his video recorder, Chris who played about with his computer, and she herself went on pressing switches, dialling programmes, saving herself time when time weighed heavy on her.

What would David think of the house, with its luxuries, its gloss, too big and showy for two women on their own? Neil had certainly been generous – left her everything, when other wives were stripped and plucked. He even paid the mortgage and the rates still, had arranged the settlement as if he were still the householder, who had gone away for no more than a short spell. She had offered to move somewhere smaller, find a flat or maisonette, but he seemed strangely loath to cut all ties with his first middle-class exclusive property, the first proof of his success, the bricks-and-mortar evidence that he had outgrown his lowly origins. He appeared to want to keep the place as a sort of monument, a milestone on his way to even better things. Yet it made it harder for her in a way – at least emotionally – more difficult to accept that the real and more important ties were broken.

'You're really very lucky,' friends had said.

'Yes,' she nodded, 'lucky,' hoping at least that the endless whirr and chunter of machines would drown out the howling in her head.

She washed the salads, peeled the vegetables, prepared the fish and meat; then flicked around the house with a duster, seeing it through David's eyes, not Neil's – a snob suburban villa with too much of everything. She walked upstairs to the so-called master bedroom. The master was there still, had chosen the bed himself, insisted on kingsize. 'To match me,' he'd said, grabbing her hand and clamping it round his . . . his . . . She had never known what to call it, not even in the privacy of her own mind. The nuns' *Shorter Catholic Dictionary* had emphatically excluded the male organ and all its more familiar forms. Neil had solved the problem for her, christened it Big Sam. Big Sam ruled, OK. He was Neil's spoiled and darling child who must never be denied, always petted and indulged. Morna found him ugly, red-faced, greedy and demanding. Yet if he ever dwindled, things were worse – a Small Sam could ruin a whole day. Any threat to Neil's virility and he would sulk or storm, lose his temper over trivialities, blame his wife. Perhaps she was to blame. She had read once that some men were so sensitive to their partner's mood, that a woman could make them lose their erection just by willing it. She *had* willed it – often – turned over when she saw Sam swelling, tried to pretend she was already asleep, even thought murderous thoughts about castration.

If Neil had been less insistent, she might have found some pleasure in it. But sex was a second career for him. He brought the same ambition to it, the same ruthless dedication. Once, she had started adding up all the hours and hours she must have spent on top of him, or under him, or side by side, or kneeling, during their fourteen years of marriage, and realized that if she had spent that time at a language school instead, she could have mastered five or six new languages by now, plus all their literatures – translated the entire collected works of Racine and Corneille, turned Aeschylus into German or rendered Pliny in Serbo-Croat.

Yet, despite such diligence, she had received no diplomas or doctorates in bedroom studies, won no medals, set no records. She, who had been the convent school's star pupil and one of the brightest in her year at university, was E-stream when it came to sex. It wasn't really Neil's fault. He was as generous in sex as in everything else. Perhaps that was the trouble, though. She didn't want the things he urged on her – his wet, hurting, biting, insisting mouth, Big Sam penetrating orifices the nuns had never even permitted to exist.

In the Sixth Form, Reverend Mother herself had taken what was labelled 'Life Instruction'. She talked about 'The World', which meant anything outside the four walls of St Margaret's, warning them almost daily of its dangers; imploring them to beware especially of the letter D – D for Devil. The Devil lay waiting in the World offering Drugs, Drink, Dancing and Depravity. Sex as such was never mentioned, though there was a digression about Hands which were apparently as dangerous as the Devil, though Reverend Mother never explained quite how. She told them that they could kiss their fiancés once they were formally engaged, but only the type of kiss they would be prepared to give if their own mothers and Our Blessed Mother herself were both present in the room with them as chaperones. One of the problems with Neil had been the constant feeling that Bea and the Blessed Virgin were indeed sitting side by side on the velour topped bedroom stool, watching Big Sam going through his paces.

She found the bedroom vulgar. Neil had insisted on mirrors and a real fur rug. Instead of the antique mahogany downstairs, they had fitted mirrored cupboards floor to ceiling, reflecting and quadrupling that smug expanse of bed. She sat down on the edge of it, remembering. Four big Big Sams, four wives shrinking from them. And now she had the perversity to miss him – not just Neil, Sam too.

She glanced at her watch – already almost five – time to change. She wouldn't have changed for Chris, nor Chris and Martin, but David had never seen her in a dress. She opened the cupboards her side. Neil's side was empty. She had never allowed her things to stray from the thin brass rail which divided his from hers. He had chosen most of her clothes and in the five years since he had left, she had bought almost nothing new. No point.

She took out Neil's favourite dress – clingy scarlet with a low neck – put it back again. David was colleague and ascetic, nothing more. She fingered the brown – safe, boring, and too thick for early September. She could see Bea's old teddy-bear reflected in the mirrors, watching her boss-eyed from his chair. Bea had bequeathed him to her when she first went off to boarding school at seven. She had cried so often into his fur, she had worn him half away. He had left school with her, moved to university, been ragged by a crowd of students, introduced to Neil; even smuggled into her case on honeymoon, remained ten days under the creaking lurching bed.

On their first anniversary, Neil had been turning out his near-new suits, flung half of them into a cardboard box.

'Darling, if that little Cub Scout calls, give him these for jumble.'

Bea had brought her up never to waste. Brown paper from parcels was smoothed out, used again; string never cut but patiently untied. Thrift was a virtue, practised also by the nuns. Neil squandered everything, enjoyed it. Was that why she had married him – the first thing not on ration, the first person who didn't count the change? Even so, it hurt to hand over expensive handmade suits, hear them classed as jumble. Morna helped the Cub Scout shift the box, noticed a shabby paw protruding from the pinstripes.

Neil was in the office. She only phoned him in emergencies. She stood shaking in the hall while his secretary tried various extensions.

'How *could* you, Neil? You know what Bear . . .'

'But he's falling apart – and filthy dirty, Morna, covered in germs.'

She thought of the germs swarming on Big Sam – not only germs, but devils. Bear was holy. He had been blessed by the Pope when she took him to Rome on her first school pilgrimage in 1953. He had made his First Communion the same day as she had, his balding stomach concealed in white flounces, his veil falling over one glass eye.

Neil had rung off, arrived home that evening with a broad smile and an even larger parcel. She knew what it would be, cringed before she had even eased the string off. (She still saved string, in spite of Neil.) She stared at the thick gold plush, the satin bow, the expensive gross vulgarity of a new bear two foot tall with everything but a soul and history.

'Thanks,' she muttered, almost under her breath.

That night in bed was the first time she refused him.

Morna slammed the wardrobe door, wished she could shut Neil out as easily. She was shamefully aware how often he kept striding through her mind, or turning up in unexpected places, upsetting her, confusing her, keeping her in thrall still. In one way, it was easy to explain. Neil had been her first and only lover, had become her God and guru, the assured dogmatic Saviour who had reversed all the nuns' values and beliefs. He had thrown her a towrope, shouted 'Follow me!' Captain God. The trouble was the rope had snapped and he had cruised away to brighter warmer waters, leaving her tossing and pitching in his wake. It was her own fault, in a sense, if she refused to steer her own course after five whole years without him. In some ways, she had done so – with her job, her daughter's upbringing – but one scared and childish part of her kept clinging to that pathetic piece of rope, expecting Neil to pick it up again, pull her into safety.

She dragged off her old skirt, changed into the brown. It *was* too thick, and hardly flattering – but it seemed stupid now to go to so much trouble. It was Chris she wanted to see, wished almost she could oust the men – Martin as well as David – be just mother and daughter again as they had been until this year, on their own, exclusive. Whatever its pain, the divorce had brought them closer, changed the whole pattern of their life. No more huge cooked breakfasts with the radio booming and Neil cowering the kitchen with his rush and noise; no more grandiose dinner parties – claret breathing on the sideboard, Pouilly Fuissé chilling in the fridge, slick-suited ad-men vaunting and wisecracking till the early hours. Instead, Chris brought girlfriends home from school – still the upmarket private school Neil had insisted on to deflect attention from his own skimpy education – Emilys and Sarahs, Charlottes and Fionas, sitting in the kitchen eating egg sandwiches without the crusts, jelly and ice cream. She had sat with them, pouring tea, cutting cake, chatting about guinea pigs or netball matches, helping with homework or new maths, plaiting hair. It was Fiona, not Chris, who first had a boyfriend. Morna stayed upstairs that day, while the two girls whispered and giggled on their own. When she came down to fill the teapot, they stopped abruptly and the silence felt as cold as if someone had left the door ajar in winter. Martin came much later, just a name at first, dropped casually into the conversation. It was two months more before she was actually allowed to meet him. After that, she rarely saw Chris without him. The Fionas and the Emmas disappeared.

Morna finished dressing, started on her face. Chris should have arrived by now, hanging on to Martin's arm, looking almost identical from the back, both in matching Levis, narrow-hipped, long-legged, both with cropped brown hair. It didn't seem fair that Chris had turned out plain when she and Neil were both reasonably attractive. Or *had* been, anyway. Morna glanced at her four reflections in the mirrors. The figure which Neil had called voluptuous now needed constant watching to avoid less flattering adjectives; the hair he had praised as fiery had to be kindled from a bottle. How did David see her? Middle-aged and fading? Or pretty still? As a woman at all, or simply as a linguist whose gender was immaterial? She reapplied her lipstick, returned downstairs, stopped by the phone, willing it to ring. She longed to hear her daughter's voice – 'I'm back, Mum!' Chris had only called her Mum since Martin. The Fionas and the Carolines had Mummies.

She picked up the receiver, dialled the Euroways Head Office. No delays. The boat had docked on time, the coach discharged its passengers at Victoria within a minute of the expected time. She rang Martin, knew nobody would answer, since he had gone to meet Chris, and his mother (Mum) worked late.

It was half past six already. David would arrive in just an hour. She prayed Chris would turn up first. She had better start the cooking, anyway. That at least would stop her fretting.

By eight o'clock, no one had arrived; the fretting turned to fear. The blood from the steak was carnage on the motorway, the glazed eye of the fish her daughter's in the mortuary. Ironical to travel the seven hundred miles and more safely from Les Lecques, only to crash on the last stretch down to Weybridge. Martin's bike was old, and probably overloaded. She had warned him about the dangers of carrying too much luggage, but he'd only shrugged and said the bags were soft and squashy, would fit on easily. Martin shrugged off things too often. She glanced down at his steak, marbled with skid-marks of fat and still oozing gore, turned away nauseated. How could a sensitive vegetarian be in love with such a carnivore?

Love was dangerous as well as motorbikes. If Chris married the wrong man, she could mess up her whole life. Neil should be there to vet the men, share the responsibility. She walked to the window, stared out at the garden. The gold was beginning to tarnish now; the day no longer shining young, but ageing, turning grey.

She returned to the stove, checked on all the food. The fish looked very dead – white flesh shrinking from white bones. Chris's bones scattered in the overtaking lane. Ridiculous. A hundred things could delay her on such a long and complex journey. She was overreacting, behaving like the standard hysterical mother. The word mother had never seemed more crucial. It was her daughter she had lived for after Neil had gone; her daughter who made her still a family, gave her a rôle and purpose.

She sat at the table in Chris's place, both hands gripping the wooden salad bowl. She had made the salad a work of art – tomato flowers, radish roses, slices of apple arranged like petals with celery stalks, green-pepper leaves. She always had to tempt her daughter to get her to eat enough, offer treats or titbits. Chris had lost her appetite along with her father. 'I'm not hungry,' she'd kept saying, pushing away cheese and asparagus crêpes or lemon soufflé. She herself had eaten more – felt hollow inside, needed to stuff the gap. Nothing tasted, nothing fattened. It was the only time she had lost weight without trying. She had put the weight back on now, yet the hollow was still there, beneath the flesh.

'Please God,' she prayed. 'Let her be safe.' The retreatants were right. There had to be a God so you could pray to Him when the one thing you valued in your life was threatened. Plain, moody Chris *was* her life – her flesh, future, heritage.

When the doorbell rang, she flung herself towards it, almost wept that it was David standing there and not her daughter. He was rambling on about some hold-up on the train and how he hadn't been able to phone because they were stuck between Vauxhall and Clapham Junction.

'Come in,' she said. He was wearing a white shirt with a dark blue jacket, looked smart and yet uneasy as if he had put on clothes which belonged to someone else, was clutching a small brown paper bag. All the pleasure she should have felt on seeing him seemed now to have seeped away. She led him down the hall. It seemed suddenly too full of things – antique settle, inlaid table, framed prints set one above the other.

'I'm afraid my daughter isn't back yet. Shall we have a drink?' Her hands were shaking on the bottle. She fetched her own glass, sat down opposite. Stupid to panic. David had materialized with a perfectly routine reason for his delay – and Chris would do the same, in just a moment. She sipped her sherry, sat back in her chair. Everything was normal now, two people sipping amontillado, waiting for their younger guests.

'I'm sorry about your train,' she said. 'They can be awful.'

'*I'm* sorry to be late.' David was pulling at a button on his jacket. 'How about your daughter? Is she coming by train as well?'

'No, motorbike from London, and coach before that.' Cheaper and more dangerous. 'It takes twenty-seven hours in all, with various stops and so on.'

'She'll be pretty tired, then.'

'Mm.'

She could see him glancing round the room. It suddenly looked vulgar, like the bedroom – an uneasy mix of her and Neil. Bea had bequeathed them some of her choicest pieces – the Queen Anne sideboard, the mahogany sewing table. Neil had chosen the rest – insisted on the sort of expensive modern masculine furniture he had in his own advertising agency: leather chairs, chrome and glass coffee table, hessian on the walls, prints chosen more to tone than for any artistic merit. Antiques aged gracefully. Time had done nothing to Bea's furniture except improve its patina; had been more unkind to Neil's things. The long-pile oatmeal carpet was losing its plush like Bear, there were scratches on the glass, the leather chairs were sagging. She wondered what would happen when they got older still. Throwing them out would be like destroying Neil. She couldn't live there for ever, though, custodian of Neil's monument – especially after Chris had left. Even with the two of them, it was extravagant, unjustified. Was David judging her? One of the retreat talks had been on poverty – six or seven kids squabbling in a flyblown room, eight million Indians crammed into Calcutta, while Mrs Neil Gordon spread herself through nine *House & Garden* rooms and half an acre of velvet lawn and apple trees.

If there *had* been an accident, she would be left alone in what the estate agents described as a family home. Chris filled half the house now and even Martin had begun to take it over, left his stuff around. Without them, she would shrink to nothing. Really nothing. She glanced across at David, long legs stretched out straight in front of him, trousers slightly short. She should be entertaining him, not indulging in self-pity. She had forgotten how tall he was, forgotten the lurch of excitement and nervousness he had produced in her before, and which was returning even now, beneath the worry over Chris.

'Have another drink,' she urged.

'I've hardly started this one.'

'Fasting again?'

He forced a smile. 'No.'

'Good. I've got a lot of food out there and no one to eat it. I mean, we can't really start without them. Or do you think we should?'

'Oh, no.'

He seemed so sure, she let herself relax a little. No policeman had rung, no hospital or doctor. No news is good news, people always said. Except people said a lot of things which turned out false – 'Every cloud has a silver lining', 'Enough is as good as a feast', 'God is love'.

'Do you believe in God?' she asked suddenly, cursing herself for being so direct. She had planned to orchestrate the evening, lead only gradually and slyly to the crucial questions, maybe use her daughter as a sort of catalyst. It was a stupid question, anyway. Of course he believed in God. Hilden Cross would hardly invite a speaker who was an out-and-out atheist. And yet through the whole of his lecture on the miraculous, he had never mentioned God as such, seemed always to slip between or beyond conventional definitions.

David took a cautious sip of his sherry. '*My* God, yes.'

'What about St Abban's?'

'They're not that different.'

'Really? A hair-shirt God, then, gobbling up your penances?'

'Oh no, a *young* God. Abban's God was thirteen hundred years less old and tired than ours. He still danced and sang.'

'That sounds rather pagan.'

'Maybe. Remember how close the pagans were. And St Abban was a Celt as well as a Christian, knew the old traditions.'

'Yet he seems to emphasize denial all the time.' Morna

recalled the French professor's words – *pénitence, mortification corporelle*.

'Yes, but don't you find he does it with a . . . sort of joy? It's not a spoilsport sourboots attitude, like some of the later ascetics. I know our society shies away from *any* type of self-denial, regards it as neurotic or obsessional, but I disagree with that. Anything worth having is worth suffering for, and Abban's so . . . so eager to suffer anything. He almost burns with it, like a bridegroom going through the fire for his Beloved.'

Morna stared at him. Half a glass of sherry had loosened his tongue already. He was sounding poetic, romantic even. She tried to refill his glass, but he covered it with his hand.

'Go on, just a small one. Let's be pagan.'

David laughed, drained his glass, held it out to her. 'There you are.'

She filled it, lingered by his chair – couldn't see the clock from there, only hear it ticking through the silence. It seemed impossible to concentrate on intellectual matters or make routine conversation while Chris was still delayed.

David uncrossed his legs, cleared his throat. 'You're . . . er . . . worried, aren't you, Morna – about your daughter?'

She nodded.

'You've phoned the boat and train, I take it?'

'Mm.'

'And no one's rung you?'

'No.'

'Shall we pray for her?'

Morna turned on her heel, strode back to the chair. If he were going to behave like Father Clarke, imagining God had time to spot-check all the mortuaries or work her own personal miracle as soon as they joined their hands, then . . .

'Don't overreact. I don't mean to a God – mine or yours or anyone else's. Just hold her in our own thoughts, concentrate all our energy on her safety. It's a question of trust. We've got to *trust* she's safe, refuse to doubt it.'

'That's . . . praying?'

'Isn't it? The power of the mind's enormous – the power of faith. Just shut your eyes and concentrate a moment.'

It sounded bogus, but she shut them all the same – saw Chris at eight months trying to sit up – fierce determined expression on her face, tenacious arms. The child had mastered it, then gone on to walk, talk, add up. Amazing skills. She had trusted *then*. It had never entered her head that Chris might turn out lame, dumb, dyslexic, even dull. She hadn't. Was that the result of trusting, or just good luck?

She opened her eyes a crack to check on David. His were still closed, his whole face creased in concentration. It touched her suddenly that he should lavish such concern and fervour on someone he had never met. He had been delayed himself, must be tired, hungry – had expected dinner, not a worry-hour. Several minutes passed. She could almost feel the power and intensity of his faith, tangible and vibrant in the air; the room charged with it, alive with it. It was like a spell thawing her own worry. Her daughter would be safe – she knew it now.

'Listen,' she said, when he had opened his eyes at last. 'Why don't we go over my translation until Chris and Martin turn up, and have dinner after that – unless you're starving?'

'No, that's fine.'

'Right, bring your glass to the study and I'll show you what I've done since . . .'

Neil had called it study, kept his tycoon toys there. There was still a modern sculpture on the desk, a fancy chrome-framed calendar five years out of date. Before Neil had left, she had done her own work in the kitchen, first pushing back the toaster and the coffee pot, clearing crumbs and dirty cups. Neil didn't want a working wife. She felt less guilty playing with words at the kitchen table, like a child. 'Just keeping up my languages,' she told people.

She pulled up a second chair for David, wished the room wasn't quite so grand. You could sleep seven homeless children there, cram in twenty-seven of Calcutta's starving. Even the desk was big enough for four. She edged a little nearer David so he could see the manuscript.

'The main problem was the shorthand,' she told him. 'I don't think you realized, but Le Goff changed it halfway through. At first he was using his own brand of sort of speedwriting, leaving off the second halves of words, putting initials instead of spelling whole words out, but then it changes. He seems to have picked up shorthand proper. Fortunately my shorthand's still quite good, so I could follow most of it, but then he starts combining the two, adding hieroglyphs of his own and that's where I'm slowed down.'

David had taken off his jacket, was flicking through the pages. 'I'm sorry, I'd no idea what . . . You've done a hell of a lot, though. I just don't know how you managed it in the time. I can't tell you what a help it is. I'm absolutely delighted.'

Morna turned to the originals, checked through them for examples of the shorthand. The work had certainly been demanding. She had had to give up reading, walks, even cut her sleep down, in order to complete so much. David was right about joy in self-denial. There *had* been joy in it – not only in her achievement, but in his obvious satisfaction.

'After chapter ten, it gets much easier. In fact, what I've done is . . .' She broke off, and kicked her chair back, darted down the hall, calling out apologies to David as she flung open the front door.

'Chris!'

'Mummy!'

No Mum, no Martin, not even any luggage. They were

hugging – a pre-teens hug, fierce and unselfconscious. Morna could feel her daughter's tears hot against her neck.

'What's wrong, darling? What happened?'

'N . . . Nothing.'

Chris was thinner even than when she left, ribs hard against her own flesh. 'Where's Martin? Didn't he come and meet you? Why didn't you phone? I'd have come myself and . . .'

'He d . . . did come, he did – in fact all the way to Dover. He was w . . . waiting for me on the quay.'

'Why are you so late, then?'

'We . . . er . . . didn't start immediately, and then we . . . stopped for a bit and . . .' Chris suddenly pulled away, rocketed upstairs.

Morna swung round. David was standing tall and awkward in the kitchen doorway. She was torn between the two of them, running halfway up the stairs, then stopping, turning back. 'I'm sorry,' she called down. 'Have another drink, David. Read my work. I must just see what . . .'

'Of course.' David was putting on his jacket, making for the door. 'Look, I'd better go now. I . . . I'll phone you in the morning.'

'No, *please*. Please stay.' She was pleading with him, voice rising, felt ridiculous relief when he trailed back to the study, closed the door.

She dashed on up to Chris who was standing by the windows, staring out. Morna cursed herself for the apples and the flowers, the vulgar comic card. If Martin were lying paralysed in hospital, such things were crassly inappropriate.

'Martin's not . . . hurt, is he?'

Chris shook her head. She had removed her jacket but still had a blue silk scarf swathed around her neck, almost like a bandage. Chris never wore scarves – nor gloves and hats, despite the number Bea had given her.

'What is it, then?'

'Oh – nothing . . .' Chris still kept her back turned, shutting her mother off.

Morna felt excluded, useless, walked slowly to the door.

'We had an argument, okay?' Chris swung round, started pacing up and down. 'Two arguments, in fact.'

'Wh . . . What about?'

'Oh, everything. Him and me. The future. You see . . .' She paused, chewed her lip. 'Bunny wrote to me in France.'

'*Bunny*?' Morna gripped the doorframe. That was the new wife's name.

'Yeah. She can't spell and she uses ghastly pink paper which smells of roses. She wanted us to visit them.'

'Us? What, you and Martin?'

'No, you and me.'

'*Me*?'

'Yup. She's suggesting we go out there for Christmas.'

'You mean California?'

'Mm. Martin's furious. He says I've been away two months as it is, and we've been arguing over Christmas anyway, almost since the last one. He wants me to spend it at his place. I told him about Grandma and how she'd hate it if we broke the tradition and her being on her own and everything. So we'd agreed Christmas Day as usual there, and Boxing Day with him. But now . . .'

'But you're not *going*, are you? Not to Bunny's?' Morna was still incredulous. One of the advantages of Bunny was that she wasn't real. The name was so absurd to start with, you couldn't take it seriously. She was just a harmless pet, something Neil kept in a cage, would tire of when he grew up. But if Chris were to meet her, stay in her house, get to know her son, exchange letters on her pink scented paper, then . . .

'Look, Mum, I haven't seen my father for five whole years. If I wait for him to come back here, I'll be dead and buried.'

'B . . . But we can't afford it. The fares are . . .'

'He's paying everything. It's my Christmas present and birthday present combined. He wrote to me as well – not on pink, but a sort of grey glossy art paper with the name of his firm on top – huge. He said as soon as we let him know, he'd book the tickets.'

Morna still gagged on the 'we'. 'But why *me*, for heaven's sake?'

'That's Bunny, I suppose. She's got this thing about loving her enemy.'

'And I'm the enemy?' Morna tried to make her voice sound neutral. 'I should have thought it was the other way round.'

'Well, she wants you to love *her*, then.' Chris wiped her eyes with her sleeve. 'I wish you would, Mum. Try, at least. I hate you hating her.'

'I . . . don't.' Morna had tried for five damned years to say nothing, stay always bloody neutral, keep her racking disapproval locked up in her mind. And Chris, her shrewd and honest daughter, had seen through her all the time.

'I won't go if you don't.' Chris sagged down on the bed.

'Why not? That's ridiculous.' Unfair. A sort of blackmail. Morna resented Chris as well now. Christmas was sacrosanct. Bea in dove-grey cashmere and real pearl earrings, and Joy with a red bow on her fringe; Chris out of jeans as a concession to her Grandma, she in Chris's blusher and mascara. Four females proving that they didn't need their men. Frost on the windows, glowing fires inside.

The glow paled into the California sun – golden beaches, golden curls on Bunny's four-year-old, proving something different – that she and Neil had . . . had . . . Mustn't think about it. How could she not, when her safe and tidy calendar was disrupted? Waking on Christmas morning in an enemy house. Rose-scented Bunny gift-wrapping bitterness and resentment. Planes, packing, falseness, fear, fear.

'You don't understand, Mum.' Chris sounded close to tears again. 'I'm . . . scared of Daddy. Well, not scared exactly, but . . . I don't feel easy with him. I mean, I won't do in the States.'

'Why go at all, then?'

'Look, just because you're divorced, it doesn't mean *I* have to be as well. I *want* a father. He left when I was twelve – dying to be netball captain and doing my first-aid badge at Girl Guides. That's not me any more.'

'And supposing *he's* changed just as much?'

'He will have. That's the point. I'm remembering him all wrong – sometimes not remembering him at all. Do you realize, Mum, just before I went to France, Martin asked me what colour my father's eyes were. I said "grey", of course, like mine, and tried to picture them, like in – you know, a sort of passport-photo machine flashing little pictures into your mind when you put your 50p in. But the machine had broken down. The photos were all blank.'

'But . . .' Morna stared around the room. Neil smiling, wheedling, bare-torsoed in his swimming-trunks. 'He's *here*. You see him every day.'

'I don't. I hate those photographs. They're all sham.'

'So why keep them, darling? I'm not too keen on them myself.'

'I've got to keep them. I've nothing else. Oh, his presents, yes, but they're *his* taste, not mine – or maybe even Bunny's – and I bet he gets his secretary to send them. He'd never have the time to hunt around for brown paper and Sellotape and stuff. They're probably just a guilt thing, anyway, to make up for the fact he hardly ever writes. Even when I *do* get a letter, like the one in France, it's all sort of stiff and false. He's no idea what to say. I mean, he asks me things like how am I enjoying netball, when I gave it up three years ago.'

'So why don't you tell him in *your* letters?'

'I do.'

There was silence for a moment.

'I don't think he even reads them – not properly – just the beginning and the end. Like he used to do with books – you know, so he can *say* he's read them and feel okay about it.' Chris was tugging off her boots. 'By the way, who's that guy downstairs?'

'David Anthony.'

'*Who*? He's dishy, isn't he?'

'Is he?'

'Well, in a ravaged sort of way. Is he divorced?'

Morna laughed. 'No.'

'Mum, you're not going *out* with him, are you?'

'Would that be so monstrous?'

Chris didn't answer, hunted for her slippers.

'No, I'm not, in fact. I'm doing some work for him.'

'Work, at this hour?'

Morna had always kept her evenings free, devoted them to Chris. 'I'm sorry if he's in your way. He just came to pick up a translation. I assumed Martin would be here and we could all have . . .' Shouldn't have mentioned Martin. Chris was weeping again, silent tears which puffed her eyes. 'Don't cry, darling. You're probably just exhausted from the journey and everything seems worse. Christmas doesn't matter. We'll sort it out. Perhaps Martin could go instead of me.'

'How c . . . can he? He's got a job and Daddy's hardly likely to pay for . . .' Chris broke off, pulled out a rose from one of the flower arrangements, watched it shed its petals. She was wearing a creased and dirty tee shirt with 'MAIS OUI' printed across it in scarlet capitals. Her breasts barely pushed the letters out. Perhaps Martin wanted curves.

'Where's your luggage, anyway?'

'Still on the bike.'

'It can't stay there. What are you going to . . . ?'

'*Leave* it, Mum.'

Morna pushed the hurt down, tried again. 'How was France? You've hardly told me anything about it.'

'Okay.'

'Did *Madame* improve?'

'A bit. Could we leave it till the morning? I'm whacked.'

'Yes, of course. How about some dinner?'

'Not hungry, thanks.'

'Chris . . . ?'

'Mm . . .'

'Could I ask you a favour, darling? I know you're tired, but . . .'

'If it's "will I phone Martin and ask him to bring my luggage back", no I won't.'

'Nothing to do with Martin. It's . . . David. I wondered if you'd come downstairs, just for half an hour, and help me talk to him? I invited him to dinner, so I can't really . . .'

'Who *is* this bloke? Is he staying here or something?'

'Don't be silly.' Morna sounded sharper than she intended. Did her daughter imagine that she had smuggled David in the day she had left for France and been living with him ever since? The thought was not unattractive. Working together, as she had never done with Neil, unravelling problems of chronology, discussing shades of meaning in a single word, digging up more and more fragments of St Abban as if he were a pot or artifact.

'He's only dropped in for an hour or so. As soon as we've had dinner, I can drive him to the station, and then we'll be on our own. All right?' Morna hugged her daughter again. 'You've still got your Mum, you know.'

'Yeah, I know. Thanks.'

Chris sounded embarrassed, stood rigid, unresponsive. Morna let her go. Perhaps she should have stopped the hugging now that Martin was on the scene. Bea still hugged *her* and she had to admit she didn't really like it. The smell of dog and powder, the possession.

She stared at Chris's neck. The scarf had slipped, revealing a purple bruise. She mumbled something, escaped into her own room. Eighteen years ago, she had had a bruise like that herself, in exactly the same spot. It had been wintertime, so she had worn polo-necks and mufflers until it faded. Weeks it took, marbling purple to red to mauve to dirty yellow. A love-bite, Neil had called it. He hadn't used his teeth, more his tongue and lips, nuzzling on and on in a fierce hurting sort of kissing as if his mouth were a suction machine pulling on her flesh, leaving his mark for everyone to see – the milkman, the butcher, the lynx-eyed couple opposite, Bea herself. And then he *had* bitten – hard – her ear and then her breast. She had hated it, hated it, pushed him off. Wild beasts bit, not husbands. The nuns had never mentioned biting. 'Hands' they'd said, or kissing with Our Lady in the room, even making souls for God, but never ever teeth. She felt outraged. The bruising on her neck was like a blazon of sin, or the purple bands which the prostitutes of ancient Rome wore to advertise their services. She was now a sexual being, her loss of innocence as blatantly on show as if they had hung up the blood-stained bed-sheets outside the window.

Neil couldn't understand her upset. The marks to him signified passion and virility, proved they were adult and enjoying it. However, he didn't bite again. Tried other things instead, things which Reverend Mother would have blushed at, or simply not believed went on between a Christian man and wife. Often, she had removed her mind, so that they were happening far away to someone else, some cheap non-convent girl at the far end of the bed, while she herself lay back against the pillows and thought of Florence Nightingale.

She felt guilty now. How could she have been so prudish,

selfish, even? What was virtue in the nuns' eyes was sin in the world's – to be rigid and uncooperative in bed, to fail to enjoy it. And supposing she had passed on her antipathy to Chris? Was her daughter outraged because Martin had given her a love-bite which perhaps he had intended simply as a welcome-home gift, his equivalent of apples, flowers? Had it been more than just a love-bite? What had they been up to all this time? Booked into some hotel in Dover, made babies there together?

She had always tried to blot out what her daughter did with Martin. People said it was impossible to imagine your parents having sex. She hadn't had to deal with that. Bea had dodged the issue by remaining a widow and a staunch Catholic. But it was equally impossible to imagine daughters making love. They would always be too young. Yet Chris and Martin had known each other for eight long months already. Surely they . . . ? Except where would they go? Martin worked as a printer, but his real passion was for scuba diving. That took all his wages – not hotel bills. Neil had seduced her in his car. Martin had a third-hand motorbike. Martin had stayed the night with them, but only once or twice, and she had put him up in the spare room. On the first occasion she had woken in the early hours, anxious suddenly. Had she been woken by a noise – the opening and shutting of a door, the creaking of a bed? She crept along to her daughter's room, opened the door a crack. Chris was sleeping on her back, on her own, wearing a brushed cotton tracksuit which doubled as pyjamas and made her look innocent, a defenceless child again. She had tiptoed away feeling cheap, a traitor. She had never forbidden sex, hardly ever mentioned it. She had been as coy as Bea, as naïve as the nuns. She had broached the subject once, started talking vaguely and too fast about VD, contraception. Chris had stopped her.

'We've done all that at school, Mum.' She sounded bored,

as if it were algebra or economics. 'Miss Mason told us in biology. She made the whole thing sound like some disease. Doctors before you start, to dish you out pills and things or fit you with horrible contraptions, then clinics when you catch the pox, then more doctors for the abortion . . . No thanks!'

'It's not *like* that.' Morna had started, then stopped. Wasn't it? Sex education was more or less impossible. How could you talk about release or ecstasy unless you had experienced them in person? Perhaps Miss Mason was a woman like herself – honours in her degree course, but a failure when it came to sex. Degrees hardly counted unless you had also graduated in the school of Masters and Johnson. She had read the books, worked through the syllabus, yet still failed to make the grade. The books depressed her. One was alphabetical, moved from algolagnia and anus to yohimbine (some sort of aphrodisiac). She knew what Chris meant about diseases. Half the entries had been pathological – epididymitis, pederasty, phimosis. The other half made her feel frigid and inadequate – banished to the remedial class.

'Mum . . .'

She jumped. Chris was standing at the door. The scarf was gone. She was wearing a high necked blouse now, the same dirty crumpled jeans. 'I thought you wanted dinner?'

'Yes, sorry. Let's go down.'

The doorbell rang before they got halfway. Chris nose-dived the last five steps, dashed along the hall. Morna could see a dark head blurred and distorted through the glass panel in the front door, hear Chris's shrill triumphant 'Martin!' She tried to suppress a sudden stab of anger as she greeted him herself. Did she resent her daughter's boyfriend simply because he had usurped her place as Most Important Person in Chris's life? Or because she was a snob like Bea? Or because Martin always seemed a stranger, even when he sat daily in her house? It was as if he and she were from two different countries with different languages, could communicate only in stiff and formal monosyllables – polite noises which meant nothing, hid bafflement and tension on both sides. Or was it more that she hated her daughter's submission to her man, echoing her own to Neil? Even now, Chris would probably be apologizing. They had disappeared upstairs together. She had apologized herself to Neil, even after the biting. Submission was safer.

She left them on their own, returned to the study where David was still sitting at the desk. He had never married, never known that endless game of winning points and losing sleep, or losing face and gaining approval, safety.

'I'm so sorry. My daughter . . .' David didn't have a daughter either, couldn't understand that terrifying mix of love, fury, guilt, fear. 'I think things are all right now. I'll dish up dinner, shall I?'

She led him into the kitchen, opened the oven door. She had left the gas on low, but even so the meal had spoilt – steak toughened, fish curled up at the edges; Martin's chips, once golden-crisp, now beginning to stick together in a greasy mess.

'I'm sorry, David. I cooked us Dover sole, but I'm afraid it doesn't look too marvellous now.'

David stepped back from the oven. 'I'm sure it'll be absolutely fine. Sole's my favourite fish, in fact, though I haven't had it for an age.'

She was all the more annoyed that she had spoilt it. She was normally a good cook, one who would never dream of cooking chips or vegetables in advance, then leaving them to mush and shrivel; had done so only to staunch her growing fear, keep herself busy as the mocking clock ticked on. She placed the vegetable dishes on the table, turned the oven off. She wished Chris and Martin would hurry. She had called them twice, but still no sign of them. Were they kissing again, or still fighting over Christmas? Joy with a red bow on her fringe, Bunny with a love-bite on her neck. Bunny would have graduated *summa cum laude*. A rabbit with honours, who also believed in Love and Peace and . . .

'Do sit down, David. I hope you don't mind eating in the kitchen? Chris says it's more . . . homely. No, sit there at the end. That's it. And if you'd like to pour some . . .' Morna jumped, swung round, her own voice drowned by a sudden crashing down the stairs, pounding footsteps, angry shouts. She dashed into the hall, sprinted down the passage just in time to see the front door slam. She wrenched it open again, heard Martin's Triumph coughing into life. Chris was clambering on to the seat behind him, squashed between her luggage and Martin's studded leather back, the two of them screaming insults at each other above the engine noise.

'Wait!' she shouted herself.

Chris turned round, yelled something indistinguishable as they swerved away.

'Be *careful!*'

No one heard. They had already turned the corner. It was dark now, really dark. Morna stepped back into the house, fighting tears and anger, almost collided with David who was just walking through the door.

'Look, Morna, I . . . I'd better push off now. The trains run every half an hour, so if I leave immediately I can catch the . . .'

'No.' She stood with her back to the door, barring his way. 'I asked you to dinner and we haven't had it yet.' She was using Martin's tactics, raising her voice, bullying, letting the anger oust the tears.

'No, really. I feel I'm in the way.'

'Whose way?'

'Well, your . . . daughter's.'

'She's gone.'

'But . . .'

'I'd like you to stay, David.' Wheedling now, little-girl voice. Shameful. *'Please.'*

She coaxed him back into the kitchen, back to his chair. The vegetables were cold now, as well as overcooked. She lifted up the lids – courgettes flabby, cauliflower as pappy as its sauce, peas puckering and shrunken.

'W . . . We can't eat these. *Or* the fish. Let me make you an omelette or . . . or . . .' She tried to keep her voice steady. The tears were threatening again – tears for all that wasted food, the whole botched and shattered evening. She had wanted David to relax, to see her as a successful cook and hostess as well as painstaking translator. Instead he was stuck on his own at the far end of a table set for four, looking rigid and uneasy, and probably ravenous.

'It looks quite all right to me,' he said, fiddling with his fork. 'And please don't bother with omelettes. I'm really looking forward to my sole.'

She went to check on it, fins charred, flesh dry. Was he seeking a chance of penance, or just unwavering in his endless *politesse*? 'I'm sorry, David, but it's gone all leathery. Best chuck it in the wastebin and start again.'

'No, don't do that!' He sprang up from his chair, blocked her access to the bin. 'It's a shocking waste of food and my mother always regarded waste as a major crime.'

'Did she? So did mine.' Morna grinned suddenly. She had forgotten they had things in common – even mothers, obviously. 'All right, we'll eat it for both our mothers' sake – to make us big and strong. Is that what yours said?'

'Oh, yes.' David was grinning now, as well. 'And to make my hair curl. She was right, you see. It has.'

'And allow us to see in the dark. No, that was carrots, wasn't it?'

'Yes, and spinach for iron. I could never understand as a kid how a plate of green and soggy spinach had anything to

116

do with the great tall railings round my infant-school, which my father said were iron.'

Morna laughed, dished up fish and vegetables. 'Right, iron railings coming up! We'd better open the wine to wash them down.'

She had bought a sparkling wine to celebrate. Ironic in the circumstances. She filled two glasses, watched the bubbles pop and seethe. 'Let's drink a toast to something. What about St Abban? Or would he disapprove?'

'Le Goff would be better. He left twelve crates of claret in his will, as well as all the papers.'

'You didn't get those too, did you?'

' 'Fraid not.'

'Monsieur Yves Le Goff, then.' She raised her glass. 'When was it that he died?'

'April last year. Easter Day, in fact.'

'Bad timing – to die on Resurrection Day.' She was sounding flippant, disrespectful. It was the effort of trying to play the hostess when she wanted to snatch up her car keys and hurtle after Chris. 'Though I presume you believe in an afterlife?'

As always, he hesitated. 'I wouldn't use that term. If it's after, then it isn't life. I prefer continuity.'

'Unfortunately, death breaks that.' She hacked off a piece of bread, crumbled it, sat staring at the pieces. Fragments of her father exploding over Hamburg, crashing from youth and glory into void. Chris and Martin crashing now, so busy quarrelling, they didn't see the articulated lorry hurtling towards them as they wavered out of lane.

'Only if we let it.' David was eating his fish with relish, although it had lost almost all its flavour, tasted cardboardy and dry. She had failed as cook and hostess, failed Chris as a mother.

'Look, I'm . . . I'm sorry about this evening, David . . .' Perhaps she should confide in him, explain about Bunny's invitation, her daughter's sense of being tugged between Martin and her father. But was that fair on Chris? Was it even fair on David? There had been non-stop tension since he first stepped through the door. Even now she wasn't really concentrating on what he was saying about different interpretations of reincarnation. Her mind was still on Chris. How serious was the quarrel? Would her daughter submit this time, or . . . ? If she and Martin parted, would she dare to love again? Trust? David's word. Too easy.

She glanced across at his plate – nothing left but bones now, empty eye sockets staring back at her. She passed him the salad, watched him disrupt Chris's flower-tomatoes, apple petals – her work of art a mess of jumbled colours.

She excused herself a moment, removed their fish plates. Martin's steak was lying on the side looking shrunken and neglected. She hadn't valued Martin enough, hadn't realized the hole he would rip in Chris's life if . . . if . . . All right, so he wasn't permanent, but eight months was a long time when you had lived only seventeen years. She retrieved the steak, parcelled it in foil.

David had finished his salad, pushed his chair back from the table so that he could stretch his legs a little. 'Thank you,' he said. 'I enjoyed that.'

Simply good manners again, she wondered? It had sounded genuine enough. 'There's still some cheese,' she said. 'And strawberries.' She should have made a sorbet – something cool and sharp. The Indian summer sultriness still lingered in the air; the heat from the oven doubling its effect. Beads of perspiration were pricking beneath the rough tweed of her dress; her face was flushed with wine. She filled her glass again.

David picked up one forgotten radish, put it on his side plate. 'I'm pretty full already, I'm afraid.'

Morna flounced up, kicked her chair back. The strawberries were huge, the most expensive in the shop. She had soaked them in curaçao with just a dash of brandy, sprinkled finely grated orange rind on top; made a special détour to the delicatessen for really unusual cheeses. And David hadn't room. He had stuffed himself with dried-up fish and smelly cauliflower, even tackled Martin's soggy chips, but he couldn't manage one liqueur-rich strawberry, one sliver of Doux de Montagne, imported from the Alps. She guessed it was some penance thing again. If she made a hash of the food, then David had to eat it, even press for second helpings, but if something were good – worse still a luxury – then he must refuse on principle. She had been the same herself at school – a pious little prig actively seeking out lumps in porridge or fat on meat, so that she could be top in holiness.

'This dinner wasn't meant to be a penance, David.'

'I . . . I beg your pardon?'

She fetched the tray with the four glass dishes on it, banged it down. 'Don't worry, I expect I can eat all four myself.' She heard the edge of sarcasm in her voice, went back for the cheese. 'Not to mention a pound of Dolcelatte and some Doux de . . .'

David flushed. 'Look, I . . . I can manage a few strawberries, I'm sure I can. They look fantastic.'

Morna passed him a dish, suddenly remorseful. He seemed so easily cowed, so eager to please, like an over-sensitive child on its best behaviour. She had been rude and boorish, longed to start again, put the clock back, re-run the whole failed evening – for Chris's sake, as well as hers and David's.

'Just try one or two,' she urged. 'And have a biscuit with them. They're rather special biscuits those – made with ground-up hazelnuts instead of flour. A friend of mine brought them back from Spain as a little present.'

David leapt up, as if the biscuit had burnt his fingers.

'Gosh! That reminds me . . . Excuse me just a minute, will you?'

He was back in seconds, holding out the crumpled paper bag he had been clutching when he first arrived. He pressed it into her hand. 'It's . . . er . . . nothing much, I'm afraid. I mean, I owe you such a lot and . . .'

'Owe me?'

'Well, all that translation work.'

'David, I told you, I enjoy it. I'd be most insulted if you . . .' Morna fumbled in the bag, drew out something small and hard, well wrapped in tissue paper. A brooch? A pendant? She only hoped she'd like it. It was embarrassing when people gave you jewellery and you had to pretend it was just your taste and style. She unwrapped the tissue, revealed a battered silver coin, stained greenish-brown and covered with a sort of hard and dirty scale.

'Er . . . what exactly is it, David?'

'What we call a piece of eight – eight reales. It was found just off St Abban's Island by a marine archaeologist friend of mine who was working on a seventeenth-century Dutch wreck. His divers discovered a horde of about a thousand with bits of wood around them which might have been the remains of a money chest. The rest are now in the Museum of National Antiquities in Edinburgh, but this one –' David grinned – 'got away.' He held it up to the light. 'See the date? 1687. It was minted at Potosi. Those are the quartered arms of Spain, and if you turn it over –' David did so, rubbed it up with the tissue – 'you'll see the Pillars of Hercules.'

'B . . . But David, this is . . . *treasure*.'

'Not really. I'm afraid it's less valuable than it sounds, and in pretty poor condition, but I thought it might appeal to you because of its – well – history. It's been lying on the sea-bed for nearly three hundred years, went down when James II was King of England and Charles II King of Spain, and Louis XIV still throwing his weight about. The coins were found lying around the bones of two dead seamen. They brought those up as well.'

Morna shivered suddenly. 'David, I . . . I can't take it. Even if you say it isn't valuable, it must mean a lot to you.'

He shrugged. 'In a superstitious way, maybe. I've always used it as a sort of . . . lucky charm. I've been carrying it around for the last few years.'

'Well, there you are. You can't give it away, when . . .'

'I *want* you to have it, Morna. Please.' David passed it over, laid it on her place mat.

She picked it up, cupped it in her hand. She felt excited by the gift, not only by its history, but because he valued her enough to entrust her with something which was obviously important to him. He was giving her his luck, making her part of his work. That coin was precious not just because it had been lying on the sea-bed for three long centuries, but also because it had sat in David's pocket for the last few years, so it was as if she now had part of him captive in her palm.

'Thank you,' she said. 'I . . . I hardly know what to say. I mean, it's such an unusual gift, and so generous of you to . . .' The phone cut through her words – almost a relief. David was looking embarrassed by her effusions, which only made her nervous in her turn. She got up from the table, still holding the piece of eight. 'I won't be a moment. Help yourself to cream.'

She picked up the receiver, listened to the rush of words, squeezed the lucky coin tighter in her other hand. It must be working already. 'Good,' she said, smiling. 'I'm really glad. Yes, of course it's all right. You stay. I'll see you tomorrow sometime. No, I don't mind, I'm only relieved you've . . . Daddy'll understand, I'm sure he will. I'll write myself if you like. There's always next year, anyway . . .'

She returned to the kitchen, smiling still. 'She's not going.'

'I beg your pardon?'

'To Los Angeles. I'm sorry, you don't know what I'm talking about. That was Chris.'

'Is she . . . better?'

'Mmm. Fine. She's staying the night at Martin's place.' She wished she hadn't said so. Unfair to Chris. Martin's parents had no spare room. But there were camp beds, sofas. Christmas was safe now, Chris and Martin safe. She dug into her strawberries, watched David toy with his, wave away the cheese.

'Fancy a glass of mead?' she asked, getting up to fetch it from the dresser. 'And don't say no again.' She removed the bottle from its wrappings, broke the seal. She had spotted it in the bargain bin, bought it simply because it was labelled 'Made by the monks of Buckfast Abbey', which seemed appropriate. Only when she got it home had she seen the smaller print: 'Mead, the honeymoon drink'; returned it to its paper. She eased the cap off, found two glasses. She had drunk too much already – sparkling wine sparkling in her veins, and now the mead, sickly sweet and velvety. But there were things to celebrate – a reprieve, a change of luck.

'Let's take our glasses in to the other room. It's so hot in here.'

David stood up. 'I'm afraid I'll have to be going soon.'

'Oh no, you've only just arrived.' What she meant was that she was only just beginning to enjoy him, only just relaxing.

'I asked at the station and they said the last train goes at midnight, but I'm not sure about the bus.'

'Don't worry about the bus. I'll drive you to the station. It only takes ten minutes.' Perhaps the car would refuse to start.

David was holding on to his chair-back, staring down. 'Do you . . . er . . . think you ought to drive, though?'

'What d'you mean?'

'Well, the . . .' He paused, flushed. 'You know – breath-alyser.'

'I'm not drunk, for heaven's sake.' Her elation burst like a balloon. He *was* a prig. Best to close the door on him, get some sleep. 'I'll make some coffee if you like – black and strong.'

'Have we time?'

'Yes, ages.' He couldn't wait to get away – that was obvious. She filled the percolator, switched it on. 'And don't forget your translation. I suppose you've got to take it, have you? I'd have liked more time on it.'

'There's no need, honestly. You've done wonders, as it is.'

'No, just for my own enjoyment. I'm getting quite fond of Abban.' She fought a sudden wave of desolation. She was about to lose him – lose them both. In just a few days' time, David would be at the other end of the country, following in the footsteps of his saint. Prig or no, she couldn't bear to let him go like this, remembering her as tipsy and incompetent, even rude. She got out the best Spode cups, the silver apostle spoons, refilled the cream jug.

David let go his chair. 'Could you . . . er . . . point me in the direction of the bathroom?'

'Oh, I'm *sorry*, David.' She had failed again – failed to show him what Bea described as the geography of the house. Bea was fond of euphemisms. So was Neil – strangely – not in bed or bathroom (where piss, shit and screw had shocked her profoundly at first), but in his job. Advertising was the art of euphemism. Even love-bite was a euphemism – lust and bragging ownership, rather than love. Neil and Co. had spoilt so many words, poured peace and love and happiness into face cream or detergents, used them to wrap chocolate bars or nappies.

She ushered David up the stairs. The downstairs cloak-room still had Neil's *Playboy*s in it, five years old. 'There – just in front of you.'

'Thanks.'

She went into her bedroom to fetch a jacket. It was cooler now, pitch dark outside. Los Angeles was eight hours behind – light there still, bright sunshine. Bunny in a bikini and in love. She sat on the bed. Once David left, there would be silence as well as dark, black thoughts crowding in again – Neil at Bunny's, Chris at Martin's. Martin's mother wouldn't patrol the sofas at three a.m., listen for gasps. She saw Martin's thin, pale, not-in-the-nun's-dictionary penis knifing between the gaps in Chris's ribs.

Couldn't David stay – block the thoughts out, keep away the darkness? But if she offered him a bed, he might misinterpret it, suspect that she was hoping to seduce him. Why, when you were adult, was sex always ticking away in the background like a time bomb – unless you lived in a convent and deliberately locked it out? The whole week of the retreat, the subject had been studiously avoided. All man's different facets had been mentioned in their turn – the spiritual, the rational, the emotional, the metaphysical, even the physical – but never actually the sexual. Most of the retreatants had seemed sexless, anyway, judging by their dress and conversation. Maybe Freud and *Cosmopolitan* were wrong and sexual feelings were far from universal – some people born frigid in the same way others were unmechanical or had no aptitude for music or mathematics. Was she like that herself, or just a failure when it came to Neil? No, that wasn't the right word. They had rarely missed a day. Three-hundred-and-sixty times fourteen could hardly be called a failure.

She heard David flush the lavatory, start downstairs, and sprang to her feet.

'David . . .'

The footsteps hesitated, stopped. She could always agree she *was* too drunk to drive. She had brought her glass up with her, drained it at a gulp now. No, better not say that. He would only judge her harshly.

'I'm in here. Just . . . er . . . trying to find my car keys. D'you find you're always losing yours?'

'I don't drive, actually.' He had stopped just outside the door.

'Oh, I see.' Was that privation again, or impecuniousness, or was he one of those born unmechanical? 'Come in, David. I won't be a minute. They're probably in the pocket of my other jacket. No . . . Hold on a sec. I'd better tip my handbag out. Do sit down.' She sat herself – on the bedroom stool – saw four of him behind her, still standing tall and dark against the expanse of white fur rug. 'I hate this room, don't you?'

'Well, no, I . . .'

'Not just the furnishings. They're bad enough, but . . .'

David was at the door again. 'I'd better go and check the coffee. I can hear it sort of seething.'

'Don't bother. It switches itself off.' Morna sorted through her bag, capped an unsheathed lipstick. 'I suppose it's just the . . . memories. I was sitting there, exactly there, on that side of the bed, when Neil told me he was leaving me. He blurted it out, just like that. I didn't even know the girl existed. He was often away, you see, on business trips and . . .'

Of course David didn't see. He wasn't even interested, was chafing to leave. She was blurting things out herself, letting the mead talk and the wine. She had never told anyone before, not even Bea or Chris. She, too, was good at euphemisms. ('We decided it was best to separate.')

'I didn't say a word. I couldn't. There was nothing to say. He loved her.' She broke off. The words still hurt. *'I'm afraid we love each other, Morna.'*

She was glad he'd said 'afraid'. She had said nothing still, just sat staring at his shirt. The middle button didn't match the rest. She hadn't noticed before. It was the same blue, but just a fraction larger. She was the one who always sewed his buttons, matched them perfectly. That was service, part of her marriage vows. Till death do us part.

It had been death. Darkness again, like when she had lost her first God. They had sent her to a priest then and the Jesuit had droned on and on, trying to fill her void with words – sterile proofs and arguments. But she still sat in the dark. Neil had used proofs as well – proofs that they were unsuited, would be happier apart. It had been September when he told her, September the fourth. Today was the eighth – four days off the fifth anniversary of the break-up of their marriage. Perhaps she should have drunk to it. They were happier apart. *He* was. Bunny was. It had been a warm day then, as well – tactless sun streaming into the bedroom, smirking in the mirrors. Neil's words had switched the sun off, put an end to summer.

'I'm going back with her. My firm has arranged a transfer to Los Angeles. Promotion, actually. Don't worry about money. We . . .'

'We' meant him and Bunny, though she hadn't known the name then, just 'the other woman', a woman thirteen years younger who lived always in the sun; a woman who could sew, but was something of a slattern. If you loved a man, you made sure his buttons matched.

'We decided it would hurt less if we went away. I know it's hard on Chrissie, but . . .'

Chrissie. Neil had only called her that since he met his Angeleno. *Non Angli sed Angeleno.*

'And she can always come and visit.' Five years had

126

passed and the visit hadn't happened. Chris had resented that, and now at last, when the invitation had arrived, she'd had to turn it down. Pressured by Martin, blackmailed by her mother. They would probably never discuss the matter again. Silence was safer. Five years ago Neil had been angered by that silence, sprung up from the stool where she was sitting now herself.

'Can't you *say* something, Morna? We want to know what you feel.'

'We', again. What *could* she say? He and Bunny were married already, before the divorce. Divorce was forbidden, except she had left the church which decreed that. She had stared at the button, tried to fix on something, keep away the tears. Tears were undignified and too late, in any case. It had been difficult to speak. Her lips felt dry and taut, her mouth broken off at the hinge.

'Th . . . That button doesn't m . . . match,' she had whispered at last.

Silence again. She looked up. Neil had gone. It was David who was standing over her.

'Are you . . . all right, Morna?'

'Y . . . Yes. Fine.' Mustn't bore him, mustn't scare him off. She had learnt long ago that grief was embarrassing, cost you friends. Even at school she hadn't told her classmates how terrifying it was once you lost your God; how life closed off like a cul-de-sac instead of opening up to heaven; how morals, ritual, purpose, all collapsed. When Chris was three or four, they had sprawled on the rug together and built multi-coloured towers of bricks. Chris had laughed and clapped as each tower grew higher, brighter. 'Wait,' she'd said. 'Watch this!' And she had pulled the bottom brick out, reduced the tower to rubble. Chris had cried the first time, howled and banged her head. Morna had rocked her in her arms. 'It's all right, darling. We can build it up again.'

David couldn't say that. He wasn't saying anything, just standing by the mirrors looking anguished – shoulders hunched, eyes lost beneath a frown, as if he were reliving that bitter scene five years ago. She could feel his sympathy, expressed if not in words, then in his stance, his whole demeanour, yet she somehow shied away from it. One teenage outburst was enough. She must keep her own control.

'Right, time for coffee,' she said, snapping her handbag shut. 'My keys must be downstairs.'

David followed her down. 'Perhaps we should skip the coffee. We're cutting it a bit fine, aren't we?'

'No.' Morna didn't know, refused to look at her watch. 'Unless you want to stay, of course?' It was easier to say it when she wasn't in her bedroom. 'I've got four spare beds, counting Chris's.' After Neil had left, she had tried them all in turn, to see which was the least lonely. In the end she had returned to the fur rug, loneliest of all. '*And* a sofa,' she added. Stupid. She was alienating him. Of course he wouldn't stay – alone in a house with a divorcée and a bungler.

'I'd . . . er . . . better get back, Morna. I told my cousin I wouldn't be too late. He's a bit of an old woman and if I simply don't turn up, he might . . .'

'Don't worry. Your chauffeur awaits. She's even found her keys. Right, a quick gulp of coffee.' Morna had poured it into the old mugs by mistake – sheer force of habit – felt embarrassed by the mocking empty Spode.

'Got your work?'

He nodded.

'Jacket?'

'Mm.'

'Right, let's go then.' She picked up the lucky silver coin, slipped it in her pocket. 'I'll just lock up. Weybridge is prime burglar country.'

She let him into the car, wished it were smaller and less flash. Neil's choice again. David was right – she wasn't fit to drive. It wasn't just the alcohol but grief, loss, regret, all curdled and mixed up with it. She had better not talk, but fix her whole attention on the road. They didn't want any more disasters. She eased into the street, cruised in silence for a while. 'Well, I hope you enjoy your time on the island, David.'

'Thanks. And thank you for the dinner, too. I really enjoyed it.'

The last polite and painless clichés – before goodbye. One more right turn, two more lefts and they would be at the station. Unless she went the longer way. Pointless, though, to make him miss his train if he didn't want her company and when she couldn't stop him leaving in the end. Too late. She had taken the left-hand fork instead of the right, was skirting the river now. She slowed a little, waved a hand.

'That's the Wey. It was made into a canal in the 1650s – one of the earliest canalized rivers in the country.' Nice to be telling him something for a change, instead of the other way round. He seemed interested, was peering out.

'A Sir Richard Weston was the man behind it, a local man from Guildford. He'd travelled on the Continent and seen the locks and sluices on the Dutch canals, introduced them here. It's quite a story, actually – endless quarrels and double-dealing, which went on for years and years, long after Sir Richard himself had died.'

Morna wove in a few more names and facts before driving on again. Best not to delay too obviously. There was still half a mile to go, and if they took it slowly . . .

There was a rhythmic rumble in the distance as they reached the station car park. The noise crescendoed, rattled through their voices.

'That's it!' David shouted, leaping out.

She followed, jumping down the few stone steps which

short-circuited the path, and dashing into the station after him. 'Got your ticket?'

'Yes!'

He flashed it at the ticket collector, took the stairs three at a time.

'Goodbye, Morna. I'll phone . . .'

He was almost on the platform now. She could no longer see him, only hear his voice. 'Goodbye!' she shouted back.

She heard the train pulling out, gathering speed, stopped halfway down the stairs. She couldn't wave goodbye, let him see how stupidly upset she was. She trailed back to the top, stood looking out at the track where she could see the train cutting through the darkness in a blaze of lighted windows, a shower of sparks; watched it grow smaller, smaller, until it was swallowed up and the night closed in again. She glanced at her watch. What an irony! That train was seven minutes late.

He should have missed it.

7

'I missed it!'

'*What?*' Morna swung round, came face to face with David – a David out of breath and panting, puffing up the last stair.

'I got to the platform just as it was pulling out. I dashed across and tried to grab a door-handle, but the damn thing must have been jammed or locked or something. It wouldn't open, anyway. Just my luck! By the time I'd tried the next one, the train was moving so fast, I . . .'

'You're not hurt, are you, David?'

'No. I just feel a bit of a fool, besides having a stitch . . .'

Morna touched the lucky coin in her pocket. A delightful fool – tie awry, one hand smudged with oil, the other clutching at his side. 'I'd *drive* you to London, David, but I don't really think . . . I mean, if I lose my licence . . .'

'Of course not. I wouldn't hear of it.' David was attacking the oil with a hankie and some spittle. 'It's just my cousin . . . He was decent enough to offer me his sofa for the night and if I don't show up, he might start dragging the river or something.' He gave an awkward laugh.

'Can't you phone him? Tell him you're okay?'

'It's midnight, though. He could well have gone to bed.'

'David, honestly . . .' Morna gave an exasperated shrug. 'If he's sound asleep, he'll hardly be dragging rivers.'

'No, I s'pose not. I think I'd better phone him all the same, though.'

'There's a call-box over there. Got some change?'

'Yes, thanks.' David jingled the coins in his pocket, returned with most of them unused. 'That was short and sweet. He *was* asleep and he wasn't worried. In fact he couldn't wait to get back to bed. Well, now we've settled that, perhaps you'd show me Weybridge.'

'What, in the dark?'

'Why not? We've got the streetlamps. I'd like a proper look at that canal. You seem to know quite a bit about it.'

Morna paused at the station entrance. Not enough to fill a night, she thought. He was obviously reluctant to return to her house, face those five free beds. Yet she was surprised how cheerful he appeared now he had made his phone call. She had expected irritation, resentment even; feared he would blame her for making him miss the train. Or was he glad to miss it, preferred her company to some nervy cousin's? She watched him stride out of the station, gaze around.

'All right,' she said, catching up with him. 'Walk or drive?'

'Oh, walk, I think. It's a lovely night.'

'It's quite some way, though. Weybridge sort of wanders.'

'We can wander too, then, and you show me all the sights. We've got the time. The next train's at 4.22, the porter said.'

'There aren't many sights. This isn't Paris, you know.' Morna giggled suddenly. More than four whole hours' reprieve and the night and Weybridge to themselves. The road was deserted, the heath deserted, the trees dark shapes in the gloom; the moon thin and near-transparent like the last sliver of a well-sucked sherbet-lemon. She looked up, serenaded it.

' "*With how sad steps, O Moon, thou climb'st the skies!*
How silently, and with how wan a face!" '

David chimed in, word-perfect:

' "*What! may it be that even in heavenly place*

That busy archer his sharp arrows tries?"
That's thirty-one, isn't it? I used to know them all, once, off by heart.

"*Come, sleep, the certain knot of peace,*
The baiting-place of wit, the balm of woe,
The poor man's wealth, the . . ."

No, I'd better not start on that one or I'll have you running for your bed.'

'Let's stick to the moon, then.' Morna smiled up at it again. 'I know – we'll play a game. I start a verse and you continue it. If you know how the lines go on, then you begin another one and *I* have to take it up. If not, then it's my turn again. Okay?'

'Okay. Is it only Sidney, or anyone we like?'

'Oh, anyone. Right, I'll start again.' Morna struck an attitude, spoke in a false baritone.

' "*By heaven methinks it were an easy leap*
To pluck bright honour from the pale-fac'd moon . . ." '

David hardly let her finish:

' "*Or dive into the bottom of the deep,*
Where fathom-line could never . . ." '

'You're good at this, David. Your turn now.'

'Still the moon?'

'Why not?'

He paused a moment, grinned.

' "*O the moon shone bright on Mrs Porter*
and on her daughter . . ." '

' "*They washed their feet in soda water,*" ' Morna shouted. 'Easy! Chris was doing that for A level. My turn again.'

Fifteen minutes later, she was flummoxed for the first time.

'Say it again – slower.'

' "*The moon on the one hand, the dawn on the other:*
The moon is my sister, the dawn is my brother."

You *ought* to know it, Morna – with your Catholic school and everything.'

'No, I'm really stuck.'

'It's Hilaire Belloc – "The Early Morning" . . .'

'Oh, *him*. We never did him, actually.'

'What, a good orthodox Catholic writer like that! We were brought up on him – and Chesterton.'

'I suspect he was too frivolous for our Reverend Mother – all those Cautionary Tales and Bad Child's Books of Beasts and things. Reverend preferred the real solemn Catholics – Gerard Manley Hopkins and George Herbert and . . .'

'We had those as well, and a lot of other much less defensible ones. It's funny, isn't it, how they push the Catholic writers? Our school library was packed with third-rate books by first-rate Catholics, but lacked half the first-rate books by unbelievers.'

'So did ours. We even had bits snipped out of books. The tiniest hint of anything – well – risqué, landed up in the waste-bin.' Morna laughed, longed to take his arm. They were sister and brother, weren't they, pooling childhood memories? David seemed to have opened up, relaxed. She turned round suddenly, heard a soft pattering behind them. 'Oh, look – a dog! I wonder where he came from.'

'It's a she.' David stooped down, stroked the squat brown head. 'Without a collar. Must be a stray.'

'You don't get strays in Weybridge – nor blacks, nor unemployed. All forbidden.' Morna giggled again. Nice to be just slightly tiddly, legs floating under her, showing off her poetic repertoire. 'Get off home, there's a good boy.'

'*Girl*.'

'Girl, then. Drat! It seems to have attached itself to us. Go on – shoo!'

'Oh, let her stay. She's rather sweet.'

'Sweet! With a face like that?'

'I've always had a weakness for ugly dogs – you know, bull terriers and pugs and . . .'

'She looks a quarter pug and a quarter sort of beagle, with a large chunk of dachshund thrown in, too, judging by those sawn-off legs.' Bea had had a dachshund once, with the same waddling gait, the same black-treacle eyes. She didn't want to be reminded of her mother – not now – didn't need a chaperone, was reluctant to share David with anyone at all. She turned her back on the dog.

They had reached the junction with Church Street and Bridge Road. The streets were deserted, the day's heat and grime quenched in the cold stare of the moon; the softer light of the lamp-posts flattering ugly shopfronts, pointing silver fingers at their own distorted shadows. The place looked almost exotic without the usual press of shoppers, purr of cars. Or was it simply that she had David with her, was seeing it through his eyes? She felt strangely light and free, as if by divesting herself of house and car, she had changed her status, become young again and footloose, without the weight of Neil's possessions; playing truant with a man who was still a student, who had never set up house, never tied himself down with children, chattels, vows.

'The shops start here,' she told him. 'The High Street's just ahead. And that's the parish church. Not one of ours, as my mother would say.'

'They *stole* them from us, those Protestants – that's *my* mother's line.'

Morna laughed. 'Isn't it crazy – all that fighting for religion – sects and schisms and bloody wars and things.' She stared at the poster in the churchyard, 'JESUS SAVES', shivered suddenly. 'I'd better own up now, David. I've left it all. You know, the classic lapsed Catholic thing, except I've always thought that "lapsed" is completely the wrong word. It's too passive – a sort of sliding, drifting, gradual word, whereas what I felt was a sudden shattering fall, like

135

Lucifer's out of Heaven.' She was being grandiose, expressive, and enjoying it.

David nodded.

'Are *you* still a Catholic?' she asked him. 'I know you said you believed in God, but that's not the same, is it?'

He paused to check on the dog, seemed unwilling to commit himself. 'I'm . . . er . . . still redefining all my terms. That can take a lifetime.'

They had stopped outside a boutique – Neil's type of shop, chi-chi and expensive, everything matched and toned, beads and ostrich feathers strewn between designer clothes. Morna pressed her nose to the glass.

'It's funny, though, how one's Catholic training sticks. I mean, is that chiffon dress there a vain and worldly bauble or something to be saved and slaved for?'

'Oh, a vain and worldly bauble, definitely.'

They both laughed this time. 'It was even worse at school,' Morna went on. 'I remember coming home in the Christmas holidays and feeling a real aversion to all the loaded shops and fancy decorations, seeing them through the nuns' eyes, I suppose. Then, just when I'd softened up a bit and was actually enjoying things, I'd be dragged back to school and have to change attitudes again.'

'I know exactly what you mean. Our form master told us we should try and squeeze a penance in, even on Christmas Day, so when I was thirteen, I went the whole hog and refused to touch the turkey at all or even try a mouthful of mince pie. My mother was dreadfully upset and thought I was sickening for something. It ruined the whole Christmas.'

Morna said nothing. It still seemed amazing that they had shared a similar sort of childhood, an identical type of school, that David understood conflicts which Neil had laughed to scorn. She shouldn't be disloyal, though. Neil had saved her, in a sense.

'Actually, I . . . I think I only married Neil because

I'd . . . lost my faith.' They had crossed the road to the churchyard, were wandering among the graves, feeling the chill of clammy marble, moss-encrusted stone; watching their shadows dart before them and seem to bring the tombs to life. It was easier to talk there, in the gloom, with a sheltering wall around them, guardian trees. She longed to pour out everything, felt David would understand as no one ever had yet. He had turned towards her, as if to fix his whole attention on her words.

'It was like . . . like marrying on the rebound – you know, leaving God and finding someone else. Neil made quite a decent substitute, in fact. He had tremendous energy – was very ambitious, very much a presence. That sort of man's easy to worship, especially when you're young. I replaced the old Catholic sacraments with new ones – rituals like home-making and cooking, service to a provider instead of to a Creator. It gave life point again and a sort of axis. Neil was always *there*, like God had been – if not actually in the house, then in my thoughts or phoning me or planning our lives or shoring up the universe. That was important. On my own, I didn't feel quite . . . real, hardly seemed to exist – not without a religion. If God had created me in the first place, then when He disappeared, so did I. I felt this sort of . . . terror, that I was shut up in myself, and so infinitely small, I was like one of those microbes which live on your eyelashes and can't even be seen without a microscope.' She paused, peered down to read the inscription on a tombstone, '*beloved husband of* . . .' David was still silent, frowning in total concentration, seemed to be encouraging her to continue.

'When Neil left, those feelings all returned, got so bad sometimes I'd wake screaming in my sleep. And yet it seemed ridiculous, out of all proportion. I had friends who were divorced and separated. They weren't exactly over the moon, but they groused about the simple things – lack of cash or having to move to a smaller place or . . . I was lucky.' Morna stooped to avoid a trailing cedar branch. That word again. 'I kept telling myself how much worse it would be crammed into a bedsit on Social Security, but it somehow seemed irrelevant. The terror was so . . .' She broke off. 'D'you know what I'm even talking about?'

David nodded, called the dog to heel.

'I'm sorry, I'm boring you. Other people's divorces *are* a pain. I learnt that soon enough. Actually, I've hardly ever mentioned this before. Yet it astonishes me sometimes that *more* people don't feel fear – fear of being here at all, when everything is so fragile and mysterious and we don't know where we come from or where we're going and we've only scratched the surface of any knowledge and we're going to die and after that . . . God! It all sounds so adolescent – what Chris should be feeling at seventeen. I *did* feel it at her age, but I haven't grown out of it. Retarded, I suppose!' She laughed. She would regret it in the morning, letting out that secret tortured teenager whom she had always kept strictly caged before, strictly private. Damn the morning! It was still night-time, time for indiscretion, mead-talk.

'Yet how can people be so . . . so happy-go-lucky, David – even people with no beliefs or philosophy at all? It's different for you. You've still got a faith – even if you've had to redefine it.'

He stopped by the cedar, ran his hand across its scaly bark. 'I . . . I know what you mean by the terror, though.'

'Do you?'

'Mm. The trick is to move beyond it, *accept* the terror as part of the whole scheme of things, part of God, if you like.'

'Isn't that a bit . . . heretical?'

'Yes, probably. You can't avoid heresy. Things are too damned complex to get all our answers right.' He leant against the tree trunk, face shadowed by its foliage. 'One of the problems is that we try and stuff fear and evil out of

138

sight, pretend they don't exist. Those dark forces need facing and propitiating. Abban understood that. So did the pagans. Perhaps they weren't so wrong in seeing evil spirits in storms or draughts, or waiting to snatch their children away or punish them with plagues. There *is* evil in the world and we have to deal with it.'

Morna jumped as he snapped off a twig, broke it in half again before continuing. 'There's a bit in Abban's life when they'd had a terrible summer on the island with all the harvest ruined and boats wrecked, and Abban stayed up all night and did battle with the demons. It was an inward battle, of course, with Abban using prayer and penance, but in the morning, the sea was like a village pond and the sun was shining and all the islanders knew that Abban's God had vanquished the demons. *We* need rituals like that. Even if they're not true in the literal sense, they're still psychologically valuable. We have to slay our dragons and see them slain.'

'Well, at least we're staying up all night. That's a start.' Morna was suddenly reluctant to get too intense again. She had started it herself, but now she wanted to change the mood, return to the games. She led him out of the graveyard, along the narrow path which skirted the church, the dog still following, their footsteps echoing in the silence. The stars looked weak and very far away. A faint scent of honeysuckle smoked from the hedge beside them, though it was too dark to make out any flowers.

'Oh, look!' said David. 'A recreation ground – and with a really decent slide.'

'Want to go in?'

'Yes, *please*.'

He was suddenly running, heading for the slide, the dog bounding after him, yapping at his heels. He clambered up the metal steps, settled himself on the chute, seemed to stick there.

'Damn! My shoes are catching.'

'Pick your feet up then,' Morna shouted from the ground, dodged as a worn brown shoe came bouncing down the slide, followed closely by the other, then by David himself. She stared at him, astonished. He was running in his socks towards the steps again, had reached the top and was manoeuvring on to his stomach, shooting down head first this time. She could hardly recognize the David of the retreat, the Father Anthony, as he crawled up from the ground, rushed back for another go.

'Come on, Morna. Your turn!'

'No, thanks! *Hush*, boy.' She tried to quieten the dog who was near hysterical, front paws on the bottom of the chute, stump of tail quivering and throbbing. 'You'll wake the whole of Weybridge.'

'*Girl*,' insisted David, as he crash-landed between them. 'She wants her turn, if you don't.' He swooped up the plump brown body, climbed the steps with it, held it on his lap as the two of them whooshed down, the dog silent now as if in sheer astoundment.

'David, you . . . you're crazy.'

'Want a swing? I'll push you.'

'Not too high!' she yelled, as he crouched down on his heels to get more leverage, seemed to fling her towards the sky. She was still marvelling at his mood, his sudden burst of vigour and high spirits, as if his nanny-in-attendance had slackened his usual tight-held reins, let him run wild for once. He was walking the seesaw now, from end to end, springing from there to the climbing frame, still shoeless. He had even changed the weather. A sudden bray of thunder shocked the sky, a spat of raindrops whimpered against the slide. She stuck out her legs to slow herself, jumped down off the swing.

'Quick! There's going to be a storm. We'd better shelter.'

David was hanging upside down, blue-socked feet entwined. 'No, let's stay out in it. I love storms.'

'But you haven't got a coat.' It was raining harder now, the sky rumbling and belching as if it were in pain.

'Doesn't matter.' David thumped down from the climbing-frame, held up his face to the rain, tongue out to catch the drops.

'Oh God! I've just remembered . . .' Morna struck one hand with the other in annoyance.

'What?'

'I've left the car unlocked. I'll have to go back and check it. We can shelter there, if you like, or drive to the house and fetch some waterproofs.'

'The storm will be over by then.' David sounded crestfallen. He had retrieved his shoes and was lacing them up, sitting on one end of the seesaw.

'I doubt it,' Morna had to shout against the thunder.

'Race you, then!' he yelled, suddenly getting up and darting through the gate.

'It's miles,' she shouted, panting after him, shoes squelching on the muddy path.

'Keep you warm!' He slowed for her a moment, then hurtled off again, the dog following so close it seemed sewn on to his heels.

Morna put a spurt on. She could run as fast as any bloody mongrel. She was catching up now, drawing close, ignoring slippery pavements, lashing rain. She had never made such speed before. It was as if David's own energy were an example and a challenge, spurring and inspiring her. She wasn't even tired. There was some crazy elation in pushing herself past the limits of her usual spoilsport body; in feeling the rain soaking through her clothes, yet her skin triumphant warm; hearing the thunder rumbling all around her, being part of it, part of the night, the storm.

She pounded on and on, her breathing loud and laboured,

heart thumping its objection, dress flapping wet against her calves. Lightning lasered through the sky, kindling the dark in a sudden flashing strobe of blue and silver. She didn't stop, didn't slacken, reached the car only minutes after David, collapsed against him.

'You're incredible!' he said, opening the door for her. 'And in those shoes . . .'

She had hardly noticed the shoes, had been only thudding heart, racing blood. She sank on to the seat, listened to the kickback of her breathing, relished the 'incredible'.

'Wow!' she said when she had recovered her voice at last. 'I'm starving.'

'That's because you didn't eat your dinner. Mortal sin!'

'D'you mind if we go back and raid the larder?'

She saw his face change, the guarded look return, cursed herself for spoiling things. Hadn't he already made it clear he didn't want to be in the house with her alone? Perhaps he had a girlfriend, a jealous clinging one who kept him on a ball and chain. What about that cousin? David had already referred to him as a bit of an old woman. Supposing she were a *young* woman – a stunning blonde – furious at his casual midnight phone call, pacing up and down the bedsit? When she came to think of it, he'd made quite a song and dance about the cousin. A female would be more likely to be frantic, dragging rivers.

'Tell you what,' she said, switching on the engine. 'Let's drive somewhere – anywhere – till we find an all-night café. I could just do with egg and chips.' She towelled her hair with the car duster, turned up the heater to dry their sopping clothes.

'We haven't seen the canal yet.' David's voice was wary again, controlled.

'We can see it on the way. I'll stop. And if you're worried about my driving, I'm totally sobered up now. Even Sebastian Coe couldn't run like that while squiffy.'

142

'What about the dog, though?'

It was sitting on David's lap, had followed him into the car, uninvited. His girlfriend was bound to be that type – overbearing, pushy, refusing to let go. Morna watched the pink tongue lick his face, the soft brown head nuzzle against his chest. 'We'll take her,' she said, curtly – had to humour him. 'Buy her a sausage, if you like.'

They had to drive for an hour before they found the sausages. The dog diverted them, had been turfed into the back from David's lap, but kept trying to clamber over, or bark a descant to the radio. Morna drove fast, enjoyed streaking through the darkness with David as her passenger, their damp clothes steaming in the fug, a German station broadcasting Tchaikovsky. She had headed away from London, away from the cousin's bedsit, even avoided the motorways, wanted him private and alone.

He seemed relaxed again, had regained his good spirits in exploring the canal. They had found another Weybridge – not Neil's fey and fancy suburb with its ritzy houses sloping to the river, Mercedes moored in front, cabin cruisers behind; expense-account restaurants and exclusive land-scaped golf clubs; but a world of marsh and wasteland, gravel pit and millpond, lonely meadows, silent rippling water. They had poked around a rubbish tip, sheltered in a deserted barn. At last even David decided he could eat something, agreed to hit the road. That was about two-thirty. It was a good hour later now, the air colder, cleaner, the stars looking nearer and newly shined. He hadn't mentioned his early morning train – seemed to have forgotten all about it. Morna braked suddenly as she saw a neon sign, pulled into a layby with a straggle of parked lorries.

'Where are we?' David asked.

'No idea. At least it's open, though – and food.'

They pushed at the door of the café – a run-down looking

place in weather-beaten wood, with one window boarded up and even the sign missing half its letters; were immediately engulfed in glare and noise. A jukebox was thumping out hard rock, cutting off the last bars of the Tchaikovsky Serenade for Strings still cadencing in Morna's head. The place was thick with cigarette smoke, loud with lorry drivers.

'What d'you fancy?' Morna asked. 'Egg and chips?'

'Yes, fine, but let me get it.' David had removed his tie and was turning it into collar and lead.

'No, it's my treat. You stay and dog-sit.'

'Please, Morna. You've already cooked me dinner and . . .'

'Sorry, I insist. I'm the one in mortal sin.'

He laughed, found a table furthest from the fruit-machines. She walked up to the counter, embarrassed by the scrum of men joking with the waitress.

'Egg and chips twice,' she said. 'Oh, and sausage,' she added, remembering the dog. 'And one lamb chop.' A bone would keep it quiet, stop it slobbering over David.

'How about fried bread and tomaters, while yer at it?' joked a driver.

'The beans is good,' chipped in another.

'All right, beans as well.'

'You want the mixed grill, do you?' asked the waitress.

'Er . . . what d'you get in that?'

'Egg, sausage, bacon, chips, steak, chop, peas, tomatoes, mushrooms . . .' The waitress paused for breath.

'Yes, please. Twice.' Morna was ravenous. She had left more than half her dinner as well as skipping lunch, but it wasn't only that. She had to cram in everything while she had the chance, while David was still with her, stuff the gap already threatening. She wanted to feed him up as well, pile his plate so high that he would miss his train just wading through it all. They would never catch the 4.22 – not with the long drive back – and could miss the next few after that

144

if they really span their food out. She must somehow keep him with her even after the meal, drive further and further from London, from duty, commonsense. It was already Saturday – holiday – when you were allowed a break from normal tedious routine. They were students anyway, still on vacation, with neither job nor timetable to tie them down. True, he had planned to return home on the Saturday, told her originally that he would be leaving for the Midlands first thing in the morning. But couldn't his parents wait a few hours longer – or even till Sunday? They had had him to themselves for thirty-five whole years, she but half a day.

'*Money can't buy me love,*' the Beatles were insisting from the jukebox. Morna scrabbled in her pocket, touched the silver coin again. Some currencies were love. She heard her order shouted to the cook, returned to David, sat beside him on the rickety chair, trying not to notice the frieze of naked breasts and bums around the walls. She bent down to ease her shoes which were still soggy-damp and hurting, saw a pair of denimed legs pass their table, stop. A tall man with tattoos all down his arms touched David on the shoulder.

'Excuse me,' he said. 'Your missus dropped her scarf.'

David flushed as the wisp of yellow silk was dangled in front of him. Morna stayed crouched down, fiddling with her shoe – glanced at her third finger still circled with Neil's wedding ring. She wore it for convention's sake, her daughter's sake, but now it had bonded her to David in these strangers' eyes. They were a couple, a family – dog and all – she with the purse strings, feeding up her bloke. The Beatles were still pleading.

> '*I'll get you anything, my friend,*
> *If it makes you feel all right . . .*'

She eased up straight again, retied her scarf. 'Hungry?' she asked.

David nodded. 'What did you order?'

'Oh, a bit of everything.'

'Is this breakfast or a second dinner?'

'Both. Neither.' Morna didn't want things labelled, longed to banish all categories, break all moulds; felt crazily elated. She tapped her foot, drummed her fingers to the rhythm of the song.

> *'I'll give you all I've got to give*
> *If you say you . . .'*

'Two mixed grills,' shouted the waitress from the far end of the room, raising her voice above Paul McCartney's. 'Come and get 'em!'

Morna jumped up. 'I'll go.' She felt as if she were on a spring, throbbing with coiled-up energy which had to be held down. If she wasn't careful, she would burst right through the roof, zoom on to hit the moon. This was her usual sleep-time, yet every cell in her body was shoutingly awake. She bounded up to the counter, took the two overflowing plates. She could eat both meals – and then another one – could sprint a hundred miles, swim an ocean. She forced herself to slow down so that she wouldn't spill the piled-up chips and peas, glanced across at David. He looked tiny, suddenly, dwarfed in his corner as if the room had expanded and he was miles and miles away from her; a pinprick figure sitting on its own, staring out of the small and smeary window, face closed, brows drawn down. She stopped in her tracks, confused.

'David!' she called with a sudden twinge of fear. He hadn't heard her. It wasn't just the music. He seemed to be slipping from her, as if he had already crossed to the island. She had to bring him back, make him lifesize once again.

'No, no, no, no . . .' the Beatles interrupted.

She ignored them, strode up to the table, put the plates down. She must have been imagining things. He was there, real, solid, tall – one sleeve trailing in a pool of ketchup, the dog still anchored to his chair-leg.

'We'll never eat all that,' he said, exclaiming at the size of the grills.

'Yes, we will,' she said. 'We've got to.' To make us big and strong, she added silently, and bit into her steak.

8

Pierre *Chéri*,

I can't write in French. It's more difficult now I'm back in England, but it's not just that. What I'm going to say is very important and it might come out differently in French. Actually, now I've written that, I realize it's hopeless. Because what I say in English will come out differently for *you*. My mother once said that foreign languages are like electric fences. If you do get through, it's not without some pain or even shock. I'm rambling on and I haven't said I miss you. I do. Terribly. I can't tell anyone, but . . .

Chris stopped at the 'but'. It was the 'but' which was so difficult. She had planned the rest, made it sound impromptu and spontaneous, through seven different drafts – ripped them into pieces. Her mother had never mentioned electric fences. She had made that up herself, was rather proud of it. It sounded sophisticated, dashing. Pierre was sophisticated himself – still a student (post-graduate) but at least twenty-five; a man, not a boy, who wore tight white jeans and drove a Porsche and had a real moustache. None of her friends, not even Emma who slept with everyone, had ever had a man with a moustache. The first time he kissed her, it had prickled. She pulled away, stuttered '*J . . . Je ne peux pas. J'ai un ami.*'

'*Moi aussi. J'ai une amie anglaise, qui est très belle et très chic.*'

Nobody called her chic, let alone beautiful. No one that

experienced and sort of decadent had ever looked at her before. She smiled. '*Non, c'est sérieux entre nous.*'

'*Entre nous aussi.*' He held her close again, opened his mouth. He kissed differently from Martin – wetter and much longer. Madame Dubois was often out. That's what she was there for, to look after *les petits* when their mother was at work, teach them English. Pierre taught her French – words they hadn't bothered with at school. *Zizi, enculer.* The youngest child had seen them kissing in the garden. Fortunately, Marie-Claire's vocabulary was limited, so she couldn't blab even if she wanted to. *Maman, chat, encore* – not *baiser*.

It was always *encore* for Pierre, always more he wanted. He had tried to undress her, feel her breasts.

'*Ils sont tout petits,*' she murmured, shy.

'*Juste comme je les aime.*' He had found the nipples now.

Martin liked them small as well. She had tried to shut him out. This was just a holiday, didn't count. Anyway, she ought to have experience. She hadn't felt really guilty until she was on the coach for home. What you said in French wasn't real. You were just practising the language. If she had whispered '*je t'aime*' to Pierre, it was only because she was trying out the verb like they had done in the third form, '*J'aime, tu aimes, il aime.*' *Aimer* meant like, as well as love. Nothing wrong in that.

As the Townsend Thoresen ferry heaved across the Channel, her guilt blew up like a storm. Martin loved her in plain no-nonsense English. She would have to lie to him to explain the mark. The mark had ruined everything, not just her and Martin, but her and Pierre. Up till her last night, she hadn't been to bed with Pierre – not bed. They had done things standing up, or hidden in the bushes, but never gone the whole way. Martin had always stopped her, sitting in her head and muttering 'cut it out', like he did when she messed around with his diving gear or recording equipment.

But that last night she had left Martin behind, eight hundred miles behind. Pierre had bought her Cognac, taken her to a party, and then upstairs, three floors up to a tiny attic room. The noise of the pop group faded, the thud of her heart took over.

'*Non*,' she said, as he pushed her to the floor, started to undo the buttons on her blouse. When she said 'no' again, in English, he cried, really cried. She had never seen a man cry. Martin would have died rather than blub in front of her. Yet it didn't seem gormless – not at all – rather dramatic and sort of doomy as if she had the lead rôle in a wide-screen movie and could drive men to extremes. He told her he would miss her and that he couldn't live without her, which sounded far less hackneyed than in English, and then they'd had more Cognac and . . .

It was only later she regretted it – when she saw the mark – was furious and frightened. He had branded her, like a ewe in his flock. Of *course* he had a flock. A man like that would hardly stick to one boring-looking bit-part with bad French and no breasts and who was leaving anyway. That was the horror of it. If she'd had just one week more, the mark would have faded, before she faced Martin and her mother. Perhaps she could stay, send a telegram, invent some language course or sick child or coach drivers' strike. Impossible. Her ticket was booked and paid for, and it was back to school on Monday. Anyway, she didn't want to stay. If Pierre could do a thing like that, he was just a selfish boorish bragging lout like all the rest. He knew she had a boyfriend. That's why he'd done it, probably – to break it up with Martin, ruin everything.

No, that wasn't fair. It had been very, very special in the end. The floor was hard and she kept worrying that someone might come upstairs and find them, but soon she forgot even where they were. It wasn't just the Cognac, though she could taste that on his kisses. It was the fact that he was old and rich and French, and sort of sobbed when he came, and didn't jump up afterwards but lay there looking smug and swoony as if he had died and gone to heaven, and then kissed between her fingers very very gently as if they were made of glass or lace or something. Except it was all a con, in fact, because he had already made the mark by then. Twenty-three hours on the bumpy stuffy coach with a hold-up in Aix and a stop in Grenoble hadn't faded it. She ordered a glass of Beaujolais in the Channel-ferry bar, hoped it would inspire her to concoct a convincing lie: she had hurt her neck and had to wear a bandage; or met a school friend on the boat who had asked her to stay a few days down in Kent; or decided to do a project on the hop fields or the Cinque Ports . . .

When the boat docked at Dover, she still hadn't finalized her story. But Martin had a surprise for her – himself on the quay with twelve red roses. He had never done a thing like that before. Extravagant, romantic. She burst into tears, sobbed like Pierre. It was while he was trying to comfort her that he discovered the mark. She had to comfort *him*, then – or rather lie to him. Much more difficult to lie in your own language and she didn't want to lie. She loved Martin (well, almost. At least she wanted to, and he loved *her* which was nearly the same thing). She stuck to the truth, with variations. The party on her last night, but no Pierre. The Cognac, drunk not willingly, but slipped into her Coke when she wasn't looking by a drunken lout who later took advantage of her when she was too far gone to know what she was doing.

It was an hour at least before Martin stopped shouting and creating, or agreed to start for home, and even then she wasn't all that sure if he believed her. Then, when they were just about halfway, she suddenly remembered that she had left his roses behind. He refused to go back, said someone would have nicked them long ago, and serve her right since they obviously meant nothing to her. That set off *another* row and she was fool enough to drag in her father's invitation to Los Angeles, as if they didn't have enough to spat about already. Martin was so rattled he all but roared away without her, there and then, and she had to almost grovel before he let her clamber on the bike again, and then he only dropped her at the far end of her road, careered off round the corner, still with all her luggage.

She felt rotten about the rows, rotten about the roses – though they would never have fitted on his bike, in fact, and they'd have had to leave a bag behind instead, which would only have peeved her mother. Her Mum was upset enough already. Couldn't blame her – what with them slamming out before they'd even eaten, and embarrassing that David bod who was obviously someone special since her mother had put on eye-gloss in his honour, when she never normally wore it. They had upset Martin's Mum as well, and in the end she'd felt so knocked out with guilt and misery that she had apologized to everyone in turn, agreed not to go to Los Angeles, divided Christmas with a slide-rule between his family and hers, and even eaten Martin's mother's steak and mushroom pie, picking out the steak and shifting it to Martin's plate when his mother had her back turned. By the time they had reached the Arctic Roll, Martin had relented, even promised her more flowers.

Chris got up to stretch her legs, prowled around his room. He had new posters on the wall of groups she didn't know. Martin never played top-of-the-pops stuff, but discovered bands for himself who were foreign or unorthodox or unfashionably way-out. Chris moved round to the table where he kept his diving treasures, objects he had brought up from the bottom – old bottles, lumps of coral, multi-coloured sea urchins, and his two prize exhibits centre front – a First World War brass shell-casing, and an eighteenth-century cannonball which he had found when he was only fourteen and snorkelling in Devon, and had managed miraculously to conserve with the help of an older friend and several coats of thick black varnish. Diving was Martin's life. He had a job in printing, but that was only a means to an end, a way of paying for his equipment or covering his expenses when he went on new and advanced courses underwater. He was an instructor already, at nineteen and a half, had impressive plans to dive wrecks, join expeditions, travel the world, even run a diving school himself, one day, somewhere exotic like Bermuda or the Red Sea. He needed time, that's all – and cash. He already had the skill, the passion.

She was lucky, really. Many divers were loners, or kept their women as sandwich-making landlubbers whom they fitted in if and when they could. But Martin had insisted that she learn to dive herself, wanted her to join him, become part of all the plans. He had bought her the equipment (secondhand), supervised her training in the local swimming baths. She had stopped at F-test. The next test after that was in the open sea, and she had to admit she was scared. Stupid, really, because she longed to go down with Martin and the crowd, share the life he dreamed of rather than settle for a boring job and never see the world except for a fortnight in August in some tame and crowded resort.

She was meant to be trying for Cambridge, embarking on a career, but career was only a fancy name for a more serious sort of boring job, which took longer to get and was harder to hold down. She wasn't even sure she wanted to go to Cambridge in the first place. Everyone would be clever there and cultured like her mother. That's why she loved (loved?) Martin. She could be brilliant in his company without even trying, without having to borrow ideas from books or spout other people's opinions from the heavy Sunday papers when she'd rather be reading the *New Musical Express*. And

Martin had taught her other skills – not just the whole diving thing, but how to service a motorbike, catch and cut a bass, change a wheel, handle a boat; made her one of the boys. She was happiest when riding pillion behind him, speeding down to the coast to meet Tony, Rob, Scott and all the rest, drinking draught Guinness with them, discussing the newest equipment, the latest expeditions; making herself useful filling cylinders or repairing wet suits. It didn't matter then that she wasn't blonde like Claire or busty like Fiona. In fact it was actually an advantage to have no curves – at least in one way. Excess fat was more likely to retain the dreaded nitrogen bubbles which could give you the bends, even paralyse or kill you. Anyway it was fitter to be slim, meant you were more agile. Even though she hadn't braved the sea yet, Martin and his mates respected her because she had done well in her pool tests, knew her stuff. She had mugged up all the diving books and could talk intelligently about air embolism or nitrogen narcosis; had even helped Martin plan and write the lectures he had been asked to give this autumn at the club. There was his name in bold type on the programme which he had pinned up on his notice-board – M. J. Brett; Martin Brett again in a newspaper cutting which reported how he had towed a yacht to safety when it was headed for the rocks – a swanky thirty-footer saved by his old and patched inflatable.

She was proud of Mr Brett. Most of her girlfriends' boys were feeble in comparison; wimpish public school types (Grandma's type), still fretting through their A levels or planning to do boring standard things like accountancy or law. Only Martin had real guts – not just physical courage, though he had enough of that, all right, but the sheer determination to get there on his own. He didn't have rich and doting parents or a posh supportive school, just nerve and dedication. She felt guilty, sometimes, about her own fancy education – all that cash lavished on her when Martin had been at a dump where one or two of his classmates had fathers who tore up their books to light the fire, or kept them out of school so they could run errands to the betting-shop. She didn't even *believe* in private schools. Martin would have made it if he'd had all the perks she did. He'd make it, anyway – wasn't just the duffer her Mum and Grandma assumed. He was even reading things like history and archaeology to help him in his wreck-diving, and was doing an extra printing course at night school so he could take exams, earn more cash.

Chris plumped back on her chair. She would fail her own exam if she didn't settle down to work. It wasn't easy to work in Martin's room. The house was on a main road, trembled with the lorries. She couldn't use the table when it had half the ocean bed on it, and there wasn't a desk, only a chest of drawers. If she wanted to write, she had to pull the middle drawer out and put a board on top, so that at least she had something to lean on. She returned to her board, re-read the last draft of the letter, tore it up like the seven attempts before it. It was probably wrong to try and write to Pierre in Martin's room. And yet her own room was just as dangerous. If her mother saw that 'Pierre *Chéri*' . . .

She ought to be reading, anyway, not writing. School in two days' time, and great chunks of Racine and Thomas Mann to plough through. She glanced up at Martin's scanty shelf of books – half on diving, half on printing, with a motor cycle maintenance manual at one end and a few dog-eared thrillers at the other – wished she could put her feet up with a thriller. She took down the fattest one, with handcuffs on the cover and a pool of unlikely looking blood, found her *Four Quartets* skulking underneath it. She must have left it there last June, when she was cramming T. S. Eliot for A level. She had done well – got an A – which only went to show how crappy the system was. She didn't understand Eliot, not really, not if she were truthful. Oh, she could write the essays, discuss his use of imagery or analyse his sources, but underneath she wasn't sure if she knew what he was on about. And she didn't like him enough – not with the undivided passion her English mistress had, or Anne-Marie who had won the English Prize each year since she was twelve. Perhaps she *couldn't* love – not anyone, not wholly – not Martin or Pierre or Anne-Marie or Thomas Stearns or even her mother.

She opened the book, turned to 'Burnt Norton'. Eliot depressed her.

> *'Timid apathy with no concentration*
> *men and bits of paper, whirled by the cold wind . . .'*

She felt her own bits of paper crumpled in her pocket, bits of Pierre, the cold wind on the Channel-ferry blowing her lies back in her face. Mind you, there were some things in Eliot which were really great, got you where it hurt. *'The still point of the turning world'*. That was wonderful, though still depressing, mainly because she had never known it, probably never would. Things were rarely still for her, always churning, breaking into pieces. There were yards of footnotes after it, ruining its perfection. She hated footnotes, making things too complicated, showing up her ignorance – references to Dante and Heraclitus whom she had never read, probably never would. Strange that Grandma should have a romantic name like Beatrice, when she was so down-to-earth and strict and all her church friends had stuffy saintly names like Agnes and Edwina. Dante's Beatrice had died at twenty-three – younger than Pierre. Probably best to die then, when you were unhaggard and still loved. She couldn't be a genuine intellectual because she didn't worry about death like her mother did. It seemed so far away. Even twenty-three seemed miles off, especially when one night could drag on and on for ever, as last night had. It was always difficult to sleep in Martin's bed, but when you were missing the man you resented and resenting the one you were meant to love, sleep was more or less impossible. And then guilt had kept exploding into excitement. She couldn't be that boring if two men wanted to sleep with her. Fiona had always stuck to Paul, and Claire was still a virgin, and although Emma did it with anyone who asked her, they were all mostly teenagers and hardly even shaved.

She turned back to the *Four Quartets*:

> '*Descend lower, descend only*
> *Into the world of perpetual solitude.*'

The trouble was, every bit of life was in a separate box – Eliot and Thomas Mann and sex and school and France and diving and . . . Everything had little fences round it like the school timetable itself. 9.15, English I; 10.30, French drama. If you brought sex into literature at all, it was only Sexual Imagery In Shakespeare or John Donne's Love Poetry Compared With The Holy Sonnets. Had Eliot actually fucked? He hadn't any children, so you couldn't prove it. She had read somewhere that his first wife was mad and poured melted chocolate through people's letter boxes. They didn't tell you things like that at school, just discussed his religious conversion or digressed onto the footnotes. Had he been unfaithful? He'd never use a word like that, in any case. It was too open-ended and not obscure enough. Unfaithful to whom, to what? There'd be acres more footnotes, charting every stage of the affair – Heraclitus at foreplay, Dante at climax.

> '*Only by the form, the pattern,*
> *can words or music reach*
> *the stillness, as a Chinese jar still*
> *moves perpetually in its stillness . . .*'

That was beautiful. Grandma had a Chinese jar standing on the piano which she never played. Grandma had a stillness.

It seemed to come from her religion. Nice to have a God, though He would probably turn out crackpot like Eliot's first wife, and all Gods made Commandments which meant she wouldn't be able to go to bed with Martin, let alone Pierre; and if it were Grandma's kind of God, then there'd be a kid each year with no chance of contraception. Religion hadn't done much for Eliot, despite the fact he was always on about it – nor for her mother, either. Probably best to follow Martin and refuse to worship anyone.

She could hear him now, the motorbike crescendoing as it skidded to a halt, the slam of the front door, his heavy thudding footsteps on the stairs.

'Finished?' he asked, as he burst into the room.

'I'm never finished.' She should have said 'Yes' and hugged him, but thinking of God upset her, and since Pierre she felt irritable, defensive. The mark was still purple, fading into yellow at the edges. She hadn't even *started* her work. That was Pierre's fault, too.

Martin was kicking off his trainers. 'You said you'd be undressed.'

'I am – well, underneath.' She slipped her sundress off, stood naked, stooping. Pierre had undressed her himself, sliding both his hands down inside her knickers before he eased them off, kneeling while he unbuckled her sandals, kissing up her thighs . . .

Martin couldn't even see her. He was struggling out of his sweatshirt, head down as he tugged it off, then turning away to lock the door.

'I thought it was your Mum's late Saturday at work?' Chris closed the Eliot, crossed her arms across her chest.

'It is. But in case she breaks her leg or something and the boss-man sends her home.'

'She'll hardly come upstairs with a broken leg.'

'Sshh. Get on the bed.'

He smelt different from Pierre. She hadn't really realized

until she'd had another man, that every naked body had its individual odour – not a bad one – not sweat or nicotine or obvious things like different brands of aftershave, just the intimate smell of skin and hair and hands. She had noticed it last night. It had been very brief last night. Martin's mother didn't object to sex, only to disturbance. The walls were thin, so they had done it sort of gingerly and in total silence. It was another sort of branding, a deliberate solemn one, so that Martin could overlay her body with his own fingerprints and monogram, in place of the drunken lout's who had spiked her drink. He'd been rougher than he ever had before, left marks himself, faint bruises.

This time it was better. Martin was less angry, spent longer turning her on. The Frenchie bloke was still in bed with them, but instead of thrashing him, Martin was trying to prove he was every bit as good. She lay back and enjoyed it. Emma had had two boys at once, or so she claimed. She could hear Pierre murmuring *'mon chou, mon petit lapin, ma minette'*, as Martin thrust into her. The bed was creaking – didn't matter when his mother wasn't there. Marvellous creaking. They had broken a spring once and Martin had spent ages mending it, still naked, and then insisted they do it again, to try it out.

'I love you,' she shouted. 'I *love* you, Martin.' It didn't count in bed. You said crazy things – anything – couldn't think. 'It's wonderful! I love you. Hey, come *out*!'

He almost didn't. She loved that, too. The danger, the excitement, his come spurting on her thighs while he grabbed his thing himself, pumped it up and down and sort of shuddered. She only worried afterwards, especially if her period was late. Martin promised it was safe. His Dad had done it all his life and only produced two kids. Pierre had used a Durex – or whatever the French equivalent was – a decadent looking black one. She was almost disappointed when he came inside her. She had got so used to Martin snatching out when they were both so frantic and worked up, then rubbing in his come like body lotion. Such a tiny drizzle after all that pounding and excitement. She was always surprised – felt there should be gallons of the stuff, streaming out like a petrol pump or one of those ice cream machines where you pulled a handle and Soft-Whip frothed and billowed into the cornets. With Pierre, she hadn't seen it at all, just a limp black chrysalis with something white and sticky at the bottom. He had left it behind in the attic and she had worried someone would find it in the morning, but what could she have done with it – put it in her handbag?

Martin's finger was stopping her from thinking. He always touched her once he had come himself. It was the best bit really, except she made him close his eyes. She knew she looked ridiculous, gasping and grimacing. Strange to think what people did in bed, when you only saw them dressed and public. Fences and boxes again. Maggie Thatcher might be the Iron Lady, but did she also like a finger? Had Thomas Stearns ever used black Durex?

    'Oh dark, dark, dark, . . .
    . . . with a movement of darkness on darkness . . .'

It *was* darkness, but bright as well behind her lids and down where Martin's finger jabbed and circled. Marvellous, bloody marvellous. Hands clenched, face screwed up.

'Oh, Martin. *Martin!*'

He was always starving afterwards. Already he was pulling on his jeans, not white, but blue and oil-stained. She lay back, closed her eyes. He would crash downstairs, bring up Mr Kipling cake, or bacon-flavoured crisps.

'Chris . . .'

'Not hungry, thanks. *You* eat.'

'No, I want to ask you something.'

She squinted through one eye. 'What?' She was still tired after her journey, exhausted from the guilt.

'Something – well – important.'

'Get on with it, then.'

'Look, Chris.' He was still hesitant, embarrassed. 'I think we ought to get . . . you know, engaged.'

She sprang off the bed. 'You mean you're asking me to marry you?'

'Yeah. Well, not exactly . . . asking. I reckoned we ought to talk about it, see how you felt and . . .'

Chris slumped against the wall. He should be on one knee, in evening dress, punting down the Cam with nightingales pouring out their love song overhead, or in Eliot's summer midnight with the music and mysterious dancers, not slouching in his bedroom with its cheap carpet and chipped paintwork and the lorries rumbling through everything he said.

'B . . . But you haven't got your exam yet. And you're saving all your money and you said . . .'

'Doesn't matter. Anyway, we don't have to marry straight away. We can have a long engagement.'

Long engagement sounded like a lead – tying you to someone so you couldn't stray. Martin didn't trust her. Why should he? She had already strayed, betrayed him. Perhaps a lead would help. If she met another Pierre, she could always say *'j'ai un fiancé'*, instead of just *'ami'*, flash the diamond to prove it.

'You mean have a ring and everything?' A ring was like a love-bite, branding and possession, bragging to the world.

'Well, I couldn't afford that yet – not a decent one. But we could get engaged in secret.'

Chris stared at her ring finger – bare. The possession without the bragging. That would be safer, easier to break if . . . She ought to be flattered, really. Half his fellow divers would rather die than get engaged. She owed him something anyway.

'Okay, then.'

He was unzipping his jeans again. The engagement had excited him.

'Lie on your front,' he said.

'No, wait, Martin. I want to ask you something, too. Not just quid pro quo but . . .' Chris stopped. He hated her using words he didn't understand, but there wasn't an equivalent and a footnote would be worse.

'I was going to ask you, anyway, but now it's more important. You know my Dad?' You couldn't call Neil 'Dad' – it was too downmarket.

'Christ! Not all that again. I thought we'd *settled* Christmas.' His thing was going limp, sort of sagging at half-mast.

'Yeah, we have, but I think I ought to see him. I mean, if we're getting engaged, shouldn't we inform him, ask his permission? He's quite old-fashioned about things like that.' Her father had never been old-fashioned. She was improvising as she went along. But why should Martin win, ban her from her father when she had waited five years two months for an invitation? It was hardly her fault if some depraved French layabout had had it in for her, taken advantage of a foreign girl. She could almost see the rotter – not dark and gorgeous like Pierre, but dark and swarthy – newspapers tied around his feet like those tramps who slept on Charing Cross embankment, a fag drooling from his toothless mouth, the reek of Cognac. No, he couldn't afford Cognac if . . . She giggled.

'What's so funny?' Martin scowled and dragged his pants back on, as if she were laughing at his fallen manhood.

'Nothing.' She forced the tramp out, her father in. 'I could go *after* Christmas. I'm free then. Well, I've got to get a job until I start at university, but there's no great rush for that. It would be the perfect time to go, in fact, when I've finished at school but not fixed up anywhere else. Then I can square things with my father, get his blessing, so to speak.'

'I thought we'd said we'd keep the engagement secret?'

'Yeah, course, but Daddy doesn't count, not all those miles away. He's good at secrets, anyway.' She had never told Neil a secret in her life, but there had to be a first time.

'But what about your Mum? She was invited too, wasn't she?'

'Mm, but she'd never stay at Daddy's. She'd rather *die*. If she comes at all, which she doesn't even want to, she'd probably book in at some motel. They're very cheap out there. Fiona's father told me. You can find quite decent places for only . . .'

'Can't *we* go, then – together? If it's so damned cheap, I could borrow some cash from Tony and . . .'

'No, it's the fares which cost a bomb. Five hundred pounds to LA and back – and that's third class or tourist or whatever they call it.'

Martin jabbed his foot against the skirting. 'I can't understand your Dad. Why should he shell out five hundred quid for an ex-wife who doesn't even . . .?'

'Oh, guilt, I expect.' People did anything for guilt. 'Anyway, I don't suppose he pays it directly. He's been working on some airline account and Mum said a couple of free tickets now and then is just one of the perks, especially in the winter when the planes are half empty.'

Martin didn't answer. It was so easy to offend him. His own father had never been further than Dungeness in the South and Whitby in the North, and got nothing free except mail order catalogues or Co-op trading stamps before they stopped them. So what? Her own father's father had been much the same – still was, in fact. Martin could outgrow him; fight his way to the top and take her with him. Her own world was so restricted – an all-girls school with a prissy uniform and a staff-room of spinsters, and Sundays eating sponge cake with her Grandma. Once Martin had his diving school, they could jet around the world, book in to any motel they pleased. But meanwhile she ought to take the only chance she had, and quite honestly, she would rather see her father than the Taj Mahal or the Bridge of Sighs or . . .

'How long would you be gone, Chris?'

'Not long.'

'Not like bloody France?'

'Oh, no. That was a *job*.'

'And you wouldn't . . . I mean, I couldn't bear to think . . .'

She shook her head. Yanks were lousy in bed. Emma had told her that. She was still undressed, pressed herself against Martin's hard and hairless chest. 'Who'd look at me in California? They're all beautiful out there and if they're not, they rip themselves apart and start again. Hey, shall I get my breasts done – come back with a D-cup?'

Martin growled. 'No, I like them as they are. They don't get in the way.'

He cupped them, tipped her head back, and she felt him rising again through his holey scarlet pants.

9

'Welcome to LA!'

Chris stared at the short, smiling, blinding blonde who had rushed towards them with a curly haired four-year-old clinging on to one hand and a huge bouquet of flowers brandished in the other.

'Hi! You must be Chrissie. Great to meet you.' The flowers changed hands. Chris was suddenly swamped in roses and carnations, choked by their scent and the reek of L'Air du Temps. She backed away.

'I'm Bunny. I knew you right away from your pictures. And this is Dean. Say hallo, Dean.'

Dean said nothing, grabbed his mother's leg and hid his face in it. It was an impressive leg, clad in real suede jeans in dusky-pink with a glimpse of well-tanned ankle above high-heeled open sandals with gold thongs. There was more gold in the dangling chains, jangling bracelets, rings on every finger.

'And there's your Mom! She looks exactly like her picture, only prettier.' Bunny darted over to Morna, shook hands across the luggage trolley, gold a-jingle, thousand-watt smile.

'I'm *so* glad we could finally meet. Did you have a good flight?' She didn't wait for an answer. 'Eleven hours, isn't it? You must be dead. Have you been over here before? Oh no – Neil said it was your first-ever trip. Well, you're going to love it – I promise you. Is this all your stuff?' She heaved a case up, dislodging the dyed mink blouson jacket flung across her shoulders, pink to match the jeans.

Chris glowered. It must take thirty or forty minks to make a jacket like that – living breathing animals with feelings of their own. Would Bunny like to be made into a coat, cut up into little pieces, dyed a different colour? She *was* dyed, that was obvious. Her hair was that outrageous shade of platinum which could only have come from a bottle and which hurt your eyes. Okay, so she had a stunning figure, but it had probably been sculpted by a surgeon. Emma said she had read about a woman in Los Angeles who'd had twenty-six separate operations. She had started with a nose job, but once her nose was perfect she wanted perfect teeth to match it, and then perfect breasts, a trimmer waist, tauter buttocks . . .

Chris watched the buttocks curvet through the automatic doors, followed at a distance, screwing up her eyes as she stepped from the air-conditioned chill of the airport to the sweltering heat outside.

'This is the hottest day we've had so far.' Bunny was boasting, as if she had fixed the weather herself – part of the welcome, like the flowers. So why wear fur jackets in eighty-two degrees? Bunny had slipped it off now, exposing a flounced top which ended in a sort of bow thing just above her navel. She had probably had a navel job, as well, and wanted them to admire the surgeon's art. Dean was pretty gorgeous, too – the sort of cute kid Chris had never been herself, with a cloud of golden curls which looked as if they had come straight off the set of a sunshine breakfast commercial, and a grin to melt your heart if you weren't actually his older, plainer half-sister. He was wearing scaled-down denim jeans with lots of fancy pockets and overstitching, and a pair of miniature cowboy boots in highly polished leather, with a belt to match.

Chris shrugged off her plain blue anorak, smoothed her

crumpled skirt. She felt stupid clutching a sodding great bouquet as if she were an opera singer, but without the glamour or the voice to match. People were already staring. She looked past them to the road, glanced up at the dingy airport buildings criss-crossed with scaffolding as if they had braces on their teeth; down again to the traffic jam of taxis. No skyscrapers, no palms, no Pacific Ocean. What was that chap's name in the Keats poem, the one who gazed at the Pacific with eagle eyes? Stout Cortez, wasn't it? She had forgotten how it went now, but he and his men had been pretty damn impressed. She had imagined she would feel the same, step off the aircraft and come face to face with a wild and crashing seascape. She squinted at the sky – or what was left of it – Cambridge blue, but mainly swallowed up in steel and concrete.

'It doesn't look like California,' she muttered.

Bunny laughed, displaying improbably pearly teeth.

When they'd first landed, it had been even worse – just grey concrete all around them like a prison. She thought perhaps the pilot had made an error, brought them down somewhere drab and unexotic like Chicago, or even doubled back to Britain and was taxying into Liverpool or Glasgow. They had all piled into a bus and then out again into a gloomy Customs building with dingy beige lino and mustard-coloured walls, and stood in a queue for hours to be questioned by bad-tempered officials, then hung around again to get their luggage. She hadn't minded at the time because she was still over the moon about seeing her father, kept imagining how he would bound towards them, clasp her in his arms, whisper, 'My darling, my own darling daughter'. All right, that was crap – pure worst-of-Hollywood – but he might at least have *come*.

Bunny was still laughing. Her laugh was like her jewellery – jangling and overdone. 'What about our weather, though?

That's Californian, isn't it? I hear it's snowing back in London.'

'I like snow.' Chris turned her back. Okay, so it was rude, but what about her father? Wasn't it equally bad-mannered to send the new-model wife to meet them on her own, when his only daughter (thank God Dean was a boy) had flown what felt like half a million miles for no other reason than to see him. It must be even worse for her mother. In fact, she was feeling pretty lousy now about the way she had more or less dragooned her into coming; really put the screws on, mooning around the house saying she would never see her father in her life again if she didn't take this chance, but refusing to make the trip unless her mother did as well. Morna had absolutely refused at first, used words like monstrous and grotesque, raised her voice, sounded close to tears, but she had gone on and on pestering and wailing until at last she got her way. She hadn't *meant* to bully – it was just some stupid fear of facing her father on her own, plus some stupid hope that if he saw his first wife again, they might all get back together. Now she realized how fatuous that had been. Bunny was a fact, not some abstract inconvenience you could spirit away if it didn't fit your scheme. And her mother looked quite awful – pale and sort of cowed, yet trying valiantly to be the perfect guest, asking polite and formal questions like was it always as warm as this in winter and when would Dean start school. (Dean, for Christ's sake! What a name.)

'He's at school already, aren't you, honey-pie? He's really smart. He could read when he was only three. Okay, you guys, you wait here with the bags and I'll go get the car.'

Guys. Honey-pie. Chris screwed up her face against the sun. It should have been dark. They had left Heathrow at lunchtime and it was still only teatime and yet hours and hours had passed – hours and hours of watching imbecilic movies and eating plastic food. It had been exciting at the time. She had laughed at the movies, scoffed the chicken and the trifle, joked with the stewardess about the picnic tea at breakfast – every meal and hour bringing her closer to her father. And then he hadn't come. Couldn't be bothered to miss a footling meeting or cancel an appointment. Perhaps she wouldn't see him at all. Twenty-one days with Bunny's five-thousand dollar smile, while he wheeled and dealed in his glass-and-concrete skyscraper and then failed to see them off because an important client (*miles* more important than a mere forgotten daughter) had just flown in from Texas and if Bunny Sweetheart would take them in her Pontiac . . .

It had driven up now, yards of it, all scarlet metal fore and aft, sort of showing off and scalloped, but nowhere much to sit. She squashed in the back with Dean and half the luggage and Bunny's fur which she tried to squirm away from, while her mother took the front seat. The two wives side by side. Horrible. There was a tiny toy rabbit dangling over the dashboard – a Bunny in a dress. Dean was staring at her with his huge cornflower blue eyes – Bunny's eyes – his lashes as long and thick as hers but without the spiked mascara.

'Know something?' he said. It was the first time he had spoken. Chris shook her head.

'You're my sister.'

'I'm not,' she muttered.

'Yes, you are. Mom said.'

'Half-sister. That's different.'

Dean pouted, didn't understand.

'Look, darling – palm trees.' Morna being tactful.

Chris peered up at the date palms, more to please her mother than anything else. Not bad. At least the place looked right now, more like California, though not exactly beautiful – garish billboards, skyscrapers soaring past the palms, a great throb and honk of freeway with seven lanes of cars streaming in both directions, a glare on everything like a sticky shimmering film. The excitement began to trickle back again, shimmering itself. They were *here*, they had made it, half a world away, with a whole ocean and a continent between them and tiny England, a different time scale, different climate. Even the cars looked different – bigger altogether with extra swanky bits, bigger rumps and jaws, even bigger lights and mirrors. All the lights were coming on now. Darkness seemed to have fallen very suddenly, not just a gradual creeping dusk like four o'clock back home, but more as if someone had got up and pulled the blinds down and then flicked a thousand switches to turn on stars, headlamps, streetlamps, neon signs. She blinked against the flicker dazzle glare, the flashing letters, fluorescent sky. Even the freeway was only streaking light now – scarlet tail-lights stretching to infinity their side, white headlamps speeding towards them on the other. It was like two battle lines – red and white – the Wars of the Roses. No, that was school and she had done with school. In fact if she lived in the States, she'd have had a proper graduation with a gown and mortarboard and a high-school diploma dished out by the Principal.

'How many cars do you have?' Dean was asking her.

'None,' she said, turning back from the window. 'Well, my mother's got one, but . . .'

'Don't you know how to drive, honey? We better teach you.' Bunny flung her a smile over her right shoulder.

'She hasn't got a licence,' Morna cut in. 'And certainly not an international one.'

Bunny hooted loudly at a bumptious truck. 'Don't worry about that. We can take her to a parking lot or . . .'

'My boyfriend's got a motorbike,' Chris said. 'A Triumph Bonneville.' She'd love to learn to drive. Perhaps she would have a word with Bunny on her own, tell her it was best to say nothing to her mother. Morna feared so many things – bikes, cars, muggers, rapists, diving. Bunny herself seemed fearless, switching lanes, overtaking laggards, following complicated signs as if someone had plugged her into a computer terminal.

'I used to have a motorcycle myself,' she said. 'A Harley Davidson Police Special.'

'Wow! That's a really big one, isn't it?'

'Sure is! I hit a hundred once, right on this freeway when I was just about your age.'

'A *hundred*?'

'Yeah. I was real wild!'

'*I*'ve got a bike,' said Dean. 'I've got three bikes. And a pedal car.'

Chris grinned at him – he couldn't be so bad if his mother had done a ton on a Police Special. She only wished her own mother seemed less strained. She could see just her back, but it looked stiff and sort of hostile and she hadn't said a word for several minutes. She was probably semi-mesmerized by the endless chain of lights, the rhythmic drone of traffic. No green fields or mountains yet, no ocean. She had better speak herself, break the silence.

'Is this still Los Angeles?' she asked.

'Yeah,' said Bunny. 'Downtown LA is pretty small, but the suburbs go on for ever. There's about thirteen million people living in the greater LA area and guess how many there were when the town was founded two hundred years ago?'

'One!' yelled Dean.

'A hundred?' ventured Chris. She was surprised that Bunny could quote statistics. If she were honest with herself, she couldn't have said how many lived in Greater London and she was considered Oxbridge material – *failed* Oxbridge material. Cambridge had turned her down.

'Forty-four,' said Bunny, with a laugh. She had made everything a giggle, even figures. 'Do you realize California is the richest state in America, yet in 1846 they said it wasn't worth a dollar?'

Chris stared at the back of her curly blonde head. Dates, too. Perhaps Bunny had had a brain job as well as boobs and navel, and the surgeon had implanted a silicone parcel of useful information.

'Everything in California is the biggest – the biggest ocean in the world, the biggest trees – you know, the giant redwoods and the giant sequoias – even the biggest strawberries.'

Chris yawned. Swanking again. Anyone would have thought that Bunny had planted the trees herself, lugged redwoods and sequoias to the forest in her shopping bag, fattened up the strawberries, filled the Pacific in person, with a jug. When it came to oceans, she could quote statistics, too. Martin had told her that the Pacific stretched almost sixty-nine million square miles, with its deepest point over thirty-six thousand feet. Figures like that made her feel small and rather pointless, like a pinhead-sized crustacean stranded on a rock. Martin knew a lot of things, especially things to do with seas. She was missing him – badly. He had seen her off at the airport with her grandmother, which hadn't really worked because the one inhibited the other. Grandma's hug had been short and rather awkward and Martin's kiss had no real juice in it. When she turned back to wave, the two of them were standing side by side, both silent, Martin in dirty Levis and leather jacket, Grandma all dolled up in a black coat and matching feathered hat, as if she were attending some VIP's state funeral.

Chris stared out at a giant palm, all trunk and no leaf, stretching up, up, as if it wished to avoid the noise and fumes below it. It was Martin's birthday in two days' time, and she wouldn't be there. She had made him a cake, left him a load of presents, and they had even had a birthday session in bed, four days in advance, but it wasn't the same.

'MACDONALD'S' screamed a billboard. 'OVER 40 BILLION SERVED.' Everybody bragged here.

'Why do they allow all those horrid signs?' she asked. 'They ruin the view.'

'They *are* the view,' grinned Bunny. 'Part of LA – like the freeways. You'll see picture postcards here with great freeway intersections on them, where other countries have photos of cathedrals or works of art. These are our works of art, I guess.'

Chris said nothing. If she had to choose between the Louvre and a fifty-foot sign for 'DUNKIN DONUTS' complete with 3-D sugared sample, she knew which she would go for.

Bunny was flirting with the driver of a Buick who was cruising beside them as they slowed for some diversion. 'I love LA,' she said, turning back to her passengers. 'You either love it or you hate it. I've lived here all my life. I was born in a hospital near Malibu, looking right out over the ocean.'

'You live in the mountains, don't you, now?' Her mother had revived, was continuing the polite remarks. Her voice sounded puny, though, as if she had left half of it in England.

'Yeah. You'll see them soon. They're stunning. It was Neil's idea. He chose the house himself. I adore it. We both do.'

There was silence for a moment, like a cold wind blowing through the car. Only Bunny appeared blithely unaware of it.

'I'm sorry he couldn't come. He was furious about it, too, but he was playing in this real important golf tournament and he couldn't let his partner down.'

'*Golf?*' repeated Chris. She felt queasy suddenly, clutched at her stomach as the car shuddered over a bump.

'Yeah. He's a fantastic golfer, and he only started playing

three years ago. I talked him into it. I play myself, only I'm not quite tournament material.'

'But it's . . . it's dark.' Chris tried to keep her voice down. Meetings were understandable, pressure of work, important clients, yes – but a *game* . . .

'Oh, they'll have finished playing now, sweetie. They'll be back when we get home – all ready to open the champagne. We got Californian champagne, to welcome you both. Pink. It's real neat. We often . . . Hey, look! See those little twinkly lights? Those are our mountains!'

He wasn't back. The champagne was chilling in the giant-sized refrigerator, but no Neil to open it. Chris felt numb inside and distanced from her mother, since they could say nothing to each other except in Wife II's presence. Bunny was showing them around the house, flinging open doors, quoting still more facts and figures.

'See that silk? It cost fifty dollars a yard, and the table top's real marble. Antique. Well, that's what the man said.'

'Yes, it's . . . lovely.' Morna, valiant still, as they were whisked from room to room, entrusted with the vital statistics of every frill, flounce, knick-knack, ornament.

It *stinks*, Chris thought. Anyone could see that. Bunny's bedroom was the worst – her father's bedroom, though how he could bear to sleep in it, she didn't understand. Yellow everywhere. Yellow floor-length curtains, draped and swathed in layers with yellow nets beneath them; a yellow satin bedspread extending into a satin padded headboard which reached halfway up the wall and was crowned with a sort of three-D yellow topknot with satin streamers flowing down and fringed. Even the carpet was yellow, a sicklier yellow still, if that were possible, with little scatter rugs in white fake fur. The bed was huge, huge. A whole family could have stretched out in it and still had room for second cousins and hangers-on. Every surface was busy – vases of silk flowers in stiff arrangements, rows of simpering dolls in twenty or thirty different national costumes. Kleenex boxes in fancy dress, flower-sprinkled powder bowls in the shape of hearts. There were a lot of hearts. Heart-shaped cushions on the bed, a red velvet heart with a broderie-anglaise backing framed and hung like a picture and clashing with the yellow wild-silk wall; a heart-shaped nightdress case with 'B' embroidered on it in a second appliqué heart.

Chris backed away. She could see her father suddenly, no longer tall and slim, but heart-shaped, cut out like a cookie with one of Bunny's pastry cutters, from an offcut of red satin.

'And this is the little girls' room,' Bunny was saying. 'We've got four bathrooms, one each and one left over. I decided the extra one would be females only. Men always *splash*, don't they? Half the time they're aiming wrong, I guess.' She opened the door on an acre or so of petunia-coloured carpet. Somewhere at the distant end, a toilet in the same unlikely shade blushed beneath its lurid pink velvet cover, which matched the covers on the cistern and the toilet roll. Pink fur mats fringed the bath and shower which had curved gold taps in the shape of outstretched swans' necks.

'Maybe you'd like a shower?' she asked. 'Or a nap? It's your night-time, isn't it? Or how about something to eat?'

How about my *father*? Chris fumed. So he splashed, did he? Couldn't even aim straight. Had to be restricted to his own inferior loo, with a black velvet cover on the offending organ so it wouldn't drip or . . .

'Come see *my* room.' Dean tugged at her hand, led her along the passage to his bedroom which was red, white and blue – blue swathed curtains over fake white wooden shutters, a scarlet bedspread piled high with plush new cuddly toys, an immaculate white carpet. White for a four-year-old and not a blemish on it! They must renew it every week. Even Dean's toys looked as if they had been chosen

175

to match the furnishings. Most were red and blue and so pristine shiny, they were obviously traded in for new ones every time they got a bash or scratch. That's what her father had done – traded in his faded ageing first wife for a dazzling new model, his drab and boring daughter for a cute curly-headed cherub. He was having second thoughts about the visit – that's why he was lingering at the golf club; couldn't face seeing her again. She would spoil his house, upset his colour scheme. Her Mum was right, as she so often was, curse her. They should never have come at all. It would only make things worse. She had been cruel and selfish and stubborn to insist on her own way, overrule her mother's sense and tact. Now she was paying for it. Neil would keep away, reject them both.

'You're crying,' Dean said. 'What's the matter? Don't you like my room?'

'Y . . . Yes, I do. It's . . . smashing.'

'Don't cry,' he said and took her hand again, sat her down on his little white chair with its blue and red piped cushion. 'I like you,' he said. 'You're my sister. I've never had a sister before.'

The kitchen table was huge – almost as big as the bed. Chris and Morna sat stranded at one end of it, facing Dean and Bunny; Neil's place empty still.

'Would you believe? Your very first night here and his car breaks down. I guess you're stuck with me.' Bunny's giggle was no longer bandbox fresh. In fact, she was looking pretty strained. Chris had noticed her constant anxious glances at the clock, her gold-ringed fingers restless on the table. *Both* the wives were miserable and it was all her fault. How could she have been so blind – not to realize that they should never ever meet, were incompatible like oil and water or fox and duck.

'You've got *me*,' said Dean, beaming at Chris and Morna as he stretched across for the bread.

They had decided on food rather than shower or nap – at least Dean had decided. It was obvious he made the bulk of the decisions when his father wasn't there.

'It's a do-it-yourself dinner,' Bunny announced. 'There's never time to cook out here. I mean, why waste precious time slaving in the kitchen, when you could be in the pool or out at the gym or . . .? Hey, would you like a swim?'

Bunny kept suggesting things, as if to compensate for the absence of her star exhibit who had broken down on the two-mile stretch of freeway which led from the golf club to his house – or so she claimed after a complicated phone call from the garage up the road. She had been jumping up and down, offering saunas, jacuzzis, even a foot massage on her latest pet machine. It had got on Chris's nerves at first especially as her mother was sitting like a corpse saying 'no' to everything, but with a fixed smile on her face which looked as if it had been crayoned on by an embalmer. Now she realized Bunny was simply nervous, trying to make amends.

Dean was tugging at her sleeve. 'No, Mom. Let's not swim. I'm starving. We've been in the pool four times today already.'

'Yeah, but Morna and Chrissie haven't.'

'Chrissie goes diving. She told me – in a wet suit. Can I have a wet suit, Mom?'

'You can have a turkey sandwich just at the moment. Or there's ham or cheese or pastrami or . . .' She smiled around at the three of them. 'Go right ahead and make your own. It's so much simpler, isn't it? Bread's right here.' She waved at seven different loaves, all sliced and packaged – two whites, a rye, raisin-bread, honey-bran, wholemeal and high protein; a cluster of butters and margarine – whipped, salted, low-cholesterol – plates of meat and cheese, and such a large array of chutneys, pickles, relishes, she could have stocked a supermarket with all the jars and bottles.

Dean had already buttered four slices of the Super-White and was piling all the different fillings between them; a dollop of relish on every layer, a dab of pickle, a slice of onion, until the final sandwich was several inches high. He opened his mouth as wide as it would go.

'A giant sequoia sandwich,' Chris said and giggled suddenly. Perhaps it was just as well her father wasn't there. He would only be disappointed in her, especially now she wasn't going to Cambridge. She kept trying not to think about it. It set up such contradictory feelings – relief, rejection, envy of Anne-Marie who *had* got in and even won a scholarship; resentment that she'd wasted a whole year. She could be up at Bristol now, just starting her second term, if she had accepted their offer last January instead of just last week. Now she had nine months to kill and she hadn't found a job yet to keep her going till the academic year re-started in October. Bristol was good, in fact, but her father probably wouldn't know that, and he wouldn't approve of Martin, that was certain. She was aware of a sort of fear, churning in her stomach, creeping into her throat – a fear of seeing him at all – made worse and contradicted by the longing. She was scared for her Mum, as well. It was bad enough her mother looking so much older than Mark II, with sort of staider clothes and hair, and her skin less well-upholstered than Bunny's pink-and-white marshmallow, but what if Neil were downright cool to her, or they even had a row?

She watched Dean dismantle his sandwich, pull out a piece of turkey from the bottom layer, shred it into pieces before finally discarding it; pushed away her own plate.

Dessert was do-it-yourself, as well. The meats and cheeses were parcelled up in clingfilm, lost in the echoing cavern of the fridge. Bunny opened a second fridge which turned out to be a freezer, removed several gallon cartons of ice cream.

'More!' yelled Dean. 'I want *all* of them.' He fetched the toppings himself – ten different syrups and sauces.

'Right, help yourselves,' said Bunny.

Dean piled coffee-pecan on top of rum-raisin, sprinkled both with nuts and chocolate flake, added two scoops of lime sherbet, awash in maple syrup, snowed the lot with desiccated coconut. He had left three quarters of his sandwich which had been tipped into the pig-bin. Chris wondered if pigs were partial to peach chutney. She couldn't eat herself. She had tried half a slice of bread, but it had lodged in her throat and scratched it, although it was the softest whitest bread she had ever seen. She was toying now with a spoonful of plain vanilla, lost in the bottom of a skyscraper sundae glass.

Both televisions were blaring, the one in the kitchen and the one in the living room. There were four in all, one each and one to spare, like the bathrooms. Dean had his own set in his bedroom (a child's model, with Mickey Mouse grinning on each dial). She had been reading about some survey in the States where half the kids interviewed said that if they had to choose between losing their father or their television, they'd keep the telly, thanks. Which just showed what a ballsed-up country it was. She would have given up everything (well, almost) to have her father back. Instead they had his video recorder. She could see now why he didn't need it. She had counted three already, along with two freezers, two cars, one dog (pedigree), one cat (Persian) and fifteen different flavours of ice cream.

'Do they *have* ice cream in England?' Dean was asking.

'Yeah – pink or white.' Chris pushed her dish away.

Bunny was on the phone again. There were four phones altogether, each one a different colour. Bunny obviously had a thing about safety in numbers. She could talk on the phone without even holding the receiver, just wedged it between her ear and shoulder and went on spooning in ice cream, or even clearing plates or walking round the kitchen. She seemed to have endless female friends, who all screamed and giggled at the other end. Each time it rang, Chris prayed it would be her father so at least she could say hallo to him. He hadn't rung himself the first time – it had been some garage bloke reporting the breakdown for him. The whole thing sounded fishy. Perhaps he was still snug in the golf club, downing whiskies or postmorteming his game, or had returned to his office for a post-golf round of business. Maybe he was dead – had collapsed with a coronary the night before and Bunny dared not break the news. But wouldn't Dean have said?

'Daddy!' Dean shouted, rocketing off his chair and darting towards the door.

'No, wait here, sunbeam.' Bunny grabbed his sleeve. 'Let Chrissie go and meet him. It's her turn tonight.'

Chris gripped the edge of the table. 'You mean, he's . . .? My father's . . .?'

'Yeah. That's him now. Go and say Hi.'

Chris glanced at Morna. Her mother's face was pale still and impassive, but she nodded.

Chris stumbled out to the hall. Her feet weren't working properly, her heart compensating by beating overtime. She could see a tall dark figure standing by the door, shrugging off its jacket. She dared not look up. Supposing he were changed – stern, sarcastic, old and grey? Two tartan-trousered legs were striding towards her, an American voice she didn't recognize saying, 'Honey, honey, honey, honey, honey.'

She shut her eyes and let herself fall into his arms.

10

Morna closed her book, switched off the bedside lamp which was in the shape of a lady in a rose-pink crinoline, her lace-edged flounces blocking off half the light. She threw the duvet back, smoothed the rumpled sheet. First she had been too cold, now too hot. She had got up at one a.m. for a glass of water, at two for a couple of aspirin; at ten past three she had started reading, was now halfway through the book. Impossible to sleep. It wasn't jet lag – that wouldn't last four days – more the fact that Neil and Bunny's bedroom was just along the passage. If she got up for the bathroom, she had to pass their door. Did she *really* need a pee now, or was it just that ghastly fascination, that cruel desire to pass it, coupled with a dread every bit as strong? The walls were thick, so she couldn't actually hear them, but silence was almost worse, left her free to imagine things – creaks from the bed, muffled groans of ecstasy, sudden high-pitched cries.

She strained her ears. Was Neil awake as well now, about to rouse Bunny for a pre-dawn session? Impossible to tell from three whole rooms away. She *did* need a pee. She slid out of bed, groped along the passage to the bathroom, stopped outside their door. She had done the same the last two nights. It was crazy, paranoid, downright bad-mannered as well as highly dangerous. Supposing one of them came out and found her? She stood paralysed, listening to the silence – total silence – fighting a desire to burst in, haul

Bunny out of bed, demand she leave immediately, restore her husband to her. Her hand reached out to the door handle, paused two inches from it. Bunny's handle. Bunny's door. Bunny's home and husband. *She* was the one who should leave. She had never planned to stay here in the first place – or only a few days until Chris had settled in. Chris *had* done – remarkably quickly in the circumstances – so why was she still here, and not in a motel?

She turned on her heel, crept back along the passage and down the stairs, feeling her way with the help of the banisters. The house was in total darkness, seemed to resent her disturbing it, resent her presence there at all. Everything conspired to make her feel an alien – the way she couldn't find the light switches, or tripped on steps she didn't know were there. Even now, the dog was growling at her from its guard-post in the hall – Neil's dog treating his ex-wife as an intruder and a threat. Neil had never even liked dogs – and certainly not unmanly ones like dachshunds. She stopped where she was, fearing it would bark and wake the house.

'Good boy,' she whispered, letting it sniff her hand, fondling its ears until it quietened.

Was she simply torturing herself by staying in a house where she couldn't escape Neil's presence – his wife, his son, his pets? Even when he was absent at the office, his possessions seemed to taunt her. A pair of golf shoes lying in the kitchen or a tie flung casually across a chair could set off a flood of memories, emotions; mix rage with loss with pain with jealousy. Even in the spare room or the lumber room, she was still aware of him, as if he had left his smell on the whole house like a dog himself, cocking his leg, marking out his territory. In fact, it smelt of Bunny – her L'Air du Temps perfume, her rose verbena talc, the joss sticks she burnt in the hall 'just for a giggle'.

Morna could smell the joss sticks now – a faint tang of Eastern incense which didn't fit the all-American décor. She stopped a moment, fumbled for the light switch which had shifted its position again as if to confuse her deliberately. There was Neil's jacket hanging on a peg – a scarlet parka with purple bands across it – ridiculous for a man of forty-five. The Neil she had known and married had completely disappeared – the City Neil with his smart grey suit and camel coat, his black calf-leather shoes. Now he wore two-tone suede loafers beneath sky-blue slacks with a white rollneck on top. And that was office gear. For golf, he went still further, dared checks and stripes, jaunty little caps with pompoms on. She had never realized that one could feel such fury for a pompom – or a pair of acid yellow socks. Men wore brown or grey socks, navy blue, maroon, but never ever yellow. She couldn't even blame the socks on Bunny. Neil had boasted about choosing them himself.

She trailed into the sitting room, which Bunny called the Den, switched on the dimmest of the lamps so that she couldn't see the photographs. They were bad enough in Chris's room back home, but here they were in every room, charting the history of the second marriage – Neil and Bunny on their own, Neil and Bunny and the baby, Neil and Bunny and the toddler, Neil and Bunny and the toddler and the puppy. She turned her back on them, slumped down on the sofa. She had sat there last night, Dean on her lap, Neil beside her, the dog at her feet – part of the happy cosy family, keeping Neil up to date with his first home.

'Oh no, the Harveys moved away some time ago. We've got new neighbours that side, and opposite they're . . . Yes, the fruit trees are doing pretty well. The wasps got all the plums last year, but . . .'

You didn't sit and mumble bread-and-butter clichés to a man you had known almost twenty years, who had pounded and thrust into you, entrusted you with his semen some five thousand times, made a baby with you, seen you young, naked, weeping, sick, afraid. Bunny was catching up with her. They had each produced a child (one all), but Bunny could go on to have a second or a third, and as far as thrusting was concerned, if she and Neil did it twice a day, then . . .

She jumped up as if to drag the two apart by force, sagged down again, confused. The problem was that Bunny was too damned kind, too bubblingly good-natured. She could have attacked a classic bitch, hated a scheming Other Woman – had one clinching row and then marched out. But it was Bunny, in fact, who kept urging her to stay. Most second wives would have shown coolness or contempt, or at least have kept their distance. But Bunny smiled and glowed, arranged treats and trips, car rides, hospitality, and seemed blithely unaware of the strangeness of the situation, accepting it as normal for ex-husband and ex-wife to sit side by side on one small sofa, partner her and Dean at ping pong, or sleep three doors down from each other.

Morna sprang up again, retraced her steps to the stairs, feeling like a burglar creeping through the hushed and shadowy rooms. Other people's houses often felt strange at first, as if you had put on a dress which didn't fit, or were wearing your shoes on the wrong feet. But that normally wore off after a day or two, as you and the house shook down a bit, eased and trimmed to accommodate each other. Not here, though. She remained continually on edge, and the house, too, seemed to hold its breath, waiting tense and rigid for some row or outburst, some blazing confrontation. Bunny might be cheerful, but was that just a façade? Did all the trips and outings have some ulterior motive – bait in a trap about to close around her? Would the rosy glow suddenly cloud over, darken into a storm?

She stopped where she was, aware that she was trembling. Stupid to get so overwrought, allow the heavy-breathing darkness to prey upon her nerves. Yet it felt so claustrophobic. She could see no chink of sky nor shred of garden.

Night and nature were both shut firmly out behind the frilled and flounced entrenchments at every window. The doors were double-locked. The dog was awake again, not growling any longer but keeping her marked, watching her every move. There was no sign of the cat. It must be out on the tiles, searching for a mate. She longed for a mate herself, someone to snuggle up to, somewhere she belonged.

She groped on towards the kitchen, paused outside. Bunny had urged her to treat the house as her own, help herself to anything she wanted. She wanted a drink, in fact, something hot and soothing to calm her down, but it still seemed wrong just to barge in and make one. The kitchen was Bunny's sanctum – her food in the larder, her weight-and-calorie chart taped above the cake tins, Dean's drawings on the walls.

She slipped through the door, shut it noiselessly behind her, checked through the cupboard for Bunny's herbal teas. She picked up a box of blueberry cheesecake mix – luscious purple topping, rich and crunchy base. The picture on the packet bore the same relation to the actual cake as a film star to a stand-in. They had tried it out that evening for dessert, after do-it-yourself hamburgers and instant chowder. Neil had gorged two helpings, both with synthetic cream on top. It infuriated her that he should demolish all that junk food and still look just as slim and actually more healthy than when she had fussed about his diet, bought him low-fat cuts of meat or low-cholesterol margarine. Perhaps it was just his sun tan, or his all-American clothes.

She had found the herbal teas now, read the blurb on all the packets, took down the camomile – for 'jangled nerves and sleeplessness'. She switched on the kettle, sat at the table waiting for it to boil, a second Morna looking down at her. Dean had chosen her as his subject in his latest work of art; showed her overweight, lop-sided, with violent carrot-coloured hair and purple eyes. 'I LOVE MONA' was scribbled underneath. (Chris had added the 'R' in a different colour and out of line.) Morna sat staring at the wobbly scarlet letters. The love was reciprocated – a painful complicated love which had something of envy in it. This was the son she might have had herself. He had taken a fancy to her, followed her round the place, joined with Bunny in begging her not to leave. Nobody was neutral in the house, nothing simple or straightforward. Chris was in her own camp, yet was fast becoming Neil's new slave; Dean was Bunny's son, yet spent more and more time with his new English stepmother. He even looked like her – fair, plump, blue-eyed. For one traitorous second, when he was sitting on her lap and had turned those huge eyes up to hers, she had resented Chris's plainness, craved a pretty child, then buried the thought as unworthy and unfair. But to have *both* of them . . .

The kettle was almost boiling. She switched it off to prevent it shrilling out, started to fill her mug; swung round suddenly as she heard footsteps at the door.

'N . . . Neil!'

'Oh, I'm sorry. I heard a noise and thought it might be Dean.' He was already backing off, the door half-closed again.

'No, wait!' she called, darting after him and wrenching it open. 'Stay a moment. Have a cup of tea. Don't go. Please don't go.' She was pleading with him, begging, almost ashamed to hear the tremor in her voice. She had to keep him there, seize this one God-sent chance of talking to him on her own. He had always contrived never to be alone with her, never undefended, using Dean, Chris, Bunny as his bodyguard. There had also been the barrier of clothes. Now he was in pyjamas, which made him look vulnerable, yet also somehow dangerous. Every time she saw him, it was something of a shock to have him there in the flesh after so long a separation – more so now, when that flesh was actually

186

so close to her without the defence of vest, shirt, pants and trousers. His hair was ruffled, his feet bare. She glanced down at the feet – dark hairs on the toes, dark hair creeping up his legs, up, up to . . . Big Sam would be hanging loose, no longer caged in Y-fronts. She could almost glimpse him through the opening in the pyjama bottoms. If she reached out a hand, she could touch his tip. She edged away, appalled by her own feelings. She herself had only a loose robe on, one made of thin material. He could probably see the outline of her figure, the dark blur of her nipples. Had he forgotten how he used to kiss those nipples, suck them into his mouth?

'S . . . Sit down,' she mumbled, pulling out a chair. Neil was still standing rigid at the door.

'It's . . . er . . . late,' he said. 'Best talk in the morning.'

'It's morning now.'

Neil grimaced. 'Middle of the night! I meant eight o'clock.'

'B . . . But you always leave so early. You're never here at eight.'

'No, it's Saturday tomorrow. I'm playing golf, but not till ten or so. We can have a chat at breakfast if you like.'

A chat, yes – pointless, idle prattle about the garden or the waffles or whether they needed more chlorine in the pool, with Dean butting in every second minute and Chris jumping up and down and the dog barking at the postman. Playing happy families again.

'Just have a cup of tea,' she coaxed. 'The kettle's boiled, so it won't take any time.'

'I . . . I don't drink tea.'

Since when, she wondered? He had drunk three or four cups a day at Weybridge, taken his own Earl Grey to the office. 'Well, coffee, then, or herb tea. I'm having camomile.'

He suddenly strode across the room, reached up for a bottle of Bourbon concealed on a high shelf, poured himself a double. So he couldn't face her without some fortification. She had noticed already how much more he drank – cocktails before dinner, whisky after it. Was that just America, the badge of wealth, success, or was he trying to drown some problem? Admittedly his job was very stressful, but there were also tensions at home. Even in four days, she had seen the tiny signs – his only half-concealed annoyance when Bunny's friends breezed in, especially the more militant ones who downed his gin and then attacked him as a chauvinist; the pacing up and down when Bunny was still fussing with her face upstairs when they were already late for some appointment; the sudden coldness in his voice if she mentioned her masseur who was twenty-five and single. If only he would talk to her, break through the superficial gloss to reach the things that mattered. Yet there they were, standing like two strangers drawn up for a duel.

She felt too tired for duelling, subsided into a chair. She could do with a drink herself, in fact, to dull the shock of being alone with him, having him so close. She glanced at his square and stubby hands, contradicted by the long torso, the tiny pricks of stubble on the usual morning-smooth chin. She had spent months and months remembering him and somehow got it wrong. It wasn't just the clothes; wasn't even the accent, although that had jolted her the first time she had heard it, and still grated on her nerves – a hybrid accent, which mixed gin-and-Jag Weybridge (fake itself since his father came from Penge) with a new Californian drawl.

'Skol!' he said, taking his first gulp of Bourbon. That was a Bunnyism. Bunny had picked up 'Skol' from a Scandinavian movie, used it ever since. Neil was always ready to extend his vocabulary. When he'd lived in England, it was *her* expressions he had cribbed, or even Bea's. Now he borrowed Bunny's, which didn't suit him, only sounded bogus.

'Do sit down,' she urged, patting the seat beside her. 'My neck's aching with the strain of looking up at you.' She tried to force a laugh, dispel the tension.

He took a step towards the door, glass clutched in his hand, glanced up at the clock. 'No, really, Morna, I must go back upstairs. Bunny will be wondering where . . .'

'Oh, is she awake as well?'

There was a short uneasy silence. Bunny always boasted that she slept like the proverbial log, claimed she would probably slumber on if they dropped the Bomb on Los Angeles itself.

'She's . . . er . . . got a bit of a headache.'

'I'll make *her* a herbal tea, then. One of them's specially good for headaches. Rosemary, I think it is.'

'She doesn't want one.'

'Have you asked her?'

'Y . . . Yes. No.' He was getting flustered, tripped on one of Dean's toy cars, swore. 'Oh, all right, make her one if you insist. But hurry up. It's cold down here.'

Stifling. Neil kept the heating on all night, although the daytime temperature was still in the seventies. The kitchen was the warmest room of all.

Morna emptied out the hot water from the kettle, refilled it with cold. That would give her longer – three minutes, at least, until it boiled. One hundred and eighty seconds to cram in five whole years, not to mention the fourteen years before that – years which needed reassessing, analysing; things she had waited sixty months to say, rehearsed over and over again, lying on her own in Weybridge. She had received her decree absolute, filed it under Finished Business. But it wasn't finished, wasn't absolute. There were addenda, emendations, which no solicitor nor judge could ever put in writing, which only she could say, and say in person. She turned to face him, cleared her throat.

'It's . . . er . . . a nice kitchen,' she stuttered. 'Nice and large.'

'Yeah. We had it extended, actually – knocked out that wall there and built the dining recess.'

'Oh, yes? Are American builders good?'

'Depends. I found this marvellous chap Greg. He had the whole thing completed in a month.'

'Really?'

'Mm.' Neil was checking his reflection in the highly polished steel of the upper oven, surreptitiously smoothing back his hair. It was still shiny dark without a trace of grey. She wondered if he dyed it. Was he wondering the same of her? He seemed to be keeping his eyes away from her, studiously observing the floor, the wall, his own hands or feet or glass – anything but her body. Was he aware of it at all, scared he might remember old desires if he so much as glanced in her direction?

His uneasiness was catching. She hardly knew where to look herself or how to keep her hands still. And why was it so difficult to talk openly and frankly, find any words at all? She had to take this chance before he disappeared, bounced back again at breakfast with his blandly public face. Yet every subject seemed embarrassing or dangerous, might frighten him away.

'Well, wh . . . what do you think of your daughter?' she asked in desperation. She used the phrase deliberately – *your* daughter. Wasn't Chris the proof they had been friends once, lovers once, a proper family?

'I like her,' Neil said simply, sitting down at last, though at the far end of the table. 'You've done a great job, Morna.'

She almost jumped up and hugged him in sheer gratitude. It was the first and only time he had acknowledged that it was indeed a job to bring up a daughter – keep her well, sane, happy and at school.

'She . . . er . . . takes after you, Neil. Don't you think so?'

He didn't answer, gave a tiny shrug as if he were embarrassed, even suspicious. She had meant it as a compliment. Had he taken it as such, or as some veiled criticism? Everything they said was somehow double-edged, the old wounds still not healed, so that even a harmless phrase could chafe or sting. He was back to the Bourbon again, topping up his glass.

'Mind you,' he said, still clutching the bottle, hugging it against his chest as if it were a shield. 'I'm not too happy about this Bristol business. I'd have preferred Cambridge for her myself.'

'It's not a question of preferring, Neil. Cambridge turned her down.'

'You should have pursued it with them – demanded to know why. She seems bright enough to me.'

Morna was silent, knew what he was thinking. 'If I'd been there, whispered the right word in the right ear, maybe a very special lunch, a memorable wine . . .' That might work with certain sorts of admen, but not with Cambridge dons – or only if Neil were a don himself, did the thing more subtly, knew the esoteric passwords.

'Bristol's very sound,' she said, feeling a sudden irrational dislike of the place. There were more crucial things to talk about than universities. She craved to go back, not forwards – back to when Chris was just an infant. They had conceived their baby when Bunny was still a child herself, a giggly kid in bobby socks and ponytail, swooning over pop-stars, playing for her high-school basketball team. They had to resurrect those years, rebuild the bridge between them.

She could see the kettle steaming. In just a few seconds it would screech its interruption. Neil was still staring at the floor, fingers clasped too tightly round his glass. He could well be feeling the same churning mix of anger, pain, remorse. They both had masks on, had worn them since that first agonizing evening when he had stepped into the kitchen saying 'Hi!', as if she were one more chum of Bunny's, or some odd neighbour who had dropped in for a snack. They could strip the masks off now. They were too small and frail, in any case, to conceal the maelstrom of emotions raging underneath.

She took a deep breath, sat on her hands to stop them trembling. 'Listen, Neil, I think we ought to t . . . try and . . .'

The kettle's low rumble crescendoed to a piercing wail. Neil jumped up to switch it off, before the automatic cut-out did it for him.

'Ah, good,' he said. 'That's ready now. I'll take it up.'

'No!' she snapped, snatching back the mug. 'S . . . Sorry, Neil – it's just that I . . . I haven't sugared it yet.'

'Bunny doesn't take sugar.'

'Well, h . . . honey, then. She's got some acacia in the cupboard – or there's limeflower if she prefers. She was telling me last night that limeflower's really good for . . .' This was Bunny's *husband*, for heaven's sake. He knew all about her honeys, was one of them himself. Bunny was always sugaring him. Honey this, sweetie that.

'Or perhaps she'd like a slice of lemon?' Something sharp and bitter to curdle all that saccharine.

'No, just the tea.'

Morna still clung on to it, stirring it, dunking it, rooting about for a quite superfluous saucer. She needed time to rehearse her next few lines.

Neil, I want you to know I didn't really . . .

I admit it was partly my fault, but if you hadn't always insisted, I might have . . .

It wasn't fair on Chris, you know. She never quite . . .

Listen, I *love* you, Neil, I do.

You selfish, bloody, self-opinionated louse!

'Thanks, Morna. See you in the morning, then.' Neil had cajoled the mug from her, was halfway to the door. He paused for one brief moment. 'Don't get cold down here. You ought to go back to bed, you know.'

Yes, she whispered silently. *Your* bed. Take me with you, warm me up yourself. It wasn't Big Sam she wanted, but reassurance; not to be the reject and the loser. He had turned his back again. She could see the outline of his buttocks beneath the blue silk of the pyjamas, suddenly yearned to cup her hands around them as he had done so often with her own curves. She hadn't liked it at the time, sometimes pulled away.

She took a step towards him. I'm sorry, she mouthed dumbly to his unseeing back. I'm really sorry. Just stay a few more minutes and I'll . . .

'Goodnight!' he called, already through the door and out of sight. 'Sleep well.'

Sleep well! Morna dragged out her suitcase from under the bed, started to pack, trying to move as quietly as she could. It was still only half past five, pitch dark outside, no sound in the house except the faint ticking of her clock. No clock had ever moved more slowly. Since Neil had returned to Bunny's bed, each second had mocked her, spun itself out in obscene and taunting images – Neil slipping off the pyjamas, giving Bunny not her tea, but . . .

She couldn't lie there another anguished moment, trying to concentrate on some paperback romance when a real-life one was in full flower just next door. She would leave in the morning, once Neil had gone to golf. Chris had been asked to caddy; Dean invited out to lunch. That left her and Bunny, which – oddly – made it easier. She had already explained to Bunny about her old school friend who had moved to California just ten miles up the coast and who had invited her, not to stay (since her apartment was too small for guests), but to take a room in the local motel which she highly recommended. She did, in fact, have a Californian girlfriend, one Chris knew about, which made it easier, since she hated lying to her daughter. What Chris didn't know was that the friend had moved to Florida just two months previously. The motel was real enough. Morna had found it in an old and tatty guide book back in England, when she was planning her escape-route, chosen it partly for its modest rates and partly for its name – Ocean View. It was time she went to admire the view, made her reservation.

Bunny had been horrified by the thought of a motel, had even invited the girlfriend to come and·stay as well, said she'd love to meet her and if her apartment were so poky, then she would probably appreciate a bit of space for once. Morna paused a moment, conscience-stricken. She would have to fabricate another batch of lies, repay Bunny's hospitality with some cock-and-bull deception.

She removed the last of her tee shirts from the drawer, found David's two letters hidden underneath them. She picked up the first one, dated October 2nd. That letter was the reason she was here – or one of them. She had been saying 'no' to Chris for almost a month, struggling between guilt and duty, mother-love and self-love, horrified by what her daughter was asking, appalled at what might happen if she went. Then David wrote – only a page, two sides – but enough to change her day, change her mind. David was missing her, and that simply stupid fact made her rush up to her daughter's room with an impulsive hug, a sudden unconsidered 'yes'. For that one strutting preening morning, she had courage enough to brazen out any number of visits to the States, any tricky encounter with an ex. Why fret about Neil with another woman when *she* had another man?

She sat on the bed, read both the letters through again. They sounded conventional now and stilted, the words sitting four-square on the page, instead of exploding off it as they had before. Could she really have allowed these shy and formal phrases to influence her decision on such a crucial matter? No. It had been far more complex – a whole seething mix of guilt and obligation towards her daughter, a fear of depriving Chris of her father even longer than the five vital teenage years she had already been without him; a desire to compensate her, do something for her, something real and tangible, even make some sacrifice. Perhaps it was David who had suggested that, unconsciously. He had used the word 'sacrifice' in his letter, though in a completely different context.

She had to admit there were also baser motives – weaker ones, but still ignoble – a sneaking curiosity to view the new ménage, despite the risks and dangers, lay eyes on Bunny, find some fault in her, plus a wild irrational impulse to see Neil again as well. She had seen him now – and all she wanted was to run away. It was too exhausting to keep battling with contradictory emotions – fury over footling things like the way he iced good wine or ate his food American-style with just a fork; anguish when he ruffled Dean's hair or played Bears with him which he had never done with Chris; murderous envy if he put an arm round Bunny. If he wouldn't talk, refused to make some overture, then better that she cut the ties completely, made the decree absolute at last.

She packed the last few items, retrieved David's silver coin from the drawer beside her bed, held it in her palm. Had it really brought her luck? She tried to think back to the evening he had given it to her, the next amazing afternoon. David had stayed all Saturday, given the day an electric blaze and flare. Or had she just been high, imagining things? The silver on her memories had somehow dulled and tarnished like the phrasing in his letters. She was confused now and uncertain, could hardly disentangle reality from fantasy. She held the coin against her cheek, felt it cool and hard; one side slightly roughened, the other worn smooth. David was as real as that, as solid. So why did he seem so strangely insubstantial, like the wraith of sea mist which shrouded his own island? The courage he had given her had vanished like mist as well, evaporated in Bunny's glow and sparkle, the flash of Neil's fake smile. She had to leave, she had to, whatever Bunny said – however much she dreaded being on her own. She would make her stand at breakfast, insist she left straight afterwards.

She wrapped the coin in a chiffon scarf, slipped it in the suitcase, added the two letters, closed the lid. In just five hours or so, she must be unpacking that case in the Ocean View Motel.

11

'You can't stay there, for Chrissake!' Bunny exclaimed, winding down her window and staring out at the dingy concrete pile with its bare stone steps and rusting railings.

'Y . . . Yes, I can. It's fine.' Morna wondered where the ocean was. The only view was of a weed-infested car park, a garage strung with a thousand coloured plastic flags as if to distract attention from the ugly petrol pumps and ramshackle buildings straggling out beneath them.

Bunny had got out of the car, was standing in the drizzle on the bottom broken step. 'It looks like some kind of prison to me, or something in – what's his name? – Charles Dickens. We've got fabulous motels. I could find you one with a pool and a sauna and free movies in your room – or better still, come back with me. Bring your buddy, too. I'd really like to meet her, though it beats me how she could recommend *this* dump. Hey, why don't we go visit her right now and I'll invite her myself?'

Morna still found the lies abhorrent, was getting flustered and confused, had to be almost rude to make Bunny accept that she was staying, shake her off, refuse to allow her to inspect the rooms or complain to the management. She watched with a mixture of relief and remorse as the scarlet Pontiac finally shot away; picked up her case, lugged it up the steps, head bowed against the rain. The blazing sun of their first few days had vanished, like a false promise

197

wrapped in flimsy golden paper, now torn off and trampled in a puddle.

The room at least was better than she had feared – shabby, yes; basic, yes, but surprisingly large – a double room or even family-sized, judging by the width of the bed. Walls and floor were both a sickly brown, carpet thin and scratchy, walls milk-chocolate-coloured with lighter mottled patches as if the chocolate were sprouting mould. Three cheap prints of the sunny Riviera were contradicted by the three windows streaming with rain. The lampshade was pink-tasselled, the bedspread purple-fringed. The wardrobe smelt musty and contained a forgotten pair of denim dungarees and a few wire hangers, most twisted out of shape. There was still no view – just a tangle of dripping roofs and garish signs.

Morna didn't unpack her case. She could still move – find somewhere more luxurious, more cheerful, except that would mean trudging around in the rain in a completely unknown area. Anyway, she had to keep her costs down and, whatever else, the Ocean View was cheap. Her translation of *Misère et Mort dans le Midi* was paying for the trip, at least this part of it. She had to retain some little independence. Admittedly, Neil had paid the fares, but since he had wangled them for free, they hardly counted. Chris was a different matter. She was still his daughter – not ex or superseded – so no reason why he shouldn't pay for *her*.

Best stay where she was, give the motel a chance. She hadn't even explored it yet – though that would hardly take her long. The place had no bar, no restaurant, no public rooms at all – not even any foyer or reception, apart from a makeshift desk stuck at one end of the ground-floor corridor, with a grumpy man behind it. Just fifty or sixty bedrooms, apparently deserted. She opened the door, stuck her head out, looked up and down the passage. No stir of life, no human face, no chirp of radio or drone of vacuum cleaner.

Perhaps the staff had gone off-duty, and the other guests were sleeping in. No – guests was the wrong word. Inmates seemed a better one, suggesting prison, deportation.

Morna shut her door again, prowled around her own room, comparing the view from the three different windows – rain and roofs, rain and garage, rain and car park. The problem was she had been spoilt by Neil. *He* had chosen all the hotels before, insisted on Michelin stars, lavish accolades. She had paid him back between the sheets (or on top of them in Mediterranean climes). Neil's appetite increased on holiday. She had often arrived at some foreign resort, exhausted by the journey, longing to sleep, and sent mental vibes to Neil that he too was flagging, so why not postpone it till the morning or even the morning after that or . . . It had never worked. Neil was never tired (enough) and hadn't she been taught at school 'not my will but thine'? In fact, the more exclusive the hotel, the more lavish the food and service, the more she felt she owed him. A two-roomed suite with a sea view and a balcony and a magnum of Moët chilling in the ice bucket merited at least a new position; and how could she guzzle *Gâteau de Homard Soufflé*, perfected by a top French chef, and then cavil at an after-dinner session?

Once she had lain recovering on her hotel bed in Malaga and suddenly imagined Sister Clare, the school infirmarian, doing a check on all the girls' pudenda, as she had inspected their hair for dandruff or their mouths for coated tongues. She could see the nun shuffling along the row of beds, stopping at Morna Conyers', peering in with torch and rubber glove, springing back in horror. Bruised, battered, over-used, chewed, abraded, sore and swollen. And all after a few short years with Neil. Perhaps she needed some of that cosmetic surgery which so intrigued her daughter – not a nose job or a breast implant, but a genital tuck and remake, to remove Neil's traces, his defilement. But what use would new pudenda be? Who would ever see them, enjoy the benefit? Below the waist she lived like a nun herself now.

Why not make the most of it? There was no debt to pay off here, no instant demands to lie on her back (or front or side or kneel or . . .). She could do what she liked, go to bed to sleep, even sleep with all her clothes on if she wanted. It was lunchtime though, not bedtime. She ought to go out and find a restaurant, get to know the district. She flopped back on the counterpane, closed her eyes. She had hardly slept at all since she had arrived in California. She would just relax a moment, have a brief nap to restore her energies before setting out again.

It was dark when she awoke. She could hear a siren ripping through the silence, the bray of a police car scorching past. She fumbled for the switch on the low-wattage bedside lamp, squinted at her watch. Three o'clock. So why the dark? She jolted up in bed. It must be three *a.m.*, for heaven's sake, not afternoon. She had slept for thirteen hours, right on into Sunday, slept fully dressed, even with her jacket on. She could hear the rain still lashing at the windows. A *wet* Sunday, on her own. She shrugged off the jacket, removed her watch and bracelet, slipped between the sheets, pulled the blanket over her head. Best to shorten the day, sleep right through it, on into Monday, Tuesday, Wednesday; remain unconscious and unthinking throughout the remainder of her stay, until her merciful plane home on January 30th.

When she woke again, she had no idea what time it was, what month, had lost track of where she was and why. She groped for her watch, couldn't find it, stared in confusion at the unfamiliar room. A mean grey light was seeping through the windows, another siren shrieking out its warning. She rubbed her eyes, tried to shake off the heavy lumpen greyness which seemed to have moved inside her head from the dripping streets outside, clogged her brain. Her stomach kicked with hunger; her clothes were crumpled and uncomfortable, skirt rucked round one leg, tights sweaty, even smelly. She reached out for the bedside phone.

'Yeah?' said the man in reception, after a delay of several minutes.

'I . . . er . . . wondered what time it was?'

'Ten after seven, ma'am.'

Morning or evening? She tried to make her brain work. Must be morning with that greyish light. It was dark by five in January. If it *was* still January.

She switched the receiver to the other hand. 'I mean the . . . er . . . date.'

'Beg pardon, ma'am?'

'Could you tell me what day it is. I imagine it's still Sunday isn't it, or . . .?'

'Yeah, Sunday – all day. Until tomorrow. That'll be Monday – if we're lucky.'

Morna heaved herself out of bed, splashed her face with water, cleaned her teeth. Every tiny action seemed to tire her out. She was still sunk in lethargy, drugged from too much sleep, yet craving more. She turned on the television, returned to bed to watch the morning show. At least it would be company, another human voice. She was missing Chris already, missing Dean. This was the time he usually padded into her room, clambered into bed with her, some truck or car or fire engine digging into her side, asked her about England and why she and Chrissie didn't live here all the time instead, so that he could see her every day, and would they still be here for his birthday in July, and why was her hair called red when it wasn't red like fire engines . . .

Morna smiled, slumped back against the pillows. The commercial break had just begun. A woman in a cowboy hat and boots was feeding four Afghan hounds and a mongrel.

'Three out of four dogs prefer Mighty Beef Dog Dinner.'
She wondered how they worked out their statistics. She had
read in the *Los Angeles Times* that even leading scientists (let
alone mere market researchers for pet-food companies) were
faking their results, some claiming degrees and doctorates
they had never even sat for. She switched to another channel.
Cops and robbers. There were enough of those outside – for
real – judging by the sirens. Twenty-three thousand murders
every year and almost a thousand of those in Los Angeles
alone. Those were the statistics Bunny *hadn't* given, nor the
fact that a horrifying proportion were domestic murders
within the family. Yet was it really so impossible to imagine
pulling out a gun and shooting Neil for no other reason than
that he regarded Bunny's little expeditions to the gym or
beauty-parlour with the same amused but weary tolerance
with which he had once dismissed her evening classes in
philosophy and politics, or her translation work? Or putting
a bullet through his yellow socks? She watched the movie
with a new interest. Criminals were always other people
until . . .

Three murders later, she was sickened. She turned the
sound down, lay back on the bed, stretching out diagonally.
She had never realized how lonely and demoralizing a double
room could be when you were just a single – the silence, the
empty space and unused drawers, the sense of time dragging,
hanging heavy. She was hypocrite enough to miss Neil now
– want to shoot him, yes, but want him all the same. She
had resented his demands, criticized his powers of conversation, but was it really any better to lie here on her own
king-size bed without the king?

She tried to swap King Neil for David, somehow found
it difficult to imagine David in America at all, especially in
the fat and whacky West. However much she thought of
him, re-read his letters, touched his coin, he remained

strangely faint and blurred, like a figure on a coin himself, flat and one-dimensional.

There was a burst of muffled gunfire from the screen. She struggled up to watch it, winced as the tomato-ketchuped corpse was prodded by a sneering sheriff's boot. She'd had enough of violence. Her head was throbbing, stomach growling. She needed food, fresh air. She switched the set off, ran a bath, rummaged in her suitcase for a change of clothes. She dressed slowly, like an invalid, the silence more oppressive now that the rain had stopped. She walked along the passage past the rows and rows of doors. Still no sign of life, no fellow prisoner emerging from his cell. The elevator was broken, so she used the stained stone staircase, crossed the road to the first café she saw, peered through the steamed-up glass. Two negroes in jeans and dirty singlets were sprawling at the bar top; the waitress filing her nails. Morna walked on. Almost every other building in the street sold food of some variety – hamburgers and hot dogs, Dunkin Donuts, Mexican burritos, Chinese takeaways, Kentucky Fried, pizza parlours, salad bars. 'Breakfast Served All Day', she read. 'Eddie's Oriental Feast', 'Try Our Buns – They're Bigger'.

Despite the early hour, several of the restaurants were already getting crowded, couples with their children, friends meeting friends. Morna walked on, searching for somewhere empty or secluded. It was as if she were infectious and had been shut up on her own, ordered to shun all normal human intercourse. She had to walk in zigzags to dodge the puddles, avoid the broken paving stones. The whole area was shabby and run-down, in sharpest possible contrast to the manicured lawns (and matching residents) of Neil and Bunny's suburb. Although it was nearer to the sea, there was still no sign of it – nor sound. Honking trucks instead of crashing surf.

She stopped at a small self-service café which looked bleaker than the rest, almost institutional with its plain linoleum floor and functional wooden chairs. Three elderly women were sitting on their own at separate tables, one in bedroom slippers, one in a rain-soaked panama, muttering to herself as she spooned in her creamed wheat. A man with a woolly hat pulled down towards his wispy silver beard was gnawing a turkey drumstick. Was this a place for old folks only, Morna wondered, or just so inexpensive it attracted the down and out? Today she felt in sympathy with vagrants and outsiders. She slipped inside, watched the four pairs of eyes turn her way, follow her as she walked up to the counter. Lunch dishes were laid out as well as eggs and bacon, pizzas and fruit pies alongside cereals and muffins. It seemed strangely early to be chewing turkey drumsticks. She could feel the four pairs of eyes still boring into her back. She was the cabaret – an over-dressed but timid stranger who looked as if she had strayed from her package tour or Holiday Inn to come and join the outcasts – yet still with nothing on her tray. She grabbed two rolls and a packet of Alphabetti Ricicles, sugar-coated rice puffs in the shape of little letters. They were Dean's favourite cereal, though more for playing with than eating. He always spelt out his name with them, and then her own, added an X as a kiss. She was tempted to spell some words herself – David (with an X), England, home, escape. She looked up, saw the eight rheumy eyes still watching her every move, tried to distract herself by reading the amounts of iron and thiamin contained in an average serving of rice puffs.

It was strange to see the old and poor in California. Bunny's charmed circle contained only the wealthy young, and those older people she had seen so far in streets and shops had all looked spruce and glossy as if they had been recycled, reconditioned, sprayed with a fresh coat of paint. These were the first old folk she had come across who had let nature take its course, allowed themselves to rust and warp. The gnarled old woman in her unseasonal straw hat was still mumbling to herself, wagging a finger at some imaginary companion. Her own mother would be horrified. She believed in constant vigilance to prevent mind or body cracking.

She had phoned Bea twice since she arrived, tried to compress California into a brief three-minute call, spent two minutes of it discussing Joy's arthritis. At least her mother seemed resigned about the trip now. She had opposed it violently at first, preferred to keep Neil safely dead and buried, feared that both granddaughter and daughter might be hurt by his sudden resurrection – correct in her own case, not in Chris's, though. Neil and Chris were pals. He was employing her not only as caddy at his golf-club, but also as human car-wash and nanny to Dean. She was thriving in all rôles.

Morna crunched up a letter C, then a B, E, A, for her mother. Bea would be at early evening Mass now, swallowing the host instead of iron-rich Ricicles. Morna put her spoon down, started on the rolls. Sundays still felt aimless without the Mass, just lazy straggling days which had once been vowed to God and were now sacred to the lawn mower or the Ford Capri or the *Sunday Times*. Here, in the States, she was deprived of those as well, had nothing but an empty stretch of time to fill. She almost envied the church-goers – the Evangelicals born again each Sunday, the Pentecostals hosannaing the day with tambourine and Gift of Tongues. Religion was a craze in California. Even Bunny had her own brand – belonged to a group who found God within – a highly elastic God who stretched to include money, food, possessions, sex.

Sex. Morna pushed her plate away. Wasn't that the secret of Bunny's glow, America's new God? The bookshops were full of prayer books – *How to Achieve Ecstasy*, *Prude to Lewd in Six Short Weeks*, *The Book of Total Love*. Therapeutic sex sessions were as common here as coffee mornings, vibrators prescribed for headaches instead of aspirin. If she were E-stream in England, then she was gravely sick in California. She drained her coffee, walked towards the door, aware of disturbing the silence, aware still of the stares. The hoot and fret of the traffic outside was almost a relief. She had better find the ocean. When Bunny next phoned, she would expect to hear accounts of long walks on the beach, drives around the coast . . .

She consulted her map, turned left into a quieter street, left again. Strange how garish billboards and cheap and ugly shopfronts could suddenly give place to elegant homes and gardens with fancy pilasters, scalloped palms; then back again to car parks, petrol stations. It made her feel disorientated, as if she were a character on television, with a director shouting 'Cut!' every few lines.

She almost shouted 'Cut!' herself when she stood at last staring at the Pacific. She had imagined it magnificently rolling, magically blue. Instead it spread before her in a flat expanse of grey, the beach a dirty brown, speckled with yellow metal litter-bins and crisscrossed with tyre marks. The sea itself looked passive and inert, as if it had fought and lost a battle and was now slumped nursing its wounds, no vigour in its slow and sullen waves.

She walked down to the beach. A cloud of sea birds flapped heavily away, their cries sounding desolate, forlorn. A girl was sitting on the sand, eyes closed, palms outstretched, communing with God and Nature. Morna envied her serenity, her faith, yearned suddenly to kneel down where she was, feel that strength she had drawn on as a child, that certainty of being heard, watched over. Yet there was no sense of God's presence here at all. God didn't live in California.

Two joggers overtook her, pounding across the sand – high priests of another indigenous religion, their vestments track suits and training shoes, their temples gym and stadium. She had already seen their acolytes exercising on the strip of green which fringed the boulevard, women older than her mother encased in tights and leotards, doing side-bends or leg-swings in the open. At school, they had worked through the spiritual exercises of St Ignatius of Loyola. Was it so different, really – the same passion, dedication, the same self-absorption, for something that turned out to be a chimera in the end? The latest statistics comparing a group of jogger-gymnasts with a sedentary control group revealed no difference at all in mortality statistics, and almost none in general health.

Morna began to run herself. The sky had clouded over again, and the first few drops of rain were spattering on her face. Suddenly it was pouring, the rain cascading down so fast she could barely see her way as she stumbled across the beach, tripping on empty cola cans tangled up with seaweed. Sunny California.

She panted back to the boulevard where people were clustered under awnings, sheltering in doorways. It was more flood than rain, water streaming down the sidewalks, overflowing the gutters. She had neither mac nor umbrella. Her shoes were squelching, her hair dripping in lank tails on her shoulders. It was at least a mile back to her motel. A bus pulled up, discharged three passengers. Almost without thinking, she stepped on to the platform.

'Do you pass Ocean View Motel?' she asked the swarthy driver.

'No, Ma'am. We're going in the opposite direction. Downtown LA.' She could hardly understand his foreign accent, especially as he was chewing gum, spoke only out of one side of his mouth. 'You'd better get off at the next stop.'

She stayed on. She hadn't seen Downtown yet. A morning's sightseeing would be better than another cops-and-robbers in her gloomy motel room. Anyway, how could she get off when rain was lashing on to the freeway, drenching anything and everything in its way? It was as if God had read her thoughts on His absence and was proving He was there, sending flood and fury to make His point. Why did she always think in terms of God when He hurt as much as Neil did? To Chris, he was someone remote and out of date, some kindly but irrelevant old codger who had made a botch-up of creation and then retired.

Traffic and buildings thickened. So did the rain. She could hardly see at all now. She asked the man beside her how far it was to Downtown and perhaps he could advise her . . . He muttered something *sotto voce*, appeared not to understand. Another twenty minutes passed. The streets were getting wider, the outlines of the skyscrapers outside the blurred and streaming windows taller and closer-packed. She lurched towards the automatic doors. She had better get off soon, before she was carried on to Covina or San Bernardino, or still further east to Oklahoma or New York.

The driver shouted after her as she clambered down, his heavy foreign accent distorted further by the engine noise. LA was full of foreigners. Over half the population were minority groups – not only Mexican, but Chinese, Arabs, Koreans, Guatemalans. She was a foreigner herself, felt both lost and dwarfed as the bus revved away and she stood in the lacerating rain, gazing round at discount houses, liquor stores, sleazy cinemas. This couldn't be the centre. A woman in a long grey coat and gym shoes, with a pair of pink silk bloomers tied around the head against the rain, was wheeling an empty pram. A younger woman, soaked and shivering, slumped against a shop-front shouting at her child. No good asking them. One looked cracked, the other yelling in a language she had never heard before.

She decided to brave the rain, dodging from shop to shop until she found one selling umbrellas. Many of the stores were open, despite it being Sunday. She bought a large black brolly and a fold-up mac which unbuttoned from a handkerchief-sized package to a full five foot of creased black plastic, complete with hood. She tried it on, grinned at herself in the mirror. She looked a cross between a gangster and a nun. She also got directions, though she was soon lost again, confused by both the traffic and the blinding rain. There was no one else to ask. Not only was it Sunday, but the weather had driven everyone inside. Some of the branches had broken off the trees and were lying on the pavement in a wreckage of leaves and twigs. She picked up a leaf, a strange one with saw-tooth edge and blotchy markings. Even the trees were unknown species here. She longed suddenly for London's familiar plane trees or Bea's close-clipped beech hedge, as tidy as her life.

She dawdled on, stopped outside a candy shop. Although it was more than a month away from St Valentine's Day, the window was ablaze with hearts. It wasn't just Bunny – this whole city dealt in hearts. Erasers, keyrings, ice lollies – all came heart-shaped, like these mammoth chocolate boxes arranged on heart-shaped scarlet cushions. 'Say "I love you" in candy!' shrieked the poster. 'I love you' was printed on mugs, tee shirts, cards, in the shop next door. The only thing you couldn't buy was the love itself.

She walked into the card shop – valentines for teachers, daughters, neighbours, parents, friends. They didn't count. A valentine meant true love from a sweetheart. She wished she could buy one, send it to David – a flimsy paper heart riding out his riptides, defying wind and wave until it was swept up on his island on the morning of St Valentine's.

Oddly enough, he had mentioned the feast – one of the myriad subjects they had tossed between them on that very special Saturday. Any other man would have landed up in her bed, at least by the second evening, whereas she and David had watched the twilight fall walking in the cool of Ashdown Forest, discussing the third-century Bishop of Rome whose feast day was on the fourteenth of February, but who was not, David claimed, anything to do with love or cards or sweethearts. Those derived from a pagan feast, he had told her, a Roman day of expiation when priests lashed people with strips of goat- or dogskin called purifiers, to cleanse them of their sins. She smiled to herself, remembering his words. Only David could metamorphose hearts and flowers to sin and scourge. Perhaps she should buy him a hair shirt printed with a heart and 'I love you' underneath.

She *had* loved him on that Saturday as they strolled together, still shy and over-formal, between the chaperone trees, watching the shadows hem them in. And then he had left. She had driven him herself, all the way to London. He hadn't asked her in. It was late by then and perhaps he feared to disturb his cousin, or had to get up early to catch his train back home. The next morning, when she woke alone in Weybridge, she thought of that train bearing him away from her; and three days later, the colleague's car clinching their separation, their divorce. Once David reached his island, there were five hundred miles between them – over five thousand now.

She left the shop without her card, seeing not concrete buildings but St Abban's lowering cliffs, hearing the boom of waves on rocks instead of the plash of rain on pavements. She buttoned up her hood again, made herself walk on. The shop next door was boarded up and derelict, stuck with posters. 'Sensory Deprivation', read one, 'For Creative Calm, Therapeutic Relaxation'. She moved closer. That would appeal to David and his saint – joy in deprivation. She read the small print underneath. The poster was advertising a Flotation Tank Studio, whatever that might mean, offering a special deal – two hours for the price of one. Two hours of what? She read on. It appeared you floated in a tank of tepid water in the dark and silence, totally alone, and by shutting off all outside stimuli, achieved a Higher State. David, definitely. The address of the place was given, but she had no idea where it was. North, south, east, west, meant nothing any more. She trailed away. It would probably be closed on Sunday, or too expensive anyway, or full of pseuds and freaks. LA was high on crazy therapies. The local paper had offered Integrated Ortho-Bionomy, Aura-Harmonization, Psychophysical Integration and Mentastics, and even an Atheist Dating Service. Yet, with so much help, people still seemed lost. Her old Catholic God had answered several of those needs at once – made His children loved, accepted, purposeful, given them hope, unwavering beliefs, a moral code, a reason for existing, made them part of a family which, if not happy, was at least secure. Religion was the Valium of the people, damping down their agonies, hushing the *non sequiturs*.

Morna yanked back her umbrella from the snatches of the wind. The rain was still as fierce. She would have to shelter somewhere. She crossed the road, turned a corner and suddenly, there was the name of the street she had seen on the poster, and two blocks along, a second larger notice above an open door: 'Our tanks can bring you peace, perception, mind-power. Please walk in.'

The room was dimly lit. Strange watery music seemed to writhe and ripple through it, never reaching any cadence but flowing on eternally, harmonized by the drumming of the rain. A slowly rotating mobile of headless aluminium birds was suspended from the ceiling, casting nervous shadows on the walls.

Morna dithered at the door. A man was sitting at the desk but his eyes were closed, palms spread upwards on the blotter. Was he meditating? Stoned? A fat red candle was guttering in a saucer, a stick of incense burning in a vase, emitting a sickly cloying scent.

Morna cleared her throat. The man remained motionless

apart from his eyelids, which slowly opened, revealing weak blue eyes which seemed to look past her, through her.

'I . . . er . . . wondered if . . .' she started.

'Sit down.' He was wearing an embroidered cheesecloth robe above grubby denims, open sandals with rough hemp soles. 'I'm Krishna.'

'H . . . How d'you do.' Morna stepped a little nearer. Krishna must be his equivalent of Anne. He could hardly be Indian with those pale eyes and freckled arms, that Middle-Western accent.

'Have you floated before?' he asked.

'Well, no. I didn't actually want . . .'

'You're in luck. First-timers get a real good deal. Your first hour absolutely free and your second . . .'

'I was really only inquiring for a friend . . .' Her voice petered out. She couldn't tell him the friend was in another country, living on a primitive island, almost completely out of touch, that she might never set eyes on him again.

'Great! You want our twin-tank deal, then. Bring your buddy and you can share a room. We do a special offer for . . .'

'Well, no. He's . . . er . . .' Morna backed away. She had come in really to shelter from the rain, just to look around. She had expected crowds of people – staff and customers – not one hard-sell pseudo-Indian. She was at his mercy now. It was miles back to the exit. She had walked down winding steps into a basement, wandered a labyrinth of dark and narrow corridors, following the signs, until the crack of light from this room had beckoned her in.

'Look, if you could just give me a brochure or a price list or . . .'

'Relax. You don't need a brochure. I'll explain the whole thing myself. We like to give you what we call an initiation before you enter the tank. Just sit down.' He gestured to the small cane chair drawn up in front of the desk. 'Sit,' he said again, as if he were commanding a recalcitrant dog.

Morna sat, seemed to have no more will-power to make excuses or a getaway. The music and the incense were spiralling around her, somehow sapping her strength. Krishna had changed his voice, made it both slower and softer so that he was talking in a near-hypnotic drone. She felt lulled by it, yet was really hardly listening, just sinking back and down, hearing certain words weave and tangle with the music – 'brain-wave cycles, creative hemisphere, mind expansion, psychic reverie.'

'It's like returning to your mother's womb,' he murmured. 'A safe space, peaceful, sheltered.'

Morna opened her eyes, hardly realized she had closed them in the first place. A return to the womb was definitely attractive – a Catholic womb like Bea's, not spotless like the Blessed Virgin's, but at least serene, secure. Why not go along with it, forget her fears for once?

'All right,' she said. 'I'll give it a try.'

Krishna seemed galvanized, sprang up from the desk to take her money – more than she had expected, considering all the special deals. His voice had returned to deeper normal.

'I'll only charge you the basic now. You can pay the rest at the end, depending how long you stay in. Right – just sign this form disclaiming all . . . That's the way. Now how about some little extras – self-motivation tapes, for instance?'

'I . . . I beg your pardon?'

'Listen While You Float. We've got over two hundred different titles here – any problem or fantasy that's bugging you, we can take care of on cassette. And there's a dollar off every one you choose. Stop Nail-Biting, Start Living, The Joy of Sobriety, How to Attract Money to Yourself . . .'

'Er . . . no thanks.'

'Or there's music if you prefer. Angel Voices – that's a

213

real gentle one. The Upper Astral Suite is more way-out, and the Pathless Path creates a sound environment which takes you right out of your body into . . .'

'No, really. I don't think . . .'

'We're offering Celestial Odyssey tee shirts at almost one third off. Red, blue, yellow, green or brown. Or there's black with a silver logo. That's ninety-nine cents extra.'

'M . . . Maybe when I get out. I'd like to try the tank first.'

'Okay, come this way. I'll take you to the shower-room. We like you to wash off all body oils and make-up before you float. Follow me, please.'

Morna followed, almost changed her mind when she saw the state of the shower-room – puddles of water on the floor, sodden towels discarded in the corner, basin stained and cracked. The lights were still dim – just as well, perhaps, or she might also have spotted a tidemark round the bath, other people's matted hairs clogging up the plughole. It was the first American bathroom she had seen which was not immaculate.

Krishna passed her two unironed yellow towels and a grubby plastic shower cap. 'Call me when you're through and I'll take you to the tank.'

Morna nodded, removed her clothes, still in a semi-stupor. She ran the shower cold across her shoulders. Perhaps that would wake her up, bring her to her senses. It wasn't too late to change her mind. She could simply put her clothes back on and march out of the place. Even if she lost her money, it would be better than enduring some damn fool or dangerous experience. She grabbed the towels, opened the door, poked her head out. 'Krishna,' she called.

He was there so quickly, suspected he had been watching her through a secret spyhole. Perhaps he turned himself on by luring women into showers and then gawping at their naked bodies.

'I'm sorry, but I've decided not to . . .'

'Through with your shower? Great! I've put you in tank number three. That's a lucky one. The last guy who went in there stayed in seven hours and saw the face of God, and the girl before that . . .'

Morna was jogging after him, barefoot and only half covered by the skimpy towels, trying to interrupt him, panting to keep up. 'Look, I didn't realize the time. I've got to . . .'

'Right. This is it.' Krishna opened the door of a small low-ceilinged room, lit only by a glimmering table lamp shrouded by a towel; the one small window totally blacked out. There was nothing in the room save the tank itself, a black rectangular box which brought to mind both a dog kennel and a front-loading washing machine, somehow incongruously fused.

The room smelt strange – not incense any more – a less pleasant smell of must and damp, stale bodies. She doubted if it had been cleaned in the last month, or even year. It was too dark to see the cobwebs, but she suspected they were there, could feel crumbs beneath her feet on the threadbare matting.

Krishna had lifted the hinged lid on the tank, revealing an oblong hole and darkness. She had been mistaken. It was nothing as wholesome and hygienic as a washing machine, or as harmless as a dog kennel. It was a coffin – her coffin – and any second she would be inside it with the lid closed, buried alive. She darted away, fumbled for the door handle.

Krishna scooped her back. 'Everybody's nervous at first. It's natural. All it means is you're fighting your own hang-ups. You should really have had a tape – one of our Fight Stress range, or a Pre-Float Relaxation Session. There's one dollar eighty-five off those. Okay, okay, we'll skip the tape, but just try and relax – like let go of the tension, right?' He looked none too relaxed himself, fingers tapping impatiently on the lid. 'Come on now. Just step in there and lie back, like I said. Get out of your fear, put your mind elsewhere.'

Morna crawled into the opening, felt blackness clutch at her hair, slimy tepid water close around her ankles. She tried to struggle up again, grab Krishna's hand. 'No, wait! Don't go. It's dark. I . . .'

'Just float. There's only ten inches of water, anyway, and it's so buoyant you couldn't drown if you wanted to. Remember what I told you – there's eight hundred pounds of Epsom Salts dissolved in there. That's better. Let your head go. You'll get a stiff neck if you hold it up like that. Great! I'll come back in an hour and see if you're doing all right. I don't want to disturb you if you're into your own space. I'll just tap on the door, okay? If you want to come out, say so. If not, I'll check back later.'

'No.' Her voice sounded muffled, strange. 'I don't want even *one* hour. You don't understand. I . . .'

He couldn't hear her, had already closed the lid, plunging her into now total darkness. The room was soundproof, he had told her, so she couldn't even hear his footsteps retreating down the passage. Her neck was stiff already, but she was scared to let it go. The water was over her ears, soaking her hair, might run into her eyes. She *was* floating, miraculously, but it didn't feel secure. She might tip and over-balance, submerge her face. She dared to swallow – the sound deafening in her throat, except she had lost her throat, lost all her boundaries. There was no hot nor cold, no night nor day – no winter, summer, outside, inside, body, mind. She was afraid of her own fear, could feel it rising like the water. It could flood her, overwhelm her. Fear of the blackness, three-dimensional blackness pressing down like a blindfold. Fear of the confinement – shut up in a box, only eight foot by four, nailed down in a coffin with no light nor sound nor . . .

No – there *was* a sound – the roar of her own heartbeat

drumming in her ears. It got louder, louder, until she was nothing but one gigantic heartbeat, rumbling through the tiny space like thunder with no lightning flash to rip apart the darkness.

She couldn't breathe. What about an air supply? Krishna hadn't mentioned that. Her grandfather had been imprisoned in the Great War. He, too, had died before she was born, but she had heard his story – shut up in solitary confinement for endless days and nights, cornered with his own excrement. She could feel his panic added on to hers. Her cell was smaller than his, further underground. She could die of panic. No one would hear her if she screamed. She would simply continue floating, a white corpse in the blackness. Krishna might never return and she would slowly rot and crumble, decay into black nothingness herself.

Almost without thinking, she crossed her arms on her chest, over-balancing a little, splashing water in her eyes. It was difficult to lie like that, made her neck ache more, but it was the pose the nuns had recommended when you went to sleep. If you died in the night, you were more likely to bypass hell if your arms formed the Sign of the Cross. Neil had hooted when he heard. 'It merely stopped you frigging, that's all.' Neil didn't understand. They had been far more interested in touching the hem of Christ's garment than in touching themselves.

She wasn't ready to die, in any case. There were things she had meant to say to Chris, hadn't found the words for yet, things she wanted Bea to understand. She groped out her hand, felt it brush the coffin lid above her, the enclosing walls each side. She could almost see the clogged earth heaped on top, levelled by the grave-diggers, hear the echoing silence as they stomped away. She closed her eyes, returning her arms to her chest, lurching in the water, feeling its strange clammy density buoy her up again. Better to accept her death. No more panic then, no more dull ache in her shoulders, no drowning, suffocation. Just gradual self-extinction. There was peace in it, a peace she was experiencing already, beginning to creep over her as she sank back, back, let her head loll free. She was still aware of the pounding of her heart, but now she *was* the pounding, was the darkness. She was seeping through her own boundaries, losing her outlines, dispersing into drops of the same black heavy water she was floating on.

The water deepened. How strange that she had felt herself confined. She was adrift now on a vast ocean, the immensity of a fathomless sea beneath her, the million million miles of sky above. Something bumped against her thigh. A ship? A meteor? Her own hand. She heaved it out of the water – the hand of a corpse, heavy, waterlogged – held it out in front of her. She could feel the fingers swelling, pulling out of themselves like the tentacled eyes of some gigantic water-snail, growing so massive, so unwieldy, she could only let them fall again. It was no longer hand but claw – the claw of some huge prehistoric crested beast dragging its cumbersome limbs across dark and silent swamps, as one endless aeon heaved into the next. Except time was rolling backwards. She was losing crest and claw, drifting back, back, until she was some watery creature with neither limb nor brain nor eye. Just a cell, a blob. The roaring noise she had mistaken as her heartbeat was the groan of the world as it crept back to primeval slime. That, too, died away. Now there was only embryonic silence, the expectant hush before creation.

Her foot touched against the edge of the tank. No foot, no tank. It was the edge of the world she had encountered, a world still cold and barren, still waiting for the flash and roar of life.

She tensed. Someone was tapping on the world, trying to break it open, hatch it like an egg. She could hear the echoes ripping up the blackness, disturbing the eternal silence.

Creation would only bring confusion – light and pain, the trap of time, the maze of consciousness. She had escaped all that, shed them like a skin.

'No,' she muttered. 'Go away.'

The tapping stopped. She let herself sink back again, realized suddenly that the world as she knew it was colossally absurdly tiny, their whole galaxy but a single microbe on the one spiked eyelash of a vaster universe, their earth's four and a half thousand million years nothing but a sneeze, a second, in its illimitable unfolding. She still had to travel backwards through countless ages where time meant nothing as millennia dwindled into seconds and seconds blossomed into slow infinity; where there was no longer any difference between air/water, sound/silence, darkness/light. She felt a perfect peace, a perfect emptiness.

She closed her eyes, felt herself falling through the lids, down down down into infinite and echoing nothingness.

12

It had stopped raining. Morna emerged into the street, blinking against the glare. Everything was shining – puddles reflecting sunlight, glass refracting light. She was glass herself, transparent, with nothing left between the two clear panes of her body. Her brain had been taken out and rinsed, held under ice-cold running water, her eyeballs polished, mouth re-hung.

She crossed the street, branched right, then left, right again. No longer lost, she was drawn towards the centre of the city, seeing not squalor now, but beauty, space. Trees were in blossom, pink and white confetti loosened by the breeze, drifting into puddles, embroidering the plain grey paving stones. Waifs and misfits had all gone home, replaced by handsome vigorous people, a newly created race with smiling faces, shimmering clothes. The sun itself was new, beaming raw and radiant in a freshly valeted sky.

She turned a corner, gasped at the upward rush of a skyscraper, the ever changing movement of the city reflected in its glass. Solid shapes were bent by it, distorted – lights, sun, flashing signs, all swallowed up, disgorged again. There were lorries in the glass, rumbling towards chimera buildings, writhing, disappearing, transmuting into cloud. A second glass-clad tower block swapped its fifty dazzling storeys with the first, merged, refracted, then snatched its outlines back again. Morna watched, entranced. She was hemmed in now by skyscrapers, magnificent – man's new cathedrals, but dwarfing man who made them.

'Excuse me.'

She swung round. One of the race of gods, dressed in silver grey and shining, had stopped to speak to her, a guide-book open in his hands.

'I wondered if you could tell me the way to the Museum of Science?'

She shook her head, unsure yet whether all her faculties had fully returned. Sight certainly; hearing yes, since she had grasped what he had said, even registered his accent as well-modulated English, but speech . . .?

'Or are you a visitor yourself? The first person I asked was Australian and the second Serbo-Croat, judging by his accent.' He laughed. 'I hoped with you I'd picked a native.'

'No,' she murmured. 'I'm English – I come from Surrey.'

'Good Lord! So do I. Godalming, near Guildford. How about you?'

'Weybridge.' Morna looked up again to where one proud building soared beyond its fellows, lost its head in cloud.

'We're almost neighbours, then.' He followed her gaze. 'Been up there yet? The view's spectacular. I did it yesterday. See the lift. It goes up on the outside of the building. You need strong nerves.'

She looked where he was pointing. A tiny black object was clinging like an insect to the sheer precipitous wall. Suddenly, it moved, as if it had sprouted wings and was soaring up, up, up, until she was craning her neck to keep track of it, reeling with the speed, watching it dwindle to a speck as it reached the dizzy top.

'You mean, you can . . . go in that? That high and . . .?'

'Oh, yes. It's one of the attractions of the city. Says so here.' He waved his guide book. 'Want to try? I wouldn't mind a second ride.'

She stood there, silent. This was a stranger, so she

shouldn't talk to him, yet a shining stranger, created out of slime, and growing wiser, purer, as he received eyes, hands, brains, tools, soul. She had watched the process in the tank.

'We could have a drink together – drink a toast to Surrey. There's a bar at the top with quite the finest view in all LA.'

She was still wondering how to refuse when he took her arm, guided her across the street and up some steps. The glare of sun on glass faded into the gentler light of silk-fringed lamps, as pavement softened into pile, trees scaled down to potted plants.

'Right, up we go.'

The lift doors closed behind them. She didn't even know his name. Supposing . . .? There was a sudden leap from in to out, wall to sky, as the lift ripped through the fifth-floor roof and catapulted onwards, on the outside of the building now. Fear fell away, her stomach fell away, as streets, traffic, trees, were left behind; buildings flashing past her, the clouds themselves looking close enough to touch.

She hardly knew that they had stopped. The stranger had to push her out and she walked in a daze towards the huge glass windows encircling her like a cage. There was no sense of being confined. She shared that cage with the whole stupendous city and its suburbs, glittering in the glass, spreading around, beyond, beneath her, in the scarlet shock of sunset. How could it be sunset, the new-born sun already dying? She had set out in the morning, lost great chunks of time, let them break off and float away like icebergs in a treacherous sea. She clutched at the wall, dizzied by the carousel of streets below, the tiny coloured cars strewn like children's toys. Skyscrapers clustered all around her. She was no longer looking up at them, but staring into their gleaming polished faces blushing in the sun. She walked slowly round the circle, each window opening up a different vista, a new slice of gold and scarlet. Beyond it shimmered haze or smoke or ocean, lost in the horizon, blurring into sky.

'Stunning, isn't it?' The man was following her, stopped when she did, gestured to a table. 'Well, how about that drink?'

She nodded, needed one, sank into a padded velvet chair. He pulled his up beside her. 'I think it's time we introduced ourselves. You first.'

'I'm M . . . Morna,' she said uncertainly. Was that still her name or had she been re-created and re-christened?

'I beg your pardon?'

'Morna. Like Lorna, but with an M. Morna Gordon.'

'Pleased to meet you, Morna. I'm David Attwood.'

'*David*?' She knew then it was meant. Not just the same Christian name, but a surname which also started with an A. She had posted him a valentine, across miles of land, endless miles of ocean, and he had received it already, sent her a reply. Even in the tank, she had felt his guiding spirit, glimpsed mysteries, unfathomables, things he had hinted at in his talk at the retreat. She glanced up at her companion. The two were in no way alike. Her David was taller, leaner, more intense. She could hardly have described this man, or reported the colour of his eyes and hair with any accuracy. It was not just that she was blinded by the sun, but her perceptions were still blurred, her mind adding a gloss and resonance to everything she saw. She must simply be still, let him talk until her world had stabilized. It was enough that he was a David.

'I don't normally drink cocktails,' he was saying. 'I'm a whisky man, in fact – but they're bloody good up here. I can recommend the Top of the Tower. That's vodka-based with . . .'

'You choose.' She didn't want to talk, rather gaze out at that astounding scarlet skyscape, that new and brilliant creation – busy freeways reaching out, doubling back, engulfed in pink-tinged cloud. The bar was revolving very slowly like the globe itself, spinning through the stars. There were no stars yet, only the tail-lights of jet planes meteoring past. Man had moved from slime to Concorde in one afternoon.

'See that building with the sort of greeny sheen? That's my hotel. I thought it was tall until I came up this high. My boss stays here, in fact, but it's too pricey for mere underlings. The only reason I'm in LA at all is that he went down with some kidney thing the day before his flight left. Rotten for him, but quite a chance for me.'

Morna forced her attention back from the still revolving world outside. 'What *is* your business?'

'Frozen foods – sales manager. Our parent company's based out here, but this is my first trip. I hope it's going to change my luck. It's a pretty tough business – too much competition.' He drummed his fingers on the table, as if recalling the strains of work. 'What are *you* doing here? Just a holiday?'

Morna nodded. 'Sort of.' She had no wish to define herself, explain. The lights were coming on now, challenging the dying sun – a blaze and storm of light tinselling the buildings, strung out on the freeways, reflected back in water, glass.

'Oh, here are our drinks. I was beginning to think they'd forgotten all about us.'

Morna turned back. She had forgotten they were in a bar at all – with other people, waitresses, the normal bustle of the cocktail hour. Even the drinks were full of coloured lights – brilliant hued, piled with ice and stars. She took a sip through her stripy straw, tasted mead, not vodka, saw David in his tiny paper boat sailing over turquoise waves towards her.

David raised his glass. 'Cheers!' he said. 'What shall we drink to?'

'Us,' Morna murmured, smiling as St Abban beached the boat, leaving the other David free to leap towards her.

Morna leant against the wall. She wasn't drunk – not really – wasn't ill. Just a little queasy. There was a lot of light and movement in her stomach which felt as if it were flashing on and off like a neon sign. The cocktails she had gulped were still fizzing there inside her, but had shifted up and sidewards to make room for the lavish jewelled dinner which had followed them. She had swallowed lobster beached on coral reefs, salads made of emeralds, desserts topped with soft white ermine scattered with jade. St Abban hadn't murmured, David not demurred. In fact, the more she ate, the closer he had pressed, kissing her fingers as she picked up lobster claws or strawberries, kneading her thigh as he replaced her damask napkin. She had made him break his vows and it hadn't mattered. Even now, his arm was round her shoulders as he led her into the lift, held her close as it rocketed down.

She had gone down down in the tank, actually let go. Her mind had said 'no', but she moved out of her mind and sunk back into instinct, reached heights and depths she had never known existed. She had even lost track of time. She had read about that in the sex-books – people experiencing such transports that time stood still. It had never happened to her until she let herself be overruled by Krishna, submit to someone else. She had always been too rigid before, too separate. She understood it now. She had fought Neil, resented him, and so stayed locked in struggle and resistance instead of flying past them, flying with him.

David would guide her, be another Krishna. He was taking her to his hotel – a slap of glare and cold as they crossed the street, zig-zagged along the pavement, tottered up some steps; a second elevator ride as they soared towards his room. An orange room, as if the last blaze of sunlight

225

had dissolved in the carpet and the counterpane. He tried to steer her to the bed.

'No, wait,' she said, recalling Krishna's words. 'You have to shower first – wash the body oils off.' She slipped into the bathroom – orange tub and basin – dragged off all her clothes, glanced at her body in the mirror. It looked better than it had this morning – breasts firmer and more rounded, thighs smooth, legs longer altogether. She needed someone to admire it. She had had no man prior to Neil and only that one brief fiasco after he had left – thirty minutes' sex in the last five years. She had to make amends. It wouldn't be sex, in any case – not fucking, screwing, all those crude and vulgar words which Neil used, just a sinking down, a floating up, a rocking to the waves of David's boat. The tank had showed her how, left her clear and pure like glass, but still too rigid. David would break the glass, find the mead inside it. She remembered the only Jewish wedding she had been to. They had smashed a delicate crystal goblet, ground it underfoot. One of the guests had told her it was a vestige of an ancient superstition, making a loud and frightening noise on a joyous occasion to scare off evil spirits jealous of human happiness. There were no evil spirits here – she had left them all in the tank. She could go right ahead and achieve her ecstasy.

She emerged from the bathroom, towelled and naked, found David swathed in a maroon striped dressing gown, monogrammed with the initials DLA. She ignored the L – the rest was right – saw his hair damp around the ends, where he had swum over from his island. She smiled, held out both her hands to him. He lurched across. Her stomach lurched at exactly the same moment. She clutched it, reeled back towards the bed.

'I'm s . . . sorry, David. I'm not feeling too good. Give me a moment, will you?'

She lay down on the counterpane, closed her eyes to blot

out its orange glare. No good. A kaleidoscope of even cruder colours was flashing behind her eyelids, strobing in her stomach; a hot and heavy hand crawling clammy down one breast. She tried to push it off.

'No, wait. This awful pain . . . My tummy's sort of churning.'

She heard him mutter something, tried to shut him out along with the furnishings; turn him into just a picture on the wall, something with no needs, no hands. She could hear his voice still rasping on, but couldn't make the words out. Too many other sounds were crackling in her head – ugly, painful sounds like static on a stereo. She had to rest, sink down down down again; lose time, body, boundaries.

When she opened her eyes, the noise was different – muffled gasps and moans. They appeared to be coming from several yards away. Had she parted from her body, floated off from it, so that her mind and consciousness were separate from her limbs? Were those *her* groans, her still churning rumbling stomach gasping out its pain from the opposite side of the room? She groped out a hand, touched the curve of a breast, the bulk of a thigh. No – she was lying on the bed still – all of her together. How long had she been there – hours or minutes?

The gasps were getting louder. The room was in semi-darkness but she peered in their direction, saw a flickering screen. A man was slumped in front of it, sprawled out on the carpet, his head blocking half the figures on the screen. She moved her own head, tried to make them out. *Naked* figures, male and female, writhing in a sort of dance. The man was moving with them, rocking back and forth. There were two different sorts of noises now – grunts and squeal-ings from the screen, and a heavy panting breathing from the man in front of it. What was his name – something special – a name she could never forget?

'David!' she cried, struggling to sit up.

227

He sprang to his feet, clasping the dressing gown around him, tripping on an ashtray. 'I . . . I thought you were asleep.'

'I was, I think.'

'H . . . How you feeling?'

'A little better now, thanks. What are you watching?'

'Oh, nothing. It was . . . er . . . just to pass the time until you woke.'

'What is it, though?'

'What they call a . . .' He paused, shrugged, laughed embarrassedly. 'An adult movie. You can hire them from reception. I got it yesterday – didn't know I wasn't going to need it.' Another awkward laugh.

Now that he had moved, she could see the screen more clearly. Everyone was naked, as she'd thought, but it wasn't a dance. She glanced back at David. His knee-length dressing gown had lifted a little at the hem, levered up by something. He touched the something, tossed the robe behind him, lunged towards her. His flesh looked very white in the gloom. A lot of flesh, and closing in on her.

She fell back, shut her eyes, felt folds of flab lap against her own flesh. She was lost in smells – a whiff of nicotine, a blast of garlic brandy, a faint undertone of sweat – all contradicted by a sharp imperious aftershave.

'Are you okay?'

Morna didn't answer. He was pressing on her windpipe, which made it difficult to breathe.

'Or would you rather lie on top?'

She shook her head, too tired to move or even speak. There was silence for a moment. She jumped when he spoke again.

'It's my first time with a redhead. I always wondered if they matched – you know – down below. You do. It's stunning! A burning bush.'

His laugh re-echoed in her stomach. She tried to pull free,

dislodge the dogged finger he was jabbing up inside her. There were noises as well as smells now – the squelch of flesh on flesh, both their breathings out of sync, a sudden rattling from the street outside, constant yelps and giggles from the video.

'Bring your knees up.'

His voice was urgent now, impatient, but she couldn't concentrate. The video was too distracting. A huge pout-lipped negro was head to tail with a schoolgirl in a gymslip – a gymslip but no pants. They moved to close-up – quivering crimson depths probed by pink pulsing tongue. Morna felt the twenty-dollar lobster shift inside her stomach, jostle with the strawberries. She assumed she had digested them by now, but they were still sitting whole inside her gut – strawberries with hairy stalks and leaves on, lobsters with sharp claws. She seemed to be all stomach, had lost the bits below. She wasn't even sure if David had entered her or not. If he had a Big Sam, she couldn't seem to feel it. Their bodies didn't fit.

'I'm sorry. Am I hurting?' David paused a moment, changed the pressure of his finger. 'Better?' He stopped again, tried a different angle. 'Morna, is that *better*?'

'Wh . . . What?' She had thought it was the negro who had spoken. He was using both his hands instead of just one finger – huge black hands spreading the schoolgirl's opening as if it were elastic, turning it almost inside out, exposing the raw red swollen depths inside.

She suddenly jerked up, pushed David off, dashed into the bathroom. Girl, negro, lobster, strawberries, spewed into the basin. She ran the taps to drown the noise, stood leaning against the wall, one hand pressed against her head, the other nursing her stomach. It was minutes before she dared to move, and only then to stagger back to the basin, wipe her mouth. David's matching toiletries were arranged on the shelf. She sprayed on his cologne to drown the smell of vomit, gargled with his mouthwash.

There was a hammering on the door.

'J . . . Just coming,' she called, swabbing down the basin and almost colliding with a white and naked body as she emerged.

'What the hell . . .?' David grabbed her arm.

'I'm sorry. My bladder's a bit . . .' Morna forced a laugh, a lie. 'It must have been all those cocktails. I'm all right now.'

'Well, you don't look it.' David let her go, slumped down on the bed, swatted irritably at the sheet. He *did* have a Big Sam, a tiny tiny one, like a baby shell-less snail which had curled for safety between the slack folds of his thighs.

'S . . . Sorry,' she said again.

He was still glancing at the video, then looking back at her, as if uncertain which was the better bet. The negro and the schoolgirl had gone – or come. Two older girls were soaping each other in a bubble bath. The blonde leaned across and sucked the brunette's nipple. David crawled towards the set, squatted on the carpet, nose to screen. 'I've taken my contact lenses out and I can't see a damned thing back there. Come and sit beside me.' He patted the orange pile.

Morna lowered herself gingerly to the floor. Everything was faintly hazed and blurred as if she, too, had removed her contact lenses – except she didn't wear them. She let David take her hand, felt its growing hurting pressure as he watched the blonde part the brunette's thighs. His nails were digging into her as the blonde probed deeper, deeper.

'Quick!' he said. 'Lie back. No – where you are.' It was the blonde he was instructing, slavering over her slim and eager thighs as he rearranged her own sluggish heavier ones. She lay torpid, as if dead. The girls in the bath were doing the work for her. The fair one had manoeuvred the long-handled bath brush between the dark one's legs. She could feel it now, just the tip of it – wobbly for a bath brush. She tried to firm it up, grip with her muscles, used her hands to help. Too late. It was already slipping out, dwindling away to nothing.

'Hell's teeth!' David heaved off, stalked away, sagged down by the desk.

She knew she ought to follow him, but she felt too weak and queasy. Everything was tipping, including the screen. The two girls in the bath were rocking back and forth in a sort of writhing agony, mouths open, eyes closed, slopping turquoise-tinted water over the sides of the marble tub. They must be ill as well, judging by their groans. She wished she could turn them off, turned her back instead, crawled towards David in his corner.

'I'm sorry,' she said. Third time.

'No, it's *my* fault.' He shifted round on his bottom, fumbled out a hand. 'Bit out of practice, I'm afraid. The . . . er . . . wife walked out six months ago and you know how these things affect one.'

She nodded. 'Mm.'

'It's worse for a bloke, though, don't you think? A girl can always pretend.'

'Oh, no.'

'Are *you* married?'

'No . . . No.'

'Divorced?'

'Er . . . no.' Three 'noes' now, and two of them straight lies.

'Just my luck! A cracker of a girl and single on top of it, and I balls it up.'

'It doesn't matter – honestly.' She wished he would stop talking, stop pawing her with that damply heavy hand. He got up for a moment, but only to fetch his Marlboros, plumped down again beside her, offered her the packet.

'No, thanks.' She had already told him – twice – she didn't smoke.

He puffed in silence for a while, using his cupped palm as an ashtray.

'You won't understand about the kid then,' he mumbled at last, almost to himself.

'I . . . I beg your pardon.'

'If you're single – never had a kid – it's difficult to realize just how it cuts you up. I've only got the one – Michelle – haven't seen her since the wife left.'

Morna forced her attention back. She was trying to find David – the other David – slip off somewhere colder and more bracing where her brain would work again, her stomach stop its shuddering.

'H . . . How old's your daughter?'

'Two and a half. Go on – say it – I know what you're thinking: what's a middle-aged bloke like me doing with a toddler? I was always a late starter – late getting married, late producing a kid, and still waiting for promotion. Christ! That reminds me . . .' He stubbed out the fag end on the desk-leg, scrambled to his feet. 'We've got our sales conference tomorrow – all the big guns there – and I haven't finished my report yet.'

Morna struggled up as well. 'Don't worry, I've got to get back myself. It's quite a distance and I'm not even sure which bus . . .'

'Oh, don't go. Please. You'll never get a bus this late, and taxis cost a bomb, if the driver doesn't mug you first. Stay the night. Go on – be my guest. I'd like to make it up to you – have another stab – if you'll forgive the pun. I'm always better in the morning, and once I get that homework off my chest . . .' He was dragging on his pyjama top, hunting for the bottoms. 'I suspect that was half the trouble, actually. I'd planned to work this evening, you see – miss dinner and tie up that report as soon as I'd done my hour or two of sightseeing. Unfortunately' – he laughed – 'I met the best sight last of all.'

Morna trailed towards the bathroom and her clothes. If only there weren't so many explanations, so many strings of words. Each one hurt her head, left a stain on her mind like a blot from a leaky pen. He was tagging after her, pulling at her arm.

'What d'you have to leave for if you're on your own? It's damned lonely on your own. I ought to know.' He tied his dressing gown, too tightly, round his middle. 'I feel bad enough already, going off the boil like that, and if you push off now before I've had a chance to . . . Hey, perhaps you're hungry, are you? I can order you anything you want, you know. It's twenty-four-hour service, direct to the room. I just charge it to the firm. How about a nightcap, or a milk shake, or a nice club sandwich?'

She shook her head, heard her stomach snarl its own refusal, flopped down on the bed.

'Great! You've changed your mind. That's it – have a little shut-eye. I can see you're tired. I'll creep in after you, as soon as I've got shot of this lot. Don't worry – I won't disturb you. Let's save it for the morning, shall we? I'll set the alarm for six. That'll give us time before my meeting – even time for breakfast, if you like. Is that light a nuisance? Tell you what – I'll switch it off and just use this desk one – shade it with a towel or something. How's that? Better? If you turn the other way, you won't notice it at all.'

She turned to face the wall, heard David creak his chair back, rustle papers. Blessed silence otherwise, though it made her feel uneasy. Was he watching her, creeping up on her? She humped back the other way. His head was bent across the desk, shoulders tense, legs stuck out at an angle, huge grey shadow spastic on the wall. A plume of smoke was coiling up above his head as if he were on fire. Smoke and shadow merged. The light was so dim, he was only a

233

shape, a blur. If she closed her eyes, she could turn him into David Anthony. *He* would be working, too – one small square of light beaconing from his cottage, her letters on his table. She could already hear the faint roar of the sea, feel the swell and slap of the waves against her body. The orange blankets paled into silver sand; the glimmer by the desk was the waning moon.

'David,' she whispered as she sank back in the water, tried to swim towards him against the rolling threshing waves. 'Shout louder. I can't hear you.'

The alarm was a quiet well-mannered one. Morna reached out automatically to turn it off, then spent some minutes groping for the light switch, blinked in surprise when at last she jabbed it on. She was lying in a bed she had never seen before, in a room completely strange to her, with a man she had never laid eyes on in her life.

The man was snoring, snoring very loudly, mouth open, the sound vibrating through his chest. His breath smelt of nicotine, the lower teeth stained brown with it, the upper ones crowded with bad bridgework. His hair was sandy, sparse, his face slack-jowled, shadowed with gingery stubble. A button was missing from his pyjamas, revealing a strip of pallid chest, grizzled with coarse hair. One hand was flung towards the wall. It wore a wedding ring.

Morna edged away a little. The man stirred, muttered something in his sleep. She held her breath. The snoring resumed – rumbling, regular. She inched out of bed, made contact with the floor. Her legs felt strange, unsteady; the pain in her head seemed three-dimensional, the wrong shape for her head yet forced inside it, a sharp-edged pain made of solid steel. She swallowed, tasted something foul and slimy adhering to the lining of her mouth.

She stood shaky in the centre of the room. The desk was strewn with papers, Hershey chocolate bar wrappers, an empty cigarette packet. Six or seven fag ends had been stubbed out in a saucer; a grey chrysalis of ash lay trembling on the cover of a glossy colour brochure on frozen strawberries. The lamp was muzzled with a man's string vest, not quite Persil-white. Morna backed away. Two shoes with gaping mouths, kicked off beneath a chair, seemed to be crying out for help as she tiptoed to the bathroom. The bathroom stank. Flecks of dried-on vomit were sprayed across the mirror; transferred themselves to her face as she peered at her reflection. Why was she naked? She never slept with nothing on. She looked around for her clothes, found them jumbled in a corner when she always hung them up. She dragged them on, fighting with buttons which didn't seem to fasten, tights which had shrunk and twisted in the night. A black plastic raincoat was lying at the bottom of the pile. She slipped it on, shivered suddenly.

She crept back to the bedroom, shoes in one hand, bag in the other. The stranger hadn't stirred. He was no longer snoring, but making a harsh snuffling sound as if his sinuses were blocked. He looked old and tired, in need of sleep. Gently she tucked the sheet around him, switched the light off so it wouldn't hurt his eyes, then groped towards the door and out along the passage labelled 'Ground floor, exit, street'.

13

'Would you mind stopping here? I'll walk the rest.'

Morna paid the cab driver, then turned the corner to Neil and Bunny's avenue. She didn't want to be seen arriving in a taxi instead of in her imaginary friend's imaginary Buick.

She screwed up her eyes against the sun, which had returned again after a week of rain and storm. Late January seemed more like early June now – apart from the icing of snow on the magnificent mountains rising in the distance. The trees were green, the gardens lush, sprinklers rotating on velvet lawns; exotic palm trees shading more familiar flowers such as pansies, antirrhinums. Butterflies were sporting in the sunshine, the lemons on the leafy trees turning from acid green to shrillest yellow. Palms and lemon trees apart, the atmosphere was not that different from Weybridge. Neil had swopped one lush exclusive suburb for another. There were the same stone lions and carriage lamps, wrought-iron gates, English-style house names – the same absence of weeds and litter, the same smug luxuriance. No one poor, coloured, disadvantaged, could ever debase or taint this mini-Eden. Each house had its burglar alarm, its stern notice advertising fully-armed security patrols operating round the clock. Morna felt an intruder herself, neither rich nor glossy enough to fit her impeccable surroundings.

She slowed her pace to a dawdle. She had forgotten the curdling mix of fear, exclusion, envy, which even the street itself could rouse. This was enemy territory. Yet her daughter was living here and how could a daughter be an enemy, or Dean, who was far too young to be blamed for anything, or even Bunny who had issued the invitation to come today? She walked on again, passing a house with giant Corinthian columns flanking its triple garage, a Greek god posturing naked by a fountain. The house next door resembled a mausoleum with its marble façade and heavy double doors, its gloomy Cyprus trees and two bronze sphinxes.

The street was deserted – no jogger on the pavement, no child in any garden, not even any animal except for one clipped and tonsured poodle which yapped hysterically as she passed. Everything was clipped – hedges, trees, lawns, shrubs – nothing permitted to grow tall, wild, unwieldy, or even natural.

She stopped at Neil and Bunny's house. She had hardly had a chance before of studying it dispassionately. There had always been someone with her, whisking her in or out of a car – Bunny distracting her with chit chat, Dean tugging at her hand. She gazed up now at the fussy tiles, fake pillars. It looked like a cross between a mock-Italian *palazzo* and a curtain showroom. Every window was in fancy dress – nets and drapes swathed, pleated, beribboned, frilled. The driveway was patterned with paving stones in pastel shades of pink and green. A stone replica of Bunny's golden labrador (now deceased) stood in the porch complete with stone collar, lolling stone tongue, even a stone bone at its feet. 'Whispering Trees', read the wooden plaque suspended from brass chains above the door.

Morna stood and listened. It wasn't whispering trees she could hear, but giggling girls, clinking glasses. The noise was coming from the patio at the back of the house. She stood motionless a moment. Had she been foolish to accept Bunny's invitation? She couldn't even argue that it was a chance of seeing Chris again. Chris was out with Neil all day, not just caddying, but having the first of a course of lessons from the pro. As Neil's daughter, she had to share his passions, take up his pursuits. Anyway, this was Bunny's show, her equivalent of church or synagogue. She had phoned to ask Morna and her buddy to come and share their weekly service of light and love. Morna had swiftly made excuses for the buddy, but accepted herself, surprised at her alacrity. The last few days had dragged, the nasty taste in her mouth not disappeared.

She shut her eyes, fought a wave of nausea. Orange carpet was taunting on the driveway, lobsters sprouting hot-pink in the flowerbeds in place of red geraniums. She had tried to cancel out that shameful Sunday, fill the days which followed with healthy walks, constructive sightseeing. It had been lonely on her own, wandering aimlessly through galleries, museums, shrugging off all overtures in case they proved a repeat of David Attwood. Yet at least it had been safer, removed from new wife, ex-husband, almost-son.

It was not too late. She could still escape, creep away to the nearest call box, phone Bunny and tell her she was ill, then order a cab to take her back to the Ocean View motel.

'Hi, Morna!'

She jumped, swung round. Dean was standing on the path grinning at her, naked save for the briefest pair of swimtrunks. 'Why did you go away?' he asked, springing into her arms. 'I *told* you not to. You didn't see my goldfish and now it's deaded.'

'Oh, I'm sorry.' Morna hugged him. 'What did you call the fish?'

'Jane. That Chrissie's second name.'

Morna laughed, put him down. 'I know. I chose it.'

'You *did*?'

'Well, Chrissie's Grandma did.'

'Is Chrissie's Grandma coming to stay as well?'

'I shouldn't think so – no.'

Dean stared up at her, silent for a moment. 'I like you, Morna,' he said.

'Do you, darling?'

'Yeah. You're Chrissie's Mom.'

And if Chrissie was his sister, then . . . Strange to have a son – the opposite sex, sharing your body, feeding from it. Why opposite at all, then, when it began as symbiotic?

'Hey, Morna, I want to show you something.' Dean patted the step. 'Don't go away. You promise?'

She nodded. He was back in minutes, dwarfed by a giant-sized paper bag.

'No wonder your fish die if you keep them in paper bags.'

He giggled. 'It's not a fish. It's a chocolate bar – the biggest biggest chocolate bar in the world.' He drew it out, two foot of chocolate three inches thick, boasting its dimensions on the gold and scarlet wrapper. 'Isn't it great? Daddy bought it for me. I'm never going to eat it. I'm going to save it for ever and ever and ever.'

'It'll go bad, then.'

'No, it won't. Here, *you* hold it.' He took her free hand, led her round the back of the house towards the patio.

'We're going to have a barbecue. Do you have barbecues in England?'

'Sometimes. Not as often as you do.'

'Why not?'

'We don't have so much sun.'

Bunny had seen her, rushed towards her, crushed her in a hug. 'It's so great you could come! I've told everyone about you. Girls, this is Morna. I hope you're good at names, sweetie. That's Angie in the pink, and Bella next to her, Lee-Ann with the gin bottle – typical! – and Beth over by the . . .'

Morna murmured hallos. All the names were jumbling together, all the bodies tanned and over-dressed, several overweight. Bunny herself was wearing a full-length emerald

239

kaftan with two matching green hair-slides, one trimmed with a bow, and her usual tangle and jingle of jewellery. Lee-Ann's coppery hair clashed with her purple knicker-bockers and scarlet halter top. Several of the girls were wearing tracksuits, but exotic ones in jewelled colours with knotted scarves. Morna felt more and more drab, in plain blue skirt and toning blouse, the merest dab of lipstick. She had dressed for a church service, yet this looked more like a picnic or a party.

The patio was huge and busy with so much equipment it looked like a second kitchen. The barbecue unit had a stainless steel sink built into it, and a rotisserie, extractor fan and plate-warmer, as well as the central charcoal grill. There were two white wrought-iron tables piled with food and wine, and six matching chairs, besides the flowered and padded recliners on which most of the girls were sprawled. There was even a mini-bar in fake wood, with three high bar stools; the counter hung with Chianti bottles and raffia dolls, college pennants and silk rosettes, and every brand of gin, bourbon, vodka, ranged along the top. To the right was a lily pond with an electrically operated waterfall which turned on and off at the touch of a switch. A red wooden bridge traversed it, with two scarlet-jacketed gnomes fishing from its summit and four plastic ducks swimming underneath. The lilies themselves looked plastic. On the other side stretched the glittering turquoise swimming pool, small but luxurious, with more chairs, tables, lilos, clustering round it – a diving board, a water chute, a small straw raft floating in the centre.

'Right, Morna honey, pick your steak.' Bunny pointed to the pile of raw pound-sized T-bones basking in their marinade of oil and wine. That was the extent of Bunny's cooking. Every guest was to choose and grill her own.

'We like to eat first,' she explained. 'It helps to relax us before we start the meeting. Angie here was brought up a

Catholic too, the same as you were, and she always used to pass out cold in church because they wouldn't let her have her breakfast before.'

'So did I,' said Morna. 'Our Reverend Mother asked me once would I please stop fainting as it was most embarrassing for the priest.'

Everybody laughed.

'Well, we don't believe in all that crap. We don't even meet on Sunday, because it's got bad vibes for most of us. You either spent half the day on your knees or it was Sunday school or prayer meeting or . . . We chose Saturday instead. That's fun night, party night. After all, Christ said we should live life abundantly and abundance includes food and funsers and . . .'

'Gin,' Lee-Ann chipped in, pouring herself half a tumblerful. 'What'll you drink, Morna?'

'Just wine, please.' Morna felt confused. They had discussed religion on her very first morning in Neil's and Bunny's house, and Bunny had said distinctly that she believed in neither God nor Gospel, yet here she was misquoting Christ.

Martha waddled over, fifteen stone of flowing scarlet robe, flung a hot arm round Morna's shoulders. 'You see, dear heart, we formed this little group ourselves and it takes a bit from everything – Zen, Christ, Dale Carnegie, Carl Rogers, Maslow, Germaine Greer . . . We actually met at Weight Watchers – well, three of us fatsos did. That's almost like a religion itself and, boy, is it strict! Every pound a mortal sin. But then Angie read this book about women's bodies and how they're *meant* to be fat . . .'

'Not fat,' corrected Angie. 'Voluptuous.'

'Yeah, sorry – that's crucial. See how I'm conditioned, Morna? Fat is yuk. But it's *not* – it's womanly. But we're all so mad at our mothers for denying us the breast, or love, or slapping us down when we were small and powerless, that we try to stunt our bodies so we won't grow into women or mothers ourselves, but stay like adolescent boys with no hips or boobs or . . .'

'It's all unconscious,' Angie explained. 'You may not even know you're feeling it, but the rage is there all right. We're mad at our own bodies, so we starve them and deny them or truss them up in corsets or panty girdles or . . . Men feel just the same about their mothers, so they join in the conspiracy. In fact, the guys are worst of all. It's males who run this whole diet thing, males who wield the power in the fashion industry, males who . . .'

'That's what pornography's all about,' Beth added. 'Little men tying down their big fat powerful mothers, or whipping them or putting them in chains . . .'

'We decided to keep our group all female, at least at present.' Ruth was speaking now, a dark intense woman who looked older than the rest. 'There's no hostility intended, but until men are more enlightened . . .'

Martha speared her steak, transferred it to the barbecue. 'This is the age of the female, but she'll only come into her own if she can accept herself the way she is, flab and all. We're not against fashion – far from it.' She patted her own exclusive designer robe. 'In fact, we always dress up for our meetings. That's part of the whole deal – celebrating ourselves and our own beauty, making every day a party, refusing to slop around in any old thing because we're trying to hide away from life, or are ashamed to show our bodies off. God gave me this shape so I rejoice in it, see it as part of His fullness.'

'I . . . don't quite follow,' Morna put her glass down. 'I thought you didn't believe in God? Bunny said the group was . . .'

'We're *all* gods,' Beth cut in. 'God's just another name for the Good in each of us. That's what we focus on, not sin or guilt or . . .'

'We decided to quit Weight Watchers for just that reason.' Martha continued, smearing butter on her steak. 'It was fixing on the bad, the fat, but we turned that round and saw ourselves as beautiful – temples of God or the Good or whatever you like to call it. Words don't matter, actually. No – let me finish, Morna. We started meeting in our own homes instead of Diet Centres, and eating and drinking rather than weighing ourselves, and then . . .'

It was Bunny who interrupted, frowning, shaking her head. 'You're giving Morna the wrong idea. This isn't just an anti-diet thing. It's serious. It's . . .'

'Sure it is. I'm getting to that.' Martha turned to Morna again, gesturing with her fork. 'The more we talked, the more we realized how woman has been made the scapegoat in *all* religions. Christians say man only fell because of wicked Eve; Jewish women are regarded as unclean every time they menstruate or give birth. God! If it was the fellers who had the kids, they'd think they were fucking marvellous. They'd award themselves medals, not soak themselves in tubs like dirty laundry. And look at Moslems! All those women bundled into purdah because they're considered so lewd, they can't even be trusted to . . .' Martha paused to swallow a mouthful. Bella continued for her.

'You see, our group's a sort of celebration of the *good* in women generally. Woman has never gone to war or taken over other people's countries . . .'

'Or raped people.' Martha again, still chewing.

'Or enslaved the other half of humanity.'

Morna sucked the ice cube in her glass of Californian Chablis, tried to concentrate on pacific woman – saw the Amazons rushing into battle with shields protecting naked breasts; Catherine of Russia condemning each of her lovers to a grisly death once she had exhausted him in her bed; Boadicea, Joan of Arc, the more unsavoury of the Ancient Egyptian queens. Women had rarely had the power to go to

243

war, annex colonies, enslave. Given that power, might they not prove themselves as violent and exploitative as the men? It was a tricky question, one she had often debated with herself.

Bunny was also still uneasy, though on different grounds. 'You're telling it all *wrong*. This isn't just a peace movement or a feminist thing. We've worked through all that stuff at high school. This is different. It's a new religion, Morna – a religion of riches and abundance.'

Morna glanced round at the sizzling steaks, the pink champagne, the pool reflecting its tide of consumer durables. 'But what about the poor, those without a . . .?'

'There aren't any poor people,' Lee-Ann retorted, topping up her glass. 'It's all a question of attitude. Abundance is a state of mind. If you think poor, you stay poor. We can all attract riches to ourselves just by willing them. I took a course once on just that subject and you should have heard the stories! One man was starving, I mean literally starving, and he prayed for more money in his life, and within a week – just seven little days – he received a cheque for fifty thousand dollars, and he didn't even know the guy who'd sent it.'

'B . . . But *can* you pray for things like that? I mean, surely . . .'

'You can pray for anything – bigger boobs, a smaller overdraft, your number coming up in the local lottery, even . . .'

Angie interrupted. 'Prayer is simply getting in touch with the good in yourself and in the world, and making it increase. I can say "Angie, you're the greatest", and that's a prayer in itself. It's helping me believe in myself and love myself and then I can go out and love others. Hey! Watch your steak, honey, it's burning.'

Morna retrieved it, helped herself to salad, went and sat down next to Dean who was squatting on the steps playing

with a bowl of cherries. He seemed suddenly so innocent –
small, simple, clad only in his skin, not gilded or bejewelled
or clogged with theories, sticky with self-love.

'Do you know "Tinker Tailor"?' she asked him, turning
away from the rest.

'No, what is it?'

'Well, let me see your cherry stones.'

'What's stones?'

Bunny laughed. 'Pits, sweetheart. "Stones" is the English
word. Neil said it once and it really cracked me up. Imagine
stones in cherries!'

Dean laid the stones in front of Morna's feet.

'Right,' she said. 'We count like this. Tinker, tailor,
soldier, sailor, rich man, poor man, beggarman, thief. Wow!
You've got a lot. We'd better start again. Tinker, tailor,
soldier, sailor, rich man, poor man, beggarman . . . That's
it. You're going to marry a beggarwoman.'

'What's a beggarwoman?'

'A very poor lady who hasn't got any home or food, so she
has to sit out on the sidewalk and ask people for dimes.'

Dean stared at her, disbelieving. 'And what's a tinker?'

'Someone who mends pots and pans.' Morna paused. The
perils of translation. No one mended anything in America
– not even marriages – just chucked away, bought new.

Dean was making patterns with the stones. 'I'm going to
marry Chrissie, not a beggarwoman.'

Bunny scooped him up. 'Hush, sweetheart. Morna's
steak's going cold. She can't eat if you keep hassling her. Go
play with Sausage.'

Sausage was the dachshund, no longer puppy save in
ways. He was fawning round the group, scrounging titbits
from each overflowing plate. Morna was glad to give him
half her steak. It was burnt outside, bloody inside. Since
Chris had turned vegetarian, she felt uneasy eating meat
herself. Chris was a clever propagandist. The intimate details

245

of the abattoir at lunch could soon make you long for bread and cheese. She was surprised that Bunny's group were not vegetarian too. Shouldn't so much love spill over to sheep and cows?

Bunny was clearing plates. 'I suggest we save dessert for later and start our sharing now. Gee! It's hot.' She slipped off her kaftan, revealing a minuscule bikini in what looked like silver lurex string. 'Why don't we all get comfortable. Morna, honey, can I lend you something cooler?'

'Er . . . no . . . I'm fine.' She and Bunny were a different shape entirely. It would somehow seem obscene to be wearing Bunny's clothes.

'You brought your bikini, did you? We'll be swimming later on, but put it on now if you prefer.'

'No, really . . .' Morna didn't own a bikini, had dashed into a chain store the day before her flight, found nothing but boring one-piece costumes in schoolgirl navy, grabbed the last one in her size. She couldn't wear it here when most of the girls were changing into gaudy frills and flounces, displaying acres of bare flesh. Even stripped off, they still looked exotic with their huge coloured sunglasses, their ankle chains and turbans. They all refilled their glasses before lounging over to the lawn, arranging themselves in a circle on the grass.

Lee-Ann took Morna's hand. 'Don't be nervous, sweetie. You'll love it. I was real screwed-up before I joined the group. I'd been divorced three times and I was living on my own. Now that I've learnt to love, I love the world and everybody in it.'

'Everybody?'

'Yeah, including all my exes – *and* my first ex-mother-in-law. That took some doing!' She laughed, revealing well-capped teeth. 'It'll happen to you, too, if you don't resist it. Our theme today is Love. Bella's been to a Making Love Workshop and she's going to share it with us.'

Morna tensed. Not sex again, she prayed. Orange bed-spreads, frozen strawberries. She couldn't bear to hear Bunny talking about letting go or total giving, when the reality had proved so sordid, sordid and debasing. How could she have been taken in like that – a smarmy stranger asking her the way when he already had a guide-book in his hands? She had lain awake the following night in a fret of shame and guilt, torn between remorse, disgust and pity; had accused herself for joining him – and equally for failing him. Two nights later she had dreamt about his daughter, a tiny child with haunted eyes and straight dark hair like Neil's, howling for her father on the topmost storey of a huge white frozen skyscraper. She had woken trembling, leapt out of bed as if David Attwood were still sweating and snuffling beside her. She was in need of help, obviously, should have joined Bella on her course. She had seen those workshops advertised – five hundred dollars for one weekend and that didn't include meals or accommodation.

'It's . . . er . . . some sort of Masters and Johnson set-up, is it?'

'Oh, no,' said Bella. 'Much more spiritual than that. We're all conditioned to think love means simply screwing. But there's other sorts of love – love like Christ said – love thyself and love thy buddy. Jesus didn't mention bed.'

Nor did He charge for love, thought Morna – take money at the door when He preached and taught, add a service charge to the loaves and fishes. A hundred dollars for each Beatitude – special deal for the set of eight. Even His miracles came free. You would need top-rate Blue Shield cover for Californian miracles.

'Ready, girls?' Bunny was presiding – priestess in a bikini. She had switched off the waterfall, covered the barbecue, and was now sitting cross-legged in the circle, her wine glass at her side.

'What we do first, Morna, is a Self-Esteem and Happiness

247

Check to see how we're making out. I call out the numbers from zero to ten and you put up your hand when I reach the number you feel you're at. Zero means you're suicidal and hate yourself, ten is cloud nine and you're the greatest. Don't worry if you're low to start with. Lee-Ann was stuck on one for weeks and weeks, but last time she reached nine. Hush, Dean, I can't talk now. Go watch Superman. No, you *can't* bath Sausage, chickie, not now. I told you, Mommy's busy. Okay, everyone?'

The girls shuffled, fidgeted, finally settled down. A Boeing 747 ripped across the silence. Bunny waited till it had passed.

'Zero,' she said, in a softer and more solemn voice than usual.

No one stirred.

'One.'

No hand went up.

'Two.'

Still no hand.

'Three, four . . .'

Morna bit her lip. Supposing there was some sort of built-in lie detector? If she didn't put her hand up soon, she would land on cloud nine with all the rest.

'Five.'

Two hands went up, Morna's just a fraction behind. Most of the others scored seven or eight, Bunny nine, only Bella ten.

'That's great. Only three fives and you'll probably find you're up at least two points by the time we're through. Now, I'll just explain to Morna about our meditation. What we try to do, honey, is get in touch with the good in ourselves, find our inner beauty. We just close our eyes and sit in silence and concentrate on all our skills and strong points, all the neat things we've ever done, all the . . . Be quiet, Dean. You know you mustn't talk once we've got

248

started. Yeah, you can have ice cream, but mind you shut the freezer. And take Sausage with you. He's yapping.'

The group seemed unaware of child or dog. They already had their eyes closed, palms spread upwards on their knees. Morna glanced around at the ring of faces, rapt, expectant.

'Close your eyes, Morna, honey. It helps the concentration.'

Morna didn't want to close them. Once she turned inward, tried to find her inner beauty, she was scared it might rot beneath her scrutiny, or – worse – be simply absent. All the good she had done . . . But what about the bad? Her boringness in bed, her impatience and irritability with Bea, her jealousy of Bunny – worst of all, last Sunday night. To have got drunk like that, staggered through an evening in a dazed and queasy stupor, not known what she was doing, even risked a pregnancy. Someone like herself who had nothing to excuse her – no delinquent parent nor latchkey mum, no lack of principle nor neglected education. That flotation tank seemed to have had some strange effect on her, broken down her defences, made her less rigid, less responsible. She had welcomed it at the time, but now . . . She forced the memories down, tried to fix on something simple. Tinker, tailor, soldier, sailor. Someone should have updated it. Astronaut, gay libber, sales manager for frozen foods, blue-movie-watcher, pick-up . . .

An insect was buzzing near her face. She wondered if it were the stinging kind, and if she were allowed to open her eyes to check. Perhaps she should try to see its inner beauty. She squinted through her eyelids. It *was* beautiful, with slender steel-blue wings, surprising scarlet eyes. Supposing Bunny's friends were right and it was her own mocking, judging, overcritical mind which needed changing? She kept her eyes half open, stared at her outstretched leg. She had always regarded her figure as too plump. 'Beautiful leg,' she told it. 'Voluptuous leg. Truly feminine, Rubenesque, lovable.'

The leg looked better. Her mind returned to Sunday last. 'Good encounter,' she insisted. 'Letting go, reaching out to someone new and different, losing inhibitions . . .' She could smell vomit mixed with aftershave, see the tiny padded box with the contact lenses in it – two spare eyes swivelling round to watch her as she made her getaway. She closed her eyes again, jumped as the insect bit her leg.

'That's it, girls.' Bunny's voice intruding, still churchy and low-pitched.

'Take your time to finish, then slowly bring your minds back to the present.'

'Swollen leg, itching leg. Red lump on untanned flabby flesh. Ache in the back from sitting on the ground, grass stains on blue boring skirt. Indigestion. Guilt still.'

'Beth, go get your guitar and we'll have our chant.' Bunny turned to Morna. 'This works like a sort of mantra. Mantras are very powerful. Even doctors say they can lower the blood pressure and change the brain waves and all that stuff. *We* use them to help us relax and release the love in ourselves. It's only four lines, so you'll soon pick up the words. Okay, Beth?'

Beth played a chord or two, then broke into a simple melody. All the girls joined in with a rhythmic chant, mainly on one note.

> *'I love myself*
> *the good in me*
> *the good in you*
> *the whole world too.'*

'I love myself,' they began again.

Angie nudged Morna. 'Join in, honey,' she whispered. It's very simple.'

'The good in me,' Morna wavered, keeping both eyes and

voice down. Supposing the neighbours were watching, or Neil and Chris returned from golf? She tried to shut her mind off, blank out the imbecilic words. They meant less and less, anyway, as they were endlessly repeated – round and round, round and round. At least it was warm and the wine was good. She felt herself relaxing, her voice rising and falling with the rest, the sun hot and numbing on her back – was almost sorry when the final chord sounded and the chant died away like the rumbling of a plane.

Bunny's voice seemed to come from some great distance. 'Right, girls. Now we start the sharing.' She leant across, touched Morna's hand. 'What we're going to do, sweetie, is go round the group in turn and everyone tells us where she's at. Okay? Bella, why don't you start? And let's say our names as a little gift to Morna, in case she's having trouble sorting them out.'

Bella rose, another of the fatties, but short and mousy-haired where Martha was dark and Junoesque. 'I'm Bella and I'm real excited because I've just come back from a terrific workshop which I want to share with you later, but right now I'd like to say how thrilled I am to have Morna with us today.'

Bella walked across to Morna, squatted down in front of her, reached out her arms. Morna felt herself pressed against hot and sticky flesh, a scratchy rhinestone brooch digging into her neck. Everyone was clapping.

Lee-Ann waited for the applause to subside before scrambling to her feet. 'I'm Lee-Ann and I'd like to share with you that on my way over here I saw a dead tree struck by lightning, with a new green shoot growing out of it, and I thought, "That's me, I'm growing again. I've cut away the dead wood." '

More applause. Angie next. 'I'm Angie and I'm the greatest.' (Laughter). 'Last night, I cooked dinner for myself – a real good dinner with roses on the table and chilled wine, and I sat down, just little me at that whole great big table and I said, "Angie, you deserve this." And I didn't gobble or read a book or wallow in self-pity because I was all alone on Friday night. I relished every mouthful and sipped a brandy afterwards, and I saved you this –' She held up a long-stemmed scarlet rose, turned to Morna. 'I'd like to give it to you, Morna, as our guest today, to share my love with you.'

'Th . . . Thank you,' Morna mumbled, as her hand closed on thorns. It was her turn now, as she was sitting next to Angie and they were going clockwise round the circle. She struggled to her feet, feeling absurd, superfluous, with a rose stuck in her hand and nothing to say.

'I'm Morna,' she started. That at least was indisputable, but what did she say next? Everyone was looking at her, the circle of smiles like handcuffs. She longed to turn tail and bolt for home, but real home was half a world away, and lonely. At least these girls were friendly, had done everything they could to make her welcome. In one way, she yearned to share their simple-minded faith. They were like the retreatants, needing a faith and so creating one, in this case tailor-made, throwing out what didn't fit – men, sin, guilt, the poor. It was a strictly local religion, would hardly fit Calcutta. You loved your fellow leisured woman, shared your T-bone and champagne with her, and let a non-existent deity take care of the lepers and the starving.

Yet who was she to be so supercilious? All her agonizing about the Third World's poor had not actually alleviated one millionth of their problems. Her plate had been as loaded as the rest, her glass still three-quarters full beside her. She was leisured herself, a lotus-eater, swanning about on holiday while Ethiopians gasped for bread and water, Indians died in gutters. Neil was still partially subsidizing her while she mocked his house and wife, abused the friendship offered her. It *was* true friendship, real concern.

She could feel these women's warmth, integrity, however much she winced at their jargon, criticized their crazy rituals. Did jargon really matter? She was a translator, so she could find her own equivalent, try and understand what they were saying beneath the catch phrases, find the kernel in the shell.

Even now, they were trying to help, squeezing her hands, whispering suggestions, and she stood there silent, rigid, spurning what they offered because she was an intellectual snob, too damned superior to do anything but scoff.

'I'm . . . er . . . not much good at loving,' she stuttered at last.

'Oh, but you *are*.' Bella sprang up out of turn to hug her. 'Everybody is. It's a natural thing. Look at kids! It's just blocked in you, that's all. At the workshop, they told us there's only one door to the heart, and it's either shut or open. If you keep it shut with hate or bitterness, then you're not free to love. But if you just turn the key, then you can embrace the whole wide world. You see, we can't love again until we've cleared out all the shit – all that negative stuff we cling to – revenge, resentment, envy. We've gotta let it go and allow the new love in. People cried their eyes out at the workshop – you could have stuffed a mattress with all the wet and sodden Kleenexes. But they were tears of joy. Realizing that they could heal themselves and love again.'

'We've always been taught that love is rationed,' Martha broke in, levering herself up on one plump and dimpled elbow. 'That we can only love one or two people in our whole life – and always *men*, of course. If those relationships break down, then we think we have to live alone and loveless, or we start frantically searching for some new replacement guy. But we can love women, too – children, neighbours, everybody – the girl who waits table, the mechanic who fixes our car. They're all people craving love like us. If we give it out, we receive it back, and the world becomes a loving space. But first we've gotta love ourselves. Morna, honey, do you think you love yourself enough?'

'Well, I . . . er . . .'

'What you've got to remember is you're special to start with.' Martha wiped perspiration from her neck. 'You won the sperm race, didn't you? We all did. Just think – only one in four hundred million spermatozoa gets fertilized. The other three hundred and ninety-nine million poor suckers never made it here, but *you* did, Morna. That makes you a winner and don't forget it. Tell you what . . .' Martha turned back to the group. 'Shall we tell Morna how we love her?'

Everybody nodded, clapped.

'Sit in the centre, honey, and just listen. We're going to beam back at you all the good we see in you and how we relate to your inner beauty. We'll all speak at once, but don't you worry, you'll get the message.'

Morna was blushing before they had even started. If her friends back home could see her now, squatting on the grass in the centre of a circle as if they were playing some kid's game, clutching a rose like some pampered prima donna . . .

'Shut your eyes if you prefer,' said Beth. 'It makes your hearing sharper.'

Morna shut them, more to block out the eager friendly faces, make-up running in the heat, grass stains on shorts, gigantic fleshy thighs, the babble of voices rising round her.

'Morna, we love you for your gentleness.'

'Morna, we love you for your love.'

'Morna, we love you for your openness.'

'Morna, we love you for your beauty.'

'Morna, we love you for your . . .'

She could hardly make out all the different voices, caught words and phrases here and there which she would never have applied to herself in a thousand years – not just beauty, openness, but courage, loyalty, selflessness. 'Stop!' she wanted to shout. 'You've only met me two short hours. You

254

know nothing at all about me. I could be a murderer, a pervert. If you really love me, let me out of this, close your eyes while I slip away, spend the rest of the day on my own with the paper and a stiff drink.'

The voices had died down. Arms reaching out towards her now, fingers touching, hands squeezing. Someone was massaging her back, finding the exact spot where it ached, easing away the pain. Someone else was stroking her hair, gently, rhythmically as if she were a child. She had never been a child – not really – only a soul for God; had never been cuddled, petted, not since she started school. From the age of seven, the nuns had forced her into a mould, tried to stamp out childish weaknesses, substitute the Host for sherbet dabs or Crunchie bars, replace Noddy books with missals. When she cried for Bea at night, they had pointed out that God's love was a Higher Thing than mother love, that evening prayers meant more than goodnight kisses. The nuns never kissed, never touched at all. Physical contact could be dangerous, even with a child. They had to guard against it – encase themselves in full-length black armour, all their vital organs caged in chain mail, helmets on their shaven heads, hearts blocked off with heavy metal crucifixes. They tried to arm their girls as fully – high necks, long sleeves, hearts and larynxes cut out, feet hobbled, hands tied down. St Margaret's girls never ran or shouted, never crossed their legs, never touched each other, never drew attention to themselves. St Margaret's girls were taught to bow to Reverend Mother, curtsey to the priest, submit to grown-ups' judgement, kneel up straight in church, curb their appetites, never skimp their darning, be on constant guard against their bodies, punish them, deprive them, sleep without a pillow.

Martha's chest was a pillow – soft, supporting. Morna longed to sink down into it. That was self-indulgence, though – a weakness, like self-pity. 'Don't touch me,' she whispered silently. 'Please I beg you, don't be kind.' It would only make her cry and crying was another form of selfishness. God hated tears; so had Neil.

She scrubbed at her eyes, tried to pull away from Martha's arms. 'I'm s . . . sorry. I'm so sorry.'

'You go right ahead and cry, honey. You gotta wash the pain out before there's room for love.'

'No . . . No, please. I ought to get back. I t . . . told my friend I . . .'

They didn't understand. They would undo all the good the nuns had done, all those years of self-control, offering up one's grief for God; later years when she hid the pain and shame of divorce behind an impassive wooden mask. Even with David Anthony she had managed not to cry – confessed her loss and misery for the first time in her life, but not all of it, not the cruellest childhood part – then changed the subject, anyway, tried to shrug it off. Better that way. You only embarrassed people by pouring everything out, wallowing in 'poor me'.

'Morna, doll, try and just let go. You're so goddam stiff, it's like someone's encased you in a straitjacket.'

A straitjacket, yes. Punishment for that self-indulgent child who still whimpered for its Daddy, still craved cuddles and attention. She had attention now – more arms than she could count, a circle of bodies pressing warm and close. Dangerous. If she let go, lost control, where would it ever end? Once she started crying, she might never stop. There were years and years of tears to shed – all those cold nights in the dormitory, frightened of the Devil, mornings at breakfast starving herself to free a soul from purgatory; the teenage years when purgatory went up in smoke, along with hell, heaven, God Himself; the whole world as she knew it blown to pieces, leaving her trembling at the crater's edge, staring into void.

She could feel the darkness now. They had locked her in

the Penance Room, Mother Michael switching off the light, turning the key as she stalked away.

'If you doubt God, Anna, you need time on your own with no distraction, nothing to eat or drink, no one else to talk to. You'll find Him then, soon enough.'

'No,' she had pleaded, hammering on the door. 'Let me out! Please, please let me out.'

No one heard. No one came. She could feel the tears sheeting down her face, shaking her whole body.

'I *do* believe!' she shouted. 'I do, I do.'

'Of course you do.'

She stopped in shock. The voice was gentle – not Mother Michael's sackcloth rasp. Someone had unlocked the door, switched the light back on. The dark gloom of the Penance Room was bathed in brilliant sunshine, Mother Michael's scratchy serge transformed to scarlet silk. People were streaming in, kind and careful people with velvet arms scooping her off the cold stone floor, holding her tight so she couldn't fall; soft fleshy people who had taken off their armour so you could sink right into them. She felt herself pressed against bosoms, folded into laps; heard that swansdown voice again.

'You cry, Morna honey, you just cry.'

She cried. They had called her Morna instead of Anne. School must be over, then, Mother Michael dead and buried now, but she went on crying still. She was crying for her father, and her mother who had lost him, too; crying for her daughter, and David Attwood's daughter, for the other David and the miles between them, for the down and outs in Downtown, the old crones in the café, all the old and sick in California. She was unravelling like a piece of knitting, losing her edges and her shape so that she flowed now into everyone, could feel their grief as keenly as her own.

It hurt to cry. Her body was cramped and shaken, legs twisted underneath her, nose blocked, eyes sore and swollen.

She could hear strange animal noises rasping from her own throat, ugly noises which mixed pain and fear.

At last she mopped her eyes, raised her head from the soft and squashy pillow of Martha's chest, stared appalled at the crumpled silk. Her nose had run on to a five-hundred dollar outfit, her tears had spotted it. She tried to find her voice.

'I . . . I really am so s . . . sorry.'

'Don't be sorry, sweetie. We're *glad* you've opened up.'

'Crying's like a safety valve. If you don't let that stuff out, it gets all blocked up inside you.'

'We understand. We've all been through it, too, all cried oceans here.'

Morna blew her nose. They were only being polite. Whatever they said, she must be boring them, embarrassing them, snivelling like a dead-end kid, holding up their meeting.

'I'm all r . . . right now,' she faltered. 'I'm quite all right.'

'Sure you are,' said Martha. 'You're absolutely fine. No, don't move. You've finally relaxed and it feels a whole lot better.'

'B . . . But isn't it time for . . .?'

'It's time for *you*, Morna, honey. We've got all the time you need – all the love you need.'

Morna sank back down. It *wasn't* just politeness. Easy to wince when they used the word love, threw it around so indiscriminately, but now she was experiencing it for herself. Love had always been conditional before – God's love, lost if you transgressed; Neil's love, a four-letter word, animal and urgent, demanding entry, demanding a response. Strokings and caressings had been only strictly sexual, part of a cold-eyed contract. 'I'll hold you if you let me . . .'

These girls voiced no 'ifs', asked nothing in return, got nothing back save aching arms, mussed clothes. They had accepted her completely, messy and dishevelled as she was, a total stranger they might never see again, and who had criticized their theories as mawkish and naïve. She was crying for them as well now – for their naïveté, their simple generous warmth, for Lee-Ann's three failed marriages, Angie's Catholic childhood, Martha's flab. She didn't have a monopoly in grief. They had suffered, too, wept as much as she had. Beneath their bounce and sparkle were the scars of failure and rejection. They simply refused to pick at the scars for ever. Wounds healed, tears dried. She could feel her own slowing up, easing into quiet exhaustion.

'Better?' Martha asked.

She nodded. Vastly better. The nuns had called her rebellious and self-willed. She was also warm, loving, courageous, open, beautiful. These girls had told her so. A winner. A survivor. One in four hundred million.

She sat back on her heels, smoothed her damp and crumpled clothes. One last hand was still stroking her hair – a smaller lighter hand than Martha's. She scrubbed at her eyes, looked round. It was Bunny – her rival – the girl whom Neil loved, who had broken up her marriage, left her daughter fatherless; Bunny tanned, glowing, radiantly young, where she was fading, ageing, tear-stained, superseded.

Morna reached out her arms and hugged her.

The girls didn't leave till nearly dark. Neil and Chris returned from golf soon after, found Morna and Bunny still stretched out on the patio, surrounded by empty glasses, Morna resplendent in the silver string bikini, Bunny in a second one made of tiny shiny beads and strictly not for getting wet.

'Mum, you look obscene!' Chris was wearing Bunny's clothes herself, white jeans and a sweatshirt with HARVARD printed on it, both too big for her. 'You're far too fat to wear that.'

Morna stretched out her legs, admired them. 'No, I'm not, I'm beautiful.'

Bunny giggled. 'Your Mom's as high as a kite.'

'Mum, you're not *drunk*, are you?' Chris snatched up her mother's glass – sniffed it. 'What's this?'

'My second Harvey Wallbanger – what's left of it. They're fabulous! Want me to make you one?'

'No, thanks.'

Neil was already fixing drinks. Morna took her refill, kissed his hand. There were no exes any more. They were all one big happy family. She was merely the old wiser wife, Bunny her kid sister. She had a whole bevy of new siblings – not just the group who had left offering love, support, addresses, invitations – but girls who waited table, mechanics who fixed your car. Men, women, children – she embraced the world.

She stumbled to her feet, squeezed between Neil and Bunny. It was only convention which decreed they should be enemies – just as convention said that January should be cold. Snow was muffling London, but here the warm nuzzling evening caressed her naked skin. Even the dark was made of velvet. She was basking in the stars.

'Do you realize, those are the first stars I've seen since we arrived? The sky seems full of lights from aircraft, but never a single star.'

'I guess you weren't really looking.' Bunny got up to put her robe back on. 'The stars are huge here and fantastically bright. Just look at that one! It's like a frisbee.'

'That's Venus,' Neil said softly.

There was a sudden silence as they all looked up. They could hear the faint plashing of the pool, its silver water reflecting Venus back.

'Just imagine,' Bunny whispered, still gazing at the sky. 'The very same energy that holds those planets up, keeps them going around and around, is inside of us too. We're

260

part of the whole goddam thing. Doesn't that just freak you out?'

Morna nodded. The same energy which had made her win the sperm race – made them *all* winners – Chris, Neil, Bunny, Dean. She could hear Dean pounding down the stairs, bursting on to the patio in blue pyjama bottoms, top still bare. He flung himself at Chris.

'You're back, you're back! You're going to be a beggar-woman.'

'What you talking about?'

'Well, you know I'm going to marry you . . .?'

'You don't let me forget it. I've almost bought the dress.'

'Well . . .' Dean broke off suddenly, rushed across to Morna. 'Can we do it again – Tinker Tailor?'

'You've eaten all the cherries.'

'No, I haven't.' He went to fetch a second bowlful, carried it unsteadily down the steps. Morna got up to help him, took the bowl and placed it on the table, hugged him suddenly, lifted him off the ground and swung him round.

'Again!' he shouted. 'Do it again!'

Twice more and the two of them collapsed dizzy on the lawn. She held him on her lap, felt him warm, clinging. *Her* child. She sorted through the bowl for double stalks of paired cherries, hung them across his lobes as cherry earrings. He tugged them off and ate them, spitting the stones out in her hand.

'Tinker Tailor,' he prompted.

'Tinker, tailor, soldier, sailor, rich man . . . You're going to marry a rich girl, Dean.'

'Sure,' he said. 'She'll be so rich we'll go to Disneyland every single day. Last time I went, Daddy let me go on Space Mountain. It's great. Have you been on Space Mountain?'

'No, I've never been to Disneyland at all.'

'You've never been to Disneyland?' He stared at her, incredulous, a cherry frozen halfway to his mouth.

He wriggled off her lap, rushed across to his mother. 'Mom, can we go to Disneyland with Morna?'

'Yeah, sure. When do you want to go?'

'*Now*!' said Dean, jumping up and down.

'It'll be closed, stupid.' Chris yawned, grabbed a cherry.

'Tomorrow, then, tomorrow.'

14

'*Our hero, Mickey Mouse,*
Our hero, Mickey Mouse.'

Over and over, the loudspeakers thundered out the chorus, which was taken up by the clapping cheering crowd; Mickey Mouse placards processing down the street, Mickey Mouse banners screaming 'Yea, Mickey!' in white and scarlet, Mickey Mouse hats on half the spectators, Mickey Mouse balloons with their hero's ears and smile. And now King Mickey himself, star of the procession, capering on his float, black-ringed pop eyes, white-gloved hands, huge bow tie, spindly legs.

Fifty thousand people worshipping a mouse, a cartoon mouse with fat belly, little brain. Girls turning cartwheels in his honour, men blowing trumpets, bashing drums. A whole army stepping out, uniformed and braided, marching to his tune. Floats before him and behind, bearing all his retinue – his consort Minnie, his acolytes, his outriders – Pluto, Goofy, Donald Duck, Peter Pan, Pinocchio, glass-slippered Cinderella; cheer-leaders, dancing girls, acrobats and clowns, all singing, skipping, cavorting down Main Street, Disneyland. Cameras flashing, balloons popping, streamers tangling in the trees; crowds pushing from behind to get a better view, children hoisted on to shoulders or crawling between legs. Oompa, oompa from the tubas, clash and jingle from tambourines, amplified by brash loudspeakers;

Mickey Mouse's praises echoing through Disneyland's exotic playgrounds – Frontierland, Fantasyland, Bear Country, Adventureland.

Morna mopped the perspiration from her neck. She was wearing a Pluto hat with huge hot ears. Dean had insisted. He had ears himself, Mickey Mouse ones, a Mickey Mouse balloon. He tugged at her hand.

'Isn't it *great*?'

She nodded. It had been – the first three hours. She had been surprisingly impressed with Disneyland, expected a vulgar funfair strewn with litter and reeking of chips, found instead a place so clean and swabbed you could have performed an operation in it. Its paths were shaded with green luxuriant trees and bright with beds of flowers – scarlet cyclamen, blue and yellow pansies, magnolia trees in pink and perfect bloom. Everyone was friendly – guides with names on their lapels – Andy, Cindy, Sue, all with non-wilt smiles; Disney characters wandering around amongst the visitors – Donald Duck stretching out a wing to shake, Snow White blowing kisses.

They had arrived early, seen it at its best, the day still cool and breezy, not a speck of litter in all seventy-seven acres. The crowds soon surged and thronged, the sun began to glare instead of smile. The place was impressive but exhausting. Whichever way you turned, something screamed out its attractions, dazzled your eyes, assaulted your ears, insisted you admire it. They had been on a score of rides already, been snapped at by crocodiles, wrecked by pirates, rocketed into other galaxies, paddled down tropical rivers or ventured into rain forests, screamed with terror in the Haunted Mansion, clung to their hats and stomachs in a runaway mining train. In the space of one short morning, they had moved from night to day and back again, from submarine to moon rocket, from the silent films and gas lamps of Main

Street, 1890, to the twenty-first century's mind-chilling Mission to Mars.

Now Morna felt sated, like a spoilt and fractious child whimpering for its bed. No chance of that yet. Dean seemed indefatigable and Neil and Bunny were obviously determined that she shouldn't miss a thing. It was only early afternoon and the crowds were swelling even thicker, the sun melting ices, faces; trumpets blasting, drums pounding, as the relentless song pumped out. *'Our hero, Mickey Mouse, Our hero . . .'* A new group of cheerleaders kicked and pirouetted along the street, their white frilled panties flashing beneath scarlet mini-skirts.

'I ought to get a job here,' Chris grinned. 'Imagine that on my CV. Pre-university experience – drum majorette to Mickey Mouse!' Chris was walking arm in arm with Neil, relishing her official role as daughter, stockpiling all the goodies he had bought for her and Dean – Snow White pencil sharpeners, fluorescent Goofy golf balls, garish tea towels – trash she would have tossed aside if anyone else had dared insult her with it. Morna had never seen her eat so much before, downing everything Neil bought her – ice-cream cornets, popcorn, frozen banana lollipops on sticks, hot dogs, bags of chips. She tried hard to be glad that they were getting on so well after all the years apart. There was a danger in their closeness, though. In eight short days Chris would be parted from the parent she had only just refound. How would she cope?

It was strange to be with Neil at all, particularly in public – one united family to passers-by – except now it included two children and two wives. He had renounced golf in their honour, bypassed both bar and tennis club, and had been acting full-time father since seven a.m. As far as Wife I was concerned, his mask was still as firmly in place as her own Pluto hat and ears. He spoke to her in clichés, never probed beyond the surface, avoided any reference to the past. Had he *always* worn a mask, she wondered, even when she was the one and only wife, and had she ever really glimpsed the man beneath it? She glanced at him now, immaculate white shirt setting off his dark and well groomed hair, smile vitamin-enriched. Supposing there *wasn't* a man beneath it, just stick-on clothes and features covering a hole? Big Sam had been real enough, but even he existed only an hour or less a day.

She clutched at the post beside her, feeling suddenly disorientated. Fourteen years married to a cut-out, five further years mourning and missing a mask?

'Hey, look!' Neil cried, pushing Dean to the front. 'Snow White and the Seven Dwarfs. Aren't they cute?'

She turned away. Cute was Bunny's word and did he have to laugh so loudly? She didn't even look at the approaching tableau, scared she would yell abuse at an enigma of an ex-husband rather than simper out her praises of Snow White. A week ago, she had contemplated shooting him, struggled with a mixture of angry resentment and aching loss. Now she felt simple irritation. Stupid things had set it off – the way he had bounced up that morning at the crack of dawn and started giving them their orders, masterminding a pleasure trip as if it were a business project, a time-and-motion study; the casual jaunty way he drove his silver Jag – only one hand on the steering wheel, the other tapping out the rhythm of the radio; the fact that he had switched on the radio at all, without checking first that anyone objected to that tumpty-tumpty music, those breathless commercials.

Bunny was right – it was good for exes to meet – not as she thought to heal the scars by grafting new love, but to lance the old wound, drain off any festering love which remained. It was easy to pant for Neil, foment jealousy and passion, when he was completely out of reach and not actually offending her by wearing lemon-tartan trews, or saying 'garbage' and 'bullshit' when he meant 'nonsense' and 'not true'. She realized now she had made her ex-husband increasingly desirable the longer he stayed away, fabricated a subtly different model from the one who actually existed.

She forced her attention back to Mickey Mouse. The procession was almost over now, the last float rumbling down the street, the last tangle of Pied Piper children running and cheering after it, gathering up the streamers, joining in the song.

'That's it,' said Neil, already consulting his guide-book for the next attraction. He had been marshalling them all day, following his master-plan, keeping strict control. 'Right, we've done everything but Fantasyland. This way, kids.' He frisked ahead with Dean and Chris, Morna and Bunny bringing up the rear.

'Isn't this the greatest?' Bunny exclaimed, gazing round at the gold and silver turrets, purple flowers. 'I've been here at least twenty times, but I never get tired of it.'

'Yes, it's . . . fantastic.'

Too fantastic, Morna thought – too much of everything, like the banana splits Neil had bought them all – four scoops each of different coloured ice cream, two whole bananas apiece, hot fudge sauce, swirls of sickly cream. She had closed her eyes a moment, seen David sitting in her Weybridge kitchen, toying with his strawberries, refusing cream and sugar. He would be working now, elbow-deep in books while they stopped to fondle Goofy or have their photos taken between the Mad Hatter and Pooh Bear. She longed to join him, swap this world of candyfloss and sunshine for the bracing cold and spartan regime of his island. Was she just a spoilsport? The others were laughing and joking, trying on each other's hats, acting out the Seven Dwarfs with gestures, jokey voices – Dopey, Sneezy, Sleepy, each in turn. She had larked herself yesterday, but only with the help of Harvey Wallbangers. Walt Disney banned the hard stuff in his dreamland. Just as well, perhaps. She had been drinking far too much since she arrived in California, criticizing Neil for his recourse to the bottle while following his lead. Bunny could fizz without the bubbly, get high on hot fudge sauce or soda pop.

She was fizzing still as they passed through a fairy castle into Fantasyland, exclaiming at everything she saw, as excited as her four-year-old. She and Dean were even dressed the same, both in expensive-looking blue jeans and shirts with tiny hearts on. Bunny had added her usual treasure-trove of rings and chains, dramatic-tinted sunglasses, and a heart-shaped scarlet badge shouting 'LOVE'. They all bore Bunny's stamp, Morna realized, as she glanced around the group. She herself was wearing Bunny's sneakers and had borrowed both a sweat shirt and some socks. Chris was dressed completely à la Bunny, in the Harvard tee shirt she had more or less appropriated and a pair of navy clamdiggers cut off beneath the knee; while Neil was draped with Bunny's jacket and loaded down with her cache of souvenirs.

'I can't see, Daddy! I can't see.' Dean was tugging at his father's arm.

Neil returned the jacket, dumped the souvenirs on Chris, swung Dean up on his shoulders, denimed legs clinging round his neck.

'I'm the king of the castle!' crowed Dean, jigging up and down. 'I'm taller than you now, Chris.'

'No, you're not,' grinned Chris, leaping up on a bench and standing on tiptoe.

Morna yanked miserably at her Pluto hat. Neil had never carried Chris like that, complained she was too heavy when she was a tiny tot of two or three, half the size of Dean at nearly five. He was more indulgent to Dean in every way. Was it because he was a boy, or simply because he was Bunny's child? Both hurt.

'Race you to that flowerbed!' Chris shouted to her father, sprinting off before he could refuse.

'Faster, Daddy, faster!' yelled Dean, drumming his heels against Neil's chest and pretending to ride him like a jockey.

'We won!' he lied, as his father sank panting on to a bench beyond the flowerbed.

'You little pig, you didn't.' Chris was jogging still, round and round the bench, as if working off an excess of energy. She seemed to have become a child again, full of bounce and zip.

'*Did*,' insisted Dean.

'Dead heat,' Neil adjudicated, fanning himself with his map. 'Sit down, Chrissie. We'd better wait for Mummy.'

Which one, wondered Morna, who had caught the remark as she drew level with the bench. Bunny was still chatting to her, explaining how Fantasyland was her number one favourite, except perhaps for Bear Country, and that reminded her – did Morna like zoos, and if so, perhaps they'd take a trip next week to Griffith Park which was the largest municipal park in the whole damn country and had two thousand different animals, not to mention golf and horseback riding and bars and restaurants and an Olympic-sized pool and a real Greek theatre and . . .

Morna mumbled something noncommittal. There was enough to look at here, without a zoo and Aeschylus thrown in as well. The animals in Fantasyland were more the plush or plastic variety – a huge green Dumbo with aerodynamic ears, the Three Little Pigs dressed in caps and britches. Morna glanced around her – comic-hatted grown-ups spinning round in giant-sized cups and saucers, the Mad Hatter's Tea Party brought to crazy life. Above them towered the Matterhorn, fourteen storeys of concrete, five hundred tons of steel, yet looking like another enchanted castle. You could bob-sled through its icy caverns, the brochure promised, race past glaciers and waterfalls, meet the Abominable Snowman.

'I'll sit this one out, I think,' said Morna.

'Chicken!' Chris accused.

Morna found a bench while the others joined the queue. It was true that she was scared. She had already lost her nerve in hair-raising Tomorrowland, found herself gripping the edge of the rocket ship or submarine, praying for deliverance, while everyone around her revelled in the thrills, Chris shouting louder than them all. She had never seen her daughter so relaxed before. She envied her, envied Bunny, envied the whole happy carefree crowd. Was she the only one among the hundred thousand visitors who was locked in her head instead of joining in the fun, checking her watch rather than letting time fly by as Peter Pan was flying over Disney's version of romantic moonlit London? There were queues for everything (including Peter Pan) – slow and shuffling queues which seemed to move as slowly as the prehistoric monsters they had seen in another part of the park. Yet no one else appeared to mind. Queues were part of the excitement, building expectation in their inch-by-inch approach to some new wonder or sensation. Only Morna Gordon found them tedious.

Was that why Neil had left her – not just the sex, but her poker face, her endless analysing, her refusal to unbend in bed and out? She tried to push the thought away. Disneyland was the Happiest Place on Earth – she had seen it written on a poster in huge official letters – so how could she be anything but happy? The trouble was they had tried too hard, laid on too many goodies and distractions. The guide-book was full of figures – boasting firsts, five-star superlatives. A thousand candles in the Christmas Day procession, three thousand lights on the sixty-foot Christmas tree, over three hundred thousand vinyl leaves and blossoms on the Swiss Family Robinson Tree-House, twenty million dollars to construct the two-hundred-foot Space Mountain.

David had one sleeping-bag, one rusty paraffin lamp, one

staling loaf, two pairs of jeans, and a stretched-to-the-limit research grant. She shut her eyes against the three-billion-watt sun. She would spend the next half hour with him in a cooler, quieter place.

'Did you see us? Did you see us?' Dean came racing, shouting back. 'We went right inside the mountain. Look! I'm all wet from the waterfall.'

'It was great,' said Chris, still shadowing her father. 'Really fast and scary. You'd have hated it. Right, Mum, your turn now. What d'you want to go on?'

'Something quiet and gentle, please.'

Chris consulted the guide. 'How about Storybookland? "Wish upon a star," it says, "and your wish comes true." Yuk! Or how do you fancy Sleeping Beauty's Castle? "Wake the princess with a kiss." '

Morna made a face.

'Wait – I've found something really gungy. "It's a Small World", it's called. Listen and I'll read it out. "Join the world's enchanting children on the happiest cruise that ever sailed. All the wonder, excitement and happiness of youth overflows in a musical fantasy trip around the globe, as these gay and carefree youngsters bring a smile into your . . ." '

'Oh, it's absolutely darling,' Bunny interrupted. 'I went on it last summer. You ride in a boat, and hundreds of little puppets dressed in national costume sing this real cute song in all the different languages. You'll love it, Morna. Quick – let's get in line.'

The queue was the longest yet. They snailed towards the white and golden castle, its gleaming turrets banked with flowers, its hedges and bushes cut in the shapes of animals and birds – waltzing hippos, waddling ducks. Morna checked her book again. More statistics. Three hundred handmade toys decorated with a hundred and ninety-five pounds of glitter, fifty-seven gross of jewels, three hundred and seventy yards of braid; every costume authentic; every detail researched. Neil was explaining the wonders of the clock which flanked the entrance. It almost deserved a guide-book to itself with its parade of toys, its pulsating springs and cogs, its drum tattoo and trumpet fanfare.

'After this,' he said, 'we'll see if we can get in for Fantasy Follies. Right?'

'Right' was another of his catchwords. Everything was right so long as he decided it. Dean was still sitting on his shoulders, cock of the walk.

'Quick! Put me down,' he shouted. 'It's our turn now.'

They had reached the entrance and the string of boats, clambered into the first one, were swept along a winding riverway which washed through the castle itself. They had entered a new world – a world of greenish light and turquoise water, flanked by fantastic coloured vistas of lakes and mountains, flowers and fiords. Shrill and piping voices rose from every side where smiling puppets twirled and pirouetted, jerking to Walt Disney's string as the boat meandered through the Seven Seaways, cruising first to Europe, then on to all the other continents and countries.

> '*It's a small world,*' they warbled,
> '*A world of laughter, a world of tears;*
> *A world of hopes and a world of fears.*'

A pity, Morna reflected, that they hadn't spent less on the glitter and the braid, and more on a decent lyricist. The song sounded better in Norwegian, when she couldn't understand the words. Not that they needed a translator, the sentiments were obvious – cosy joy, universal brotherhood, hands joined across Berlin Walls and barbed-wire boundaries, a smile on every face, be it black or brown or yellow. Piccaninnies beamed among woolly lions and papier-mâché tigers; bewitching Russians in brilliant national costume banged nothing more dangerous than drums;

Chilean tots in ponchos sang of peace and plenty as they bobbed and curtseyed; Pole and Russian, Jew and Arab breathed concord and fraternity.

She had heard on the news that morning of fresh fighting in Beirut, more deaths in Afghanistan, an international squabble over the administration of famine relief while famine itself increased. The enchanting children of Chad and Ethiopia, Bangladesh, Brazil, were squalling with hunger in mosquito-infested slums, not singing and dancing in universal harmony. Disneyland had cost two hundred million dollars to set up, enough to feed those gaping mouths. Over two hundred million people had already visited it, but that still left the other four thousand million of the world's groaning population, who might find more pressing uses for the fifteen-dollar entrance fee. And what about America's own poor, the ones queuing now outside a soup kitchen for a plate of cabbage and a hunk of bread, rather than waiting in line for a magic castle ride?

'Oh, look!' cried Bunny. 'Isn't that just darling?'

A cluster of crocodiles were snapping their lethal jaws in winning smiles, a man-eating tiger in spats and fez strumming a banjo. Morna tried to force a smile herself. Couldn't she just enjoy the ride, for heaven's sake? She was becoming a bore, a prig, if not a downright hypocrite. She was one of those two hundred million visitors herself, so what right had she to pontificate or criticize? She let the sugar-plum world slip past – flowers which never faded, years with no winters and no droughts; a small world where only children lived, only pretty happy tots. Up and down they glided, round and round, the song near-hypnotic now as it was repeated over and over.

> *'There's so much that we share*
> *That it's time we're aware*
> *It's a small world after all.'*

273

Morna winced at the limp scansion, began to recompose the words herself, was interrupted by the second verse.

'There's just one moon and one golden sun . . .'

That at least she couldn't dispute. She let her hand trail in the water. Why did she keep mocking? Dean was revelling in the ride, jumping up and down on his seat, shrieking with laughter at duck-billed platypuses or purple kangaroos. Couldn't she follow his example, become a child again? Yesterday she had wept for her lost and loveless childhood. Here was a chance to savour an enchanted one, if only for ten minutes – all the wonder, excitement and happiness of youth as promised in the brochure, without sin or rules or devils; a united singing world free of poverty and war. Disney had created an ideal, one which she could share if she left her carping mind behind. At the opening ceremony, real-life children from around the world had each brought a jug of water from the seas and rivers of their native lands to pour into his symbolic Seven Seaways. Her hand might be floating now in water from the Nile or the South Pacific, a Venetian lagoon or the ice-bound Arctic Ocean, even from the straits near David's island.

'Though the mountains divide
And the oceans are wide
It's a Small World after all.'

She shut her eyes as the song began again, warbled now by the children of Japan. All the waters of the world were merging into one another, tropical rivers thawing northern seas, tiny streams swelling into huge and boundless oceans. God (or Walt) was rubbing out the boundaries between all the different countries, as if they were mere pencil marks in a child's school jotter instead of gun-defended battle lines.

Dean submerged her hand with his own, splashed her face with water. 'Wake up, Dozy! We're almost at the end.'

Morna looked up, saw all the world's children coming together in a final curtain call, no longer divided by colour, race or creed. She watched cowboy dance with Indian, Turk line up with Greek, Iraqi woo Iranian. Dean was humming the tune – Neil's and Bunny's son, her son, joined with every other child on earth.

'Know what?' he said, breaking off.

'What?'

'Daddy's going to buy me the record. If you stay at my house, I'll play it for you every single day.'

'Gee, thanks,' said Morna, as they emerged from the green glow of the water to the blazing sun outside – from Utopia back to Anaheim.

'Where next?' Chris asked, before she was barely out of the boat.

'The Fantasy Follies,' Neil reminded, consulting his map so that he could frog-march them towards it. 'There's a show beginning in just about ten minutes.'

'No!' yelled Dean. 'Not yet. I want to go to the Tinkerbell Toy Shop first. You can buy Pluto suits there and . . .'

'*I* need the ladies' room,' said Morna.

'It must be all that water,' Bunny giggled. 'We'll meet you in the store, okay? I don't mind waiting in line for rides, but not for calls of nature.'

A whole hour later Morna was still standing in the toyshop, on her own. Bunny and Co. had vanished. She had searched every inch of the store for them, scoured the other shops in Fantasyland, returned to the Matterhorn, scanned the queues of people, wandered round the Sleeping Beauty's Castle, checked the canal boats, motorboats, every ride and stall.

Once again, she retraced her steps to the rest room in case they had gone to find her there. The usual press of people, but only strangers. She pushed forlornly through the milling crowds. How could you believe in one small united world when you were lost in a huge and alien one? The barbed-wire barriers were up in place again, not only between countries, but between individual groups. 'Keep off! You don't belong,' Disneyland was built for happy families, not for jaundiced singles. No one else appeared to be alone, no one anxious, fretting, traipsing back and forth. She remembered an actress friend remarking once that every individual was only an extra or a walk-on in everyone else's play. She was no more than just a blur, a splash of colour, to all these passing faces, a minuscule fraction of one of the tiny noughts in that tramping two hundred million.

She spotted a blonde head, raced after it shouting 'Bunny!' It turned round. A wrinkled face of fifty-odd, bleeding fuchsia-coloured lipstick on to a vanilla ice-cream cone. Morna muttered an apology, stumbled on again. Anger began to jab between the worry and fatigue. Were they making any effort to search for *her*, or too busy making whoopee, buying trinkets? She turned on her heel, walked the other way, checked Main Street once again, clambering up on a bench so that she could get a better view of all the faces. Every type of hat, every colour of skin and cast of feature except the ones she sought. She glanced down at Disney's own face grinning on the cover of the brochure. He was shown amongst a group of kids, hugging the smallest and cutest, smiling on the rest, the universal uncle dispensing human happiness. The reality was darker. Walt had been something of a tyrant, his successors more so – benevolent dictators who insisted on rewriting history. All biographies of their chief were censored, the slightest breath of criticism expunged. When one irreverent writer dared to reveal that Disney couldn't draw his own Mickey Mouse, or reproduce the famous signature, his book was refused the imprimatur. Even the Disney 'villains' were sweetened and sanitized. Bad-tempered ducks or buck-toothed hounds posed no problems, but to suggest that the Queen in *Snow White* might be sadistic or castrating would be blatant heresy. Both sex and sadism were forbidden entry here. It was like Bunny's group – all saccharine and silver linings. She had let herself be taken in by them in a storm of self-indulgent tears. Their whole religion was self-indulgent – self-growth, personal development, the well-fed God inside. It was too narrow, too excluding, like Disneyland itself.

Yesterday she had seen it very differently, had floated off to bed in a blaze of light and love. Perhaps she was just suffering from a hangover, the Harvey Wallbangers exacting their revenge. No – she had woken up feeling bright and energetic, newly born, glowing with the group's good vibes; had stayed the night at Neil and Bunny's so she would be ready to set off early in the morning; had even cooked the breakfast for them all – waffles swamped in syrup, eggs sunny side up.

So what had soured the sweetness, fused the light? Why this adolescent change of mood, this growing desolation, when the sun was still shining, the playground in full swing? True, it was no fun to lose one's party, but it wasn't tragedy. They would hardly drive off without her, so she could always return to the car, wait for them there.

She doubled back to Tomorrowland. That was Dean and Chris's favourite, with all the hairy rides. She would have one last look and if she didn't find them there, she'd make her way to the car park. She gazed up at the purring monorail, the white cathedral spires of space mountain, the rocket jets whirling up and round. Tomorrowland – and not a bomb in sight. Rockets here meant kiddies' rides, not weapons of extinction. Walter Elias Disney had wanted people to forget the real world when they walked into his wonderland. But wasn't that a sham? LA was built of sham – a city of façades with its false stucco porches and pseudo-Grecian pasteboard pillars concealing violence and squalor.

More murders in a week in Tinsel Town than Japan had in a year, and Japan had a population of one hundred and eighteen million. Yet this was called the Happiest Place on Earth – just twenty miles from Downtown's screeching sirens and bloody gunfights. If you dropped your candy wrapper, it would be picked up in an average time of one minute forty seconds, but who picked up the casualties outside these seventy-seven acres – the butchered bodies which Uncle Walt preferred you to ignore?

Nothing was what it seemed. She had gone on a tour of a Hollywood film studio, seen portable trees which could be 'planted' anywhere, portable lampposts plugged in like bedside lamps, the Red Sea parting at the flick of a switch, blazing houses which never actually burnt down, fake floods, fake storms, fake earthquakes. She had left the place in the pouring rain, emerged into a real flood. The weather itself was crazy, changing from storm to sun and back again, the whole Pacific area in flux, beaches swept away, piers snapping in half like chocolate bars, crops ruined, homes dumped in the ocean.

She trudged on, searching every corner, seeing every child in the world save Dean and Chris, every entwined and happy couple but Neil and Bunny. Perhaps they were *glad* to lose her, had slipped away on purpose. She was hardly the best of company, surrounded as she was by Disney's wonders, yet focusing only on her black and bitter thoughts. California was beautiful, a playground and a paradise, and she could only grouch, revile it as an Armageddon. No wonder Neil had left her, replaced her with a fun wife, someone simple and spontaneous who wouldn't know what Armageddon was and certainly couldn't spell it if she did.

Bitch, she accused herself. Okay, so she could spell, but she didn't have a scrap of Bunny's kindness. Even Chris had warmed to it, had made a friend of Bunny despite her initial reservations. She herself had hardly spoken to her daughter

– not in private, anyway. There wasn't any private now. Chris had changed camps, joined Neil's new family – the young and pretty wife and two standard sun-kissed children of the television commercials. Why should they need *her* in tow – a sourpuss and an ex, unbalancing the numbers, clouding over the sun?

'*Stop* it!' she almost shouted at herself. Self-pity was worse than bitchiness and she was so absorbed in it, she was blind to her surroundings, had come to a halt in the middle of a busy thoroughfare, people bumping into her, a woman with a pushchair trying to squeeze by. She forced herself to wander on, keep her attention focused outward. She passed the Circle-Vision Theatre and the Peoplemover, found herself standing in front of a ride they hadn't sampled yet – Adventure Through Inner Space. Dean had dismissed it, preferred outer space to inner, had been begging for a second dose of Space Mountain.

'Travel through a microscope,' she read. 'Discover the thrilling world of the atom.' She joined the queue, intrigued. Something small for once. She would leave the biggest and the brightest and crawl inside what had once been considered the ultimate particle of matter – a truly small world, not a pastel-coloured bogus one full of simpering marionettes.

Chris had studied Physics up to O level and she had dipped into her daughter's text-books with a sort of chastened astoundment at what she found. The tiniest speck of dust visible to the naked eye contained more than a thousand million million atoms, and the nucleus of each of them, while taking up ninety-nine point nine five of the mass, occupied only $1,000,000,000,000,000$th of the volume.

Noughts like that almost brought her God back, or suggested a different sort of God, white-coated with a test-tube in His hands. And yet for all the statistics, there was still nothing you could grasp. Atoms had no substance, no appearance – not in the usual sense of the words. David had said that modern physics was seen to be drawing close to Eastern mysticism – elusive, paradoxical, with more questions than answers, and inapprehensible concepts which left you both marvelling and aghast. It was the same with modern mathematics. Easier really to be a Sister Cyril, believe God made the world in seven days, and that heaven was up, hell was down, and science dangerous if it made you doubt your faith.

The queue was moving faster now. Morna had almost reached the string of little cabs.

'It's not scary, is it?' she asked the man in charge. That was Dean's word.

'No,' he drawled. 'You could take your great-grandmother on this one.'

The cabs were made for two, joined one behind the other like a train. She stepped in on her own, the only single, gripped the pushbar as they began to move away.

They clanked up an incline and into the gaping mouth of a huge black microscope which plunged them into darkness. The cab was gathering speed, hurling along its roller-coaster rail, a deep distorted voice booming from the soundtrack. Morna could hear only a disorientating roar, with no coherent words. Surely something had fouled up – the electronics shorted, the mechanics about to fail? She clung to the bar in fear. In some of the other frightening rides, she had cowered damp-palmed and quaking, realizing that if she fainted, panicked, no one could get her out until the ride stopped. But there, at least, she had had the others with her – someone to grab her if she lost consciousness or . . . Here she was alone. The people in the cabs in front and behind had simply vanished, been swallowed up in the darkness and the roar. She was truly lost now, had entered some dark underworld. The soundtrack was still jarring on, but she could hear mainly echo and vibration, a rude backfire of sound. She forced herself to concentrate, caught

280

a few discordant phrases. 'Single crystal', 'a snowflake's perfect symmetry . . . something, something . . .'

She shut her eyes a moment as the cab made a sudden lurching dive, opened them to dazzling white. She was staring into the shining blinding faces of a hundred snow-flakes, growing slowly larger as she herself shrank in scale.

The disembodied voice was coming clearer now. 'Still we continue to shrink,' it said, and the snowflakes expanded even further until they were towering all around her in a glittering wall of ice. Despite her own dwindling size, her sight appeared to have sharpened so that she was aware of details never glimpsed before; gazed astounded at every multi-faceted crystal of each gigantic flake.

'And now,' boomed the voice, 'we go right inside the snowflake, enter one of its water molecules.'

Morna clung to the side of the cab, surprised to find it solid. She had lost her own solidity, lost her shape and outline as they zoomed into a world of orbiting spheres, hazy whirling patterns. She heard the voice explaining, caught the words 'nucleus', 'electrons'; lost them again as she seemed to spin and circle with the ever-changing spirals. Words were losing their shape as well; were too trivial, too earth-bound, to have any relevance to this dizzying dance of the spheres.

'Smaller still,' the voice continued. 'As we enter the oxygen atom within the molecule, pierce its wall, go right inside of it.'

Morna gasped as she was rocketed into an entire new solar system, a huge red sun blazing in the centre with countless tiny stars shooting and sparking round it, confusing the mind as they dazzled the eyes. This soaring cosmos was in fact so minuscule that it would have made a pinhead look like St Peter's dome, yet it had dwarfed her into nothing, dazed and overawed her. In the flotation tank, she had seen the world as infinitesimally small. Now she saw that every one of its trillion atoms was ineffably vast, and yet the two were indistinguishable. Small and large had somehow merged, defying definitions – infinity not in a grain of sand, but in the millionth part of a millionth of a grain; mocking fractions with its complex teeming nothingness. This was the Order in the world, this whirling turbulent confusion; this was omnipotence, one single atom in a single molecule. She shaded her eyes against the seething ferment of the red-balled sun. She had found the time which she had lost in the tank, except it wasn't time, but distance, force. And now there was only distance, the vast unfathomable distance to that red sun of the nucleus from the smallest electron-star, a journey across endless space and void.

She heard the voice again, faint and puny now as if it were already light years distant. 'We dare not enter the nucleus,' it warned, 'as there can be no return from there.'

She ignored the warning, slumped back in her seat, let her hands relax. She had to be comfortable for so long and strange a journey.

15

'Mix 8oz suet with an equal quantity of breadcrumbs moistened with milk. Stir in 6oz of raisins and as many nuts as you can spare and . . . and . . .'

And *what*? Bea peered closer, took her glasses off, polished them on the corner of her apron, then put them back again. The recipe seemed blurred still. She would have to make an appointment with the optician, get some stronger lenses. She stirred in chopped cashews and hazelnuts, a dash more milk. So many things blurred as you got older – even God. His photo frame was empty still, had remained so since the operation. She had been doing exercises to make her bladder stronger, but her faith was still weak and saggy. She went to Mass as always, said her prayers, but there was an increasing frightening sense of no one there. She hadn't breathed a word to any of her friends. How could she? They were God's friends first, would all be horrified. She was horrified herself – kept trying to suppress the doubts. If God really wasn't there, then all those years and years of chatting to Him, serving Him, building her life round His, had simply been a delusion. Worse than that – there would be no afterlife, which meant no chance of being reunited with her husband. She had always lived in hope of that, old age not feared or dreaded because it would bring her nearer to him, was only a passing stage in any case. They would rise again with young and shining bodies, Edward's shattered bits made whole, she a girl again, blushing as he took her arm, led her round the tranquil paths of heaven. No fighter planes. No war.

Now things looked rather different. Old bodies getting older, rotting away in the cold and lonely earth. No – mustn't think like that. It was probably just a stage, a sticky patch, perhaps a trial sent by God Himself. Father Clarke had preached once about the dark night of the soul when God kept His distance and everything seemed flat and pointless. It wasn't just a night, though. Over half a year now since she had first felt that emptiness. It had been worse at the retreat house, way back in July, surrounded by all those kindly pious people who were still in touch with God, walked arm in arm with Him, shared meals and news with Him, and she a fraud amongst them. She had taken to her bed – not just with post-operative depression as she had let Reverend Mother think. A few stitches in a womb or bladder wall were nothing compared with a whole lifetime cut away. Her new friend, Madge, had had a total hysterectomy, ovaries as well. She and Madge had met at the retreat, first got friendly swapping operations, then gone on to swap addresses, found they lived quite close. Now she saw Madge every week. They had discussed most things except the most important one. Madge's life was set in God as firmly as a gemstone in a brooch, so how could she confess that her own brooch had lost its pearl, was only an empty metal clasp? They had been back to the retreat house at least a dozen times for days of prayer or weekend scripture courses. She felt more and more uneasy being greeted as a friend there, valued as a regular, had tried to find excuses not to go. Madge had also roped her in to parish work – running church bazaars, organizing missions, visiting Catholic children in hospitals and orphanages. She would have to put a stop to it. It was hypocritical playing the pious committed Catholic and crusader, when she wasn't even sure if . . . The trouble was it would leave a gap, a hole she couldn't fill. She

284

had to admit she'd been enjoying the activities, the sense of being busy, even needed. Life without God was like a cake without fruit – dry and savourless. She had her daughter, of course, and granddaughter, but they were busy with their own lives. Dreadful to be a burden. That was the advantage with a God. You could never be a burden to Him, however old you grew.

She stoned some dates and chopped them, sprinkled them with flour, added them to the bowl. She had been worrying over Morna. She hadn't been herself for weeks, seemed restless and unsettled, didn't always answer when you spoke. And now she was away on that crazy Californian trip, which was undignified as well as dangerous, and very bad for Chris. She would have to keep an eye on Chris, with her mother so distracted – though she saw less and less of the child. She was always out with Martin, or busy with her books, and if she were going to start commuting to America to see a father who couldn't be bothered to do the travelling himself, then they would be parted still more often. That was the trouble – people didn't need her now, and if God also kept His distance, then . . .

Damn! She had added too much milk and the mixture had gone soggy. She crumbled in more breadcrumbs to soak up all the liquid, lined a tin with greaseproof, scribbled 'greaseproof' on the shopping list. The roll was almost empty. She had used it up last week making twenty quiches for Madge's charity bazaar. Father Clarke had bought a couple himself, complimented her on the lightness of her shortcrust. He was the one she should confide in. 'Go to your priest,' people always said when you had some spiritual problem. Father Clarke was a friend and guest as well, though. How could you admit that you thought you'd lost your Faith to a man who praised your pastry? Anyway, he would never take it in. She had been a pillar of his parish for as long as she remembered, couldn't pull that pillar down, watch his face collapse – especially now, when he'd only just recovered from a cancer scare. The cyst had proved benign, in fact, but he still looked pale and drawn, as if the week of uncertainty had aged him several years. He was older than she was anyway, perhaps already thinking about leaving to join his Maker. How could she suggest that there might not *be* a Maker? It would be cruel as well as tactless. He had always comforted *her*. '*He that believeth in Me, although he die, shall live* . . .' She had often imagined the three of them – Edward, herself and her favourite priest – lazing in deck chairs on the lawns of heaven with someone else to weed the beds, make the tea and cakes. But what if she *didn't* believeth?

She had chatted with him that morning after Mass, but not about faith or afterlives – only about the value of including recipes in the parish magazine and whether the tea urn in the church hall had sprung a leak or not. He had been leaning on a stick, his frail white wisps of hair no longer covering the patch of shiny scalp which looked pink and flushed like a well-scrubbed baby's bottom. 'God bless you,' he had said, and she had almost cried wishing that He would – or even curse her. Anything to prove He was still there. Doubts felt worse on Sundays. There were more people in the church, more false smiles to hand out with the pamphlets on Church Aid and Foreign Missions; all the congregation flocking out asking how she was, having no idea that everything had fallen – not just her womb, but her whole world.

She gave one last stir to the mixture, then transferred it to the tin, put it in the oven, removed her apron. Now what? It would take at least an hour to cook and she couldn't sit there in the gloom fretting over God, worrying about Morna. She fetched Morna's letter, Chris's cards, sat down in the drawing-room, re-read them for the twentieth time. Chris was all right, Morna not, though her daughter had pre-

286

tended. All those 'fines' rang hollow – she knew that from her own case. Ironic, really, that she was experiencing her daughter's doubts, only at the age of nearly seventy instead of seventeen. Twenty years ago she hadn't understood, had been angry, even, censorious, labelled doubt as sin. Now she realized it was more a sort of illness, something which just *happened*, had to be endured – the pain, the fears about the future, the sleepless nights. She glanced at her watch. A quarter to eleven. She ought to be asleep now, not making cakes – but no point tossing and turning when sleep was so unkind, kept away.

She buttoned up her cardigan, pulled the sleeves right down. It was chilly in the drawing-room. She had to economize, keep the heating low, light the fire only for visitors. It was the worst part of winter when they had already shivered through three months of cold and dark, with another two to come. The cold made her arthritis worse, stiffened up her joints. Pain was like the doubts – always there, always nagging, sharper sometimes, and occasionally so bad she almost panicked. Pain and God were linked. You bore it for Him willingly because He had died for you. But supposing He . . .?

She fetched another woolly from the hall, put it on. It would be warm in bed, of course. But she hated lying in the dark, trying to pass the time by saying the rosary – decade after decade, every Hail Mary sounding more hollow and hypocritical than the last. Mind you, it was gloomy even here, with half the lamps turned off. She could hear the wind whining outside the windows like a dog shut out. They had forecast gales tonight in the South, snow in the North. She hated wind – the way it blew the walnut tree against the kitchen window, made the front door rattle. She glanced around the room. The furniture was closing in on her, dark and heavy pieces inching closer. Ridiculous! She was just imagining things. Strange, though, how after ten o'clock the

287

house appeared to change its usual sunny character, become gradually more sullen and bad-tempered the longer she stayed up. She wished she could phone a friend, hear another human voice. They would all be in bed by now, or getting ready for it; Madge at the retreat house sharing a room with a stranger. She should have gone with Madge, booked a double room as she'd suggested. Easier to lie awake when someone else was there, even someone snoring. But she couldn't face ten days, half of them in silence; a retreat called Taking Stock. She had been Taking Stock for far too long, not finding any answers. And Hilden Cross seemed more and more depressing. Bad food and shabby rooms were of no importance so long as God were there. But if you were simply filling time, filling holes . . .

She refolded Morna's letter, returned it to its envelope. Morna was clever and hadn't found the answers, so what hope was there for *her*? She had never been a brainy type and the world had grown increasingly confusing. First they had changed the money, then the weather. She still thought in terms of shillings and half-crowns. And when that chappie on the forecast said six degrees centigrade, it always sounded colder than it would in Fahrenheit, and by the time she'd worked it out, she had missed the 'general outlook' and couldn't plan her clothes for the next day. And as for those new thermometers – well, you never had a fever on them, however ill you felt. Schools were different, too. Boys and girls in tee shirts and blue jeans, and chips for lunch or Mars bars instead of grey flannel and rice pudding. And the things the children studied had never even existed in her day and no one learnt their tables any longer. It was all machines and calculators, or worse still, those computer things which they kept warning you would change the world and were probably dangerous anyway. She didn't *want* her world changed, preferred the old and safe one where God pressed all the switches and the only printout was the Ten Commandments.

The clock struck the quarter-hour. Still eight hours till dawn – four hundred and eighty minutes. At least she could multiply without a calculator – couldn't be senile yet. She stretched her legs in front of her. Not bad, either. Still slim, still decent shaped. She could hear Joy snoring in her basket on the stairs. She snored like Madge, unevenly, with little rasping grunts every second snore. Nice to have her there, snuggled on her lap – Joy, not Madge. Madge was too big and bony for anybody's lap. She smiled to herself. 'God bless Madge,' she whispered. 'Keep her safe.' Maybe He was listening. Somewhere. She had to believe for Joy's sake. A heaven for dogs with not just lawns and deckchairs, but a whole wild park beyond, nonstop trees and lamp-posts, new exciting smells, and her own legs and heart rejuvenated so a walk could last two hours or more, instead of a puffing twenty minutes.

Well, she had better check her cake, turn the oven down. She eased up, smoothed her skirt, jumped when the doorbell rang. No one called this late. Best ignore it. You read so much about muggers – people pretending to read meters or sell brushes who coshed you on the head just as you were picking out your matching dustpan. No one sold anything at eleven o'clock at night, though, and the electricity board never worked past five. Bea stood stock still where she was, closed her eyes. She could see that picture in her prayer book of Christ standing knocking at the door, holding a lamp, His brown eyes sad, yet very bright like a bird's. Morna had told her that it had been painted by Holman Hunt, which hadn't meant a lot, except she discovered later he wasn't a Catholic which seemed a pity when the picture was so good. Underneath was written 'Behold, I stand at the door and knock. If any man hear My voice and open the door, I will come unto him and sup with him.'

That would be nice – to have Christ turn up for supper. Not that she'd got much food in. No point when she was on her own with Chris and Morna away. She had always given Father Clarke plain and homely food – Irish stew (he came from Donegal), apple pie and custard. But you couldn't serve Irish stew to God and certainly not custard. He'd be used to more elaborate fare – salmon trout or crown roast of lamb, with profiteroles to follow and a decent pâté to start with, maybe duck or chicken-liver. She had a *tin* of pâté, but that really wasn't the same. She also had eggs and bacon. If she added Joy's lamb chop and piece of kidney, she could call it Mixed Grill. Mixed Grill was on the menu of even the very best of restaurants and they had served it in Edward's Mess (with English mustard in a solid silver jar and cranberry sauce for the Group Captain who was known to be eccentric).

The bell rang a second time. She *was* getting senile, planning a meal for Jesus with a mugger at the door. Christ had knocked, in any case, not rung. Mind you, it was a very gentle ring, what you'd call a meek one, not a mugger's brazen peal. It hadn't even woken the dog, though she had to admit Joy was going deaf. Between the two of them, they were losing all their faculties. Maybe it was Madge, come all the way back to fetch her. Well, she wouldn't go. She had made a decision and she was going to stick to it. In fact, she would have to pluck up courage and speak to Madge as soon as she returned – admit her doubts, cut down her activities to strictly non-religious ones, refuse to play the hypocrite. She would lose a friend most likely – a dear and valuable friend who had a car and two adorable Skye terriers as well as a loving heart. She would also lose the whole shape and point and purpose to her life. But what was the alternative?

She inched into the hall, saw a head silhouetted in the pane of glass set in the front door. Not Madge's grizzled dishmop, but a man's head, dark and sleek.

'Joy!' she called, trembling. The dog might be deaf, but she wasn't dumb, could still scare a postman or a thug.

'Who's there?' she shouted, above the crescendoing bark.

No answer save for a second round from Joy. This was when you really longed to pray, to have a God to call on to save you from a flick knife or a cosh. 'Lord, I am unworthy. I know I doubt You, but if You're there, please send the brute away.'

Everyone was deaf – God, the mugger, the nice young couple next door. The face was pressed against the glass now, nose squashed like a mongol's.

'Wh . . . Who is it?' she called again, cowering in the shadow of the tallboy, voice trembling now itself.

'Only me, Martin.'

'*Martin!*'

Martin never called without Chris, and even with her, had been there only twice, sitting silent both times with his back hunched and his long legs stretched in front of him, so that she had almost tripped on them bringing in the tea. Bea opened the door a crack. Perhaps it was a trick, or a different Martin, a Jack-the-Ripper Martin.

No. It was Chris's Martin, dressed in that strange black leather thing he always seemed to wear and holding his crash helmet by the strap as if it were a pail.

'Wh . . . What's wrong? Is Chris all right? There hasn't been an accident? You haven't come to tell me . . .?'

'Course not. I was just passing on my way back from my mate's. Saw your lights on, so I thought I'd . . .' Martin's voice tailed off. His face was pinched with cold, his nose red and running slightly.

'Come in, dear. You look half-perished. Like a cup of tea?'

'Yeah, I'd love one. Thanks.'

'Come into the kitchen and I'll put the kettle on. Leave that thing in the hall. Down, Joy! *Friend*, Joy. That's right, let her sniff you, and she'll settle down. You like your tea strong, don't you? With two sugars?'

'Please.'

291

She wondered why he had come. He couldn't just be passing when her house was in a cul-de-sac. She wished he would fill the silence, say something, anything, not just sort of stand there, shuffling from foot to foot and blowing on his fingers.

'Sit down, dear. It's warm in here. You shouldn't drink strong tea at night, you know. It stops you sleeping. I've got Ovaltine, if you prefer. Or Horlicks. No? I'll have Ovaltine. I've stopped drinking tea in the evenings – not that it seems to help.'

She was rambling on. Shy or silent people always made her garrulous. She must be boring him. But what did you say to nineteen-year-old boys? Or was he twenty? He'd had a birthday, hadn't he? Yes. She remembered Chris telling her she'd miss it.

'Happy birthday, Martin, for last week. How did you enjoy it?'

'It was all right, I s'pose.'

'Did your mother make you a cake?'

'No. Chris did.'

'What, before she went away?'

'Yeah.'

'That was kind.'

'Mm.'

Silence again, save for the spasms of the kettle as it panted to the boil. Martin suddenly lurched up, joined her at the hob.

'That's . . . er . . . really what I came about. I mean, I . . . wondered if you'd heard from them?'

'Oh yes, dear. Morna phoned the minute they arrived and I had a card from Chris within the week. A pretty one with palm trees and an orange sky. She said they're really orange over there, the sunsets.'

'C . . . Can I see it?'

'Of course. I've got another one as well, from Chris.

Malibu, it says. Odd name, isn't it? They went there for a visit, saw the house where Bunny lived as a child. Her mother bred dachshunds, so Chris said. They had eight at one time, all living in the house. Isn't that nice? I'll just fill the teapot and I'll get both the cards.'

She wished Chris had written a letter, a long one like she used to as a child, not just those few scrawled lines. She checked the cards before showing them to Martin, to make sure there was nothing private or embarrassing. She didn't really like him reading them at all. They were all she had of Chris at present, and the boy had dirty hands.

She passed them over, wondered why he took so long to read four sentences. Mind you, Chris's writing left a lot to be desired. Perhaps he was having trouble in deciphering them.

'What did *you* get, dear?' she asked at last. 'A beach scene or . . .?'

'I . . . er . . . didn't.'

'You mean you haven't heard?'

'Nope.'

'What, not at all?'

'Well, she phoned. That was on my birthday, but I was out and my mother took the message – she said she'd ring again, but I wasn't to ring her.'

'And what did she say when . . .?'

'She didn't.' Martin had both hands on his cup, holding it so tight, she feared he'd crush it. 'I was getting worried, tell the truth. That's why I called round.'

Bea felt a dart of triumph. She had imagined Martin with a ten-page letter, when the score was in fact two–nil – to her. She had always been Chris's favourite until he came along. They had been on holidays together, endless outings to puppet shows and parks, pet shops and sweet shops, cinemas and zoos. Now Chris went to discos which only made you deaf, or went diving with that rough unruly crowd, which was unladylike as well as dangerous. Horrible to gloat, though. No wonder God had gone – walked out in sheer disgust. Love thy neighbour as thyself, and Martin was a neighbour – almost a relation. She tried to reassure him.

'I expect you'll hear tomorrow. Weekends are always bad. The post mounts up, you see, and by the time they've . . .'

'When did yours come?' Martin tried his tea, blew on it. 'The second one, I mean.'

'Let me think.' Bea dithered, lied. 'Only a day or so ago. Postmen are quite dreadful nowadays. I even heard of one who threw half the letters in a hedge so he could get round in quicker time.'

Martin put his cup down – still too hot. 'Did Mrs . . . you know – Morna – phone again?'

'Well, yes, she did, in fact.'

'Did you . . . er . . . speak to Chris, as well?'

'Just a few words, that's all. They're very expensive, those transatlantic calls.'

'Yeah, I know. What did she say?'

'Let's see – she was having a lovely time and she'd been to Hollywood and . . . and . . . some other place I can't remember now – oh, and she's learning golf and . . .'

'*Golf*? She . . . er . . . didn't mention me, did she – I mean, give you any message or . . .?'

'Well, no, she didn't, Martin, but they only had three minutes, dear, and that was between the two of them. Morna took up most of it. Anyway, Chris wouldn't have known I'd be seeing you, so why should . . .?'

'No, I s'pose not.' Martin sagged back in his chair, chewed his thumbnail. Another minute took its time to pass. 'She's all right, is she, though? I mean, well and everything?'

'Oh *yes*, dear. Absolutely fine. She sounded really bright and cheerful.'

Martin picked up his cup again, stopped with it poised halfway to his mouth, sniffed the air. 'Something's burning.'

'The cake!' Bea jumped up to save it. 'I had the oven high to start with, just to brown the top, and forgot to turn it down.' She whipped out a blackened mess. 'There – I've ruined it!'

'You can cut the burnt bits off. My mother always does. I'll eat them, if you like. I like burnt cake.'

'I shouldn't do that, dear. It's bird cake.'

'*What*?'

'I make it for the birds – once a week in winter. I got the recipe last year from that television programme – what's it called? You know, that chap with the moustache. He's got a bird's name himself. Trilling, isn't it? Yes, Robert Trilling. I often wondered whether they chose him for his name. Mind you, *Robin* Trilling would have been even better. "Birds in Your Back Garden" – that's it. Six o'clock on Thursdays. I expect your mother watches it.'

'She's hardly ever in at six.'

'Well, she ought to make the effort. It's very good. They've had several different recipes. There was one for water birds – a sort of mixed grain loaf with sunflower seeds. I made two of those, in fact, took them to Black Pond. It's especially important to help out in the winter when they're cold and short of food.'

Martin still looked cold himself and famished, gulping the bits of blackened cake she had cut off round the edges.

'I've got some other cake – human cake – date and walnut. Would you like a slice?' She owed him that at least. It was a sin to crow, count points.

'No, thanks.'

'Well, how about a biscuit or a sandwich or . . .?'

'No, really.'

She wished he would accept. He was probably just being polite. He still seemed ill at ease, the sort of thin and restless type who found it an effort to keep still. Even when he was sitting down, he looked ready to take off, perched only on the edge of his chair rather than settled into it, one foot tapping nervously, the other doubled under him. She felt very old and heavy in comparison, as if she were screwed down on her seat and would need a crane to winch her up again. No – they couldn't be relations. Chris was far too young to marry, anyway. Morna had married young and look where that had got her. Yet how could she interfere? Chris was stubborn. Morna always said she got that from her Grandma. Bea smiled. Or Grandpapa. The Conyers were all obstinate.

Silence again, save for Martin's tapping, Joy's snuffly wheezing snores. The dog had returned to sleep, but now curled up at her feet instead of in her basket on the stairs. Martin couldn't be that bad, not if Joy were sleeping. She never slept in front of tricky people, but stayed on her guard and growled. She wondered if he had a God. Funny how you couldn't ask, as if it were something private and embarrassing like bodies. Chris had said his parents were vaguely C of E, but never went to church. Mind you, they had given him a saint's name. She had always liked St Martin – the Tours one, not de Porres (who was a mulatto and illegitimate, which only went to show how broad-minded the Church was, in that it could overlook his birth and canonize him). St Martin of Tours was a different type entirely – a man of power and breeding who had gone on to be a bishop. Before his conversion, he had met a naked beggar on a winter's night and cut his cloak in two, handed over half of it. The beggar had been Christ, of course – or so the books all said. Now she was less certain. Would people be allowed to walk around stark naked, even in those early days? She couldn't remember what century it was, didn't know St Martin's dates at all. Dates were worse than centigrade.

She glanced back at his namesake. If Martin cut his jeans in half to help a naked tramp, neither he nor tramp would be warm or even decent. The jeans were so skimpy, they were pulling at the seams, revealed a gap of flesh between his sweater and his belt. It wasn't fair on Chris to dress like that. Young girls were susceptible and he was showing off everything he had. She fixed her eyes on his cup instead – empty now, save for a few last grains of semi-dissolved sugar which he was laboriously spooning out.

'More tea?' she asked. He really did look hungry.

'No, thanks.'

She drained her own Ovaltine, racked her brains for something interesting to say. Surely he would be going soon, now that he had heard her news of Chris. He had picked up the postcards and was reading them again, seemed reluctant to be parted from them. If she were kind, she'd say 'Take them with you, dear', but Chris might not write again. She had sounded very busy on the phone – strings of names and places. It took time to buy a card, find a post office.

She jumped. Martin had dropped his spoon on the floor, alarmed the silence. He kept shifting on his seat, casting nervous glances round the room.

'Is that Chris?' he asked, suddenly, pointing to a photo of a scowling baby in a smock.

'No, Morna. Chris is in the other room. I've got several of her as a tiny tot. You must have seen them when you came before.'

Martin returned his gaze to Malibu. 'I don't remember.'

'D'you want to see them now, then?'

He nodded, followed her into the sitting room, stood by the piano.

'That's the first. She was just a few days old then. Neil took it in the hospital. And this one's six months later. See her first tooth? She was a bit swollen and bad-tempered then. Oh – and look at this! Isn't she a darling?'

Martin said nothing, was just tagging after her, staring at each infant, his face impassive. He stopped in front of

Edward – the largest of the photographs, which showed him in his best blue uniform with his DFC and DSO.

Martin touched a finger to the glass. 'Did he really win those medals, or were they just – you know – decoration?'

'Of *course* he won them, dear. He was very brave indeed, Chris's grandfather. Well, she's like him in that, isn't she? Chris always had great spirit, even as a baby.' Bea sat down on the sofa. She could smell Edward's pipe again, the strong sweet fumes of Capstan Navy Cut, flaring into the reek of scorching fabric, the stench of charred flesh. 'On his . . . his last operation, he sacrificed his life. His Lancaster was hit by an anti-aircraft shell and he tried to keep it airborne while all the crew baled out. The last man had just jumped free when the thing blew up. One of the young airmen told me the whole story. He'd been taken prisoner of war, but when he got back home he came to see me. He said my husband showed outstanding courage and they'd never forget what he did that night. Apparently, he was even joking with them – right up to the end – you know, to try and keep their spirits up, stop them panicking.'

Martin slumped down opposite Bea, postcards on the chair-arm. He kept jabbing at the palm trees with his finger, then glancing back at Edward. 'I don't know how you managed,' he muttered, almost to himself. 'You know – with him dying when you'd only just . . .'

Bea tensed. Her own friends had been more tactful, used words like 'loss' and 'shock', never death.

'I mean, how on earth did you cope? I feel bad enough with Chris away for three short weeks, and even when I know she's coming home.'

Bea thought back. She *had* coped. There had been no alternative. She took the photo down, sat with it on her lap, ran a finger along the fine arched brows, traced the generous mouth. He hadn't changed.

'I . . . I just carried on as if he were still there.' Bea laid

Edward face-down in her lap. Martin didn't understand. She could see that from his expression. She tried again. 'I just . . . refused to be a widow. It's so depressing, isn't it, moving to some poky house and letting yourself go, living on toast or ginger nuts, and joining those dreary groups like Cruse or . . . or whatsitsname. I can't remember names, dear – not these days.' Bea winced at a sudden stab of pain, eased her neck and shoulders. 'No, I stayed where I was and behaved exactly as I had before Edward . . . passed away. I ran the house the way he liked, cooked regular well-balanced meals, including his favourite dishes, wore the clothes he'd chosen, kept to his routine.'

'Yeah, but if he wasn't there to . . . ?'

'It didn't matter. It was a way of coping. A sort of . . . game if you like.'

Martin crossed his legs, uncrossed them, stretched them out in front of him. 'It doesn't sound much fun to me.'

'It wasn't. It wasn't any fun at all. But it gave me something to hang on to, something to live for. I'd always ask myself "What would Edward have done if . . . ?" And then I'd do it anyway.'

She and Edward had planned to send their child to boarding school, since they were frequently abroad. She hadn't changed the plan, though she had never once left England after her bereavement. It had proved a strain, both financial and emotional, to send her only child away. But if it was what Edward had decided . . . Perhaps she *should* have changed the plan. Morna hadn't really been happy at that school, especially in the later years. She rubbed at a tiny mark on Edward's cheek. It wouldn't budge. She tried a drop of spittle, scraped it with a fingernail – still there.

Martin was fiddling with the postcards, making a roof with them, an L-shape, laying them back to back, then face to face. 'Yeah, but how could you keep going if you never got anything back? I mean, if your bloke never bothered, or wrote letters or phoned you up or . . . ?'

'I didn't need letters. Well, I had his old ones, anyway. But I just believed he was there. Don't misunderstand me, Martin – I wasn't dotty, seeing ghosts and things. It was more a matter of his *presence*, refusing to let go of it, refusing to give in or wallow in self-pity. It's all to do with will-power – or maybe even . . . obstinacy. You can play the widow even when you're married, you know. It's a question of attitude.'

She polished Edward up, put him back on his shelf, remained standing there, staring at his picture, hearing her own voice – 'a way of coping, something to live for, a question of attitude'. She gripped the shelf, closed her eyes a moment, felt a sudden rush of blood to the head as if somebody had hit her. Not somebody, but something. Wasn't that her answer, her way of coping with her new bereavement, her loss of God? She had been weeping and wailing, wallowing in self-pity, indulging in doubts and fears – all the things she had despised and fought against when she'd first been widowed. Here was her solution – one she had just spelt out to Martin. All she had to do was carry on as if God were there, refuse even to think about the doubts, or waste her energies on ifs and buts. It wouldn't be a bed of roses – she knew that from her first attempt. But she also knew it worked. It kept you going, gave you purpose, saved you from despair. You slept, worked, trusted, and you kept your sights on the Beloved. Never mind if he were faint or blurred or deaf or even cruel. Will-power was enough. Spirit, obstinacy. She was a Conyers, wasn't she? Edward would have been ashamed of her these last few months, behaving like a raw recruit, wavering and bleating, almost deserting ranks.

'What, dear? Yes, I used to play. Not so much these days, though. My fingers are too stiff.'

Rude to ignore a guest, yet she could hardly concentrate. She could see herself kneeling at the altar rails, receiving the Host from Father Clarke. 'The Body of Christ,' he murmured, placing it on her tongue. No more need to doubt it, spend the rest of Mass agonizing, wondering if her doubts showed up like tumours on an X-ray, visible to all the congregation. And of *course* she could continue with her church activities, in Madge's parish as well as in her own. It was the work itself which mattered, not her puny fears and scruples. Those were to be banished now, replaced by acceptance and obedience – all the virtues Edward's men were trained in – courage, loyalty, unquestioning submission to one's Leader.

'No, Chris never cared for music much. She had lessons for a year or two, but then she gave it up.'

The poor boy couldn't get away from Chris. That at least they had in common – both of them missing her, longing for a letter. Lovely eyes he had – sad and brown and very bright like that picture of Christ in her prayer book. Funny how she had never noticed – thought him rather plain before. Joy was lying almost on his foot now, which proved he was a decent sort.

His stomach gave a sudden growling rumble. He flushed, clapped a hand on it, as if frightened it might show him up again.

'Er . . . pardon.'

'You sound as if you're hungry, dear. How about that piece of cake?'

'No, really, Mrs Cony . . . I ought to be getting back. I haven't had my supper yet.'

'You haven't had your *supper*? But it's getting on for midnight.'

He shrugged. 'I never bother much with meals when Mum's out.'

'She doesn't work on Sunday, does she?'

'Yeah, sometimes. Not today though. She's gone to Woodford.'

'*I* could always cook you something.' His eyes really were exceptional, kind and gentle as well as bright. 'How about a nice mixed grill?'

'Won't it – you know – keep you up too long?'

At least he was polite – and thoughtful. She could hear his stomach saying yes, the flush deepening as it growled again.

'Not at all. I'm feeling a little peckish myself, to tell the truth. I'll light the fire and we'll eat in here.' Why not be extravagant for once, switch on the electric heater, too, build up a real fug? She never ate this late, but just an egg or something couldn't hurt. She'd make another pot of tea, have a cup herself. She would sleep tonight, she knew it, tea or no. She felt better than she had for months. They ought to celebrate. There were peaches bottled in brandy in the larder. She had been saving them for years – for something special. *Now* was special. All you needed was a plan, a way of carrying on, making sense of things.

The fire was laid already. She always lit it when Chris and Morna came, or Father Clarke. She struck a match, watched the bright flame lick along the newspaper, burning out her doubts, her futile barren questionings. God was there – as Edward was. She had both their photographs – the picture of the Sacred Heart which Madge had bought for her just a month ago from a convent in East Grinstead, smiling down on Edward and his medals.

'Can you lay tables, Martin?'

'I'll have a bash.'

'Knives and forks in here. Wait a minute, I'll get a cloth. Careful with it, dear. It's very old, that one. I embroidered it myself the first year I was married. Lupins were Edward's favourite flowers.'

'I never know the names of flowers.'

'You must know lupins.'

'Nope.'

'Well, you do now.' Bea touched a clump of silky purple ones. 'There are ninety-eight exactly on that cloth, and every one has a good two hundred stitches. It took me eight solid months to finish, working every evening and all weekends.'

'My Mum won't sew a button on.'

Bea said nothing. Chris certainly shouldn't marry into such a family. She was already far too casual – blamed it on Martin, said he liked things homely. Mind you, if someone took some trouble with the lad, he could be trained the other way. He was doing quite a good job on the table, smoothing out the cloth, setting the knives and forks down very carefully. He weighed one in his hand.

'Are these real silver, Mrs Col . . . ?' He seemed to be having trouble with her name. Found it a mouthful or had forgotten it, most likely.

'Oh yes, dear. They belonged to Edward's grandfather. See the initial on the handles? C for Conyers.' She spelt the name out slowly and deliberately as if teaching a small child.

He followed her out to the kitchen, the fork still in his hand. '*I*'d like stuff like this – something with a history. I've been reading this book about a wreck they've just discovered off the Lizard. The divers found pewter plates and a battered silver tankard and a dagger with a real ruby in the hilt and great gold chains which men wore round their necks and . . .'

'*Men*? I thought it was only nowadays that men wore jewellery. Do you know, even my butcher wears a gold earring in one ear and he's six foot tall and bearded.'

'No, blokes have always worn it – though, actually, those chains were used as sort of ready cash, to escape the tax due on minted gold. They'd break off a link or two to settle some account – only noblemen, of course, not the proles. I've seen portraits of lords and people wearing them. They could be really heavy sometimes and up to eight feet long.'

'You know a lot about it.' Bea was trimming the chop, removing bacon rinds.

'Yeah. I read all the books I can. I hope to dive a wreck like that myself one day, so the more I know, the better. I've done a bit already – nothing very grand – only brought up rusty nails and broken bits of pottery and things. But actually, it isn't just the treasure, it's . . . I don't know –' He shrugged. 'I can't put it into words. But imagine turning up a tankard which some bloke actually drank from centuries ago, and feeling you're sort of . . . linked with him, that he isn't entirely dead and gone, because . . . well –' He broke off, embarrassed, traced a pattern with the fork prongs on his palm.

Bea snipped off three pork sausages, put them under the grill. The boy had real potential. All right, she wouldn't want him for a grandson-in-law, but then if Chris were cooling off him, hadn't even sent a card, then that wouldn't be a problem. Just as well with all that dangerous diving. She felt sorry for him, really. Chris could be cruel – not intentionally, just casual over things, making people feel they didn't matter when once they'd been kingpin.

'One egg, dear, or two?'

'Two, please. What are those things?'

'They keep the eggs a nice neat shape, stop them running.' She melted oil and butter in a second pan. 'And I always use a clean pan for the eggs. There's nothing worse than bits of black on egg whites.' He might as well learn while he had the chance. He'd be someone's husband, one day, not Chris's – not someone quite that special – but a nice girl, certainly. He deserved a really nice girl.

'Thanks,' he said, as he put his knife and fork down, pushed his plate away. 'I enjoyed that.'

'Well, it was only very simple, dear.'

'No, it was great. I like the way you – you know – make

things look so nice. I mean, taking all that trouble with the table and the serviettes and that silver mustard thing – just for me.'

Bea swallowed her last bite of crustless toast. *'If you do it unto the least of My brethren, you do it unto . . .'* She had that text safe back now, together with all the other precious texts. Everything and everyone rooted in God again. Order again, peace again; not a sparrow falling without her heavenly Father's will, not a water bird starving without Him there to thaw the pond.

Martin was still speaking, seemed less tongue-tied now. 'I hated school dinners because everything was so grotty. They fed us like pigs, sloshed the food around. If you weren't careful, you'd get gravy down your arm or custard on your cod. And we had plastic knives and forks.'

'Plastic!'

'Yeah. The boys were always nicking the metal ones or trying to bend them – you know, like Uri Geller. Not that it was difficult. They were so cheap and tinny, they'd bend on a fish finger.' Martin picked up his knife again, admired the crest. 'Chris says you fuss, but I like that. It makes things sort of special.'

'Fuss?' Bea flounced up to fetch the peaches. Of *course* it made things special. Edward had said the same himself, in different words. 'You've got a great gift, Beatrice.' He had always called her Beatrice – took the trouble, just as Father Clarke did. 'A gift for making things and people happy.'

Then he had gone and blown himself to bits, so that she couldn't use the gift – well, not as fully as she might have done. They had planned a nice big family, at least four or five children to keep her busy, test her skills. She would have dearly loved a son, another Edward – maybe even Edward Martin. She had always liked the name. When St Martin cut that cloak in half, he hadn't known it was God he was keeping warm, hadn't asked for His identity, demanded proofs or documents – just clothed a naked wretch. There weren't many naked wretches in stockbroker Surrey – the rates were too high for that – but it was the principle which counted. Madge herself was a bit of a St Martin – generous to a fault (and bossy with it) – didn't waste time asking God to prove Himself, just got on with His work.

She spooned peaches into cut-glass sundae dishes, giving Martin the lion's share.

'What's that sort of winey taste?' he asked, as he swallowed his first mouthful.

'Cognac. A very good one. They've been steeping in it for over two years.'

'Two *years*?'

Bea nodded. She must steep herself in God, soak Him up like brandy, serve His family if her own were too small or didn't need her now. The retreat house was a sort of family. They even talked about themselves as brothers and sisters, sons and daughters of Christ. She could be useful there, not just Taking Stock, praying with her eyes closed and her hands clasped, but helping out as Madge did. There was enough to do, for heaven's sake – a rambling house and garden with only a handful of nuns to keep it going, and Mother Michael not the best of organizers. St Martin had been a soldier's son, an officer himself; she an officer's wife. She knew about efficiency and service. She mustn't interfere, of course, but there were things she could do almost unobtrusively. Little things. St Thérèse of Lisieux had become a saint on Little Things and St Martin himself had worked all the hours God sent, founded his own retreat house – a score of them across the whole of France.

'Have an almond finger, Martin. They go nicely with the peaches. I made them myself.'

He took a couple. 'Thanks.'

She sat staring at the rose-sprigged plate of biscuits, saw herself baking almond fingers for the nuns, shining up that brass umbrella stand which they had allowed to get so tarnished, pruning roses, embroidering altar cloths. She had kept house and garden for Edward even after he had gone. She could do the same for God – at least one day a week. Madge never missed a week in her trips to Hilden Cross, sometimes went more often. All she had to do was beg a lift with her, say she had changed her mind about the place. Madge wouldn't bother asking why. She was a Martha, not a Mary, too busy to keep questioning or examining people's motives when the office needed manning or two hundred letters had to be sent out. In fact, if she were going to live as if God were there, then the retreat house was the perfect place to start – surrounded by believers, people whose faith and ardour would rub off on to her; nuns praying for her, with her, every moment of the day; a constant stream of clear-headed clever priests who weren't friends like Father Clarke or entangled in her pastry – perhaps one she could confide in if things got bad again.

No – she wouldn't *let* them get bad. If God chose to keep His distance, well that was His privilege. The lower ranks couldn't expect to hobnob with top brass. It was enough that He was there, running the whole show.

Martin had finished his peaches, made inroads on the biscuits. He folded up his napkin, pushed his chair back. 'I really must be going, Mrs Conyers. My Mum'll be back by now and she'll wonder where . . .'

'Off you go, then. And mind you wrap up warm. That wind's really whipping up now. Can I lend you a woolly scarf?'

'No. I'm okay. And thanks for the meal and everything. Can I . . . er . . . help you with the – you know – clearing up and stuff?'

'Good gracious no! That's my job. I like to keep busy, Martin. If you want those postcards, by the way, you're welcome to take them with you.'

'But . . . I thought you always kept your cards? Chris said you've got hundreds – all the ones she sent you as a kid.'

'Well, I don't need any more then, do I? The cloakroom's down the passage, if you want it – second door along. That's it.'

She went to fetch the cards, slipped them in a carrier bag with the last few almond fingers and three quarters of the date and walnut cake swathed in one of her lupined damask napkins; pushed it into his hand as she waved him off. Charity was easy, faith harder. Hope she had almost forgotten these last few months. Now she had it back – hope in God, in heaven, in being reunited with her darling Edward. She ought to be prepared – just as she was always ready for an accident, wearing decent underclothes with no safety pins or ladders, so that if a doctor scooped her off the road, she wouldn't feel ashamed. The rest of her life – and there wasn't that much left of it – must be a training period, to make her worthy to meet her two Beloveds.

She returned to the kitchen, filled the sink with soapy water, started on the dishes. It was nearer one than midnight now, but first things first.

'I'm ready, Lord,' she said, scrubbing at the stubborn burnt-on cake tin. 'When You are.'

16

The cab was still roaring, lurching on. Morna shifted position. It was the longest ride she had been on in the whole long day at Disneyland, except time was lost, meant nothing. She had pierced through the smallest smallest scintilla of a snowflake, come out the other side, still reeling at its vastness, stunned by worlds she had never glimpsed before. She rubbed her eyes. Strange shapes and patterns were flickering in front of her, not snowflakes any longer, but distorted human figures. The soundtrack had fouled up again, jarring even more now that new voices had joined in, discordant, overlapping, shuddering through the cab. She covered her face with her hands, tried to block her ears. She couldn't take in any more. She was exhausted by the queasy swooping motion, the insistent whining roar.

When she opened her eyes again, the shapes had disappeared, the flickering stopped, the voices silenced or blurred into the roar. It was darker now, save for tiny points of light above, like stars, except stars had never been that close before. She tried to reach up and touch one, but her arms seemed padlocked to her side, her whole body weighted down. Perhaps they were going from inner space to outer space. But wouldn't she be weightless, then? Her limbs felt heavy, leaden, as if she had changed her density, been given a transfusion, not of blood but mercury. It was hard to breathe, impossible to think. The reverberation of the cab was throbbing through her ears, dulling her whole body.

She let herself sink down, woke again to voices – different voices, softer and more distant, soothing like a chant or lullaby. Someone had nailed her eyelids down, but she was aware of a bustling around her, people stirring, getting up. The ride must be over. Time to get out, join Neil and Bunny, Chris and Dean. Was that Bunny she could hear – a female voice with a Californian accent, speaking very loudly above the rest?

'Snow,' Morna heard. 'Something something snowing.' Surely not. They had already had the snowflakes. The ride was finished now. Or had she missed the exit and been carried round a second time? A third?

She groped for the push-bar, felt something soft instead, fuzzy like a rug. This couldn't be the cab. There were no rugs on rides in Disneyland and the seat had been harder and more rigid than the one beneath her now. She forced her eyes open, stared at the fistful of red blanket glowing in her fingers. They'd had red blankets in the infirmary at school. Blue on all the ordinary beds – blue for the Blessed Virgin – red when you were ill.

She must be very ill. You were only allowed in the infirmary if your temperature was 102 degrees or more. With mere colds or minor flus, you stayed on your feet and suffered. She felt her head – it was clammy hot, throat parched and dry, eyes closing down again. She could hear footsteps coming closer, the clink of something on a tray. A bedpan, a thermometer? She squinted through her eyelids, tried to see which nun it was.

'Breakfast time.'

Morna sank back. It wasn't a nun at all – not in that swingy pleated skirt, that dapper little jacket edged with scarlet braid, and speaking with a Californian twang. Anyway, she couldn't be at school. Even in the infirmary, you didn't get your breakfast before prayers – prayers for the sick, followed by a long Latin blessing, and, only then, your bowl of tepid porridge.

She struggled up, clutching at the blanket, gasped at the sudden dazzling light streaming through the windows, cutting golden swathes across the padded seats.

Windows? Padded seats?

'Er . . . where are we?' she asked, confused.

'Right over the Scottish Highlands. That's the sun shining on the mountain peaks. Aren't they pretty? There's no sun in London, though. They had gales last night and now they say it's trying to snow. There was an announcement earlier, but I think you were asleep. You slept all through the movie and . . .'

'Movie?'

'Don't worry, you didn't miss much. It was kind of a boring one, to tell you the truth. Anyway, we'll be arriving at Heathrow in less than two hours now, so you better sit up and have your breakfast.'

Morna rubbed her eyes. Heathrow. That was in London, wasn't it? London, England. Place names hurt her head. They were too big, too full of jostling crowds and booming traffic.

'Wh . . . What time is it?' she faltered, above the traffic noise.

'Quarter of two.'

A.m. or p.m.? Neither was breakfast time. She glanced at her own watch. Almost six o'clock. It hadn't stopped. She could see the second hand circling slowly round. A yellow plastic tray was slotted in across her lap, trapping her in her seat. The tray was confused as well – breakfast, lunch, tea, all jumbled up together – orange juice and croissants, a dish of tinned fruit cocktail, a slice of cheese with three cheese biscuits wrapped in cellophane, a sickly looking cake. She sipped the juice. It tasted sharp and sweet at once, cold and clean on her furred-up palate. She had better try and eat.

311

She bit into the cake – cream oozing out like the clouds outside the window, whipped-cream clouds sprinkled with a pink and golden topping. How could there be snow in London when that blazing sun was turning the yellow tray to topaz, the sky to knickerbocker glory?

Perhaps it was all a trick again, a staged effect like Hollywood? Except things were coming clearer now – other people with proper faces, working hands; rows of seats with heads above them, rows of letters which spelt words she could understand – 'NO SMOKING', 'PUSH FOR STEWARDESS'.

'We're nearly there,' said someone. She turned to her right. A frail old woman, with thin and papery skin stretched across the skull beneath, was buttering a croissant with a veined and bony hand.

'You've been sleepin' for a good wee while.' The accent was Glaswegian, the voice not frail at all, harsh and almost mocking.

Morna nodded. She remembered now, she had taken sleeping pills. Wasn't used to them. A giant gin-and-Mogadon cocktail gulped down after take-off.

'Are you on a visit to London?'

'Er . . . no. I . . .' Morna put her cake down. She had been visiting California, not London, seeing the sights. Disneyland. Adventure Through Inner Space. She shut her eyes, stepped trembling from the ride again into a world she didn't recognize. The sun had gone down, natural daylight faded into fluorescent glare, fairy lights twinkling in the trees.

'Chris!' she had shouted, panicking; was answered by the laughs and shouts of strangers. A hundred thousand strangers. She had lost her party, would never find them now with all that razzle-dazzle spangle swamping individual faces into a general glow and sheen. She struggled along the path, out of Tomorrowland and into Main Street, all firm outlines blurring into iridescent mirages, illuminated façades. Trees were coloured cutouts, water only ripple and reflection, buildings one-dimensional. She had blinked against a burst of neon flowers. Every bloom was breaking into molecules and she was being whirled into the centre of each shining blinding atom – new galaxies in a millionth of a pollen grain, a cosmos in a sliver of a stamen.

She had tried to walk straight, kept tripping on debris – suns, planets, bits of star. A band was playing in Main Street Square, adding to her confusion. Tubas in her stomach, drums inside her head. Even the music was splintering into atoms, every demi-semiquaver exploding in its own symphony of ever-crescendoing blare. She had to get out, escape from Disneyland. She fought her way to the car park through the clumsy sluggard crowds, found Neil's silver Jaguar among a galactic waste of cars – all empty while their owners orbited the rides. She scribbled a note, secured it under the windscreen wiper, fled towards the exit and the bus stop.

The high-speed bus swallowed up the darkness, spat out lights both ends. More lights stretching out each side, cancelling the horizon, distorting shapes and distances. No band now, only the judder of the engine, the roar of passing cars. A sudden burst of fireworks as they passed a motel and someone's private party. Rockets exploding in her skull, catherine wheels spinning her round and round with them, the Big Bang throwing up creation, then scattering it to the winds, the whole heaving universe burning out like a squib.

At last, she had reached the Ocean View Motel. An ambulance was throbbing just outside, with its gaggle of voyeurs. An accident, a mugging. Blue flashing lights breaking down the blood into whirling scarlet corpuscles, a murder in each congealing drop. She pushed through the crowd, panted up the stairs. She had to get away. It wasn't safe. She flung her clothes in her case, phoned for a cab, directed it to Neil and Bunny's house. No key, no one back yet. Dark windows, yapping dog. They must still be in Disneyland, still searching for her, still plunging up and down on all the rides. They would never find her – she was breaking down herself – cells, pores, corpuscles, hurtling around a central sphere of panic. Swept by the panic, she raced to LA airport in the cab. More confusion. Wrong ticket, wrong day and only one last flight to London, almost leaving. She had to catch it, had to. She begged, stormed, changed the ticket, checked in, dashed through the departure lounge and out to the waiting plane.

A huge plane – huge and noisy. People pushing down the aisles, folding coats, stowing luggage, clambering over each other to find their seats. She collapsed into her own seat, heard voices babbling round her – laughing, chatting, Captain Brady speaking, safety regulations. Nothing safe. A great hurting lurching shudder in her stomach as they gasped into the sky. She peered out of the window – a dizzy tipping world, shrinking as she looked at it, falling away into only roar and light. Squares of light, strings of light, a city built of neon. Even that fading as the plane climbed steeper, was swallowed up in cloud. She could feel the cloud choking down her throat, clammy on her face.

'Are you all right?' asked someone – later – although time had disappeared still.

She nodded.

'Like a glass of water?'

She sipped it, heard the liquid slurping in her stomach, changed the glass for gin when they brought the trolley round. A double gin. Another. She needed a drink to wash down the sleeping pills stolen from Neil's bathroom. The last thing she remembered was holding the second pill between her thumb and index finger before she swallowed it – a tiny white pill swelling vast, immense, as she transferred it to her mouth, as if she were face to face with one gigantic snowflake. Then piercing through the snow-flake, shrinking smaller smaller as she burst into its atom, was swallowed up in its deafening roar.

The roar of the plane. Morna surfaced to it again, opened her eyes. The mouth on the right was opening and shutting, the same pumice-stone Glaswegian voice.

She tried to find her own voice. 'I'm s . . . sorry, I didn't quite hear what . . .'

'Och! You're English, are you? I thought you looked like an American.'

Morna glanced down at her feet. *Were* they her feet? They were wearing bright pink sneakers with Snoopy laces, stripy socks. American feet. She remembered now. Those were Bunny's socks and shoes. She had borrowed them for Disneyland – something comfortable and casual – hadn't changed her shoes since Sunday morning. Was it Sunday still? Or Monday? Tuesday morning?

'I'm Scots myself – aye – born and bred in Langside.' The wrinkled mouth paused to swallow fruit. 'I've been stayin' with my daughter in Santa Barbara. I only had the one wean. Wean!' She made a face, spat a piece of peach into her hand. 'She's sixty-nine now and has mair aches and pains than I've got, and then she's the cheek to say I'm too old to fly. I may be eighty-seven, but I'm strong as a horse. Feel that.'

Morna's wrist was gripped in cold but steely fingers. This woman was close to ninety, close to death, yet had more strength in her arm than she did. She turned to look at her – near transparent skin, age spots on her hands, gaunt body in its chain-store frock, one cheap brooch in the shape of a black cat with a fake gem studded collar. The grip was hurting still, the grey eyes challenging – keen unfaded eyes, not even wearing spectacles. She let go of Morna's wrist, clawed the biscuits from their cellophane.

'Those cracker things. I'd rather have had the sweet ones.'

She picked one up and sniffed it, turned to Morna again. 'Have *you* got any weans?'

'Yes, just one.'

'A boy?'

'No, girl.' Morna stared down at her own dismembered cake, jam bleeding into cream. How could she have left her daughter, run away on impulse like a child herself? Chris would be upset – worse, contemptuous. She had left a note which no one would believe – flimsy lies, excuses – told them not to worry.

'My daughter never married.' Gnarled and yellowed fingers dunking salt biscuits in a sweetened cup of tea. 'She went to California with some man she met at her work. He talked her into it with a few vague promises. It didn't last though. He soon dropped her for a native. Is your girl married?'

'No. She's . . . er . . . only seventeen and a half.' More stable than her mother, though. *She* was the adolescent – moody, mixed-up, acting like an irrational impetuous fool. How could she have done it, given way to panic, let a kiddies' ride unhinge her?

'*I* got married at sixteen and a half. Two years later, my man had scarpered – run away to sea.'

'R . . . Run away?'

'Aye. Though my old mither used to say that people never run away. They run *to* something – something else, something they think is more important – love and adventure, mibbe, or security and home. Anyway, I never mourned him. Nae regrets, as the song says.'

Morna glanced down at her stupid pink-striped knee-socks. Her own regrets were swarming as the haze of drugs and alcohol receded; shameful distorted snapshots rushing in to take their place – her vomiting and naked in a garish hotel bathroom, sobbing like a booby in Martha's fleshy arms, slurring her words on Bunny's patio, bolting out of

Disneyland. The whole time she had been in California, she had acted out of character, lost her inhibitions, almost lost her mind, bared first her body and then her soul to total strangers, spewing up emotions she had kept down for twenty years. Always before, she had believed in self-control, even bottling up her grief at the time of the divorce. But now she had poured out everything – grief, tears, panic, pain – reached the gritty dregs. Was it still the impact of that strange flotation tank, or the fact she was abroad, freed from her usual restraints, cut loose from home and friends? It was David she was missing, not her other friends – which hardly made much sense, since she hadn't even seen him since September, had spent only a few short hours with him in total. Yet she found herself clinging to his memory, as a sort of anchor, a shaft of hope and strength, despite the fact he still seemed so remote, not only in terms of miles, but in the way his frame and features had faded and receded. She longed to lay eyes on him again, see him sharp and solid in the flesh; let his own steady seriousness calm her down, set her an example. But he was away for months yet, committed to his work and to his island, and even when he did return, there was still no guarantee that they would meet.

She took a sip of tea, already tepid and curdled by the creamer. It was Chris she should be concerned about, not David. So what did she do now? Board the next plane back to California, tell her daughter it was all a joke – an April Fool in January – that she had merely caught a local bus to Long Beach, rather than a jumbo-jet to Heathrow? Impossible. She had no more money for transatlantic fares, no more strength.

'Are you no eatin', hen?' The old lady peered across at Morna's almost untouched food. 'If you don't want that cheese, I'll take it with me. I've got another flight after this – the shuttle up to Glasgow. It's on and off that quick, I didn't even get a drink last time.'

Morna passed the cheese across, let her hand linger on the other's tray. Wasn't there some bond between the two of them? Both leaving only daughters on an alien continent, both returning to cold and empty houses. Glasgow. That was on the way to David and his island – except he had gone by road, not air, then crossed over from the mainland in a tiny fishing boat. He would be hard at work, not wasting time and energy rushing around in circles. She must return to work herself, go home and settle down. The lotus-eating was over. That old mither had been right about people running away. All she was doing was running to something safer, bolting back to England before the Californian fever tightened its grip. Los Angeles was dangerous. Glaring bright or throbbing dark. Never tranquil, never neutral. Sirens ripping up the night, never-never promises writhing in flashing lights in the advertisements, paint and pasteboard pretending to be gold; birds-of-paradise flowers blooming out of blood and smog, menacingly exotic with their fat and fleshy stalks, their gaudy colours, their blue and pointed tongues.

There would be no flowers back in England save the odd wan and shrinking snowdrop, a spray or two of chilly winter jasmine. She must return to cold, to commonsense, merciful routine. Four hours' translation work each morning, long bracing walks to clear her head; housework, gardening, shopping, before peaceful evenings reading with a single glass of wine. She was right to leave. Chris could cope without her. It was only one short week, for heaven's sake. The old Scots dame had been married at that age, with a baby on the way. Chris wasn't even alone, but staying with her adored and indulgent father in a family home with every material comfort.

'She didn't want me there, you know.' The old woman swilled her tea, wiped her mouth.

'I . . . I beg your pardon?'

'My daughter. I was in the way – I see that now – just a pest.'

'Surely not?'

'You needn't humour me. I may be old, but I'm no fool.'

'N . . . No, of course not. I didn't mean . . .' Morna picked up her own cup, tried to cover her embarrassment.

'And what age are *you*?' The questions were still rapping out.

'Er . . . forty-one.'

'You're halfway through, then. Mibbe. You cannae tell, can you, when your time's up?'

Morna didn't answer. Her own mother might be saying much the same, telling some stranger she was a nuisance to her daughter, in the way. Had she made Bea feel that? She tried to think coherently, but Bea seemed very faint. She must make her stronger, reforge their ties. She would go straight from Heathrow to Oxshott, bring Bea back to stay with her, offer her the little things she valued – company, Scrabble in the evenings, proper home-cooked meals. Suddenly, she bundled all her remaining food in her paper serviette – croissant, biscuits, butter, jam – pushed it into the old woman's scrawny hand, found room on her tray for a second dish of fruit. It seemed imperative to feed this body up, keep it going, keep death away at least a little longer.

The woman said nothing, just unwrapped the serviette, peered closely at the biscuits, poked a bony finger into the croissant as if checking it were fresh. She tore a piece off, crammed it in her mouth.

'Are you dietin'?' she asked at last, still with her mouth half-full.

'N . . . No.'

'Och, they're all dietin' nowadays. My daughter's skin and bone – lives on fruit. Strawberries for her breakfast. It was porridge and a fry-up when she lived with me.' She

319

swallowed the last butt-end of croissant, wiped her mouth.
'And where do *you* live – North or South?'

'South. Weybridge, actually.'

'Never heard of it. Have you got your own place?'

Morna nodded.

'House or flat?'

'A house.'

'I'm in a tenement myself – the bottom floor of one. They
keep tryin' to shift me, though. When you're old, they're
always meddlin' – wantin' to cage you up, shove you into
hospitals. But I'm set on dyin' where I was born – safe in my
own home.' She laughed, transferred the biscuits to her
handbag, snapped it shut.

Morna glanced out of the window. The sun had disappeared, the sky a leaden grey. They were clearing away the
trays now, in preparation for the long descent. Thirty
minutes later, the first glimpse of patchwork land was
blurring through the clouds. She squinted down at it. This
was her country, temperate and staid, where old people
laughed off death, allowed themselves to age and fade
without face lifts or false hopes; where men wore sober suits,
not yellow socks or pompoms; where women hid emotions,
respected the word love; where funfairs were restricted to
Bank Holidays, buildings to a dozen storeys, and trees were
bare and brown in the five-month winter.

She needed cold and cure. Her body might be numb, but
her emotions were still raw, reacting over-violently to every
smallest thing. She was close to tears for no other reason
than the anonymous old duck beside her had a daughter
who'd been jilted, a second tiring flight ahead without a cup
of tea.

She turned back to the window, stared out at the grey and
sullen skyscape. Fields were swallowing up in urban sprawl,
tiny cars on toytown roads, Lego shops and houses looming
larger as they swooped lower, lower. Morna closed her eyes,

felt a sudden thump and lurch as the plane touched down. She reached across, fumbled for the old lady's hand, gripped it for a brief embarrassed moment until the screeching whine of the reversing engines had shuddered into silence; opened her eyes again to see the first flakes of dazzling snow starring the drab grey concrete of Heathrow.

There was a queue for passport control. Morna joined it, shuffled inch by inch towards the desk, her legs stiff and aching under her. Everyone looked tired – a line of pale and faded faces, crumpled clothes. They were like refugees arriving at a prison camp. She was almost surprised when the official at the desk merely checked her passport rather than branding a number on her arm.

She walked on towards the baggage hall, found a phone booth, and some coins. Her Scots neighbour had disappeared – too old for all the queues. She had been collected by a stewardess as soon as they touched down, given special treatment. She must do the same for Bea, make her feel she mattered, wasn't just someone on the sidelines who had been shunted into a rusty shed marked 'Death'.

'Hallo Mummy darling. I'm . . .' Morna broke off. Not her mother's voice but Vera Grant's – fussy little woman who divided her time between the Legion of Mary and the Women's League of Prayer.

'It's Morna, Mrs Grant, Bea's daughter. Is my mother there? Oh, I see. How odd. She didn't *tell* me she was going.' Mustn't sound so curt. It was hardly Vera Grant's fault that her mother was away. She was only there to feed the dog, keep an eye on things. Why should she mind in any case? Having Bea to stay was usually a drag and now she was reprieved. Reprieve felt leaden like her legs. She had decided on a week of service and her mother had eluded her, proved she didn't need her, had returned to Hilden Cross for a whole ten days.

'When exactly did she leave? I mean, I only phoned three days ago and she didn't mention it. This morning! What, just like that?'

Mrs Grant sounded slightly peeved herself. Bea had apparently decided that it was absolutely imperative that she leave for the retreat house right away. She had been fetched at noon by a Miss Madge Parkin and her very ancient Morris, leaving Vera Grant to hold the fort – and Joy – with only two hours' notice. Morna's commiseration was cut short by the pips. She inserted two more coins.

'Mrs Grant? Could you let me have her number there? I haven't got it with me. Yes, I'll hold on. Thanks a lot.' It was bound to be that wretched Father Clarke again, interfering because Bea was on her own, probably suggesting a retreat because he was running it himself. 'Yes, I've got a pen. That's the code from London, is it? Thanks, Mrs Grant. Sorry to have bothered you. Yes, I'm fine. Yes, I did enjoy America – just left a few days early. Are *you* well? And Joy behaving herself?'

Strange how exhausting small talk was. Morna rang off, slumped against the coin slots, closed her eyes a moment to rest her throbbing head. She felt like David's silver coin, covered with a stubborn gritty scale. Concretion, he had called it – a good word – hard and clogging. If someone scooped her up from the bottom of the ocean, the bottom of a phone box, they would find her whole body caked with that concretion, her usual sharp-edged self dulled and grimed. It was an effort even to pick up the receiver. But she ought to phone the retreat house, tell her mother she was back, find out how she was, maybe even coax her home again. She fumbled for more coins, winced at the high-pitched female voice which answered.

'I'm sorry, but we don't take messages except in an emergency. The retreatants are here for spiritual peace and growth, you see, so we try and block off all distractions.

They're in the chapel, anyway, for Father Malachy's talk. He's come all the way from Dublin and . . .'

Morna swore under her breath, pocketed the unused 10p pieces. Priests again. Her mother would hardly need company or service when she was surrounded by eminent clergy, eating three good meals a day, and with a non-stop cabaret in the form of talks and Masses.

She walked across to the baggage carousel, watched the cases gliding round and round, was tempted to pick up someone else's luggage, steal not their goods but their identity, return to a different house and rôle. If she selected the right suitcase, she might be wife of judge or pop star, muse to a poet, boss of a chain of factories, mother of twin prodigies. Her own home seemed too empty, milk and papers cancelled for another seven days, no friend or client phoning since they all assumed her absent; her doubts and regrets breeding in the silence.

She checked her watch, still set to LA time. Half past eight. Neil would have already left for the office, having breakfasted with Bunny. Would they have criticized her rude bizarre behaviour as they downed their bacon and hash-browns, worried over Chris? Was Chris herself annoyed, or lying sleepless? She ought to phone immediately, reassure them.

She asked three other passengers for change, rehearsed her stock of lies as she sorted through the coins. A crucial job of work with a two days' deadline, a sudden stupid worry about burglars or a break-in, an urgent appointment she had only just remembered, an agonizing toothache. Chris would explode them all. Why not tell the truth? She had pierced inside the atom, glimpsed the structure of the universe, fled in panic. Impossible, ridiculous, and not the whole truth, anyway.

It was Bunny who answered, far too soon. How could you be connected to Los Angeles quicker than to Oxshott?

Morna held the receiver at a distance from her ear. Bunny's voice was loud, swamping her in great washes of concern, uttering little squawks of worry and surprise, pouring out endless frenzied questions. Morna half-answered the first few, used the pips as an excuse to ask for Chris.

'She's not here, Morna honey.'

'N . . . Not there?' Chris was rarely even up at half past eight, unless it was a school day, let alone dressed and out of the house.

'She's having her second lesson with the pro. He had to make it early. It was the only space he had. Neil dropped her on his way to work. But listen, honey, I still don't understand how this French bureau of commerce or whatever could phone you with a job when you were out in Disneyland all day. I mean, even if . . .'

Bunny's voice seemed to be booming round the airport, boomeranging back. There were other noises – a baby crying, a crackling announcement of some hold-up with the luggage on a flight from Ottawa, the man in the phone booth next to her talking very fast and loudly in a foreign language – all the sounds fusing and distorting, breaking into fragments which felt like sharp glass splinters in her head. She forced her mouth to work. Forming words had always been a simple skill before, almost automatic. Now it needed effort, and at a time when her whole body wanted only to sink down. She hacked out a few more sentences, blessed the second set of pips.

'I'm sorry, Bunny, I've run out of coins.' She still had a handful, but what was one more lie? 'I'll write, okay, but do give my message to Chris as soon as she gets in, and special love, of course, and tell her . . .'

She had already been cut off. She picked up her bag, mooched away from the phone booth. So Chris was at a golf lesson, learning to improve her swing, not lying sleepless with anxiety on account of an absent Mum. She tried to force a grin. That put her in her place. Neither her mother nor her daughter was exactly counting the days till they laid eyes on her again. She had been stupid to imagine that Bea would even have welcomed her return. Her conventionally pious mother would hardly approve of her beloved only granddaughter being left on her own in what she considered a distressingly irregular *ménage* in a distinctly foreign country. She had never sanctioned the visit in the first place, loathed the thought of her dead-and-buried son-in-law being rudely resurrected, along with a new necrophiliac wife. She would only fuss and fret, ask too many questions, conclude that Neil or Bunny had driven her out of the house, bite back 'I told you so.'

Why not just go home? Even without Bea, there would be plenty to keep her busy – unpacking, washing, shopping, sorting through the mail. Perhaps a letter from David, a gust of cold clean island air. Cold! It was stifling here in this airless hall with no windows and no view. She took a deep breath in, trudged back to the baggage carousel. Her suitcase was now circling with the others, dented in one corner, scratched along the top. Well, there was her dirty washing. She had better get on with it. She grabbed the case, walked towards the channel marked 'Nothing to Declare', passed a group of Customs men who barely glanced at it, went on towards the exit. Her holiday was over. Back to work. She slackened her pace, changed arms on the case. Strange how work seemed less compelling in an empty echoing house with no one to distract her from it, no one to look after. She was tempted simply to camp out where she was, find a seat or stretch out on her suitcase until the seven days were up. At least she would be on the spot, ready to meet her daughter's plane as soon as it touched down. Chris might be upset at leaving Neil, need a mother's comfort. Except Martin would be there as well, offering rival consolations. Strange to play second fiddle after years of . . .

She swung round. Someone was calling out. It was the old Scots crone, sitting huddled with her luggage on a little motorized buggy. As the oldest passenger, they hadn't let her walk, but were driving her to the transfer-bus which would take her to the terminal for Glasgow.

'What did you say?' Morna had to shout. The buggy was moving faster, the woman almost out of sight.

'Just good luck!' The voice was swallowed up in the general stir and bustle of the airport.

Morna snatched up her case, sprinted after the buggy. 'Wait,' she shouted. 'Wait! I'm coming with you.'

17

'Anyway, I can't. I've got my . . . period.'

'That doesn't matter.'

'It'll make a mess – everywhere.'

'We can put some paper down. There's an old *Reveille* here.'

'I don't want to do it on a newspaper.'

'Well, towels then. I've got a red towel upstairs in my locker. Nothing'll show on that.'

'Yeah, but . . .'

'What?'

'It's . . . embarrassing. Let's leave it, Gerry.'

'We can't. I'm going East tomorrow – for the trials, and by the time I'm back, you'll be gone.'

'You can always visit England and we'll do it there.' Chris shifted position on the dusty floor. Where? England would be still more difficult – with Martin and her mother hovering over her and no handy basement storeroom in a sports centre, open until midnight. The storeroom was officially out-of-bounds, but Gerry had a part-time job in the centre as a security officer, and so had access to every part of the building. Gerry lived, breathed sport. Athletics was as crucial to him as diving was to Martin. Chris glanced across at the muscly legs, emerging from the brief white running shorts, the broad and powerful torso. Why did she always go for sportsmen? Gerry wasn't even handsome, but an achiever, a success. He had the fastest speed in the under-twenties' hundred yards, the highest score in target shooting, and had beaten his personal best in the high jump just last week. All pretty powerful turn-ons. Perhaps she ought to go to bed with him just to see if his decathlon coaching had paid off, if he broke any more records in the sack. Why did she have to have the curse the very day he had invited her to lunch? If men had periods, they would probably have invented some way of switching them on and off at will, or making them last just half an hour instead of five endless draggy days, or turned the blood white and sort of invisible like rain, instead of shaming red. Actually, this period had been the easiest one of her life – no pain, no floodings, not even any cramps – more like Bunny's periods which were so light and hassle-free, all she needed were a few midget-sized tampons, instead of stuffing half a chemist's shop up inside her and still being scared she'd leak. Bunny talked quite freely about things like tampons and the curse – even sex – yet somehow it was never squirmy or embarrassing. Her mother put on a special voice for sex, like those God-men did for Jesus in 'Prayer For The Day', whereas Bunny made it sound down to earth and basic like a grocery order.

She and Bunny had sat up several evenings, sprawling on the floor with mugs of coffee, discussing men or life or lib or God, as if Bunny were a girlfriend her own age rather than a stepmother. Sometimes she felt guilty about her own mother, especially now, when her Mum had gone rushing back to England and she'd felt a whole confusing tangle of contradictory emotions rather than simple loss or worry. Bunny and her father had been frantic, spent the rest of the day at Disneyland searching the crowds for her, which was just about as futile as trying to spot a currant in her school's so-called steamed fruit pudding. Then they'd hurtled back home and found her second note, which didn't say a lot more than the first one, but which had kept them up all night analysing and agonizing. She herself kept seesawing from guilt to irritation. Her mother's running away was a sort of melodramatic proof that she had been wrong to make the trip at all, that her daughter was a bully to have talked her into it. It was like rubbing her nose in it, shouting out, 'I told you so' to the whole of Disneyland, the whole of LA airport. Yet she also felt a sense of sheer relief that her mother wasn't there, that the tension in the house had dropped and she no longer had to fear some terrifying scene. Even at the Ocean View Motel, Morna had somehow been far too near, weighing on their consciences, arousing guilt again. The whole motel thing sounded fishy, anyway. Who was that mysterious American girlfriend who had booked her into the place, and why was no one ever allowed to meet her? Her Mum went tense and sort of flustered if they so much as mentioned it.

Chris clutched at the wall beside her. Could the girlfriend be a boyfriend? She had never thought of that. Had her Mum shacked up with someone, left the Ocean View and gone to Miami or Florida (via Disneyland) for a veteran honeymoon? She had been pitying her mother back at Weybridge, slaving away at some tedious translation in a cold and empty house, yet she might in fact be sprawling on a sun-kissed beach beside a naked male in swim-trunks, rubbing oil into his back, sipping passion-fruit cocktails through one shared straw. Okay, that was embroidering it a bit, but even so, why should she torture herself with scruples over Gerry when her own self-styled virtuous mother was screwing around with some hermaphrodite?

The scruples had got her nowhere – that was obvious. Gerry appeared to have forgotten all about her, turned his attention to more important things. He had cleared a space on the floor and was doing a series of sit-ups, face screwed up, eyes bulging, as he levered up down, up down, sweat beading on his forehead. Nice to come first for once, know you counted more than athletic trials or diving tests or golf medals or board meetings, or even mysterious girlfriends. Only Bunny put her first. Funny, that. She had been wary of Bunny before she had even met her, hated her on first acquaintance, yet now she was confiding in her, divulging things she had never told her mother. That made for guilt as well. Even moaning about her periods to Bunny was somehow disloyal and ungrateful when Morna had taken her to two top men in Harley Street, as well as their own G.P. Bunny distrusted doctors and had suggested a Women's Centre staffed by lay women therapists. They loved the word 'therapist' in the States. Everything was therapy – art, religion, screaming the place down while you bashed a pile of cushions with a tennis racket. (That was called Controlled Rage Therapy, though she couldn't see where the controlled bit quite came in.) Even keeping pets was therapy – something about Dependency Relationships and Learning Trust from Faithful Friends. She had refused to go at first, feared they'd make her scream or pray, do ink-blot tests or buy a Pekinese. Bunny didn't argue, just trotted out a few more of her famous statistics.

'Listen, sweetie, the average age for the menopause is, say, forty-nine to fifty. You're seventeen and three quarters – right? That's roughly four hundred more periods, not counting gaps for pregnancies. If each one lasts five days, you've got two thousand days of pain and cramps and . . .'

That clinched it. They had gone a week ago, when Morna was still at Ocean View. The Centre was new and glossy with pamphlets on contraception contradicting the pictures of smirking chubby babies on the walls, and luxuriant leafy plants which looked as if they'd been dosed with fertility hormones. Their (foreign) therapist, who had cold hands and a name out of Isaac Bashevis Singer, didn't seem to match the place. She was far too tired and jaded, as if she had lost both her leaves and her reproductive organs long ago.

'You like being woman?' she croaked, once they had stripped her naked and stuck her on a couch, her feet yanked up and out so she was showing everything she'd got.

'Yeah,' she had answered, wondering if she did like. You didn't have much choice.

After half an hour's grilling on subjects which seemed to have more to do with philosophy and politics than with menstruation, the therapist concluded that the painful periods were a result of anger at enforced submission and subservience, and a secret desire to be a man.

'Balls!' Chris had muttered, stomping to the door. She wasn't submissive. Was she? Often scared of Martin, though. Well, not actually scared, but always worrying about what he'd say or think, and feeling she ought to be faithful to him – like now. Stupid word. Sounded like a spaniel. Men were never faithful. Look at Gerry. He already had a steady – a blonde called Shirlee (with a double 'e'), and here he was trying to lay her too. He saw all women as subservient. They had only been created to be the chauffeurs or the cheer-leaders, or to keep the dinner hot if you played extra time. Martin wasn't like that. Martin wanted her to dive with him, hating leaving her behind on the beach or in the pub, only sharing the experience in fumbling words or out-of-focus photographs. It was she who had resisted – through sheer craven fear. Fine to dive in Putney baths with blue tiles underneath you and fully trained instructors all around, but the wide open sea . . .

She ought to have phoned him again, or at least have sent that letter, but every time she scrawled another paragraph, the ones before seemed wrong – either sloppy or too cool, or plain untrue. She kept crossing them out and starting afresh, writing two or three more pages, only to tear them up the next day, then deciding to phone instead. That wasn't simple, either. She had to find a call box somewhere private and make sure she had lots of change and that she'd worked

331

out the time difference so that it wasn't three a.m. in Wandsworth. The second time she had rung, Martin was out again, and she'd got his kid brother, Phil, who probably never passed her message on, since he regarded girlfriends in general as pure Yuk and Slop, and Martin's as Betrayal. So she had gone back to the letter which was now ten and a quarter pages and every page more fatuous than the last. The trouble was, the longer she was away from him, the more distant Martin seemed, so she wasn't sure who exactly she was writing to, or even why it was so damned important that she did write. *He* had written to her, though – three times in a fortnight – intense impatient letters which didn't seem to fit their cheap lined notepaper and which had left her so confused, she'd only sort of skimmed them, then shoved them in a drawer, tried to pretend they'd never come at all.

She checked on Gerry again. He was doing leg-bends now, grunting with exertion. It made her tired to hear him. She slumped against a crate to rest her back, stared down at her hands, waggling the fourth finger of the left one – wedding finger. She was engaged to Martin, more or less, and had let fifteen days go by without contacting him. Worse than that, she was locked in a room with another man – one she had met just three short days ago and who might leap on her at any moment if he could spare the time from his workout. Was it really wrong, though? Bunny said she needed more experience, owed it to herself, and that she shouldn't say no to sex just because of guilt, but only if the encounter wouldn't nourish her – which made it sound like vitamins. The whole subject was confusing. Half the world made you feel a monster if you went to bed with more than just one bloke, and the other half kept urging you to try out every possible man and variation. She had only slept with two men – Pierre and Martin – and Pierre didn't really count because he was what the women's magazines called a holiday romance. Girls like Bunny had probably had *dozens* before they settled down. She ought to make it three. Three would be more representative.

'Gerry!' she called. He was back to sit-ups now, but he turned the last one into a stand-up, vaulted over a box of light bulbs to reach her side.

'Changed your mind?'

'Uh-uh.' That was Bunny's phrase and actually meant 'no', but sounded far less final than a straight refusal. She stared around at the brooms and brushes, the cartons of toilet paper and crates of detergent. The room smelt musty with a faint whiff of disinfectant. Why were men so unromantic? She might have said yes if he'd booked a suite at the Biltmore and was wearing a black tuxedo instead of a white singlet soaked in sweat.

'Come on – just a kiss.'

'Okay.' She owed him a kiss at least. He had bought her two Budweisers and a king-size hamburger for lunch – even offered her crabs' legs as a starter, although they cost six dollars for just four. She opened her mouth. The kiss went on so long, she had paid him back for double crabs' legs, plus fillet steak and cocktails and was still in credit. He kept pressing himself against her through the running shorts. It wasn't fair to get a man excited and then let him down. Martin had told her that. And Bunny had urged her to feed herself and love herself and give herself permission to enjoy things, so long as they were enriching. This was. They were on the dessert kiss now – triple scoops of strawberry ripple with whipped cream and cherries.

She pulled away. Strawberry was Martin's favourite flavour. Martin was saving for their future. Hell, though, a kiss was nothing really, and she owed it to her father to give Gerry some encouragement. It was Neil who had introduced them in the first place. Gerry belonged to his tennis club and played in all the tournaments. His own father was an attorney and his mother shopped at some place in Beverly Hills which was so damn swanky you had to have an appointment before they even let you in and then they bought you cocktails on a silver tray to help you endure the tedium of trying on thousand-dollar dresses.

Chris glanced down at her own bargain-basement jeans, touched the shabby leather belt she'd nicked from Martin before she went away. She had tried to tell her father about Martin, though she had seen from his expression that he wasn't all that thrilled. She'd decided to leave out the engagement bit, rambled on instead about the diving, and how Martin would make it in the end, even though he'd left school at sixteen and had lumpish sort of parents. Neil hadn't said a lot, in fact, but the next day he had invited her to the club for drinks and somehow hoovered Gerry in, until he was sitting at their table listening to how smart she was and how she had turned Cambridge down (instead of vice versa) and was more or less trilingual. She had felt a perfect fraud, but Gerry seemed impressed and had then started on his own achievements which were still resounding when her father sort of slunk away and left them on their own.

Gerry hadn't mentioned touching in his list of accomplishments, but he was good at that as well. He had found her nipples and was rubbing one broad palm up and down against them, down and up. He didn't seem to mind small breasts. Perhaps he was used to female athletes who were on those drugs and things and were probably semi-bearded as well as flat up front.

'Want me to get that towel?' he whispered.

'N . . . No.' If he went away, she might lose her nerve again, lose the erection in her nipples. She pushed her shirt up. 'The . . . er . . . newspaper will do.'

She could tell he was a hurdler by the speed with which he dashed across the room, leapfrogging bales and boxes in his way and returning with the paper. She squinted down at it as he spread it on the floor.

'Redskins Fight Back All The Way,' she read. 'Return match draws six thousand.'

'Take your jeans off.' Gerry made it almost like an order.

'Y . . . You take your shorts off first.'

She hadn't realized how tanned he was until she saw the pale private strip the shorts had hidden. He was big – bigger than Martin. That made it worse, like stealing a million bucks instead of a dime. He was pulling off his singlet now, revealing blondish chest hair tangled with two silver chains. She looked away.

'C'mon,' he said. 'Your turn.'

'Close your eyes, then.' Somehow, she had to get the Tampax out and then dispose of it. There wasn't room for both of them inside her. It was worse than trying to get rid of a mouthful of chewing-gum when a boy suddenly decided to kiss you. That had happened too, with Gerry – the night they met.

'And turn your back as well.'

'What you doing, for Chrissake?'

'Never mind. Just promise not to look?'

'Okay, okay, but don't take all night.'

She didn't answer. She ought to clean herself up before they started and she had only one mingy Kleenex in her bag. She slunk across to the carton of toilet-rolls, reached up on tiptoe, tried to ease one out without him hearing. At least he had his eyes closed. The rolls were jammed tight together and all she succeeded in doing was breaking a nail. The box was too high up, piled on three other crates and set at an awkward angle. She tried to tug it towards her, dodged away as it suddenly keeled over and fifty toilet rolls cascaded to the floor, some of them unravelling in a tangle of pink ticker tape.

'Jesus Christ!' said Gerry.

Chris lunged to the floor to stop them rolling further, leapt up again as Gerry strode across. She was naked from the waist down, with bloodstains on her thighs. She snatched up her jeans, used them as a loincloth.

'Don't look!' she cried. 'You promised.'

'What d'you mean, don't look? I'm in charge of all this stuff. They'll take it out of my wages.' Gerry was swearing to himself as he righted the box, a shit for every toilet roll. Chris tried to help with one hand, still clinging to her loincloth with the other.

'Fuck!' said Gerry, which was at least a change from shit, though they seemed further from actually doing it than they had been all afternoon. 'Some of this paper's dirty from the floor. My supervisor's gonna go out of his mind.'

'Tear it off, then,' Chris suggested, ripping off a few grubby sheets herself. She made Gerry close his eyes again while she mopped between her legs with it, hid the debris in an old tin bucket, dragged her pants back on.

'Ready?' Gerry asked. He didn't look ready himself, not any more.

'You mean you still want to . . .?'

'Sure I want to. Let's go, okay?'

Chris removed the pants, lay down gingerly on the *West Coast Reveille*. If she moved too fast, the bleeding might set off again. The floor felt cold and hard. She was lying on two Redskins in full gear.

Gerry crouched beside her, touched her breasts. 'You're beautiful.'

'I'm not.'

'I've never done it with an English girl.'

'Don't worry. I doubt if God made us all that different.'

'You're quite a tease, aren't you?'

'Am I?' She suddenly wanted to call it off. She didn't like the feel of his skin, the stupid things he said. Anyway, she was worried about the blood. She had never done it with a period before, not even with Martin. That made it more of a betrayal. She pushed his hands off, struggled up.

'Look, I . . . don't think it's going to work.'

'You *what*?'

'I've . . . er . . . changed my mind.'

'You're kidding.'

'No, I'm not.'

'Christ almighty! Listen, nobody fucks me around like this. I take you out to lunch, I take time off without pay, I'm risking my job by even bringing you down here, and then you have the nerve to say . . .'

He had grabbed her by the arm. She tried to shake him off, but he was far too strong for her. They were wrestling now, she a flyweight, he a slugger. It was terrifying, terrifying. She hit out as hard as she could, yet even her fiercest blows hardly grazed his steel-hard muscles. She kicked, punched, let fly with arms and legs, hardly caring now that she was naked so long as she could hold her own. She wasn't doing badly. In fact, shouldn't he be hurting more, have her down by now? She stopped for a moment. He stopped. He wasn't even fighting. All he'd been doing was dodging her blows, kidding her along. He ran a hand along her thigh. She took it off, enraged. He was just using the tussle as an excuse to touch her up.

'Fight properly,' she shouted. 'Fight me as if I'm a man.'

'Want me to kill you, then?'

'Yeah.'

He suddenly pitched her to the ground, sat on her feet to stop them flailing, pinioned her arms. 'I'll kill you *afterwards*,' he whispered. 'Okay?'

'O . . . Okay.'

He seized both her wrists in just one hand, used the other to steady her face while he lowered his lips towards it. Both hands were hurting now.

'Still want to chicken out?' His lips were almost touching

hers. She could feel his breath, hot and lager-flavoured, smell the rank sweaty odour of his armpits.

'N . . . No.' A drool of blood was seeping out between her legs. She tried to press her thighs together, trap it somehow. 'Just d . . . don't be too long. I'm worried about the mess.'

He kneed her legs apart. 'Okay, if you want it quick . . .' He was big again, big and red, as if he had swollen up in anger. He climbed on top, forced in.

'Ow! You're hurting, Gerry.'

He took no notice, just went on thrusting, circling his body at the same time as he pistoned up and down. She closed her eyes, moved with him.

'Hurting now?'

She didn't answer. It was fantastic, but she wasn't going to tell him that. He had forced her, more or less, so she shouldn't be enjoying it. If she were a true feminist and believed all that stuff they'd spouted at the Women's Centre, she should be kicking him in the balls rather than stroking them with her one free hand and making grateful gaspy noises underneath him. She couldn't stop herself, that was the trouble. He was sort of corkscrewing on top of her, jab-jabbing his body right against that bit of hers which counted. The blood made it feel different, wetter and more slippery, and with a bit more room inside her as if someone had stretched her to fit another prick or two. Not that she could cope with more than one. Gerry's was in training like the rest of him, super-fit and tireless, showing off its paces, winning medals. She was winning them herself, part of the act, his team mate, his goalkeeper. Yet one part of her was horrified, shocked that she was cheering him on, shouting 'Yeah!', 'More!', 'Great!' as he pounded into her. If only she could stop thinking, be just a body and a hole, a dumb broad without a conscience who could shut out all the accusing voices.

'Be greedy,' Bunny was urging. 'Feed yourself.'

'Men men menace!' shrieked the Women's Lib badges.

'Promise you won't . . .' Martin was imploring, leaving her to fill in the words – screw around, betray me.

Why were all the messages conflicting, all the words mocked by her wild and gasping breathing, her sudden yelps of pleasure?

'Sssh . . .' hissed Gerry suddenly. 'There's somebody out there.'

Heavy feet were echoing down the passage. She tried to lie still and silent as the footsteps stopped. Gerry froze. Someone was rattling the handle on the door.

'Did you lock it?' she whispered, aching with the strain of having to stop.

'Yeah, I did, but . . .'

She heard the footsteps plonking off again, giggled suddenly. 'Perhaps they were desperate for some loo paper. We should have pushed some under the door.'

'Hush up.' Gerry was back on form again, she moving with him, shouting.

'Don't make so much noise. If the supervisor finds us, we're in trouble.'

She'd bloody shout if she wanted. It was a yell of triumph, anyway. She was coming – NOW – without even the help of a finger and before him. Her climax spurred him on. He had really got a speed up, ramming back and forth. That excited her in turn again. She ground her body into his, gripped him with her thighs. 'Yes, *come*,' she shouted, 'come!'

He couldn't not. His eyes were closed, his face screwed up, nails digging into her flesh.

'Shirlee!' he shouted, suddenly. 'Christ, I love you, Shirl.'

There was a sudden silence. Thirty seconds passed before she freed her face from his, wiped her mouth. 'The name's Chris, actually.'

'God, I'm . . . I'm sorry. I . . . er . . . don't know what I'm saying.'

'Don't you? Shirlee's your girlfriend, your steady. The blonde with big boobs – remember? You told me all about her over lunch.'

He bit his lip, looked down.

'No sweat,' said Chris. 'We're made the same, I told you.'

He was limp now, sagging out, his thing dripping blood, his thighs red and shiny with it. She eased up from the newspaper with its spreading scarlet stain, pummelled it into a ball, fought an urge to aim it at his head. She had no right to be angry or vindictive when she and Gerry were quits – both cheating on their steadies. If Martin slept with another girl, would he call the creature Chris? Martin *wouldn't* sleep around. Martin was faithful. It no longer seemed a stupid word at all.

'Hey, you've got newsprint on your bottom.'

'Where?' She twisted round to try and see her buttocks, glimpsed only a patch of floor. 'What's it say? "Bomb Scare" or "Win For Redskins"?' He was probably simply trying to change the subject, deflect attention from his own embarrassment.

'I can't read it. It's just a splodge. D'you want to clean up? There's a shower room upstairs. Wait a minute – I better check if the coast is clear.'

This was the time for afterplay – staying close and cuddling, winding down, whispering sloppy things. Instead, Gerry was crouching by the ventilator, mopping himself with spittle and a dirty handkerchief, dragging his clothes back on. He tossed her the hankie and her jeans, went to check the corridor.

'Okay – nobody there, but hurry. Up the stairs and first door on the left.'

She turned the shower to hottest, tried to wash him off. He was stubborn like the newsprint. It had been good, damned good – the first time she had come without a finger. So why did she feel so rotten? It wasn't just the guilt. It was more complicated than that. Sex meant Martin – all of him – his smell, his voice, his holey pants which no one ever ironed, the way he bounced and whistled afterwards, fed her with chocolate biscuits or bacon-flavoured crisps. She missed the crisps, the bits of salty crumb which tickled in the bed, the way he blew the bag up and then burst it like a kid, the sort of crazy specialness between them.

She dawdled over dressing, praying Gerry would be gone by the time she emerged. He wasn't. He was waiting by the exit doing side-bends.

'Time for a Coke?'

'No, sorry. We're going out. My Mum flew home the night before last – back to England. She just suddenly left without telling anyone, and my father's worried that I'm still upset about it. I suppose I am in one way . . . Anyway, he's taking me out for a meal to – you know – cheer me up.' It had been Bunny's idea, in fact, but it still gave her a kick to say 'my father' and she wouldn't have the chance much longer.

'Where you going?'

'Somewhere called "The Queen's Head" in Hollywood. It's an English-style place, my father says, where they all . . .'

'I know it. It's great. You'll love it there.'

'Well, I'd better make a move or I'll be late. I'm late already. Thanks . . . for everything. And give my regards to Shirlee.'

She was glad he had the grace to blush.

'What kept you, sweetie?' Bunny was already in her wrap, red ruffles underneath, and all the bracelets.

'I was playing . . . tennis with Gerry.'

'Who won?'

'We . . . er . . . drew.'

341

'Congratulations.' Neil was wearing a seersucker jacket in gold and navy stripes, a navy polo-neck to match. 'He's a damn good player. Why didn't you go on and play a tie-breaker? You might even have beaten him.'

'I was . . . um . . . too shagged.'

'Well, hurry up and change, honey. We reserved a table and they'll think we're not coming and give it away to someone else.'

Chris put a dress on, the only one she owned, went to say good night to Dean. He wasn't in his room.

'He's staying with the Bradleys,' Bunny explained. 'We thought we'd have you all to ourselves tonight.'

They were trying to make it up to her, assumed she was missing her Mum. It seemed crazy now that she should have brought a chaperone, felt she needed Morna there as confidante and buffer, someone to hold her hand and field the blows. In fact, she felt far better on her own. Martin and her mother were the two people closest to her and for that very reason, she was glad they weren't around. They loved her, yes, but their love was like a wooden fence caging her in, blocking out the view. Bunny and Neil were different, didn't keep watching her every move or patching up the fence with extra boards if she so much as pawed the ground.

The restaurant was a sort of Tudor palace with huge gilded axes which served as handles on the studded doors. 'The Queen's Head' was starred in all the guide books, a top tourist attraction, where you had to book at least a week ahead, unless you were someone like her father who Knew People. He was already deep in serving wenches, all dressed as Nell Gwyns or Anne Boleyns or something, with flowing velvet skirts and lots of cleavage. The place looked distinctly schizophrenic. The dartboard and the draught bitter belonged in a British pub, whilst the court jester and the wenches had been imported from some MGM period spectacular. Except they had got their periods mixed.

Sixteenth-century madrigals thundered from a twentieth-century synthesizer. The long wooden tables were mock-Jacobean, the suits of armour pseudo-Cromwellian, while both Victoria Regina and Queen Elizabeth I frowned down from the panelled walls, surrounded by a bodyguard of stags' heads.

They were ushered to their table, knocking elbows, tripping over expensive feet. Neil and Bunny hardly had her to themselves. Half of southern California appeared to have joined the party, dinning out the music, dressed to kill. Her own frock looked poorhouse by comparison and clashed with the padded purple covers of the menus which were so large and springy Gerry could have used them as a trampoline. The lettering inside was gold italic, while the food itself ranged from King Henry VIII's Roast Sucking Pig to Lancashire Hotpot (anon).

'Fish and chips for me,' said Bunny, once they had sampled their Freedom of London cocktails, which came in pewter goblets with miniature Union Jacks stuck in fat red cherries on the top. 'It's out of this world.'

At twenty dollars a portion, so it should be, Chris thought, twirling her little flag – and that probably didn't include the newspaper. She couldn't get away from newspaper today. She could feel the blood still seeping out of her, mixed with semen now. How long did sperms survive? Supposing they were still alive and kicking when Martin met her plane in six days' time. Would he guess, sniff out Gerry's traces? She tried to banish both of them, decipher the Olde Englishe spellings on the menu. 'Meade', she read. 'A fertilitie drink, made with honeye and rare spices'. She slumped back in her seat. Fertility. Gerry hadn't used a Durex. She had been so concerned about her period, she had totally forgotten contraception. But weren't periods themselves a sort of Durex? She was sure she'd read somewhere that you couldn't get pregnant when you had the curse.

Except there was also always the exception which broke the rule, broke your life apart. Imagine having Gerry's baby. She could see it in its cradle wearing running shorts above its nappies, flexing its biceps on the feeding bottle, practising its sit-ups. She gulped her cocktail, wincing as the ice cubes froze her teeth. Maybe Bunny was wrong about sex. It couldn't just be kicks (or vitamins) when there was a chance of making kids. Kids made it sacred. She was old enough to have a kid already. Dean could be her child – just. She'd like that. Or Martin's child – who'd be born with fins and a snorkel and drink bacon-flavoured milk.

'What d'you want to eat, honey?' Bunny asked, passing her own menu across and shouting above the clatter of plates, the cackle of conversation and the strains of 'Where the Bee Sucks' recorded on electronic sackbut. 'The vegetarian dishes are down the side – see? There's Shepherd's Pie and . . .'

'That's not vegetarian.'

'It says it is.'

'The shepherd must have lost his sheep, then. I don't think I'll risk it, anyway, just in case one or two slipped in. I'll have Anne Boleyn's salad, please.'

'Sounds dangerous to me,' said Neil, slipping an arm across her shoulder. She still felt shy of him. Odd to think she was actually made of the same flesh and blood and genes and things (well, half at least). It didn't feel like that. If you shared your building-bricks with someone, shouldn't you be closer, be able to see into their soul or communicate without the need for words or the constant worry that you wouldn't quite come up to scratch? There were new lines on his face, disguised by the smile, but remaining there after it had faded. He had always had frown lines, as far back as she could remember, but she didn't recall those two deep furrows running from nose to mouth. She felt angry with them suddenly, as if they marked her five long years without

344

him, like those rings on tree trunks which grew one for each new winter.

Bunny was still poring over the menu, holding it up to the light of the (all-electric) candles. 'We'll have the Poacher's Broth first, shall we? It's very good.'

'Okay.' Chris traced a G with her fork prongs on the tablecloth. Poachers meant snares and traps and meat again, no doubt, but she couldn't be worrying about fur and feather when Gerry's naked kid might be taking root inside her, building cell by cell.

'What's the matter, hon?'

'Nothing.'

'Missing your Mom?'

'A bit.'

'She's just fine. She told me so. She was real glad to get that job.'

Chris was silent. There wasn't any job. Her mother was hardly so important that clients phoned around the world for her. They just passed the work to someone else. There were enough out-of-work translators, for heaven's sake, panting for a crust.

Neil snapped his Union Jack in half, jabbed the broken ends against his palm. 'She should have turned it down. I mean, dashing off like that in the middle of a vacation and changing all the plans . . .'

'Leave it, Daddy, can't we?' Chris couldn't understand why her father should object to Morna's going. Unless it were just pride. No one ran away from Neil, and the things he planned must always prove an unqualified success. Her Mum had kiboshed that. Or maybe he was jealous – had somehow sussed out that boy/girlfriend in the Ocean View Motel.

'Let's put our crowns on,' Bunny smiled. 'Be kings and queens tonight.' She was papering over cracks. Each person's place was set not only with olde worlde knives and

345

forks in pseudo-pewter, but also with a paper crown. Bunny reached across for Neil's, set it on his head at a rakish angle, removed a rosebud from the vase, stuck it in the band. Neither matched his frown.

Chris picked up her own crown, rammed it on her head. Her Mum had left because she couldn't stand the tension, the frowns beneath the rosebuds. There wasn't any boy-friend. The whole idea was quite absurd. Her mother didn't go for men, or only ones like Rilke or Sainte-Beuve who were safely dead and buried. Even in the States, Morna had started on the culture thing, bought poetry books and tried to foist them on her – American stuff to match the trip – Ezra Pound, Robert Lowell. She had dipped into them both, in fact, found them difficult, depressing. Poetry didn't seem to belong in California. Even back in England, it was all a bit of a con – one of those things the adult world approved of, like drinking orange juice instead of gin, or going to the Natural History Museum or early bed, but which the adults never bothered with themselves. If you took all the people in this restaurant, for example, you could bet your life not one of them chose Pound or Lowell as their bedtime reading. Literature was something Important like Church or Freedom or Equality which all had capital letters but which didn't get much of a look-in compared with lower-case things like stuffing yourself or getting laid or making money or merely making out. Most of the grown-ups she knew spent their reading time on newspapers and magazines, business reports or recipes, or even cornflake packets. Perhaps the whole thing was the wrong way round. Wouldn't it be better to save your studies for later on, when you were settled or married or resigned, or at least less confused about all the basic things like being faithful or submissive, or whether you wanted a career or kids, or neither. They could invent new A level courses in Knowing Who You Were, or at least finding out whether you meant yes or no and then not regretting the one you had plumped for. And with that weight off your mind, you might have energy enough to tackle *Leaves of Grass* or *Life Studies*.

If you hadn't died first, of course, of syphilis or AIDS. She had probably caught both from Gerry. America was famous for VD. Herpes was so common, there was a special dating service for people who were infected, and you could even buy plastic models of the virus to offend your friends. She'd pass it on to Martin and then he'd *know* she'd been unfaithful (that word again) and she would have to keep grovelling and letting him win arguments in order to make up.

'Ah, here's our first course.' Neil shook out his napkin, spread it on his lap. The Nell Gwyn waitress had paused to flirt with him, her cleavage plunging so low, you could almost see her navel. Chris tried to keep her attention on the soup. It had come with English muffins which were neither English nor muffins, but so big and soft Anne Boleyn could have slept on one and still room to spare for some of the other wives. It had been worse for Anne Boleyn. She couldn't even *choose* about babies, just lost her head for not producing a son. Chris let out a sudden nervous laugh.

Bunny squeezed her arm. 'That's better. You've been looking as if you'd lost twenty bucks and found a dime.'

Hadn't she? Martin was worth two hundred of Gerry, at least, yet she had valued him at nothing, kicked him in the gutter. Bunny would say 'Enjoy them both, honey child. A dime-store's fun as well as Saks Fifth Avenue.' She snatched a glance at Bunny, who was giggling with the waitress, mopping butter off her chin – having a ball, to use one of her own phrases. Bunny was always cheerful, always having a ball – the only person she knew, in fact, who seemed genuinely happy, not merely coping or content or not complaining. And it wasn't just because she was an uncomplicated type. So was Martin's mother and yet *she* had grievances. She didn't like the Council or the milkman or the neighbours opposite or the way they timed the coffee breaks at work. Why didn't they have A levels in Happiness? It was obviously quite a skill, yet seemed as scorned as subjects like Home Economics or Dressmaking. In fact, half the writers they studied at school had lived thoroughly miserable lives and the American ones were worse. Pound had landed up in an institution, branded as a fascist and a traitor; both Lowell and Roethke had been in and out of mental hospitals all their lives, and . . .

'How's the soup?' asked Bunny.

'Great.' Chris picked out a scrap of chicken and discarded it on her side plate, swirled the rest with her spoon so she could spot any further offerings from the poacher.

'Good God!' said Neil, pushing back his chair. 'Look over there.'

Chris looked, couldn't see anything new – just another troop of people frothing through the door, adding to the crush.

'It's Irving Stroud, would you believe?' Bunny was goggling now as well.

'Who's he?'

'You *must* know Irving Stroud, honey.'

Chris blushed. He was probably some top movie star or leading politician, the sort of Shining Light who made the cover of *Newsweek*. What was the use of her lousy prissy school if all it taught was nineteenth-century fogies?

'Is he that . . . er . . . you know . . .?' She wasn't even good at bluffing. Neil wasn't listening anyway, was already on his feet, striding to the door, where a slight man in his early sixties with flabby skin the colour of stewed onions and eyes like two black peppercorns, was shrugging off a fur-lined overcoat.

'Irving!'

'Neil!'

Their voices carried, even over 'Greensleeves' amplified on lutes and viols. Neil had meant them to.

Bunny turned back to her soup. 'He's one of Neil's old clients. He was big then, but now he's very big. His last party made all the headlines. Everyone was there.'

'Were *you*? I mean you as well as Daddy?'

'Oh, yeah. I bought a whole new outfit. Shocking pink. Everyone wore pink. You had to. It said so on the card.'

'What, the blokes as well?'

'Sure. It was a Pink Party – period. All the food and stuff was pink and there was pink champagne and pink flowers everywhere and . . .'

'I *loathe* pink.'

'So does your Dad.' Bunny giggled at the memory. 'You should have seen him!'

Chris checked on him now, his hand on Irving's arm, their shoulders almost touching, the other hangers-on standing back in awe. His face was pink beneath the tan. Pink with triumph. She turned back to Bunny. 'Don't you get to say hallo, as well?'

'Oh, no. It's man-talk only here. Big-man talk.'

Chris ripped a piece off her muffin, crammed it in her mouth. Big-man talk. So Bunny was the little woman, the original dumb blonde. Is that why her father had married her – someone less threatening than her own Mum and who was content to play foil to Mr Big? Morna was disqualified twice over. Not only was she clever (a crime for wives), she was also far too old. No self-respecting he-man in LA would be seen dead with a woman over forty. Bunny was Neil's advertisement for himself. 'Look at me! I made it. Isn't she cute? And only last year's registration plates.'

Martin wasn't like that. Martin could have picked a blonde as well – gone even further, insisted on crap like waist-length hair or natural curls, instead of a standard-issue makeshift like herself. Martin loved her for that self – not just her face or bum or what she did for his standing with the boys. She had never really realized that before, nor valued the fact that he didn't mind her being what he labelled brainy – brainier than he was – was proud of it, in fact, didn't keep trying to put her down or shut her up, to make sure he stayed top dog.

She checked on her father again. He had competition now – had been swept into the crowd of Irving Stroud fans, all vying to buy him drinks or touch his garment as if he was Christ Come Back and could heal their leprosy. They *did* look leprous in the strange light of the bar which seemed to leach the colour from their faces and dump it in their garish-coloured cocktails. Martin wouldn't leave her on her own if some big-wheel wreck diver swaggered in. He'd take her over, introduce her, show his pride in her. Didn't Bunny *mind*, for God's sake, sitting there in front of an empty soup dish with a few shreds of mangled muffin on her plate, whilst her husband fought to be the one who bought Irving's second Tequila Sunrise? Their own glasses were empty. Neil had been about to order the wine when Jesus Stroud dropped in. Maestro Stroud? Senator Stroud? She still hadn't worked out who he was.

One of the Nell Gwyns had come up to their table, her own two plump peeled oranges strapped high up in front. 'Shall I bring your main course now, or wait for Mr Gordon?'

'Oh, *wait*,' said Bunny, shocked.

Chris removed her crown. So now they had to starve, suck their ice cubes. She was ravenous, despite the soup which had been only flavoured liquid. The whole place was something of a con, failed to live up to its five-star adjectives. The man at the next table had ordered the roast suckling pig which sounded both cruel and grand and was described on the menu in such high-flown prose that she felt it called for footnotes like her Eliot. Yet what actually arrived were thin anaemic slices of the same boring pork they served up at school, but heavily disguised with cherries and bits of green stuff and even a paper frill or two, as if it had been sent straight from the knacker's yard to the gift-wrapping department. The party opposite were already on dessert, and were tucking into Sir Roger de Coverley's Syllabub which looked suspiciously like Bird's Eye lemon mousse and only owed its knighthood to the fancy dish it came in. Even the Nell Gwyns were sort of bogus – all panstick and hair-pieces and push-up bras – smiles stuck-on like the beauty spots. The one by the window wasn't even smiling but carrying on a quarrel with a down-at-mouth court jester, hissing out insults from the corner of her mouth.

'Don't you just love those costumes?' Bunny said, following her gaze. 'See the one with the fur all round the hem?'

'Yeah. It's dragging in the dirt.' Chris rocked back in her chair. Bunny was only trying to fill the gap, distract attention from the fact that Neil had forgotten all about them. Was she really so damned cheerful? Or was that a con as well? The trouble with the adult world was that everyone pretended – all smiles and smarm, bill and coo. It made you uncomfortable when you didn't know the language, when 'Divine' or 'Great' could mean 'Horseshit' or 'Fuck off', and all those hugs and handshakes hid rage and jealousy. She was guilty herself to some extent, angry with her father, contemptuous of Bunny, yet concealing it, dissembling. What if they were angry with *her*, and the whole two weeks' hospitality had been simply a load of humbug, plotted in advance? Neil might have decided to do his duty by her just the once, more to still his conscience than for her sake; offer her this one short trip, then cut all ties completely. Easy for Bunny to charm the arse off her if it were only for three weeks in a lifetime and she could bar her doors for ever at the end of them.

She picked up her empty glass. 'C . . . Can we have a drink?'

'You're thirsty, are you, honey? Want a Coke?'

'I'd rather try that mead stuff.' Fertilitie drink. At least if she were pregnant her father would take notice of her. He wouldn't have much choice. She'd refuse to go back home until the kid was born, dump it on him wet and screaming, call it Irving.

'D'you think you should? It's very potent. Even one small glassful makes me tiddly.'

'Let's have a bottle, then. Two bottles.'

Bunny forced a laugh. 'Why don't we wait until your father. . .?'

'*No.*' Chris snapped her fingers at the beefeater-cum-wine-waiter, as she had seen Neil do earlier. She was frightened at her anger. If her father felt like that inside, then the past fortnight had been fraud, he and Bunny slapping whitewash over rust and stain.

'Bunny . . .?'

'What, sweet?'

'Did you and Daddy . . .' Chris stopped, changed tack. 'I'm *not* sweet, Bunny. I'm horrible. I wish we could be . . . real – you know, say what we think. I mean, are *you* sweet – right inside, where it counts? Truly? Cross your heart?'

'Well, I . . .' Bunny broke off, seemed relieved to see the mead arrive, sidetracked on to the cuteness of the bottle.

Chris moved it out of range. 'Take now, for instance. Aren't you annoyed with my Dad, at least a little bit? Okay, so we had him for the soup and I suppose we have to be grateful if he comes back for the After Eights, but . . .'

'It's . . . only business, honey.'

'Business! What, holding up the bar and all fawning on each other?'

'Irving Stroud's worth a hundred million bucks, at least, hon.'

'And what are *we* worth?'

Bunny was silent, looking down, fiddling with her glass.

'What's he *do*, anyway?'

'Well, he made his money originally with a chain of laundromats . . .'

'L . . . *Laundromats*?'

'That's right. He started with regular ones and then he had this idea of building them up into like pleasure palaces. You can spend the whole day there. They've got video games, vending machines, sun-beds, everything.' Bunny paused to sip her mead. 'He came from nothing, you realize. His father was a Jewish immigrant who arrived in the States with only the clothes on his back.'

Chris banged her glass down. 'Stroud's not a Jewish name.'

'Oh, he changed it, hon. They often do. It's the classic story – second generation son makes good. Irving left school at fourteen and got his first job in a Chinese laundry. By the age of thirty-four he was a millionaire. That didn't really make him, though. So who *isn't* a millionaire in California?' Bunny shrugged. 'But he was sharp enough to make the absolutely right kind of marriage – a starlet who went on to be a star. That gave him the entrée to the movie world and . . .'

Chris stabbed her hand with her fork, winced at the four red weals. So there was her own father paying court to a chain of laundromats, licking the boots of a scullery boy who didn't even own his name, but who'd made sure he married right. Blonde again, most likely, and under thirty. She refilled her glass. The noise level was rising – 'O Mistress Mine' in quadraphonic sound, guests guffawing and cackling as the liquor flowed, the clatter of knives on platters, the tread of wenches' feet. Yet she was more conscious of Bunny's silence, a terrifying silence. Bunny was happy, right? Full of jokes and chatter. So what had snapped?

'Y . . . You're angry with me, aren't you, Bunny?'

'Angry?'

'Why don't you admit it? I'm sick of all this crap, pretending we're bosom pals when . . .' Chris stopped. Bunny looked older suddenly. She had eaten off her lipstick; the make-up on one eyelid had smudged into an age-line. What when she was *really* old – like forty? Only eight short years to go. Dean would be twelve by then, the same age she had been herself when her father ditched her own Mum. Bunny didn't even have a degree to fall back on, a job to tide her over. She was unravelling already. A blob of grease had dribbled from her soup spoon to her ruffles, the giggles had dried up. It was *her* fault. She had tried to break the rules, probe beneath the surface. She was beginning to understand now. If you didn't keep the pretences up, everything might smash to smithereens – families, marriages, even meals in restaurants. She snatched up her glass, used it as her anchor. The mead was sweet and sticky, uncomplicated, comforting. She tried to think of nothing but the steady trickle down her throat.

The music was different now, no longer a choir with lutes and viols, but a harpsichord and solo countertenor – a strange, forced, strangled sort of voice. Chris recognized the song from *Much Ado*. '*Sigh no more, ladies, sigh no more, Men were deceivers ever* . . .' What about women, though? Weren't they as bad, or worse? She was a deceiver herself.

> '*One foot in sea and one on shore,*
> *To one thing constant never* . . .'

She tried to block the words out, glanced across at Bunny – silent still and drinking. 'Speak,' Chris prayed. 'Call me "sweet" again or "honey-pie".' Bunny said nothing, just refilled her glass. The record shrilled and quavered on, reached its final refrain: '*Hey nonny nonny*', repeated over and over and over until the last sighing cadence. There was a sudden roll of drums, a trumpet fanfare, and two Elizabethan lookalikes looped back the heavy velvet curtains on the stage.

'Hey, look!' said Bunny. 'They're starting the cabaret.'

'So early?'

'Oh, they go on practically all night. This is just the warm-up.'

Chris giggled suddenly. 'I'm pretty damn warm already.'

'It's the mead, hon. I warned you, didn't I?'

'I like it. I feel better, actually. It's only just hit me now – sort of all at once, slap bang. You're tipping, Bunny. The whole room's tipping.'

'Don't say that or you'll make me dizzy, too. I've had quite a bit myself.'

'Have some more. Go on, let's be dizzy. Instead of angry. Right?'

'Right.' They clinked their glasses, settled back to watch the show. Henry VIII had strutted on to the stage and was marshalling his wives. Jane Seymour had gone missing. An MC in a black tuxedo and emerald cummerbund seized the microphone.

'Okay, guys, we like to start the show by getting everybody relaxed – which means you folks joining in as well. We're gonna need some volunteers, okay? Are there any guests from England here tonight?'

There were a few embarrassed titters, but the only 'yeahs' were Middle West in accent.

'No cheating, please. I want only genuine born-in-Brits this time. Right, here's our first one. What's your name, pal? Stuart. Great! Hi, Stu. Say "Hi" to Stu, everyone. *Louder!* That's better. Now, how about a lady? We need a girlfriend up here for Stu. Don't we, Stu? No, sorry, Ma'am, Vancouver doesn't count. Yes, Sir, Dublin does. Is your wife Irish, Sir? Bring her up then. What, Denver? Denver isn't Irish, for Chrissake. Come on, now. I can't believe we haven't got one single English girl out there.'

'Go on, Chris,' Bunny urged, pushing her almost out of her seat. 'This is your big break.'

'I can't. I'd rather *die*.'

'Course you can. It's only a bit of fun.'

Chris stole one last glance at the bar. Her father wasn't looking, wasn't even listening. The whole damned restaurant had its eyes turned to the stage – except for one Neil Gordon who was still in the laundromat.

'Okay, okay, I'm going. You needn't dislocate my arm, Bunny.' Chris snatched up her crown, marched onto the stage amidst shouts and cheers. Those would make Neil turn round. She couldn't see him now. She was blinded by the dazzling lights, confused by the strange floaty feeling in her limbs. It was difficult to stand straight and they wanted her to dance – join a chorus line with Stu and Henry Tudor and all six wives and a dancing bear or two. Okay, she'd dance – sing as well. Who cared? Course she could sing, yeah, loudly. No, she didn't know the can-can, but she'd have a bash. High kicks? Okay, high kicks. Careful . . . No, she couldn't fall. Two arms linked through hers, bodies pressing closer. More bodies behind. Feet kicking up all around her, froth of petticoats. She had got the hang now, got the beat. Easier when they played the music. Smashing music – wild and fizzy like she felt inside. Kick kick kick. Hoped she had clean knickers on. No, mustn't giggle – it would only spoil her singing. Singalong along along along. Henry VIII was losing half his padding. Roars of laughter, more applause. Stu had sweaty hands. Didn't matter. Nothing mattered. Kick kick, can can can . . .

'You were great,' said Neil. 'Absolutely great!'

Chris didn't answer, just forked more salad in. A fantastic salad, with loads of nuts and fruits and swanky things like avocado chunks and hearts of palm. The meal was looking up, no doubt about it.

'And she tried to kid me she was shy,' grinned Bunny. 'They ought to sign you up, hon.'

'It was only a bit of fun.' Chris picked up an asparagus spear, waved it sort of nonchalantly. Several people had come up to their table, told her she was great, pumped her by the hand, offered to buy her drinks. There was someone coming now, a friend of her father's, judging by the way they leapt upon each other – but not that Irving creep – no, someone much much younger and really rather dishy. Neil made the introductions with all the Cambridge spiel again, and she didn't blush this time, just smiled her best light blue smile and murmured '*enchantée*' which was probably phoney but fitted the trilingual bit. His own name was Derwent which was frightfully chic and seemed to match his dark hair (longish for America) and mulberry-coloured jacket. Did they mind if he joined them? No, of course they didn't mind, and how about some champagne? Yes, absolutely fine, and would it mix with the mead? Well, who cared if it didn't, so long as he filled her glass like that, sort of gazing into her eyes and asking her questions about Granchester and Rupert Brooke and bluestockings, and to hell with herpes, all she had was a double first from Emmanuel and an MGM contract for the lead rôle in a musical spectacular . . .

Derwent edged his chair a little closer. 'And how are you enjoying California?'

'Oh, it's *great*,' she said, sipping her champagne. Of course it was. She'd been jaded before, blasé, clinging on to boring old England instead of grabbing the new country with both hands.

'Have you seen much of it – been along the coast yet?'

She shook her head. Perhaps he was planning to ask her out, take her for a spin in his Tornado. She might not have a cleavage, but she did have orgasms (two with Gerry and both without a finger) and she could do the can-can and make people laugh – even make her father laugh, prise him away from multi-millionaires. She'd like to see the coast, maybe take in Santa Barbara or even San Francisco. The trouble was, she only had a week left, and if the Derwent thing developed, they wouldn't have much time. She could always stay on, of course.

She gulped her champagne too quickly, sneezed into the bubbles. That wasn't such a bad idea. All she had to do was change her ticket, buy a few more clothes. Okay, so there was Martin, but it was obvious her father didn't like the sound of him, and just being Neil's daughter counted over here, meant she met a different class of person, sort of supercharged and swankpot. If she hitched herself to Martin, she might turn out like his mother who expected nothing and spent her weekends mowing their scrap of lawn or washing the loose covers or scouring out the saucepans after the same heavy greasy lunch they'd been having every Sunday since their twenties. Californians took their food and selves out, went surfing, golfing, water-skiing or just soaking up the sun. True, Martin had ambition and the Diving Club, but half the year the weather loused things up – freezing sea or gale-force winds or pea soup visibility, and once they were married, they probably wouldn't go at all, but spend their Saturdays in Tesco's and their Sundays in the launderette. England killed ambition, so her father said. It was Americans who made it, turned dreams into hard fact. You were freer in the States, not tied down by class or convention or lots of footling rules. You could earn more and do more – and do it earlier – not wait until you were ninety before you could afford to buy an underwater camera or a car. Most Yanks learned to drive when they were still at school – and the schools were far less hidebound. You could call your teachers by their Christian names and wear jeans to class, and make-up, and if you needed an abortion, there

358

were walk-in clinics and special counsellors instead of all the forms and frowns back home.

Not that she was pregnant – not with Gerry's kid. Absolutely not. She would save the baby thing for someone more like Derwent. Derwent Lester Waldo – it really was a very classy name. Mrs Derwent Waldo. Derwent Junior. She ought to stay on ages if she planned to get to know him, get to see the country. California was the third biggest state, and then there were the other forty-nine, not to mention Mexico and Canada and . . . In fact, what was the point of going back to England at all, slaving away at some second-rate university only to be unemployed at the end of it and spend the rest of her life cooking cut-price steaks for a non-vegetarian chauvinist who didn't even trust her? Back home she was no one, sort of anonymous like the hotpot, but garnished with her father she could move into the Michelin class – two rosettes at least. He might even find her a glossy job in his office with wall-to-wall secretaries and mink-covered telephones until her society wedding to some Derwent-clone who would fight off all the beauties in homage to her torrid sexuality. She giggled into her glass.

'How long are you here for?' Derwent was leaning on her chair now. His mouth was full and what the women's mags called sensuous. He was probably an ace lover, could teach her things Martin hadn't dreamed of.

'My plans are very . . . er . . . fluid,' she drawled, and drained her third glass of champagne.

18

Morna stared at the mist-shrouded hump of land emerging from the grey and wind-torn sea around it, growing slowly larger as the boat lurched south of it, seeking shelter in its lea. Waves were slapping at the prow, cascading over, sending up rocket showers of spray. Her feet were soaked, still in Bunny's sneakers, the rest of her dry but freezing beneath the filthy yellow oilskins which flapped around her ankles, engulfed her hands.

'Is that it?' she shouted, pointing to the island and trying to project her voice above the engine noise, the bellow of the wind.

The boatman shook his head, bawled back something indecipherable. He was a sullen man, heavily built with greyish stubble dirtying his chin, grizzled brows above granite-coloured eyes, his torn black oilskins covered with a fine white film of dried-on salt and spray. He was steering a course between the hump, which had turned from speck to blur to rock to island, and the chain of smaller islets clustering round its southern tip. The sea was calming as they reached the shelter of the cliff-face which broke the rude force of the wind.

Morna dared relax. She had been gripping the side of the boat since they pulled out of harbour and hit the open sea. The craft seemed so tiny – twenty feet of tinderwood tossed on the waves, dwarfed by the vast sea surrounding it, the deep vault of the sky. It seemed hubris to attempt a crossing in an open boat with no cabin, no shelter, nothing but a rough wooden bench to sit on, a couple of ancient life-jackets flung on the deck with a tangled pile of waterproofs, a coil of rope, and a few rotten stinking fish.

Yet St Abban had made a longer crossing still, in a rowing boat with one rudimentary sail, twelve centuries before motors were invented. He'd had neither chart nor compass, only the occasional miracle to save him from disaster. Her own miracle had been to find a boat at all. She had arrived in Glasgow on the Monday evening, too late to catch the last train up to Oban, had spent the night in a cheap hotel, caught the first train in the morning, travelled in pouring rain through bleak and hilly moorland, expecting to wait days, at least, before she could persuade a boat to take her over. Hadn't David said the tides were treacherous, the local fishermen unwilling to make the crossing even in the summer? She had made inquiries at the pub, was told to speak to Ruari who was drinking in a corner, his shapeless trousers tied with a piece of string, his jersey stained with oil. He seemed as reluctant as she had feared to take his boat out, shy of her, suspicious, a man who hoarded words like coins, doled them out grudgingly. Even when he did speak, she could hardly understand him. His accent was so broad, he appeared to be talking in an alien tongue, one which she could translate only piecemeal.

She spent that night in a room above the pub, begged the landlord's wife to help, act as go-between. She had to bribe her, bribe Ruari, too, the following morning, when she approached him for the second time, tipped out the entire contents of her purse into his broad and calloused hands. He kept shaking his head, muttering to himself, his mood only changing as she added still more notes. The tide had changed as well, the fierce wind moderated. He stood on the quay, gazing out to sea as if forbidding it to challenge him or thwart this godsent chance of making money.

They had set out at lunchtime, when the tide was right – she, scared at first by the pitch and toss of the boat, frightened she would disgrace herself by sicking up her breakfast. Now her stomach had adjusted to the motion, was even declaring it was hungry. She broke off a corner from David's crusty loaf, crammed it into her mouth. She had brought him presents, precious things – fresh vegetables and salads, French bread, French cheeses, fruit – rare treasures on his small and barren island. She tossed a piece of crust to one lone gull, hovering over the boat, watched the huge span of wings descend, soar up again with a screech that ripped the sky. She wanted to shout herself, with sheer relief. All her worries about making the trip at all, her concern over Chris, her fear that David wouldn't welcome her, even her dismay at her own impulsive behaviour in bolting out of Disneyland, giving way to panic, had been blown clean away by the purging wind. She was healed now, back to normal, with a whole wide ocean to herself, the first land rising out of it, not David's island yet, but one equally mysterious, its black and brooding cliffs embroidered with the white of countless bird droppings.

Black and white were new. Everything had been grey before – slate sea pearling into gunmetal sky, gulls' wings shadowing silver-dappled clouds, grey blur of the horizon. She herself felt anything but grey. If one's mood were an organ like lungs or liver, something with shape and colour you could take out and examine, then hers would be plump and healthy pink. She had phoned America that morning, finally got through after seven 'no-replies' at what was the early hours for them. Chris sounded high, even tipsy, had just got in from a dinner and a cabaret.

'Don't *fuss*, Mum. I'm fine. You do your own thing and I'll do mine, okay?'

Morna recognized the Bunny jargon, felt a stab of guilt since her garbled evasions of the truth were transgressing

Bunny's philosophy of openness and trust. She tried to steer closer to the facts. The French job had . . . er . . . fallen through, but when she got back to Weybridge, there had been a letter from David ('*Who?*') waiting on the doormat, begging her help with some difficult translation work. She had decided in the circumstances, with both Chris and Bea away, to join him on his island since he couldn't leave himself and there were tricky matters of interpretation, problems with the shorthand and . . .

Would Chris see through the intellectual padding, suspect some crass liaison? Her daughter seemed hardly to be listening, was carrying on a conversation with someone in the background. Morna could hear whispering and giggling, a deep male voice which wasn't Neil's.

'So, you don't mind if . . .?'

'Why should I? It's your life, Mum. Bunny says oughts really foul us up and . . .'

'*What* do? This line's awfully bad, darling.'

'Oughts. You know, shoulds, musts, duty. We've gotta sling 'em out with all the other mental garbage. Stay as long as you like, Mum. I might stay on here, in fact. We've just been discussing it.'

Morna replaced the receiver as if it were a heavy load she had been carrying for too long. She was free – free to take a real vacation chosen by herself, not inflicted on her by Father Clarke or Bunny. She almost believed in that fictitious letter waiting on the doormat. After all, she had David's other letters, and unlike Bea and Chris and the French bureau of commerce, he *did* need her help. She had still not completed his translation nor totally solved the mysteries of the shorthand, and there were parts of the work she longed to discuss with him, especially now that she had read more widely, deliberately swotted up his subject and his century so that she could be of more use to him, understand the issues which concerned him, grasp the problems of the early Church.

And now she was actually on her way to him, to a once-famed cradle of that early Church, crossing the same stretch of sea which he had crossed four months earlier, marvelling at its beauty. The wind had dropped a little, the first glint of sunlight changing sullen grey to turquoise, the clouds gold-flecked and parting, and every subtle gradation of green and blue gleaming beneath the surface of the waves. She could see a trawler on the skyline, a froth of gulls streaming behind it like a wash, the sea scored and furrowed as it dipped towards them. She waved to the boat, the only craft but theirs, the only sign of human life on that endless expanse of water.

No wonder David had described St Abban's Island as a fortress when it was so difficult to reach. Two centuries after Abban's death, the Vikings had descended, sacked the monastery, slaughtered all the monks, held the place as a base for other raids, been succeeded in their turn by waves of rebels. Pirates had used it as a hide-out, warring clan chiefs plotted there against the Scottish king, ruling it like kings themselves, free from interference. Jacobites had fled there, been hounded out and brutally attacked by English redcoats. Ships had foundered on it – over fifty since records had been kept, and who knew how many before that? The islanders had got fat (and drunk) on wrecks, had even prayed to God to send them a ship or two in lean times, especially one with hard liquor in the hold.

Morna stamped her feet to warm them up, blew on her freezing hands. She could do with a tot of something strong herself, to help thaw her out a bit. The cold was getting fiercer as they left the chain of islets behind, hit the full force of the wind. She tried to duck away from it, shut her eyes against the drenching spray. Ruari rummaged in a locker for a piece of heavy canvas, flung it over her.

'Thanks!' she shouted, but the word was blown away, shredded into spume.

He was obviously contemptuous of her clothes, had glanced at her with something like derision when she first stepped into the boat in a cream cotton jacket and the sneakers. She had rifled through her case to find something warm and waterproof, but she had packed originally for sunny California, not winter in the wilds, and half her clothes were still at Bunny's anyway. In the end, she had dressed in layers – a summer dress on top of a pair of linen trousers, two blouses over that, and then the jacket. She felt stiff and cumbersome, like a bulky parcel wrapped too tight, yet still unprotected from the groping wind. Ruari had prodded the pile of oilskins with his boot, jerked a thumb at them. Now nothing showed beneath the yellow waterproofs except half her face and that was numb. She had never imagined that cold could be so violent. Spray was lashing at her face like hailstones, her eyes streaming from the sting of salt, her lips white and crusted with it. She was swallowing salt, breathing it, fighting blindly with the flapping corners of the canvas as it was tugged and tortured by the wind. She snatched it back, wrapped it more tightly round her so that even her face was covered, huddled in the bottom of the boat, hardly daring to look out at the huge troughs and towers of waves seesawing around them.

How could the boatman remain so calm, impassive? He was drenched himself, water running down his oilskins, struggling to stand upright at the wheel, yet his countenance devoid of all emotion. He had hardly said a word since the moment they set out – needed all his concentration for the shift of the tide, the swiftly changing currents. Would he die like that, go down without a cry? His leather face was crisscrossed with a maze of tiny lines, his mouth a black hole where he had lost more than half his teeth. She guessed he was an islander himself, since David had told her that none of the smaller islands had resident doctors or dentists, and that trips to the mainland cut into precious working time. Easier – and cheaper – to lose one's teeth. Some had lost more than that. One of the few remaining inhabitants on David's island had been crippled for over sixty years – had broken her leg as a child, let her mother set it as best she could, and had been hobbling around with sticks and grim endurance ever since.

Ruari had a limp himself. She was totally in his hands, this gammy-legged, probably near-illiterate man who was king of the ocean. David had said that the local boatmen were often more skilled than the captains of vast transoceanic liners, had frequently to pit their tiny craft against riptides, whirlpools, submerged and hazardous rocks. Only now did she understand the dangers, begin to realize what courage Abban had shown, bobbing around in his nutshell of a boat amidst what he saw as sea monsters and demons. She had been amazed to read what distances those early monks had sailed, fighting hunger, thirst, fatigue and every hazard, yet trusting God to bring them safe to port.

Ruari was shouting something, gesturing out to sea, pointing at a smudge of land emerging from a cloud bank, the faint outline of a cliff-face dark against white cumulus. That must be it – St Abban's Island, David's. She crouched in the prow of the boat, her eyes just above the gunwale, so that she could watch the cliffs take shape – cliffs more than three hundred million years old, so David had said. On such a time scale Abban was almost a contemporary. She liked the thought of that. She had come to love the saint – slight of stature, the chronicler had written, but great of soul; a man with the courage of a lion who could weep for an injured spider, and who saw both lions and spiders as proof of the craftsman God's inspired invention.

She wished he were sailing with them now, as they drew closer to the island and she began to make out the sharp skewers of rock standing up around it like a fortification. They had somehow to steer a passage through that ring of sword points and on a sea already seething from their impact, as if furious that brute and solid rock should interrupt its sway. The boat was bobbing like a flimsy paper cup as it hit the currents ripping out like snares. There were also reefs, submerged beneath the water, showing as dark stains as the waves hurtled back from them.

Morna held her breath as the boatman steered a zigzag course, judging his distances so finely it seemed that they were missing destruction only by a hair's-breadth. The water looked as if it were boiling in a kettle, smashing on to the rocks, hissing and sucking into crevices, exploding in sheets of spray. The cliff face was now rearing up in front of them, growing taller and more menacing as they heaved towards it – the granite sculpted into twisted crags above, hollowed into caves below, clawed and pummelled by a fuming sea. The boat was so close now to the barbed and barnacled sheets of rock, it seemed that the cliff itself was plunging up and down, rising and falling with the waves, spray whirling through the air, seabirds blown and battered by the wind, the whole scene in violent motion. One false move and their tiny craft would be driven on to those knife-edged crags, grated like a nutmeg against their jagged surface, splintered into firewood.

St Abban had reached the island in a raging storm, circled it a dozen times with no hope of landing, his few brave monks faint from hunger and already reciting the prayers for those drowned at sea. He had viewed the storm as the work of devils or perhaps a Sign from God that this was not to be their chosen resting place. He fell to his knees as twenty-foot waves crashed across the boat, begged God to reveal his Holy Will. Immediately, the storm abated and a friendly seal led them to a calm and sheltered inlet. They landed. Abban prayed again, this time for sustenance, since he could see neither blade of grass nor scrap of soil. Instantly a flock of mysterious white birds metamorphosed into angels who fed the monks with heavenly ambrosia.

No such miracle for them. Wind and wave were both relentless, the dark shadow of the cliff falling on them like a pall, as one black cormorant flapped frantically away, as if warning them to make their own escape. Morna could see no proper harbour, only a small grey slash among the darker rocks, which grew slowly larger, revealed itself as a crudely fashioned wedge of stone and concrete running into the sea. A few old car tyres had been suspended along its sides in a pathetic attempt to make it safer, break the impact of any craft skilled enough to reach it. But that craft had first to escape the pincer-claws of rock which fringed the narrow inlet, seemed to have been placed there by some vindictive god demanding his toll for landing. There was no guiding seal, no angel, just one lone boatman adjusting speed and engine within the few feet of safety which marked survival from extinction. Morna's hands were trembling as she gripped the gunwale, struggled to keep her balance against the pitch and judder of the boat.

Suddenly, their speed increased. They appeared to be charging towards the concrete wedge, the engine revving up as if gasping its distress. She was jerked from her seat as Ruari wrenched the wheel round, thrust the lever into reverse. The boat slowed, shuddered, turned half circle, then miraculously moved parallel to the landing slip.

He ripped away the sheet of canvas, picked up her suitcase, flung it on to the roughly concreted stone and gestured after it, yelling above the engine noise. Even without the rant of wind and wave, she couldn't understand him. She stared, bewildered, trying to lip-read, realized with a sickening dread that he wanted her to jump. He hadn't even secured the boat. It was still plunging in two directions at once – thrown up and down on the swell while threshing backwards and forwards from the quay. Even as she dithered, she could see the gap widening, the surging expanse of wave between her and safety.

'No!' she shouted. 'I can't. I *daren't*. The sea's too rough. I'll never . . .'

Her words were flecks of spray, empty froth. Ruari was shouting again, more urgently, grabbed her arm, pushed her to the edge of the boat. She tucked up her oilskins, stared at the tiny landing point, now level with her, now rearing up above her, as the waves hurtled back and forth. Supposing she missed it, fell into that sea to be pounded against the cliff face like a piece of jetsam?

'I c . . . can't,' she yelled again, felt a sudden jab from behind as Ruari shoved her out. For one terrifying moment, she felt nothing beneath her feet; empty space whirling round and past her, the slang and heckle of the wind outshrilling her own shriek of fear. She reached out her hands to break her fall, landed with a thud on solid ground, remained sprawled on all fours, shaken and disorientated, uncertain whether she was lying on the quay or on some lower slab of rock from which the sea would prise her like a puny crab. Her hands were grazed and throbbing, something warm and sticky trickling down her leg. She ignored the leg, dared to look up; the pain of the grazes fading into staggering relief as she realized she was safe, spreadeagled on the quay, the sea roaring at her sullenly as if galled that she'd escaped it.

She had to thank Ruari, share her relief with him. She turned slowly round, still crawling on her hands and knees, watched the boat in horror. It had already reversed and was edging its way back between the obstacle course of rocks, which seemed to be closing in on it as waves and currents fought each other in a seething churning brawl. It looked pitifully small, a bobbing cork, a paper toy which could be crumpled up, submerged. Its owner had risked his life for her, and she had been petty enough to resent the sum he charged – a sum which had seemed excessive from the snug safety of the mainland, but which now she saw was trifling when set against the dangers, the fact he had to face them all again. She clutched at a stump of metal, barnacled and rusting, tried to stop her trembling, shout her belated thanks. But her voice was as weak and feeble as her legs, fell like a small pebble into the sea. Anyway, Ruari had already dwindled to a pinhead, dwarfed by the cliff which reared above them both. She had assumed he would escort her to David's cottage, at least point out the way; had imagined a safe and easy stretch of beach, or the secure refuge of a harbour like the one they had departed from. Nothing had prepared her for this wildness, desolation – only rock, crag, cliff, sea, sea.

She struggled to her feet, wincing at the pain from her bruised and bleeding knee. Her case was soaked, broken at one corner. She picked it up, tried to lug it up the steep and stony track which led off from the quay. Impossible. She needed both her hands, would never keep her balance against the wind. Even the string bag of provisions was proving an encumbrance. She hooked it over her shoulder, concealed the case in a cleft of rock. It was unlikely that anyone would steal it. There wasn't anyone – or no one human. One black shag was perched on the rocks beneath her, a shrill of gulls wheeling overhead. A rabbit darted away as she climbed to flatter ground, pulling herself up on the handholds of rock. A white stone scared her by turning into a sheep. She gasped as she reached the top, gazed around her. On all sides pounded the wild and braggart sea, slamming at the rocks, stretching to infinity, moat to her island's castle.

One used the word island so indiscriminately. Greenland was an island – all eight hundred and forty thousand square miles of it; so was New Guinea, and Britain itself. The dictionary definition was bald and unimaginative – a piece of land entirely surrounded by water. Yes, here was the piece of land, and an unimpressive piece in terms of size or fruitfulness, bare granite grimacing through its thin and stony soil. And there was the water entirely surrounding it – as grey and bleak as the land itself – the swirling Atlantic, youngest of the oceans, according to Martin, a mere one hundred and fifty million years old. Yet the two together, scrap of land and greenhorn sea, could produce this sense of awe, this wonder smudged with fear. You could shout or rant up here, dance naked on the cliff top, sing paeans to the seals. No one would complain or lock you up. No one would even see you. This splinter of land was like a fragment which had fallen off and got forgotten, while the rest of planet Earth was being planted, painted, civilized. No crops, no colours, almost nothing to show man had ever been here. And yet there must be dwellings somewhere, since six islanders still eked out an existence. Crofters, David called them, but what could they harvest beyond peat and stone?

The wind was so strong now she could barely stand against it, strands of salt-stiff hair flailing at her face, oilskins bellying out like a ship under sail. She struggled on, bent half double, turning left along the sheep track which followed the line of the coast. David's cottage was on the west side of the island – that she knew – close to the ruins of St Abban's monastery. The whole island was barely two miles long, so even if she had to check every dwelling on it, the task was not impossible. She walked faster, trying to thaw her stiff and frozen limbs, stumbled down an incline, pounded up again, glimpsed a house on the far side of the hill. Could that be David's? She jogged towards it, dispersing frightened sheep, admiring its position – sheltered in a dip, yet fronted by the sea, crowned by a vast and rolling sky. She drew nearer. The cottage looked sturdy – strong slate roof, low-set like frowning brows, walls dungeon-thick, windows small and sparse to bar the elements. It would be warm and dry inside – a fire, perhaps, a cup of tea. She panted up to the door, peered through the tiny window on the right. The room was bare, totally deserted, no stick of furniture, no covering on the rough earth floor; only cobwebs, an empty lemonade bottle mouldering on a shelf, a few fragments of peat in the cracked and rusting fireplace.

She backed away. Where was the family who had bought that lemonade, laid that fire? Dead? Drowned? Mouldering themselves? The harsh cry of the sea birds sounded like their requiem.

She returned to the path, tramped on, admiring each new vista as she followed the curve of the island round, she and the sheep continually startling each other as she came upon them huddled beside boulders or sheltering in dips. The colours were unchanging – dark cliff, grey sea, white and dazzling spume – but the rocks themselves were endlessly varied in their twisted shapes, sculpted by the waves into proud distorted heads or milk-plump breasts.

She could see a second cottage, set back a little from the path, half a dismembered wheelbarrow rusting in front of it. That one couldn't fool her – it was obviously a ruin – its door-frame black and gaping like Ruari's toothless mouth, its only garden a bent and stunted gorse bush. Even the granite had succumbed to wind and weather; the toughest rock in the world reduced to a pile of scattered stones.

She stopped to rest a moment, tired already, tried to block off memories of cushy holidays – smiling couriers holding open taxi doors, obliging drivers whisking her to the most luxurious hotels. Here, she was on her own against the elements – no transport, not even any road, no shelter, no Mediterranean market stall selling *pain sucré* or *dolmades*. Her stomach growled with hunger. Where were the angels, the ambrosia? She broke off another hunk of bread, frowned at the mangled loaf. Supposing David were fasting? And even if he weren't, would he really welcome a soggy loaf with all four corners missing, two squashed misshapen cheeses, a pound of pulped bananas? Would he even welcome *her*? She stared down at the torn and flapping oilskins, her sodden trouser-legs in their squelching pink-striped shoes. A scarecrow, and a female one. St Abban would have fled from her as a demon. Would David feel the same? She had come to help him, but how could she be anything but a hindrance when she had arrived with no warm clothes, no wellingtons, not even any warning; inflicted herself on him when he was still little more than a stranger, and one who valued privacy?

She put the bread down. She must be crazier than she realized, not only doing a bolt from California, but now compounding folly and impulsiveness by chasing a man who had deliberately chosen to live in peace and silence. She had craved that peace herself, but how could she have been so crassly confident that he had any wish to share it? Yet what could she do now? She was stranded on this chip of rock, might be trapped for weeks. 'Stay as long as you like,' Chris had urged so blithely, meaning a week or two at most. And what about her mother, who would be counting on seeing her when she returned from Hilden Cross?

The only boat was Cormack's – the crofter who rented David his cottage, fetched his supplies. But he was elderly, suffered from bronchitis, might resent her, a stranger and a southerner, appearing out of nowhere, barging into his day. Even if she made it worth his while to take his boat out, the wind might well have changed, the tide be wrong. She had heard all the stories of those capricious winds. St Abban's could be cut off from the mainland for a month or more, especially in the winter. Anyway, she might not even find the crofter. He lived up in the north end with the five inhabitants, quite some way from David who had com-plained in his letter that it was a hell of a tramp to ask a simple question or borrow a twist of salt. Not that they were free with anything, be it provisions or advice. David had described them as wary and suspicious, and knowing his politeness, that might well be translated as downright hostile.

She picked up her bag, trudged on. She couldn't face hostility, and at least David's would be tempered by good manners. She would have to lie again, invent some story about being in Scotland anyway, on a visit to a relative, deciding to surprise him. She hated lying, most of all to David; somehow wanted him to know she had travelled all that way on his account alone. If he were threatened by that fact, angered by her presence, then he would have to help her leave, go grovelling to Cormack for a boat.

The path was steeper now, and harder going. Icy blasts of air were knifing down her neck, sneaking up her trouser-legs, flaying every inch of flesh which they could reach. Morna thrust her numbed hands into the folds of her oilskin, pulled the hood right down; strained against the hill, caught her breath as she breasted it and gazed down at the scene below – St Abban's monastery spreading in a heap and haunt of stones.

She had seen David's photographs, made copies of his sketchmaps, but nothing had prepared her for the wonder of the place, not even for its size – especially considering the confines of the island and its early date, when building was still simple and austere. At Lindisfarne, the Early Christian monastery had been built in wood or wattle, a huddle of rough and primitive huts which centuries ago had rotted into the ground. St Abban, not long after, had built in rugged stone. Most of the dry-stone wall which had once surrounded the site had fallen into ruin or had been carted away to build walls or houses elsewhere on the island, but one stretch of it remained, standing almost waist-high in places. The remains of three or four monks' cells, now worn by wind and weather and open to the air, were still defying time, protected by the shelter of the hillside. The foundations of the oratory had been buried beneath a succession of later buildings, themselves a waste of scattered stones, but if you shut your eyes you could almost reconstruct the site, your inner eye completing its fragmented geometry.

Morna kept her eyes closed. She could see the monastery inhabited and working, the monks filing in to worship after hours of lonely prayer in their tiny cells; breaking bread together, planting grain, harvesting and threshing; Abban himself gaunt and haggard as he goaded his frail body past its limits. She could hear chanting from the oratory, deep male voices mingling with the bleating of the sheep, the more profane babble of the pilgrims who had arrived in their jostling hundreds to beg for cure or favours, the sudden shout of triumph as a festering limb was healed or a dying child revived.

She opened her eyes, looked down. No one. Nothing babbling but the stream which wound between the fallen stones at the bottom of the slope; the only disturbance two black-backed gulls tussling over a mouldering rabbit carcass. She jumped as a sheep lurched up from its knees, lumbered bleating past her. They were the only congregation now, those black-faced, white-cowled munchers – they and the lonely sea birds perched like statues on their plinths of rock. She scrambled down the slope, picked her way between the butts and bones of granite, Abban's last remains. The saint would have been shocked to see the place deserted, his monastery in ruins when he had raised it as a proud and lasting monument to an immortal faith; the faith itself, then fresh and green, now considered fusty and irrelevant by the blasé inheritors of its near two thousand years. Yet the holiness was there still, lying so thickly on the stones you could scrape it off like lichen. There was some presence here, some power, which made the place the centre of the island, not geographically but in some more vital sense. It seemed wrong to wander as a tourist, trying to date walls or reconstruct the site; rather she should be on her knees.

She walked towards the holy well – once famous as a place of miracle in Abban's time and centuries afterwards – knelt beside it. Defeated kings or barren queens, wounded heroes, women with sick children, had all braved the stormy crossing to drink its waters, bathe their limbs. Now rabbit droppings clustered where they had lain their offerings, left their bandages. Just six months after Abban's death, a wealthy noblewoman possessed by seven devils had been totally immersed, held down by force as she kicked and screamed; emerged so purified she went on to endow a monastery herself. Another woman, blind since birth, had had her sight restored. The first thing she laid eyes on were two huge white sea birds which opened their beaks and joined with her in singing God's praises and whom St Abban identified as cherubim.

Morna plunged her own hands in the icy water, wincing as her grazes stung and smarted. She, too, was in need of cure, or at least of rest. Her whole body ached with tiredness, her bruised knee throbbing, her feet swollen and rubbed raw. She sank back on her heels, let the peace of the place engulf her, its magic go to work. Those miracles no longer seemed so far-fetched. David might regard them as metaphors or symbols – inner blindness healed by faith, devils as one's doubts or faults of character, yet, for all his caution, his world still soared beyond the rough-hewn stones of dates and facts. He refused to live blinkered in just one single creed, or tied to one interpretation. In fact, the island attracted him because it had been a cradle and a cemetery of many different beliefs, had been considered sacred, numinous, centuries before St Abban's time. There had been two archaeological digs in the 1920s which had discovered extensive remains of early Bronze Age cist burials. They had even found a skeleton buried knees to chest in the small stone cist with his dagger and his wrist-guard and a ritual beaker containing an alcoholic drink flavoured with meadowsweet. There had also been a later Bronze Age settlement which had left arrowheads and traces of post holes and another impressive grave containing a decorated food vessel. David had told her that all these primitive peoples believed in an afterlife and this could be the reason why they were buried with their possessions and some sustenance to keep them going, equip them for the other side. The strength of their faith seemed to linger in the air, intensify the light; the strength of all the faiths since man first landed here was almost palpable, as if it, too, had left its traces, charged the whole atmosphere.

Morna picked up a loose stone, one of the ancient weathered ones which edged the holy well, held it in her palm. Its history weighed heavy. This well had been sacred to the Celts before Abban Christianized it, pagan legends of death and resurrection fusing with his own miraculous cures. David had shown her all the papers, let her read the excavators' notes, tried to share his own excitement with her. But it was only now she fully understood his awe and wonder at the place, could actually experience its strange other-worldly quality which seemed to take it out of time. She gazed around her at the sweep of the horizon, the stark glower of the cliff standing guard above the lonely broken splendour of the worship stones. The monks had built simply – no soaring arches, towering walls, but the grandeur of the buildings was supplied by sea and sky, which could never fray or fade – a vast painted mural of white-stippled waves, silver-shadowed clouds. There was nothing of the twentieth century here, nothing which marked the passing of the ages. St Abban himself would still have felt at home; even Bronze Age man perhaps recognized the landscape.

She walked on to the largest of the cells, stood within its

crumbling circle. A circle within a circle. David had explained how an island could be seen to symbolize the closed nature of a soul like St Abban's vowed to God. All he had ever told her now seemed to crystallize and kindle, as if the stones themselves had power to teach. She stooped down, ran her hand along the rough uneven surface of the granite. The stone seemed darker now, shadowed by the huge clouds brooding over it; the oyster-coloured sky smirched with purple. She had lost all track of time, hardly realized that light and day were fading. She sprang to her feet, strode back up the slope. The hill had served as windbreak, the stretch of wall protected her, but now she hit the full force of the wind again – a bad-tempered wind which made rude swipes at her clothes, tried to push her over. She stood her ground, watched the changing colour of the sea, the dense sky pressing down on it like a piece of blotting paper mopping up any excess gleam or colour. She ought to hurry. It would be dark in half an hour or less.

She sprinted back to the path, tried to put a spurt on. Dark! The word was terrifying, meant something entirely different from the cosy well-lit dark of Weybridge. Here, there were no lampposts, no car lights, no electricity at all; not even any lighthouse to throw its reassuring beam across the ocean. She plunged along the path, watching the soft purplish gloom begin to shroud both land and sea. She was powerless, could no more halt the stealthy tread of night than dry up the ocean bed. If she didn't find David's cottage soon, she would be left floundering in the pitch black on a treacherous cliff with a sheer drop to the ruthless depths below. Perhaps she shouldn't chance it, return to the monastery, shelter there till dawn.

She glanced behind her – ghosts of buildings, ghosts of monks. In David's view of things, ghosts were not simply white-robed spooks from some haunted house or Disneyland to be denied or laughed to scorn, but real presences confounding reason, confounding time, suggesting some mysterious continuity between age and age, mind and mind. Was ancient man in some way present still, his soul surviving like a standing stone? And what about Abban and his monks, buried higher up the slope, where the soil was fractionally deeper and where they were closer to the heaven they aspired to? Did they wander earth as well, haunt their former cells? She shivered. There were more recent deaths. A wreck had foundered here, just yards from the monastery ruins, the bodies of the Baltic sailors smashed on to the rocks, never buried. She tensed, stood petrified, hands damp with sweat, every nerve and muscle strained. What was that strange shadow, that whitish blue just ahead of her? She stifled a scream, tried to calm her breathing. She could hear someone else's breathing, slow and laboured, a faint whistling sound as each heavy breath was haltingly let out. Was it just the wind, or . . .?

'Don't touch me!' she shouted, fled along the path, tripping on loose stones, fighting off the shadows with her hands. She ditched the bag, needed all her strength just to keep pounding on. Her feet burned, her legs ached; her heart was thudding so loudly it sounded like some madman on her trail, his heavy footsteps drumming in her ears. She lost her balance suddenly, sprawled full-length on the ground. The path had descended sharply and she hadn't even seen it. She hauled herself up, touched her forehead gingerly, flinching at the pain. Another bruise. She would have to go more slowly, despite her fears. Things were blurring now, losing their clear outlines. Soon nothing would exist at all as grey deepened into black, kidnapping all landmarks.

She paused a moment, listened. The wind was still heavy-breathing, the waves prowling to and fro with their dull and rhythmic roar. But other sounds were muted – the bleating of the sheep thinner and more mournful, the cries of the gulls only ghosts of ghosts of cries. There were no human sounds at all. Yet six islanders still lived here, must have voices, radios, doors which slammed, dogs which barked. Had they all turned to stone?

She picked her way along the path, peering through the gloom. Still no sign of any cottage. Should she shout for help, hope that someone somewhere was still made of flesh, had ears? She stumbled to a halt. The path had divided, a second rougher track leading off inland to what looked like a house. Was it just a ruin? A shadow? Chimera? She dared not hope, stood dithering, unsure which way to go.

Suddenly the darkness was alive – and conquered. A light was flickering in front of her, showing up a curtained window, a sturdy door. No one would hang curtains in a ruin. Whoever had lit that lamp – be it David, grudging crofter or crippled crone – they were flesh and blood, not ghost of monk or sailor, wandering spirit. The light spilled across the path as if beckoning her forward. She fell against the door, beat with both her fists on the weather-beaten wood, laughed with sheer relief as she heard slow and heavy footsteps echoing towards her.

19

Morna reached out for the bedside light, couldn't find it, shivered. Cold for California. The motel was always either stifling hot or freezing cold. She had better complain in the morning, try and find the manager. Her hand groped further, knocked against something hard. She traced four corners, a rough and splintery surface, fingers closing on a torch. She switched it on, its feeble beam lighting up an upturned wooden crate beside the bed, a swathe of dusty floorboards, the black and gaping mouth of a long-dead fireplace. Where were the sickly browns of the Ocean View Motel – the dung-coloured carpet and mouldy chocolate walls, the blank face of the television screen staring into hers? She rubbed her eyes, glanced around again. The room contracted, the ceiling lowered, turning from smooth plaster into blackened board; the roar outside no longer traffic but howling wind and wave. This was ocean view for real.

She sat up slowly, kicking off the strange assortment of covers heaped on her bed – three Boer-War-vintage blankets, a piece of dirty sacking, two thick and musty curtains and a duffle coat. *David's* coat. She was in David's cottage, in David's bed, and wearing his pyjamas. She flung the last cover back, revealing two blue-striped baggy legs, the trouser hems reaching well below her ankles, swallowing up her feet. David's *only* pair of pyjamas. He was sleeping in vest and cords downstairs, on a battered sofa which looked older than the blankets.

David downstairs! It seemed absurd, miraculous – as miraculous as when his tall and stooping figure had appeared at the door of the cottage. She had stood staring like a ninny. He had grown a beard which completely changed his face, made him look less priestly, more foreign and exotic. The hair was strong and coarse, not grey to match his head hair, but the darkest shade of brown; seemed to be alive in its own right like some wild dark-pelted animal. The beard had made her shy, turned David into stranger, someone slightly threatening, too male, too primitive. He had said nothing at all, just motioned her to enter, stood holding the door for her, shaken, almost stunned, gazing at her as if uncertain whether she were real or not. She, too, had lost her voice. All the explanations she'd prepared, all the apologies, excuses, seemed to have crumbled into shale. All she could do was stand shivering and trembling, exhausted by the sea crossing, the long stumbling walk across the island, the sheer relief of finding him at all.

'Are you all . . . right?' David asked at last, staring at her bruised and bleeding forehead, her filthy oilskins. He had both his arms hugged across his chest, as if he were holding himself up, holding his emotions in.

'C . . . Cold.' Her teeth were chattering, legs numb and clumsy so that she tripped on an uneven piece of lino, almost fell.

He seemed to come alive then, started boiling kettles, brewing tea, fetching dry clothes and blankets, as if he had suddenly remembered Abban's own example. The saint had urged his monks to treat every visitor as if he were Jesus Christ Himself, to turn no traveller away, however poor and lowly. On one occasion, a young man, starving and in rags, had arrived shivering at the monastery door. Abban had given up his bed to him, shared his scanty meal. In the morning, the man had disappeared, but an intense golden light was shining over the cell he had vacated. The saint had fallen to his knees, giving thanks and praise. It *had* been Christ.

Would David hope to wake to a Shining Light rather than to an inconvenient woman? Had he slept at all on that lumpy springless sofa? Morna sat back against the bedhead, pulled the blankets round her. She was wide awake herself now, hunger and excitement both churning through her stomach, precluding further sleep. She had been excited last night, had to try and hide it with David still so tense. There had been constraints between them, sudden awkward pauses in the conversation, embarrassments over things like non-existent lavatories. She longed to know what he was feeling – resentment, irritation, or something of her own strung-up elation. It had been impossible to eat. Despite her hunger, she had refused the meal he offered. There wasn't room. Someone had tanked her up with brightly coloured soda pop which was fizzing and exploding in her stomach. She had gone to bed at seven like a child, with just a cup of tea, a stale digestive biscuit, had collapsed on to his box bed with its thin and scratchy mattress which rustled when she moved, its one misshapen pillow which smelt of paraffin and woodsmoke. He hadn't even changed the sheets – maybe hadn't changed them since September. She didn't care. It was a way of getting closer to him, sharing his space, his smell.

She hauled his duffle coat further up the bed, pulled it right across her face. It felt heavy, rough against her cheek, pressing down on her like the dense and muffling darkness which pressed down on the island, on the house. She no longer feared the dark. David had lent her his torch, left it by her bed like a magic charm to guard against the demons of the night. He had stood at her door, rigid, over-formal, as he mumbled good night. She had almost expected the words to be in Latin; he the abbot of the monastery, she the novice, newly admitted to his rule. She had listened to his footsteps receding down the stairs, heard the faint noises from the kitchen, noises tangled with the wind outside, rattlings from the roof, whistlings down the chimney; tried to keep awake so she could think, found herself drifting on a sea again, rocking back and forth, lulled by the waves until they turned into the mighty shipping lane of Ocean View.

She pushed the coat off, rolled over on one side and then the other, sat up again, restless like a child on Christmas Eve who couldn't sleep because of all the treats downstairs. Could she not wake David, go and say good morning? She fumbled for her watch, shone the torch beam on it. Five past three. Barely morning yet. Impossible to bother him so early. His own watch had broken. He had dropped it in a rock pool whilst hunting limpets, hardly seemed to miss it. She counted back the hours to Californian time. Chris would be sitting down to dinner – Bunny's help-yourself or Loo Fung's takeaway. She felt starving now herself, would never last till breakfast. Perhaps she could creep down to the kitchen, raid the larder. She ventured one foot out of bed, wincing at the cold. She was already wearing two pairs of David's socks, his warmest sweater underneath the pyjama top. She struggled into his jeans which were too tight around the waist and far too long, rolled the bottoms up, added a second sweater and an old suede jerkin which stank of tar and fish. It couldn't be easy to wash your clothes out here – or yourself – needed courage to undress at all.

The door whimpered as she opened it, each wooden stair grumbling at her tread as if she had woken it from sleep. The torch sent startled shadows up the bare stone walls. She stopped stock-still as she heard a sudden noise, shone the torch beam down. A tall dark shape was emerging from what Cormack called the parlour, a gloomy room where damp seemed spread on everything like a dank and clinging dustsheet.

384

'Morna . . .?'

'D . . . David . . .?'

Silence. She manoeuvred the last few steps, stood gripping the banisters, staring down at the strip of floor between them. 'I'm sorry, David, I didn't mean to wake you.'

'You didn't.'

She could feel her heart thumping its excitement, struggled to sound casual. 'You d . . . don't get up at three, do you?'

'Is it three?'

'Mm. Ten past.'

'No, I'm quite a layabout, in fact. It's a matter of saving fuel. I tend to get up when it's light and turn in when it's dark.'

'Bed at four p.m., you mean? That's worse than me last night.'

David smiled. 'Not much good if you couldn't sleep.'

'Oh, I did. I went out like a light.' Morna cleared her throat. Embarrassing to be caught like a thief halfway to the larder. 'I was . . . er . . . just going to try and find your biscuit tin.'

'It's empty, I'm afraid. Anyway, biscuits won't fill you up. You must be really starving. How about some supper?'

'Supper? Now?'

'Why not? We haven't had it yet.'

'Well, I . . . er . . . wouldn't mind a snack.'

'That's all it'll be, I'm afraid. What d'you fancy? I've got almost everything in tins – soup, Spam, sardines, corned beef, even mixed fruit cocktail.'

'I don't mind. What do you eat usually?'

'It was baked beans for the first month – breakfast, lunch and tea. I was dreaming Heinz in the end. Then I got more adventurous – tried my hand at home-made bread. That's what Abban lived on – soda bread and seaweed.'

'*Seaweed?*'

'Mm. You ought to try it. It's meant to be nutritious – you know, roughage and minerals and all that sort of stuff.'

'No thanks.'

'It's not bad. The Welsh and Irish have eaten it for centuries. And in Japan it's as basic as our chips and peas. They have hundreds of varieties – arame and kombu and nori and mekabu. One of the Japanese scribes was praising it as a delicacy as far back as the sixth century BC. Abban ate it stewed with roots. In fact, it's amazing what you can do with it. In the last war, when most foods were short or rationed, the Aran islanders got together and cooked a sort of banquet based entirely on different types of seaweed. They had laver salad, devilled dulse, carragheen purée, and heaven knows what else besides. I've only tried dulse, so far, but I've made dulse soup, dulse pancakes, dulse salad, dulse . . .'

'Okay, dulse dinner for two. And a cup of standard supermarket tea, please.'

She was glad when he laughed. It helped to break the tension. She was still standing at the bottom of the stairs, he a yard or two away, both stiff with cold.

David was the first to move. 'I'd better light the lamp. We'll break the rules for once. Light and heat at three a.m. By the way, have you seen the moon?'

'No.' There had been no moon when she went to bed – only cloud swatched over darkness.

'Come and look.' He led her into the parlour. A piece of crumpled fabric had been tacked up in front of the small and deep-set window to form a makeshift curtain. He swept it back.

The sea was so close, she gasped – a whole ocean trapped in a foot or two of glass, with a lumpy three-quarter moon pouring down its light so that the water looked alive, glittering and rippling. Neither of them spoke. She had always felt impatient with the language. You couldn't say 'It's beautiful.' It was too banal. Anyway, *was* it even beautiful? The moon was a cold, dead, dusty chunk of rock tagging after planet Earth. So how could it move you so profoundly, make you want to coin new words? David was so close now she could feel his elbow brushing hers. A man and a woman, shoulder to shoulder, gazing at the moon. It was a setting for a story, a Mills and Boon romance. David wasn't wearing a cloak and ruff or thigh-length riding boots, would never have made the book jacket with his ancient corduroys, his three bulky shapeless sweaters. But what about the romance? His bed was just behind her, the rumpled sofa where he had been sleeping – or perhaps not sleeping – thinking of her, maybe, as keyed up and excited as she was herself. Couldn't she try and tell him what she felt, break down his reserve? They couldn't hide forever behind formalities, decorum. She turned to face him, dared to touch his arm.

He stepped abruptly back, let the fabric fall. 'Well, I'd . . . er . . . better get that range going. It's damn cold down here.'

Morna flushed, followed him into the kitchen, a cramped low-ceilinged room which she had seen only in the tactful light of the oil lamp. David was lighting it now, striking four damp matches before the fifth took him by surprise, jumping back against the sudden burst of flame. The flickering shadows unwove the solid walls, embroidered the rough stone floor with gold. She suspected harsher daylight would reveal the room as dirty, even squalid. Everything was improvised – the waste bin an empty oil-can, the toaster a rusty fork with half its prongs missing, the fridge a packing case set outside the back door. Fridge! She shivered. The whole kitchen was a fridge. She moved closer as David struggled with the range, feeding it with driftwood or bits of flotsam thrown up at high tide. Fuel was a prize, the reward for patient scouring of the beaches – a gift from a fickle sea which might withhold its bounty. He had told her already how he went out twice a day to collect every stick and scrap he could find, then rationed it to tide him over empty-handed days. Water, too, was precious, collected in a rain butt, or lugged in a bucket from the stream. Yet there was some new and raw excitement in living rough, struggling for every basic need. A simple cup of tea became a challenge, an achievement. As a child, she had always longed to go back-packing or pony-trekking, escape her mother's timid holi-days, where they sat it out in genteel guest-houses with antimacassars on the chairs and board games for wet and endless afternoons, and where no one ventured further than esplanade or tea-rooms, and lights were out at ten. She had often resurrected her father, invented expeditions for just the two of them – canoeing down the Amazon or sleeping under the stars in the Gobi desert. When she grew up, Neil imposed his own timidities, always splashing out enough to ensure unruffled luxury, keep away danger or adventure.

David was still coaxing the range. The wood seemed damp, slow to kindle. When at last it caught, his face and hands glowed orange suddenly, as if they, too, were on fire; she still in shadow, separate.

'Can't I help?' she asked. Best to stick to practicalities, avoid all personal subjects for the moment.

'You could make the tea.'

She quarter-filled the heavy iron kettle from the pitcher of water, put just one tea bag in the cracked and lidless pot. There were barely a dozen left. David's supplies were scanty altogether, although he was emptying his larder in her honour, spreading the table with a sort of picnic tea – bloater paste and cupcakes, a knuckle of stale soda bread, a tin of pineapple chunks, a jar of cut-price strawberry jam without the strawberries. It was like those midnight feasts she had read about in Enid Blyton and never had at school – weird food at a weird hour, when the rest of the boring world was fast asleep and you had to whisper. They had been whispering themselves. She hardly knew why, except the night seemed so private, so huge and overawing, it was as if they had no right to intrude into it, assault it with their noise. The wind was a constant presence, ranting outside the cottage like the roar of the range inside. She moved from the front window to the tiny makeshift side one which had been inserted at a later date and faced inland. No curtain here to hide the dark hulk of a hill, further hills beyond it, merging into sky; the two almost indistinguishable, the darkness as solid as the land it swallowed up. The moon's light barely reached there, or only as a thin and watery milk drizzled on to granite cloud. The few faint stars looked timid and uncertain as if they could be brushed away by the first impatient hand.

Morna turned back from the pane, attracted like a moth towards the lamp. That tiny pool of light was challenging the vast black uncertainties outside, the kitchen range crackling its defiance of midwinter. She went and sat beside it, warmed her hands. David was pressing some black oozy substance between a plate and a saucepan lid, to squeeze the liquid out. The seaweed, she presumed. It looked worse than she had imagined, its cloying smell hanging in the air as if he had uncovered a haul of long-dead fish.

'I think I'll stick to bloater paste.'

'No, wait a bit. I'm going to make dulse fritters. The batter disguises the taste.' He drizzled oil into a huge black frying pan which looked as old and battle-scarred as the cottage itself. 'They may be a bit heavy, I'm afraid. I haven't any eggs. Cormack offered to sell me pickled gulls' eggs, but nothing from his hens. He told me they'd stopped laying in the tone of voice which implied I was personally responsible.'

'Why is he so hostile?'

'Well, I'm English to start with, which is enough to damn

me anyway, but even if I weren't, I'd still be an outsider and all the islanders are suspicious of outsiders. You can hardly blame them, I suppose. Life's damn hard out here, so they're bound to resent softies or townies, or people who stay a week or so and think they know it all.'

'That's not you, though, David.'

'I don't know. My life's pretty soft compared with theirs. I'm living on a grant, sitting at a desk and . . .'

'Where's the desk?'

'Well, metaphorically. Cormack and his wife have struggled to bring up seven children who've all left without a thankyou and now he's lucky if he can scratch a living from a patch of stony soil and a leaky fishing boat. In a few months, I'll be back with all mod cons. They won't. Anyway, my work isn't governed by the weather like theirs is. Farming's a constant battle here. The north end's less barren, but even so, the soil's either so shallow you can hardly use a plough on it, or else completely waterlogged. And the wind can drive you mad. It never seems to drop. Everything you do is against that wind or in spite of it. It's fine for me, calling it exhilarating while I sit inside sipping my mug of tea and listen to it holler down the chimney, but Cormack's out in that gale watching it batter down his miserable potatoes, or tear the roof off his byre.' David was beating long-life milk with flour, making batter. It seemed too tame an occupation for his wind-torn words.

'He's getting on, in any case, hasn't got the strength now. They're *all* old, the handful who still live here, eking out their pensions with a few hens and sheep and a cabbage patch. Most of the crofts have just been left to rot. The soil's worked out, or the sheep have ruined it, or they've simply given up. You need incredible endurance on an island, not just guts and stamina to accept the weather, work along with it, but psychological strength. There's no escape from anything, including yourself. You can't just pop out to see a film or a friend or buy half a pint at the local or . . .'

Morna tensed. Was that a subtle dig at her? No escape from a woman who inflicted herself upon you, even woke you up? David was still talking. At least he had an audience, something he had lacked in the last four months.

'Everything takes forever on an island. If you need a loaf of bread, you have to make it yourself, or take a long and dangerous trip to the mainland and then maybe find you can't get back again until your precious loaf's gone stale. If you want a bath, that's several hours of boiling kettles and collecting wood just to plunge your bottom half in an old tin tub while your top half freezes. Actually, Cormack's got a generator, but it's always going wrong. He's never had a bath in his life. He boasts about it – says baths are bad for you, weaken the blood. I doubt if his wife bathes, either. She wears so many layers of clothes it would take her half a day to get them off. She's not a bad old thing. In fact, she was the one who told me about the fritters. She's got a book of recipes dating from the last war – eggless this and meatless that. It adapts quite well to the island. Right, eggless fritters going in!' There was a splutter of fat as he coated each shaped and floured seaweed-cake with batter, transferred them to the frying pan.

Morna watched, admiring. It seemed strange to sit useless in a kitchen while someone else got on with preparing the meal. She couldn't even make the tea. The kettle was still nowhere near the boil. She yanked at David's jerseys which felt itchy and uncomfortable. It was an effort not to scratch. Or *was* it just the jerseys? Perhaps she had caught fleas from that unconventional bedding. You couldn't mention fleas, though – not to David – or only Neolithic ones. He had found a flea-comb once on an archaeological dig.

'Is there nothing I can do?' she asked.

'You could lay the table. Hold on a minute. I'll just remove those books.'

The table was piled with books, strewn with notes and papers. So *that* was David's desk. Morna suspected he never ate there normally, never laid it up – just grabbed a snack or sandwich, ate it while he worked. She helped him stack the books one end, cleared a space the other.

'Cutlery in here.' David jerked open a warped and sticking drawer. Cutlery sounded too grand for what she found – two rusting forks, a penknife, a kitchen knife, a handleless potato peeler and four stained plastic spoons. She searched in vain for mats, side plates, or a salt and pepper set.

'You won't need salt,' he told her twenty minutes later, as he dished up his fritters at the head of the rickety table. 'It's built in, so to speak. Actually, they're nicer with eggs and bacon, but I couldn't get bacon, either. In a couple of months, I'll be able to collect gulls' eggs from the cliffs.'

'Isn't that cruel?'

'Gulls are pretty damn cruel themselves, so you could say it's a mercy to their prey. They gulp down young chicks whole – even their own species. The parents have to stand guard or they could lose a whole nestful to what could well be an aunt or uncle. And I've seen them grab young puffin, devour the carcass and leave the skin completely whole and clean like a glove turned inside out. They're also fond of seaweed, by the way. The males bring fronds of it to the female when they're courting, like a sort of engagement present – a brown shiny necklace or a boa.'

Morna smiled down at her fritter. Nice to see it as a courting ritual, except men like David didn't court. Was he simply bashful, or just not interested? She wished she had a present for him. The provisions she had bought would have disappeared by now – gobbled by those scavenging gulls, and the few trinkets in her suitcase would hardly be appropriate. It was almost a relief to be without her luggage.

What use were flimsy dresses, trashy souvenirs? There wasn't even room for them. The wardrobe in her room was two stout pegs, the chest of drawers a single wobbly shelf.

'Well, what do you think of it?' David was watching as she swallowed her first small and wary mouthful.

She could taste oily batter, not quite disguising an undertow of rotting fish, with a strong kickback of salt. She put her fork down. 'It's . . . er . . . unusual,' she said.

'Is that high praise?'

'Mmm.' She tried again, swilled the fritter down with watery tea. 'Quite unique, in fact,' she added, seeing how intense he looked. She had almost forgotten the high seriousness he brought to everything, including seaweed. He looked tireder than he had done in September, his face almost gaunt in the shadows, with its bones and hollows emphasized, except where the beard concealed them. The light struck one hunched shoulder, wove a pattern into the dark wool of his sweater, then faded into the soft blue of his corduroys.

She dared another mouthful, checked her watch. 'It's nice to be having dinner in the early hours. I feel I've caught up with Chris at last. I lost her in Disneyland and I've felt out-of-sync ever since.'

'Did she enjoy it?'

'What?'

'Disneyland.'

'Oh yes. I think everyone did except me. You'd hate it, David.'

'I loved it, actually.'

'You mean you've *been* there?' Morna rubbed her itchy back against the chair.

'Mm.' He nodded. 'Though it seems like a hundred years ago. I was invited to give a paper at UCLA by an American professor who was interested in a project I was working on.

When we'd finished all the heavy stuff, we took a break at Anaheim. Three whole days of the Magic Kingdom.'

'Three *days* and you enjoyed it?'

'You couldn't drag me away. I've always loved funfairs. I remember once going to a conference at Sussex University – some archaeological thing. I was absolutely whacked. We'd been arguing for hours about the interpretation of Silbury Hill – you know, the man-made hill in Wiltshire – why it was built, what it signified . . .'

Morna mumbled something. She *didn't* know. They seemed to have lost the funfairs for the moment.

David cut off a piece of fritter, moved it halfway to his mouth, put it down again. 'Archaeology can be pretty damn frustrating, especially in matters of religion. You can't excavate beliefs, you see, and even with prominent remains like standing stones or megalithic tombs, you still don't really understand their meaning. It's like trying to grasp all the depths and complexities of the human mind from just an empty skull. We try and guess, of course, but half the time I suspect we're way off beam, even with all our so-called scientific methods. I'm not slamming science, mind you. It can tell us what Neolithic man ate for his dinner three thousand years ago. That's fascinating. What we *don't* know, though, is whether he said grace or not beforehand.' David picked up his fork again, but only to gesture with. 'Anyway, I'd had enough of Silbury Hill, so I sneaked off before the last evening lecture, drove into Brighton instead. It was winter, so the place was half-deserted and a lot of things shut down, but I saw this helter-skelter – two slides for 20p. I took a pound's-worth. It was marvellous – completely changed my mood. I had the whole thing to myself – king of the castle. After about the fifth time, I got the hang of it, tucked my feet in so they wouldn't drag, really got a speed up. It was like flying.'

Morna heard the excitement in his voice, saw him again

in the Weybridge recreation ground, a boisterous madcap child. She was still sitting with the adult, the solemn high-souled scholar, but at least he had relaxed now, opened up a little.

'That's the only thing I missed at Disneyland – a real English-style helter-skelter with those scratchy doormats and the bump on the concrete when you touch down on your bottom.' David drained his mug. 'Any tea left?'

'Yes, course.' Morna fetched the kettle, refilled the pot. 'It'll be weaker still, I'm afraid but . . .'

'I like it weak. Anyway it's quite a treat to have it made for me at all. Thanks.' He sat warming his hands on the mug, a coil of steam pluming up between them. 'I wish I'd met Walt Disney. He was one of the world's great men. Obstinate, maybe, but a real individualist who'd move mountains if he had to. He was like Abban in that respect. In fact, they were alike in several ways. They both worked like stink and made everyone else around them sweat their guts out – but all in a cause. They both refused to compromise or use the word impossible and got quite upset if people thwarted them or tried to cut their ideals down to size. In fact, they both had quite hot tempers and then felt remorse when they let fly. They both . . .'

Morna interrupted, almost choking on her fritter. 'I can't think of two men more different. Walt Disney was a family man with a wife and children, a showman making films in Hollywood, a big tycoon who . . .'

'He wasn't a tycoon – not really. He never put money first. He was surprisingly naïve about it, actually, and in horrendous debt for most of his life. Basically, he was quite a homespun man – like Abban. But they both had a vision – that's what marks them off. They both took a strip of wasteland and transformed it – Disney at Anaheim and . . .'

'It was an orange grove, David. Stick to the facts.'

'Well, metaphorically a wasteland. I mean without him,

there would have been nothing but orange juice and marmalade. He used very high-flown language, you know –
talked about other worlds and works of love, and Disneyland
being a source of joy and inspiration to the world. That's
Abban's sort of language. They were both Utopians, determined to make a better world – Walt's on earth, Abban's in
heaven. And even Abban's set-up here was a struggle against
the odds, the result of one man's vision and sheer bloody-
minded persistence. He changed a desert island into a centre
of learning, a sort of spiritual Disneyland where miracles
happened and people could forget their earthly cares
and . . .'

'You're bending the facts, David. It's nothing like the
same. Disneyland is non-stop consumption – eat, buy,
spend, indulge. Hell – one of the restaurants we went in
looked like a palace inside, with fifty-thousand-dollar chandeliers. St Abban lived in a rough stone cell and ate once
every two days, and even then he . . .'

'Hold on a minute. Those chandeliers are important, part
of the whole ideal. Disney believed you could bring out the
best in people if you gave them the best to start with. He
and Abban both believed in man's perfectability. That's
crucial – a lot of people don't.'

'But Abban was concerned with the *soul*, David, not just
mindless pleasure or . . .'

'It isn't mindless. Disney was a moralist. He wanted his
park to be an education as well as just a playground. He
always stressed that aspect – and it *is* that. I learnt a lot
myself. Do you realize Disneyland's been called the greatest
piece of design in the whole of America, and that was praise
from the Harvard School of Design, not just some biased
press agent? And look at EPCOT – that's truly visionary.
It's funny, really. Neither Walt nor Abban were intellectuals
themselves, yet Abban's monastery became famous for its
scholarship, and people flock to EPCOT now to learn about

town planning and conservation and . . . Walt would be thrilled to see that. He was a pioneer and an innovator – yet also quite old-fashioned in a way. He believed in the importance of the family, even saw himself as a bit of a social worker, holding families together and spreading happiness and . . . You can scoff at that, Morna, but it went deeper than mere whoopee. He understood fantasy and the need to escape or become as little children. He was a simple man at heart – they both were – and very emotional. Disney often cried in public – even at his own films, however often he'd seen them. And look at Abban! He was always weeping with joy or sorrow and breaking down in his sermons. And yet they both had the same sort of humour – whimsy, if you like, but very appealing. *Any* sense of humour's unusual in a Celtic saint. They're often gloomy souls obsessed with judgement and retribution like . . .'

'But Abban *was* obsessed with hell. I mean you said yourself that . . .'

'He also made people laugh. *And* brought them hope. Remember the last line of his Life?' David was brandishing his fork, his voice rising as he quoted. ' "And the fame of his miraculous doings spread far and wide, bringing joy to all God's people." Well, that's Disney, isn't it? I mean, look at the Mickey Mouse Fan Club. It spread like wildfire, with new groups springing up in all the different countries – just like the early Church roping in new converts. Walt even worked the odd miracle. My American friend told me a story about a little boy with terminal cancer who wanted to see Disneyland before he died – a matter of six months or so, the doctors reckoned. Walt not only laid on a VIP visit with himself as personal guide, he was still writing to that boy eight years later, when he was a healthy strapping lad with no trace of a cancerous cell in his body. Maybe that's apocryphal, but then so are a lot of stories about St Abban. I suppose all I'm really trying to say is that both men had a special sort of power – the sort that gets things done, changes people's lives. It's a funny thing, but that sort of power is far more common in evil men – Hitlers and Caesar Borgias. When I was a boy, I was always reading history books and they seemed chock-full of baddies. I used to get frightened I'd turn out like that myself. I had a devilish temper and I was very greedy and . . .'

'Greedy?' Morna stared around at the bare and ill-stocked kitchen. No coffee, butter, booze. Even the strawberry jam had not been opened.

'Actually, I realized later, saints are greedy, too. Having ideals at all is a sort of greed, I suppose. You're not content with a mediocre world. You keep grabbing for perfection. Abban was greedy for solitude. The more that people flocked to him, the more he longed to slip away and be a hermit. Well, he did, of course, the last year of his life – moving to that rockstack and living like a bird perched on a reef, with only a patch of nettles and a couple of shrivelled onions to keep him going. He refused to return even when one of his monks fell and broke his leg. You could say the hermit's life is very selfish – or at least a form of deferred gratification for the greatest lollipop of all.'

'You mean heaven?'

David nodded.

'Let's hope there is one.' Morna tried to picture it – a sort of non-stop playground to out-Disney Disney's, with Walt and Abban as joint directors. 'With an English helter-skelter – just for you.'

'Yes, please.' David stretched his legs out under the table, drew them quickly back as they encountered hers. She shifted position too, hooked her feet safely round the chair-rung. Why was he so nervous, scared of half a second's contact?

'I often wonder about Abban,' he said, forking in a mouthful of his now congealing fritter. 'Where he is now, what he's doing. *And* his biographer. Have they met at last? Were they disappointed in each other?'

Morna smiled. 'Well, they *ought* to be in heaven – I mean, one a saint and the other signing off the Life with a plea that all his readers pray for his eternal soul. I love that bit – the way he puts his own name in – "Pray for me, Dubhgall" – as if to try and make sure no one will get muddled and waste their prayers on the wrong chap.'

'Biographers often did that. It became a standard form. In fact, Dubhgall seemed to crave a double immortality, to live through his work – Shakespeare-and-his-sonnets-stuff – and then the heaven bit. Perhaps I ought to take that line myself when I come to end my own book. "Pray for me, David, so that I may win eternal life." ' He laughed, took one last mouthful before collecting up the plates; opened the tin of pineapple, dividing the chunks equally, then taking three from his dish and putting them in hers. Chris had done that as a child, but the other way round – first measuring meticulously, then nicking two or three when she thought nobody was looking.

Morna downed hers quickly. They were refreshing after the salty fritters. She wished they had stones like cherries. Tinker, tailor. What could you call David? A rich man in his learning; a poor man in his life? He looked more like a beggarman in his stained and balding corduroys. She hadn't spotted a mirror in the whole of his house. Just as well, perhaps. She couldn't see her own tousled hair or borrowed makeshift clothes. They hardly seemed to matter. To David she was Morna first, woman second. Or woman at all, she wondered? It was a relief in a way, afforded her a certain peace and safety, and yet how could they be distant on this island? It was as if the encircling sea was pushing them towards each other, throwing them together like pieces of flotsam tangled on the tide line. Did David feel the pull, or was it only her weaving empty fantasies? Perhaps it was the clothes which put him off. She was hardly at her best, bulked out like the Michelin tyre man, and smelling of salt cod. Yet Neil had been excited if she ever wore his clothes – liked the thought of her breasts beneath his sweaters, his shirts against her flesh. Was David even aware she had a body, as she was aware of his – the strong line of his beard, the dark matching hairs on wrists and hands which disappeared beneath the sleeves of his three jerseys? How far did it spread, that hair – to his chest, his stomach, further? He still hadn't mentioned any girlfriend. If he did have one, a serious one, then why wasn't she with him on the island? Couldn't she simply ask, make it tactful but direct, find out where she stood with him herself?

'D . . . David . . .'

He looked up, met her eye. In all the time they had been together, he had always looked past her, or away. For one brief moment they were joined, she reflected in the dark lens of his pupils. He turned his head, embarrassed, broke the contact. There was a sudden awkward silence.

'H . . . Have you always been a medievalist?' she asked. 'Is that the right term, by the way, or is the seventh century too early for "medieval"? I always get a bit confused. It's "Dark Ages", isn't it, the bit before the Conquest?' She was spinning words, trying to plug the silence.

'I hate the term "Dark Ages".' David rocked back on his chair. 'Okay, I admit they were dark in the sense that we don't know much about them, and also dark in that Roman civilization was obviously in decline then, but there was a genuine sort of flowering in the Celtic West – a new start, if you like. And by Abban's time, you can even talk about a golden age, when the Church was still relatively pure and simple, not corrupted yet by power or property or greed. Everything seemed to blossom then – not just the whole monastic thing itself, but art and learning, too, I mean, look at the Book of Kells and the Lindisfarne Gospels and even

400

some codices before them, and the amazing metalwork – bells and brooches and chalices – and that incredible lyric poetry written by hermits living in the middle of nowhere with only a handful of berries between them and starvation.'

David's hands were locked together on the table. The full light of the lamp seemed to be concentrated in his eyes. His tea had gone cold, but he appeared unaware of it, unaware of the dish in front of him. Morna put her own spoon down. Wasn't it still his *mind* which turned her on – the passion and intensity he brought to everything, the way he made things live for her, could bring a seventh-century hermit or a seventeenth-century treasure ship right into the kitchen? His silver coin was just upstairs. She carried it with her everywhere she went, had done so since September. He was discussing treasure now – not silver coins but Celtic jewellery. She watched him as he talked, his whole body thrusting forward, hands still clasped, but gesturing towards her.

'It's always amazed me, really, how they did it – I mean, men with nothing to their name, following a rule which was more or less a penal code, yet still managing to produce all that art and scholarship, and travelling miles and miles taking a creed of light and love to barbarous pagan tribes who could have hacked them into pieces. They were so . . . so *brave*, Morna, so completely dedicated. That's what the Church needs now – men like that with true ideals who didn't give a fig for power or status or all the outward trappings.'

Morna tilted her dish, scooped up the last of her pineapple juice. 'But Abban *did* have power – and relished it. You told me yourself he could be something of a tyrant. Remember that story about the Irish Chief who . . .'

'Of course he had power in the sense of leadership. I'm not disputing that, or trying to romanticize. I mean, there were even feuds and rivalries between the different monasteries – bloody ones, in fact, but it was still called the Age of the Saints. Okay, I grant you that "saint" was a more general term then, meaning anyone who followed a strict religious life, but the very fact so many *did* follow it, were willing to give up everything for the sake of an ideal, makes it a special period.'

'But I thought you said a lot of them were very shadowy figures, or even sort of invented or embellished by a later age to provide an inspiration?' Morna wiped her mouth. At least she could hold her own, remember what he'd told her, what she'd read.

'Yes, that's true, but there are still enough substantial ones to prove the saintliness – well, charisma, anyway. Men like Columba, Aidan, Cuthbert – and Abban himself, of course – come over as real personalities with a sort of star quality which attracted fans and followers. Okay, they were tough, as well, and probably damned pig-headed, but they *had* to be in the conditions of their age, if they were going to achieve anything at all. And you can always see their softer side – those little quirks or foibles which prove they were human and *couldn't* have been invented.' David added powdered milk to tepid tea, stirred it with a fork. 'I wrote a little thing once on all the animal stories in the different Lives – comparing and contrasting them. All right, some of them may be standard, trotted out to edify the reader, or to symbolize some victory over paganism, like Abban clouting that boar to kingdom come . . .'

David broke off mid-sentence, tried his tea, added another scoop of milk. 'Wild boars are always cropping up, you know. They were one of the cult or totem animals of the pagan Picts. You can see them in their art – marvellous carvings of really ferocious specimens – so when Abban and Co. bumped a couple off, it was one up for the Christians.'

'David, that's the third lot of milk you've put in your tea. It was weak enough to start with.'

'Sorry, I wasn't thinking. Where was I, anyway? I've lost the thread.'

'Wild boars.'

'No, that was a digression. Ah, yes, I remember now. All I was trying to say was that as well as the standard stories you still get variations on the beasties – little individual touches where you can almost see the saint preaching to a stubborn pig or praising the fly who marked the place on his psalter by settling down on the line he'd just read. Which reminds me . . .' He paused to drain his tea, pushed the tin of milk away – 'I haven't answered your question yet. Yes, I *do* prefer the early stuff. It's a fascinating period, from the breakup of the Roman Empire to – well, say the death of Bede in 735. Most of my work has centred on the sixth and seventh centuries, and mainly on the Church. I've got the background for it, I suppose. You see, I started off doing a degree in theology. You know how it is in Catholic schools – all the girls panting to be nuns and the boys rushing off to seminaries.'

'You mean, you went to a . . .?'

'No, I just escaped. My headmaster talked me out of it – or at least told me to wait a year or two. He suggested I read theology at Oxford. I was one of the few non-priests on the course. Dazzled by the dog-collars.'

Morna laughed. 'I must have felt the vibes. Don't you remember, I thought you were a priest when we first met, even called you Father. Why didn't you tell me then?'

David didn't answer, seemed suddenly reserved again, frowning into his cup as if he already regretted his one disclosure.

It was she who broke the silence. 'I'm sorry, I'm confused. I thought you said you took your degree in history and then went on to . . .'

'Yes, I did. But I switched halfway, you see, ditched the God stuff. In fact, I always tend to hush it up. It's amazing

403

what a conversation-stopper the word "theology" is. No wonder so many priests wear mufti nowadays. It's a form of disguise, I suppose, to prevent people clamming up or getting abusive before they've even introduced themselves.'

She heard the note of bitterness in his voice. He had used the word 'escape' about the seminary, but that could be simply bluff. Did he regret the fact that he had never achieved the priesthood? If things had worked out differently, she could be Sister Anne and he Reverend Father Anthony, the two of them in full religious habits, nodding primly at each other at some solemn church convention, instead of sprawling in jeans and sweaters in a cottage in the wilds. She suppressed a laugh. Her own jeans were gaping at the waist, the zipper creeping down. Too much strain on them. Should she make a joke of it, or simply fumble surreptitiously, try to do them up again? She fumbled.

'Wh . . . Why did you change subjects?' she asked, still fighting a desire to laugh, still trying not to scratch. She would never have made a nun.

'History appeared to have more respect for the facts – though, actually, I doubt that now.' David was looking tactfully at his dish, seemed surprised to see the pineapple, although he had served it out himself. 'That's what interested me when you talked about your own work – you know, the element of distortion in it. In history, too, there's no exact translation of the past.'

'How do you mean?'

'Well, we either have too little information – say with Abban – where even what we do have is often plagiarism. Those chroniclers weren't ashamed to crib great chunks, you know. It was a form of literary showing-off – proved they knew their letters or that their subject was worthy enough to be modelled on a classic. But when you come to read it, you're never quite sure whether you're dealing with a real event or a reworked version of some earlier Life or . . .' David split a pineapple chunk in two, swallowed half, continued. 'Then, with modern history, there's the opposite problem – you're absolutely swamped with facts. New evidence pouring in and contradicting last year's theories, or new discoveries in some other field like science or archaeology suddenly upsetting all the apple-carts. There's no such thing as history, really, not in the sense of a cool objective record detached from the historians who write it. They're all entangled in their own prejudices and preconceptions, and they see another century through distorting glasses, or only select the bits they want and ignore the rest, or tidy the whole thing up so it's all defined and neat instead of a morass of contradictions and complexities. Actually, the word for history in French and German is the same word as for fiction. That's quite significant.'

David was still jabbing at his second half of pineapple, shredding it with his spoon. 'I envy you your languages, you know. They're sort of antennae into the thought and culture of other countries, and you need that for history. I've found it myself with both Scots Gaelic and Irish – the very words they have or don't have, or the way they form their words, that's all crucial, helps you understand what . . . Am I boring you?'

'No. I'm just surprised. I always thought of history as the most – you know – honest sort of subject, settled and neatly tethered down, so it couldn't blow up in your face, like physics or biology have, or even theology.'

'Oh, no. There are eruptions all the time – and not just over trivia. Look at Joan of Arc. Several historians are saying now she was never burnt at the stake at all.'

'Didn't one scholar prove she was a man?'

David laughed. 'Like Shakespeare was a woman. That's the latest feminist theory.'

'Is it? What about his anti-feminist plays, though? Like *Taming of the Shrew*?'

'Auberon Waugh wrote those, or Kingsley Amis.'

They both laughed. Morna relaxed back in her chair, cupping both hands around her second mug of tea. To hell with the jeans. If they revealed a strip of naked flesh, well – the sweaters covered that. And what were a few odd flea-bites? St Abban must have been bitten alive, especially in the summer. It was minds which counted, surely – David's mind and hers, communicating, coupled. They had broached more subjects in an hour than she and Neil had tackled in fourteen years. And there were a thousand other issues to explore. She could feel them churning in her brain, flickering into life like the endless restless shadows from the lamp. She could hardly sit still, longed to run, jump, turn cartwheels. But where and how? They were cloistered in one low-beamed room, chained to lamp and fire. The cottage had only four small rooms in all – two up, two down, and three of them unheated. She glanced across at David, still ploughing through his fruit. How could they *not* be close, sitting opposite each other, hemmed in by four stone walls, corralled by the sea? She could lean across and touch him if she wanted, stroke his beard, run a hand across his cheek . . .

'Biscuits and cheese?' he was asking. 'Sorry – no cheese left. Biscuits and strawberry jam?'

'I thought you'd finished all the biscuits.'

'The sweet ones, yes, but I've got a few cream crackers left – or crumbs of cream crackers, perhaps I ought to say. They came over on a very rough crossing and by the time Cormack had flung them ashore and hauled them up the cliff, they were done for.'

'I bought you cheeses, actually, then ditched them. We could always go on a treasure hunt – try and find half a mangled Brie and . . .'

'In the dark?'

'We've got the moon.' Morna slipped back to the window – the larger one which faced south – pushed aside the frill of

406

tattered cretonne. The view of the sea was restricted by the porch, but she could see the lights of some small craft cutting across the moonlight. A fishing boat? A coaster carrying coal, or supplies to a lonely oil rig? Only the dull and torpid were asleep. Brave souls fished and navigated, prospected for oil or new ideas, made seaweed fritters, kept the night alive; Walt Disney scribbling sketches in the early hours; Abban on his knees till dawn. The power of the individual. The Celtic Church had allowed that power to flourish – scores of dedicated men beavering away in bleak and lonely places, fostering their talents. They hadn't needed large-scale formal buildings like later medieval monks, or official written rules. Any tiny one-off settlement could achieve fame and sanctity through its individual founder, its individual work. The greatest of them had transformed their barren sites into centres of scholarship respected throughout the world – Columba on Iona, Aidan at Lindisfarne, their own St Abban here. If David's book succeeded, it could make Abban's name and island live again. And she was part of it, could be involved still further if she stayed a while, helped and supported David in his work. Couldn't they inaugurate their own mini golden age – even if it lasted a scant month or less – two scholars working for one end, following one ideal? She could rise above her usual petty concerns, do without her creature comforts, forget bodies, gender, clothes, strive for something higher, more worth-while.

She strode back to the table, cleared away the dishes, replaced David's books and papers centre-stage.

'What you doing? We haven't finished yet. I've just broken a nail opening that wretched jam.'

'We can't have jam. Abban would be horrified. It's not even a feast day.'

David laughed. 'See how he's affected you already? He

407

does that all the time. No, leave the dishes, Morna. If you're tired, you go back to bed.'

'I'm not in the least bit tired. In fact, if you wouldn't mind, I'd like to make a start on the rest of that translation – the bit I never finished.'

'What, *now*?'

'Why not?' She picked out a Biro and some paper, drew up her chair. 'It's getting on for five. Abban would have been working for an hour or two already if he'd gone to bed at all. If we're going to be saints, David, we've got to rival that.'

20

Chris put her cases down, stood blinking against the glare and noise and bustle of the airport. Crowds of people pressed against the barrier – chauffeurs with placards, excited children hopping up and down, a tiny stoop-backed nun dwarfed by her cello case, a turbanned Indian brandishing a bouquet of yellow roses. So where was Martin? Surely he could spot her. She was standing slap-bang in the centre of the concourse, wearing a crazy hat which said 'I love Los Angeles', a two-foot-long koala bear (a present from Dean) stuck under one arm. Most of the other passengers were being swallowed up in hugs and kisses as their friends and relatives rushed forward to take their luggage, fall upon their necks. She watched in envy as a dishy guy dressed all in white swung his red-haired girlfriend off her feet. Hadn't Martin made it? Been delayed in traffic? Was still in bed asleep? Okay, if that's how much she meant to him, she would make her own way back. There were buses, weren't there, tubes? It would be better anyway. If she were going to cut their ties, then best to do it right from the beginning, not let him think . . .

'Chris!'

She swung round, saw someone pounding towards her from the opposite direction – a boy – no, a man; someone taller than she'd remembered, older, better looking. He seized her in his arms, crushed her against his rough and matted sweater which smelt of printer's ink. She tried to pull free, couldn't breathe, couldn't see, but he only held on tighter, pressing her whole length against his body so that she could feel his ribs, the bulge between his legs which had suddenly got bigger. At last, his arms relaxed a little and she ducked out under them, took a step back, stared at him, confused. She had planned to play it cool, just a brief kiss and a 'Nice to see you, Martin', but how could she say that when he was obviously so choked, sort of blinking and screwing up his face and . . .?

'You . . . you're *crying*, Martin.'

'Course I'm bloody not. Is this all your luggage?' He snatched up her two cases, started striding on ahead towards the exit.

'Wait,' she shouted. 'Wait! L . . . Let's have a coffee first.'

'What for?' He paused a moment to allow her to catch up, flung an arm across her shoulders. 'We can make some tea at my place if you're thirsty.'

'N . . . No, please. There's no rush, is there?' She needed to sit down quietly and work things out. She was thrown, totally thrown by the Martin who was standing there – the strong dark wilful hair which refused to lie flat or wave, the intense and wary eyes, narrowed now as if daring her to mock them, the tall slouched figure which showed his bones through his body, his body through his clothes. The Martin she had shrugged off in America had been different altogether – sort of flabbier and slighter, with mousy hair and little piggy eyes. Had she downgraded him on purpose so she could be free to go with other men, free to find a partner her father would approve of?

He was suddenly kissing her again, had stopped right outside the bookshop, put the cases down and scooped her up instead, so that people were muttering and complaining, having to walk round them, tripping on their luggage. He had never kissed like that before – not even in his bedroom, let alone in public – so fiercely and sort of famishedly, as if he were a wild starving animal who had only just been let out of its cage. At last, he let her mouth go, but still held her by the wrists, staring into her face.

'God! I've missed you, Chris.'

'H . . . Have you?'

'Well, haven't you? Missed me, I mean?'

'Yeah, course.' Chris stepped aside to let a tall and tutting lady grouse into the shop. Of course she'd bloody missed him, but she didn't have the words for what she was feeling – a whole churning tangle of mixed and snarled emotions which had knocked her off-balance, left her floundering.

Martin ran a hand across her buttock. 'Sure you still want that coffee?'

'Y . . . Yes, please.' She had to play for time. She knew he wanted to get her into bed. Well, yeah, she'd like that, too, but she wasn't *meant* to want it. It wasn't on the agenda. She had planned to say she was tired, absolutely whacked, in fact, and if he didn't mind, she'd go straight on to her Grandma's, see him later. Then in a day or two, she would explain that things had changed, fundamental things like . . .

Things had changed again, though – back the other way. And she *wasn't* tired – well, pooped after the long flight, obviously, but sort of fizzing underneath it, so she didn't know what she wanted or where to go and what to do or . . .

'*Would the Rank Xerox representative from Kansas, please report to Airport Information.*'

'*Will Mr Albert Hamburg meeting Mr Stein from Delhi kindly go at once to . . .*'

God! Those announcements drove her mad. It was impossible to think straight when every word she said was interrupted by some disembodied voice chasing Mr This or That. The place was so damned crowded. Half the world seemed to have flown in just this morning and half of those again seemed to be making for the shop. She dodged aside as a woman with a pushchair scraped it against her leg, ducked the other way to avoid the smoke-trail of a seven-foot Nigerian and his pipe.

'*Would Dr Aziz Al-Saga of Saudi Finance please contact . . .*'

'Let's sit down,' she mouthed against the boom.

Martin stumped towards the café with the cases, found a table. 'You stay here with the luggage, Chris, and I'll get the coffees. Want a bun or something?'

'No . . . yes . . . You choose.' She couldn't think of buns when her whole settled plan had burst apart, her future changed, *Martin* changed. It was tiny things which had knocked her back – his long lean bony hands with their chewed and broken nails, the patch on his jeans which said 'Einstein's kid brother', the fact he was wearing ropy old jeans at all, hadn't bothered to dress up. All the blokes in California now seemed so damned prissy in comparison – sort of scrubbed and sanitized as if someone had put them through a car-wash, then dolled them up in button-downs and blazers, tanned them on a sun-bed, doused them with cologne – at least the types her father knew. She had never had a chance to meet the proles. Martin was pale and smelt of Martin, and one shoelace in his trainers was a piece of hairy string, and he didn't wear gold rings or After-Sun Skin Smoother, and he had actually cried – well, almost – for no other reason than the fact he had her back again. It was Frenchmen who cried, swoony Gallic lovers in white trousers and red sports cars, not trainee litho operators who still lived with their mums in Wandsworth and bit their nails. In California, she had made him out a chauvinist – boring, boorish, unromantic – and there he was, contradicting her, losing his place in the queue because he couldn't keep his eyes off her, bumping into people as he turned back again, again, drinking her up, devouring her, while all the other earthbound guzzlers grabbed their coffees and their buns.

And even back at their table, he still kept kissing her and touching her, feeding her bits of doughnut, sugaring her coffee. Had he ever done those things before? She could hardly remember, was totally confused. She had stayed a week longer in the States, just seven extra days, planned to stay a lifetime. The plan had broken down, in fact, but she had started off the week breaking the ties with Martin in her mind, told herself he was immature and scruffy and that if her father didn't like him, then best forget him altogether, make a brave new start.

Okay, so he was scruffy – okay, so her Dad preferred accountants and attorneys, but what did she do about these new sloppy inconvenient feelings which had knocked her for six, blasted everything apart?

'*Will Mrs Lois Hampton of Ontario . . .*'

The booming voice collided with the wails of a jet-lagged child. Chris blocked her ears against them both. If only there were an announcement for *her*, a voice from On High telling her what to do. She stared at the brown plastic ceiling, down again at the orange plastic table. Nothing. Only Martin's grubby hand. She could have lost that hand for ever, lost his magic finger which knew exactly what to do and where to go. It was probing the doughnut now, scooping out the jam.

'D'you realize, Chris, I didn't recognize you at first – just for a split second when I saw you standing with your cases in that hat.'

'What d'you mean?' She licked the jammy finger he was holding to her lips. 'I . . . I'm just the same.'

'No, you're not. Your hair's a different colour. Sort of two-tone.'

Chris removed the hat, patted her hair as if to make sure it was still there. 'Don't you like it?'

Martin shook his head.

'You ought to. It cost nearly sixty dollars.'

'Christ! I could have bought an underwater torch for that, one of those halogen ones with . . .'

'No, you couldn't. Bunny paid. She took me to her hairdresser. He said I had good bone structure.'

'*He?*'

'Claude. Don't worry. He's the . . . other way. They mostly are at hairdressers.'

Martin pushed his plate away, kidnapped her foot between his trainers, rubbed knees. 'I wasn't late, you know. You didn't think that, did you? I got here at the crack of dawn, hung around for hours, but I was busting for a pee and I'd just dashed off to the gents when you must have actually showed up. I could have kicked myself. I wanted to be the first. I *was* the first, for God's sake. The place was half-deserted when I got here.'

Chris swallowed the last morsel of her sugary Chelsea bun. Martin hated getting up early, loathed hanging around in crowded stuffy places. She wanted to thank him, tell him how she'd missed his finger, but a waitress was standing by the table, a middle-aged fatty in a maroon striped apron and a boater saying 'Welcome to Heathrow'. Martin didn't care, leaned across and kissed the sugar from her lips.

'Shall we make a move now?'

Chris drained her already empty cup. Supposing he smelt those other men on her, started asking questions? Supposing she were pregnant? No, she mustn't start on that again. Bunny had assured her that it was utterly unlikely and she had promised to stop worrying about it. All the same, Martin might sense that some other sucker's sperm had been inside her, when his own was always strictly banned. 'Just . . . five minutes more,' she pleaded. 'My . . . er . . . legs still feel all funny. I got cramp in them on the plane.'

He stroked them under the table. '*I'*ll sort them out. God, Chris, I can hardly believe you're here! When you phoned to say you were staying longer, I was so angry I . . .'

'Angry? But you d . . . didn't say. You didn't even . . .'

'How could I, with the pips going and my parents listening in and you sounding so damned chuffed about a still longer separation?'

'I . . . I wasn't, Martin. I *asked* you if you minded.'

'Yeah – and then rushed on to tell me you'd already changed your ticket before I had time to even answer. When you'd put the phone down, I dashed straight off on my bike – drove for bloody miles. It was pissing down with rain and I got soaked to the skin. I even blamed you for the weather – thought of you lolling in the sun, living it up with some American creep.'

Chris went on drinking non-existent coffee so that he couldn't see her face. She *had* been lolling in the sun, living it up with . . . And supposing he found out that she'd been planning to stay longer still, never return at all? She had only changed her mind because of another man, a louse – returned home not for Martin, but to run away from Al. Al had come after Derwent (who had turned out like the hairdressers). He was old – thirty-two – and they had done it in a proper bed with a proper contraceptive (which Al had called a rubber), in a snazzy sort of ranch house where she had spent the night after elaborate lies to Bunny about a girl she had met whose parents were visiting England in the summer and wanted her to meet them. She hadn't slept at all. Alan was married. She hadn't realized until they had gone upstairs and she had seen his wife's photo on the chest of drawers – a tall and scraggy blonde holding a small girl by the hand who had Al's own eyes and mouth.

'Don't worry,' he said, when he saw where she was looking. 'They're away till the end of the week – gone to stay with my mother-in-law.'

'I . . . I see.' Chris was still staring at the child. She looked four or five, the same age as Dean, but painfully plain with lank brown pigtails and a gap in her front teeth.

She'd had crappy plaits like that herself, felt sorry for the kid. She turned her back, slumped against the bureau. Bloody hypocrite. How could she be sorry and then go right ahead and have it away with the brat's own father? That was Bunny's rôle. Bunny had already sneaked into the bedroom, was lying naked on the counterpane with Neil on top of her, Dean sobbing in a corner. She kicked them all out again, bagged the bed herself, tried to concentrate on an article she'd read in American *Cosmopolitan* called 'Help Yourself to Ecstasy in Bed'. It might have been okay if Al had bucked up and got a move on, but he was obviously a soap and water freak, and even when he had showered and washed his hair in the en-suite blue-dream bathroom, he still stayed glued to the basin, scrubbing his nails and swilling out his mouth like a twin-sponsored commercial for Listerine and Lifebuoy. By the time he had climbed on top of her, smelling like a drugstore and so sterilized she was surprised he used his prick and not forceps and a scalpel, she felt nothing but exhaustion mixed with guilt. And although she kept her eyes shut, she could still see the gap-teeth and the pigtails, so she lay anaesthetized, a dumb and lumpen patient, while he pulled his rubber glove on, then made his incision, opened her up. And in the morning, after he'd performed a second op, he brought her up her breakfast on a tray – Sugar Ricicles in his daughter's Snoopy bowl.

'Had a good time?' asked Bunny, when she slunk in, pale, at noon.

'Yeah, great.'

That evening, she told them she was sorry but she would have to go back to England after all. Yeah, she realized she'd only just changed her ticket to stay on, but she was worried about her grandmother who was on her own and feeling pretty low. She had phoned Bea already (who was on top of the world, in fact – full of some retreat thing she had only just returned from), checked that she could stay with her while her mother was away. She loathed the whole stupid business of counting men like trophies (number four), wanted to be a kid again, safe and small with Grandma, sharing her bed with no one but a teddy.

Except she had changed her mind (*again*) before she had even stepped on the plane. Her father had seen her off, left Dean and Bunny in the airport cafeteria, steered her towards the departure gate, carrying the koala bear and all the other presents he had showered her with himself. He had stopped at the barrier, drawn her into his arms – not a rushed embarrassed hug because people were watching, or a rationed one because his wife and son were waiting, but a real slow-motion embrace with all the stops out.

She was the one who had cried then, really sobbed, realized she was running away, and that America didn't have to mean jerks like Al and Gerry and becoming a bed-hop and a slut, but her father and excitement and a whole new way of life. She had hardly thought of Martin, just wished Al had been single or Derwent heterosexual, or she herself less ridiculously adolescent so that she didn't change her mind and mood with every passing guy.

'I'll miss you,' Neil was murmuring, stroking her hair as none of the others had.

She put her bag down. 'Look I needn't go. I can change my ticket back again. Please. I don't even *want* to leave now. I've made a mistake, I know I have.'

Neil had gone very quiet and steely, told her he couldn't upset important clients by continually swapping tickets which they had been decent enough to provide in the first place and that she was quite old enough to stick to a decision once she had made it. She couldn't bear the farewells ruined, the last memory of her father an angry scathing one, so she had forced herself to think of all the awful things about America – the sixteen-ounce steaks oozing blood, Al's taste in bathroom fittings, rush-hour on the freeways, Bunny's furs.

'Enjoy your flight!' Neil called, as he walked away.

She *had* enjoyed it, actually – being treated as a jet-setter and using her last remaining dollars to buy American martinis and refusing to think about problems like what she said to Martin and how she got a job. Martin remained a problem until she was squeezed half to death against his grotty sweater and suddenly realized that she had been wrong (and blind) again and that his hug was more important even than her father's. Neil was a stranger still. Despite the caddying, the outings, she still didn't know her father – maybe never would. His future lay with Dean, not her, perhaps with another (ultra-gorgeous) daughter who would displace her in a year or two. They had had their time together – twelve whole years which she had simply taken for granted, then three weeks as a bonus, and a week on top of that. That was it.

She didn't regret the trip. She was truly thrilled she had seen him, had brought back the excitement with her like another exotic present, duty-free. Martin had brought her nothing – no gifts or flowers or bears – just himself and all that choked emotion. Even now, he had both his hands in hers, was gazing at her with a mixture of greed and wonder like a dog in a butcher's shop. Okay, so it was sloppy, but what was wrong with that? She had been just a body to men like Al and Gerry, a bit on the side. To Martin she was life and future. She had to make this moment last, hold on to it, not puncture it or let it fade or tarnish.

'Hey, Martin, let's find a bar, order some champagne.'

'Who's paying, chump? You're in Hounslow now, not Hollywood.'

'Well, wine, whisky – anything.'

'It's only half past nine, Chris. The bars aren't open yet.

And even if they were, it's hardly going to mix with all that coffee.'

'Let's have breakfast, then – a proper one. Not here, but in that other swish restaurant in Departures – eggs and bacon and sausage and . . .'

'We've got eggs and bacon and sausage at home.'

'Oh, Martin, you don't understand. I want to *do* something.'

'What d'you mean? You've just had a whole month's holiday and an eleven-hour flight on a Jumbo jet. Isn't that enough?'

She giggled. 'How about London Zoo? Breakfast with the chimpanzees.'

'I hate zoos.' He kissed her again, laid his hand on the inside of her thigh.

'Tell you what, then . . .' She broke the kiss, seized the hand. 'Let's whizz off to the coast and you can take me down on my first sea dive.'

'You'll ruin your new hairdo. Sixty bucks down the drain.'

'No, I mean it, Martin. I'm not joking. I really want to dive. I've been telling Dean about it and . . .'

'Are you mad?' Martin tugged irritably at his jeans. 'The sea's colder now than at any time of the year, and you're out of practice and jet-lagged and . . . Anyway, I thought you were scared of tackling the sea.'

'I was. Not now, though. I feel absolutely great – not scared of anything at all. I could go hang-gliding or parachuting or shin up Everest or . . .'

'You're high, Chris. I'd never take you down like that. You'd forget half of what you've learnt.'

'Oh, come on, Martin, don't be such a spoilsport. You've begged me often enough.'

'That was in the summer, though, or at least the spring. And on a proper club dive with all the crowd and . . .'

'I don't want that lot, thanks. I'd rather be alone with you – just you and me and the whole sea to ourselves.'

'You're crazy, girl.'

'I'm not. Look, I might never feel the same again. I chickened out all summer and . . .'

'That's the trouble. Supposing you panicked? You ought to go down in the very best conditions, when there's no wind and the sea's warmed up and with someone who isn't your boyfriend, so you stay – well, you know, cool and detached and . . .'

'I will stay cool, honestly I will, but I want it to be *you*, Martin, not just one of the others. Oh, please. Not today – I know that's mad, and we'd never even get there by the time we've ditched these cases and collected all our gear and stuff, but how about next weekend? I'll go on a refresher course beforehand – brush up all I've learnt. I could go to Putney baths one evening and Walton another and . . .'

'And supposing it's blowing a gale?'

'All right, that kills it then, but the weather's not too bad at the moment, is it? They told us on the plane that you've been having quite a mild spell.'

'It can change any day, you know that. We had snow just two weeks ago and force-ten winds and . . .'

'Right, the sooner we go the better – especially while my Mum's away. She'd only worry, otherwise. You know what she's like.'

'Where is she?'

'I told you. On the island with that bloke.'

'I can't believe it. Not your mother.'

'It's not *like* that, Martin. She's working.'

'Nice work.'

'Don't be stupid.' Chris banged her cup down. 'Okay, okay. Let's go back to Wandsworth and watch "Coronation Street".'

'I just can't understand you, Chris. I come to meet you

420

after a whole four weeks away and we've hardly had a chance to catch our breath, let alone catch up with news and things, when you suddenly want to dash down to the coast and do your first sea dive in the very worst conditions, when anyone else would be knackered and dead beat, gasping for home and bed. I mean, you've never even been that keen before. What's up with you?'

'I . . . I don't know.' She didn't. Except there was no point in arguing any more. She could feel the excitement already seeping away, exhaustion taking over. What was it that therapist had called her? Submissive. Yeah, that was it. Going back to Martin's and doing what he wanted, letting him screw her after a nice cup of tea in his mother's mail-order cups with the blue roses round the rims.

She crumpled up her paper serviette, banged up from her seat. 'Okay, boss. Back to bed.'

The next weekend was perfect diving weather – apart from the cold – as if Bea had been saying a novena for clear skies, low wind, calm sea and neap tides. Martin set the alarm for five, and when Chris had concocted an Anglo-American breakfast of waffles and baked beans, they rattled off in Tony's ten-year-old Ford Transit which doubled as hotel and carry-all. They had bundled in their sleeping bags as well as all their diving gear, Thermos flasks and sand-wiches, extra sweaters, change of clothes; speeded down the motorway to a stretch of coast further west than the usual Club venue. Martin wanted safe and shallow water in a deserted spot with no dangerous currents, no boats or sailing clubs. He was trying to keep the risks as low as possible, although he still maintained that February was one of the worst months they could have chosen, the sea breathtakingly cold.

Chris only really realized what he meant when she was standing on a shelf of rock trying to struggle into her wet suit, teeth chattering, shivering with goose pimples. No wind, he had said, yet she could feel a cruel sea breeze sneaking down her neck, attacking all her weak spots. The suit was wilful, seemed as opposed to the whole venture as Martin had been himself. Even in the baths it had been tricky to put on, but there at least it was sheltered, her hands not numb and clumsy with the cold. Martin was helping, tugging the jacket over her shoulders, easing up the zip. He seemed strangely solemn, treating her body no longer as something female which excited him, but merely item number one in the long inventory which followed – wet suit, bootees, hood, life-jacket, watch, knife, snorkel, harness and bottle, weight belt, gloves. He double-checked each item, adjusting straps and fit, inspecting the demand valve, making sure that the emergency cylinder was correctly attached to her life-jacket and the weight belt free to disengage; saying nothing, his total concentration on the equipment. He was the instructor now, the pro, not the randy whooping lover who had come three times in two hours the night he had met her plane and only changed his mind about the dive because he was so knackered after the third, he would have promised anything.

She wished to God she hadn't pushed it now. Her father was involved again, of course – always was. Both Neil and Dean had been thrilled about her diving, imagined her plunging down to wrecks, exploring the ocean bed. She hadn't actually admitted that all she had explored, as yet, were two municipal baths. Somehow, she had to prove herself, make her father proud of her by turning phoney boasts to fact. When Martin opposed her, it had become a sort of test case. She no longer really wanted to dive, especially when she felt the cold of England after cushy California, and her father was fading like her suntan. But then it was Martin she needed to impress – or at least stand up to him, disprove that word submissive, substitute words like fearless, independent.

Now she was being punished for it – by cold, discomfort, fear – clinging to her back like clammy garments, adding to the weight of her equipment. She had never felt so burdened by her gear before. In the baths, you sat on the edge of the pool to put it on, then simply tumbled in, or dispensed with half of it and wore just a tee shirt or bikini. Here, you had to pick your way across the rocks, lumbering along in what felt like a suit of armour, your cylinder digging into your back and shoulders and clanking against your weight belt, which dragged you down itself with its fifteen pounds of lead. Every step was an effort, the rubber tight and constricting against your skin, chafing at the crotch, pulling under the arms.

At least there was no one to see them, jeer in disbelief. The rocks were deserted. They had spotted one lone female walking her dog by the quarry higher up, a single jogger panting along the cliff path, but both had vanished now. The sea itself looked grim and grey, grumbling around the rocks. The sun had disappeared and although the sky was clear still, it seemed crazy to be plunging underwater into a temperature of ten degrees centigrade, when anyone in their senses would be hugging the fire indoors.

'Okay?' asked Martin, as they approached the last few feet of rock, slippery with seaweed and encrusted with barnacles. He scrambled the last bit on his bottom, sat on the edge of the rock with his feet dangling in the water. She did the same, wincing as a trickle of icy water seeped in at the seams of her suit and inched slowly up her legs. She slipped her fins on, sat upright again as Martin turned on her air, inspected the pressure on her gauge, checked that her harness was secure, the clamp on her bottle tight. The more precautions he took, the more her fear increased. She remembered all the horrors she had read about –

decompression sickness, failure of the demand valve, nitrogen narcosis, hypothermia. They had been only words before, theoretical crises you mugged up from a textbook so you could pass your theory tests, complete your training in a safe and heated pool. Panic itself was dangerous. She felt claustrophobic already and she hadn't even got her mask on yet. Martin was spitting into it, rubbing saliva over the glass, then rinsing it in sea water to clear it. She should be doing that herself, not standing like a ninny, semi-paralysed. This was her last chance to say no. Once she had the demand valve in, she couldn't speak at all, could communicate only through signs. She had learnt those, too, in her training, but they hadn't seemed so primitive then, so totally inadequate. There were no signs for terror, total funk.

'Are you sure you're all right?' Martin was asking as he checked his own equipment.

She nodded. 'F . . . Fine.'

'We can go back if you want.'

'No, of c . . . course not.' And have him say 'I told you so', label her a coward ever after.

'Right, once you've got your mouthpiece in, I want you to check your breathing for a moment before we actually go in. Okay?'

She nodded again, felt she had lost all power of speech for ever as she splashed her face with sea water, fitted the mask, pushed the mouthpiece in. She had forgotten how to breathe, forgotten everything. All those quiet steady training sessions seemed preparation for some totally different sport, one less terrifying, less sheer bloody crazy. Martin was gesturing to her. She tried to concentrate, stop shivering with cold and fear, inhale, exhale, as he had asked. He was putting on his own mask. Only seconds now and they would both be under.

Stop! I've changed my mind. She had intended it as a yell, a final shout of defiance, but no sound came out at all.

She didn't have a mouth any more, only a plug of rigid rubber. Martin had his back to her in any case, climbing down a further shelf of rock. When he turned round, it was to make the 'Okay' sign, the signal for them to ease forward and plunge in. Weakly, she signalled back, watched him push off into the water, followed herself, almost in a daze, her heart thud-thudding like a separate piece of equipment which had gone dangerously wrong.

The shock of the dive took her breath away. She had entered some strange whirling churning world where neither she nor anything else had shape, weight, direction or solidity, but everything boomed and blurred around her in a seething ebb and flow. The sound of her own breathing (too shallow and too fast) was roaring in her ears, light and dark spinning through each other, bubbles teasing and blinding in a stream of quicksilver, slimy weed entangling her hands and feet.

One sensation was gaining over the rest – cold, cold, a cruel and stabbing cold past description or belief, as freezing fingers of water shocked between her breasts, poked between her buttocks, seeped inside her suit to grope her stomach and her thighs. If she had thought it was cold before, she had hardly understood the word. She trod water, paralysed, unable to move with the sheer raw shock of it. Martin was a dark shape just beyond her. She tried to shout his name, kept forgetting she was muzzled, blundered towards him instead. He turned to face her, took both her hands in his, lining up his mask in front of hers. She felt almost hypnotized by his reassuring gaze, his solid calming presence, the steady pressure of his hands against her own. Cold and fear were there still, the sea still buffeting and slapping her, but now it had Martin to contend with.

He tapped his hand against his mouthpiece, then touched hers, motioning to her to breathe more slowly, stop panting in sheer panic. She watched the bubbles streaming from his valve, tried to breathe in time with them. He cleared his mask, gesturing to her to do the same, all his movements slow and deliberate, reminding her to relax and keep her cool. She obeyed him like a child, easing her mask and blinking the water from her eyes, feeling less confused already as her vision cleared. Martin had no words, but was using his hands and eyes to calm her down, willing her to remember what they had taught her in the training. They had warned her of this moment – how she would feel disorientated, but must on no account give way to it, just take her time to adapt to the new environment, adjust even to the cold.

Already she felt less paralysed as the world settled back in place, grey marbling into green and the first brutal wound of cold dulling into ache. At least she was weightless underwater. That clanking and cumbersome equipment seemed to have sunk without trace, leaving her light and strangely free. Excitement began to nudge aside the fear. Martin was still beside her, motioning her to follow him. She rechecked her air supply, cleared her ears, then drifted to the bottom, touched down on silver sand. She gazed around in awe at the tumbled crags and boulders – the whole strange distorted secret startling world. Everything looked bigger. The crevices in rocks were gaping mouths, the fine brown thongs of bootlace-weed twisted together like hunky coils of rope. She was blinkered by her mask, longed to have eyes in every part of her body so she could see everything at once – fish, coral, sea anemones, strands of shiny bladder-wrack threshing back and forwards on the current, finer weed sprouting like dark hair from grimacing heads of rock. She glanced back at the surface, heaving like a giant mass of mercury shot with shafts of greenish light, the bubbles from the demand valves streaming up as if they were alive.

Martin was gesturing at the bottom, pointing out a pair of staring eyes. A fish – so cleverly camouflaged, she would never have noticed it herself. Suddenly there were more fish – six or seven darting skittering bodies, flashing past so close she could have touched them, wheeling back again, their silver scales shimmering against the darker weed.

Martin was making certain she missed nothing, turning this way and that to show her a strangely sculpted rock or dark-jawed cave, a sea mouse with iridescent green and golden hairs along its sides, a hermit crab scuttling across the bottom. He pointed to a furrow in the sand, the trail of a whelk which she traced to its grooved and turreted shell. Beside it was a rusting hunk of metal, half a broken engine, encrusted with weed and barnacles. Even junk looked exotic underwater.

He led the way into a gully between two rocks, piercing the barrier of weed which swashed to and fro with the gentle swell of the waves. She could feel the swell herself, lapping against her body as she dived down after him. It was darker here, more menacing, fronds of seaweed forming prison bars above them, moss-fringed rocks encircling them below. Strange spooky objects had been trapped in the cleft, abandoned there for years – bits of ship or fishing gear, scraps of life now dead or mouldering. Martin was tugging something free, offering it to her as a souvenir. It was a dumpy little beer bottle, circa 1985, slimy brown and cracked, but the sea had transformed it into treasure. She took it from him with as much excitement as if it were an ancient drinking vessel. Martin had talked so often about wreck-diving, but only now did she grasp the thrill of it. It wasn't just a greedy lust for loot – he had told her that enough times – but the challenge of retrieving bits and pieces of the past, finding what was buried, exploring a world where everything was treasure, everything transformed.

She turned to follow him, finning from the shadows of the gully into warmer water no longer murky grey. The sun must have come out again, intensifying colours, lighting up the gloom. A bumptious looking fish, greenish-blue with darker rings marking out its fins, was swaggering through the weed, dodging away from them. She longed to ask Martin what it was, shout out her excitement. He had warned her that the dive might be a washout, in the sense that they wouldn't see much so early in the year. She had seen enough to stock an underwater museum and her eyes were still out on stalks trying to take everything in. Martin seemed to have tuned in to her mood, even without words, was showing off, trying out a somersault. She dared one herself, realized that the clumsy funky chicken-livered booby who had set out half an hour ago had vanished like the weight of her equipment, leaving behind a graceful streamlined fish as fearless in the water as the greeny one still playing tag with them.

Martin was signalling to her, 'Follow me', streaking on ahead. He must have spotted something, another treasure, wanted her to share it. He paused a moment to check his watch and depth gauge. They couldn't have much time left, but they'd come down again tomorrow, every day they could. She was hooked now, wanted only to dive and dive and dive, see more of this amazing secret world. She swooped after him through a rippling veil of weed, took his hand, tried to say with the pressure of her fingers that of *course* she would follow him, anywhere he went, to the deepest furthest ocean.

'Cod and double chips, please, a cheese and mushroom omelette, and a pot of tea for two.'

'Oh, Martin, it was *great*.'

'You've said that twenty times. And a portion of bread and butter. Chris, you don't want bread, do you?'

'Yeah, I do, I'm starving. When can we go again?'

'Tomorrow, if you like, if we can get our cylinders filled.

Make that bread and butter for two – no, three. Depends on the weather, of course, but . . .'

'What was that fish we saw? The bluey-green one?'

'Wrasse.'

'What?'

'Ballan wrasse. They're very common, actually. They're called sea swine sometimes or even sweet lips.'

'Sweet lips? You're joking.'

'No, I'm not. Sweet lips like yours. Give me a kiss.'

Chris made it a double like the chips. 'Oh, Martin, I do love you.'

'Ssh, the waitress's coming back.'

'I don't care.' Chris paused to pour the tea, filled his cup, went on pouring. 'I just can't tell you how wonderful it was. I mean, I never realized . . .'

'Look out! You're flooding the whole table. Give me that pot. I can see diving's gone to your head.'

'It has. Oh, I wish it was tomorrow and we were down again already. Can we make it longer next time?'

'No. You were perished as it was. You're even shivering now.'

Chris blew on her tea, cooled it with a dash of milk, then drained the whole cup almost without pausing. '*Now* I'm not. Anyway, it's worth it. It's not until you're that cold you realize just how wonderful hot tea is. Want a fill-up?'

Martin found her knee. 'I want *you* – soon.'

'You'll have me after tea. It'll be funny doing it in Tony's van. D'you think we'll both fit in one sleeping bag?'

'We'd better. Sssh . . .'

The waitress had returned again, banging down the plates of food, making a final slam with the ketchup bottle as she saw the pool of tea.

Chris giggled. 'D'you think she heard?'

'D'you think she's ever *done* it? Poor bloke if she has.' Martin started shovelling in his chips, offered one to Chris.

She gobbled it, stared down at her omelette, seeing not golden eggs, but silver sand, fronds of weed instead of mushroom stalks. She had cleared her ears, her eyes, rinsed out her wet suit, washed herself, her hair, but she couldn't clear her head. The sea was still surging to and fro in it, not just the tiny fraction she had explored herself, but the entire vast ocean which covered three-quarters of the world and included the deep dangerous waters of the abyss which plunged down so far they swallowed up mountain peaks and craters, drowned whole islands where dinosaurs had lived once, a hundred million years ago. She had read about those icy depths which sounded like a realm from outer space or a spookland in a saga, with their total darkness, their babel of discordant sounds, their weird blind creatures gliding to and fro in the eternal night. It had been book-learning before – astounding facts and figures which couldn't fail to move you, but which were remote and set apart. Now it touched on her own experience. All right, so she had been down only a puny thirty feet, would need not only a whole lifetime, but maybe two or three more centuries of techno- logical advance before she could ever go so deep, but at least she had made a start. She was no longer a total novice, one of those timid landbound plodders who hugged the shore, refused to get their feet wet, refused to quest or dare. Martin had turned her from funk to fish, taught her to fin, fly, defy gravity and danger, had joined her to that chain of higher souls who for twenty or thirty centuries had been battling to expand their lungs or invent new apparatus so that they could explore the whole underwater world.

She had had her initiation, passed with flying colours, and that meant more to her than any exam she had ever sat, her three A levels put together, even the acceptance slip from Bristol University. She was tempted to bypass Bristol altogether, take her exams in diving rather than modern languages, gain Honours underwater. Except it wouldn't be worth the uproar from her mother. She must see her degree as a sort of gift to Martin. He planned to travel, didn't he, so languages might help. Now she could go with him, share his diving life. Her Ma and Grandma would be shocked by that sort of life, living like a nomad, never secure or settled, badly paid, often out of work. But they didn't understand the thrills, the chance of winning fame or fortune if you were prepared to take the risks and had that crazy combination of sheer guts and dogged patience which Martin had himself. Even kids and amateurs had found amazing things. The sea was full of wrecks – four-thousand-odd off Florida alone, and further down this very stretch of Devon coast, there was said to be a treasure ship with nineteen tons of gold and silver coin spilling out among the skulls. Someone had to bring it up. Why not the new and famous duo of Brett and Gordon, the man-and-woman team whose name was headlines in the diving world? Okay, so she was fantasizing, but even if they didn't find a dickybird, there was still the excitement of the life itself, the challenge and the travel, the freedom from stupefying in some boring suburb, settling down behind their starched net curtains with nothing to survey but privet hedge and garden gnomes.

Martin speared a chip on his fork, dunked it in a pool of ketchup. 'You're shivering again, Chris. You're not cold still, are you?'

'No, just excited.' She seemed to have been shivering all day, with chill or panic, and now sheer raw elation. She hadn't admitted her initial fears to Martin, had shrugged them off, along with the resentments, irritations, unfair comparisons, petty carps and moans. All right, so Martin hadn't been to Marlborough, would never get to Cambridge (nor had she), couldn't afford to take her to the Ritz. Who cared? He was an adventurer, explorer, with more guts and nerve than any of the creeps she had met. A real man wore a wet suit, not pseud white jeans or scarlet running-shorts.

Anyone could drive a Porsche or even throw a discus. It took a special sort of skill to be a diver, an instructor – one who had got distinction in his theory tests, completed his training in half the usual time. And yet Martin hadn't been rash or taken any risks, not once been impatient with her or used his greater experience to make her feel stupid or a drag. He had treated her like glass, observed every possible precaution, shown care, consideration, even a tenderness which she had rarely seen before and which made her feel quite choked. Gerry would have left her on the rocks, twirling her baton and kicking up her frilly skirts while she cheered him on, cutting piles of sandwiches to feed him when he surfaced. Martin had shared the sea with her, lending her his eyes and all his knowledge, making her an equal and a partner. The sea had become part of them, part of their relationship, a threesome with no jealousy. She had wanted romance, excitement, and now she had them – a whole vast oceanful.

'Oh, Martin . . .'

'Eat your omelette. It cost enough. They're 30p cheaper at Roxy's and that's got class.'

Chris glanced round the shabby workmen's caff with its steamed-up windows, its scuffed linoleum, the bored and scraggy waitress smoking over the cupcakes. The ketchup had been watered down with vinegar, the bread was yesterday's, curling at the edges. 'It's a smashing place – the best meal I've ever had.'

Martin hooted. 'Better than the ones in California, I suppose, with your ice-buckets and half a dozen waiters.'

She tried to remember California. It seemed as far away, as deeply buried as the waters of the abyss. How could she have made it so important, let a month of gloss and glitter give her sunstroke, a few macho men unsettle her, so that she had forgotten the thrills of diving, the thrills of Martin's finger, forgotten she belonged here – and with him? She fumbled for his hand, laid her own palm on top of it. 'I'm glad I came back,' she whispered.

'Are you?'

'Mm.'

'You're not just saying that?'

'No.'

'Not planning to . . . run off again?'

She shook her head, said 'Uh-uh', changed it into 'No.'

'Promise?'

'Yeah.'

'Never?'

'No.'

He pushed his chair back, wiped his mouth, fiddled with his knife. He seemed embarrassed suddenly, rummaged in his pocket, cleared his throat. 'I . . . er . . . bought you this.' He drew out a twist of plain brown paper. 'Sorry about the box. I mean, there *isn't* a box. I bought it off a bloke – you know, privately. Couldn't afford a jeweller's.' He passed it across. 'It's not tat, mind you. I wanted something decent, so I mugged up all the advertisements – *Exchange and Mart*, local papers, cards in shops. I saw a lot of rubbish and a lot more cons. This was the best – no question. You may not like it, of course, but . . .' His voice trailed off.

She stared down at the ring. A diamond – a real fat swanky one. She didn't like diamonds. Never had. Didn't want a ring. She wanted Martin, but they were bonded already, didn't need the Kohinor to prove it to the world. Anyway, how in God's name had he bought it? Martin couldn't afford diamonds, even second-hand ones.

'Martin, *no*. I . . . I can't. It must have cost a bomb. And I know you're short of cash. I mean, you said only yesterday that . . .'

'It's okay. Put it on. I want to see how it looks.'

'It's *not* okay.' She pushed away her omelette. 'We'd better take it back, quickly, before . . .'

'Don't be stupid. We can't. Not now.'

'But I don't want you in debt, or paying interest to banks and things or . . .'

'I'm not.'

She tried to calm her voice, sound less graceless and ungrateful. 'Look, Martin, darling, I don't like to be rude, but I know you can't afford this. I mean I'll only keep on worrying that . . .'

He picked up the last chip with his fingers, swallowed it whole, mumbled through the mouthful. 'If you really want to know, I sold my stereo.'

'You *what*?'

He shrugged. 'I didn't need it.'

Now he was really lying. His stereo was the most precious thing he owned after his diving gear. His only rich relation, a bachelor uncle in Ilford, had given it to him on his eighteenth birthday – a Sanusi, a posh one with a graphic equalizer. All the groups who jostled on his walls would be silenced now, just one-dimensional posters mouthing word-lessly, like when you turned the sound off on the telly and singers and guitarists dwindled into dumb and jerking puppets.

'B . . . But, Martin, all your records – you've been collecting them for years and . . .'

'I sold all those as well. It'll give us a bit more space.'

She remembered now, the room had seemed less cramped, yet she hadn't realized why. She had been so self-absorbed, so busy with her jet lag, her puny little problems, she had allowed her . . . her fiancé to lop off a bit of his own life and hadn't even seen the scar. True she had gone to Bea's after that first wild night with him, slept with Madonnas looking down on her instead of Iggy Pop or Talking Heads, but she should at least have noticed that he hadn't offered to play her a disc or raved about a new one. Selfish bitch she was, when he was faithful, generous beyond belief.

Martin picked the ring up. 'Well, aren't you going to put it on?' He slipped it on her finger, hands still greasy from the chips. It jammed halfway. 'Shit! It's too small. I was scared of that.'

'You can always get them . . . altered.' Chris tugged it off again. Her words sounded reluctant, even grudging. Why should she feel relieved that it didn't fit? She couldn't explain, not even to herself.

'Yeah, but I wanted you to wear it – now.'

They stared at each other. He looked so crestfallen, Chris wanted to weep for him, felt humbled, dazed, by what he had done for her. She had thought Love was duels and violins and Shakespeare's Sonnets, and it had turned out to be a line or two in *Exchange and Mart*, a scrawled card in a window, a month of harrying and haggling to buy her a ring the hard way, wasting precious time and petrol on wild-goose cons and rip-offs.

'I know –' Martin stopped picking at his nails – 'You can wear it round your neck. Have you got your chain on?'

She shook her head, had brought no jewellery with her.

'Wait a tick.' Martin stuck his hand down the collar of his sweater, came up with a piece of string which he had been wearing round his own neck, something dangling from it.

'What's that?'

'Just a couple of O-rings, fathead. You've seen them often enough.' Martin pulled them over his head. 'I'll stick 'em in my pocket and you can have the string.'

'No, leave them.' She grabbed them from him, string and all, slipped both the washers on her wedding finger. They fitted, went right down. Engagement ring, diving ring.

'Nutcase,' Martin grinned.

She took them off again, undid the knot in the string, threaded it through the diamond, tied it round her neck, peered down at the necklace. A solitaire flanked not by useless sapphires, but by two tiny rubber pressure-seals which played a vital rôle in maintaining the diver's air supply, could make the crucial difference between going down and staying up. She wanted to go down, as often and as far as he would let her. No need to be nervous when she had had her honeymoon already, found it wonderful, ecstatic. This ring was her passport to a hundred and thirty-nine million miles of ocean, so how could it restrict her?

Martin was jabbing his spoon against the hardened rock of sugar in the bowl. 'You do . . . er . . . like it, don't you, Chris?'

She took his hand, held his own wedding finger in the encircling ring of her linked thumb and index finger – the 'okay' sign in diving. 'It's great,' she whispered. 'It's absolutely great.'

21

It was Morna's turn for emptying the privy pail. The wind was making her eyes water as she battled along the cliff path, whipping her hair against her face, tugging at the ends of David's scarf. She turned north, lugging the heavy bucket towards the jutting piece of rock which they used when the wind was a southwesterly. It seemed crass and anti-social to empty sewage into the open sea, but the ground was too shallow to dig cesspits. There was deeper soil around the stream, but they had no wish to contaminate their precious water supply. Cormack and the other islanders could dig more easily in the boggy softer north end. Not that Cormack bothered. David had told her the crofter simply squatted down behind his hen-house, or turned his own house wall into a urinal.

The whole subject was embarrassing. She hated to think of David emptying the pail. Something so crude and basic had no place in their delicate relationship, one fragile still despite three idyllic weeks together. Even using the privy had caused some awkwardness – unpleasant smells, overlapping times; things abhorrent to them both. Neil would have stated baldly 'I need a crap', and gone ahead and had one, leaving her to empty all the pails. She and David tried to pretend they had neither bowels nor bladders. It was roses she was carrying, or bread to feed the gulls.

She stopped a moment to rest her arm, gazed out at the ocean. It was the first day she had seen it blue, the sky streaked azure and white above it, despite the early hour. True spring weather, fitting for St Valentine's. Hadn't Chaucer said this was the day that the birds picked out their mates; Shakespeare, too, talked about woodbirds coupling once St Valentine's was past?

Did sea birds couple later? David had told her that several species were still wintering in mid-ocean. It humbled her to think of them – kittiwakes and petrels riding out the howling Atlantic gales, sleeping on the wing or not at all, flying thousands of uncharted miles, guided only by the sun and stars. But breeding time was coming round. She had seen fulmars beginning to gather on the cliffs, the first gannets gliding in. In a month or two, the sky would be clouded with their threshing wings, the air rent with cries of mating.

She wouldn't be there to watch, couldn't stay till then. It wasn't fair to her mother, or to Chris, if she were back. She kept worrying about them, wondering how they were, had never intended leaving them so long. When she first set out from Oban, she had planned to return before Bea's retreat was over, be there to welcome her back, the Oxshott house springcleaned in her honour, flowers on the table, all her shopping done. Instead, she had written to her mother, a brief evasive letter, which Cormack had posted when he took his boat to the mainland for supplies. She should have been on that boat herself, returning home to duty. The problem was she had come to prefer her duties on the island. There was something deeply satisfying about working with David, cut off from the distractions and complexities of home, even from the news. She hadn't read a paper since the *Los Angeles Times*, felt guilty sometimes that she had no idea how many bombs had exploded in Armagh or whether the Middle East was still a battleground. Would she even know if someone pressed the nuclear button and the rest of the world went up in a mushroom cloud? Their island was a sanctuary, a monastery. The more they worked on Abban's

Life, the more they seemed to move towards it themselves – a simple almost spartan diet, strict periods of work and rest (with work preponderating), rough and practical clothes, no luxury or ostentation, no hint of what Abban condemned as fleshly lust. Most of the day was spent in silence, though a companionable silence, while they sat together at the kitchen table – David writing up his book or struggling with problems of chronology or interpretation, while she finally solved the mysteries of the French professor's shorthand, revised her translation in light of them, helped David in the general structuring of his book. When they talked, it was to discuss the outline of a chapter or the ramifications of a word. They had worked out a schedule and a timetable almost as if they were living under a rule. But she no longer felt the novice to David's abbot. They were equals now – sharing the chores, both autonomous, yet never arguing. At first, she had tried to cushion his way of life, cook more ambitious meals, introduce more comforts. Gently, he resisted, refused to let her change his standing order which Cormack brought over from the mainland when wind and tide allowed. Instead, she had become an expert with the tin-opener – beans, soups, pease pudding, canned spaghetti, but not the Spam. Somehow they had both turned vegetarian. They hadn't discussed the issue, it had simply happened. She suspected it was Abban's influence again. The saint seemed so forceful sometimes, it was as if they were living as a threesome.

She switched the bucket to the other hand, clambered down a yard or two where there was a firmer flatter foothold. She had read about a contemporary of Abban's, St Cuthbert of Lindisfarne, who had made his own lavatory out of a driftwood plank set across a sea-washed chasm in the rocks, when he had been living as a hermit on Farne Island. It must have been risky if the waves which slapped the east coast were as insistent as the ones which thundered here.

439

She watched them smash against the cliff, froth back around the smooth black rocks like lace. In just three weeks the sea had become a presence, one you could never ignore nor overlook, like a new intractable member of a family, a mercurial adolescent quick to change its mood, always making a racket, always demanding attention. Yet you had to respect it as both provider and destroyer, supplying food and driftwood, threatening lives and craft. David had told her that one or two of the older islanders started their day by doffing their caps to the ocean, to salute it and acknowledge it. She was wearing no hat, but she bowed her head, paused a moment before moving to the edge of the ledge. She uncovered the bucket, turned her face away as she tipped the contents out. Why were human beings so defective – excreting, smelling, dragging down their higher selves? It must have been worse in Abban's time, with no deodorants, no Blue Flush. Did Abban have his sea-washed plank, or did some ministering angel or friendly seal bear away all excrement? His biographer had said nothing on the subject.

She scrambled back to the path which zigzagged steeply to the cottage, wished she passed a newsagent's en route. She hadn't missed the papers until this morning. St Valentine's day was different – she always bought *The Times*, then, read the passionate messages in the personal column, the doting dotty avowals, displaying ardour or despair, jealousy or lust; the in-jokes, the pet names, the fantastical inventions – sometimes four whole pages of them, nearly forty columns. For the rest of the year, the paper reverted to its usual staid agenda – politics and war, diplomacy, disasters; ignoring love, demoting it, despite the overwhelming evidence that it was a perennial force throbbing under wraps until St Valentine's allowed it to break out. Nice to phone the editor and spell out a message for David – a declaration of love from Walt Disney to F. R. Leavis, or from Simone Weil to a seal. *They* had their in-jokes now.

She wrapped his coat around her, ran the last few yards, stopped outside the back door of the cottage to remove her wellingtons. Cormack had bought those from the mainland (for a fee), along with woolly gloves. She was still sharing David's sweaters, even his vests. She could hardly stock up with new clothes when she kept saying every day that she must leave. It had become a sort of formula, a ritual to assuage the guilt, but which she didn't act upon. She had her reasons – kept trying to shine them up, make them sound less selfish, more convincing. No point in rushing back to an empty house if Chris were still away in California. And as for Bea, well there was always Madge and Vera, Father Clarke. And if Chris *did* return, then Bea could act mother, invite her to stay. That would take care of both of them – her mother purposeful, her daughter in good hands. It wouldn't be for long, in any case. She would leave next week, for certain, or the week after that, or . . .

She unlatched the door, sniffed the air. There was a heady smell of baking, richer than David's usual soda bread. He had got up very early, started on his cooking before she was awake. It had astonished her at first, his solemn sessions in the kitchen, the way he kneaded dough or sautéed vegetables with the same prayerful intensity he brought to his intellectual work. Now she simply accepted it, tried not to interfere.

She watched him for a second without him knowing she was there, his tall dark figure stooping over the range. Strange how every time she saw him she felt a sort of jolt, as if he were a naked cable conducting energy. On the surface, he seemed quiet and safe enough, self-sufficient, engrossed in what he did, courteous to her always, generous to a fault, yet there was some dangerous undercurrent which he appeared to fear himself, as if he might explode should she come too near or touch him. She remembered an old wives' tale which said that the first unmarried man you spotted on St Valentine's would be your sweetheart for a year. He had assured her once that old wives' tales were often true. She crept up on him, smiling to herself as she risked electric shock, grabbed him round the waist.

He swung round, breaking the circuit of her hands. 'Gosh! You made me jump.'

'What you cooking?'

'Sun bread.'

'What?'

'Well, that's my name for it. I thought we'd have a holiday today. Celebrate St Valentine's and Candlemas and the rites of spring and my birthday and . . .'

'David, it's not your birthday is it?'

'Yesterday.'

'Why didn't you *say*?'

'I forgot all about it, to tell the truth, until I was just settling down to sleep at five to midnight. I almost came and got you so that we could celebrate the last five minutes of it.'

'I wish you had.' She wondered what form the celebrations might have taken, how long he would have stayed.

'It doesn't matter. We'll keep it today, instead. In the early days, feasts were very movable. Even Christmas wasn't fixed to its present date until as late as the fourth century. Actually, I didn't celebrate Christmas this year, either. It was too damn cold. There's a whole hotchpotch of feasts piling up – St Abban's feast day, Lupercalia . . .'

'Luper – what?'

'The ancient Roman version of St Valentine's. I told you about it, didn't I? It was held on the fifteenth, not today, but . . .'

Morna made a face. 'I remember now. Priests scourging women with bloody strips of goat hide. I'd rather have my hearts and flowers.'

'I thought we'd re-enact it.'

'I can hardly wait! You the priest, I take it, and me the woman?'

442

'No, we'll both be priests. They ran all around their settlement – not just scourging people, but to keep the evil spirits out. A sort of beating of the bounds. It was mainly a fertility rite. They only beat the women to help them conceive, and it was extended to the land as well – to make it fertile, protect the sheep and cattle. I thought we could do the same – walk all round the island and . . .'

'There aren't any cattle.'

'Plenty of sheep, though. And what about Cormack's hens? We might even start them laying.'

'And who do we scourge? His wife?'

'No, we'll just carry sticks as symbols.'

'David, you're not serious, are you?'

'Why not? Ritual's important. We've lost so much of it. This is a very crucial time of year. Lent starts in a fortnight . . .' He broke off, swept flour and pastry cuttings from the ancient wooden draining board which he was using as a worktop. 'D'you know why it's called Lent?'

'No.'

'Because it falls in spring which the Anglo-Saxons called *Lencten*, since the days are beginning to lengthen then.' He turned back to the range, added more fuel, screwing up his eyes against the heat. 'It's a time of transition. Spring is on its way, but it's not quite certain. For us that's no big deal. We know it'll come sooner or later, and even if it's a bad spring, we can compensate with artificial heat and light or imported foods or processed this or that. But in the old days, it was absolutely crucial. A failed crop could mean starvation. And they were never quite sure that spring would come at all. If the evil forces got the upper hand or punished them for something, then cold and dark might last for ever. Which explains the rituals. They had to appease the gods, you see, and try and encourage the light to return. That's why they lit fires – to represent the sun or set it a good example. Fires are important. There's the cleansing purging element as

443

well. I thought we'd have a bonfire tonight, followed by a special ritual meal. We'll be disgracefully unhistorical and mix everything up at once – birthdays, Lent, spring rites, Lupercalia . . . Hold on – the sun bread should be ready now, I made it for our feast. Want to see it?'

'Yes, please.'

He picked up the piece of towelling which doubled as oven glove and dishcloth, removed a tray from the oven. On it was a flattened circle of bread, baked golden brown and with a cross cut into the top. 'It's round, you see, to represent the sun. And it's made with the grain from last year's harvest. That's symbolic, too – stresses continuity and fruitfulness and . . . I had to wangle some from Cormack. He thinks I'm a weirdie anyway, but he doesn't seem to mind so long as I pay. He charged me enough, considering he feeds the stuff to his hens.'

'You mean you ground it yourself to make the flour?'

'Between two stones, the old way.'

'David, you're amazing!'

He flushed, went on talking to disguise his embarrassment. 'I added the cross to pacify St Abban. You know how fierce he used to get about all those pagan rituals – the ones he hadn't managed to adapt to Christian ends. Mind you, the Church was always pretty good at that. Even Lupercalia was wrested from the heathen. One of the early Popes stripped it clean and turned it into Candlemas.'

'But that's earlier – February 2nd.' Morna remembered the feast from school, processing round the grounds with lighted candles in the freezing dawn, holding her fingers in the flame as a penance or bravado, messing about with the hot and sticky wax to help pass the time during the lengthy Mass which followed.

David removed his sun bread from the baking tray. 'It is *now*. But it used to be held on the 14th. It's very complex, really. There are so many layers and different strands coming from various cultures and mythologies, some of them overlapping or superseded. I mean, Candlemas itself probably harks back to the Feast of Lights, which is all to do with the return of the goddess from the underworld and the rebirth of nature in the spring and . . . Blast! Something's burning.'

He rescued a second tray from the oven. The manure-coloured dough had spread into a shapeless mass, soggy in the middle, burnt around the edges.

'Whatever's that?'

'A failure, by the looks of it. It's meant to be salt-meal cake, but I had to improvise. The Vestal Virgins offered it to their goddess at Lupercalia, so I thought I'd have a shot at it. I used ordinary self-raising flour mixed with salt. They made their salt from brine, so I tried to be clever and add some mashed-up seaweed as a sort of extra. That's probably what ruined it.' David stuck a fork in, withdrew the prongs sticky-wet and clogged. 'Never mind – I'm cooking other things.'

'What things?'

'Wait and see.' He seemed elated like a child. He must have made a second secret trip to Cormack's. There were new provisions she hadn't seen, mixtures in bowls she couldn't recognize. He had gone out yesterday, ostensibly for a walk, left her by the fire.

'Can't I help, though?'

'You can be the goddess – earth mother and provider. Or you can leap over the bonfire to keep the witches away. That's another later custom which . . .'

'I'd rather get the breakfast.'

'I don't think we should have any. We ought to be fasting for our beating the bounds, and anyway, we want to save our appetite for supper. Fast before feast – it's psychologically right.'

'Let me help with supper, then.'

'No. That's *my* thing. A little present to you, for all your help on the book.'

'But it's your birthday, David. You should have the presents.'

'Well, on *your* birthday you can cook a meal for me. I'd like that.'

'It's not for ages, though.'

He shrugged. 'Doesn't matter.'

That was a present in itself, her guarantee that she would continue seeing him. Even when she had to leave, they could keep in touch by mail, so long as Cormack fetched and posted the letters. He went once a month, at least, to collect his pension and those of the other islanders, and could usually be persuaded to make an extra trip if his bronchitis had eased up and they made it worth his while. Not that it was easy to be an ardent correspondent. She had found that with her mother. The second (longer) letter she had written to Bea was still propped up on the dresser awaiting an improvement in Cormack's bronchial tubes, which had also to correspond with a calm spell in the weather. Judging by today, though, the worst of winter was over, and even if the squalls returned, to cut off any mail – well, David would be home himself in a matter of mere months. She would make her own birthday very special, say all the things she hadn't said, give him the things she couldn't give him here.

David was still busy, seemed not to want her in the way. She had learnt when to help and when to disappear. In the same way he respected her privacy, rarely came upstairs at all. She went up now, lay on her bed in all her outdoor clothes. He had asked her to be goddess and earth mother. Was that just a joke or empty words? Why couldn't she stick to her decision, regard David as a friend – nothing more; ignore that stupid inappropriate excitement which kept welling up every time she saw him? Yet surely he had hinted at something else himself. All that stuff about Lupercalia –

446

was it just a history lesson, or had he deliberately stressed the fertility rites, the echoes of an ancient cult of Pan? Pan was a lecherous god who panted after nymphs, not a skivvy baking salt bread in his kitchen.

When she went down again, the kitchen was cleared and tidy. David had disappeared. She tracked him to what they called their garden, a stretch of bare and rocky wasteland outside the back door of the cottage. He had coaxed an impressive blaze from a few strips of broken fish box, a cardboard packing case, some washed-up plastic bottles, two stumps of twisted driftwood and a little precious peat. He had cut the peat when he first arrived on the island in September, been drying it ever since, rationing it like everything else.

She squatted down beside him. 'I thought the bonfire was this evening.'

'It is. This is just a sacrificial fire. The Luperci sacrificed a young dog and a couple of goats. We can't run to those, I'm afraid, so we'll have to improvise. I've done my best.' He gestured to a small bulge in a piece of oil-stained sacking.

'What's that?'

'A dead bird. A razorbill. I found it on the cliff path. Don't worry, it's very cleanly dead. I was lucky to find anything at all. Are you ready, by the way? I was just going to come and get you.'

'Well, yes. But . . .'

'I'll fetch the corn and oil, then. They're not really right for Lupercalia, but they're a pretty standard offering for a lot of other feasts. Can you watch the fire?'

He returned with a small box of provisions, placed it on a ledge of rock, unwrapped the sacking, revealing a large bird boldly marked, jet black head and back contrasting with dazzling white underparts.

Morna stared at the sleek white wing-stripe, the curious

but powerful bill. 'David, it's beautiful. We c . . . can't burn that.'

'Would you rather it simply rotted or was gnawed by rats?'

She didn't answer. He came and knelt beside her. 'Look, it's a symbolic offering, Morna – quite an apt one, really. It represents prosperity and light and food and . . . A hundred years ago, they used to slaughter sea birds, not just to eat, but for their feathers and their skins. They made candle oil from the skins – that's our light, you see, and then they sold the feathers – that's wealth we're offering – and wings suggest the spirit, anyway, and . . .'

'All right.' She shrugged, eased up to her feet, stood watching as David decanted oil and corn into two chipped and clumsy cups. It seemed all wrong. They should have used virgin oil from a local olive grove, glistening in a stately silver vessel, not Tesco's cheapest in a plastic bottle. The corn was cornflakes – Kelloggs' vitamin-enriched without the milk and sugar. Yet somehow David made it solemn. She could see the priest in him, the way he handled cornflakes as if they were the host, his slow deliberate movements as he circled the fire, poured oil onto the flame. She felt herself drawn into his ritual, standing straight, head bowed, as if she were in church. The island itself was the huge rock of their cathedral, grey cliffs towering like nave walls, sky overarching as its marble roof, waves booming and resounding as their organ.

The fire was really roaring now, unweaving the solid granite of the rock face, crimsoning David's hands as he offered the bird on the sacrificial pyre. There was a crackle of flesh, a reek of scorching feathers. Morna shut her eyes. A bird which had soared and freewheeled in the sky, a diving bird like Martin, fearless and courageous, now grilling like a chop. She could hear the flames licking greedily, not just from their puny pyre, but from all the

448

fires lit through all the ages stretching back to first primeval fire – Bronze-Age man anointing the earth with blood and bone, flesh and ash, to appease his gods, renew fertility; pagan Celts offering human sacrifice. She squinted through half-closed lids, glimpsed the whole unravelling horizon tinged blood-red; dark and shadowy centuries charring into ash.

'Are you all right?'

She felt David's hand touch lightly on her arm, opened her eyes to grey now, the fire dying down, the sky overcast as one leaden cloud dragged its slow and creeping shadow over them. She shivered.

'Cold?' he asked.

'N . . . No.'

They were whispering, both of them, as if David, too, felt those other presences, feared to anger them, disturb them in their rites. He was kneeling now, raking up the remnants of the fire.

'The Luperci smeared their foreheads with blood from the sacrifice. We'll use ash instead, for expiation.' He retrieved a few hot ashes, dipped his thumb in them, traced a cross on both their foreheads.

Morna's brow was burning from his touch, her legs still shaky under her. She remembered Ash Wednesdays at school when the priest had marked them with ashes at the morning Mass. '*Remember, man, that thou art dust and unto dust thou shalt return.*' All through the day they had gone about their business – arithmetic and hockey, embroidery and choir practice, eating bony black-skinned cod at lunch, bread and scrape at tea – still with that black smudge on their brows, reminding them of death. It was said among the girls that if the mark stayed on until bedtime, then you were going to be a nun. Sister Anne Morna's always did.

David was damping down the embers. 'They wiped off

the blood with white wool dipped in milk. That was all symbolic. Then they had to laugh.'

'*Laugh?*' An observer might have laughed, someone not involved – laughed in sheer derision at this improvised charade – but Morna was still caught up in the ritual, still aware of powerful forces which she could hardly understand. Ancient man had believed in the living spirit in soil and rock, stone and stream. She glanced around at the craggy boulders encircling their small patch of ground, sculpted by the wind into grotesque and staring faces. The stones *did* seem alive, not just in the last flickering glimmer of the fire, but in the way they witnessed, watched.

David stood up, his movements slow and solemn still. 'We'll build our bonfire from the embers later on. That links the sacrifice with the feast. Right, I think we ought to get off now, start our beating of the bounds. Got your stick?'

She nodded. In the absence of any trees, they had to make do, David with a stave from a rotten barrel, she with a wooden wardrobe-rail which she had found in the spare bedroom without its wardrobe.

'We ought to run – at least the first bit. The Luperci did.'

'They went naked, didn't they? I draw the line at that.' She heard herself sounding flippant, superficial, but she had to break the tension, escape from the black clutch of pagan hands.

David laughed, surprising her. 'Naked except for loin-cloths made of goat-skin. I'll get my jacket, shall I? That's got a very tatty sheepskin lining – the best I can manage, I'm afraid.'

'Oh, look!' she said, relieved that he could joke. 'The sun's broken through. Our rites must have worked already.'

'I hope so. This island needs a change of luck. Cormack was telling me they've had more than their fair share of disasters in the last fifteen years or so. Two fishing boats were lost and his son fell off the cliff and broke his leg and

450

then a lot of oil was washed up on the beaches and destroyed most of the bird life. And even long before that, people were starting to leave, feeling the place was cursed. Once those last six stalwarts kick the bucket, the island dies as well.'

'And you think we can halt all that by running round it in a loincloth?'

'Well, no . . .' He paused, shaking out his jacket which was flecked with ash and sawdust. 'It's a . . . gesture, like ban-the-bomb marches. Maybe they won't stop a war, but at least they're making a plea, rallying the forces of good against those of evil.' He buttoned up his jacket, turned the collar up. 'And maybe, at some level, gestures sort of . . . register – chip away at evil or . . . Oh, I don't know, it sounds crazy when I put it into words.'

'No, it doesn't.' Morna stared up at the sun, a weak, raw, uncertain winter sun, with more brightness in it than warmth, but exciting because it was rare and unexpected, stirred memories of spring. Suddenly there was colour in the grey, glints in the rock, promise in the dead brown heather, damask on the sea. The sun had energized her – or was it David's words? She was no longer just the stooge of sea and weather, but able to lift curses, weaken evil. Everything seemed easier, even running. She broke into a jog-trot, turned back to take David's hand. He didn't tug it back this time, pretend he needed the hand to blow his nose or tie his scarf, but ran beside her, keeping pace, his fingers clasped in hers. They gradually increased their speed until they were running at full pelt as they had at Weybridge. He had raced her then, kept always a yard or so in front, competing, showing off. Now they were abreast, arms and legs coordinated, moving in perfect time with one another. It felt effortless, like flying, despite their bulky wraps and unwieldy sticks. Everything was urging them on, the gold-flecked clouds rolling overhead, the sea rampaging round the rocks, their drumming footsteps re-echoed in the waves.

They were children again, haring along in ragged jeans and gymshoes, unwashed hair streaming in the wind. Or adults living when the world was still a child, before civilization, sophistication; clad in wolf-skins, eating roots and berries. She had never felt so close to him before, their palms sweating into each other despite the cold, their shadows overlapping.

Suddenly he stopped, almost tugged her over.

'What's wrong?' she panted. 'Got a stitch?'

'N . . . No.'

She followed his gaze, saw a dumpy woman dressed in layers of woollies over a long and bulky skirt, watching them from further up the cliff path. They were too far away to make out her expression, but could feel her disapproval hanging heavy in the air like the threat of rain.

'Old Nan,' said David softly.

'Wh . . . Who's she?'

'Cormack's second cousin's aunt. They're all more or less related on this island. I met her once at Cormack's.'

'Want to go and say hallo, then?' Morna had never approached the islanders herself, had glimpsed a shuffling figure once or twice, nodded at a watching head. Even Cormack was little more than a name to her, a small blurred cutout manoeuvring his boat. 'I'll come with you, shall I?'

'No, no.' David sounded shocked, stayed stock-still where he was. 'They . . . er . . . don't approve of you – us – I mean . . .' He flushed, broke off.

'*Us?*'

'You know, sharing the same cottage. They're . . . er . . . very puritanical.'

Morna said nothing. Was that why David kept his distance, feared gossip, bitchy tongues? They must have been wagging anyway, since the day she had arrived. She had compromised him, without even realizing, and whilst living like a nun. She watched the woman stomp away, disappear from sight. David was striding towards the cliff edge.

'See that rock,' he said, pointing out to sea. 'The very narrow craggy one?'

She nodded. He was trying to act the teacher, distract attention from his own embarrassment.

'That's where Abban spent the last months of his life.'

Morna stared at the chimney stack of rock, lashed by waves, guarded by one raucous gull which seemed to be screeching out a warning. She had read about Abban's last retreat, even translated the passage from the French, but the sheer brute fact of it was far more frighteningly extreme than her namby words, or the biographer's euphemisms. Dubhgall had called it a stepping-stone to heaven. It looked more like a fortress or a penitentiary, a one-man prison ship with cascades of water thwacking at its hull, breaking over the deck. How had Abban ever got there in the first place, braved that vicious sea?

She turned away, trudged on, sobered by Abban's courage, or perhaps foolhardiness. Had he deliberately courted death, in a longing to join his God?

David tramped beside her, both of them silent now, needing all their strength to battle against the wind. They were walking north along the west and most exposed side of the island where the sky was often stormy, angry violent colours daubed across the clouds. Today they were white and fluffy, innocently pale, the sea beneath them glinting in the shifting morning light. David paused a moment, drew out a soggy package from his pocket.

'I forgot the salt-meal cake. We ought to be strewing it on the ground as an offering to the soil.' He unwrapped the paper, broke the cake into chunks. 'Want a piece to eat?'

'I thought we were meant to be fasting.'

'This doesn't count. It's a symbolic offering like the host at Mass.'

Morna was already squatting on her heels, fastening a loose shoelace. Almost without thinking, she shut her eyes, put out her tongue, felt a damp and salty morsel placed upon it, gulped it down. When she opened her eyes again, David was standing over her, the vast sky behind dwarfing his tall figure. He struck her very lightly on the shoulder with his stick. Neither spoke. They could hear the fretting of the sea below them, the squall of gulls above. This blow was a cure for her sterility, not literal barrenness – Chris had taken care of that – but the years of stagnation when she had fumbled around in torpor and fatigue, achieving little, fearing everything. She would blossom now, grow towards the light instead of cowering in the darkness. She sprang to her feet, seized the cake from him, crumbling it along the path, tossing a chunk towards the sea. She wanted blessing for this place, blessing for Abban and their work on him. David followed, striking the ground with his stick, scattering more crumbs. They were walking faster now, despite the wind, the steep and rugged ground.

'This wind is nothing, really,' David said, as they stopped to rest a moment, sheltering in a dip. 'We're lucky. This time last year, they had non-stop blizzards. Cormack's wife was telling me about it. Apparently, a lot of birds had just arrived to breed and a good half of them collapsed with sheer exhaustion. They were pretty deadbeat anyway, flying all that way, and a buffeting by ninety-mile-an-hour storms was just too much for them.'

'Ninety miles an hour? Surely not.'

David shrugged. 'Easily. On St Kilda they've recorded winds of one hundred and thirty miles an hour. And at Barra Head a hurricane dislodged a solid block of gneiss weighing more than forty tons. The cliff's a good six hundred feet there, yet I've seen surf and small fish flung right up out of the sea on top of it. Hey, look!' he pointed down to a cluster of rocks. A seal was surfacing between them, swirling with the waves, its whiskers dripping foam as it paused to peer at them.

Morna sprang up. 'Isn't it seals you're meant to sing to? Let's climb down and serenade it.'

'It looks frightfully solemn. We might offend it.'

'How about a hymn, then – the sort we sang at school?' Morna was already scrambling down, her feet sliding on the slippery rock.

'Careful!' David warned, abandoning his stick so that he had both his hands free. 'Plainsong would be even better – in good old-fashioned Latin. He looks a bit like Gregory the Great to me, with that mournful face.'

Morna laughed, clutched at a ledge of rock to stop herself from falling. 'Oh, David, he's gone.'

'No, he hasn't.' David pointed to a flurry of water between two rocks. The wave somersaulted, turned into a smooth grey snout. 'He's waiting for the concert. What shall it be?'

'How about the "Te Deum", since it's a holiday and sunny and your birthday and . . .?'

'Perfect.' David hummed a few bars, broke off. 'Okay?'

Morna nodded. 'Yes, you start. I can see you're more musical than me. I'm a sort of female baritone.'

David cleared his throat, stood up as straight as he could on the jutting spur of rock, took a deep breath in. The first phrase of the 'Te Deum' soared powerful and majestic, his voice so compelling Morna was humbled into silence. She had never heard him sing before.

After the 'Te Dominum', he broke off. 'It's not meant to be a solo.'

'I'm sorry. You sing so well, I'll only spoil it. Even the seal's impressed. Look, he's brought his mate.'

Two grey heads were now poking above the waves, two streamlined bodies bobbing up and down, keeping their balance in the tumultuous sea around them.

'Well, you join in this time. We'll start at the "Te aeternum". Okay?'

Morna nodded, let her voice waver after his, less certain until they reached the 'Sanctus, sanctus, sanctus', and the words were more familiar, almost identical to the 'Sanctus' in the Mass. Strange to hear a man's voice shape those words, after all the years at school when there had been only nuns' sopranos and contraltos, backing the shrill piping voices of the girls. She remembered the little golden bell ringing on the altar, declaring the moment sacred. It was sacred now, their own religious rite, with two seals as congregation and the whole vast sea and sky as altar.

'*Pleni sunt caeli,*' David was intoning, conducting with her wooden wardrobe rail. She joined in, her voice growing stronger as they reached the end of the phrase, '*majestatis gloriae tuae*'. Glory and majesty were all around them, spilling over in cloud and ocean, grey and gold, in the ancient words themselves. '*Paraclitum Spiritum*', they sang, as a huge grey-winged gull wheeled low across the cliff. She wanted to bow down and worship it, worship something, everything, give thanks for this day, for David.

'*Tu devicto mortis aculeo.*' David made the phrase a clarion call. Their voices were circling round each other, converging, seeming to embrace; his tenor and her contralto so perfectly attuned it seemed impossible that they should still be standing separate. She took a step towards him, the power of the music throbbing through her body.

He broke off suddenly in the middle of a bar. 'Sorry, Morna, I'm out of breath – haven't sung for ages.'

He seemed in no way out of breath. 'I thought we were doing pretty well,' she said, trying to hide her disappointment. 'And the seals are loving it. They look quite rapt. They must be Lefebvrians, hungry for their Latin. Is the larger one the male?'

David nodded.

'Let's christen him Gregory, then, after the plainsong.'

'I'm not sure it's right. Seals can be quite vicious, you know – even bite your foot off. Freud would say it's maternal deprivation. The mothers leave their pups when they're only three weeks old. They have to fend for themselves then, make their own way to the sea and eat whatever they can find.'

Morna thought of Chris at three weeks old, white and fluffy, too, in Bea's hand-knitted poodle pramsuit, totally dependent on her. Still needing her now, to some extent. Supposing she had quarrelled with her father, or had got in with some wild crowd in LA, or was moping back in England. Dreadful not to know if one's only daughter were even home or not. She tried to force the worries down. Chris had *said* she was all right, told her not to fuss. And surely even human mothers could take a break after seventeen odd years?

Both seals were romping through the waves, seemingly careless of the jagged crags of rock, their blotched and mottled coats looking like clumps of seaweed rippling underwater. The smaller one surfaced again, stared in their direction as if begging for more music.

David shaded his eyes to watch it. 'The local legends say that seals were once human, but were put under a spell and forced to live in the sea. They're never really content in either element. How did Cormack put it? "Their sea-longings shall be land-longings and their land-longings shall be sea-longings." Well, that's a rough translation from the Gaelic.'

'It's . . . beautiful.'

'Yes. Cormack can surprise you sometimes. He obviously believes all that stuff about the seals. He said they can still change back into human shape. In fact, there are several stories about islanders marrying seal-wives, hiding their skins to make them stay on land. They always seem to escape, though, in the end, find their skins and creep back to the sea.'

'How about an encore, then, to lure that female back? She might be Cormack's wife from long ago, before he married his all too human one.'

'No, better not. We'll never get round the island if we stop so long.' David was already clambering back towards the path. Morna followed, silent, increasing her pace as he broke into a jog-trot.

He slowed, turned back for her. 'We're almost at Cormack's now. I think we ought to turn inland, cut across the island to the east side. If Cormack sees me, he'll only think I've come to pester him for something – and he's had enough of that the last few days. He's wheezing rather badly as it is.'

Morna said nothing, just followed David across the scrubby grass. He didn't want to be spotted with a woman – that was obvious and really rather ludicrous. They knew she was here, wouldn't stop their tittle-tattle just because she hid. She realized now he *had* been hiding her, keeping her indoors whenever he could. Easy to blame the weather or pressure of work or her lack of proper walking shoes. Those were all factors, yes, but so also was his resolve to screen her from prying eyes. She had sensed it somehow, unconsciously, even gone along with it, kept her own walks short, deliberately avoided the north end as if she were infectious. Now she was curious.

'Where *is* the farm?' she asked.

'Down there.' David clambered on to a boulder, pointed back to a dip in the hill where a squat grey cottage collapsed into the arms of a few crumbling outbuildings.

Morna hauled herself up beside him. 'But it's a *tiny* house. I thought they had seven children.'

'They did. Three or four to a bed, I suppose.'

Morna could almost see the seven, crammed into that hovel, buffeted by gales, never having glimpsed a single tree or flowerbed in their lives, let alone a shop or cinema, until they were sent away to school where the comforts of the mainland finally seduced them, so that they stayed away, leaving their parents and the island with no new growth, no promise of a future. She gazed around Cormack's boggy empire, could see no spread of crops, no new-dug soil, only a rusty plough, a pile of rotting posts, a straggling potato patch whose rickety fence had been broken down by sheep.

'This place needs blessing, David, more than anywhere. Any salt-meal cake left?'

'No.' He jumped down from the rock, struck the ground with his stick, muttered something in a foreign tongue.

> ' "Dhe fadaidh thusa am chridhe steach
> Aiteal graidh do m' choimhearsnach . . ." '

'What you saying?'

'It's an ancient prayer in Gaelic – a blessing on the hearth.

> "Bho'n ni is ìsle crannachaire
> Gu ruig an tAinm is Àirde."

It's nice, that last bit – "from the lowest created thing to the Name Most High". We've lost that view of the world – the sort of . . . divine unity of everything. Right, we really must push on. We've got the whole east side to walk yet.'

They continued across the island to the other coast, the path less overgrown there, since it was the main track to the quay, although that was still some distance further south. David was looking up, shading his eyes against the glare, following the flight of two black and white birds swooping in from the sea.

'Razorbills?' she asked.

'No, oystercatchers. They're very different. See their orange beaks and that sort of cross on their breasts? Well, it's more a white band really, but the islanders say it's the sign of the cross. The birds are meant to have received it as a reward for hiding Christ from His enemies beside the Sea of Galilee. They covered Him with seaweed.'

'We can't get away from seaweed. Do they eat it, too, or only oysters?'

'They don't eat oysters, actually. Your crazy mixed-up Yanks gave them the wrong name. They saw them – in Maryland, I think it was – feeding on crustaceans in the oyster beds and assumed they were eating the oysters themselves. It's a nice example of a mistake locked in the language, even passing on to other countries.'

'America's good at those.' Morna stopped to take a stone out of her shoe. The wellingtons were difficult for walking, so she had set out in Bunny's sneakers, now stained and waterlogged. 'David . . .?'

'Mm.'

'Did you think of me in America?'

'Course.'

'It seems so far away now. Not just another time scale, but another world completely.'

'Yet Los Angeles is almost like an island.'

'An *island*? Surely not.'

'An island on land. Someone called it that and I can see what they meant. It's cut off by the desert and mountains on three sides and the Pacific on the fourth. And then it's very much a separate culture with its own traditions and . . .'

Morna was silent. LA seemed like a prison, one she had escaped from, all seventy square miles of it confining her, while this two-mile stretch of rock promised endless space and freedom – or would do, if only David . . . She glanced up at his profile, the beard still fascinating, taunting her to touch it. Was this how Neil had felt when she herself had been undemonstrative? Was coolness a sort of attraction in itself, challenging you to change it, break it down?

David refused to meet her eye, was still gazing out to sea, watching for new and rarer birds amongst the squabbling

460

flocks of herring gulls. 'The fishermen round here say gulls are the spirits of dead seamen still following the boats.'

She mumbled some reply. He was too concerned with spirits to bother much with bodies. Couldn't she just accept that, as she'd resolved a dozen times, stop being so perverse? When men *did* pester her, she didn't like that either.

'We mustn't forget our firewood,' he was saying. 'There are some steps cut in the rock just here. We can climb down to that scrap of beach I was telling you about – the one where I found the crate.'

Morna's feet were squelching now and aching, her stomach rumbling from the fast. Yet David and St Abban had taught her greater tolerance, simply to endure fatigue or cold or hunger, to find joy in pain and hardship, if for no other reason than the sweet relief of food and warmth when finally they came. She followed David down the rough-hewn steps of rock, not daring to look down and see the dizzying drop, but concentrating on each steep step, each handhold. The sea bellowed like a wild and hungry animal, making pounces at them, licking at their feet as they jumped the last yard or two which had crumbled into scree.

David picked his way from rock to rock across the tiny sandy beach, turned back to shout to Morna. 'We're in luck! See that box? Well, half a box. That'll make marvellous fuel.' He stopped before he reached it, squatted down to peer at something else. 'Good God!'

'What?' Morna caught up with him.

He didn't answer, just stood staring at what appeared to be a boulder, half-submerged in sand. He leaned forward, touched it gingerly, grimaced. 'Feel that.'

She reached out her hand, withdrew it in shock. The rock wasn't hard, but flabby, rubbery. Its surface was mainly blackish, but marbled with different colours – purple, pink, ghoulish-green.

'It's a seal,' David muttered.

'It . . . It can't be.' Morna recalled the two lithe acrobats on the other side of the island, somersaulting, diving, vigorously alive. This was something inanimate or defunct.

'It's been skinned,' he explained. 'And washed up here by the tide. Look, you can still see a few tufts of hair, and a gash or two where the knife slipped.'

She stared in disbelief, slowly made out the bald and bloated body, its head shrunken and twisted back. The eye sockets were empty, the teeth yellowed, one small flipper curved helplessly across its chest. A piece of frayed rope was tied around its neck, entangled with necklaces of seaweed; a film of fine sand adhering to the few remaining scraps of fur.

'B . . . But why should anyone do that? I mean, I thought you said the adult skins weren't valuable.'

'They're not.' David's voice was low, but taut with anger. 'Sheer spite, I should imagine. The fishing started just this week. I imagine what happened was that a seal broke a precious net and the fisherman who owned it took revenge.'

'But those . . . those legends said they *married* seals . . .'

David shrugged. 'Maybe that's all part of it. Revenge for other crimes as well – desertion, returning to the sea.'

Morna backed off. From even a yard or two away, the seal details disappeared and the hulk turned back to rock again, a rock she could have sat on. She shuddered. The mottling on the skin had reminded her of something – Chris's love-bite – the same purplish-red, blotching into black. She clutched at her stomach. She could make out a whiff of putrefying flesh above the tang of salt and seaweed. She closed her eyes. No. It was David Attwood's sickly after-shave. She could feel his rubbery flesh against her own, his bloated body beached on orange carpet. The ground was tipping, quicksanding beneath her feet. She lost her balance, stumbled against David's blurred and shifting form.

462

'I'm s . . . sorry,' she muttered, clutching at his arm. Even her voice sounded faint and indistinct.

'My fault. I shouldn't have mentioned the seal. You look quite pale. Want to sit down?'

She didn't answer, just clung on to the arm. The roar of the sea was still too loud, seemed to have burst inside her skull.

'There's a ledge of rock back there. Why don't I take you over and . . .'

'N . . . No.' She couldn't move. He had to heal her first, remove the bruising on her neck, erase the teeth-marks made by those grinning orange blankets. She had never been so close to him before, slumped against his chest, sheltered by his body. He was standing rigid as a post, obviously embarrassed, but she didn't pull away, stayed absolutely motionless. The sea was moving for her, crashing on the rocks, thrashing up and down against the steep slope of the beach. All the tension of the last three weeks seemed to have compressed into this moment, screwed so taut she could feel it as a pain constricting in her chest.

Suddenly, he shifted, withdrew his arm, took a step away. 'Morna, look, I . . . I think we ought to . . .'

'No, please. I'm all right now. I just felt . . . faint.' She couldn't bear to hear his fumbling frigid words – excuses and rejections which might distance him still further. Safer to say nothing, leave things as they were. 'It was . . . a dizzy spell, that's all.' She shook her hair back, wiped her face with her sleeve.

'I walked you too far, I'm sorry.'

'Not at all.'

They were back to the stilted phrases, the careful wary distance measured out between them. She kicked at the sand, dislodging pebbles, shells. Two guillemots were shadowing each other, two cormorants preening on a rock, spreading out their ragged wings to dry. Everything in pairs.

David moved away, picked up his half-box, poked among the flotsam with his stick for other fuel.

They climbed back up the rocky steps in silence, trudged on more slowly now, weighted down with wood. David tried to take the largest pieces from her.

'It's all right, I can manage. You're loaded down yourself.'

'Sure you're feeling better, though?'

Morna muttered something, unsure what she felt. Confused, put down, rejected. Restless. Even angry. Angry with herself. Why did she have to spoil things, risk a confrontation? She said nothing more until they reached the wreck. They both stopped then, instinctively, walked to the very edge of the cliff. David had told her about the ship, how he had clambered down the steep cliff to explore it, even walked the green and slippery deck. She had no desire to make the climb herself, inspect that grim hulk still clinging to the rocks as if not daring to let go and be submerged. From where they stood, she could see only the mast, looking as small and insubstantial as a straw.

Morna turned away, dizzied by the plunging drop, her thoughts with the floundering crew. Two only had survived. They had been lodged in David's cottage until a boat arrived to take them off, had slept in the very bedroom she was sleeping in herself. The day he had told her that, she had lain awake all night, imagining their swarthy limbs crowding the tiny bed, afraid to close her eyes in case she should dream their own pitching tossing nightmares, or touch in sleep the bloated stinking bodies of their mates. It still upset her that in the past the islanders had furnished their homes from wrecks, fed their children on plundered stores, retrieved the spoils from corpses.

They were nearing the concrete landing slip. Morna dragged her feet as she recalled her first sight of it, her whole impulsive escape from California. Perhaps she should have stayed there, sat out her last week, instead of barging into hermit David's life. She had been female in America, not neuter, someone men noticed and admired. It wouldn't hurt to mention a few details.

'I . . . er . . . met this guy in Los Angeles,' she said, staring intently at her wood, trying to sound casual.

David said nothing, was waiting for her to finish.

'He was called David, actually.'

'Oh, yes.'

'We went for cocktails.'

Silence. David hated small talk.

He fucked me. I was drunk. We watched porn movies together. Of course she couldn't say it. David would be deeply shocked. Yet she wanted him to realize she was woman – flesh and blood, legs and breasts, which other men desired. He was stooping down now, examining the markings on a striated rock, more interested in geology than in her sexual exploits. She really ought to get out of his life, stop torturing herself, leave him to his fossils. She couldn't stay in any case. For days and days now, she had been saying she must leave, concerned for Chris and Bea, then shrugging off that worry, kidding herself they were both absolutely fine. She had no proof of that at all. Her daughter might have returned from California upset and miserable, missing her father, needing a mother to replace him instead of just a Grandma. Bea herself could be lonely or unwell. It was time she thought of them for a change, stopped being so damned casual.

She stopped abruptly, put down her stick, her firewood, stared out towards the frail and makeshift quay. 'David, look, be honest. Would you rather I left – soon, I mean – the minute Cormack's better?' She couldn't see his face; it was hidden by his load. 'Go on – say. I shan't mind.' She minded already that he hadn't answered, had said nothing yet at all. 'I mean, I realize I just turned up, without an invitation, when you might well have preferred to be on your own.

Anyway, it's not just that. I ought to get back for Chris and my mother – check that they're all right. I can't help worrying. If I could phone or something, it wouldn't be so bad, but I've never been out of touch before. I know I've written to my mother, but it's not the same. It was a scrappy letter, anyway, and the second one isn't even posted. She's used to just picking up the phone and . . .'

David put his own wood down, fumbled for her hand, held it so tightly the nails dug into her palm. 'No,' he said. 'No. No. No.'

She left her hand in his, wincing at the pain, yet feeling a shock of triumph at the vehemence of his 'noes'. She tried to change tack, convince herself that Chris and Bea were fine, started rambling on again, trying to keep the excitement from her voice.

David wasn't listening. 'No,' he was still saying, as if she were a dog or stupid child who hadn't understood the first and second times, had to be told 'No' again, again, held on a short constricting lead.

He seized her other hand, crushed the two together in his own two. 'No,' he said once more, looking anguished, almost desperate, his knuckles white from the fierceness of his grip. 'You mustn't go, d'you hear me, Morna? You really mustn't go.'

22

'Right, you can come down now,' David called from the foot of the stairs.

Morna adjusted her belt, gave a final towelling to her hair. It was the first time she had really missed a mirror, the first time she had clad her legs in tights instead of David's jeans, replaced his thick sweaters with one of the silky dresses from her suitcase. She had even washed her hair, though it had taken so long and proved such a major task that she had given up halfway. It now felt stiff and soapy, clean, but still not dry, curling in damp tendrils round her shoulders.

She walked down the stairs, her high-heeled sandals (packed for Los Angeles' beach restaurants) echoing on the wooden steps, flimsy summer dress fluttering in the draught. She heard David gasp as he caught sight of her, saw him look her up and down, his eyes finally stopping at her neckline which plunged low and was emphasized by a fine gold cross and chain.

'Morna, you look absolutely . . .' He flushed, broke off, staring down at the floor now like an awkward teenager who had gone too far.

Morna laughed. 'So do you.'

They were both transformed, as if they had changed not just their clothes but their whole species – no longer coarse and clumping bipeds lumbering about in boots and water-proofs or muffled in pelts and hides, but slimmer, finer creatures with necks and curves and naked flesh. David seemed half a stone lighter without his bulky jerseys and baggy corduroys. He was dressed all in black, as he had been the first day she met him at the retreat, but in tight new jeans which she had never seen before, which clung to his buttocks, revealed slim hips and narrow waist. A heavy leather belt accentuated the waist. He had even trimmed his beard which looked almost rakish, cut to a point like an Elizabethan gallant's.

He was holding open the parlour door. It had always been out of bounds before, save for that one brief glimpse of the moon her first morning in the cottage. The room where David slept was somehow inviolate, and always freezing cold. She had tried to persuade him to bed down in the kitchen which was warmed by the range and had become their main living-room – refectory and study, scriptorium and den. But he seemed shy about sleeping in a room so public where she might slip in unexpectedly, late at night or early in the morning, catch him half undressed. They couldn't waste fuel on two fires, so he slept like Abban in the cold and dark.

Now, however, the parlour was transformed. A fire was crackling in the black iron fireplace, its blaze augmented by a score of candles ranged all around the room – plain white candles set on plain white saucers, but transfiguring the room with their flickering light. David had pushed back the battered furniture, disguised the threadbare matting with a purple velvet curtain which he had spread as rug and tablecloth and laid with plates and dishes. At one end he had built a throne of pillows, collected from beds and chairs and draped with another curtain in poppied chintz.

'Sit down,' he urged, gesturing to the throne.

She sat unsteadily, almost over-balancing, yet feeling like a queen.

'Presents first,' he said.

'Presents? Oh, David, I haven't got you anything.'

'I didn't want you to. Not until *your* birthday. They're only bits and pieces anyway. Flowers . . .' He picked up a jam jar which held a single sprig of gorse, one drooping yellow coltsfoot. 'I reckon that's the one and only flower on the entire island. And the gorse is the first green shoot I've seen since winter. All the rest is dead still and will probably stay that way till April.' He shook water from the stalks, held them out to her. 'There you are – a promise of spring.'

Morna touched a finger to the coltsfoot, still not fully open and with no leaves yet on its stem, but the colour of the sun; admired the glaze of green on the tiny twig of gorse. Back home, there would be sticky buds and catkins, primroses and snowdrops, jasmine, aconites, even the first dog violets. There were two thousand species of native plants in mainland Britain – David had told her that – less than sixty here, and none of them in evidence this early. She hadn't seen a single bud or flower on their entire morning's walk around the island. David had ventured out a second time, must have searched every sheltered dip and southern slope.

He had also scoured the beaches. Arranged in a pattern round her plate were a dazzle of coloured shells – limpets, cowries, periwinkles, one large scallop shell – interspersed with mottled pebbles, stones of curious shapes and markings, a piece of green glass abraded by the sea. She picked them up, admiring, one by one.

David shrugged. 'They're just nonsenses. But here's something precious – well semi-precious.' He handed her a package swathed in three or four pink tissues borrowed from her Kleenex box.

She unwrapped it, revealing a rough piece of stone with some brighter near-transparent mineral embedded in the centre.

'It's beautiful. Wherever did it come from?'

'It's a piece of quartz. You find it sometimes in granite

cliffs. There's only one vein I know of on this island – right on the southern tip. You have to climb a hundred feet or so, down a pretty horrendous drop, and hack it out with a chisel.'

She shuddered. 'You could have broken your neck.'

'No. I used to do a bit of climbing once, and I took it very carefully. Anyway, with no jeweller's shop on the island, what else could I do? I wanted to get you something really nice.'

She held it up to the light, its milky crystals glittering and flashing, contrasting with the brute grey stone. Neil had given her fourteen years-worth of jewellery, for Christmases and birthdays, promotions, anniversaries – showy stones in padded velvet boxes with the name of some Bond Street jeweller swanking on the top – jewels to give her status which then reflected back on him, rings to prove he owned her, gold to show he had made it in the world. She had felt weighted down by stones, padlocked into his necklaces and bracelets. He had spent a lot of money on her presents, but little time. He would dash out in a lunch hour, the day before her birthday, sign a credit card, leave his secretary to do the wrapping and choose a birthday card. Sometimes he bought her things he wanted himself – an Olympus OM I when he was going through a camera craze, a top professional racquet when he'd started playing tennis after work. Both gifts ran into three figures. David's quartz came free – except he had risked his neck for it, given up his precious working time in trekking there and back. It was the same with the shells and flower – all had cost him effort, needed patience.

'Thank you,' she said, still fingering the quartz. 'I'll keep it on my desk at home, use it as a paperweight and a sort of inspiration.'

'Just two more crazy things.' David had got up again. 'Shut your eyes and hold out your hands. Left one first.'

She waited like a child, eyes screwed up, palm cupped. A round and scratchy object prickled into it. She opened her eyes, squinted down at a purple sea urchin with a thick halo of spines.

David touched it gingerly. 'I tried to find you what they call a heart urchin. I thought it would be appropriate for St Valentine's. But no luck, I'm afraid. I don't think they have them on this coast.'

'It's gorgeous. Such a stunning colour. If it were still alive I'd keep it as a pet.'

He laughed. 'Now the other hand. Be careful, though. It's fragile. Shut your eyes again.'

Something cool and heavy plopped into her right hand. She knew already what it was, cupped her fingers round the speckled shell.

'Oh, David, you really are a wizard. I grumble about no eggs and the next moment you've produced one. Did you lay it yourself?'

'It was almost a case of that. But one of Cormack's stubborn hens actually did its stuff – the first time in six whole weeks, he said. He's threatening to wring all fifteen idle necks if they don't start laying soon.'

'So how did you prise it away from him? I bet he charged a king's ransom.'

'Only a princeling's one. And it was worth it. I was determined to get you an egg. Apart from anything else, it's important for our ceremony. Eggs represent the universe and new life and resurrection and the union of opposites and creation itself and . . .'

Morna let out a mock groan. 'And I was stupid enough to think I could simply eat it boiled for breakfast.'

'Oh, you can – afterwards. If we ever get round to dinner first, that is. You hungry?'

She nodded. 'Starving. It beats me how St Abban managed all those fasts and still worked an eighteen-hour day.'

471

Though David had done almost as well himself. He had been out again after their lunch break of a glass of water and ten minutes with their feet up, and had then continued his cooking for the remainder of the afternoon and early evening, taken over the kitchen, banished her upstairs for a read and a rest in bed. It was now almost nine o'clock – late for dinner.

'Can I help?'

'No, you sit tight. It's all ready anyway.'

He returned with an old and blackened saucepan, set it on the floor, steam rising from the top. 'Sorry about the pot. You'll have to imagine the Royal Doulton soup tureen and the solid silver ladle.'

'Soup. Lovely. Dulse soup?'

'Not a single morsel of dulse tonight, I promise. If it tastes fishy, that's because it *is* fish. It's got everything in it I could find.'

'You mean you caught the fish yourself, David?'

'No questions. This meal is a joint effort – Cormack, Mrs Cormack, a bit of begging, borrowing and poaching, the odd miracle thrown in, and a few mountains moved by our ever-obliging Abban. What do you think of it?'

'It's . . . good.' Morna tried a second spoonful. It was salty – saltier than the seaweed. David could hardly help that. Fish were scarce in winter, difficult to catch without a boat. He had probably used salted cod and herring. But she could also taste fresh mussels, other shellfish. He must have gathered those himself, prised them from the rocks, spent long and patient hours shelling and cleaning them. Like the presents, the soup was a labour of love. She cleared her plate.

'Want some more? Or would you rather save room for the rabbit stew?' He saw her frown. 'Don't worry – even Abban ate fish and flesh on feast days, so I thought we'd relax our own rule just the once.'

He removed the dishes, brought the same two back again, newly washed and dried. They had only three between them and two of those were chipped. He made a second trip for a handsome cast-iron casserole which was either Mrs Cormack's or one of Abban's miracles, since the cottage boasted nothing so spectacular.

Morna tried to look eager as David lifted the lid and spooned a thick brown viscous mixture onto her plate. They had seen rabbits on their morning walk, sunning themselves in sheltered spots, their white tails beaconing as they streaked back to their burrows in fear of human feet. Had David actually killed one, skinned it with his bare hands? She prayed not. David's hands had become important to her – the only part of his body she ever saw unclothed. They were labourer's hands confused with scholar's hands – long slender fingers, broad calloused palms, broken dirty nails – hands always busy, bringing things to life – books, bread, shelves, biographies. She didn't want them smeared with blood, taking life instead. She only hoped Cormack had done the dirty work, shot the rabbit, sold it.

She swallowed the first mouthful – salty again, but rich and gamey. 'It really is good.'

'Well, don't sound so surprised.' David was struggling to remove the cork from what looked like a giant-sized medicine bottle, the liquid inside the same murky brown as the glass. He poured out two half tumblerfuls, passed one across to her.

'What's this?' Morna sniffed the sticky liquid – a tarry smell with a whiff of liquorice.

'I wish I knew. All I can guarantee is that it's highly alcoholic. It's Mrs Cormack's home-made tipple – but she wouldn't tell me made of what. Best not guess, perhaps.'

Morna sipped it. It tasted sweet and fiery at once, seemed to sting and shock the tongue, cutting through the salt, the lingering taste of fish. She was surprised to see David drinking. He lifted his glass, touched it against hers.

'Happy Valentine's,' he said.

'Happy belated birthday.'

'Happy Candlemas. I'll bring some candles over, shall I? Then we can make out what we're eating.'

He fetched the two largest, already half burned down, placed them one each side of the casserole. She could see his face more clearly now, his eyes reflecting back the restless orange flame, light gleaming on his cheekbones. The whole room was made of flame, shadows from the candles leaping on the walls, the red glow of the fire thawing the cold sober stiffness of the parlour. Wind and cold and night were all shut out, the booming of the sea lost in the crackle of the fire, the sudden hiss and splutter as the flames licked against a damp patch in the fuel. Morna sipped her drink, felt her own edges blurring into warmth. David was sitting at her feet, her full skirt overlapping his right knee. She longed to move closer, reach out and touch the knee. Better be careful. The drink must have affected her already. He would only flinch away, repulse her. She latched her fingers safely on her glass, forced her attention back to safer subjects.

'Er . . . when was it they changed the date of Christmas?'

'542 AD. The Emperor Justinian ordered it as a thanksgiving after a plague. That was in Constantinople, though. I'm not sure about Rome. In any case it doesn't bear much resemblance to the Lupercalia.'

Morna put her glass down, returned to her stew. 'I wonder who we'd be worshipping now if Christianity had simply fizzled out – you know, just a flash in the pan like the flower-power thing in the sixties – whether we'd still be pagans, or offering human sacrifice to computers, or . . .'

'I don't think it would have fizzled out. The Church won through because it had a total system. Okay, paganism had its rituals, so did emperor-worship, but neither had a real moral or theological base. The philosophical sects gave you guidance for life, but hadn't much to say when it came to an afterlife. Mithraism threw in initiation rites and even a bit of mysticism, but no coherent world view. Only Christianity promised the whole damn lot – a reasoned philosophy and theology, a complete moral system, a united Church offering real spiritual sustenance, salvation after death, unity, brotherhood . . .' David's plate was spilling in his lap. He mopped his jeans with his paper serviette, licked his fingers, went on talking. 'And it appealed right across the board, you see. For the intelligentsia it blended Greek and Roman thought, so was far more acceptable than many of the woolly pagan rites, and for the peasants and the downtrodden it offered compensation for the hardship of their lives – you know, hell down here, but paradise to follow. That made the injustices more tolerable, gave them something to live for. Above all, it answered the big questions, combined certainty with hope.'

'So why is it declining now?' Morna removed a rabbit bone, put it on the side of her plate.

'If I tried to answer that, we'd be sitting here all night. The world's changed, for one thing. It's bigger now – or smaller, if you look at it another way – and far more complex. And then there's ritual itself. We've lost so much of that, or it's become a dead-letter thing, worn out and formalized, just empty words and gestures cut off from people's real gut-needs and feelings. They've tried to tinker with things a bit – give us new translations or throw us little sops, like the priest facing the people instead of turning his back, or Communion in the hand or . . . but that's just window-dressing.' David paused to swallow a mouthful of stew. He had been eating with more eagerness than usual, had downed a brimming bowl of soup and was now halfway through his rabbit. 'Even the sacraments have become sort of standard formulae without much charge left in them.

475

Take Communion itself. It should be a proper meal like this – a sharing, with people sitting down at table eating real coarse grainy bread, not a prissy little wafer, and drinking rough red wine which warms them and relaxes them.' He drained his own glass, refilled them both.

Morna cupped hers in both hands. 'You surprise me. I'd have thought you'd have stressed the substance, not the accidents. Weren't those the terms they used at school?'

He nodded. Strange how she hadn't forgotten – all those tricky technical terms like transubstantiation or temporal punishment, which they had mugged up at their daily doctrine lessons, while other fifteen-year-olds were learning the names of pop groups or make-up ranges; Mother Annunciata fielding all awkward questions into the confessional box, labelling them pride or heresy, never the sign of intelligence or independent thought. Judging by his words, David was an original, if not an outright rebel, and both rebellion and originality were ruthlessly suppressed in Catholic schools. She watched his fingers restive on the glass.

'You're not even much of a drinker,' she said. 'So why all the poetry about rough red wine?'

'Oh, I could be a drinker – very much so. In fact, I often fear I could turn into a full-blown alcoholic, if I didn't watch it.'

'David, that's the first drop you've touched all the time I've been here – and knowing you, probably since September.'

'Only because it interferes with my work.'

'There you are, you see – work first. You're a natural puritan.'

'Yes, but puritans are the worst. Don't you suspect they only make such a song and dance about other people's pleasures because they're racked with desire themselves? You can see it in Abban – all that flogging himself with thorns and sitting naked up to his neck in icy water to calm what he called his lusts. They must have been some lusts.'

Morna said nothing. 'Lusts' was a word he had never used before, one which made her feel uncomfortable. Was it only safe to desire him because he revealed no desire himself? 'Racked with desire' was a Catholic expression, the sort of phrase Mother Michael favoured. But David had used it with an almost relish. She glanced across at him. He had picked up a bone and was gnawing the meat off it; suddenly looked too animal, too pagan, despite the fact he was still talking about the Church.

'Penance became a continuous way of life. There's a story in Bede of an Irishman called Adamnan who ate and drank only two days out of seven. He'd been instructed by a priest to fast for several days a week, to atone for some sin he had committed in his youth. The priest had promised to return to review the situation, but he was recalled to his native Ireland, where he died. So his poor obedient penitent continued to eat on Sundays and Thursdays only, for the entire rest of his life, until he passed away himself.

'That was at Coldingham – you know, one of those double monasteries I was telling you about, with nuns as well as monks – the only one, at that date, with any hint of scandal. Well, more than just a hint. The place burned down, in fact, and Bede viewed the fire as a punishment for sin. It seemed that everyone but Adamnan had become really lax and negligent – holy virgins enticing men into their cells, or monks carousing in the wee small hours, or snoring through the night instead of praying. Adamnan was so saintly by this time, he even received a sort of heavenly visitation warning him of the fire. When he told the community about it, they tried to mend their ways – at least for a few days – started fasting themselves and . . .'

Morna put her fork down. It wasn't easy to eat with all this talk of sin and fasting.

David wiped his fingers, took another draught of wine. 'Sometimes you could commute a long penance to a shorter sharper one – something like the Black Fast.'

'What was that?'

'Three days without eating, drinking or sleep, plus three nights of mortification – the first immersed in water, the second naked on stinging nettles and the third naked on a bed of nutshells.'

'You're joking.'

'I'm not. That's absolutely factual. You can get all the details from the Irish Penitentials which list every sin, venial or mortal, with its corresponding penance. Just one lustful thought could mean a month of bread and water or sleeping on bare rock.'

Morna stared down at the purple tablecloth, the colour of penance itself. Was David getting at her, aware of all the lustful thoughts she had been trying to suppress for the last three weeks? Or hinting at his own desire again? She felt suddenly uneasy, pushed her plate away.

'That was . . . er . . . lovely, David. Thank you. A really special meal.'

'We're not finished yet. There's still the sun bread. I've been saving that for last. I was planning to have Angel Delight for pudding – I thought Abban would get a kick out of the name, but Cormack said the grocer didn't stock it, only Instant Whip, which didn't sound quite in the same class.'

Morna laughed. 'I used to make it for Chris – Angel Delight, I mean – and I was the one who was always licking out the bowl. I love it. That's what I'd have really missed if I was a seventh-century monk – the sweet things.'

'They had honey sometimes. Wait a sec.' David sprang up, returned with the sun bread and a large square honeycomb. 'There you are – I bought you some – to eat with the bread.'

'David, you're a wonder, but I don't think I've got room for it. I'm pretty full already.'

'You must have just a slice. It's the most important part of the feast. We're eating the sun, you see, which fills us with light and warmth and fruitfulness and . . .'

'All right, cut me just a sliver – though it seems a shame to cut it at all. It looks so pretty.'

David had pinched and fluted the circumference of the loaf to represent the sun's rays, brushed the top with milk so that it had turned a glossy gold. He cut two slices, passed her the smaller one along with the Cerebos. 'You're meant to eat your first mouthful with salt.'

'No thanks! I've consumed enough salt from three solid weeks of seaweed to last me the whole year.'

David shook out a few grains. 'Please. Salt stands for friendship. It binds us together, means we trust each other.'

Morna dipped her bread in the salt, swallowed it in silence. There were other forms of bonding besides symbolic rituals. Was David not aware of them, or leading up to them in his own subtle tortuous fashion? He had hinted at a lot of things tonight – lust and greed, wild unbridled appetites. That scared her somehow, made him someone different from the David she admired. For days and days (nights and days), she had wanted him to want her, but now that he appeared to, she had lost her nerve.

'Salt for immortality, as well,' he said, mopping up a few spilt grains. 'And wisdom and truth. They put it on the baby's tongue at baptism.'

Morna sagged back on her pillows. Chris had been baptized. Another sham – the worst one – except it had been done to placate Bea, like her own white wedding.

> *'Do you renounce Satan?'*
> *'I do renounce him.'*
> *'And all his works?'*

> *'I do renounce them.'*
> *'And all his pomps?'*
> *'I do . . .'*

She shivered suddenly. The room no longer looked so cheerful. The candles were guttering, some burned down completely; the fire slumping into ashes. Darkness coiled heavy in the corners of the room, pressed against beams already blackened from a hundred years of smoke. David's features were smudged together now, his hands and feet lost in shadow. She could hear the wind again, reminding them of winter, danger.

The nuns were right – sex was dangerous, led to sin and hell. It wasn't sin she feared, but the hell of it not working, the shame of failure. Supposing David made advances and she couldn't respond, stayed dry and tense, or put him off his stroke as she had with David Attwood. Why risk a second fiasco, some sordid grope or scuffle which could ruin their whole friendship? All right, so she had tried to rouse his interest, spent three whole weeks contriving to get closer to him, but she realized now it was his very distance and aloofness which kept her safe, protected her. As a simple friend and colleague he admired her; as a lover, he might not.

Safer to renounce sex and all its works and pomps. The nuns had known best, but had got their definitions wrong. Sin wasn't sex – not today – but just its opposite: frigidity and prudishness, lying passive, failing to respond. She was already nervous, David more so. If things went wrong, resulted in some bungling flop, she couldn't even sneak away as she had with David Attwood, but would have to sit out here until wind and tide and Cormack agreed to let her go. How could she and David continue with their peaceful way of life if they had let each other down, made fools of themselves in bed?

She reached forward for the bread, cut another slice, sprinkled salt on top. They would be bound, yes, but only by the ties of friendship, and she would risk absolutely nothing which might spoil or strain that bond. She broke the bread in two, passed David half. That would be their sole Communion.

The cold clean midnight air cut across the heavy pall of candle grease and wood smoke as David opened the front door. Morna slipped out first, groped her way to the cliff path, gazed down at the sea. It always seemed more menacing at night-time, its black swirling water refusing to lie quiet or hush its voice, even while the rest of the island slept. David was lighting the bonfire in the shelter of the cottage. She used its flame as a beacon as she picked her way back across the rocky stretch of ground. He had lit the fire to stimulate the sun, but it was the moon which was watching him thin-lipped in the sky, his tall figure tagged by a grotesque and taller shadow. Her own shadow lurched towards his, merged.

'Marvellous fire,' she said.

'Yes. I saved the fish and rabbit bones to burn. That's how bonfires got their name – from bones. They make a rather nasty smoke which drives away the demons. Are you ready to make the offering?'

Morna stepped forward, poured out the libation – the last dregs of Mrs Cormack's brew. The flame was quenched a moment before flickering back to life. David had banked the fire with gorse, dead and brown, but another ancient charm against evil spirits. He took her hand.

'Now we dance round it. That encourages the sun.'

Morna felt not quite real. The heavy long-fermented wine had split her head off from her body, made her legs clumsy so that she was shambling rather than dancing, steered by David, barging into him as they went round and round, round and round; their elongated shadows tripping a second unsteady circle beyond their own. Despite the rawness of the night, David was still in his shirtsleeves, she wearing just a light wool cardigan over her thin dress. Yet neither felt the cold. The fire was flushing their faces, scorching the fronts of their legs, while the wind whipped them from behind, tugged at their hair. Morna could hear the sea nagging at the rocks, a steady threatening boom beyond the crackling of the flames. The bright sun of the fire lit up only one small circle of the night, an enchanted circle which haloed them with gold, but outside it sea and sky were black, merging in one huge and potent darkness. Morna's heart was pounding, her breath coming in gasps, yet she didn't, couldn't stop. This was a rhythm dictated by something outside her, the orbit of the sun itself. Her hand was locked in David's, his body part of hers, so that they were no longer separate, but had become one strange four-legged creature with one set of lungs, one heartbeat, which could spin only round and round. It was endless summer because they had devoured the sun, yet winter darkness loomed beyond the fire, encroaching now as the flames began to weaken, feeding on themselves.

Their pace slackened, as if it were the fire itself which had been fuelling them as well. They slowed down to a walk and then a stumble, finally collapsed on the ground, dizzy and out of breath. Morna still clung to David's hand, while the island whirled and spun.

Gently, he freed it, struggled to his feet. 'We'll light our candles from the fire before it dies completely and process around the house with them. That's the very last rite, I promise. You must be dead.'

'No, I'm fine. Anyway, I've got to jump across the fire first.' She paused a moment, until the ground had come to rest, then sprang to her feet, leapt across the flames, feeling their hot breath pant against her legs, landed safely on the other side. Now she had ensured fruitfulness twice over, the morning's rites clinched by these midnight ones, the demons doubly banished.

She turned back to David, his dark form crouching down as he held his candle to the last faint tongue of flame. He passed her a second candle, lit it from his own. Their eyes met for a second and this time he didn't look away. If the eyes were the window of the soul, then she was embedded in his soul, a tiny flickering figure staring out.

He held his candle high, led her slowly, solemnly, back into the house. The rooms were all in darkness, the other candles distorted stumps of wax, the parlour grate a tomb of dying embers. They processed from parlour to kitchen, then up the stairs in silence, in and out of the second bedless bedroom, shadows leaping from the stacked and ghostly jumble, and finally into Morna's room. There they stopped.

The silence seemed wrong now, awkward and unintended rather than part of a solemn ritual. Morna shifted from foot to foot. This was the finish of the ceremony, the end of the feast day, yet there was no final rite to mark it, no fitting culmination. She could mutter good night, close the door on him, but that would ruin the whole day, make him feel she hadn't valued it. Anyway, how could she simply settle down to sleep, switch off the excitement?

She blew out her candle, let his light them both. 'David . . .'

'Mm?'

'Thank you – for everything. It was a wonderful day. I'll never forget it – ever.'

He mumbled some reply, embarrassed as always when she tried to praise him. She sat on the edge of the bed, willing him to stay a little longer; wished there was a chair, a pair of chairs, so they could both relax, settle down more casually, simply talk a while. Why was it so difficult to talk now? David seemed completely tongue-tied and she herself could think of nothing to say which wasn't either stupid or provocative. Silence seemed to clog the room, fill all the space between them. The half-light made it worse, suggesting an intimacy which simply wasn't there. Perhaps she could praise the meal again, thank him for his trouble.

'David, that . . . er . . . rabbit stew was quite . . .'

He suddenly blundered towards her, blew his candle out, dropped it on the shelf, grabbed her round the waist, pressing his whole body against hers. She fell back on the bed, banging her head on the wall. He seemed not even to notice, just plumped on top of her, hugged her so fiercely she could hardly breathe. She tried to free herself, break the tight noose of his arms. She could hear him muttering something, the words indistinct, as squashed and bruised as she was.

'Stop, David, you're hurting.'

He snapped back to his feet, let her go as abruptly as he had seized her. 'I'm sorry, I'm sorry.' He was shouting now, stumbling to the door.

'It . . . It's all right. It's just that . . .'

'It's *not* all right. I hurt you. I always get it bloody wrong.'

She could hear him fumbling for the door handle, groped after him, laid her hand gently on his arm. 'David, listen – let's not spoil things.'

'They're spoilt already. *My* fault, sorry.'

'Don't say that. You just . . . took me by surprise, that's all.'

'I thought you *wanted* me to . . . Oh, forget it.' David had his back turned, was hunched against the door, mumbling into the wood. 'I tried to warn you, tried not to . . . to start things, but you kept leading me on, encouraging me . . .'

'I . . . I didn't.' She could feel herself blushing in the darkness as she fibbed.

'Of course you did. Oh, I didn't mind. I was flattered, actually.' His voice was muffled, indistinct. 'Trust me to mess things up, though.'

'You haven't, David. I mean, I . . .' The flush was deepening. Why were words so difficult, even one's own language?

484

'What I'm trying to say is I don't mind your . . . I even quite . . . but you mustn't be so sort of . . . violent.'

David kicked at the door. 'Don't say that.' He was shouting again. 'Don't use that word. I *feel* violent, that's the whole damn trouble. You don't understand. I tried to explain but . . .'

'How can I understand if . . .'

'Leave it, Morna. I've said enough – more than enough. You've told me I've as good as botched it, so we might as well . . .' He was through the door now, halfway down the stairs, tripping in the dark.

She fumbled for her torch, darted after him. 'Wait, David. You . . . You don't understand me either. I feel just as . . . screwed up as you do. If you really want to know, I'm a . . . washout in that department myself.'

'Y . . . You?' He stopped, swung round, blinking against the sudden beam of light.

'Well, N . . . Neil always said so. He spent fourteen years telling me I was cold and prudish and . . .'

David walked slowly up three steps, stopped again. 'I can't believe it. I always thought . . .'

'Why don't we talk? We never have, you know – not about you, not really. Always me.' She backed into the bedroom. David followed cautiously, remained standing at the door, hands clenched, one foot jabbing at the floorboards.

'Look, David, I don't quite know how to put this, but what I feel is . . . we – you . . . don't really trust me – not completely. It's not just a matter of touching or . . . or . . .' She stared down at the torch beam which was trembling with her hand. 'I want to know you better. I've told you a lot about my own life, but you never seem to . . .' The words gave out again, stumbled into silence.

'We talk all the time,' he muttered. 'I've probably told you more than anyone else I've ever met in my life – name, age, address, religion, father's occupation. What more do you want to know, for heaven's sake?' He was trying to make a joke of it, but she could hear the tension in his voice, arms folded tight across his chest now.

'It's only because I'm . . . I'm fond of you. Perhaps I shouldn't be, but . . .'

'I'm fond of you, too.' David sounded uneasy with the admission, head turned half-away. 'I'm sorry I shouted, Morna. I behaved very . . . stupidly – like a child in a tantrum.'

'Come and sit down.' She patted the bed beside her.

He sat reluctantly, said nothing for a while, rubbed his eyes, crossed his legs, uncrossed them. She could feel him fidgeting and shuffling in the darkness, his nervousness infectious.

'It's funny,' he said at last, one hand across his mouth so that the words were muffled and distorted. 'When I *was* a child, I never felt like one. My brother was much older – very quiet and serious. I worshipped him – tried to model myself on him – you know, be another Dominic. It didn't work. Everyone in my family was very . . . good. Stupid word.' He laughed, more harshly this time. 'Except me, that is. I always felt I'd let them down. I was the only one who ever lost my temper or had punch-ups or black moods or . . . When I was thirteen, I was sent away to school. I'd won a scholarship, in fact, but I saw it more as a punishment. Dominic was a dayboy – good enough to stay at home, but *I* had to be disciplined, beaten into shape.' David was tapping his feet, picking at the blankets, a moody, restless thirteen-year-old again.

'I was a great gangling thing by then, the tallest boy in the class and the first one to shave. I hated that, hated what I looked like. Dominic was smaller-boned and fair, and never swore or shouted or used his fists, and although he was quiet, he wasn't shy. I was. It was agony to meet people, especially new ones. Girls were worst of all. I blushed if a female came within ten yards of me. My form master was always going on about body and soul, sort of splitting them off as if they were quite separate – soul good, body bad. That appealed to me because I could send the bad bit packing. The body was the big feet and the blushes and the scruff of beard covering the acne, and the soul was the real me. I became a sort of disembodied spirit – all fire and air, who had a fantastic time chatting up female spirits and never sweated or got tongue-tied or cut myself shaving and then had to go around with bits of cotton-wool stuck on to bleeding pustules. I began to change – read more and argue less. I swapped beer for books and . . .'

'Beer in a Catholic boarding school? We'd have been expelled for less.' Morna tried to lighten the mood. David was talking too loudly and too fast, one fist hammering the palm of the other hand.

'Well, it wasn't allowed, obviously. But one of my friends brewed his own in the science lab and kept it hidden in his empty trunk in the luggage room. I broke with him as well, went back to plain Thames Valley water, started attending church three times a day and serving Mass. My form master was thrilled. He saw the whole thing as a sort of conversion like Saul on the road to Damascus. He was always on the lookout for budding priests – replenishments for the order, you might say – and I seemed a pretty good bet. A stormy youth is often a good training for a saint – look at Augustine, or Francis of Assisi carousing with the lads. Anyway, I threw myself more and more into religion, with my form master whipping me on and lending me tracts on dangerous things like spiritual ecstasy or self-denial or vocations to the priesthood. I didn't see it then, but I was as violent and extreme in trying to be holy as I was in everything else. I felt if I once let up, I'd be in danger of . . . I don't know – but the school was always preaching hellfire and my mother was as bad.'

She squeezed his hand. 'I know.'

'I'm not sure you do. Forgive me, Morna, but the sheer force of sex when you're a sixteen-year-old boy . . .' He pummelled the bed, as if he were still battling with that force. 'I'm sorry, but we can't avoid the word for ever, and at school I felt it was scrawled over everything in Satan's red. Maybe it's the same for girls. I doubt it. It *is* a sort of violence. It seems to drive you and possess you. You can think of nothing else, yet everything's forbidden. There weren't any girls, not even any women staff, except a matron with a fuller moustache than mine.' He gave another bitter laugh. 'The only way out was to be a priest, take vows which saved you from yourself. I saw those vows as sort of iron chains holding me down, stopping me exploding. Does that sound crazy?'

Morna shook her head. She had never felt that violence, that intensity – hoped she never would – but she understood the fear, the distaste for the body. At thirteen and a half, she had stared with dismay at her own budding breasts. Mother Michael had told them that no man, not even a good Catholic, could withstand the temptation of a woman's naked chest. '*Never, never draw attention to it, never wear your blouses tight, never ever, under pain of mortal sin, let a member of the opposite sex . . .*'

David's urgent caustic voice cut through Mother Michael's. 'I felt better once I'd decided on the priesthood. It seemed to solve everything at once – save me from the flames of hell, placate my mother, give me the edge on brother Dominic. He'd left school by then, and gone to be a missionary – but only a lay one, luckily. That was no real competition. *I* was the special one, consecrated, set apart, and a Jesuit of course. *Crème de la crème*. I suppose the abbot was right to suspect my motives, but I was furious and hurt when he advised me to wait a while, test my vocation, as he put it, get some other experience. I didn't take much notice, spent the whole of Oxford fawning round the Jesuits, still avoiding women. I told myself if I was planning to take a vow of celibacy, then I might as well start as I meant to go on.' He kicked out at the floor. 'Or maybe I was scared.'

'Scared?' Morna felt a stab of fear herself. She had complained that David had told her nothing, yet contrarily admired him for just that restraint. Now he was pouring out a lifetime's pent-up anger and frustration, turning into someone else, someone she wasn't sure she even liked.

'Not of women, but of my own feelings. They were still too damned strong. I was right to fear them, actually. When the Jesuits turned me down the third and final time, after I'd been begging cap in hand for five whole years and missed other decent openings and mucked up my career, I had my first affair – deliberately. Tit for tat, you might say.'

Morna bit her lip, tried to interrupt him with hollow reassurances. 'But that's quite understandable. After all, you'd waited long enough. Most men . . .'

He sprang up from the bed, clutching at the wall, leaning down to face her. 'I'm not most men. I'm a bloody brute. I forced the girl – all but raped her. I didn't even know her name. I wasn't fucking a woman, I was fucking Holy Mother Church, getting my own back, making up for all the years and years of . . .'

Morna shrank away, shocked by his language, and his hectoring voice. He started pacing up and down, the torch beam throwing his shadow on the wall, an angry lurching shadow which seemed to cower the room.

'The next time – oh, yes, there was a next time, but with a different girl – I tried to make amends.' He broke off, stopped his prowling.

'What . . . What happened?'

'Nothing. Bloody nothing. I couldn't do it at all. I'd become a priest, in fact, but without the trappings.' He was talking to the wall, shoulders hunched, head down. 'It's funny, soon after that, my hair started going grey. I was only in my twenties, but I took it as a sort of . . . sign that life was over – that side of life, anyway. I'm sorry, Morna –' He turned to face her. 'I don't know why I'm drivelling on like this. I told you

I shouldn't drink. So long as I keep control of everything, I can live my life as I want. But as soon as I break a single rule . . .'

'There aren't any rules, David, not now – not as such. You sound as if it's school still. Everybody drinks too much at times, or has an off day.'

'You don't understand. It wasn't just an off day. It happened again – several times, in fact. I began to realize I was afraid of my own body. I'd tried to split it off, but it was still there. The trouble was I'd given it such a beating, it was all but paralysed. The cure had killed it, I suppose. Or perhaps that's just an excuse. I don't know. Maybe I was a . . . duffer in that department. I loathe being bad at things – anything – tennis, women, maths. So I gave it up, decided I wouldn't compete, took my own private vows and . . .'

'You mean, ever since then, you haven't . . . ?'

'There you are, you see – you're shocked. That's the normal reaction. I'm a freak – like you said.'

'I *didn't* say, David. I'd never say a thing like that.'

'Well, you thought it.'

'David, please don't tell me what I think.'

'I'm sorry, I don't know what I'm saying. I've never talked like this before to anyone, least of all a woman. Put it down to Mrs Cormack's brew.' He plunged towards the door again. 'I'd better go and sleep it off. I'll be my normal self in the morning, I promise you. Only please don't . . . you know, bring the subject up again, or I'll become the blushing shambling idiot I was at sixteen. Let's forget the whole thing, can we?'

'No, I don't think we can.'

'Oh, you're going to throw it in my face, are you?'

'David, please don't be so touchy. I wouldn't dream of doing that. What you still don't seem to grasp is that I . . . I've got just as many . . . hang-ups myself.'

'You're only saying that to make me feel less bloody.'

490

'I'm *not*, David. After Neil left, I almost took vows myself.'

'And broke them, I presume?'

'Only once – no, twice – and the second time I was blotto.'

'Blotto?' He sounded shocked himself now.

She nodded. 'I don't know why you keep idealizing me. I often drink too much. In fact, I was so far gone, I tried to turn a balding middle-aged creep of a frozen-foods salesman into you.'

'*What?*'

'I'm sorry. That sounds insulting. It was actually a compliment. I was missing you, you see.'

'You mean, it was . . . recently?'

'Four weeks ago.'

'So I was right, then. I imagined you making it with half America.'

'*David!*'

'I'm sorry – that was crude. But I was missing you as well, and feeling pretty jealous and . . .'

'Jealous? But we'd hardly even . . .'

'I know. That made it worse, though. I felt I had no right to . . . In fact, I made another vow – that I'd never touch you, ever. You'd confided in me, proved you'd trusted me, and I wouldn't take advantage of it.'

Morna said nothing. He sounded so . . . so old-fashioned, so out of touch with his own needs, and hers.

He was still standing by the door, hand on the knob as if ready to escape. 'You . . . You're laughing at me, Morna.'

'I'm not. Of course I'm not. It's just that . . . well, I think you've got it wrong. You can't base your entire life on something you decided years and years ago when you were angry and mixed up, still an adolescent more or less, and influenced by teachers who were in a mess themselves and saw the world as a sort of . . . cess-pit. I know what that does to people. It ruined things for me, as well. Even when I was married, I saw the . . . er . . . physical side as doggy and dirty, something

491

you did as a duty, not because . . .' She was blushing again, relieved now that the torch-beam was so dim. 'I never actually . . . refused Neil, but he picked up the vibes, called me frigid and . . .'

'I just can't understand that. You seem so . . . well – sensual to me. The first time I set eyes on you, I assumed you were very – you know – experienced. That made me shy, of course, but . . .' He shambled back towards the bed, sat on the very edge of it, reached out one arm, put it on her shoulder, held it there so tentatively, she felt he was ready to snatch it away again if she made one wrong move. It wasn't easy to stay still. It excited her to be thought experienced, described as sensual; made her feel quite differently, about herself as well as him. The pressure of his hand had switched her body on. She hadn't been aware of it before with all that talk and tension, all the problems. She brushed her own hand down across her breast, wished he would do the same. Her dress felt too tight, confining, as if begging to be taken off. She shifted on the bed, uncrossed her legs, let her thighs fall apart a daring inch or two. David's thigh was nudging into hers now, his dark form hunched so close she could smell bonfire on his clothes, the strong male carbolic soap he had used to wash his hands.

She edged still closer, dared to lean her head against his chest, leave it there a moment. They sat in silence, neither moving, until suddenly he slumped back on the bed, she falling with him, her body sprawled on his. He made no move to touch it or explore it, just lay passive underneath her. She feared she was too heavy, crushing him, tried to shift her weight, shivered in the draught.

'You're cold,' he said, extracting his left arm and rubbing it.

'And you've got cramp.'

'Only pins and needles.'

She helped him rub it, shivering still, as much from fear and excitement as from cold. Even massaging his arm seemed far too dangerous, only the light silky fabric of his shirt between his flesh and her own. She could feel his muscles hard and taut, his whole arm tensed. 'Shall we . . . er . . . ?' She cleared her throat, tried again, made her voice more casual. 'W . . . We could always get under the covers. I mean, there's no point freezing, is there, with all these rugs and things?'

He didn't answer, just unlaced his shoes. She heard them thud on to the floor, her heart thudding even louder as she kicked off her own shoes, pulled the blankets back, squeezed into the narrow bed, still fully clothed but trying to make herself as small as possible so there would be room for him as well.

'Bit of a squash, I'm afraid.'

'At least it's warmer that way.'

They were both whispering, both lying absolutely rigid. Morna's arm was hurting, doubled back behind her, her head uncomfortable without the pillows which were still down-stairs in the parlour. David seemed larger than he ever had before, taking up three quarters of the bed, yet still trying not to touch her.

'Are you all . . . right?'

'Mm. Are you?'

'I'm . . . er . . . nervous. Stupid, isn't it?'

'No, it's not. I'm nervous, too. Terrified, in fact. I keep worrying whether you want me to . . . to . . .' He stopped.

'Yes,' she whispered, brazen suddenly. 'I do.'

His silence seemed an instant reprimand. Why ever had she said that? She reached out and switched the torch off, felt less flagrant in the dark. 'I . . . I've shocked you now, haven't I?'

She heard him clear his throat. 'Course not. I . . . I'm just scared that if you say yes, I'll be sort of . . . paralysed.'

'All right – no, then.' She forced a laugh. 'Better?'

'No, worse. That's rejection.'

493

'David, you're impossible.'

'I know.'

They both laughed.

'We could just go to sleep.'

'Yes, I suppose we could.' David sounded unconvinced. 'Except I can't sleep in these jeans. They're far too tight.'

'So you expect me to say, "Take them off," and then when I do, you'll complain I'm trying to seduce you.'

He laughed again, more easily. 'Okay, I deserved that. Though actually, I don't know what we're worrying about. It's pitch dark, so you couldn't see me anyway.'

'All right, let's both get undressed – purely for comfort.'

'Purely.' David was already kneeling up, tugging at his belt. She wondered if she ought to help him, or take her own clothes off. She squirmed out of her cardigan – that was fairly simple – but the dress was stubborn, seemed to fight her. She hit her hand against the wall as she struggled with the zipper, fingers clumsy as seal's flippers; almost panicked as the skirt caught over her head and she was blinded for a moment by choking folds of turquoise silk. She tugged it off, released herself, wished she was wearing a few more clothes – petticoat or vest or girdle – anything to cover up that nakedness, slow the whole thing down. She unhooked her bra, felt her breasts spill out, covered them with her hands, wincing at the cold. There was too much of them, too much of her body altogether. If David had admired it, touched it, made some comment or some overture, she might have felt less ill at ease, but he had slipped off the bed, retreated to the door again. He wasn't even looking at her, had his back turned, seemed equally self-conscious as he struggled to unpeel his jeans. All she could hear were furtive fumblings and rustlings, a sudden clink as his belt dropped on the floor. She longed for music – some romantic serenade to fill the silence, charge the atmosphere. The present mood was so solemn and constrained, David might have been unvesting after Mass.

494

She turned her back as well, to take her pants off, hadn't hands enough to cover both breasts and pubic hair. Even in the dark, the hair seemed too bushy, too flauntingly red. She felt blatant, whorish, standing there stark naked. She stole a glance behind her. David was naked too, now, his body a pale blur in the gloom. He seemed suddenly too vulnerable, as if his clothes had been a form of armour and he was now totally defenceless. Perhaps they should call the whole thing off, get dressed again, be safe and simple friends once more. But how could she suggest it? She couldn't even reach her clothes which were scattered on the floor. It would mean pushing past that huge male naked body which was now shambling towards her, bearing down on her, no longer vulnerable but dangerous. Somehow, she managed to keep her eyes only on his top half, but even so, the shoulders looked too broad, the hair on the chest too dark and animal. He might grab her, hurt her . . . She slipped between the covers, pulled the blankets right up to her chin.

'May I get in too?' He was standing right beside the bed, leaning down. She could hear his breathing, heavy and too loud.

'C . . . Course.' Her voice sounded odd, cracked and rusted up.

A freezing foot shocked against her thigh, a hand like ice put goose flesh on her stomach. She tried to edge away, although she was already pressed right against the wall. Her heart was pounding so violently she feared it would start shaking the mattress like those Magic Fingers massage beds you could set off in America by inserting half-a-dollar in a special slot in the headboard. Should she touch him, make some overture? She was terrified of everything – rejection, failure, violence, disapproval. She hadn't cleaned her teeth. Her breath might smell fishy from the soup, or reek of Mrs Cormack's vicious brew. Why had David made no move himself? Was he copying those medieval saints who went to

495

bed with women only to prove their strength against temptation?

'Well, at . . . at least we're not lying on a bed of nutshells.' The joke sounded lame, her voice still strained and forced.

'N . . . No.'

'Nor stinging nettles.'

'No.'

Silence again. She'd *tried*, for heaven's sake. If he wouldn't even respond, just lay there in that total rigid silence, they might as well go to sleep and be done with it. At least she was warming up. She could feel his body clammy with heat (or fear?) thawing the chill from hers. Cormack had told him that in the old days he and the other crofters had often slept with their animals for warmth, and that his father's father owed his life to the fact that after a near-drowning, he had been laid to sleep in the byre between two cows, so that the creatures' body heat revived and warmed him. Morna raised her head a fraction, rubbed an aching arm. If only they were simple cows or sheep, so that mating was just a natural bodily function, no more embarrassing than eating. But both their schools had downgraded the word animal. Animal passions threatened the eternal soul. She froze. David was moving, levering up on one elbow.

'Look, Morna, this sounds absolutely crazy, but c . . . could you take that . . . cross off?'

'*What*?'

'That cross and chain. It . . . It puts me off my stroke.'

She let out a great nervous gasp of laughter. 'Oh, David, you are funny.'

'I'm sorry. It's just . . . just . . .'

'I understand.' She was already fumbling for the clasp. 'What *I'd* like to remove is the Blessed Virgin and both our wretched mothers. The nuns used to say that we must never do anything with a man which we would mind our mothers or Our Blessed Lady witnessing. I keep imagining the three of them standing in a huddle by the bed, looking absolutely shocked.'

David gave a strangled laugh. 'Don't! That'll really finish me. *We* were always told to treat our girlfriends like our sisters. But as I didn't have a sister, it wasn't a lot of help. In fact, it set me off thinking wickedly incestuous thoughts, which only led to more guilt. My mother's line was safe at least. She said never to go out with anyone unless she'd come from a devout Catholic family and had been a Child of Mary at school.'

'*I* come from a devout Catholic family and was a Child of Mary at school.'

'That's all right then, isn't it?'

It was easier to laugh now. David seemed emboldened, wiped his palms on the blanket, cleared his throat.

'M . . . May I kiss you?' he whispered.

She wished he wouldn't ask. Neil had never asked for anything, just gone ahead and grabbed. She realized now it had solved a lot of problems.

He didn't kiss like Neil did – slowly, expertly, bringing in first lips, then tongue, then teeth, alternating slow with swift, hard with soft, orchestrating the kiss – but just pressed his mouth roughly against hers. She had never kissed a man with a beard, wasn't sure she liked it – rough coarse prickling hair chafing her lips, choking in her mouth. She pulled back, began the kiss again, moving her lips so gently towards his, they were barely touching, letting the tip of her tongue flick slowly round the outline of his mouth. The mouth opened and relaxed. She probed it with her tongue, gently explored his teeth, found his own tongue. She suddenly realized she *was* experienced. David was the novice, not herself. She had become the expert, the teacher, taking on Neil's rôle, displaying skills she had picked up over fourteen years but never really owned. She wanted to show them off now, earn that label 'sensuous'.

She moved her tongue to David's ear, slowly traced its

coils, acted the voluptuous daring female. Neil had used his hands as well. She stroked her own down David's chest, heard him let out a huge great shuddering sigh as if he had been holding his breath for three whole weeks, or since he was a wild lad of thirteen, and had only now expelled it. Yet he was passive still, leaving everything to her. She remembered what he had said – 'Nothing bloody happened'. Was nothing happening now, Big David small? God! If he stayed soft as David Attwood had, she would have to judge herself a total failure, someone men found boring or repellent. She dared not feel, or run her hands that low – let them stray instead on to his stomach, then down a little further, felt the rough grin of a scar beneath her fingers.

'How did you get that?' she whispered.

'Peritonitis. As a child. I almost died.' He said it so flatly, so matter-of-factly, she wanted to shake him, tell him he had to live, love, get up off his back. Months ago, he had been urging her to trust life, yet he mistrusted it himself – at least the physical side of it – mistrusted even her. He *was* limp – she could tell now. The Catholic Church had done that, as it had ruined her own sex life. She would kick out every bloody priest, every straitlaced monk and nun, the Blessed Bigot Virgin, all those smarmy squeamish saints, those smug self-righteous celibates. Bea had better go as well, and prissy Mrs Anthony and every ice-cold Child of Mary who had ever simpered in her pale blue sash. And David Attwood, too, while she was about it – shaming her, reminding her of failure, making her scared ever to try again.

'Get *out*,' she muttered under her breath. 'Get the hell out of here and don't come back.'

She kicked the blankets off, struggled up, knelt across David, one leg on either side. Okay, so she was risking her eternal soul. She didn't care. It was her instant immediate body which concerned her. It was warm now and wet now and it bloody wanted him. She was an animal with appetites, and no castrated Pope or cuntless Reverend Mother would muzzle her or make her keep her legs crossed.

The mattress was rustling, the bed making obscene outrageous noises. Too damn bad. She had to get David stiff, turn his tiny cowering child's prick into a grown man's. Those sanctimonious monks had ruled him thirty years. It was her turn now. She rubbed her breasts against his chest, pressed her whole body down on his, felt something stir and twitch beneath her thighs. She had to win, she had to. She used her hands – both hands – slow, then faster, tight, then gentle, used her mouth, her tongue, her will.

She was winning. He was larger now, much larger, still not fully stiff, but big enough to chance it. Slowly, she lowered her body onto his, inch by gradual inch, until they were almost making contact. She didn't want to rush him, make him feel she was frustrated or impatient. They were almost almost there. She let out her breath, closed her eyes.

He gave a sudden gasping cry, his whole body tensing in a shudder. She felt something warm and sticky spurt against her leg, dribble down. She lay absolutely still, listening to his breathing, the excited wind outside, her own heart pounding out its crazy smirking premature elation.

'Stupid, stupid, *stupid*,' he was muttering, pounding his clenched fist against the mattress.

'Hush.' She kissed his neck. 'It's not stupid.'

'You're right. It's worse than that. It was pathetic, completely and utterly pathetic.'

She squeezed his hand, tried to find some words which didn't sound too patronizing. 'Y . . . You could regard it as a sort of . . . compliment – to me.'

'What d'you mean?' His voice was gruff, almost unintelligible.

'Well – you know – you found me . . . exciting, so . . .'

He groaned. 'That's true.'

She took his other hand, kissed them both. 'Don't worry, then.'

'Yes, but, *you* . . . I mean, you haven't . . . I didn't even . . .'

'I'm fine. I feel absolutely wonderful.'

'How can you? I was hopeless – a total washout.'

'I . . . liked you coming like that.'

'You're being sarcastic now.'

'I'm *not*, David. I did like it. I can't explain, but it was so sort of . . . *real* – you know, surprising and spontaneous and . . .'

'A bloody let-down.'

'David, stop it. Why keep judging yourself? I know I do the same, but why *should* we? Who said we had to live up to some mythical five-star standard just because the sex books tell us to? I loathe those books. They're all foreplay drills and performance-checks and homework, as if making love was a very difficult subject which . . .'

'Isn't it?'

'Look, David, according to those books, what we've just done would be judged a . . . well, not exactly a rip-roaring success. Okay, I admit that. And yet I feel marvellous, really marvellous. How do you account for that? Are *they* wrong, or am I?'

David rolled towards her, unclenched his fist. 'You . . . You're not just saying that – to be . . . kind or something?'

'No, I'm not. I can't explain it really, even to myself, but I can honestly say it . . . it never felt so . . . good before – never in my life.'

'You mean, I pleased you more than . . . ?'

'More than anyone.'

He grabbed her, started kissing her – neck, throat, down towards her chest, still too roughly, still holding her too tight.

'Gently,' she warned.

'You see, I can't even kiss. Will you teach me?'

'Mm.'

'Every night?'

'Mm.'

'Whose bed, yours or mine?'

'You mean the sofa?'

'Yup.'

'Or the floor. There'd be more room on the floor. We could make a sort of double bed downstairs – bring the mattress down and take the sofa cushions out and lay them alongside it and then pile rugs on top and . . .'

'You're shameless, Morna. Father Burnett would have put you on the Index.'

'Who's he?'

'He's dead now. My old form master. RIP.'

'We'll be spirits then. To please him. Or angels. We could go down there now. At least it'd be warmer in the parlour, even with the fire out.'

'Spirits don't feel the cold.'

'This one does.'

'Shall I carry her down, then?'

He rolled out of bed, hauled the blankets off, wrapped them round her, picked her up like a baby, groped his way in the dark towards the stairs.

'Careful!' Morna giggled. 'You'll fall.'

'No, I won't. I've got wings.'

She kissed his shoulder. 'Lovely wings.'

It was more lurching than flying as David clumped down the stairs, she half-clinging to his neck, half-grabbing at the wall, both of them laughing like a pair of school kids. He laid her on the sofa, picked up the pillows, propped them behind her head.

'I'll go back for the mattress now.'

'I'd better help. You'll never manage on your own.'

'Yes, I will. You stay put. Want me to light the lamp?'

'No, it's nice like this.' The embers of the fire sent out only the faintest reddish glow, but their eyes had grown accustomed to the dark. Morna lay back, thighs parted slightly, one hand resting on her breast. She was a success, a sensual woman. All right, so David had come in fifteen seconds, before he had even entered her, but they were spirits and spirits did things differently. She could hear David manoeuvring the stairs, weighed down with sheets and mattress; got up to help him through the door. Together they constructed a bed more original than comfortable, piled it with an assortment of covers including the purple velvet curtain-tablecloth.

Morna frowned at the result. The mattress was higher than the sofa cushions, so the bed was on two levels. 'We'd better start again. There's a ridge right down the middle.'

'No leave it. If you go to all that trouble, I'll probably find I can't even . . .'

'Stop worrying. We're going to go to sleep.'

'Are we?'

'Yes. So long as you don't mind a bed with a ridge.'

'And you don't mind bed with a failure?'

'David . . .' Morna hugged him for a moment, fiercely, let him go. 'Let's never use that word again. Banish it. Put it on Father Barnett's Index.'

He didn't answer, just eased into the makeshift bed, taking care not to dismantle it. 'This will probably sound even more pathetic, but it's the first time I've ever . . . shared a bed with . . . I mean, the others weren't . . .' He broke off. Morna imagined cars, park benches, alleyways. He cleared his throat, embarrassed. 'Stupid, isn't it?'

'No. It makes it special. To tell the truth, I was always a bit jealous of that cousin in the bedsit. I suspected you were sharing a couch with her.'

'*Her*?'

'Well, I know you called him "him", but I reckoned that was just a ruse to put me off the scent.'

David laughed delightedly. 'I'll have to introduce you. Colin's six foot six and balding, with a bushy ginger beard.'

'Colin? And there I was imagining a Samantha or a Jezebel.'

'No, the last time I stayed there, it was Morna I was sleeping with. I took you back to bed with me after our marvellous day together.'

'And what . . . er . . . happened?'

'I'd blush to tell you.' He leaned over, touched her cheek. 'It *does* mean beloved.'

'What does?'

'Your name. Beloved and beautiful and sensual and special and . . .'

She was blushing now herself. 'And what does David mean?'

'A crazy nervous fellow who's in too much of a rush, but may improve, given time and a loving woman. No, actually, David means beloved, too – in Hebrew. Isn't that strange?' He sat up, dislodging half the covers. 'The root is DWD which probably means "to love", though it's a bit obscure. As a noun, it definitely means "the beloved" and is used that way in "The Song of Songs" at least a score of times. And as a proper name . . .'

Morna hid a smile. Even *post coitum*, David couldn't resist a scholarly digression.

'So we're both beloveds,' she whispered, when he was silent again, lying back beside her, one arm across her body as if to make sure it couldn't stray.

'Yes.' He kissed her, very gently, on the mouth. 'Good night, beloved.'

'G . . . Good night.' Morna could hardly get the word out. He was going so fast, had promoted her from colleague to beloved in just one evening. She settled herself against him, closed her eyes. How could she ever get to sleep with that 'beloved' dazzling in her gut as if she had swallowed a spinning sparking firework, or taken a pep pill which made her gloriously uproariously awake? She shifted position, felt the warm and solid buffer of his thigh.

'David . . .'

'Mm?'

'I'm not sure I can sleep. I'm flaked out physically, but . . .'

David half sat up. 'Shut your eyes and join your hands.'

'What for? We're not going to say the rosary, are we, or an Act of Contrition? I draw the line at that.'

'No, just an ancient prayer for peace and sleep.' He joined her hands for her, stroked her eyelids shut, recited some words aloud. She recognized the strange guttural softness of the Gaelic.

'Want me to translate?' he whispered.

She nodded.

He took her hand, kissed the palm, clasped her fingers round the kiss, then held them in his own. 'May the peace of the tallest mountain and the peace of the smallest stone be your peace. May the stillness of the stars watch over you. May the everlasting music of the wave lull you to rest.'

'Amen,' she whispered, drawing him down towards her. 'Now we'll sleep.'

23

Morna stood pressed against the wall, watching the crush and press of dancing bodies, wincing at the insistent beat of the record, angry drums and shrill guitar. She could hardly make out the words, but those she caught seemed anything but sweet. She wished she could choose a record – something passionate, romantic – moons and Junes, whispered vows of love on lonely beaches, long lingering kisses as the wild waves crashed and foamed – something to match her mood, her thoughts of David. She tried to remove the smug contented smile. She was meant to be the chaperone, the stern and watchful parent, not just another party guest mooning around singing vacuous love songs in her head.

A saxophone yelped and sniggered, bawled out by the drums. The photos on the bureau were trembling with the beat, the whole room vibrating, thick with cigarette smoke. Morna picked her way between the couples – girls in spangled minis or junk-shop dinner jackets, boys with earrings and dyed hair – edged into the hall. A new squall of guests had just arrived – the front door jammed with bodies, people hugging, handing over bottles, one girl carrying a huge home-made birthday card for Chris, the figures 18 cut out in red felt and glued with sequins. The girl herself had a V of sequins stuck on to her neck and pointing down her cleavage; her purple plastic eyeshades clashing with the hot-pink micro-skirt which barely skimmed her crotch. Morna glimpsed a flash of black lace knicker as the girl reached forward to hug a friend. When *she* had been that age, she had worn Terylene pleated skirts with pastel-coloured home-knits, one daring pair of slacks. Yet the clothes had seemed exotic after years and years of frumpish school uniform. She remembered her first thrilling dab of lipstick, her first pair of shoes not regulation brown, the almost sinful ecstasy of dangly rhinestone earrings borrowed from her mother for a dance. Even today she was sedately dressed – the only female present in a classic navy two-piece with the hem below the knee, the only over-twenty-five at all. Yet if they could see beneath the clothes, pare away the conventional outer shell, realize how like a kid she felt herself – a lovesick teenager waiting for the postman, replaying all the love scenes of the last few weeks, continually sneaking back to the island in her head. It was good to be eighteen again at forty (well, forty-one) – enjoying the excitement without the fears and shyness, the kisses free of guilt. She longed to be dancing like the other couples, arms around David's neck, their two bodies touching all the way down.

'Hi, Mrs Gordon! How you doing?'

Morna jumped. It was Anne-Marie who had come to tea a year ago in pigtails and gymslip, now squeezed into a tight and tarty skirt and tottering towards her on three-inch scarlet heels.

'I'm great.' Morna borrowed Chris's word. 'Absolutely great. Know where Chris went? She was here a moment ago and . . .'

'Yeah. She's in the study.'

Neil's ex-study was barely recognizable. The desk had been pushed back, the bookshelves hung with streamers and balloons, the thick-pile carpet lost beneath sprawling arms and legs. Morna couldn't spot Chris at first, finally made her out at the far end of the room, sitting on the window seat, squashed between Martin and another boy who was sporting a black tail coat over denim dungarees. Her daughter hadn't bothered to dress up, was wearing her third best jeans with one of Martin's drabber shirts. Her only concession to the party was a pair of grey suede buttoned ankle boots which she had bought from a stall in the Portobello Road and treasured as genuine Victorian. The clothes which Neil had bought her or Bunny bequeathed had been pushed to the back of her wardrobe, the blonde streaks in her hair fading, growing out. The diamond looked too opulent against her drab and boyish clothes. She kept glancing at it, twisting it round and round, moving her left hand stiffly and self-consciously as if she had injured it, could no longer really trust it. It was the first time she had worn the ring in public, on her finger rather than concealed around her neck. Morna felt a pang of guilt and envy every time she saw it – envy because she was romantic (and stupid) enough to want David's diamond on her own third finger; guilt because a daughter's ring spelled a mother's freedom, and she feared she had agreed to the engagement partly to liberate herself. Chris was now Martin's responsibility which left her free to live her life around David. If there hadn't been a David, would she have put up more objections, played the heavy-handed parent? Yet what good would that have done? Sowed anger and resentment, turned Chris into a Juliet.

Morna glanced across at the two dark heads, the almost matching grey-blue shirts. Strange how Chris and Martin seemed better matched all round now. It was only David who had made her see it. Always before, she had ignored the simple fact that her daughter went to bed with Martin, had a whole complex secret bond with him beyond the one she showed the world. It was the same with her and David. They might seem incompatible to those who judged them just from the exterior. But now she knew David from the inside out, knew his body in all its tiny details – the damaged nail on the third toe of his left foot which a shire horse had trod on when he was in his teens and staying on a farm; the way the hair on his chest and stomach seemed to grow in two different directions – that above his navel springing up and out, that below softer and less curly, running down to his shock of pubic hair. She liked to touch the hair, groom it, comb it with her fingers, stroke it flat or ruffle it up, even tug it, tease him. Those were the sorts of crazy things which bonded you – together with the words you coined, the silly games you played. She and David were seals one day, Abelard and Héloïse the next. How could she ever say that Martin was wrong for Chris when she saw only half of their relationship, the public, superficial half? She had been unfair to Martin, anyway, judging him by Neil's standards, expecting a different sort of son-in-law – Neil's sort – with a briefcase and a diploma in business management and bridge-playing parents who would vote Conservative and invite them round for canapés.

She watched him kiss her daughter on the forehead, whisper in her ear. They both giggled and touched noses before Martin got up, stepped across the tangled arms and legs, making for the door. He stopped when he saw Morna, reverted to his usual awkward self. He was still shy with her, had been almost tongue-tied when he had tried to discuss the engagement earlier that week. Neil should have been present, laying down conditions for his daughter's hand in marriage, driving a hard bargain as he did with all his clients. She hadn't even told Neil; nor had Chris. That was wrong. Yet he had walked out on his daughter, stayed out of reach during all her vital years, so why should he start interfering now? She would inform her ex-husband when it suited her, present the engagement as a *fait accompli*, something decided by his legally adult daughter and her fiancé. All she had said to the fiancé himself was 'Look after Chris. Make her happy, Martin. Please.' No point hassling the lad again. Bea had upset him quite enough and she herself had been through all the arguments already – in private – with her mother first, and then with Chris.

'Congratulations,' Martin mumbled now, hands thrust in his pockets, shoulders hunched.

Morna tensed. Why congratulations? Had he somehow guessed that she and David . . . ? 'What d'you mean? The congratulations belong to you today – and Chris, of course.'

'You as well. I've got this mate in Holland who told me it's the custom there to congratulate the parents if it's their son or daughter's birthday – you know, for having produced the kid at all, brought it up.'

'That's nice. Thank you, Martin.' She longed to say more, but somehow all her effusions about future happiness or marital bliss came out pompous, sentimental, however much she meant them genuinely. She had even searched the other languages to see if there were phrases which went deeper, sounded less pretentious. There weren't. She still felt a vague sense of unease. Martin was now permanent, official, would become woven into the fabric of their lives, sharing Christmases and birthdays, taking over Chris.

The silence was uncomfortable. She tried to fill it, stick to safely trivial subjects. 'You look a bit loaded down, Martin. All your worldly goods around your neck!' She gestured to the chain which was dangling down his shirt-front, hung with keys and penknife, dog whistle, mini-compass.

Martin grinned sheepishly. 'I don't like my pockets bulging.'

'Why the whistle, though? You don't have a dog, do you?'

'No.'

'Planning to call Chris to heel?'

'You'd need more than a tinpot whistle to do that!'

They both grinned, then, both relaxed a little. She had feared once that Chris seemed too submissive, but maybe that was only in her mind, the submission of all females to all males, which the priests had urged, the Blessed Virgin typified. She mustn't confuse her own case with her daughter's, Neil with Martin.

'What's that?' she asked him, pointing to a small piece of dull grey metal which had been drilled with a hole and was hanging from the chain with all the other things.

'Grapeshot. I found it on an eighteenth-century wreck. There was a whole mass of it lying on the sea bed. I nicked this piece and cleaned it up a bit. Don't worry – it's worth nothing, really. I just like the thought of it being – you know – old and . . .'

She nodded. It was battered like her silver coin, dented on one side. Had she been blind as well as stupid not to see that Martin and David shared vital things in common – a curiosity, a love of history, a determination to find the things it hid? Chris had told her often enough that Martin was pretty damn sharp as well as brave, had a whole deeper side they rarely saw, but somehow she had never quite accepted it. She reached forward, hugged him suddenly, his narrow boyish body tensing in embarrassment.

'I think you deserve a hug today, don't you?'

He looked pleased, despite the flush, didn't pull away. It was she who stepped back, a red mark on her neck where the keys and grapeshot had pressed into her flesh. Okay, they were too young, but were you ever *not* too young, even at forty-one? If she and David made a go of it, there would still be problems – scores of them.

Martin was trying politely to get away. 'Well, I'd . . . better help John out with the disco. I promised I'd relieve him half an hour ago.'

'Off you go, then. And try and play something with a few less decibels!' Morna squeezed past a kissing couple, both stretched out full length on the floor. Should she try and part them, suggest food or some distraction? After all, she was meant to be in charge. The man had a scruff of beard. David's beard was fuller, felt incredibly exciting when he scratched it down her breasts. She had taught him that, taught him to rub it hard across her nipples. Shameless, he had called her again. The stupid grin returned. 'Shameless' had become one of their joke words, especially when he said it in Father Burnett's shrill falsetto voice. She left the couple kissing, edged round the side of the room, joined her daughter on the window seat.

'All right, darling?'

'Yeah, great, thanks. You don't have to stay around, you know, Mum.'

'I know.' Morna got up again. The dismissal hurt. She was too old and square for an eighteenth birthday party, should be strapped safely in her bath chair, or banished upstairs with her ageing mother. Bea had long ago retreated to the bedroom to escape the noise, was hoping for a comparatively early night in the peace of her own home.

'I was just wondering when you'd planned to cut the cake. Grandma's leaving soon, you see, and she'll be disappointed if . . .'

'*You* cut it, Mum.'

'No, you and Martin must. It's your engagement party. And it's bad luck on your birthday not to blow your candles out.'

'Oh, no, Mum,' Chris wailed, still fiddling with her ring. 'I don't want all that fuss – speeches and things, and everybody gawping. I didn't even want a cake.'

Bea had spent three days on the cake – an impressive creation in the shape of two interlocking hearts, iced in red and white and with rosettes and lattice-work piped all along the sides. Chris had been embarrassed by it, complained in private that it looked like one of Bunny's more outrageous cushions. She would have preferred a simple party with a few crisps and Twiglets or hunks of bread and cheese, whereas Bea had made vol-au-vents and quiches, soufflés, mousses, flans – her recompense to Chris for opposing the engagement in the first place.

'They're *far* too young,' she had objected, shouting down the mouthpiece to make herself heard above the crackling and interference on the line. Morna had been phoning from Oban, the first time she had been able to reach the mainland for well over a month. She and David had been literally cut off. Cormack was still nursing his bronchitis and refused to take his boat out. Four whole weeks had passed since that enchanted Valentine's – weeks in which delight had fought with worry in her mind, both jostling and tussling to get the upper hand. Delight had won, in fact – at least until the last week. She had somehow managed to stuff her fears about her daughter and guilt towards her mother under the makeshift double bed, or keep reminding herself that Bea wasn't senile nor Chris a silly child. That was the trouble, though. Chris's eighteenth birthday was approaching – official adulthood – a red-letter day, a landmark. She couldn't be away for that, had to plan a party, buy a present.

She had persuaded David to walk up to the croft with her, to inquire how Cormack was. They found him quaffing whisky, his breathing back to normal, and looking generally so robust they suspected he'd been malingering for some time. He had already arranged to fetch the pensions either that week or the next, agreed to take her with him the first day that the wind dropped. She had still not planned to leave. She would have to make the trip, of course, just so she could phone, find out how things were. But if Bea were well, and Chris preferred a quiet and simple birthday, perhaps a meal *à deux* with Martin, or a disco with a few close friends, then no point rushing home to arrange catering or guest lists. She could go back again with Cormack on his boat, enjoy a few more weeks of David and the island, return to Weybridge in time for the birthday itself.

David had gone with her on the boat, bought her a pie

and coffee in Oban to help her thaw out after the wet and blustery crossing. It was raining by the time they found a phone box. He waited outside while she dripped and shivered in the booth. Bea's voice sounded very far away, muffled in a sort of droning hum.

'I'm sorry, Mummy. I can hardly hear you. The line's absolutely terrible. Can you shout? That's better. Yes, I see, but did they *admit* they were engaged? I mean, maybe the ring was just . . .' Morna dropped her glove, swore. She was shivering as much from shock as from cold. Bea seemed so distraught, had found a diamond on a piece of string, started firing questions at her granddaughter. She was acting mother in Morna's absence and therefore felt it was her duty to know exactly what was going on. Chris had slammed out, accused Bea of snooping, interfering, threatened to run straight off with Martin there and then, write to Bristol and tell them they could stuff their place and she would rather be married anyway than slaving away at stupid languages which no one even . . .

The pips had gone mid-sentence. Morna had no more coins, and an old man was waiting to use the phone box, huddled against the sleeting rain. She found David sheltering in a doorway, clung to his arm, poured out the whole story – irrationally angry with both her mother and her daughter, even with Cormack who was pressing to get off, wouldn't give her time to phone again, sort things out long distance. There was no way she could go back with him and David – not now. All the guilt and worry she had been suppressing for the last six weeks and more, had come surging, churning up. She had never left her daughter for that long before, nor behaved so irresponsibly. Chris might have eloped, thrown away her future, turned her back on a decent education while she played Seals with David. She caught the train alone. A journey had never seemed so long and arduous – not even the rough crossing in Cormack's tacky boat made just a few hours before. That had been an adventure, exciting and exhilarating because David was beside her, pointing out the landmarks, bringing Dubhgall's words to life. Now every mile she travelled took her further from him, broke their precious bond.

'I'll come back,' she had whispered, still clinging to his hand, standing on the quay as Cormack threw the shopping in his boat, cranked the engine into life. 'As soon as I've sorted things out.'

David hadn't even kissed her. Quays were too public, he still too shy. She *hadn't* come back, had been swept into the riptides of her own world – chores and duties, sullen daughter, disapproving mother, endless arguments. The house was dirty after her long absence, the garden choked with weeds. There was a pile of mail to answer, three meals a day to cook.

David had written – an eight-page letter which combined shyness with ardour, scholarship with lust – promised to return himself, sooner than he had planned. He was missing her, a lot. She made a calendar like the ones she had made at boarding school – end of term ringed and starred in red, each slow laborious day before it crossed off at bedtime. Twenty-seven and three quarters more to go. She and David had no plans. Living on the island had been not quite real. They needed something more practical, more permanent. He was still too diffident to suggest sharing a place, shacking up together, to use her daughter's term. She would have to make the overtures herself.

'Look, David, this house is far too big. Once Chris has gone to college, I'll have either to sell it or let out rooms. Perhaps you'll need somewhere to stay yourself when you're back in London working in the libraries . . .'

No. She hadn't got it right yet. That would be too blatant, scare him off. And would David really fit in a plush suburban villa? She couldn't see him discussing brands of coffee beans or paté with the dapper little snob who ran the local delicatessen where she still had an account, or joining the Residents' Association to oppose high-density housing or some other outrage which might lower the tone of the area. And what about her mother? Bea had met David for a scant ten minutes when she introduced the two of them at Hilden Cross, way back in July. He was just a name to Bea, some highbrow scholar who had subsequently asked her daughter's help with translation work or some such. Morna had deliberately kept their relationship a secret, felt like a guilty child still, hiding sweets from Mummy. Bea might approve of David as a person – a well-spoken and well-mannered man coming from a solid Catholic background – but she would never approve of *any* man living in her daughter's house, unless he were her legal wedded husband. She had already expressed concern about Morna's mysterious absence.

'I was really worried, dear. You've always phoned before.'

'There *wasn't* a phone. I told you.'

'Yes, but you should have warned me you were racing off somewhere else. That letter from the island took ages to arrive, so all that time I had no address for you at all. I phoned Chris in America and even she seemed vague about your plans. I mean, if anything had happened . . .'

Blackmail. 'I could have died,' Bea was really saying. 'And you wouldn't have even known, left a not-quite-eighteen-year-old granddaughter to arrange the funeral.' Ridiculous. Her mother was in perfect health, apart from her arthritis. Arthritis didn't kill. She had seen her mother every single week when she was married, two or three times a week since her divorce, phoned her every other day. Bea assumed that as her right now, would expect it the rest of her life. Even her opposition to Chris's engagement sprang partly, she suspected, from fear of losing her one and only grandchild. Bea *wanted* Chris as a child, someone she could cook for, invite to stay, take away on holidays as she had done in the past. Children with fiancés weren't the same.

Morna fought her way back across the study, slipped into the dining-room. That was less crowded, the food hardly touched as yet. Bea had been cooking for a week or more, fiddly food which took patience and hard work. Morna bit into a prawn and asparagus tartlet, felt a rush of shame. She *had* neglected her mother, accepted all her help while still resenting her. It was David who had changed her, David who had made her ache to cut her ties, forge a new one.

Fortunately, the rows had all calmed down now. Father Clarke had helped, tried to talk Bea round. The priest believed in marriage, if only that it prevented fornication. 'Better to marry than to burn,' he thundered with St Paul. But it was a second minor crisis which had really solved the first – an accident at Hilden Cross, where Bea had been helping out, accompanying Madge on all her rounds of mercy. Just two days after Morna's return, Sister Ruth had slipped and broken her leg, was told she would be several weeks in hospital. The community was stunned. They were short enough of nuns, and Sister Ruth had been something of a workhorse, mopping up several full-time jobs at once. Madge and Bea between them had stepped into the breach, taken over Sister Ruth's domain. Bea had bloomed notice-ably – no longer on the sidelines doing merely trivial chores, she now had an official job – her first in seventy years. She had suddenly become important, on first-name terms with nuns and priests, displaying talents she had kept hidden all her life.

Morna had driven down one evening to pick her up when Madge was out of service, at home with a sick dog; found her mother in the office, talking on two telephones at once, working out rotas, checking mail; Joy snoozing at her feet while she hummed in the hot seat. She seemed transformed – younger, more alert. Even the way she sat or walked was different, as if her arthritis had gone into remission. She was no longer a stiff and creaky pensioner, a lonely widow living for her dog, but an administrator, organizer, working in a house which boasted its own chapel, its own resident chaplain – a Jesuit who had spent eleven years in Rome. Chris's engagement no longer loomed so large. After a full week in harness and a daily lunch with Father ('Do please call me Michael') Holdsworth sitting right beside her at the table and a Reverend Mother opposite, she not only apologized to Chris, but promised to make the wedding cake, embroider all the linen.

'I can't see Martin with daisies on his pillowcase,' Chris had grinned, relieved to find the arguments were now about where and when rather than if and should. 'How about a spanner in satin stitch, or a couple of spare wheels?'

Morna smiled to herself as she circled the buffet table, trying a spoonful of the salmon mousse in aspic, a sliver of the pâté. Someone ought to do justice to the food. She picked up Bea's ivory-handled cake knife, plunged it into the larger of the hearts. The cake needed cutting or nobody would touch it, scared to disrupt a work of art. She arranged the slices on a plate, fanning them out in a pattern, wrapped the largest in a paper serviette, took it up to Bea who was still ensconced in the sanctuary of the bedroom. She had greeted the first guests, Chris squirming with embarrassment while she asked them if they liked school and what subjects they were studying. Most of them had left school and the few who hadn't loathed it on principle. She had finally been detailed to babysit. Sarah, seventeen and unmarried, had brought her baby with her, a bald and mournful-looking infant whom everybody called Fez. Bea was giving him his bottle, rocking him to and fro in the brocaded bedroom chair.

'What's his real name, darling? I can't call him Fez.'

'I don't know. Chris never even told me Sarah was

pregnant.' Morna sat down on the bed, stared at the pale and ugly child, his face squashed and puckered up as if he were continually about to cry. Perhaps it was just as well that her own daughter was engaged. There were worse things, definitely, and although Chris was young, she wasn't actually tying the knot for another eighteen months. They had finally compromised. Chris would complete the first year of her degree course before getting married, by which time Martin would have taken his exam and could move up to Bristol to be with her. Chris would still have her grant for her two remaining years and Martin would be earning better money. They would rent the cheapest flat they could find, save all they could towards their future. That future remained vague – although exciting – included treasure-ships, world travel, instructing on underwater courses, and, one far-off day, a full-fledged diving school run by the famous team of Brett and Gordon.

'You can come and stay if you like, Mum, help out in the office. If it's somewhere like the Med., your languages will come in very handy.'

'Thanks a lot.'

Did her daughter see her as she saw Bea – someone spare without a job, who had to be kept busy, kept an eye on? They didn't know she already had a rôle – two rôles – as mistress and translator. She was glad her daughter was doing Modern Languages. That at least would be a bond between them, pull them both together when other things were drawing them apart. She could relive her own student days, be young again, in love.

Bea had winded the baby, changed his nappy. 'I really ought to be getting back,' she said, as she replaced him in his carrycot, tucked the blankets round him.

Morna stood up herself, stretched her legs. 'Sure you won't change your mind and stay the night?'

'Not with this noise, dear, if you don't mind. I'd never

sleep a wink. I'm sorry to drag you out, though. If it's a nuisance, I can . . .'

'Course not. I'd like a breath of air, to tell the truth, and I don't really think they'll miss me for half an hour. You get your coat and I'll just tell Chris we're off.'

She went downstairs again. The lights seemed lower now, the music even louder, the thump-thump of a bass guitar throbbing through the house. Chris and Martin were dancing, self-enclosed, both his hands cupped around her bottom, her arms around his neck. She squeezed her way to them, shouted above the noise. 'Just driving Grandma back. Okay?'

Chris focused on her briefly. 'Yeah, fine. Take your time.'

Stay away, Chris meant, then we can relax. Would they all break out as soon as she had gone, start an orgy, unwrap the syringes? Unlikely. She squeezed her daughter's hand. 'Love you,' she whispered.

Chris frowned, embarrassed. 'Bye, Mum.'

Morna closed the door on a tiger-roar from the vocalist, took in great gulps of silence along with the cold night air.

'When will they be leaving?' her mother asked, as they turned left by the pillar box and on to the main road.

Morna shrugged. She had been wondering that herself. If she had to stay up half the night, she wished she had David with her. Wished she had him anyway. Thank God Bea couldn't see into her mind, see the constant thoughts of David, thoughts which should be censored – David naked, David fumbling with her buttons, David blushing when the sofa bed came apart and beached him in full thrust. She kept the images simmering, wove a counterpoint above them more suited to her mother – dogs, babies, the necessity (or otherwise) of pink hair on either sex.

'Thank you, dear,' said Bea, as Morna pulled up outside her close-trimmed beech hedge. 'If you'd like to come and fetch me in the morning, I'll help with the clearing up.'

'Don't worry. Emma's staying the night. She'll help me – and Chris and Martin of course.' Morna followed her mother up the path. 'I'll come in for a moment, see you into bed.'

'No, really, dear, you ought to go straight back. You shouldn't leave them on their own. And what about the baby?'

'His mother's there.'

'Yes, and not been up to see him once.'

'Only because we told her he was in expert hands.'

Bea smiled, mollified. 'All right. Come on in. I'll make you an Ovaltine. Actually, I wanted to talk to you and I suppose now's as good a time as any.'

Morna tensed. Had Chris been rambling to her Grandma about David, or Bea jumped to her own conclusions? Was she about to get a wigging, a dressing-down? She followed her mother into the chilly sitting room, left her coat on, perched on the edge of a chair. 'Well?'

'It's about the . . . er . . . future.'

Morna eased her left shoe off where it was rubbing at the heel. The word future was better left alone. Her own future lay with David – that she knew – but she wasn't sure if *he* knew. Despite his ardent letter, he was too scared, too solitary, too unconventional for formal commitments, vows.

Bea settled back with her Ovaltine and Joy. 'I've been thinking, dear. I can't keep up this house for ever. Already it's a strain to keep it clean and . . .'

Morna kicked the shoe off, massaged her foot. She had been dreading this. Whether Bea moved in with her or she with Bea, both would outlaw David. It was *him* she wanted as lodger and companion, not her mother. Bea had always been a problem hanging over her head. What happened when she got too old to manage, couldn't run her own place?

'I love my home, of course,' Bea was saying as she sipped her drink. 'But I've been lonely here, you know.'

'Yes, I do know.' Morna glanced at the photos of herself in christening gown, herself in frilly tutu, herself in fancy dress – all costumes courtesy of Bea. Lear was right. All children were ungrateful – took half their parents' lives and then begrudged a few years of their own. But she didn't *have* a few years. David was here right now. If she said 'wait' or 'not just yet' or 'I've got to put my mother first', he might slip away, elude her.

'So I thought I'd make a change. Well, it's only an idea as yet, but if my Job goes well . . .' Bea paused, as she always did when she mentioned her new rôle, gave the capital J its due solemnity. 'I might be able to move in permanently.'

'What d'you mean?'

'Well, live in the retreat house as a resident.'

'But I thought it was a . . . convent.'

'It is, but the number of vocations has dropped so sharply recently, that they're taking in lay people. You can actually join the community without taking vows – rather like a Third Order. I wouldn't do that myself. Well, maybe later if . . . when . . . That's quite a step, you realize – almost like being a nun yourself, in some ways, and I'm not ready for that – nowhere near. I've got a long way to go, in fact, a long long way.' She broke off.

Morna noticed her mother's hand gripping the chair too tightly, the sudden look of fear. What was wrong? She tried to lighten the mood. 'So I don't call you Mother Mary Beatrice yet?'

'No. No. No.' Bea rapped out the noes with a sort of desperation, slumped back in her chair. 'Hope,' she said, almost to herself, taking off her glasses and polishing them up. 'That's the vital thing, you know.' Her voice was softer now, barely audible. 'More important than charity – or even faith.'

'That's because you've *got* faith. You just take it for granted, as a gift.'

'Oh, no, I don't, Morna. You know nothing at all about it.'

Morna put her cup down. Bea had sounded peevish, almost fierce. Her mood had changed entirely. Were the nuns overworking her, putting her under strain? She reached forward, touched her mother's arm. 'You mustn't let them treat you like a slave.'

Bea shook her head impatiently. 'You don't understand. It's nothing like that at all. I *love* the work.' Joy shifted on her lap, turned round suddenly and licked her mistress's face. Bea smiled, relaxed a little. 'Anyway, I can probably stay free in return for my help. Mother Michael's already suggested the idea and I must admit it would be a lot more convenient than all those journeys back and forth and having to rely on Madge and . . .'

'I thought you liked Madge?'

'Oh, I *do*, dear – I love her – but she's got an oar in lots of other things besides just Hilden Cross. She's been taking me there some mornings and driving straight off somewhere else. That's very sweet of her, but I can't rely on it. I mean, it's not fair, is it? And then Charlie's ill and . . .'

'Who?'

'Charlie, her dog, the elder one. He's going blind, poor darling, so she's not as free as she used to be. But apart from all that, there's a lot to be said for actually living in the place. I mean, all my meals provided, and no long tramp to Mass on Sundays in the cold and wet, and the company, of course.'

Morna stared down at the carpet. All the time she had been away, in California as well as on the island, Bea had been fighting loneliness, cooking meals for one, struggling through rain and snow with no daughter to give her lifts or do her shopping. Bea had no David, had only enjoyed a man in her life for a few short years way back in her twenties. She had been living since then for her daughter and her granddaughter. Now the one was getting married and the other planning to escape. Here was escape made easy, her mother off her hands, fed and occupied. She should have felt relief. She *did* feel relief, nudging and hymning underneath the guilt. She took a sip of Ovaltine. Bea had made it with the top of the milk, given her the best bone china cup. Tiny things which counted. Could she really let Bea go, see her own mother become an unpaid drudge, living in an institution, giving up her property, her privacy?

'But supposing you don't like it?' Morna tried to keep her voice as flat as possible, suppress any hint or spark of the relief.

'Of course I shall. I'm enjoying it now.'

'Yes, but you're only there part-time and with your own home to return to in the evenings. I mean, you're used to being on your own. It might be noisy in a community.'

'Noisy? It's utterly peaceful. It's a holy place, if you know what I mean.'

Morna didn't answer. Her own memories of the retreat house were rather different. And yet she had first met David there and that made it holy, in a way. If Bea were off her hands, she could sell her own house, buy something smaller, simpler, without Neil's imprint on it, where David would fit in.

'Someone's always praying at every moment of every day. That makes a difference. You can . . . feel it, in the atmosphere. I *need* prayers, Morna.'

'Don't we all?' Morna sank back in her chair. If her pure and pious mother needed prayers, what hope was there for her – a pagan and a fornicator? She grinned, remembering David's take-off of the abbot at his school, smacking his lips over words like fornication, while damning any boy who dared so much as think about it. She was free to be with David now, free to fornicate. She kicked her other shoe off, wiggled both her feet. Freedom felt intoxicating.

'What about dogs?' she asked, trying to return to earth. She couldn't see Joy in a convent. Her mother's dog was neither meek, chaste, abstemious, nor community-minded.

'They don't encourage them, but I've been taking Joy with me every time I go, so the nuns get used to her, and Father Clarke's promised to speak to Reverend Mother. He's going to say I've had her thirteen years and she's very well behaved.'

Joy woke up when she heard her name, yapped, scratched her underparts, pawed at the upholstery. Bea tipped the last of the Ovaltine into her saucer, held it on her knee for Joy to lap.

'Anyway, there's something else. I want to do a bit for Chris. After all, she *is* my only grandchild. If I sell this house, I could give her and Martin part of the proceeds, help them buy their own place, get them off to a decent start instead of camping in some squalid bedsit or student hostel or whatever it is they're planning.'

Morna got up, removed the empty saucer, squeezed her mother's hand. Bea had her priorities right – giving thought to where Chris and Martin would live, instead of dreaming up idyllic little love nests for herself. The hand was cold, twisted with arthritis, the blue veins raised and swollen. She could see it, suddenly, clasped in her father's hand at the Nuptial Mass, smooth and straight and flawless then; a young girl's hand emerging from its sleeve of ivory satin. She wanted to weep for the change in it – the now marked and freckled skin, the bony wrist, the wedding-ring worn thin as if it had failed and sickened after the bereavement. Yet what was the use of empty sentiment? It was pure hypocrisy if she didn't back it up with some real action, say 'Don't go. Move in with me. I'll do the cooking, provide the company, drive you where you want.'

The words refused to come. She could have said them to David, but not to her own mother. And if she tried to please them both, neither would be happy. She was thinking too much of David, far too much. He had become like one of those bouncy Russian dolls with rounded weighted bottoms instead of legs, which bobbed up again in her mind however many times she knocked him down. Except David had legs, long amazing legs which . . . Her mother was speaking still. Morna forced herself to concentrate.

'I'll have to keep enough to pay my way – for when I'm older, I mean, and not able to help out, but their rates are very reasonable. They don't aim to make a profit, you see, just keep out of debt. I shouldn't think they'd mind a dog, would you? Joy's no trouble, after all.'

Morna stared down at the snuffling, twitching dog, greying at the muzzle, growing old with Bea. 'I think I'd better talk to Reverend Mother, check there'll be no problems – not just with Joy – all round.' The dutiful daughter, still with an eye on her own interest, wanting to be certain her mother was fully off her hands, with no chance of a return. She leaned down and hugged her mother, a Judas hug. Bea felt slighter than she had before, or was that only compared with David's bulk? It seemed suddenly unfair that the two of them should be competing for her loyalties. How could David not win with all his strengths?

Yet Bea had brought her up, alone, with no husband, no support; had taken over Chris when she was shocked by the divorce, had put her always first. Even now, she was probably planning to live at Hilden Cross only to release some money for her granddaughter, avoid being a nuisance to her daughter. When Sister Ruth returned from hospital, would they even need Bea any more? She might become a nuisance, an embarrassment, someone with no purpose who had now also lost her home. Bea's house had always been important to her, something chosen by her husband, which bore his stamp, perpetuated his memory. She had refused to move when she was widowed, keeping up the place almost as a shrine to him. Yet now she was ready to let it go – for Chris's sake.

Morna's palms were clammy suddenly. She wiped them on her skirt. Something sharp and jagged seemed to be pressing on her larynx. She tried to clear her throat, make her voice work. 'Y . . . You could always live with me, you know. I mean, I'd . . . like that, Mummy. It would be company for both of us and . . .' The words tailed off, but at least she had got them out.

Bea was silent, no emotion whatsoever showing on her face. Morna hardly dared to look at her. One simple 'yes' and she would have to give up David. With another man, a different sort of mother, she might have invited both of them to share her life and home, but with Bea and David it simply wouldn't work. She couldn't see David ploughing through his Sulpicius Severus or Acta Silvestri with her mother's constant chattering, Joy's barking, Chris and Martin's radios competing with each other. And how could she ever creep into his bed with Bea sleeping just along the passage?

She pulled at a button on her suit, twisted it round and round, locked her hands together to stop them fidgeting. Bea had still said nothing. 'M . . . Mummy, did you hear?'

'Yes, I did, dear. I'm very touched, very touched indeed that you should want me.' Bea removed her glasses, rubbed them up, put them back again. 'But no. You've got your own life.'

'There's . . . room in it for you, though.'

'I know. That's nice. That's very nice, Morna, darling. But I'm enjoying it at Hilden Cross, you see. I feel I can be . . . useful there. I've already had some really lovely letters from people who've noticed the improvements. Do you realize, the cook they had was never really trained?'

Morna thought back to the eggless batter pudding, the synthetic cream. 'It doesn't surprise me, no.'

'It wasn't her fault, poor dear. She was an elderly nun who somehow got drafted to the kitchen because there was no one else. I've been giving her a hand myself and now I've found this girl who comes in from the village. She's been wasted all these months, just peeling vegetables and scouring pans. But she's a natural cook with a marvellous knack for pastry, so with a bit of swapping round of jobs, we've managed to . . .'

Morna noted the 'we', a regal 'we' – Bea and Reverend Mother, Bea and Father Holdsworth. Well – it had done her mother good, made her feel important, maybe even improved the batter pudding. Best of all, it spelled her own release – at least for a year or two. She could always review the situation later, when her mother was older and might need her more, but for the moment she had her all-important respite – now – when she craved for it and when David was ardent and available. She drained her Ovaltine, relished the sweet and frothy taste of freedom.

Bea got up to take her cup. 'I don't want to rush you, dear, but shouldn't you be getting back? I'm worried about that babe. No one'll even hear him with all that racket.'

Fez was dead to the world when Morna returned, lulled to sleep by hard rock. The whole party had relaxed – girls with their shoes off, the lights turned low, the buffet table a wreckage of crumbs and crumpled serviettes. Morna checked that there were no crises before creeping back upstairs, feeling still more of an intruder. She sat on the bed, poured herself a glass of wine. She had commandeered one of the bottles from the party – a sparkling white from Waitrose – cheap, but full of fizz. She needed bubbles to celebrate. She wasn't like her daughter, content with a low-key party with no centre to it, no real celebration, no announcement of the engagement, champagne toast. She wished she could make her own announcement. 'David and

I are . . .' What, though? Not engaged, not even formally committed to each other. Yet their bond was real and solid, went right back to their childhood – shared Faith, shared restrictions.

She picked up her book, a Life of St Cuthbert which David had recommended as a contrast to St Abban, tried to concentrate. She was working through his reading list – scholarly studies on the date-of-Easter controversy, or the Desert Fathers' influence on Celtic monasticism. None of it was easy, especially with music pounding through the floor, the words of the lyric tangling with the print – hot uncensored words. She lay back on the pillows, let her hand stray towards her breasts. 'Shameless', David was saying. She liked the word, especially compared with Neil's censorious 'frigid'. David had changed her simply by being shy and inexperienced himself. She had remained the teacher, playing Neil's old rôle. Neil had become an invisible third party in their bed, exciting her in memory as he never had in fact. Things she had objected to with him, she had been trying out with David and enjoying. Was it just perversity, or because everything felt different – not better – often worse from the point of view of mere technique, but somehow sacred, special? For David, she was never just a body or a hole, as she had so often seemed to Neil, but an individual person with a soul as well as genitals. Sometimes David treated her as if her soul were actually located between her legs, worshipped her like a madonna even while profaning her. It was hard to describe. He made love to the whole of her with the whole of himself and that included mind, brain, spirit and . . . and . . . There was still no word for what Neil had called Big Sam. She had been too shy to christen it, and David himself spent longer railing against its inadequacies than rewarding it with pet names. They needed more time. He was still nervous of her, frightened of himself, too used to being alone and womanless.

528

Morna could feel her nipples hard. The chaperone and babysitter had no business to be exciting herself, especially when her charge had started whimpering. She got up and checked his nappy, settled him more comfortably. Two months ago she would have censored Sarah for her casual careless pregnancy, used words like irresponsible. Now such words applied to her as well. The first time she had gone to bed with David, she hadn't even thought of taking precautions. Her mind was too full of other fears. He had brought the subject up himself the following morning, when he woke beside her and found Big David big.

'It's . . . er . . . okay,' she had said, as embarrassed now as he was. 'It's what Holy Mother Church used to call the safe period – still does, I suppose, unless you've got one of those progressive parish priests who say "follow your own conscience" and really mean "take the Pill".'

'You're . . . not on it, I suppose – the Pill, I mean?'

'No. Why should I be?'

He still assumed she was a sort of scarlet woman. It both annoyed her and excited her. Strange how you fulfilled other people's expectations, became what they decided. With Neil she had dwindled into a boring married woman; with David she was avid mistress. When he proved clumsy and inept, she truly didn't mind, not because she was noble or ignored her own let-down or frustration, but because it enhanced her own position, made her the one without the problems. David was sharp enough to see that. What he didn't see was that it also made him vulnerable, and lovable, less threatening than Neil ever had been. David left her to take the decisions and the initiative, in contraception as well as in bed. That wasn't easy when the nearest chemist shop or clinic was a storm-tossed sea away.

'Are we still . . . er . . . safe?' he had asked a few days later, throwing back the cover on their sofa bed.

'No, we're not. Getting rather dangerous, in fact.'

They had decided on a week or two of celibacy, making jokes about how St Abban would have approved, amused to realize they were following the Church's teaching not through conviction, but through circumstance. Morna thought back to the fertility rites of Lupercalia – eggs, rabbits, lecherous Pan – and there they were sleeping in separate beds again in fear of that fertility. After seven days, David crept upstairs to her room.

'It *must* be safe now.'

'Not quite. Just a few more days.'

'I feel pretty dangerous myself. Which do you think is worse in the eyes of the Church, rape or abortion?'

'Abortion, no question.'

'What if it's both, though?'

'It won't be. I'm going to banish you, this instant – up to your neck in icy water and then a flagellation with prickly gorse twigs as soon as you get out.'

David groaned. 'I know how Abban felt now.'

The abstinence had been like an exotic game – increasing the excitement, creating a tension which made the mere touch of a hand both dangerous and provocative. The first day she was safe again, David woke her at five o'clock in the morning, came two minutes later, inside her – just – kept apologizing, did the same thing in the evening. Half those kids downstairs were probably more experienced than he was, would scoff at his brief and artless efforts, mock their slapdash and old-fashioned contraception when they were all coolly on the Pill, their rough and ready bed when they were saving for whole bedroom suites. It would be nice to lie with David in a king-size bed with freshly laundered sheets, proper bedclothes, bedside lamps instead of just a torch, central heating set at 75°. She had to admit she did enjoy her comforts, now she had them back.

She got up to check the baby again, refill her glass of wine. Fez was sleeping now, making little snuffling noises similar to Joy's. If David stayed around, he would become a sort of grandparent when Chris and Martin had children of their own. She didn't want that rôle for him, even less so for herself. She had to grow younger, not older, so she was more of a match for him. Forty-one already sounded ancient compared with his just thirty-six. She had better *stay* at forty-one until he had caught up with her, then they'd both go backwards.

The phone shrilled across her thoughts. Late for anyone to ring, unless it were a guest who'd been delayed at another party or the pub, checking if it were still all right to come. She picked it up before it woke the baby, winced at the raucous rendering of 'Happy Birthday to You' hollered down the line in a Californian accent – Neil and Bunny in duet, with Dean providing a backing of excited whoops and giggles. She waited for a pause, cut in.

'It's not Chris, it's Morna. I'll give her a shout and you'd better start again. How are you all?'

A trio of 'fine's, Bunny's loudest. 'Sorry, hon, we didn't wake you, did we? It's only afternoon out here. We're all in our bikinis.'

'*I'm* not,' Dean objected.

Bunny's giggles sounded newly minted. 'Well, Morna, hon, it must be really great to have your little girl grown up. Congratulations!'

'Thanks.' Morna flexed her toes. Two sets of congratulations in the space of just two hours. She was aware of Neil listening in, yet saying nothing, Dean on a third extension, maybe some friend or house guest on the last remaining phone. It made it difficult to say anything at all. She still felt embarrassed by her escape from California, the way she had repaid their hospitality by bolting blindly home. Bunny had already written her two anxious puzzled letters which had been waiting with her pile of other mail when she returned home from the island. Was Morna hon okay? Had the

French job turned out fine? She had also sent a valentine – a lavish one in the shape of an old-fashioned wicker flower basket which opened up to reveal a heart in real red satin and said 'Sharing my heart with a friend'. Dean had sent her one, too, enclosed in the same envelope – a home-made card which showed a matchstick man and woman holding hands, with a purple fire engine zooming up behind them. Not a word from Neil, though.

'N . . . Neil . . . ?' she said now.

'Hi, there!'

'H . . . How are you?'

'Fine. Just rang to say "Hi" to the Birthday Girl. If you'd like to go and fetch her, and tell her her Dad's got a really exciting present on its way and . . .'

'Yes . . . yes, of course. Hold on.' Morna put the phone down, walked stiffly down the stairs, tried to tell herself that he wasn't freezing her off, that long-distance calls cost money, that it was Chris's birthday, not her own.

'Chris! Chris – quickly, darling. It's your father on the phone. Hurry now.'

Chris gave a shriek of triumph, leapt up from the sofa, grabbed the phone in the hall. Morna watched her face, a mixture of excitement and embarrassment, pleasure and surprise. They must be singing 'Happy Birthday', since Chris was saying nothing, just grinning foolishly. Morna toiled back to the bedroom to replace the receiver there, listened in for a moment, feeling both guilty and excluded from the whole happy bubbly chat show – banter with Bunny, silly jokes with Dean, Chris's adoring replies to her father's platitudes. Why should she care? How could Neil upset her when she had seen through him in America, realized she was mourning an empty shell? She had David now, in any case, a whole new life ahead of her. The problem was the new life hadn't started yet – not really. She was still trapped in the old one, still living in Neil's home, still dependent on him. If she left to live with David, she would no longer be cushioned by Neil's largesse. Could she really cope with all the bills herself? David's meagre research grant would hardly pay a mortgage. Those few brief words with her ex-husband had brought back the spectre of divorce. About one in three marriages ended in the courts now, more still in America, where almost half broke down. Terrible to have another failure, her idyllic new relationship with David coming to grief over things like rents and rates.

She forced herself to go downstairs again. She would start the clearing up, wash the dirty glasses. Better to keep busy than give way to stupid fears. She dodged into the kitchen, trying to avoid the entwined and dancing couples. A boy and girl who had been sitting on the table slipped down and slunk away at her approach. It was as if she were infectious, had a disease called adulthood, which was all too catching. Up to the fourth form, mothers had been welcome – solid useful people who made chocolate cake or drove you to the riding stables and always had money and clean hankies in their handbag. Now they were superfluous, embarrassing.

All the work-tops were piled with dirty plates. Morna stacked the dishwasher full to overflowing, switched it on. She would do the glasses by hand. She had come to enjoy the ritual of washing-up, at least when David shared it. It had become their substitute for port or brandy after dinner. They talked over the dishes, spun them out, took turns to wash or wipe like a married couple. It *had* been like a marriage – a happy marriage – so why should . . . ?

'Mum!' Chris burst into the kitchen, grabbed her round the waist. 'We got cut off. Daddy was just telling me how he'd bought this really fantastic camera for my birthday, and then the line went dead. It's a German one, he said, with a telephoto lens and everything. He ordered it from Harrods, so it's coming direct. I don't know when, though.

533

I didn't have a chance to ask – or even thank him. Can I ring him back?'

'No, better not.' Morna ran some water in the sink. 'He'll be trying us and only get the engaged tone. He's bound to phone again.'

Chris perched on the kitchen stool, swung her legs. 'Gosh! I'm so chuffed he remembered. When there wasn't even a card this morning, I thought it might have slipped his mind. You know how busy he gets with golf and meetings and everything.'

Morna said nothing. Why the hell *shouldn't* Neil remember? His only daughter's eighteenth birthday was surely as important as a round of golf or some so-called creative meeting to work out a headline for a dog-food or detergent.

Chris scooped a swirl of icing off a plate, licked her fingers. 'He said he's missing me a lot. They *all* are. They want me to go back for another visit – maybe in a year or two.'

'Yes. Well, you must.' Morna tried to sound less grudging. Stupid to let one three-minute phone call spoil the party for her. She was probably just tired. She had been up at dawn, cleaning the whole house, doing last-minute party shopping, helping Bea with the food. Bea . . . Morna put her dish-mop down, slumped against the sink. Wasn't that the crux? Bea had given her her freedom and unconsciously she feared it. She longed for David, yet was terrified of any formal tie. Ties could break, commitment end in failure.

She squirted Fairy Liquid into the water, frothed it up with her hands. David had always used too much, said he liked the bubbles. It was the only thing he didn't ration – was almost reckless with it – sculpting the foam into shapes and towers, playing like a child. She copied him now, trying to make a man as he had fashioned a woman once, with curves – christened it Morna, pretended to be cross when it capsized, then turned round and kissed its more substantial

534

namesake. By the time the kiss had finished, his water had gone cold.

Things had been good between them, genuinely good. Why not simply trust? After all, they had already proved that they didn't have the problems which had divided her and Neil. Neil had been always absent, overworking, yet resenting her own work, making her feel guilty if she tried to be a linguist as well as wife; whereas David respected and encouraged her intelligence, shared his work with her, welcomed all her help. Neil's ambition had always been too large – material ambition which stressed status and possessions. Her simpler life with David was less stressful, more fulfilling. Most important, she didn't feel a sexual failure, sore and shagged, oppressed. She was the one who had outlawed words like failure, poured scorn on all the sex books. It had been only fake bravado when she said it first, a way to comfort David. Now she meant it. Why should everybody conform to some mythical standard set by the examiners, as if sex were an academic subject, the Common Entrance to Adulthood, the touchstone of existence, the standard by which everyone was judged? If David came too quickly, he was sick, disturbed, in need of therapy. If she remained nervous about oral sex, she was immature, inadequate. According to the books. Yet she had never felt less sick lying close to David in their lurching sofa bed. There were other things besides anatomy or superbly functioning apparatus. Things like closeness, trust, or their crazy games where they hymned each other in Latin or made love as seraphim. That wasn't totally a joke. There *was* some spiritual dimension which she could hardly analyse. David believed passionately in souls, but called them an endangered species like osprey or the blue whale. The twentieth century had allowed souls to waste away, devoting its attention to the body, the bit between the legs. She wasn't sure if she could define the word soul at all. All she knew was that when she was with David, the pat phrase 'body and soul' suddenly had meaning.

She let the hot tap run, luxuriating in water which ran boiling from the tank rather than being coaxed via a kettle from a slow and moody range. It still seemed strange to have instant light and heat. Her first week back, she'd had to stop herself pouncing on stray sticks, collecting scraps of firewood. She pushed the curtain back, peered out – a grudging moon in a dark and windy night. Already April, yet the air was cold and sharp. There would be gales around the island, rattling David's windows. Would he be looking out himself, missing her, her breasts?

'Mrs Gordon . . .'

She swung round. Chris had wandered off again, but someone else was standing at the door, a girl she hardly knew, a friend of a friend of Martin's, with long mousy hair and a camouflage of freckles. 'Sorry, but I've smashed a glass.'

'Don't worry.' Morna dried her hands, went to fetch a dustpan. 'I expected to lose one or two.'

'There's red wine on the carpet, though.'

'Doesn't matter. We'll squirt some soda water on it. That's meant to stop it staining.'

She followed the girl into the study. The wine had stained already, a dark patch on the pale carpet. She felt a sudden irritation. It *did* matter. The mark was right bang in the centre of the room, would still show when they pushed the furniture back. The girl had tried to rub it, made it worse, damaged the pile. Easy for David to shrug off spills in an old and shoddy cottage where stains hardly noticed against the general squalor, but a top-grade Wilton carpet, the newest and most expensive in the house, which she and Neil had bought a year before he left . . .

Hypocrite. She had just been extolling the simple life, inveighing against Neil's materialism. She was a materialist

536

herself, had helped Neil choose that carpet, trudged from exclusive store to exclusive store, comparing quality and price. It hadn't been mere service to her husband, submission to his taste. She herself had cared about her home, spent time and effort touring showrooms, planning colour schemes, insisting always on high standards. Only now did she realize that she had more in common with Neil than she had ever dared admit, even to herself. She had been running him down, trashing their years together, years she had been indulged by him, swaddled in his luxury, taking things for granted she would probably miss if she had to give them up too long.

She stared down at the stain, felt it smudging her own self, that soul which David valued. Did she really have a soul, or was she more interested in maintaining bourgeois standards, keeping an elegant home? She had berated Neil for conserving the house as a sort of monument, but wasn't she as bad? She might be less concerned with status, more with comfort and security, but both still tied her to Neil's values. On the island, she had revelled in the spartan life, where nothing was easy, let alone luxurious. Now she was less sure. Easy to play ascetic for a month or two, when she had a warm and cosy bolt hole to run back to. But supposing David wanted to live that way for ever, not on an island, but in some run-down place which to him was just a shelter or a shell, but to her was home, one she craved to polish and transform, fill with Neil-like trophies. How could it work with David, when she and he were so different in their lifestyles, expectations? Wouldn't they resent each other – he regard her as acquisitive, she depressed by the squalor he called austerity? She had used the word 'play' – in bed and out of it. Had the whole thing been a game, something temporary and childish which couldn't last beyond a few short weeks?

She trailed back to the kitchen to fetch a newspaper,

spread Friday's *Times* across the stain. The freckled girl was still hovering in the study muttering apologies. Morna edged her out of the way. 'It's all right – really. I'll take care of it.'

The other guests, sensing her annoyance, had already disappeared – slipped into the hall or joined the dancing couples in the sitting room. Morna picked up the fragments of glass, doused the wine with another squirt of soda water. The phone was shrilling again.

'Chris!' she shouted through the open door. 'That'll be your father ringing back. Take it in my bedroom, will you?' She didn't want to overhear another round of whoopee, feel excluded again, childishly resentful. She relaxed as the phone stopped ringing, mopped gingerly at the stain.

Chris came padding back, breathless from the stairs. 'Quick, Mum, it's for you.'

'Oh, no . . .' Morna crumpled up her cleaning-rag, sat back on her heels. She couldn't face Neil again, and why should he want her, anyway, when he had been so cool the first time? 'Look, tell him I'm . . . tied up – er . . . dealing with a breakage.'

'What d'you mean "him"? It's a her – some female who asked for Miss Gordon. I told her that was *me*, but then she said she wanted Morna Gordon. She sounded rather odd, Mum – sort of all bunged up as if she had a cold.'

'Didn't you get her name?'

'She wouldn't give it – said you wouldn't know her anyway. Look, if you just pick up that phone there, you'll solve the mystery.' Chris went to fetch the phone herself, passed it to her mother. '*I'll* deal with the carpet.'

'No, leave it, darling. You'll only make it worse.' Morna remained squatting on her heels, put the receiver to her ear. 'Hallo, Morna Gordon here. Who's speaking, please? I beg your pardon. Who? I'm afraid I don't quite . . . Oh, I see. You mean David's . . . ? H . . . Hallo, Mrs Anthony.'

She clutched at the chair-leg for support. It *couldn't* be

David's mother – not with that flat provincial accent, the mistakes of grammar. She had always imagined Mrs Anthony as upper class, refined; kindly, yes, a good provider, but something of a snob, the sort of person who would censure anyone who didn't treat the language with as much respect as David did himself. And why in God's name was she phoning – and so late? As far as she knew, Mrs Anthony was unaware of her existence. David, like herself, was forced to be cagey when it came to the opposite sex. He had admitted that his mother was exceptionally strait-laced. He would never air the fact he had a mistress, let alone divulge her name and phone number. Morna tried to concentrate, block out the burst of music from the hall. 'I'm sorry, I didn't quite hear what . . . You . . . you found my *suitcase*?'

Morna could feel the blush burning in her cheeks, creeping down her neck. So David's mother had come snooping to the island, impounding his possessions, checking up on him. She *had* left her suitcase there, had travelled to Oban to make her phone call with only her handbag and her waterproofs, still hoping to return to David's cottage. She hadn't packed on purpose, couldn't face the fact she might actually be leaving. And now David's prissy mother must have come across her things, pounced on make-up, frilly pants and bras – damning evidence that some shameless female was undermining her son's precious Catholic chastity.

'Yes, I . . . er . . . do know David – slightly. I'm just a . . . colleague. I did a bit of work for him, translation work. I . . . had to take him a lot of books and stuff – things he needed for his own book. I . . . er . . . brought them in a suitcase and . . . left it there for him – easier then for him to pack them up and . . .' Pathetic. She sounded as unconvincing as Chris had done at ten, lying about the strawberries she hadn't stolen from the next-door neighbour's garden when her whole mouth was stained red. She would hardly bring books to David from five hundred miles away and not stay a night or two at least. And what about those frilly pants? Hell, though, why should she defend herself? David was a grown man in his thirties. Was he still forbidden girlfriends, still answerable to his mother? Mrs Anthony sounded near-hysterical. She knew the type – those narrow Catholic females, married, but still old maids, who regarded bodies with a squeamish distaste, refusing even to acknowledge the bits below the waist, and who were obsessively determined that any child of theirs be kept pure for God and Mother. So what else had she found? Contraceptives? They had never used them. Dirty magazines? Unthinkable with David. Love letters? The only one which fitted that description was safe in her drawer upstairs.

'Yes, I understand. Y . . . You got my address from the label on the case – and then phoned directory inquiries.' Mrs Anthony had already said that twice. She kept repeating things, then breaking off mid-sentence. Half her words were lost, in any case, swamped by an ancient record of the Beatles. Morna shifted the receiver to the other hand. 'Could you talk a little louder. It's difficult to hear. There's a party going on and . . .' Why didn't she stand up to David's mother, refuse to be terrorized, instead of blushing and prevaricating as if she'd been hauled up in front of Reverend Mother herself? The problem was people were listening in. One or two guests had drifted back to the study and Chris was still hanging around, obviously intrigued. Morna covered the mouthpiece for a moment, gestured to her daughter. 'Chris, will you go and turn that record down, and shut the door while you're about it, please.'

Morna waited till she had gone, took a deep breath in, tried to steady her voice. 'Now look here, Mrs Anthony. I don't want to be unpleasant, but . . .' She broke off. David's mother had interrupted her, suddenly cut short all her blathering and blurted something out. Morna swallowed, steadied herself against the chair. The words made no sense.

She couldn't have heard them right. That music was distorting everything. No. Chris had turned it off. There wasn't any music. Only silence, shrieking silence. She tried to find her own voice. 'I'm s . . . sorry, Mrs Anthony. I . . . I didn't quite catch . . .'

The same words repeated, though less coherently, broken up with sobs. 'No,' Morna whispered. 'Don't say that. Please don't say that.'

No good. She couldn't stop the words. Wild words flooding out now, disgusting shameful details – things she didn't want to hear. 'Stop,' she shouted. 'I don't believe you. You made the whole thing up. You're a liar. You're a *liar*, do you hear?'

Morna sank back on the carpet, stared down at *The Times* spread out on the floor. Sweat was beading on her forehead, bowels and stomach churning. '*Minister resigns*,' she read. '*Less beef on British menus*'. She turned the page, hand trembling. '*Record price for painting*', '*Prison plan delayed*'. It couldn't be true, it couldn't. It would be in the paper otherwise, splashed on the front page, columns and weeping columns of it, blurred and bleeding photographs, headlines, horror stories. She scrabbled through the pages, ripping one or two, fingers clumsy with shock. Arts news, foreign news, '*Favourite falls at Cheltenham*'. Nothing. Nothing else. It was all a lie, a lie. So why did she feel so sick? She clutched at her stomach, dizzy, out of breath, as if she had run round and round, round and round, like a dazed rat on a treadmill.

'Are you okay, Mrs Gordon?' Someone squatting down beside her. She didn't answer. Impossible to speak.

'Hey! You've cut your finger. Careful now, there's still a bit of glass around. I'd better get a Band Aid. You've gone quite white.'

White. Morna watched the scarlet blood trickle onto the paper, obliterate the words. All words lied, were never what they seemed. Strange how a tiny cut could hurt so much, make you feel nauseous and faint. A tall fair girl had gone to find Elastoplast – and Chris. She could hear music, laughter, voices, all mixed up and booming like the sea, yet somewhere far beyond her. Two scuffed suede boots were tracking across the carpet, closing in on her, grey suede boots with buttons, her daughter's boots. Her daughter's shadow blocking out the light.

'What happened, Mum? Are you all right?'

'Y . . . Yes. Fine.' Mustn't spoil a birthday. No, it couldn't be a birthday, not today. She must have got confused again.

'Who was that weird woman on the phone?'

'Oh, just some . . .' Who? She wasn't sure herself now. David's mother? No. Impossible. David was . . .

'Are you sure you're okay, Mum? You look quite shaken up. If it's a deep cut, you ought to go and bathe it.'

Bathe. Water. Morna shuddered suddenly. Water drowned.

'I'll go and get some water, shall I – put some disinfectant in?'

'No.' It came out as a shout. Morna covered her mouth with her hand, didn't trust it. If she wasn't careful, it might scream or cry, betray her.

'Well, at least lie down and rest a bit. Come on, I'll take you up to bed.'

Morna let herself be led away. Safer to lie down. She couldn't fall, then. Quieter in the bedroom, away from all the uproar. She leant on her daughter's arm. Old now, a grandmother already, shambling, tripping on the stairs, being taken to a rest-home. Two girls now, one chopping off a length of sticking plaster.

'It's not deep, actually. Only a tiny nick.'

They didn't know. Too young to understand. It was very deep, the sea, deep enough to drown.

'Will you be okay?' That was Chris, aching to return to Martin. She had been the same, panting for her man, punished for it now.

'Y . . . Yes, of course. Just put out the light, would you. I think I'll close my eyes for a moment.'

'You do that, Mum. We'll be fine – honestly. You don't have to stay up.'

Morna listened to the footsteps retreating down the stairs. Darkness now. Real darkness. One she could never switch off. It could be just a hoax, though. People made joke calls. Little boys, cruel tricksters. The police would have phoned her, wouldn't they, got in touch, asked questions? Death didn't happen in that casual way, sneak up on you at parties, mixed up with stained carpets, broken glass. Death was dignified, momentous. Requiems and lilies. The word was wrong itself. Too mild, too puny. No sting in it, no horror. It wasn't death – not strictly. Drowning was different, two syllables instead of one. Eight letters. Eight hours his body in the water. Or longer still? Eight days?

Ten years ago, Chris's tortoise had drowned in the garden pond. Neil had fished it out, stiff and bloated, eyes staring, a smear of dried-on blood congealed around its mouth. A human body would look worse. No shell to conceal the middle parts. The sea was crueller than a garden pond, could maim a body, strip an arm or leg off, dash it against rocks. She could see the Russian doll again, still bobbing up and down, but on the waves now, floating face-downwards, tossed by the pitiless tide.

She tried to struggle up. What was she doing, lying useless on her bed? She had to help him, pull him out. It might not be too late. Doctors could be wrong, mistake a coma for death. When had the whole thing happened? Hours ago? Weeks ago? Had David been dead all the time she had been remembering him alive, sleeping with a corpse in the double bed of her mind? She could feel his hands clammy on her body, cold against her breasts. No. Impossible. He wasn't dead at all. Couldn't be. You didn't think of someone all month, all day, miss them, fantasize, then have them die on you. She would have known. Something would have warned her, stopped her planning and exulting. Unless it was a punishment. *Because* she had planned, fate had paid her back. This was the reprisal for abandoning her mother, shrugging off her daughter so she would be free to live her own life.

She slumped back on the bed, groped out her hands. Nothing there. Only empty space. Strange when she could feel blackness pressing down on top of her – thick black choking blankets, deep black choking water. Listen. She half sat up again. Someone was crying, a thin frail watery cry. Water. Too much water. Was it her? She touched her cheeks, found them dry. Yet the noise was growing louder. It sounded like a baby. She switched the light back on, blundered to the carrycot, picked the infant up. Yes, the child was crying – crying instead of her, howling out her own grief.

'Cry,' she whispered. 'Cry.' She couldn't weep herself. Nothing there. Numbness. The baby's feet were flailing against her stomach. Rage as well as grief. She switched on the bedside light, fingers trembling, every smallest action needing skills and strengths she lacked. The child had ceased its sobbing, almost in surprise at the sudden startle of light. 'Don't stop,' she muttered, shaking the small damp body in her arms. 'Cry for him. Please cry for him. Cry all night.'

She put the baby back, sank down on the bed again, confused to see a bottle on the bedside table. Sparkling wine. That was for marriages, not funerals. Bubbles. Bubbles streaming from a drowning man's last shout. She tried to pick the bottle up. It felt heavy, waterlogged. Message in a bottle. 'Help me. Save me.' She hadn't seen it, let him drown. She filled her glass, hand unsteady, spilling half, watched the tiny bubbles pop and fizz to nothing. Nothing. That was right – nothing had happened, nothing terrible. She was celebrating Chris and Martin's engagement, dressed in her smart two-piece, pink-pearl lipstick, silver glitter eye-gloss. She ought to go downstairs and have a dance, pass Bea's cake around. No. The cake was shattered, mutilated, two hearts a mess of crumbs. It wasn't safe downstairs. That phone was there, heavy with black words – mortuary, postmortem, pathologist, police. She would never want to pick it up again. The entire study was tainted now. She had been fussing about some footling little wine stain while David's body was lying blotched and bloated, bundled into a sack, tipped out on a mortuary slab, poked and prodded by callous men for whom dead bodies were just wages, part of the day's work.

She reached out her hand, felt the hard cold smoothness of another phone. She ought to get the facts, contact the pathologist, question the police. She groped for the receiver, put it down again. You didn't invite the police to an engagement party, mix dead bodies up with streamers and balloons. Better to ring his mother, speak to her again, make sure she hadn't heard wrong. Or father. Mr Anthony. That was David, wasn't it? No. Couldn't speak to Mr Anthony. He was dead, lying on a slab. Anyway, his father might accuse her. '*You* killed our son. You were the last to see him.' Why were her teeth chattering like that? It was stifling in the bedroom. Neil's oil-fired central heating. If they were in the cottage still, they'd be wearing three thick sweaters each. Three sweaters on a corpse. She clawed at David's sweaters, had to get them off. They were dragging him down, water closing over him. Her hand knocked against the phone. She was meant to be ringing someone. David's mother? No, no. That hadn't been David's mother, just a joker, an imposter.

545

Why not phone her own mother? Bea would be asleep, but you could always wake a mother. That's what made them special. You screamed out in your sleep and they came running with their solid bodies and their soothing hands. 'It's all right – only a bad dream.' Nice to be a child again. Her finger was throbbing underneath the plaster. A deep cut to the bone. Mummy kiss it better. Mummy bring iodine and bandages, rock her in her arms. She dialled the first two digits of the Oxshott number, stopped. She could see her mother lying on her bed, face pale, mouth half open – not asleep, but dead. She had killed her mother, wanted her to die instead of David. Only a second's fleeting thought, a fraction of a second, but wicked, nonetheless, unforgivable. Proved what a monster she had become. Monsters were always punished, paid for things.

Anger was choking now, as well as darkness – anger with herself, with the police, the pathologist, the stupid blundering editor of *The Times* who filled his columns with trivia and trash when a tragedy had happened which should stun the whole front page; anger with her mother. If Bea had been less hysterical about Chris and Martin's engagement, kept her cool, kept her head, then she wouldn't have come dashing back herself. If she hadn't left the island, David would still be alive. Maybe. Probably. She would never have allowed him to go out in that . . . Mustn't think about it. Only a nightmare. Bea would bustle in soon, straighten out the covers, make a nice hot drink. 'You're safe now. Mummy's here.'

She picked up the baby again. '*Your* Mummy's here,' she told him. 'Downstairs. Dancing. Drinking wine. You haven't got a father, have you? Nor had I.' Had Bea felt like this herself when she was widowed? Must have done. Bereavement. Peculiar word. Three syllables. They should have had a child, she and David – something left of him. A relic, a piece of his body washed up on the shore of hers. All that fuss about the safe period. That was a lie, as well. Nothing was safe. Nothing lasted.

She banged the baby back into his cot, listened to him wail. Didn't care now. He had no right to be alive when David was dead, their child dead, never conceived. Safe. What was safe? Safety belt. Safety razor. Slashed faces, smash-up on the motorway. Safety glass which you broke when flames were licking at your feet. *Sauf. Sûr. Sicher.* All languages were lies. *Mort. Tod.* Stupid little words, not big or dread enough for what had happened. Dead. Death. She tried to spin the word out. *'The wages of sin is death'.* Why did they say 'is' instead of 'are'? Made no difference. She had sinned and David had died. The nuns were right. They had warned her she would go to hell. This was hell, this darkness, despite the deceitful light of the lamp which only hurt her eyes; this scorching heat which made her teeth chatter, put gooseflesh on her arms. Dead cold arms like David's. Hell wasn't fire, but water. Water over you and under you, surging into your mouth and ears and eyes, tossing you up on the strand with half your pieces missing. Hell was a soft cream carpet under your feet, your ex-husband's precious Wilton carpet which you had decided you preferred to a scrap of tatty matting and a man with soul and genius who was now a piece of jetsam. She had doubted David, criticized, feared he would deprive her of her piddling little comforts. She had those comforts still. She touched the plump pink duvet – goose-feathers from Harrods – real down pillows. David was only a mass of drifting feathers, scattered on the wind, no shape to him, no warmth.

She stopped at the door, heard a fractured burst of music. What was she doing, skulking upstairs when there was a party going on? She was neglecting Chris again. They would punish her a second time, snatch Chris away as well. She pushed at the door – heavy, very heavy – took her first step down the stairs. They seemed steeper than they ever had before, the staircase dangerously long. It made her dizzy to see it plunging down down down . . . Mustn't look. Stairs could drown. She clung to the banisters – one step, one step – stopping at each one. Two couples were sitting at the bottom, arms twined around each other. She squeezed her way between them, dazed by the noise, the glare. Chris had spotted her, was darting over.

'Are you okay now, Mum?'

Morna nodded, didn't trust her voice yet.

'I was just trying to find the sausage rolls. Grandma said she made some spares, but I can't see them anywhere. Know where she might have put them?'

Morna faltered into the kitchen. Sausage rolls. The words meant nothing. She looked in the fridge, shivered. Ice-cold like the mortuary. David stored like a hunk of frozen meat. She searched all the cupboards, tried the oven. Yes, there they were, a tray of sausage rolls waiting to be heated. Little boats with drowned pink bodies in them. She moved them to a higher shelf, switched the oven on. Cremation. Was David cooked already, a jar of ashes on the mantelpiece? Had she missed the funeral? All his relations there, but not his mistress. Useless as a mistress. Not only inexperienced but cowardly. She had run away, left her man to drown.

No, it was a lie, a lie. David was returning in twenty-seven and three-quarter days. She had marked it on the calendar and calendars weren't wrong. They were all worked out by proper official people, followed religiously by governments and churches, schools and farmers, law courts. 'David back', it said, scrawled in huge scarlet letters across 7th May. 'Meet him St Pancras.' She had planned the reunion already – the swift drive home, the special meal, their first night together in a proper double bed. She could see the figure 7 in her mind – king-size like the bed – towering over all the other dates. That calendar had never lied before. It had been right about today, Chris's birthday. The cards had all arrived, plopping on the doormat. That proved it, didn't it? And then they'd opened presents, decorated the house. She had put the streamers up herself, wobbling on the ladder, laughed and joked with Chris, hung balloons in bunches.

She stood at the door, watched the crowd of guests. It *must* be a birthday because everyone was dancing – some crazy modern dance where you clapped and shouted, clicked your fingers, swayed your hips. Someone grabbed her, a tall lad with a navy headband lassooing long and lanky hair. 'Come on, mate, join in.'

She was 'mate' now, one of them. She had wanted a dance and here it was; longed to be young again and now she had a partner under twenty. His hand was hot and sweaty, but at least it stopped her falling. Her body was powered by his, supported by the crowd of other dancers pressing round.

'Follow me,' he shouted. 'Do what I do.'

She followed, clicked her fingers, swayed her hips.

'Bravo!' someone yelled. She whirled faster, stomped her feet, clapped her hands. She could smell sweat and scent curdling on hot bodies, fumes of wine and garlic breathed into her face. The floor was swaying with her, tipping up, then swerving down again. She couldn't fall. Too many people jerking, spinning close. Thump of feet, whine of electric guitars, glow of fag ends, a curling plume of smoke. The boy had lit a cigarette. He was reaching up, popping balloons with it. Shrieks of laughter. Bangs. More balloons let loose in the study. Neil's study. Sacrosanct. Wild girls whooping after them, dance breaking up in chaos.

'Here, Mum, one for you.' Chris flushed now, flushed with wine and dancing, darting towards her with a green balloon. Green for safety. Morna held it on its string, went on dancing. Easier not to stop. She had lost her partner, but still she couldn't fall. She was buoyed up by an air balloon. The music made her strong. It was strong itself, pounding, vehement, throbbing through the floor and through her body. She could float on it and fly. The balloon was a kite keeping her in motion, towing her along. Careful, though, the floor was treacherous, kept tipping all the time. Couldn't trust it. Couldn't trust that boy. He was lurching towards her with his lighted cigarette, face in close-up, laughing. She swung away, too late, felt the shock right through her arm as the balloon exploded and she was left clutching a piece of string with nothing on the end of it but a piece of punctured rubber. She stared at the remains, the limp and ragged fragment, unclenched her palm, let it fall.

'Time to go,' she whispered. They ought to leave now. It was late, very late indeed. 'Time to go,' she said again, except nobody was listening. She stepped over bodies, tried to find the staircase. 'All over now,' she murmured to herself. 'All finished.'

24

They shouldn't be sleeping on the sand. It was too cold, too uncomfortable. The tide was coming in, showering them with spray, creeping over their ankles, soaking their shoes. Morna tried to drag David up the beach. His body was chilled, heavy, wouldn't wake from sleep. She had to rouse him so that they could make love, conceive their child. She kissed his lips. His mouth was empty – no tongue, no teeth, just a gaping hole. No eyes in the sockets, only sand. She climbed on top of him. He was always shy, needed her to get things going. She lowered herself on his body, plumper than she remembered it, with little tufts of hair sticking up where the knife had missed a patch. Spite, he had told her, revenge for a broken net. The skinless body stank. It had been around too long. Inquest on a dead seal. Coroner's report. 'The skin has been removed, the flesh beneath marbled green and black with purple splodges. Putrefaction has begun. There is a frayed rope round the neck.'

Morna grabbed the rope, pulled herself up on it, squatted down on his loins. They still weren't making contact. She laid her cheek against his chest. Cold, cold as granite. She wished he would put his arms around her, but they seemed too short to reach. Black claws instead of hands, seaweed wreaths around his neck. Seals shouldn't drown. Seals could swim, dive a thousand feet beneath the water and still bob up again.

'Gregory,' she whispered. Was that his name? Difficult to

know now. He seemed so changed. If she didn't move up the beach, she would drown herself. She could hear the waves pounding on the sand, feel the salt spray of their breath flicking on her face. She made one last effort, pressed her body full length against his, felt the flesh flabby, decomposing under her weight. He was breaking up beneath her, bits of his body dragged away by the tide. Waves were crashing over both their bodies now – or what was left of his. She swallowed a mouthful of water, choked, tried to spit it out, clutched at a rock, opened her eyes on darkness and dry land.

Her eyes were streaming still and she could taste salt on her lips. She had never cried in her sleep before, although she had woken screaming the previous two nights, struggling with the same horrific nightmares. She mopped her face with a corner of the sheet, could feel the sea still throbbing in one finger. She switched on the bedside light, examined the cut. The dressing had slipped off, the fingertip oozing pus. Cuts had always healed before. Not this one. It had festered, swollen, the skin around it blotched and bloated. She had to keep it bandaged, had lost the use of that hand. David had lost a hand, a whole arm, perhaps. She still didn't know how much of him remained. Half his body? Less? It hardly mattered, really, when all the bits were dead. She ought to be used to death by now. Her father had died, then God, then her marriage. Why make such a fuss about it? All she had to do was stuff the pain back under the bandage, confine it to one fingertip.

She eased out of bed, fetched lint and antiseptic from the medicine chest, returned to the bedroom. Difficult to bandage your own finger. You needed someone else to tie the ends or insert the safety pin. She couldn't do it on her own, sat on the edge of the bed, cradling the finger in the other hand. So much pain.

She got up again, paced to and fro, to and fro, stopped at

the dressing table, opened the top drawer. She took out David's letters, touched his silver coin – all she had left of him. The quartz, the shells, the sea urchin, were still in his cottage on the island. The coltsfoot he had given her had withered the next day; they had shared the egg between them for their breakfast. There was nothing else – no ring, no outward bond.

She picked up the card which Chris had made for her – a sort of mourning card with a double-edged black border, crayoned in, verses printed neatly in the centre in her best italic script. Her daughter was embarrassed by death and grief, didn't have the words for them, had used T.S. Eliot's, instead.

> *'Also pray for those who were in ships and*
> *Ended their voyage on the sand, in the sea's lips*
> *Or in the dark throat which . . .'*

Morna replaced the card, face downwards. The sea was in her eyes again. She dabbed them with the bandage, smelt antiseptic, pain. Since David's death, she was terrified of water. Chris and Martin went diving in that same ruthless sea which had coffined David. She longed to implore them never to go under again – but that would be another sort of death. Water was power and joy for them, not terror. 'Accept the terror,' David had urged her, months ago, when they were walking in the Weybridge cemetery. Strange that they should have had their first deep conversation in a graveyard. *'And we all go with them, into the silent funeral . . .'* She remembered the lines her daughter hadn't copied.

> *'We cannot think of a time that is oceanless*
> *Or of an ocean not littered with wastage*
> *Or of a future that is not liable*
> *Like the past, to have no destination.'*

Eliot knew that April was the cruellest month. April 14th

today, day of the funeral. She hadn't missed it. Things had dragged out – hold-ups, complications, practical problems of sending the body back. Corpses hanging around for days and days, outstinking Eliot's lilacs. She walked across to the window, pushed aside the curtain, watched the first grey film of dawn curl like smoke beneath the edges of the darkness. British Summertime had started just three weeks ago, the clocks gone forward, giving the world an extra hour of light. Not her world, though. She could feel only darkness, the darkness of the island moved to Weybridge. Here she had electric light, every type of lamp – table lamps, bedside lamps, reading lights, Anglepoises, even spotlights in the garden. Yet the dark gloom still pressed down. On the island, David had been her light. Despite the total blackness of the nights there, the swarthy sea, often starless sky, short days, early dusk, her fear had disappeared. Now it had her trapped again; here, in this cosy suburb where the lampposts came on almost before the sun went down, the close-packed houses beamed back light at them; headlights swivelled across well-lit roads; shops and restaurants made bright squares in the streets. The darkness had moved inward. If a surgeon were to slice her body open, he would find nothing but an empty shell. Someone had already removed her lungs and stomach, so that she could no longer eat or breathe. Her body felt bruised and sore as if it had been shoved about on the operating table. It hurt to swallow. All noises seemed too loud, especially laughter. Laughter was extraordinary and blasphemous. Why should anybody laugh?

She let the curtain fall. Might as well get dressed now. She had to start early if she were going to make the funeral. She hadn't been invited – didn't exist for David's family except as an ugly rumour, a rude voice on the phone – but she had managed to discover all the details: time, place, date. First a Requiem Mass in a church called The Holy

554

Redeemer in the faceless Midlands town where David's parents lived, followed by cremation. The police had finally sent the body back, released it to the local undertaker who had shoved it in a transit coffin and driven it by van to a funeral parlour nearer David's home. She could feel the bumping of the van in her wounded finger, the throbbing of the engine, the lurching of the coffin over uneven pitted roads.

She opened her wardrobe, took out a plain grey skirt. Her two black dresses were both too party-ish. She should be wearing widow's weeds, tearing out her hair. Her hair was newly waved, glossy with conditioner. Chris had set it for her last night. She glanced in the mirror. She looked too spruce and healthy for a funeral. Outward mask covering a void. She sank down on the bed. Her bandage had come undone again. Impossible to fasten it, impossible to make the sun come up. Darkness would overwhelm her like someone going down down down under an anaesthetic. Whatever time the clock said, it was always the middle of the night; hours to go to morning which never came. *'O dark dark dark. They all go into the dark . . .'*

'Mum . . .'

Morna jumped, sat up. Her daughter in blue-striped man's pyjamas and bare feet was manoeuvring through the door with a heavy tray. 'I brought your breakfast up.'

'Th . . . Thank you, darling.' Mustn't cry. What was so tragic about toast and marmalade? Chris had boiled an egg as well. No eggs on the island, or only one.

'Are you all right, Mum?'

Morna nodded, then shook her head. The breakfast had confused her. Her daughter couldn't talk about the death, but she boiled eggs, copied verses. She had forgotten to bring a spoon. Impotence again. How could you eat a runny egg without one? Yet she couldn't leave it. The breakfast was an offering, like the card.

'Have a piece of toast,' she offered. She wanted Chris to stay. So long as her daughter stood there, blue-striped and tangible, she blocked out some of the darkness, filled the void.

Chris shook her head. 'I couldn't eat this early. It's hardly light.'

'You were sweet to get up at all.'

'That's okav.'

Silence. Morna cut her egg in half, dripped it on to the toast, sprinkled salt on top. Eggs for new life and resurrection, salt for immortality. She shook out more salt. Chris had put the two-pound carton on the tray instead of the dainty silver cruet. She watched the tiny granules pile and overflow, submerging egg and toast.

'Stop, Mum. What you doing? You can't eat it like that.'

'Yes, I can.' Morna forced a mouthful down. Had to eat, or Chris would think she was grieving too intensely. Must think that anyway. The mouthful tasted bitter. Too much salt. Salt for friendship, David had told her, salt to bond them. Salt tears seeping into the corners of her mouth. Salt sea dividing them again.

'Listen, Mum.' Chris squatted on the bed. 'Are you sure you don't want me to come with you? I mean, you haven't changed your mind? I can easily take the day off. Work's so dozy at the moment, they'd hardly even miss me.'

'No, really . . .'

'You're not driving, are you? It's dangerous, isn't it, when you're taking pills and things?'

Sleeping pills, round and shiny-bright like Smarties, except they tasted bitter underneath their coating. 'No, I'll go by train. Day return.' Cars were too vulnerable. Empty shells which you sat in all alone. Trains were more substantial and someone else looked after you – solid men in uniform. Timetables. Routine.

She knew the timetable almost off by heart, had studied

556

it for hours, working out trains and times, planning to go up earlier in the week. She owed it to David's parents to introduce herself, apologize for her rudeness on the phone. In a way, she longed to become one of the family, part of the death, recognized and valued as his closest friend, his . . . That was the trouble, though. They wouldn't want a mistress for their son, least of all one who called them liars, banged the receiver down. Anyway, she somehow feared to meet them, feared their weight of grief which, added to her own, might crush her altogether. Better, perhaps, to go back to the island, talk to Cormack, make an appointment to see the mainland police, ask all the questions festering in her mind.

The trains had left without her. She couldn't face either island or police, didn't trust herself. She might spring at Cormack, hit him, disfigure him for life for lending his dinghy to a man who couldn't cope with riptides, sudden squalls; attack the pathologist for not calling her to lay out David's body, save it the indignities. She had phoned the local newspapers, wormed the story out of them, pieced the bits together, pretending to one to be a journalist herself, telling another she was an old school friend of David's. There were still gaps in the account, but she had got the gist of it. David had made an expedition to the lonely rockstack where St Abban had spent the last months of his life, wishing to include it in his book. It was almost impossible to land there, since the seas were even more treacherous than round the island proper. Abban had managed with a second miracle. David, less blessed, had foundered. Cormack's boat was spotted the next morning, floating upside down without its oars; David discovered later, and further out, without his . . .

Morna put her toast down. She could never have made it to the mortuary. It hurt enough, for Christ's sake, when the images were only in her mind, without fleshing them out in bloody mangled fact. The funeral would be kinder – flowers and hymns and hats; polished wood confining anything putrid or unpleasant. She had agonized about whether she should go at all. One part of her craved to stay safe at home, hands clamped over her ears and eyes, seeing nothing, hearing nothing, denying not just the death, but the whole relationship. She was just a woman living quietly on her own, living for her mother and her daughter, someone stolid and sedate who had never experienced ecstasy or passion or that terrible despair which clawed you into pieces. The other part knew she would go, had to go, alone.

The train was late. Strong winds and sheeting rain had brought trees down on the line. Morna sat in the crowded carriage – windows steaming up from hot bodies and wet macs – watched children arguing, clambering on and off the seats, a toddler struggling with the wrappings on a tube of Polos, a woman knitting a huge hairy sweater, stopping every few minutes to puff at her cigarette, dropping ash and stitches. They had been delayed about an hour now. A few people were fidgeting and tutting; one man kept checking his watch and muttering to himself, but most of the other passengers merely slouched or dozed, accepting a cloudburst and a hold-up as simply bad luck. Only she was missing a funeral, the man she loved gliding through a trap-door in a crematorium and she not there to witness it.

She walked along to the toilet, paced to and fro in the tiny space outside it, wrinkling her nose at the smell which wafted out. Delays and children had made it foul, clogged it up. She almost lost her balance as the train lurched suddenly, started to move on again. She let out a brief prayer of relief, remained standing between the doors, thrown from side to side as it gathered speed. She couldn't return to the carriage and face those chatting yawning clods who were behaving as if nobody had died, as if the world was just the same as it had been a week ago. She had felt irrationally angry with them, especially those in couples, furious with the way they took everything for granted – their lives, their happiness, their living breathing partners.

She slumped against the door, stared out through the glass. The train was streaking past a lake. Water again – but still and glassy water, not the seething boiling currents which lashed around the rockstack. How could David have dared to make that journey? Had he been seeking a hermit's life himself, regarding the bare necessities of the spartan cottage as still too soft, too cushy? Or testing himself, punishing himself – a perilous crossing as a penance for the sex? Or simply following the demands of scholarship? If he were writing about Abban, then he had to experience all the saint had known – or all that was remotely possible. David always stretched the possible. He had told her once that one must give everything one had to work, hold nothing back at all.

She rubbed roughly at her eyes, slapped the tears away. They were almost there, thank God; the train slowing down again, but this time at a station, *her* station – David's. She leapt out, sprinted past the barrier, cursed when she saw the queue for taxis. She was tempted to jump it, dodge past that line of bumbling dodderers and nip into the first cab she could find. She could be at the church by the time they had struggled with their umbrellas and their pushchairs or given their slow laborious instructions to the drivers.

'There's a queue,' someone said, stepping out of it to confront her, a large bossy woman loaded down with bags.

Morna slunk back to the tail end of the line, glancing round at the dingy station forecourt. This was David's country – grimy buildings, wet and weeping roofs, a factory chimney pointing like a dirty finger on the skyline. Her own finger was neatly bandaged, tied and pinned by Chris; Kleenex in her pocket, aspirin in her handbag. Everything under control except the time.

'Can you drive as fast as possible?' she asked the driver fifteen minutes later, as she climbed into a cab, sat on the very edge of the seat as if trying to urge it on.

He didn't answer. His radio was blaring, a phone-in problem programme. Someone's son refused to pay towards his keep, although he was twenty-five and took all his meals at home. Morna checked her watch again. Wait until he's drowned, she thought. You'll save on food bills then. She rubbed a hole in the blurred and dripping window, peered out on a street of shops – Tesco, Woolworth's, Fine Fare, Boots – all the familiar names, yet looking alien and foreign here; rain beating at the windows of a travel agent plastered with posters of the sun.

'Is it far?' she shouted, over a commercial break for Berni Inns.

'Depends on the traffic.' The driver coughed his fag end out, pulped it in the ashtray, lit another.

The shops petered out, replaced by mean and close-packed houses, then a strip of wasteland overgrown with weeds; next to that a garage with a 'closed' sign. The cab pulled up just beyond it. Morna grabbed her bag, jumped out. The church was thirties' yellow brick facing directly on to the street as if no one could spare the room for a garden or a graveyard. No tree, no blade of grass.

'Can you wait, please.' She was so late now, the Requiem Mass must be almost at an end. She would need transport to the crematorium.

'Okay. It'll cost you, though.'

'That's all right.'

Morna slammed the door, stood motionless a moment. Now she was here, she could hardly bring herself to enter the church at all. It looked so ugly. No spire, no soaring arches, but everything cramped and skimped; black streaks on the brick as if the church had been weeping, a child with a dirty face which no one had time to wipe.

She pushed the heavy door, heard it grumble open, stared in shock at the empty interior. No one there at all. Nothing but plain wood pews, a simple altar. Perhaps this was the wrong church, even the wrong town. Had she somehow missed her station, got out too early or too late, muddled up the day? No – there were traces of a recent service, the smell of sweaty bodies and hot wax, the candles on the altar only recently extinguished, one still exhaling a thin blue wisp of smoke.

A glove was lying in the aisle, a woman's glove in brown wool, without its fellow. She picked it up, felt it damp and limp, stood there with it dangling from her fingers. She ought to hurry. The taxi was waiting. She could still make the crematorium if she didn't hang around. She took a step towards the door, stopped, swung back again. She felt sick, faint, hot and chilled at once. David had been here. His coffin had rested on those trestles, his friends and family gathered in the pews. Almost in a daze, she walked slowly up the aisle, knelt in the front row, the one reserved for closest kin, chief mourners. A Mass book was lying on the bench, still open at the funeral service, and on top of it, a pale pink handkerchief edged with lace, sodden and screwed up. Morna smoothed it out, found an 'M' embroidered on one corner. 'M' for Mother – relic of David's mother's grief? What was her name? Had David even told her? A Catholic name for certain. Margaret, perhaps, or Marion, or Mary. Morna held the hankie in her hand, tried to weigh the sorrow in it. How could such a flimsy scrap of fabric ever staunch such grief? 'M' for Morna. She dropped it in her handbag with the glove. Bits of David's funeral – the nearest she could get to bits of David.

She glanced down at the Mass book. Paper thin as airmail, print so small it hurt your eyes. '*May perpetual light shine upon him . . .*'

Perpetual light, perpetual light. What did it mean? She

had never known at Junior School, thought it was a technical term describing the type of light – paraffin lamp, electric light, perpetual light. Now it was simply lies. David was in the dark beneath the sea. Even this church was dark, rain drumming on its narrow grudging windows, shadows furled in corners like old rags. She went on reading, *'The Lord is compassion and love . . .'* Why did they keep fibbing? Eternal life. Eternal rest. Impossible to rest on a raging sea with only the wind as lullaby and the cruel white fingers of the waves rocking you awake again every time you closed your eyes. Eternal rest. Eternal pain. She squeezed her septic finger, went on pressing, hard. Must localize the pain.

She longed to be a Bea so that the words should have some meaning and she could pray, beseech a merciful God to turn death to sleep, death to victory. When she was a child, God had lived in churches, answered prayers, or at least referred the problems to His saints. The saints were all around her – the same standard ugly statues she had known at school. There was St Anthony, who shared a name with David, complacent on his pedestal with the Christchild and a lily. He was the patron saint of finding things, had often helped at school, bringing to light mislaid history books or sweeping gloves and fountain pens into the safety of Lost Property. Could he not assist again, bring David back, locate his missing pieces?

She closed her eyes, saw Cormack's dinghy, still wrong way up, but nailed down like a coffin. Too late now. She stumbled to her feet. No time to pray in any case. That meter in the taxi was ticking over, counting out every wasted minute. There would be nothing left at all of David if she didn't rush to the crematorium, catch the last part of the service.

She slid out of the pew, genuflected, remained on one knee, staring at the small dark circles soaking into the floor. Her own tears staining it. She tried to disperse them with

562

her shoe. Nothing left of David anyway – only scars and tears. Empty rituals couldn't bring him back. She stared at the Paschal candle with its dead black wick. It would have been alight throughout the Mass, three foot of white wax sham, blazing by the coffin – the symbol of resurrection now itself extinguished. David had lit candles on the island as emblems of the sun, representing the victory of light over darkness, spring over winter, life over death. Spring had come – daffodils and catkins flaunting in soft Weybridge, the convalescent sun growing stronger every day – but he himself had perished, making mock of his own ritual, confusing all the seasons as she, uprooted, sank back into winter dark and cold again.

'David,' she said, aloud. She had to try her voice out, make sure it was still working. Nothing was certain any more. Things could disappear, disintegrate, simply drift away. There was an echo in the church which pounced on the word, distorted it, turned it into a booming like the sea. 'D . . . aaa . . . v . . . i . . . d.' Empty endless sound.

She got up from her knees, walked right up to the altar. You could never pass that barrier at school, not if you were a woman and a secular. The little gilded rail kept you back, kept you humble and unsanctified. No rails now, though. Only wooden trestles for a coffin. She stared at them in shock. They had supported David's body. David dead. Dead body. Had he *wanted* to die, perhaps? She clutched at the wood, mouth dry. The thought was horrifying. She had suspected it of Abban himself, but never ever of David. Yet wasn't he the same intensely spiritual type who might weary of this mundane imperfect life, long for transition to some higher state? Her legs seemed shaky under her. She crouched down with her head between her knees, frightened she might faint. Better rest a moment, try and calm herself. She stretched out her legs, let her head fall back, lay flat on the floor between the trestles. Her breathing quietened. She was lying where David had lain only moments before, occupying his space, soaking up the last dregs and crumbs of him. She closed her eyes, saw dark again, dark ocean. Perpetual dark. She could feel herself sinking back and down, returning to the dark womb of the sea, the troubled self snuffed out. Merging. Nothingness. End of grief and striving. 'Their land-longings shall be sea-longings . . .' Is that what David had craved – to lose his restlessness, the sharp and jagged corners of his individuality, his impatience with himself, his frustration with his gross unruly body?

'Good God! Whatever happened? Are you all right?'

Morna opened her eyes. A dowdy woman in a blue nylon overall and fingerless woollen mittens had entered from the sacristy, and was standing over her, carrying a vase of tulips and forsythia. A church worker. Morna knew the type. Many of her mother's friends spent half their lives in the service of the church, women betrothed to God, wooing Him with Brasso and Quickshine and endless flower arrangements, rewarded with smiles and titbits from the priest. She forced a smile herself, tried to struggle up. The woman only frowned.

'Shall I call a doctor? Are you *ill*?' The voice was sharp, officious, made the word 'ill' sound culpable.

'No, no. I'm quite all right.' Morna half sat up, fell back again. She had died a moment, still felt weak and dizzy. 'I'll be . . . okay in a second.'

'You gave me quite a turn, stretched out like that as if . . . Did you faint or something?' The mittened hand yanked roughly at a tulip which had fallen out of line.

'No, I . . . er . . . didn't. There's . . . nothing wrong with me. I'm . . . absolutely fine.' It had become automatic now. 'How are you?' 'Fine.' There weren't words for what death did to you, and 'fine' was no more meaningless than any.

'Well, you've no right to be lying there, in that case. What

564

do you think you're doing, sprawling on the floor right up near the altar? Kindly get up at once.'

There was no kindly in the tone. Morna used the wooden trestles as a prop, pulled herself up against them. 'I'm sorry,' she mumbled, smoothing her crumpled skirt. Best to placate this martinet. A church worker could be useful, would know the details of the funeral, had probably cleaned the church for it herself, set out the hassocks and the service books.

'Is . . .? Was . . .?' The words died on her lips. The woman had put her vase down and was standing four-square in front of her, blocking her way, her breastless chest blazoned with a medal of the Sacred Heart dangling from a heavy silver chain, symbol of her authority, her piety.

'Father Stroud's not here at the moment, but I'll have to report this, you realize. We can't have people just . . .'

'No, no, please. I'm leaving now.' Morna dodged round one side of her, stumbled back along the aisle, not daring to run until she had actually closed the door, put a shield of solid oak between her flimsy self and that woman's laser eyes. She fell into the taxi, urged the driver on.

'The Queen's Road Crematorium, please, as quickly as you can.'

The driver turned the sports news up, made a lurching u-turn.

Crematorium. Morna tried the word again, whispering it to herself. Odd how words she had hardly used before seemed now so full of pain. Strange, too, that a devout Roman Catholic family should have decided on cremation at all. It had been forbidden in her own day on the grounds that it denied the Resurrection. She wished it were forbidden still. It was wrong for David – too modern and too final. Barbarous to burn bodies, reduce someone you loved to a handful of cinders. At least with a grave there was something you could visit, some spot you could hallow with your tears or flowers. David's ashes would be his parents' private property, interned in their small sitting room, sharing the mantelpiece with his boyhood photographs. She would be shut out – was nobody up here, just a slumped anonymous figure in a taxi, distorted by the smeared and dirty glass.

She tried to distract herself. Wolves were tipped to win away; the three-thirty had been scrapped. The streets were emptier now. They were winding through the outskirts of the town, half-built housing estates, still bleeding at the edges, blocking out the bleak brown hills beyond. The driver turned off left, jolted through tall iron gates, gleaming in the rain. There was a patch of garden, sodden grass, one shivering tree imprisoned in an iron cage, one bare and gaping flowerbed. All the flowers were blooming on the hearse instead, growing up from the black and shiny roof, ranged all about the empty space inside it. Minutes ago, that oblong had been David. Was he burnt already, raked and poked by careless crematorium staff? Bunny had told her that all the different bodies were often burnt together, to save time and fuel, so that the ashes you received might be mixed with someone else's. There were scores of current lawsuits in the States, she'd said – outraged people objecting that their loved ones might be fused with whores or murderers. Did it happen over here as well – David's unique and special self profaned?

The driver had stopped, was waiting to be paid, but Morna still sat motionless. How could that glossy swanky funeral car have carried David – David who rode an ancient bicycle or went everywhere on foot, David who loathed show and ostentation?

'£5.30, please,' the driver said a second time, making the 'please' sarcastic now.

Morna stared at the contents of her purse – silver, coppers, notes. It meant nothing any longer, as if she were in a foreign country where the currency was alien, or like a child who had not yet learnt to count. There was only feel and weight – heavy silver, flimsy notes. How much did £5.30 weigh? She stood dithering, trickling coins from hand to purse and back again, dropping one or two. Suddenly, she thrust the whole purse through the window, pressed it into the driver's hand.

'Could you take what I owe you? And a tip, of course. And the waiting-time. Or is that included? Take whatever you want.'

He stared at her incredulously, cigarette drooping from his lips.

'Go on,' Morna urged. If he grabbed too much, who cared? Perhaps his wife had died, his son drowned.

'Thanks, Miss.' He started extracting notes. 'Thank you very much indeed.'

He was right – she was a Miss – unmarried, without a man. David was an oblong edged with flowers. She turned her face away as she passed the funeral cars, their drivers smoking and chatting as if this were just a tea break. A dark-suited official was standing at the entrance of the chapel.

'If it's Mrs Carter's funeral, would you please wait in the waiting-room.'

Waiting-room. Doctors, dentists. Extractions. Pain and loss.

'No, it's Mr David Anthony's.'

'I'm afraid you're late, then.'

Far too late. A month late. If she hadn't left the island, he . . .

'You'd better just slip in and stand at the back.'

The man was holding open the door for her. She stepped inside the chapel, stifled a cry as she saw the coffin resting on a platform in the front. Six foot by two of chipboard, veneered to look like oak, plastic handles simulating brass. That was David. No. No . . . It couldn't be. She shut her eyes, appalled. What would she see if she wrenched that wooden lid off? Would David be wearing his old and balding corduroys, or wrapped in a winding sheet? Had the gulls pecked out his eyes? She took a step towards the coffin. She had to get him out, warm him up, give him the kiss of life. Even bits of him would be better than nothing. Nothing.

She couldn't seem to stand straight, sagged back against the door. It appeared to be still raining, even inside, things blurring, misting up, her clothes damp and sticking to her, water dripping down her face. Must keep still. It would clear up soon if she didn't lose control. This was a public place. Mustn't shout or sob or she would disturb those people in the pews. Why were there so few of them, and why such dowdy creatures, fidgeting and shuffling in their dripping macs, gabbling the responses as if they were multiplication tables? A man turned round to glance at her – watery eyes, nicotined moustache. The woman next to him had an insistent phlegmy cough; the hem of her black dress undone, dipping down beneath a shabby coat. This couldn't be David's funeral – this smell of damp humanity, this cramped and stifling chapel with its shiny khaki paint, its old-fashioned water pipes lumbering along the walls. It might have been a waiting-room itself for all that was sacred about it. Even the priest, droning at the other end in a flat South Midlands accent, looked somehow wrong. He had no majestic vestments on, just a creased white surplice trimmed with lace, too fancy for the grey serge trousers and butch black shoes protruding from it. A purple stole hung around his thick bull neck. His jaw was heavy, stubborn. You could hardly imagine him holding God in his hands each day – more likely a pickaxe or a shovel. Perhaps he wasn't a priest at all, just a stand-in or an understudy. Maybe the whole thing was a play, the coffin just an empty box, the mourners hired. If they were really David's friends, they should be ascetics, intellectuals, high-minded scholars beside themselves with grief and loss.

She peered towards the front row – David's parents, or their understudies. She could see only their backs – a slight stooping man with thinning hair, a woman in a navy Crimplene trouser-suit with a cheap scarf at the neck, printed with poodles' heads. 'How *dare* you,' Morna muttered, pummelling one clenched fist in the palm of the other hand. 'How dare you dress like that and look like that or . . .' She watched the woman's shoulders heave, her hand keep dabbing at her eyes. No, not an understudy. That five-foot-nothing female with her pathetic poodles, her over-permed and brittle fizz of hair, had been summoned to a mortuary, made to peer at the remnants of the body she had given birth to, identify the pieces as her son.

There was an older woman beside her, with grey wisps of hair straggling from a black felt hat, a shapeless coat reaching almost to her ankles. A grandmother? David had never mentioned one. Even from the back, Morna could see her grief – the hunched and hopeless shoulders, the face stifled in her hands. She could feel her own eyes stinging, the anguish of his family streaming down her cheeks. There was no sign of the brother, that fair, solemn, small-boned, brilliant brother whom David had worshipped half his life. Perhaps he was too busy with Good Works overseas to come home for the funeral. No sign of anybody young. Where were David's own friends? Was she the only one?

The only one crying. She jabbed fiercely at her eyes. The others were more controlled, reciting the responses, joining in the service. She forced herself to concentrate. The priest was still droning on.

'We commend to you, O Lord, the soul of your servant
    David . . .'
'May his soul and the souls of all the . . .'

Here, they believed in souls, but not the sort she knew. Soul had become a sexual word for her. Body and soul, with the body coming first. Body in a coffin now. Bits of body. She heard a sobbing choking sound. Someone turned round and stared at her. Had *she* made that noise? She bit her septic finger to confine the pain, stop her crying out again.

The priest was sprinkling the coffin with holy water. '*May your holy angels take him and lead him home to Paradise . . .*'

She was David's seraph, his holy angel sporting in a double bed. The only one he had ever shared a bed with. Punished for it now. At her own wedding, she had knelt right up in the front near the altar, near the trestles. Nuptial Mass, Requiem Mass. Labels which meant nothing. The sacrament of marriage had been just a charade to placate her mother, to please a God who had already jilted her. This was a sham as well, this hollow dreary service for a man who believed in ritual. The words were empty formulae, worn out, as David had complained himself – symbols which had lost their power, phrases which had frayed to platitudes. This was a standard service. Nothing unique in it, nothing tailor-made. Tinker, tailor, beggarman, corpse. David loved music and they had sung no hymn. David had drowned in his prime, in a daring selfless quest for knowledge, and they had buried him with the same stale and sluggish words they might have used for a ninety-year-old dotard who had shrivelled in his bed.

She stared in horror at the coffin. It was moving, moving. She hid her face in her hands, tried to calm her breathing, before daring one more look. Still moving – steadily, remorselessly – gliding on those bland oiled automated rollers through ice-blue velvet curtains.

'Stop!' she shouted. The shout aborted, hurt her throat. She tried a second time. No sound came out. She was dumb, dumb, impotent again. Why was no one else objecting, rushing up to snatch his body back, save it from the fire? Why were they all so passive and accepting, even his parents just standing there, heads bowed, while their son slid inch by inch away from them? Only the last two corners of the coffin showing now. Then nothing, nothing. The play was over, the curtains drawn again. Everyone leaving before the curtain calls, shambling out through the side door near the altar while she stood, broken, at the back.

She stared at the floor. Must control herself. Polished wooden floor. Straight lines of the floorboards. Parallel lines. Order. Everything all right. 'How are you?' 'Fine.' The black-suited official hovering again.

'Could you please vacate the chapel. We need it for another service.'

Vacate. Empty. Void. *Vacare. Vider.* Only words. Someone else had died. Production line. Strict appointment system. She could already see the second hearse, the new knot of huddled mourners. *'God is compassion and love.'*

She slunk out, concealed herself behind the angle of the wall. They mustn't see her. She was a mistress – worse than that, a murderer. Might they not suspect her? Cormack must have told the police about the woman who turned up at David's cottage, stayed with him all those weeks, the woman he had seen himself, had taken back on his boat. The police would have told the parents in their turn. Had they gone further, speculated, connected the woman with the death? There had been no inquest, no fatal accident inquiry. It was a case of simple drowning and she had long since left the island when the accident occurred, but all the same . . .

She stared at David's mother, eyes red, trousers mud-splashed, arm in arm with the confused and shaking grandmother who was mumbling to herself, her wrinkled mouth opening and shutting, her weak blue eyes unfocused. The father stood apart, picking at a loose thread on his coat, screwing up his face against the fine but steady drizzle which still slurred the sky. People were crowding round, entangling their umbrellas, offering sympathy. Fine, fine, fine.

Resurrection. Death as sleep. Morna longed to go up herself, add her soft lies to the rest, but she had left it far too late. She should have phoned back immediately, when Mrs Anthony had first reported the death. David's mother had been hysterical with grief and all she had done was shout abuse at her, refuse even to believe her. She could have found her number, tried to make amends, explained her own state of shock. But she had remained out of touch, aloof.

Even now, if she made some overture, she would only embarrass the poor woman. She was not only a mistress and a suspect, but a stuck-up southern stranger. She had heard their accents, the father's broad Stafford, the mother's softened with a Shrewsbury burr. How could accent still divide people; how could it even matter on a day like this? Yet *they* might be upset by it. Their backgrounds were so different, they might think she was affected, some snobbish phoney female who had provoked their son, driven him to . . .

It must have been hard for David, caught between two worlds, changing his own accent as he changed his school and status. Scholarship boy, he had called himself so casually. It was only now she saw the pain in it. David had been educated out of his class, remodelled, alienated, wrenched away from all that was familiar. That would explain his guardedness, his lack of social ease. Public school boys were cruel, could pounce on a provincial accent or a Crimplened poodled mother as a serious lapse of taste. David had groomed himself to fit their standards, made himself a hybrid, concealed his humble origins even from her, presuming she would mock them in her turn. How wrong he was – and how ironical that she had found out after all. A scholarship boy killed in the cause of scholarship.

She watched his parents climb into the funeral car, their figures reflected and distorted in the black gloss of its flanks. They were probably squandering all their money on David's death, as they had spent their last penny on his education. Undertakers growing fat on corpses. Death as cash. Death as profit-sheet. The cars purred away, making room for the fleet drawn up behind them. The second coffin was carried slowly out, almost identical to David's – the same shade and stain of wood, the same toupée of stiff flowers. Morna stood and watched. Should she return to the chapel, attend another funeral? She could spend days and days up here, mourning strangers. Nothing else to do now. The official was eyeing her again, suspicious like the church worker. She had become a down-and-out, a vagrant, in just a day, the sort of rootless aimless person who had to be kept tabs on, shooed out of public places.

She removed herself from view, turned towards the covered passageway where they displayed the wreaths and flowers. The colours were so bright they hurt her eyes. The central exhibit was three free-standing letters made of garish yellow carnations and spelling D-A-D. *Dad*? David? She peered closer, saw the label on the roped-off square of concrete – 'Mr Colin Thorpe'. Mr Thorpe had many wealthy friends, judging by the banks and banks of flowers – exotic swathes of hothouse blooms and fern, bravura displays with satin streamers and silver lurex ribbon. David had far fewer. His smaller square of concrete was also labelled like a showcase with name and date. In the centre stood a three-dimensional cross of amputated gold and white chrysanthemums edged with laurel. Morna bent to read the card, neatly typed in black. 'A small tribute to our son.' Why should that make her cry again? Was it the formality, the lack of personal signature? Tribute was a formal word – suggested submission as well as homage, payment from vassal to lord. Had David been his parents' lord, their clever special son who had put himself above them? And why the cross? To express their burden or his holiness? Morna brushed mingled rain and tears from her face, turned up the collar of her mac. She hadn't known their son. Whole areas had been hidden, whole chapters closed to her. Yet they, for their part, hadn't known *her* David, would never have understood him.

Morna turned back to the flowers. Next to the cross was a cushioned heart sculpted from red carnations, the card written in a frail and spidery hand. 'Have a nice rest, dear. You deserve it, Gran.' Morna laughed out loud, wiped her eyes. Laughter hurt more than crying. Why had David buried his grandmother? Was she too dowdy in her old felt hat, had left school at fourteen, perhaps, didn't understand Irish palaeography or Celtic symbolism, wouldn't know what to say if she met graduate Mrs Gordon?

The flowers looked too gaudy to be real, too ornate for this dingy crematorium. Out of their element, like David. Two months ago, he had ransacked the whole island to find her just one bloom. She had sent him nothing in return, no wreath, no smallest posy. She walked towards the patch of grass, hoping to find some flower or spray of foliage, something to leave behind. Nothing but weeds – a patch of groundsel, a stalk or two of plantain, a dead brown thistle. Plain and prickly plants to suit a scholarship boy. She trudged further on towards the gates, found only a skeleton leaf, one of autumn's cast-offs, a few stray petals from someone else's wreath. She couldn't insult him with such tribute, such small change. It was too late for flowers, in any case. She slipped through the gate, turned into the puddled street outside it, broke into a run. The funeral was over.

25

It had stopped raining, but the air was still damp and heavy, showers of raindrops strafing from windowsills and shop fronts with every gust of wind. Morna tramped on. She was back in the centre of the Midlands town again, a dirty sprawling town packed with shoppers. She had no idea where the station was, hardly cared. Why go back home? She preferred to linger where she was, here, in this town where David had grown up, try to make him whole again, find those missing parts of him which she had never known – the clever moody boy, the tortured adolescent, the would-be priest channelling violence into prayer.

It seemed an unlikely setting for him – a modern shopping precinct with garish supermarkets and greasy burger bars, sleazy fashion boutiques squeezed between unisex hair stylists and cut-price drugstores. She kept bumping into people, stupid people who wouldn't look where they were going or blocked the pavement by strolling arm in arm, or ate bars of chocolate in the street then threw the wrappers down. She had eaten nothing since her mouthful or two of salted toast at dawn. The funeral guests would be guzzling at the Anthonys', drowning David's memory in tea. She stopped, leant against the steamed-up window of a snack bar, stared in at fish paste sandwiches, cheap iced fancies. She could see David's mother spreading sandwich fillings, passing trays of cakes. A son died and you opened bloater paste, stuck cherries in pink icing. She jabbed her grubby bandage against the glass.

A woman passed her, striding purposefully, turned into Fine Fare, dumped her handbag in a shopping trolley. Morna followed, did the same. Almost a relief to have someone to copy, someone brisk and busy who seemed to know what she was doing, had a man to shop and cook for, wasn't just a stranger wandering through wet streets. She stepped from grey drizzle into fluorescent glare; products and promises shouting from all sides. *'This month's bargain offer . . . Bigger bottle, lower price . . . New meatier recipe . . . 6% more fruit.'* Everything too bright and big. Man-size, family-size . . . Now she knew what her mother felt – must have felt for a whole lifetime – nothing widow-size. She stared at a two-pound tub of margarine, a bag of two dozen apples. She had no one to cook for tonight. Bea was eating at the convent, Chris meeting Martin at Roxy's after work.

She trailed up and down each aisle, round and round the entire store, walking very slowly as if she were convalescent, had been cobbled together with only paste and string. She stopped at the packet desserts, heard David's deep wary voice again. 'I was planning to have Angel Delight for pudding – thought Abban would get a kick out of the name.' She picked up the strawberry flavour, put it back again. Bloody stupid to blub over a 35p packet of starch and sugar, prettied up with chemicals. The whole place was too garish, insulting after a death. They were unpacking party cakes, playing schmaltzy music. She had craved a hymn for David and here it was – a jolly tonky tune which told the same old lies. The Bird's Eye Promise, the Kellogg's guarantee – bigger, brighter, cheaper. Live for ever. Rise again.

She trudged back towards the eggs, shelves and shelves of eggs – sized, graded, boxed, labelled. She put a box in her trolley, Grade One, largest size; added a second box, a third. Her tears were soaking into the cheap brown cardboard. A fourth box, a fifth. Eggs for new life and resurrection, eggs for fertility. Her hands were shaking, but she still took down more boxes from the shelf. Eggs as source and symbol of creation. Eggs for spring, hope, youth, continuance. Her trolley was loaded now. She wheeled it to the checkout, joined a queue. This town was full of queues. It queued to be cremated as well as for its taxis, probably queued to be born. The woman in front of her was unloading a week's supply of food. Morna felt suddenly nauseous as she watched the mounting pile of cans and cartons, the jars of strawberry jam and mango chutney, the sticky buns in cellophane, the bloody hunks of meat. This was the time to fast, not feast. She glanced at her own trolley. Why so many eggs when she and David had been content with one between them? She was following Neil again, shoring up her ruins with produce and possessions. David had tried to point her out a different way; had died before she'd grasped it. Now she was caught between the two of them, no partner left, no path.

She left her trolley where it was, drifted away, heard a girl shout after her, took no notice, walked on through the exit, round a corner, out of sight.

The shops were closing now, people struggling home. She ought to ask directions to the station, go home herself, escape. Yet how could she leave when she hadn't found David; no trace of him, no memory? Had he shopped in that supermarket, walked up this hill which led off from the precinct? She tried to picture him twenty years ago – a lad of just sixteen, already too clever and too tall. She would have been still single then, free to court him. She could see herself strolling hand in hand with him, laughing at nothing, sharing chocolate bars, blocking the pavements for boring middle-aged women like the one she had become. She was walking faster now. It was easier with him there, someone to lean on, someone to help her up the hill. She stopped at the top to thank him, stared in shock. There, on the other side, striding down the incline, was the real David, the adult David – David with his grey hair contradicted by his young lean shoulders, strong determined walk; David with his shabby jacket over polo-neck, woolly scarf trailing as it always did.

'Stop!' she shouted. 'Stop, please stop.' She dashed across the road, darted after him. 'David, *wait*!'

He turned round. She saw pale blue eyes in a coarse and pitted face, someone else's face under not-quite-David's hair. She backed away.

'S . . . Sorry,' she muttered. 'I thought you were . . .'

He shrugged, walked on. Morna stood stock-still where she was, trembling with rage as much as shock. Stupid deceitful fool, pretending to be David, walking like him, wearing his clothes, giving her hope when hope had been cremated. She kicked out at the kerb, watched him turn the corner at the bottom of the hill, disappear from sight. What right had he to be alive at all with those watery blue eyes, that alien fatuous face, when David was dead?

'Bloody fool!' she shouted, tears smarting on her cheeks. He couldn't hear. Neither of them could hear. 'Fool,' she shrieked at David. 'Going out in that matchstick boat when you're not a sailor. You *knew* about the currents. The police said that Cormack warned you, advised you not to risk it.'

She was sobbing now, doubled up against the fence. How could he have thrown his life away, smashed himself to pieces like Cormack's dinghy? A woman passed her at the bottom of the hill, stopped, turned back, touched her on the shoulder.

'Are you all right?'

'F . . . Fine,' Morna sobbed. 'Absolutely fine.'

She shook the woman off, crossed the road, started struggling up another hill. Steep and pitiless town with no gentle gradients, not even any signposts. Was she walking north to David's island, or south to home and Weybridge?

It hardly mattered. Both were dark. She trudged on. Shops and houses thinned; rough wasteland on one side, empty boarded buildings on the other. It helped to keep on moving. Her back ached, her feet throbbed, but at least there was a rhythm which blocked out other sorts of pain. That was the answer, really, not to think, not to blame. Just one foot forward, next foot forward, right left right. Her shoes were soaked, silly flimsy shoes only suited to cremations. She could feel the left one rubbing into a blister, took no notice. One foot forward, next foot forward . . .

Dusk was falling, the leaden greyness of the afternoon purpling into evening. She glanced around at the shadows – shapes and colours beginning to swallow up and fade, the sharp edges of the world blurring into void. 'No,' she whispered. 'Let it not be night again. Not yet. Not so soon, please.' She stretched out her hands as if she could hold the darkness off. It lay so heavy on you, darkness, pressed down down, filling all the holes and spaces in your body. It was black dense fog stuffed into your mouth, dark heavy bandages drawn tight across your eyes. It was like living in a cellar, living in a nightmare.

Stop panicking. Right left right. Only babies feared the dark. It wasn't night yet, anyway. Still an hour to go. Half an hour. Even the birds hadn't gone to roost yet. Sparrows chattering in the hedge, a flock of starlings flapping across the sky. Left foot forward, right foot forward. No swallows yet. Still too cold for them. David had told her that the terns were known as sea swallows, joked with her once that she should have been born an arctic tern herself, since they enjoyed more daylight hours than any other creature, flying to the North Pole in the summer and the South Pole in the winter, travelling thousands and thousands of miles in search of nightless days. Only David understood her fear of darkness and he had gone into the dark himself. The terns would be flocking in to nest on David's island. New life when he was dead.

Right foot forward, left foot . . . No. Impossible. Couldn't not think, couldn't not rage and blame. Had to stop, in any case. Her blister was too painful to go on. She kicked off her shoe, crouched down on the verge, examined swollen heel with bandaged finger. One foot and one hand out of action now. That's what happened. Things fouled up, stopped working. You grew old and rotted, died. Darkness was so frightening because it was the colour of death. She had been born to death – her father's death – had it in her bones. Worse for her mother, though, far worse. Bea had been a widow almost all her adult life.

'Mummy . . .' she whispered, lying back against the verge. Since David had died, she had longed to be a child again. Mothers could make light of death, pack it away like dark and heavy winter wraps in summertime. She didn't remember a childhood draped in black, a mother always grieving. Bea had been cheerful, chosen bright and flattering clothes, stressed optimistic texts like 'God is Love', gave every cloud its double silver lining. Maybe those were lies again, but good lies for a child.

She hadn't told her mother about her own bereavement – had spared her deliberately. Forty years of mourning was enough. Why drag her down again when she had just found a new contentment in her Job, force her to reassume the thankless role of comforter? She had also warned her daughter not to mention it, though she hardly knew what Chris might think herself. It was harder to dissemble with someone who shared the house with you, actually saw the fierceness of your grief. She had confided in Chris to some extent – lame and halting phrases which hid as much as they revealed. 'He . . . er . . . wasn't just a colleague. We had a lot in common, you see, and the work brought us closer. I was . . . quite fond of him, in fact.' She had concealed the love, never said a word about the sex. Yet Chris appeared to understand without the need for words. Her daughter had been tactful, touchingly supportive, no longer prickly or aloof, but older, somehow, wiser; in fact had never been so precious.

Morna sat up, stared down at the patch of flattened grass. Precious – and alive. It was only death which made you realize how valuable things were – valuable and vulnerable. Her daughter had been spared her, was a whole and breathing person with her entire life ahead of her – and at a crucial point in it – doing her first job, soon to start at college, to be married the year after. Was she to ignore all that because her own life seemed bleak and pointless; neglect her daughter because a man had died whom she had known a few short months?

She struggled up, stood motionless a moment. It wasn't too late, wasn't even dark yet – not completely – though the street lamps had come on. She glanced back the way she had come, saw the lights of the town sparkling below her, making it look exotic and alluring, gilding its raw edges. Lies again. She had lied to herself over David, believed she could relive her youth with him, be sensual and selfish, cut all other ties. Even after the drowning, she had gone on clinging to his bloated lifeless body, filled the whole house with his death like a Victorian widow shrouding every room in black. And for five whole years before that, she had clung to Neil, refused to accept his absence as a fact, an actuality; endlessly resenting him or missing him, comparing, craving, criticizing; still following his values or mouthing his opinions, if only to refute them. Could she never let things go, start anew? Even Bunny's group had tried to tell her how negative and narrowing it was to remain locked in hate or bitterness, envy or resentment; had explained how one could simply move beyond them, turn the key. She had been too busy mocking their simplistic metaphors to see the truth in them.

Suddenly, impulsively, she tugged at her wedding ring, tried to slip it off. She pulled and twisted, but the ring had jammed just below the knuckle, seemed to have taken root on her finger like another joint, a hard and permanent growth. She had heard of rings stuck tight for ever, sawn off corpses' hands. She made one last frantic effort, forcing the gold band past her now sore and reddened knuckle; stared in shock at her naked hand. The third finger still bore the imprint of the metal, was indented round the base as if Neil had left his brand on her. She cupped the ring in her palm, surprised how light it felt after the weight of all those years. She was tempted simply to drop it where she was, lose it in the rough and scrubby grass, but that would be insulting, too extreme. The years with Neil had had their value. She had loved him – once – admired him – once – even enjoyed their pampered way of life; best of all, he had given her a child. It was over now – that's all.

She slipped the ring in her pocket, glanced down at her hand again. It looked pale and bare, devalued. Too damn bad. It had jobs to do, the first of which was to rip away the black, follow Bea's example, pack death away – divorce, regret, remorse away – and let some light and warmth in.

She forced her shoe back on, broke into a slow and painful jog-trot. There was still time, still a train. If she really pushed herself, she could catch the fifty-two, get in before her daughter did, change into something less funereal, make an effort to sound cheerful and positive for once. She increased her pace, forced herself to run. She could hear a car coming up behind her, slowing to a halt, felt a prickle of fear until she saw the female at the wheel.

'Want a lift?' the woman shouted, winding the window down.

Morna limped over, out of breath. 'Are you going anywhere near the station?'

'I can drop you fifty yards from it. Get in.'

The passenger seat was piled with bags. Morna clambered into the back, let the woman's flood of one-way conversation wash over her, up and back, up and back, like a tide.

'Yes,' she said and 'No' between the swelling waves of words. She craned her neck, leaned over to one side so that she could see in the driving mirror, could just make out a pale and faded face framed with dishevelled hair. She was no longer a wife and could never have been a mistress. No man would have desired her with those lines around her mouth, those dark ageing shadows under her eyes. It had been just a game with David. Mothers and fathers. When you grew up, you understood that fathers never stayed. Died or disappeared or went off with someone else. Mothers were more dependable – had to be – caught trains, always got back home in time to greet the others, fill hot water bottles, make hot drinks, bolt the doors against danger and intruders. Home was safe. She would go back home and take up the familiar simple things which couldn't break, couldn't let you down; live as Bea had, stitching her own fray-proof silver linings if none came ready-made.

They were back in the town again, lights less deceitful now, harsh pools of fluorescent glare, cheap and flashing neon signs. David had never lived here. She had hardly known him, anyway. A colleague. An acquaintance. Only a few months, only an illusion.

'Right, if you cut through that alleyway, it takes you straight into the station.' The woman had pulled up in a narrow street piled with overflowing dustbin bags. 'You're a stranger here, I take it?'

'Yes,' said Morna, stepping out onto the cracked and puddled pavement. 'A total stranger.'

26

Morna scrambled another few yards up the cliff, stopped to get her breath, gaze around at the springy clumps of sea-pinks, the frail green croziers of fern, young sea birds trying out their wings, young lambs already sturdy. Spring had come to the island – late spring. It was already the first week of June, Whitsun in the South; here, more like April with a teasing wind and sudden skittish showers extinguishing the sun. Green was still rationed; the chief mood and colour grey. But across and between the sombre granite rocks were splashes of colour brighter than she had seen before – vivid lime-green lichen, the shock yellow of the gorse flowers singing out of dry brown winter deadwood. Two seasons on one bush. Surprising it should flower at all when the only soil it had was a stony inch or two between outcrops of harsh rock. The birds themselves looked brighter, their black and white enamelled, their strident cries crisscrossing the sky as if they were trying to erect a barrier of sound to warn her off their breeding sites. The island had emerged from some dark chrysalis, an embryo period when winter's forces had been contending with spring's shock troops. Now spring had won, David's rituals worked; the first swanks and struts of green emblazoned on brown earth.

Morna peered down at the sea. That, too, would be exploding with new life, teeming with plankton, swarming with fish and crustacean eggs, million upon million, hatching into larvae, providing food for other fish, for birds. Fish eating fish, bird devouring bird – the food-chain of the island – the chain of life. And death.

She slumped down against a spur of rock. It was two months to the day since David's death. She had come to the island on impulse – a sort of ritual journey in his honour. She hadn't planned the trip, had been sitting quiet at home, caged in the tinselled emptiness of a Bank Holiday weekend – jolly voices on the radio, local paper packed with fêtes and shows, and she on her own doing nothing much at all. Chris and Martin had gone diving down in Portsmouth; Bea was helping to run a Whitsun Festival of Prayer and Renewal at Hilden Cross. Morna hoped they would include a prayer for those in danger from the sea, for divers, especially young ones, those still unmarried and untried. The fear was always there now – fear of the sea, its greed. She had made herself get up from her plush and idle easy-chair, work out some plan of action, something tedious but time-consuming which would stop her worrying, fill the whole weekend. She would shampoo every carpet in the house, reorganize her filing system, or have a real blitzkrieg on the garden – weed all the flowerbeds, prune the spiraea, uproot the stubborn suckers at the base of the lilac bush, grub out the plantains in the lawn.

She went into the bedroom to change into old clothes. Her oldest clothes were David's jeans which she had worn on her last crossing from the island. She sank down on the bed, buried her face in them, smelt salt herring, tar, David's smell of woodsmoke and strong carbolic soap. Suddenly, she was packing her bag, flinging in stout shoes and waterproofs, her thickest sweater, collecting up all her money, phoning British Rail. It was crazy, absolutely crazy, would cost her far too much in terms of cash and effort for just a day or two. She might not even get there – the sea too rough, the tide wrong.

The sea was calm, the tide poised between low and high,

T. S. T. D.—26

the perfect time to cross. The only problem was she had forgotten what Sunday meant to pious members of the Scottish Free Church – free, it seemed, in nothing except name. It was a sin to work on the Day of Rest – even to use a chain saw or do a bit of washing – a crime to take a boat out. She stood on the quay at Oban wondering why all the nets were empty, all the boats tied up and unmanned. When she inquired in the hotel bar if someone could take her over to St Abban's, the silence was oppressive. One man even spat. She left the bar, confused. Down in the South, the Thames would be thick with boats, commercial companies cashing in on the tourists and the three-day break. She stood just outside the open door, watching the men jostling at the counter, ordering their nips and pints, gulped one after the other, the beer washing down the whisky. Strange that the Scottish God should disapprove of boat trips on the Sabbath, yet not of getting drunk. It was four o'clock in the afternoon and most of the bars still open, at least in the hotels. Those same boatmen who had cowed her with their contempt looked none too steady on their pious Sunday legs.

A young lad sidled out to her, gestured to her to follow him. 'Try the Blackman,' he muttered, when they were safely out of earshot from the pub. '*He* disna bother aboot the Sabbath.'

'I . . . I beg your pardon?' Morna had seen no one coloured in Oban, not even an Indian or Asian.

'He's no from here – disna belong. He's an incomer, works for the money.' The lad was still talking in a whisper as if he feared a lynching should anyone overhear. 'Yu'll find him at The Clachan.'

The directions he gave were confusing as well as near inaudible. Half an hour later, Morna found the so-called Blackman who turned out to be English with blue eyes, although his skin was sallow and his hair a greasy brown. She had heard almost his whole life history by the time she'd tracked him down, learnt that he was regarded as an alien, although he had lived and worked in Oban all his life – a foreigner twice over – first in that he had been born in Newcastle, and secondly in that his mother was reputed to be a tinker which accounted for his swarthy skin. He was obviously disliked. Only an outsider and a heathen would take his boat out on the Sabbath Day at the whim of some disrespectful woman as foreign and as godless as himself. Worse still, he also took his nets with him and his eldest strongest son, planned to do a bit of fishing while he waited to pick her up again, maybe compound his crime by hawking a fat salmon round the more profane hotels.

Morna shaded her eyes against the glare of sun on water while she looked back at the boat. She could just make out the Blackman and his son, their yellow jerseys a tiny splash of colour against the smudged blue-grey of the sea. A few months ago, she had eulogized that sea, used words like majestic and sublime. Her adjectives were different now. She watched the waves breaking on the cliff-face just below her, sweeping back with a sullen roar before hurtling crashing forward again. A body would have no chance. The chain of women widowed by the sea edged the British Isles like a black border. She could hear their wailing underneath the lashback of the waves, a thin and hopeless sound.

She wiped her face with her sleeve. Spray was stinging her cheeks like tears, even halfway up the cliff. Was she crazy to return here when she had settled down so well, tried to put death behind her, devote herself to Bea and Chris? David had always made her act impulsively. She should have stayed at home, continued with her new translation work, a market research job for a German dairy agency based in Trier. She could have swamped the weekend in cream and butter, distracted herself in plotting the statistics of milk consumption in Koblenz or the rise in yogurt sales. Except she had been working at it, off and on, all week, was jaded now and stale. Even at school, Whitsun had been a holiday. They had had Battenberg cake for tea instead of bread and marge – squares of pink and yellow fenced by damp and heavy marzipan. And after tea they had gone up, one by one, to the wooden dais where Reverend Mother sat presiding over two large blue china jars – a sort of spiritual bran tub or tombola. You knelt between the jars, shut your eyes, and pulled out a piece of folded paper from each jar – the Gifts and Fruits of the Holy Ghost. Whichever Gift and Fruit you received was your personal message from God, never random but intended, pointing you in the direction of the virtue or attribute He judged you needed most. In all her years at school, she had never received Peace or Joy or Wisdom, always Fear of the Lord or Chastity, Piety or Counsel.

She clambered on up the cliff, surprised by the force of the wind as she reached the top and encountered it head on. The showers had ceased, the sun emerged from cloud, yet there was still that fierce southwesterly blasting in her face, trying to bore right through her – a wind like the one in the Epistle of Whit Sunday Mass. '*And suddenly there came a sound from heaven as of a rushing mighty wind . . .*' The new translation was tamer – '*A noise from the sky which sounded like a strong wind blowing.*' Sky or heaven – there was a world of difference. She had wrestled with that problem in her own translation from the French professor's work. '*Ciel*' meant both. She looked up. *Ciel azur.* Voluptuous puffy clouds, pawed by the wind, ogled by the sea; not a day for grief, but one for poets, lovers. They had told her in Oban that the island had been swept with storms – three days of lash and roar – but today was calm, precariously calm, what the locals called 'peace in the mouth of the beast'.

Morna took off her jersey, warmed by the climb, the spring sun on her back. Although it was now evening, the day seemed newly fledged still, the colours strong, no hint of night or shadow; only two weeks away from the longest day of the year. The birds hadn't gone to roost, nor the sheep ceased their steady rhythmic munching. One stared at her, still chewing, topaz eyes in mottled white wool face. She approached it softly, watched it startle away. Those sheep had been in lamb during all her weeks with David; everything fruitful, burgeoning with new life; only she barren, moribund.

She tied her sweater round her waist, set off across the heather. She wouldn't take the long way round the cliff path; quicker and more direct to strike straight across the island to David's cottage. She needed one last look at it, yearned to see David again in his possessions and his memories, gather up his things and make a funeral pyre of them, hurl her grief on top, hope it would burn out and leave her purged.

When the cottage came in view at last, she was out of breath with throbbing blistered feet. She had forgotten the roughness of the terrain, the sudden dips and climbs, the lack of any proper paths except the rough track trampled to the cottage door by its hundred years of tenants. She stopped to rest a moment, faint from lack of food. She had come to the island fasting. It had seemed appropriate, an offering to David, some tiny ritual in his memory. Although she was weak and empty, it would have been impossible to eat in any case – not now, when she was standing just five yards from his door and on the coast where he had drowned. The accounts in the local papers seemed to surge into her head again, the words jumbled and grotesque, the papers themselves torn and stained with sea-water. *'The stump of boat was found maimed and bloated, bursting out of its clothes . . .'* *'The stench of rotting oars, the puffy swollen life-jacket, the buckled face . . .'* No – all lies. He hadn't had a life-jacket, hadn't had a face – not when he was found.

589

She made herself walk on, crept up to the cottage as if David were working still and she feared to interrupt his chain of thought. The door was boarded, two stout planks wedged diagonally across it to form a barrier. Had Cormack assumed the cottage was unlucky, decided to lock the evil spirits in to prevent them running loose? David's spirit was in there, nothing evil. She heaved at the boards, pitting her whole strength and force against them; clawed one loose, then the other, pushed at the stubborn door, jolted forwards as it opened suddenly.

She stepped inside. Spring disappeared; winter chill took over. The rooms were cold and gloomy, smelt of damp. She had been remembering the cottage as filled with light, even in the murk of January. In fact it was dark – in June – and almost bare. Cormack had stripped the shelves and cupboards, taken down the curtains, removed half the furniture. She peered into the parlour. The sofa bed had gone, a patch of green mould sprouted on one wall. The hearth was empty save for a handful of black ashes. She walked upstairs, feet echoing on the wooden boards, opened the bedroom door. The bed was still there, but without its mattress or its covers – the bed where she and David had first . . .

She sank down on the floor, pressed her face against the bare wood frame. It reminded her of his coffin, that narrow wooden oblong with nothing in it. Worse, in one way. More final. End of hope. One stupid childish part of her had never quite believed that he was burnt. The outward casing had been confined to the flames, but David himself had escaped and slipped back here. She had imagined him lying on this bed, or wooing the kitchen range, kneading dough for sun bread. At least something of him would be saved – his shabby sheepskin jacket, his piles of papers with their energetic writing which looked as if it were leaping off the page, his scarlet toothbrush which had nuzzled hers in the mug beside the sink. But nothing. Nothing. Not an odd book or glove, not even a stray button. Not the echo of his voice or a greasy rim around a baking-tin.

She jerked up from her knees. Fool she was, thinking she could waltz in after a fatal accident and expect things to be unscathed. The police would have searched the place, rifled through David's every last possession, bundled them back with the corpse only when the case was closed. Death by simple drowning. No foul play. Body, books and clothes released, parcelled up like jumble to his parents.

She limped downstairs, blundered into the kitchen – once dining room and workroom, study and powerhouse, now coldest room of all, with its dead black range, its one broken chair left tipped against the table. That table had always been piled with books, documents and scribbled notes surrounding them even when they ate there. She ran her hand across the bare cold wood. David's work had died with him; those years of painstaking research now mouldering in a drawer with salt-stained jerseys, boyhood photographs, old school prizes, the cuttings about his death. His parents owned St Abban now and had coffined him in some chest of drawers or bureau along with the relics of their son, his Life unfinished, his miracles unsung. They would never understand the importance of the work – might revere it as a kind of fossil, something precious but dead – not as the growing budding struggling thing which she herself had helped to bring alive.

She pulled a stool up to the table, sat with her head in her hands, remembering her hours with pen and paper. Of all the jobs she had ever done, it had proved the most fulfilling, not only because it was a shared task with David, but because of its very continuity, the sense of something expanding and developing, as they laid brick on brick, line on line. They were building something which had a future and a public, unlike her own trivial translation jobs which were mostly filed into oblivion, or simply chucked into the waste-bin when they had served their puny purpose. She was part of the book herself now, her suggestions and her phrasing woven into it, her translation serving it. She had helped, in fact, not just with the French, but with the final polished version from Dubhgall's Latin. She and David had often argued passionately about shades of meaning, or word order, or even the use of semi-colons. She remembered one chapter in particular, when Abban had first landed on the island, found it barren and deserted, begged God to help him feed his few devoted monks. She could recall the passage almost word for word, still disagreed with some of the phrases David had chosen in preference to her own. She hunted around for a scrap of paper – wanted one last try, perhaps a compromise between their two contrasting styles, David's plain but never casual, hers always more informal. She searched the dresser drawers. There must be paper somewhere. David had had stacks of it – piles of foolscap, scores of virgin notebooks, jumbo-pads from Smith's. Now there wasn't a single sheet remaining, no smallest pencil stub.

She tipped out the contents of her handbag. No paper there, either, except her diary – a scarlet satin monstrosity which Bunny had given her when she first arrived in California and which she had been forced to swap for her own small and unobtrusive businesswoman's diary which was bound in neat black leather and contained useful facts and figures. (She had left that one with Dean.) She leafed through the gold-edged pages, rose-tinted Bunny style, but mostly completely blank – not just the remaining part of the year from June to December, but even April and May which had already passed. You didn't fill a diary with cooking meals for a daughter, chauffering a mother to chiropodist or pet shop, or even completing a translation on soft-spread margarine.

She turned back to the first week of January, began to

write under the few printed headings, 'New moon', 'Epiphany': *'And Abban said to God: "I have nothing to eat, but if it is your will that I remain here, I know you will provide me with food and drink."'*

David had put 'sustenance' at first. She had opposed it as too formal, since he was aiming at a simple childlike style. Perhaps too simple. She jotted down the next few lines. *'And God tested his saint, keeping him parched and hungry for three days and three nights . . .'* 'Hungry and thirsty', she had urged, instead of 'parched'. David had overruled her there, arguing that 'parched' suggested greater suffering and perhaps even a further dimension of spiritual deprivation as well as simple thirst.

Yes, he was right; she could see it now. She turned the page – no longer blank. The second week of January was packed with entries, expeditions. 'Exposition Park', she had jotted, 'County Museum of Art', 'Huntington Library'. She had gone to all those places on her own, wandered around California's tourist traps, aimless, killing time. Only David had given her life a shape and purpose. She picked up her pen, a gold-plated ballpoint which came gift-wrapped with the diary, scribbled another line beneath 'Universal Studios' and 'Forest Lawn'. *'But in the morning of the third day . . .'* David had never allowed her to miss the symbolism. Christ rose again on the third day and morning stood for light and hope, a new start. *'When Abban was praying in his cell . . .'*

Morna put the pen down. What was the point of all this senseless scribbling, this search for better words, when David was dead, the work aborted? She flicked swiftly through the pages of the diary, stopped at October – October 16th. That was her birthday, when she had promised David gifts, a special meal. Instead, she would be alone, Chris at university, her mother at the convent. Bea had already put her house on the market and Chris and Martin spent more and more time away. How could she delude herself that she was living for mother and daughter? She was simply killing time again, ticking off the days until her own death.

'Dead,' she scrawled in the diary under 16th October, turned the page. '*Mort*', she wrote. '*Tot, morto, muerto*', then tossed it into the corner where the waste-bucket had stood. She wouldn't need a diary any more. There wasn't any future.

She let herself out, banged the door behind her, dragged the heavy planks back, re-formed the barrier. Cormack had been right to board the cottage up. It *was* full of evils – lost work, wasted talents. She turned back south. Dangerous to walk the other way and come face to face with one of the islanders, even Cormack himself. She was a suspect here, intruder, had only brought bad luck.

It was warmer out of doors, the sea deceitful blue. She walked to the cliff edge, clambered down a yard or two, sat on a jutting ledge of rock. The sun was lower in the sky now, the bleating of the lambs less shrill. Still an hour or so to sunset, though, when the boatman had promised to return for her. She might as well wait here as anywhere. She had nowhere to go, nothing else to do. She held up her hand against the sun, saw the veins, blue-gold, running down her wrist. These veins were conveying blood to the heart, the arteries pumping it back again – she alive and David dead. It was the wrong way round. He had more to live for, something to achieve. She clenched her palm, opened it again, as if to prove it closed on nothing. Even the birds seemed to resent her presence here, hostile like the islanders, the grating 'kee-er, kee-er' of the terns cutting across the raucous screech of skuas. Some of those migrant birds had flown more than half a million miles in a single lifetime, taking their bearings from the sun and stars or the earth's magnetic field. David had told her about an experiment in which two Manx shearwaters had been taken to New York from a small rock island north-west of St Abban's and when released, had winged straight back in the direction of their home, reaching it in under fourteen days. He had made her see the order in the world, the amazing power of nature, the complexity of things; had told her once that if you compressed the entire lifetime of the fifteen-thousand-million-year-old universe into a span of a single year, then all recorded history would take up the last few moments of its final day – the whole chronicle of *homo sapiens* from caveman to astronaut, unfolding in sixty seconds to midnight on December 31st. Facts like that lodged in her mind, nudging and disturbing her. He had shown her a truth beyond confining commonsense and rationality, had refused to draw straight and rigid lines between earth and heaven, vision and so-called fact. Even in his book, he had speculated on the nature of truth and reality itself, using Abban as a link between two worlds, two points of view.

Morna picked up a flat and heavy stone, tossed it into the sea below, watched it swallowed up in a ricochet of spray. Suddenly she sprang up from the ground as if the stone had been hurled into her mind and the ripples were still circling, exploding out. Could she not take on David's work herself? She swung round, started scrambling back to the cliff top, clawing at the rocks, grazing her hands as she tried to run away from the idea – one so damnfool obvious she was surprised she hadn't thought of it before – weeks and weeks before. No. It wasn't possible. Obvious, yes, but quite impractical – even frightening. She wasn't qualified. It wasn't even her field. She might make errors, miss crucial points, reveal herself a bungling amateur. She didn't have the stamina, let alone the scholarship. It would take years and years if she worked to David's standards but without his skills, laboriously double-checking every phrase, scouring all his sources, cross-referencing each footnote. There would be problems, endless problems, not least of which was that she would have to brave David's parents, wrest all the books and papers back. They might even suspect she was trying to steal his work, make capital (and cash) out of a dead man's name and status.

She stumbled on along the path, blind to everything but the conflict in her mind. Why prejudge his parents? Might they not be glad that their son, their scholarship boy, could live on in his scholarship? After all, the basic work was done. David had planned and structured the whole book, written a good half of it already, discussed its aims and outline many times. She needn't do it entirely on her own. His publishers would help and she could always beg support from one or two of the historians who had been in correspondence with him, fellow scholars who knew the period, were conversant with its problems. It would take time – but she had time – had often longed for some real work of substance, something to fill her life. She had always respected David's view that one should give everything one had to work; admired his own patience and perfectionism, shared something of them herself. They had both been raised to discipline, schooled from earliest childhood to do every task as well as possible, as if they were doing it for God. Couldn't she do it not for God but for David – the gift she had promised on her birthday? By October, she would at least have made a start, have something to offer him, and by the October after that . . .

She already felt excited, her strides getting longer and more vigorous as the idea took shape, seemed less impractical. In some ways, she was ideally suited to the job. Her training as a translator had made her used to working on her own in the absence of the original author, yet striving to be faithful to his aims and style, serving his work with her own. She would be translating not only Abban and Dubhgall, Yves Le Goff, but also David himself, searching out all his subtleties of meaning, scrutinizing her every phrase so that it should reflect what he intended, yet adding perhaps a lustre of her own. All right so she didn't have his intellect, his depth and breadth of knowledge, but what was the alternative? To leave his work as dead and cold as he was; go on translating trivia for those dairy con-men in Trier who were quite happy to twist the facts about the rôle of saturated fat in heart disease, in order to sell more butter? That was what Neil had done as a career – earned his suburban villas selling lies. At least there were no deliberate distortions in David's work. In fact, he had spent his life quarrying for one small grain of truth in one tiny fragment of history, aware of all the problems in history itself, aware that truth was elusive and subjective, changed its shape even as he tried to sketch its outlines, yet never giving up.

She tripped on a rough patch in the path, stumbled to a halt. How could she kid herself that she could interpret all those subtleties, even detect them in the first place? Every discussion she had had with David had thrown up more uncertainties, increased her awareness of the hazards of the task. The very first time she had met him he had emphasized the problems – made her realize that myth and miracle were often masquerading as fact in Abban's time, that evidence of any sort was scanty; that you had to search for jigsaw-puzzle pieces, not only from history, but from related fields such as archaeology and palaeography. Wasn't it presumptuous to assume that she could cope when David himself had found the going tough? Any scholar she approached would soon point up her own inadequacies. Better, surely, to entrust the work to one of them, or leave it to the publishers to find another author, one with some of David's expertise.

Anyway, she couldn't really afford to do the job. David's research grant would hardly revert to her, and he had long since spent his small advance. She would be paid if she completed the book and if the publisher accepted it, now written by two hands, but both those ifs were uncertain. She could continue with her own work, subsidize David's that way, but then she wouldn't have the time to lavish on it, the energy and freshness it demanded.

She missed her footing, almost fell. The path had petered out, blocked by fallen scree. She had blundered right across it, stubbed her toe on a piece of jagged rock. She eased her shoe off, remained crouched down on the ground, rubbing her bruised foot. Why not simply accept that she was beaten? She limped over to a boulder stained green and brown with lichen, sat on the damp stone, seeing nothing but the bare kitchen table in the cottage, cheap wood like David's coffin, empty like his bed. She looked back in the direction of the cottage, as if to see that bed, reach out and touch that table. Nothing there. Nothing behind her but the pale grimace of rock in scrubby grass, the fold of hill on hill, the scimitar-curved horizon of the sea. She was astonished at the distance she had come. She had been walking like a robot, lost in thought, while her feet tramped on towards the monastery as if pre-directed there. Only one last hill to breast and she would see its stones – ruins like David's book.

She jammed the shoe back on, trudged on again, shading her eyes against the reddening sky as she panted up the slope. She hadn't even noticed her surroundings, yet the setting sun was scorching the whole hillside, as if someone had lit every lamp and fire and beacon-flame in heaven and left them blazing until they licked down and kindled earth. She pulled herself up the last few yards, stopped stock-still at the top. The stones were no longer grey, but glowing pink and gold in the fierceness of the light, the granite softened, the whole site flushed and flaming. She had only seen sunsets as fierce as that in California, sun on glass fifty storeys up. She could feel that sun flooding through her body as if she, too, were glass, stained and coloured glass, letting in the light. She *was* the colour, *was* the light. She sank down on the grass, stunned by the stab and shout of red. The sea breeze was tugging back her hair, tempering the hot fire of the sun. Wind and fire. Pentecost. She closed her eyes, watched David's sacrificial fire leap into flame behind the lids, the fires of every rite and every century blazing back to prehistoric man, further back to the first kindling of creation. She could hear creation crackling into life, she part of it, no longer separate, pointless, random, but burning with its force and power.

She opened her eyes a crack, glimpsed only gold and scarlet, the whole sky ablaze around a raw red molten sun. She reached out her hands to try and block it off, seemed to lose her balance, was suddenly plunging round and round on a roller-coaster ride, spinning in its orbit. The sun was too close, swelling even brighter as the ride lurched on and down, piercing through inner space. That was the red sun of the nucleus, infinitesimally small, yet huge, overwhelming, as she herself shrank in scale. She could hear the booming voice again, distorted on the soundtrack, could make out no clear words. She tried to grab the rail, feel the reassuring confines of the cab. Her hand closed on nothing. Nothing above her or below her but spinning whirling void. Million upon million of orbiting electrons were vibrating all around her, their glowing hazy paths tangling and interweaving until she was dizzy from their endless dance. She was part of that dance, her own boundaries dissolving, every atom stretched and magnified to its smallest smallest particle, yet one unbroken whole. She could see the entire universe in one plane, in one dimension, yet with no planes, infinite dimensions, as if the gum of time and space had melted, everything fused, merged, co-existent, unified. David's fifteen thousand million years were no longer laid out chronologically, but formed one unending present. The caveman was venturing out to stalk his prey at the same moment as the astronaut took his first tentative step on Planet Mars. The sun was rising on Ancient Greece, Abban quarrying stones to build his cell, David bawling into slippery life in the midwife's hands.

Morna groped out her own hand, touched the hard rim of the earth's crust, felt the tailwind of its satellites blow back in her face. Naked earth. Naked mind. Everything had fallen away – fear, flesh, granite, sea. She held infinity in her hand, felt its lightness, its simplicity; knew she was part of it, woven into it; that light-dark, life-death, were all one, all one.

She breathed in the silence, the silence before creation, the silence after the last y of history had crumbled into dust. She herself was history – evolving, growing, overthrowing, shifting and in flux, yet unchanged and ever now. This was the eternal now, this one astounding moment out of time, this joy, this lightness, all-embracing being. No shadow and no end . . .

Morna opened her eyes, blinking against line and shape again as the world shook back in place. Sunset. Long shadows trailing like pennants from the pink-tinged stones, sky stained gold and purple, damask sea reflecting it. She stared at her shaking hands. How much time had passed – a second or a day? She tried to struggle up, aware again of ordinary sensations – the brash wind in her face, the booming of the waves below. Her body was returning, cramp in one leg, both feet sore and aching, her stomach rumbling vulgarly. Had she merely fainted from lack of food, lost consciousness a moment?

She groped to her feet, walked slowly down the slope, still half-dazed and stumbling, stopped at the circle of St Abban's cell. The rays of the setting sun cut it like a radius. She could see the other cells clustering around it, the oratory set back a little. The buildings were still whole, still proud. Only time had blocked them from her view, as just one branch of one bowed and stunted tree could block out the whole sun or moon. There were other worlds, other modes of being, which she had fathomed for that one stupefying instant before time and space closed in again. She couldn't explain it, didn't have the concepts. If she were a philosopher, a physicist, she might have tried to coin them, but if she compromised with suspect terms like vision, revelation, most people would scoff, tell her she was imagining things, going out of her mind. Or make a joke of it, defuse mystery and immensity with a guffaw or a jeer.

Not David. She clutched at the crumbling curve of stones. Had David known what she had sensed just now, grasped it all along, been struggling to put it over to her, somehow find the words? There *were* no words. Yet he had done his best to grope towards them, find vague approximations like grandeur, terror, unity – which she had failed to understand.

She picked up a loose fragment of the granite, held it warm and solid in her hand. This was a stone which Abban might have laid himself, part of a cell which had stood for thirteen centuries. Stones lived on. So did words. She could see Dubhgall's words on the last page of his book. 'Pray for me, Dubhgall, that I may have eternal life.' His prayer had been granted, not only through his Life of Abban, but through the chain of scholars after him – scribes and copyists, historians and scholars. David was one more in that chain. She had to complete his book – she knew that now – join the ends of the chain to form a circle, a circle like the soul, this cell, this island – the structure of life and time itself, revealed to both of them. All the conflicting arguments had faded, the problems somehow dwindled. She had received the gifts she needed for the task – Gifts and Fruits of the Holy Ghost – no longer cloistered Modesty or Mildness, but Understanding, Fortitude, Patience, Longanimity; the Gift of Tongues. That last she had already – the gift of languages – the power to bring a book, a work to life.

She looked towards the sea, still gilded by the sun, its glaze of colour seeming to calm its swell, turn it into a lake of golden oil. Further up that coast, she and David had sung to the seals when they beat the bounds of the island. She could hear the echo of his baritone carrying her weaker voice along with it. '*Tu devicto mortis aculeo*.' That was the only way to overcome the sting of death, to make David and this island live again.

She walked towards the holy well, tossed the chip of granite in, heard the splash of healing water. The grass was lusher here, fulmars nesting in one crumbling cell. She sat by the stream, dabbled her hand in the water – a ringless hand which still looked strange without its wide gold band. The mark had disappeared, though – the third finger no longer different from the rest. She was single again, free to work, to lavish time and love on a project she believed in, without Neil's imprimatur. She was also free to finance the work any way she chose – sell her house and buy a smaller one, maybe not buy at all, just rent a place, live simply, even frugally, by willing to experiment, reforge all her values for herself. She grasped one hand with the other, as if to test their strength. Her septic finger had healed, new pink skin formed around the nail. She hadn't even noticed till this moment. She squeezed it, felt no pain.

The wind had dropped, the air almost still in the shelter of the ruined wall, and scented from the clusters of wild thyme which pushed between the stones. Medieval herbalists had prized the plant, believed thyme inspired courage, banished melancholie. She picked a sprig, stuck it in her buttonhole. She needed courage. Her doubts might well flood back once she started on the book, her loneliness return. Yet there was no more hesitation in her mind. David's work was hers now.

She could feel his presence still, not only in this spot along with Abban's, but woven into the whole vast chain of being, transmuted from life to death to life again. She hadn't been hallucinating. What she had witnessed had left faint traces in her mind like the streaks of palest amethyst still bruising the sky after the wound and shock of sunset. She glanced around her. No flame left, no breath of wind. The terror and the grandeur had both diminished now – stones solemn grey, hills turning from burnished gold to pewter.

She eased up to her feet, walked slowly back up the slope, waves breaking on the shore again, soft shadows smudging sea and sky together. Dusk was falling, birds gliding in to roost like shadows themselves, floating on the air with no sound, no movement of their wings. She swung south along the cliff-path, watched the sea submerge the sun, water closing over fire, the last glints and sparks extinguished. The waves chafed up and back, up and back, hissing into the crevices of rock, sucking out again with an ugly grating noise as if one rock were grinding on another. The light was fading as she rounded the southernmost tip of the island, turned northwards to the landing point. She could see the boat veering towards her, cutting a sharp white furrow through the flagging blue; watched it grow slowly larger, hatch two yellow daubs, and then two faces.

She used both her hands to scramble down the cliff. She was chilled now, damp with the spray that exploded from the charge of wave on rock. Even in June, this sea could not lie still, was bullying the boat, trying to turn it back. She jumped the last few steps of rock to the concrete landing slip, waves pummelling and pouncing at it, the whole wild expanse of water ripped by currents. The steep curve of the cliff-face lowered like some huge dark beast from another ruder age. Darkness was closing round her – vast night, vast sky – she only an ant beside an Everest, a matchstick on an ocean. She felt no fear. Great and small were mistranslations, meant nothing any longer, darkness only the underside of light. The nuns had taught the Order in the world, but had seen only a narrow and restricted world, every part of it nailed in place and labelled – good or evil, past or present, true or false. How could she ever explain to Mother Michael the simultaneous wave of creation, transformation, annihilation – all things interacting, no either-or, life-death? Even now, the faint pattern of the ever-changing motions of the electrons' dance still circled in her mind – a circle which enclosed and defined all things.

She stepped forward as the boat nudged between the molars of sharp rock, the retch of diesel engulfing the rank smell of rotting seaweed. The Blackman's son was standing on the gunwale, gesturing to her to jump. She paused a few seconds to judge the swell of the waves, sprang towards the deck, was steadied by a tanned and tattooed arm. The deck was slippery, stank of fish. The boy said nothing as he helped her in, he and his father talking only between themselves, as they had done on the outward journey, in a dialect she couldn't understand. She stared down at their catch – writhing silver mackerel, one large salmon, bloody at the mouth, a few smaller fish she didn't recognize. The Blackman was steering out between the skerries, working with the currents, his full attention on the wind and tide. He jerked a thumb towards the tiny cabin where there was bread and tea, an ancient wood-fired stove. Morna shook her head, lurched forward, clinging to the side as the boat pitched and rolled beneath her. She stood in front, bracing her feet against the wind, watching the prow cleaving through the swell. Despite the cold, it was almost mesmerizing, wave following wave as the boat ripped and broke each curve, the backwash billowing out along both sides of the boat. Sea and sky were grey now, yet every wave erupted in glints and strobes of green, purple, turquoise, fringed with white, before rolling on to grey again.

Morna tried to bundle her hair beneath the collar of her jersey, to stop it clawing in wet strands at her face. Her shoes were soaked, her feet numb. A damp and heavy chill clung around her body like a sodden blanket. Yet there was exhilaration in the speed and heave of the boat, the tugging wind, the sense of space shouting all around her. All one. All one. She looked back at the island – only a blur now, the jagged cliff softened into shadow, the churlish rocks swallowed up in mist. It was as if someone were rubbing out its contours even as she watched. She strained her eyes, could no longer tell cliff from cloudbank, land from sea; even the far horizon lost in dark and haze. One bird was still following the boat, flying from the direction of the island – a white bird with wide wings, keeping pace with them. She scrabbled in her pocket, found David's silver coin, rubbed it up on her sleeve. She could just make out the Pillars of Hercules, beneath the encrusted grime and scale – regarded by the ancients as the ends of the known earth. Hercules had won immortality – at last, at cost – in return for all his labours, found a new earth and heaven with no known ends. She smiled to herself, held the coin to her lips a moment, before tossing it into the sea. She must return it to David, as her tribute to him. The bird swooped down, thinking it was food, soared up again, flew higher, higher, until it seemed to touch the first faint stars strung like harbour lights on some second darker sea. She peered towards the stars, trying to pick out Venus as they had done in California on Neil and Bunny's patio. *'The same energy which holds those planets up, keeps them going round and round, is inside of us as well. We're part of the whole goddam thing. Doesn't that just freak you out?'*

She heard Bunny's raucous laugh puncture the silence like a rock thrown in the water. She laughed herself, out loud. The boatman's son slouched over.

'All right, Miss?'

She nodded, let him guide her down into the cabin, back to light and warmth.

MORE ABOUT PENGUINS, PELICANS, PEREGRINES AND PUFFINS